RUINS OF THE VAMPIRE

Ruins of the Vampire

SEQUEL TO DAWN OF
THE VAMPIRE
REVIVED

William Hill

Kat Hill

Otter Creek Press

Acknowledgments & About Characters

A special thanks to my proofreaders in Bristol, Bessie McCracken and Brenda Dunn. This book would have been riddled with errors about the Tri-Cities without their revisions. Even when I lived there the roads could confuse me. As always, I appreciate my mom for proofreading a final copy especially since it isn't her cup of sweet tea. I am fully grateful to my amazing wife, Kat, for the many times that she has perused the manuscript and deployed grammar and spelling checks to edit and typeset the book.

Digital artist extraordinaire, Pete Pilcic, created an eye-catching cover. Thanks again, PT.

I really appreciate the long-time followers of Dawn of the Vampire, published in 1992. Here we are thirty years later in real-world time but not in fiction. I am especially grateful to those who were dying to be a part of the tapestry of DOTV and responded to the advertisement for unpaid fictional work in the new novel. They offered their altered egos and oddball ideas for characters to add color and personality to Ruins of the Vampire. These folks who weren't wary enough to heed the advice: Be careful, or you'll end up my novel, and still volunteered have been treated far better than

Ruins of the Vampire

SEQUEL TO DAWN OF THE VAMPIRE REVIVED

William Hill
Kat Hill

Otter Creek Press

Acknowledgments & About Characters

A special thanks to my proofreaders in Bristol, Bessie McCracken and Brenda Dunn. This book would have been riddled with errors about the Tri-Cities without their revisions. Even when I lived there the roads could confuse me. As always, I appreciate my mom for proofreading a final copy especially since it isn't her cup of sweet tea. I am fully grateful to my amazing wife, Kat, for the many times that she has perused the manuscript and deployed grammar and spelling checks to edit and typeset the book.

Digital artist extraordinaire, Pete Pilcic, created an eye-catching cover. Thanks again, PT.

I really appreciate the long-time followers of Dawn of the Vampire, published in 1992. Here we are thirty years later in real-world time but not in fiction. I am especially grateful to those who were dying to be a part of the tapestry of DOTV and responded to the advertisement for unpaid fictional work in the new novel. They offered their altered egos and oddball ideas for characters to add color and personality to Ruins of the Vampire. These folks who weren't wary enough to heed the advice: Be careful, or you'll end up my novel, and still volunteered have been treated far better than

most Red Shirts in the following pages. I hope y'all's
faith in my imagination is rewarded.

Rebecca Arnold, Julie Rosenbalm Bailey, Kathy
Barlow-Weaver, Tasha Barnes, Carolyn & Sabrina
Barnett, Doris Arnold Bays, Sheilah Blankenbecler,
Randy Bennett, Ben Bonds, Becky Boyer, Chris Brown,
Robert & Roy Burress, Mary Canter, Al & Sandee
Clyne, Pam Combs, Joanie Cox-Smith, Levi Cross,
Sonja Crowe Cox, Donna S. Cunningham, Brenda
Dunn, Raymond Dzek, Marcine Eastridge, Johnny
Faidley, Darlene Flick, Donna Flowers, Ben Frizzell,
Kim & Mike Hampton, Patti Henegar, Andrea Helton,
John Hogan, Justin Hobbs, Christine & Jason
Humphrey, Sharon Humphreys, Missy Kegley, Teresa
Kilian, Bill Lancaster, Alan Linkous, Sabrina Lopez,
Jen Lyons, Bessie & Dennis McCracken, Darlene
McCracken, James & Jamie McGill, Charlotte Mackey
(RIP), Bill Martin, Damean Mathews, Jani Meyers, Kim
Mickow, Tammie Miles, Marybeth P. Moore, Timothy
Motter, Bonnie Naimo, Amanda Nutter, Chance Oliver,
Anna Owens, Angela Page, April N. Parris, Tammy
Stallard Patton, Rhonda & Emmett Powers, Alesia
Quillen, Kathie Reeves, Jami Tuesday, Todd Saddler,
Stephen Semones, Dr. Steve Sikora, Ken Siksay, Ron
Sneed (RIP), Carol Ray Snow, Whitney Tomlinson,
The Haint Mistress, Christopher J Williams, Andrea
Wilson, and Todd Young.

This is a work of fiction. The geography of Sullivan County, Tennessee, and Washington County, Virginia is real and mostly accurate, as many of these places can be visited, but I have taken poetic license and liberties with the terrain, its historical figures and the local landmarks. Permission was never asked to use the actual places of this story, whether they are South Holston Dam, East Hill Cemetery, Sugar Hollow Park, or the Bristol Regional Medical Center, and those who own The Bristol Hotel and the Down Home of Johnson City will likely be surprised to find their properties involved here. Furthermore, all the people living, dead, and otherwise are fictional or used in a fictional context, although they might wish otherwise.

One

―――

The Vampire Hunters

Vampires hunting vampires, Dillon mused as he mulled over these dangerous times. What had happened to his hometown and surrounding Appalachia? He and the love of his nights had spent the last month tracking down and slaying feral bloodsuckers. They were currently staking out the interior of a concert venue.

Since dying, Dillon Urich's life had become surreal. He felt like he was walking the razor's edge of normal and the supernatural, trying to live in two worlds and by night. Any mistake could lead to his permanent death and worse for loved ones.

Welcome to my world, Dillon thought. He was an investigative journalist and one of the recent undead, a grayling vampire for almost three months. He had hunted stories for years, but this gruesome culling of reckless, bloodthirsty vampires was entirely new to him. From what he had learned, it wasn't unusual for vampires to prune the family tree of the wild ones that might expose their secret. Vampires didn't want people to know that they existed. There were more hidden aspects of the Seen and the Unseen worlds than he had ever imagined. He was learning surprises nightly, and he expected to continue discovering more in the coming years, if he lived so long.

The Down Home was decorated with pumpkins and cornstalks for the Oktoberfest Music Festival, giving the venue less of a haunting feel and more an air of early Thanksgiving. The attendees acted excited, but many hid their fear behind cheerful facades. He could taste the sour and salty scent of stewing panic. These people were ready to let loose, to get out of the house and get down, despite there being a serial killer who had slain three, leaving blood-drained corpses. Two had been found nearby in recreational areas. A third had been murdered in nearby Shady Valley, Tennessee.

The continuous, repetitive media coverage of the Oktoberfest Vampire and lack of breaking developments kept a lot of folks in a tizzy and easily startled. Citizens' trepidations over the last week had surged along with the number of deaths and media vans. Any death at first was connected to the Oktoberfest Vampire until it wasn't, and then there was doubt. Dillon's human colleagues were heightening fears. Not that their warnings weren't justified, but it was past the point of being helpful, like being nagged until it became background noise. There were so many lights turned on in the Tri-Cities that it glowed like an East Tennessee version of the Grand Ole Opry in Nashville.

Between acts, Alter Bridge's lyrics played over the Down Home's speakers and seemed appropriate to his situation. "In your head, monsters call. In the air, you find no one is there at all. But you keep them alive. Paralyzed you cannot run. You only crawl. So, find a new way to live, before you die in the cold. And though the sky's caving in, the fear must not gain control."

Sometimes Dillon felt that eternal darkness had fallen upon him, and except for Elke, he was surrounded by monsters and strangers. There was plenty to fear, but he had been trained to handle and channel fear by his education in the martial arts, plus Elke's love brightened his outlook. She inspired him to optimism.

People would panic if they knew there were vampires among them, both good and bad. Fear ruled so many lives. It was Dillon's gift or curse to see the root of fear in their eyes. As a predator, he could use it against them. There was a fine line between terror and titillation.

Many of the attendees were college students, so of course, the fear of failing classes and not getting into the graduate school of their choice was prevalent. Oh, the end of the world it would be. Since many were young, only a few were truly concerned with the serial killer called the Oktoberfest Vampire. What were the odds? That couldn't happen to them. But being alone, that could happen to them. The eyes were truly the gateway to the soul, and vampires used them to read people's history. It helped when predators knew what tactic would help them seem friendly and attractive to their victims. Skilled vampires could transform to look like someone the target knew and trusted.

Normal human fears included heights, lightning, loud sounds, falling, people who looked different, and public speaking. Glosso-phobia was the number one fear in America. People were fright-ened by a variety of creatures, from snakes and spiders to cats and dogs, and doing things like crossing bridges, flying in planes, riding on escalators, being in small spaces, being in open spaces and seeing their own blood. Some were afflicted by cherophobia: the fear that bad things were bound to happen any moment. People attended this show because of their love of live music, despite their paranoia, fears, worries and concerns. A positive passion brought them to-gether. Joy and love inspired people, making their auras brighter, like they were larger than their life suits. With all that was going on in the world, people didn't need to know that vampires were real. There were already too many bloodsuckers in the world.

Of course, what the world needed was more love. It wasn't as easy for him to see, but he was beginning to search people's eyes and faces for their joys and passions. If fear stemmed from an absence of love, he should be able to identify people's loves by their fears.

Elke said that vampires, in general, enjoyed hunting prey during concerts because people let down their guards, ignoring fear's warning signs. So, he and his lady were attending a performance at an eclectic music hall in Johnson City, which was also the home of East Tennessee State University. The Down Home had been designed in the typical but well-kept roadhouse style with rustic, wooden tables, a long L-shaped bar, and low-framed booths. The place had opened in 1976, making it the longest running setting of its kind. When he lived in Bristol, Dillon had come here for concerts, the last likely ten years gone. Recently, the *New York Times* had featured the Down Home in its entertainment section. The superior quality sound system energized customers while the cold drinks and ceiling fans kept them cool.

The spinning breezes tugged at the concert goers' masks and costumes, as well as ruffling the wrappings and faux hair of broom-wielding witches, big-eyed werewolves, creepy clowns, and wannabe superheroes. They celebrated this time when the supernatural and natural realms overlapped. Dillon should feel at home. Even if he had worn classic Hollywood bloodsucker attire, he would blend in.

He spotted a pretend vampire with a cape, face paint, faux fangs, and a living aura. Actual vampires didn't emanate such a glow since they weren't alive in the natural or normal carbon-based life way. Come to think of it, that might have been the craft artist, Angel Jackson. Some were wearing her Gruesome Twosome masks with two faces or the faux, color-changing fangs. True vampires, like himself, Elke, and the ones they hunted, possessed dark auras that they could draw around them as a cloak for concealment at night or in shadows

One fellow stood out among the rest. Perhaps that was the point of dressing like a Nazi. He had an arrow through his head. On his back, there was a sign reading: *Always the villain.* The costume was a mockery but the look on the Nazi's face was stone. His eyes were hard as agates and shone with disdain. He had a life glow, so he wasn't a vampire. He was being stared at by many people, including a tall, skinny young male with a long scar on his left cheek and wearing an E on his chest to go along with shorts, tights, and boots. Elastic man, Dillon thought, and the costumed hero might be a thrall. His aura was dimmer and pockmarked. If there was a thrall nearby, there was a decent chance his master was here or near. But where?

Dillon thought he caught a glimpse of a red-headed woman without an aura of light. She was a slim, dark knife cutting through the radiance of living, flesh and blood people. It could be the Oktoberfest Vampire, or it could be one of the other feral graylings.

"Would you care for a dance, my dear?" Dillon asked as he turned to Elke and offered his hand.

His love of his nights had dressed to unimpress. Elke Swearington didn't want people to notice her, so she wore a floor length, figure-concealing black robe and a high priestess mask. It hid her drop-dead gorgeous beauty, often compared to the sex goddess, Marilyn Monroe, if she had been a fitness freak. Elke's blond tresses were tucked away, too. If left exposed, her supernatural sensuality would awe anyone who saw her and demand unwanted attention. Even so, men drifted toward her as if they could sense what they couldn't see. Fortunately, they avoided Dillon.

He understood the attraction. Elke was the key to his existence, his reason for being and motivation to continue to be. Even with her mask on, he could get lost in her soulful eyes. They might not be soul mates, but their kindred spirits were intricately linked to each other. He would die for her, if necessary, but she had brought him back from the dead to live for her. He had never felt this fiercely about anyone or anything. Elke figuratively and literally ran through his veins. She had lived a long time, coming up on her 100th birthday, according to her housekeeper, Doris. Elke looked young yet ripe as if she had only lived twenty-some years. He smiled, thinking she had grown up during the era of flappers, had survived World War II, witnessed the Tri-Cities' growth through the train era, and so much more.

"Of course. I would be delighted to dance with my dreamboat. It will be more heady than giggle water," Elke smiled. She enjoyed using outdated terms with him. She was delighted that he was a jive bomber instead of a cement mixer. They weren't the only ones dancing to the recorded tracks as they moved through the crowd and between tables while searching for anyone without an aura. It would be wonderful to go on a normal date, some day.

"I saw Cane Concannon. So, behave yourself," she said.

Dillon had the unfortunate displeasure to know the obnoxious, caffeine and nicotine-fueled reporter. A werewolf attack had left him in a coma until two weeks ago. Nobody believed him, either, yet. He had opined that the city council was influenced by vampires in approving Bristol Virginia's dump and the new casino. His most recent op-ed, widely circulated locally and on social media platforms, had called the people of Bristol and Johnson City scared and shaking in their boots. He listed all the paralyzing fears holding them hostage since the events of August.

"I saw a thrall. He was a tall, skinny guy with dark hair and eyes. I don't see him now, or the redhead. She's a carrot-topped, female without an aura. She could be hiding her light under a bushel, but I doubt it," Dillon said.

"Good eyes, Indy," Elke replied. She adjusted his hat. "Can you even see, my dear?"

"No. I'm distracted by you," Dillon replied. He was dressed as Indiana Jones. He even carried a whip without causing a stir. Security had checked his holster to find it empty. Guns were not the danger tonight. Dillon could make sure of that. He was less certain that they could deal with a vampire without innocents being involved. Last night, Elke had to compel a witness to forget what he had seen.

Dillon had tried to forget that they had made the same decision with the blood brothers who had survived. Their knowledge of the supernatural was dangerous and driving them crazy. So, Elke had helped them forget the worst of it. It was normal to suppress trauma.

Elke nodded to her night hounds' wonderful vet as they danced by the smart, funny, and pretty Marci Mays, appearing younger than her fifty-some years and dressed as a dog catcher, and her man who wore a wolf costume but looked more like a werewolf. In further small world encounters, he spotted Elke's accountant and Mom's neighbors, the Hamptons. Every time Dillon turned around, there was someone he knew from growing up and going to school in Bristol. Earlier, he had seen Todd Young who he had known since elementary school when he was drumming on everything. They had missed his opening act with The Coveralls.

Closing his eyes, Dillon breathed in the room, taking in too much perfume and aftershave. More than a few could have used a shower. There were times that heightened senses weren't a bonus. Many of the concert goers had worked up a fresh sweat, warmed up and ready for Justen Hobson who gave you happy feet. Dillon could sense the adrenaline levels rise, and all his predator perceptions heightened. He and Elke together might be causing a stir, mixed emotions in the people around them.

When he opened his eyes, he looked straight into the lovely blue eyes of elfin Jami Saturday. At least that's who he thought the diminutive woman was, since the pink-haired gal seemed startled to see him. He had heard she had sold her tat shop, Asylum Studios, and split town, so he was surprised to see one of his best gal friends from high school. She had actually believed him about his encounter with the Dark Lady, as she had also encountered Elke one night at a South Holston beach.

A Frankenstein and a Maleficent strolled between them, and when Dillon looked for Jami, she had disappeared into the crowd. She possessed a life aura, a potent one, so she was well.

"Do you remember this woman?" Dillon asked, thinking of Jami.

Elke saw her memory in his eyes. "Yes, a diminutive young lady. She gave me a little blood. She knew you so well that it was like I was meeting you all over again. Thank you for the dance, but I think we're sending out too many good vibrations," she said and nodded to the crowd.

Couples around them were kissing. Some of the dancing bordered on erotic.

"Oh," Dillon said. He let go of her hand and hip and stepped back.

"We could just be adding to what another has started. Or not. I'm distracted. How about you? Now back to business, dear. This is deadly serious," Elke said.

Dillon regained his focus and visually searched for the redhead. A raven tressed Wonder Woman strode languidly by and caught the attention of The Bloodlust. She had exceptionally long legs and an elegant neck. He could see her carotid artery pulse with excitement. Her aura of life blazed like a star, brighter than anyone else in the room, vitality enough to share. They exchanged a lingering glance. She feared cancer, it having taken her mother and her grandmother. The clock ticking, so she wanted to live, and she loved to dance.

Abruptly, the crush of bodies, of meals on two legs that would slake Dillon's hunger and strengthen him, overwhelmed him. The spacious yet sardine-packed venue was like wading through a smorgasbord. He held himself rigid, afraid to move, frightened over the consequences of his instincts. He had thought himself in better control of his desires and hunger. The Bloodlust threatened to break loose and rampage. It would be a blood bath.

The crowd's hearts beat with excitement like a drumming session. The brilliance of their life forces radiated through his closed eyelids. He clenched his jaw and pressed his lips together. He didn't trust himself to speak. He realized he had just growled, though. No! He refused to go feral. He was more will than The Bloodlust. He had been trained that the brain, as well as the body, was a weapon. That mastery over the body started with mind and will. Right now, his body was in attack mode, and he hung on by his fingernails.

Elke had noticed his reaction, the flaring of his nostrils, the flushing of his face, the clenching of his hands and jaw, plus the tension in his shoulders as he held himself back. She stepped closer to dominate his vision, thankfully drawing his eyes and riveting his attention. She called to a different kind of hunger. She took his hand and smiled comfortingly. He only had eyes for her, the rest of the world fading away. She kissed him, and he breathed in her calming scent. She knew what he was enduring. She had thought him ready for this, too.

"I'm losing a grip. I need some air and space," he said through clenched teeth.

"That's a marvelous idea. Let's go outside," she said.

"Yeah, we're here to save people," Dillon muttered. He blinked, doing a doubletake when he caught a glimpse of the flame-haired female without an aura. No life light glow surrounding a body meant she wasn't human, a dead giveaway, so to speak.

"Target four o'clock," he told Elke. As Dillon whirled to follow the feral vampire, he bumped into someone.

It was Jambo, one of his blood brother's, he realized. No wonder his danger sense hadn't sounded at the presence of his friend. The tall, former ETSU yell leader now dressed as a knight hugged him. Dillon managed to freeze his reactions, holding back The Bloodlust, and keeping himself still when what felt like overwhelming hormones wanted to rip, tear, and taste the blood of Jamie Boy. Dillon's body leapt into attack mode, and yet, he leashed it with his mind. His deadly hunger would wait on him.

For now! The Bloodlust roared back at him. It would inevitably prevail.

"Hey, Dillon! Good to see you, man!" Jambo said. His smile was broad and friendly, his baby blue eyes bright. He loved his music.

Dillon was still a neophyte, but he could read thoughts and memories in people's eyes. He was glad to see that his friend's encounters with the supernatural hadn't screwed up his life. That made one. Married life to a college professor had been great for the Jambo. A healthy glow surrounded the McGillises who were clad as a knight and the glittery, Glenda the Good Witch of the North.

"Good to see you and be seen. How's the grease monkey business?" Dillon asked, his voice rough.

"Great! I restore more than I fix, so I'm a bondo and paint monkey. Sometimes I miss Wild Bill's, but I like being my own boss now. I owe Denny . . ." he began, and his voice caught. Silence hung between them. They missed their blood brother.

"You make a dashing Indy, Dillon. And the tan looks great. Are you feeling better?" Jane said.

"I have good days and bad," Dillon managed. He could feel The Bloodlust surge. Using an old technique, he focused on his breathing.

Elke put a hand on his lower back, calming him, and stepped in. "Peace, my love. It's so good to see y'all, again. Jane, you look fabulous. Are y'all big Bethany Moore fans?"

"Yes, we are. I love her songs *I Never Should Have Left*, *It's Not Just Another T-Shirt*, and *Too Many Shoes to Choose*. Hobson is great, too," Jane replied.

"I like his *I Started in Fast Food (Where Fate Found Me)*. A lot of us started there. It's funny and folksy. You know, I think it's been since Denny's funeral since we saw y'all. Man, Denny would love to be here tonight doing his funky chicken dance," Jambo said. Although he smiled, there was a heavy, resigned sadness in his eyes. He had developed the start of a fear of dying young.

"Was Denny a ducky shin cracker?" Elke asked Dillon.

He smiled. "No, I don't think Denny would qualify as a great dancer." Dillon missed their blood brother, too. Denny had sacrificed his life to save many. "As would Spider, John, Pete, Walt," Dillon said, adding more dead friends that he dearly missed. So much had changed. Many had died. Dillon lived in twilight. Why was he still alive? Luck? Fate? Love? Destiny? A second chance? His best friend, Troy, would say he still had purpose, a divine mission, something he had been left to do. He never would have expected it to be killing feral vampires. "Sorry, I'm being maudlin, Jambo. I'm feeling good as long as I stay out of the sun. My tan is cosmetic. Well done, Key," he said and kissed Elke on the cheek.

"Aw, you two make a lovely couple," Jane said. Dillon didn't dare meet her gaze for long. He knew he was being rude, having darting eyes, but it was safer at this moment. He would apologize later.

The roadies testing the sound system messed up and set off feedback. The screech and wail caught everyone's attention, bringing frowns, winces, and hands to ears. Dillon shook it off. The blast of noise jarred him and helped him recalibrate so he could center himself. He had a grip, now.

"That might contribute to my future deafness. Hey, the boys are meeting at the marina later tonight. Marader's got some kind of big news. Y'all should come by, unless you're worried about the Oktoberfest Vampire, that is," Jambo said.

A meeting of his friends tweaked Dillon's curiosity. With that change in focus, he was able to function. He also wondered what they recalled about August. "We just might do that. I haven't seen everybody in a while."

"Come find out what kind of whopper Marader has to spin this time," Jambo said.

The lights dimmed. Justen Hobson, hands held high, led the second band on stage to applause and cheering. The McGillises wished Dillon and Elke well and hurried to their table and seats.

Elke kissed Dillon, changing his attention, and guided him to the nearest exit. With another kiss, she shoved him outside. "I have this. I love you, Dillon Urich. Go find a peaceful place to watch the back entrances. There's usually a door open so people can step out for a nicotine fix. If I don't spot our target here, she might show up there with a victim. The buses would afford privacy, too. Now, don't get in a rhubarb without me. Signal me and wait."

Once outside in the night, Dillon could breathe easily and focus. He was going to have to feed the hunger and appease The Bloodlust, but he refused to hunt people. He had been weighing his options. If he did nothing, he would go crazy and tear into people. He didn't want to become a stereotypical bloodsucker.

In his head, he could hear the voice of Master Cosmo telling him that he needed to practice his relaxation exercises. Dillon smiled. He needed to get in touch and in tune with his body, such as it was now transformed. His sensei would say that he was always undergoing growth, that life was change. And yet, it was with the mind that he managed change, using Thought to reach No Thought, the Mind to perfect No Mind. He would need to master being whatever he was becoming. In doing so, second nature became natural.

He had changed. Life was dynamic. Death was transformation. He must change with it, but where did he stand with Life and Death? As he walked around to the back lot, the matter preyed on his mind and vied for attention. He couldn't let it. He must be in the Now because there were newborn and experienced vampires running amok.

Turning the corner, he reached the Down Home VIP lot where two luxury liner buses owned by the performers sat parked with their running lights on. Tendrils of fog wafted through like ghostly claws. The mists seemed to thicken with every step as he skirted the barriers. In the loading dock, he found a concealed spot with a view of the open back door. Two of the three lights flickered as if they were in the throes about to expire. The jerky play of light and dark gave the place an eerie feeling of spastic movement.

The area behind the building had the sense of finality, the ambiance that death had taken a life here more than once. Ghosts seemed to linger on the grounds. Dillon caught a glimpse, a flash of insight of the past: a homeless man getting hit by a truck, a load falling onto a young man, a knifing during an argument, and a euphoric death at the hands of a vampire. He was sure of it, as certain as he was of the history that he had experienced first-hand.

From inside, the country music of Justen Hobson rolled out like a wave of force, especially as the crowd joined in and sang, *Kicked Back, Laid Back, in East Tennessee.* People sought light, company and music, even sharing the blues, to escape the predators in the darkness. Dillon knew that he must ultimately fight through any personal blues to find light in the darkness; otherwise, he would succumb to it. He was a creature of two worlds.

It was normal for new vampires to have anger issues. What a nice euphemism. He must be a writer, he thought bitterly. He worked to control his heart rate. Vampires had superior mastery over their undead bodies, especially their hearts and lungs. Some could significantly change shape. As a neophyte, he was still working on control. Strong passions connected directly to The Bloodlust in all its forms, sex, hunting, hunger, and violence.

It seemed appropriate for him to be at a university hangout. It wasn't on ETSU property but nearby enough to seem like it. As far as he knew, there wasn't a vampire academy despite what the cartoons and movies showed. He must admit that he relished being privately tutored by Elke. With enemies everywhere, he needed to learn as much about being a vampire as soon as possible so he could protect Elke and those he loved. He didn't feel he was learning adroitly enough. He wasn't allowed to keep notes, either. Fortunately, the axioms were easy to remember like bullet points.

> Don't let The Bloodlust you devour.
> To live, shun flowing water and sunlight.
> Embrace the night as darkness is power.
> Never reveal the truth to human sight.

It boiled down to the last. The Rulers of Night were a loose association of vampires that enforced those points and prohibited truthful media, written or otherwise, about them. Newbies like him were to slake their thirst in any way that didn't attract attention.

The biggest danger to the locals came from the vampires of Von Damme's inner circle, three of The Five, named Goran, Destrange, and Butcher. All were dangerously lethal, could survive the sunlight, and were far more adept than Dillon at being supernatural.

Together, Dillon and Elke had already slain a dozen feral vampires created during Von Damme's rise from the depths and return to power. Any one of them might have been the Oktoberfest Vampire. The master vampire and his followers had feasted without care, wanting to turn hungry predators loose on the towns of Appalachia. Dillon thought back as he recalled earlier hunts, where Desiree had acted as bait. She had wandered through the local parks and downtown streets of Bristol, Kingsport, and Johnson City in an attempt to draw out hungry and reckless vampires. Desiree had handled her human attackers with swift, efficient ease and pressed charges so they were incarcerated.

Dillon and Elke had intervened when the supernatural predators appeared. Key cautiously and respectfully carried a sealed, killing blade of quikmar. Of course, the Rulers of Night didn't want anyone to know about the lethal mixture or how quikmar worked. There was a lot that he didn't understand, but he shouldn't be surprised that vampires had crafted a weapon to destroy each other. After all, they had been human once. It wasn't like vampires could carry around sunshine in a bag or drop into a church for a pitcher of holy water.

He pulled up mental images of the life-like sketches that Elke had drawn of the three vampires, both full-bodied and headshots of Goran, Butcher and Destrange. She had written profiles and then burned them after he had memorized them. Going over the details in his memory helped him prepare and push The Bloodlust into the background.

Clad in black, including a wide brimmed hat, Destrange was as pale as an albino with soulless black eyes narrowed in a bitter scowl against the light. The Parisian vampire's skullcap of dark hair descended into sideburns, a pencil thin mustache, and a pointed beard. It accentuated his aquiline nose, sharp chin, and skeletal cheekbones. Destrange was skilled at creating shadow gates and known to use the denizens beyond to do his bidding. If any of them could step out of what appeared to be thin air, it was Destrange, the shadow walker.

For the next forty-five minutes, Dillon remained motionless in a mental lotus position while he scrutinized the shadows and listened to happy feet music. His body wanted to dance, but he remained still even as his soul rejoiced. The music stopped with a long, mournful riff, as if the guitarists were sad to finish the set. Dillon had a sinking feeling, a premonition of something dreadful happening any moment.

"Y'all are in for a real treat, no tricks, with Bethany Moore coming up next. She should've never left the Birthplace of Country Music, but she did, and now she's back!" Justen Hobson announced before he thanked everyone.

Dillon sensed movement nearby. He spotted a large spider crawling down the wall. He didn't detect any heat or heartbeats, just a feeling of something entering into his presence and encroaching upon his personal safe space. A chilling breeze arrived to lash about the alley as if it had been trapped and just escaped to frenetically play. The scent reminded him of his last visit to the Shadowlands.

The flickering lights finally died, going dark, leaving only one. Even so, Dillon caught a glimpse of a figure sliding out of the shadow. In that brief moment, Dillon saw the cruel visage of Destrange. His eyes seemed to peer everywhere at once and his thin mustache twitched as if he could smell Dillon.

Was Destrange alone? Dillon wondered. The Bloodlust wanted to attack the shadow walker, as vampires could feed on and sustain one another. Dillon ignored that want, overwhelming it with a desire to protect Elke.

The shadows shifted restlessly as though they were eager to rush, overwhelm and blot out the light. Dillon eased back into a recessed doorway, taking him out of Destrange's line of sight, and sent the pre-typed text with a press of a button to alert Elke. Just that action caused Destrange to look his way. Dillon didn't dare move again. He already had his hand on a flash grenade, ready to use it to surprise and blind his assailant, but it was smarter to wait for Elke. It was imperative that Dillon remain calm now. He knew he was inexperienced and overmatched.

The shadows rippled like water as Destrange slid closer. A master of shadows would likely pick him out, except Dillon also had cover. Even so, the shadow walker crept nearer, and Dillon prepared to toss the grenade if Destrange took another two steps toward him.

"I know you're here. I can smell your fear, you feral beast. You have no hope," Destrange said, his voice flat, devoid of emotion.

It might have given him away, but Dillon resolved that his fear would neither paralyze nor rule him. Instead of frightening him, he felt an odd kinship with the shadows. Those that were animated emanated a resonance of the Shadowlands and undulated darkly.

"To be honest, the shadows give you away. Even your very own shadow gleefully points you out as an oddity and stranger. He's here. Supper is here, it tells me. From now until Halloween, all of Bristol and the Mountain Empire will know terror in much the same way as you are about to experience it."

Dillon felt movement in the shadows around him. Although he sensed nobody, it seemed as if they were a suffocating mob closing in around him. A rush of unusual anxiety washed over him. What would happen to Elke if Destrange destroyed him? Or Mom and Silke? Dillon's fears tried to hurry him into crazy decisions. He would do what he must, face what he must, to protect those he loved, even if it meant facing down the shadow walker.

"I do so revel in an unhealthy widespread panic, which is something RON frowns upon. The common bloodlusters have no idea how to savor fear. And yours is quite... wan and unsatisfactory," Destrange said. Despite the monster's bold words, his next step was hesitant.

Around Dillon, the shadows flickered with dark energy. It tasted like bitter and acrid blood. The shadows sprouted fangs, claws and elongated tails ending in clubs. He had no idea what Destrange might be capable of pulling off, such as causing his own shadow to assault him. He smiled when he thought he was undefeated at shadow boxing. Bring it on, Dillon thought. Destrange took a step closer. His long-fingered hands moved as a conductor's exhorting a funeral dirge from his orchestra.

Unexpected company and light interrupted everything. Dillon closed his eyes to save his night vision. Light almost as bright as day filled the back lot.

High beams leading the way, a tow truck sped into the lot where it braked abruptly and parked. The driver turned off the engine and all the truck's lights. He stayed inside and waited patiently. Dillon wondered if the driver was a wheelman. Who was making a fast exit? And why in a tow truck with a bumper sticker reading: *My other car is a vampire killing machine.*

The whirlwind briefly returned as Dillon sensed that Destrange was departing. The shadows settled. The malevolent, bitter air faded into that of exhaust, beer, and barbecue.

***

Josh Pokushevski believed that he was lucky, first to be born in Bristol, Tennessee, next to graduate Sullivan East High in nearby Bluff City, then Heaven on earth, the U of Georgia, Go Dawgs! and fourth to have been playing a gig in the Moon Dog Cafe in Abingdon, some fifteen miles northeast of Bristol, Virginia, when a lanky ghost writer had strolled up. The handsome stranger had offered to compose songs for silently sharing fame and fortune. Josh had listened to the tunes and immediately recognized that they were surefire hits. He had been born under a lucky star. He had asked the man his name.

"Justin Hobbes, the Masked Singer," the stranger with the riveting eyes and craggy voice had replied.

"Cool. I like it. Can I use it?" Josh asked and chuckled. Pokushevski sounded like he played Polka music. That wouldn't do. He had been laughing ever since and calling himself Justen Hobson.

It was fabulous to be back near home. He had been on a long, whirlwind road trip opening for Bethany Moore. Yes, they were lucky to be born in the Birthplace of Country Music. He had loved rock, too, and played a hybrid fusion with a touch of blues inspired by his parent's lives.

When he saw the titillating, green-eyed redhead, he knew his lucky streak was truly on a roll. Her hair was the hue of fire and her lips the color of passion. She followed him on his way out back to breathe in some foggy night air where he fired up a cigarette.

"What's your name?" he asked. He offered her a smoke. She shook her head.

"Hope Charity," she said with a laugh.

"No, Faith?" he asked.

"Faith has led me to you," she replied.

He was lost in her eyes and overwhelmed by the scent of her. His body reacted like a dog in heat. She couldn't get close enough, and he was impatient to taste those lips.

Luck be a lady tonight, he thought as they pushed through the back doors. She immediately slid into his arms and kissed him. He almost forgot his name, losing his sense of when and where. Only her kisses mattered as they savored each other.

***

The nearest building exit opened, the door smacking against the wall. Dillon blinked. Light spilled out the back of the Down Home, along with waves of conversations as two people stumbled out into the night. They were laughing and leaning on each other. As the door closed behind them, they started kissing.

"Mmm, baby, just another fifty feet to the bus," the man in the hat murmured.

It only took moments for Dillon to identify the female vampire. The redhead might be in lustful heat, but she gave off virtually no thermal radiation, especially compared to the masked young man who blazed like a bonfire. Dillon recognized Justen Hobson. The vampire drew up his shirt and kissed her way up his belly to his chest, up his neck to his face. She pushed him back against the exit door, pinning Hobson there. Her lips slipped from his to slide down his neck.

Dillon couldn't wait any longer for Elke and prepared to spring.

The driver turned on the tow truck's headlights. The flood of brilliance changed night into day. Even off to the side, Dillon could feel the strength of the illumination. It was far greater than normal lumens, and the power, the radiant flux, felt closer to daylight.

The red-headed vampire screamed as she jerked back away from the young man. He cried out as well, not understanding. He reached for her, and she flailed, backhanding him, and sending him sprawling.

The truck's door opened, and a tall, slender man wearing a hat jumped out. He carried some kind of futuristic-looking gun and turned it on the writhing vampire. Dillon squinted, thinking the weapon might be an automatic paintball gun. He didn't understand until the hat-wearing man opened fire.

Whatever he had loaded into the balls blew holes into the vampire like he was using dumdum bullets. She stumbled and staggered unable to escape the barrage. As he continued unloading the hopper, the shooter stalked closer to his target.

On the breeze, Dillon smelled garlic and the stink of charred flesh. He immediately texted Elke: *Stay inside!! Vh!* He couldn't help but imagine her showing up right now. Surely, she would notice the carnage on the night air. That would warn his beloved. He began to grow sick with worry and once more had to set aside his emotions. If he didn't, he would die.

The vampire hunter continued shooting until he ran out of ammo. The vampire burned like a wicker cabinet, fast and hot. The country singer hopped up, whirled around to run inside, slamming face first into the closed door. He slumped to the ground, stunned.

"I just saved the music lovers another untimely star's death. You aren't twenty-nine, are you? You look younger. Anyway, there's been too much death already this year. You're fortunate Grace guided me here. I'm only guided to places that have become dark, dangerous, and bloodthirsty," the vampire hunter told Justen Hobson.

The singer held his head and moaned. "What's happening to where I grew up? It used to be such a simple, wonderful place," Hobson said.

Dillon thought he smelled Elke's scent. He held down his panic. To make any move now might be the death of him. He would wait to attack the vampire hunter until he noticed Elke. His world would end if she met her final end. He didn't want her to wind up in Oblivion but in a better place. That required time to make up for the sins and errors of the past. He prayed that she was intuitive and sent her strong stay away signals.

The vampire hunter took a moment to look around. His dark eyes narrowed to the size of BBs as he surveyed the back of the building and its lot. His gaze stopped and fixated on where Dillon hid. "Yes, something wicked this way comes. I can feel it."

Dillon didn't want the vampire hunter to sense his dread, so he slowed his heart's beating to a virtual stop as he let his fear wash over him and away like a tide. The only thing to fear was his own fear killing him. Fear slew the rational mind and gave rise to the irrational. Courage was pushing past fear. He remained motionless, emotionless, and held his breath and heartbeat, such was the power of vampires. If anything, the vampire hunter would sense Dillon's agreement with what he had just seen. In an odd way, they were kin, as both were slaying evil vampires. Oh yeah, Dillon was one of the good guys, and he planned to stay that way, Lord willing and the creeks don't rise. Oh yes, he had more than one to worry about. He envied those with only a single possible source of flooding.

"Hmm. I guess that evil came and went. That's a fresh but not lingering scent. Grace willing, I'll come across it again before it's too late. I can feel the clock ticking. See a doctor, Mr. Hobson. Farewell, and *Don't Take No Wooden Nickels*," the driver said with a chuckle. That was one of Hobson's hit songs. He finally shrugged, gave a grunt of satisfaction and tossed a handful of jellybeans into his mouth before climbing back inside his tow truck. He backed the wrecker out of the alleyway and drove off.

Dillon felt like he could breathe again, even if he didn't need to, but it relaxed him. He texted his beloved: Vh gone. Slew feral vamp then drove off. Dillon wondered if that was the end of the Oktoberfest Vampire.

Justen Hobson moaned. Dillon checked on him, touching his shoulder. "Are you okay, Justen?"

He groaned. "I think, so. She was gorgeous, irresistible. She reminded me of . . . Wait, you're not with The Paparazzi, are you?" he asked.

"No. I'm a music lover. I'm a fan of: *If I'm Lyin', I'm Dyin'* and *Finer Than a Frog's Hair Split Four Ways*," Dillon replied.

"That's kind of you to say. I hope you're not one of those over-zealous fans."

"I can leave you to pick yourself up, if you'd like."

"Did you see her?" he asked.

"Yep. Never grope a groupie. She might be a bloodsucker. It's a Me Too Movement kind of song," Dillon suggested. He had resisted referring to the redhead as a hot date or a beauty to die for.

"Yeah? Yeah. Yeah! Never grope a groupie, 'cause you never know if she's a vampire."

"Sounds like a hit, especially around Halloween."

"I'll work on it. Did she really burst afire? I mean, I felt the heat," Justen said. He had lost his left eyebrow, and his hair was charred, melted and matted in spots.

Dillon shrugged. He actually knew the creative writing force behind Justen Hobson. The vampire Justin Hobbes was staying at Swearington Lodge as a guest of Elke's.

"Do you think that's what happen to Elvis?"

"Why?"

"He sang about a hunk of burning love," the singer said.

Dillon almost laughed despite the moment. "You sound concussed."

"My head does hurt. I better write down the lyrics for this chart topper before I forget. Most of the great songs come from the heart, you know, based on one's rough and tumble life experiences."

"And near-death experiences. Nice meeting you, Mr. Hobson," Dillon said. He smiled as he opened the door for the dazed singer.

"Never grope a groupie, 'cause you never know if she's a vampire. One too many heated kisses, and soon your fate is dire, your life of joy and bliss, all too soon it will expire! Or should it be, you'll burst afire from the bonfire of desire? Never grope a groupie," Hobson sang his way down the hall.

"Hey, Justen Hobson! I'm Cane Concannon, reporter. You gotta minute?" Concannon asked.

Dillon immediately shut the door and sighed. Mere moments later, he sensed his beloved. She dashed into his arms, and they kissed, repeatedly, sensing how close the final end had been for him. "I was worried I was about to lose you," Elke said.

"I was worried I was going to lose you. I'm so delighted you waited," he said and kissed her again, drawing her into the shadows. It felt safer than being in the light. "I met the human Justen Hobson, saw the shadow walker, Destrange, and hid from him and a vampire hunter," Dillon told her.

She tightly hugged him. "I was as nervous as a long-tailed cat in a room full of rockers, my love. You are both wise and doubly fortunate."

"Yes, I have you," he said.

"It is wonderful that we have each other because our world has just grown far more dangerous. We need all the help that we can get."

"Let's get out of here. I saw Cane Concannon cornering Hobson," Dillon said. Neither of them wanted to get entangled with a crackpot who believed that vampires and werewolves were real.

At Elke's car, a 1958 convertible Corvette, a raven dropped out of the sky to land on the top frame of the windshield. It flapped its wings to settle, and then it stared at them with mismatched eyes. Its right one was green while the left was purple.

"So far so good," Dillon said. It hadn't pooped on the car or turned into a monster to attack them. Shapechangers could be friends or foes. This raven had no living aura, so it was more than a bird. Many vampires could change their appearance. Less could alter their body into that of an animal, what the First Americans called Skinwalking.

"With those eyes, it must be One Feather Many Colors, or as I call her, Carolyn Cherokee," Elke said.

The raven swallowed, cleared its throat with a clucking and then said, "Attend me, Elsa Swearington. I am the voice of Judge Executor Vlade Dragomir. You have been summoned to the top of

The Bristol Hotel. Bring Dillon Urich. I will listen and then pass judgment on the wordsmith. Be there before sunrise or suffer the consequences," One Feather said.

Elke blanched for a moment. "I hear and will abide by your requests," she replied.

"Nice car, Elsa. Stay well. See you later. Don't be late!" the raven said before it launched airborne. It flew off to return to its master. Elke hadn't time to correct the bird on her changed name.

"Judge Dragomir? It all sounds serious," Dillon said.

"It is. He's an executor. He oversees issues concerning the Rulers of Night, including Von Damme's entrapment. The Rulers of Night judge all graylings," she said sounding worried. Only Von Damme had elicited this type of negative response. "I love you, and as your mentor, what happens to you during your grayling time happens to me. Our fates are intertwined. That's the way it is. If they judge you lacking and kill you, they will also physically destroy me."

Dillon was shocked. He was a danger to his love. He hugged her. "No pressure to make a good first impression. I'm somewhat relieved that you said executor and not the executioner. I'll be on my best behavior. Or should we run?"

"No. They would find us. Besides, we have loved ones to protect. The Oktoberfest Vampire might still be running amok, and he isn't the only problem," Elke said.

They had to worry about the ferals, Von Damme's cronies, keeping his friends and family safe, and now judgment by the Rulers of Night who already didn't like writers and journalists.

"It's time to go to Abingdon. You must sustain yourself before we face Judge Dragomir. He will test you, and you must be at full strength," Elke said.

Dillon had dreaded this coming moment. Elke's love and blood, plus vulture bee honey, had been enough to sustain him up to this point, but now he needed more. The Bloodlust, his body, and his sanity craved fresh blood. For him to live and continue this super-natural journey, someone was going to die.

Two

Deadly Catch

Rixs one-hand steered his john boat through the night and patches of dense fog spread across South Holston Lake – shortened to SoHo by longtime residents. Earlier, around sunset, they had launched ole' Johnny at the nearby Lakeview Marina ramp. Rixs kissed his crucifix then tucked it back under his flannel shirt while he motored toward haunted Cemetery Ridge.

A spine-chilling breeze slipped under his jacket and hat. He rubbed his neck and found a spider. He squished it between his fingers and shook off the shivers. Now he kept wondering if there were more spiders. He checked for those and ants. He didn't find any, but he still felt crawling on his skin.

He sighed. He wanted to haul in more than catfish, more than trout or bass, as he was seeking fortune and treasure where he heard others had found it. He didn't believe the story of curses. He had been hearing stories about the Dark Lady for decades and never seen her. Maybe that reporter who was investigating what happened in August was scaring her away. Rixs had seen Dillon

Urich fight long before he'd gone soft and gotten sick. Now he had to fight with words, Rixs mused. Life could suck.

Rixs Frederick certainly needed a change of luck. He hadn't caught anything his last two times out, leaving him hungry with gas but no gasoline, and his unpaid bills were piling up. He glanced at Mac, head on his chest, and toasted his buddy with a sip of Rickey's Private Reserve Whiskey. Rixs knew his boating partner didn't like to fish atop the ridge, especially in the dark, but Mac was sawing wood. It sounded like the boat had two motors, at least one running smoothly, Rixs joked to himself. What the man from Beidlemans Mill didn't know wouldn't hurt him, would it? Rixs was concerned, though, that Mac's snoring might scare the fish away. They didn't like loud noises, either.

Born and raised near here in Paperville, Rixs knew the 7600 acres of reservoir like the back of his scarred hands. He knew it better than nearby Bristol, that's for sure. He could find his way to antique shops when he made a find. He had fished all the coves and their nooks, creeks, and crannies, as the land changed with the seasons, the rains, and the rise and fall of the water level. Before becoming a guide, he had worked for Sneed Welding but an accident had dimmed his vision, and it wasn't safe for him to handle a blow torch. A fishing pole was more his speed. He could only do limited damage with a fish hook.

West of the bridge and east of the dam, the Cemetery Ridge portion of the lake was a great area to catch trout, sunfish, and bass. Plenty of places to hide, Rixs figured, which is why the Bassmaster had been fishing there when he had been murdered a couple of months ago. At that time, with the drought and historically low water, the Fishing League professional had parked on the tip of the exposed ridge. Supposedly, there had been open graves. Some claimed zombies killed him, although they had left his brain. Leveler heads gave the nod to cult members of a group called either The Six

Fingered or The Appalachia Vampires, take your pick. A pickled brain doesn't know what to call itself. This area had long been a home and hiding place to a lot of supernatural things.

He had seen a few during his nearly forty years, including Big Foot, a three-legged werewolf, and too many ghosts to shake a stick at. To him, they were no more legends than the six and a half-foot catfish that he and Mac had reeled in. It had taken them for a long ride before Mac had gigged it.

Rixs took a sip of whiskey. It was always the things that you loved that killed you, Rixs thought. He mentally listed them: boating, fishing, women, Krispy Kreme donuts, and too much home-brew. The last was an oxymoron if he'd ever heard one. There was no such thing as too much homebrew.

The Bassmaster had been the first of many funerals. The black day occurred late in the summer. The weather had certainly changed from those hot, dry days when a massive wildfire had rampaged through the woods to the south in the Cherokee National Forest. It had rained a month of Sundays since then and drowned out the hardiest of embers.

Despite the higher water level, most folk refused to fish the graveyard. There were spooky tales of hearing snatches of country music, the spinning of a reel, the plop of a lure hitting the water, or even the Bassmaster's whop 'n holler when he hooked a big'n. More than a few had claimed to spot a ghost boat in the fog. Rixs had heard train whistles, blowing from the past when there had been the small towns of Big Creek, Friendship, Wreythville, and Jacobs Creek lining the Holston Valley in the decades before the dam. His great-grandfather had worked at the short-lived Summer Creek Resort. Lord Almighty, the stories he used to tell Dad who passed them onto son. Rixs poured a drop of whiskey over the gunwale in honor and remembrance of Buzz.

So far, Rixs hadn't seen Buzz's ghost, nor, thank God, that damned screaming-monkey poltergeist. He checked the fishfinder, looking at the bottom terrain on the screen's sonar device. He thought that might be the ruins of the mansion with the tall thin spike being the chimney. For so long he had thought it was a dead tree. Based on the clusters of objects, supposed to be fish, he decided to fish deeper than usual. He steered and worked around the snoring Mac to adjust the lines, letting them trail closer to the bottom. There was treasure in them thar ruins!

Soon, a couple of sips worth of patience, a heavy tug gave him the hope that he'd snagged a whopper. Even a blind hog found an acorn now and then, he mused. Two of the lines stretched taut. Bonus! Rixs wondered and rejoiced before cautioning himself. Better not to count the fish before he had netted them. Still, he looked forward to telling that to John Hogan and Chance Oliver. They were always bragging and showing off their catches. It seemed they caught a hell of a lot more fish than he did. That stuck in his craw. They and Tommy from Maraders Marina were pulling in more than their share.

Well, boy howdy, maybe it was finally good ole Rixs' time. He slowed the boat, put on his gloves and reeled in one line. It bent with his catch. Green, fuzzy and spiky, it looked like the severed arm of one of those living trees that he'd seen in The Lord of the Rings movies. Crap, he thought, so much for a big catch. Something dark was draped across the driftwood like a trash bag or a towel, but he had wasted enough time on it when there might be a fish on the other line. Hoping it wasn't another branch from one of the trees on the lake bottom, he wrestled with the pole as he cranked on the reel.

He realized that his efforts had awakened Mac who had stopped snoring and asked, "Hey, what ya got there? Did ya catch somethin'?"

"I don't know. Another branch, maybe. Ha! Let's hope it's not a tire," Rixs said. He kept reeling while the boat puttered on. Unlike the last, this catch didn't seem like dead weight. He felt a beast of a fish swim under the boat. He maneuvered the line around the stern and the motor to the port side. He let it play for a while before he would reel it in a couple of turns before allowing the fish to pull away, again, hoping it would tire itself out.

Mac reached out with the net, ready to haul in the fish. "Hey, it's a big one."

Rixs finally reeled the fish to the surface. Out of the corner of his eye, he glimpsed movement in the boat. He chuckled at himself, startled by his buddy's shadow.

"I may need a bigger net," Mac laughed. He scooped down into the water to lift up a gorgeous small-mouthed bass trapped in the net. The catch looked to be twelve or more pounds. "Snap a photo!"

Rixs leaned over to reach for his phone. Suddenly, the boat shifted, rocking wildly. He dropped the pole and fell to all fours even as he heard Mac scream. It was swallowed by a splash.

Once he regained his balance, Rixs crawled to the gunwhale. "Mac! Hey, old buddy, old pal! Are you okay?" Rixs yelled. He expected to see Mac, but there was no sign of him among the chop. The air smelled oddly, as if he had been dumping chum. He searched for bubbles but saw only dark, oily splatters on the surface. His gloves felt cold and wet, and he noticed the dark stain spreading through the leather and turning it black. Was that blood?

"Mac?!" Rixs called. He didn't know where to start.

The water swirled. He thought he saw movement underneath. He prepared to jump into the lake to save his buddy.

The fear slithered up his ankle and along his legs. A cold lump dropped into the pit of his stomach, the pain spreading up and down his back. The spasms spread through his body and seized his lungs so he couldn't breathe. A black curtain fell over his eyes, and he lost his balance to tumble into darkness.

*****

Nearby on the lake, Charlie Clarke was sprawled out reading a book, enjoying being away from it all and retired on his houseboat at Painters Creek Marina. He was lost in the story when he heard a thump, startling him. Miss Lucy barked in his ear and briefly deafened him. Charlie dropped the book and almost knocked over his hot chocolate. He glared at the too cute Yorkie. "Was that really necessary, Miss Lucy?"

His lap dog didn't look regretful in the least. She cocked an ear and wagged her stubby tail.

"I heard it and felt it, too, and I didn't jump up shouting and dump you on the floor, did I?" he asked. Miss Lucy barked, again. Out of the corner of his eye, Charlie thought he caught movement on the deck. Was something on the boat? He chided himself, currently reading a scary book taking place on this very lake, SoHo. He had never been a reader before he married his beloved, Estelle, God rest her soul. He kissed his wedding ring. She had loved this houseboat, too. He could imagine her spirit fishing off the back. There were photos of her all over, including them getting married at Steele Creek Park.

A second thump caused Miss Lucy to burst into rapid-fire barking, and the houseboat to shudder, making Charlie think something had bumped into the hull. He grabbed his shotgun and a flashlight. Sure, he was overreacting. It had nothing to do with the book he was reading or the Oktoberfest Vampire, he assured himself. Desperate and addicted people could act as monsters, too, and a shotgun could deter them. If not, the silver shot would.

He just needed to ensure he didn't kneejerk react and blow away one of his old friends from Eastman Kodak trying to scare him for Halloween. One year they had put a life-sized cutout of a snarling bear on his deck. He had been fit to be tied. Come to think of it, he had threatened to shoot his fellow retirees if they did it again. He turned on the exterior light, and it died with a flare of light.

Darkness returned. He muttered an oath. "Let's go take a look."

When Charlie pushed open the door, letting in chilly, damp night air, he thought he saw a shadow jump to a stop. He whirled to train his gun on where its owner should be and found nothing. His heart hammered. Nothing like scaring yourself to death, he groused.

He didn't really see anything, no surprise, and continued outside onto the back deck. The folded chairs hadn't moved. Miss Lucy didn't bark at shadows. Noises were a different matter, and once she got worked up, she would grumble, woof, chuff, and yip until her motor cooled down. He turned his flashlight beam on the stern and found the culprit, a floater. "Look, Lucy, a dangerous piece of driftwood." It bobbed and repeatedly nudged the hull and motor. That wouldn't do.

Miss Lucy sniffed the large, sodden branch, and found it of no interest. Charlie didn't want the hunk of wood to damage his houseboat, or anyone else's, so he set down his shotgun, pulled on gloves, and opened the back gate. The driftwood rolled, spooking Miss Lucy who leapt back to unleash scathing barks.

After visually inspecting the log for hooks, Charlie grabbed the length of branch. Something touched his neck, and he let go, swiping at it and knocking away the moth. The small log splashed back into the water, sending his houseboat rocking. He kept his feet unsteadily, lucky to not fall on his butt. The ripple in the big pond caused nearby boats to rock and roll. Miss Lucy gave him admonishing looks.

"Feel free to help. I could hook up a line to your collar, and you could haul it out," he suggested.

She retorted with a snarky bark and retreated into the doorway. Princesses were not work animals and certainly not beasts of burden. What might be next? A plow?

The second time, Charlie had a better grip and dragged the driftwood aboard. For whatever reason, he mused fondly on the weekends of the Downriver Raft Race sponsored by WQUT. Ah, the good old days before arthritis. With his shoulders the way they were now, he couldn't row to save his life. He closed the gate and returned to the cabin and his book. He hoped this guy wrote a sequel someday. It had been long enough. He might die first. Life was fragile. Once Charlie sat down, Miss Lucy settled in his lap, and offered a few loving licks before she napped, letting him read. The hero and his buddies were trapped on a burning marina and surrounded by hungry wolves. Somebody was going to die.

A hollow whump caught his attention, pulling him from his story. Miss Lucy sprang apaw and hopped to the floor where she barked at the door and beyond. A chilly breeze crept around it. This time, Charlie grabbed a jacket and a shotgun. Out of habit, he flipped on the exterior light, and then he recalled it was burnt out. Getting old messed with your mind.

Miss Lucy dashed outside into the darkness where she found and berated an orange bucket bobbing against the hull. Charlie snagged the handle, emptied it, and examined it. Since it didn't seem to leak, he used a bungee cord to lash it to the rails of the porch. The wind had shifted. No telling what might float in next.

Sometime later, Charlie heard a thud that awakened him and felt the houseboat dip as if someone had stepped aboard. Again, no movement or noise escaped Miss Lucy's sharp hearing. Her barks probably had the same response on an inanimate object as before, but he readied his shotgun anyway. He opened the door, the breeze biting at him, and searched with a flashlight, discovering an old john boat sporting fishing poles pressed against the stern. He heard flopping inside and turned his light on it. Each bark causing her to back up, Miss Lucy doggie-lambasted the floundering bass. Or was it something more? Charlie smelled it now, an unpleasant mix of the stink of warm motor and the reek of blood. One side of the boat was a splattered mess of gore. Were those fingers he saw atop a bottle of whiskey?

He breathed a sigh of relief. Nope. It was just spilled worms sitting atop a pint of Rickey's Private Reserve.

Only months had passed since the Bassmaster had been murdered. It had never been solved. Most people thought it was connected to the terrorists. Had he discovered something? Or been at the wrong place at the wrong time? Had the same happened here?

It was obvious that boat had been occupied. A cooler and a hunk of driftwood sat in the bottom. It had a bolt stuck in it. Miss Lucy growled fiercely, a full body rumble and fearful shout.

"It's okay. It's not us," he told her. She growled her way backwards into the houseboat's cabin.

"You're right," Charlie replied. This was a job for the sheriff's department. Charlie drew his phone from his pocket. Suddenly, he felt someone behind him. As he turned, he heard a thump. The boat rocked.

His flashlight failed. The lights inside had died, too. Darkness descended like a freefalling theater curtain. His dog let out a yelp that was cut short.

"Lucy?" he called. The abrupt blackout surprised Charlie. Night-blind, he was confused. He lost his balance, stumbled and fell. He reached out, fearing he might tumble over the side and into the lake. Cold seized him, paralyzing so he couldn't draw a breath as something dragged him down. He tried to scream, but it died on his lips.

Three

========

Floaters

On her evening drive home to her houseboat, Deputy Marge Cantrell sang, and Boomer howled until they saw the emergency lights flashing off the fog and the leafy trees. They had just passed the turnoff to Laurel Marina and neared the American Legion Memorial truss bridge on Tennessee Highway 421. The brown-goggled German shepherd had been trained in scenarios using such lights, and he knew that it was time to go to work.

"Well, what do we have here, Boom? A vehicular accident or a jumper?" Marge wondered. Less fools jumped into the SoHo from the 2014-built bridge since it had replaced the old, closer-to-the-water 1935 original. Raising it had cut down on the number of drowning victims and floating bodies, what they simply called floaters.

Even off duty, sometimes work found you. She always thought it meant that she was supposed to be there, and if that was true, her presence would make a difference. She could be the solution, or it could be that simply one more willing person could tip the scales. As a Sullivan County deputy, Marge was always there for the community. These were her people. She also knew strange happenings and the worst things humans could do often occurred after dark. With Halloween near, an extra dash of macabre was added to human perversity and mental instability. Being on the fog-shrouded roads of Appalachia was one way to encounter backwoods oddities.

Flares lit the way to the truss bridge. It was partly open with single lane traffic controlled by deputies with illuminated batons. Sullivan County sheriff's cruisers, ambulances and other official vehicles were parked in a gravel pull off on the south side of the asphalt. She figured she would know just about everyone here. It would be folks from Sullivan County, Tennessee Wildlife Resources agents and TVA deputies. The Adventure Diving's van was parked next to the county ambulance. That meant it was likely a drowning victim, and Alan Linkous was on the job. For several decades, he had worked Search and Rescue, as well as recovery missions on South Holston and other nearby lakes.

Deputy Burleson recognized her and deployed his flashlight to usher her into a parking spot among the official vehicles. Ron Burleson was a broad-shouldered, square-chinned guy who had once played linebacker for Tennessee High and served as a military police officer in the armed forces. His nose had been broken, but his smile remained unchanged, wide and friendly. He hated to be teased about his dimples, so she didn't. There was no reason to turn friends into enemies. A woman working in law enforcement needed any and all the support she could get.

Those that she worked with fell into five categories: beyond duty helpful Godsends, solid job doing Pluggers, the Unhelpful, the Incompetent, and Pains in the Backside, PIBs, or PINS, Pains in the Neck. The last was usually reserved for administration. The sheriff's department was a political animal, too, since sheriffs were voted in.

Ron Burleson was a Godsend, a people first, safety first, public servant and all-around good guy who had backed her up more times than she could count, and yes, she could count very high without a calculator. She had been a sergeant and detective before leaving the town for county patrol and the country life.

She climbed out of the cruiser without her utility belt and vest since she wasn't on duty. Batman's belt weighed a little over twenty-five pounds with handcuffs, a camera, pepper spray, baton, taser, radio and cellphone. She pondered donning her gear. This was a simple rescue or recovery. And yet, her sister had died in such a place several miles from here. That reminder changed her mind, and she dressed for work, adding her vest and utility belt to her holstered, department-issued Smith and Wesson. Boomer waited patiently and then bounded out behind her. He stopped and studied the people in uniform.

"Good to see you, Marge. I heard you were on vacation, running around with your new partner," Ron said.

"We decided for a change of venue. Boomer needed some new trees to mark his territory, you know how males are," Marge replied.

"Yes, I do. By the way, I used a pocketknife to carve blazons," Ron replied.

"That's why you're special and an Eagle Scout. How's the family?"

"They are doing great. The kids actually enjoy school, and they're buzzing with excitement about Halloween."

"That's wonderful to hear. I hope neither of them wants to dress like a vampire. How's the hunt for sprinkler heads coming along?" she asked. He had been going on about their home having irrigation issues.

He laughed. "I found three more. That makes fifty-seven. The prior owners thought that there might be sixty or so. I wish they'd made a diagram. I don't understand how people can just wing it," he bemoaned. Along with being a MP, Ron had been a strategic planner in his previous life in the military.

"I have days where I resemble that remark. I go where God's guidance and my angels take me. Meet Boom. Boomer, this is Ron. He's aces. I'll let you decide on the other guy," she told Boomer.

He whoofed softly in reply. Ron gave her a skeptical look. Boomer sniffed his hand and then panted and smiled.

"He's just sniffing for drugs. Aces means you're one of the good guys," Marge teased.

Boomer made a quizzical noise toward Warden Boatwright. Like father, the son worked for the Tennessee Department of Wildlife. He looked like a chip off the old block. She had met his papa one day after a bear had wrecked their camp."

"Warden Boatright. You're so stealthy and one with your element that I thought you were a tree," Marge joked.

"Heya, Marge. Good to see you back in action. We had another jump'ah this afternoon. The div'ahs finally found 'em all tangled up in fishin' line caught on an old wooden train trestle. Either Dan or Alan will be bringin' 'em to shore. Cole Dare was sixteen," the warden said. His Appa-latch-shun accent was more pronounced than any of the others present. It was a unique dialect that she could slip into when she needed to sound homey, or she was surrounded by people speaking Appalachian.

"It's already all over the news," Ron said. He knew that she avoided the news and didn't own a scanner because he was much the same. "I was hoping for some good news to edge out the Okto-berfest Vampire blitz, not something like this."

She had learned from eight years as a member of the Bristol, Tennessee PD and two as a county deputy sheriff that bad news traveled fast. Someone was always eager to share news of a disaster or tragedy. She wondered if it was their way of seeming pertinent or feeling alive. If you had survived enough of either, you dreaded the news, wanting to bury it instead of sharing it. The train trestle would have been used to cross the south fork of the Holston River before they dammed and let water fill the valley. "And he jumped on a dare?" Marge asked. People in emergencies needed some dark humor to lighten the load. It was dad humor with a cop or EMT twist.

Boatwright nodded. "I see whatcher sayin'. Some people are too damn literal," he said.

"That's an interesting statement coming from a man named Boatwright who works around water and watercraft, despite living inland," Marge said.

"She was a detective before she came to work with us," Ron reminded the game warden.

"What can't be cured gotta be endured," the warden said, poking back. "Can that dog hunt?"

"Oh yes, this is Boomer. He has an expert nose for finding drugs, firearms, and fugitives," she replied.

"If he can fetch fowl outta water, he's my kind of hound," Warden Boatwright replied.

"Hey, look who's here, Deputy Marge! I see you finally got a partner who will work with you. Are you here to take charge, Cantrell?" Hardaway asked. Some called him Hardass, and he liked it. God, the High Sheriff, and Hardaway knew best. He had worked in Philly, so he considered himself better trained and top shelf, at least a tier above most of them, supposedly two above Marge 'In Charge' Cantrell. He had given her the moniker, claiming she was always trying to take over the scene of an incident.

"Not if you're almost done here, Hardy. I'm off duty, and I don't want to take the blame when you can get the credit," she replied. It took the deputy a moment to figure out what she meant. Gary Hardaway wasn't a deputy because of his sharp wit or keen, insightful mind. Nepotism could be found anywhere, just like incompetents and Pains in the Backside, regardless of the company, business, or event. God put them on earth to test people's patience, see if it was up to snuff, and to show that there were consequences to decisions made in life. Some also needed help. It was another reason people were put here: to help each other.

Marge tried to focus on the good people. She recognized one of the paramedics. "Genny, is that you, girl?"

The pretty lady in the blue scrubs turned with a generous smile. Her dark eyes glittered in the night adding to the sense that she enjoyed seeing and helping people. "Marge Cantrell, how are you doing, sister with a badge? It's been a coon's age since I've seen you," Genevieve Lionel asked. She had been Marsha's partner. Genny had been knocked unconscious during the fatal attack and didn't remember it. Marge had thought about becoming a nurse, but she had decided on trying to prevent harm instead of helping to heal it.

"I'm hanging in there. I just got back in town. Meet Boomer. Boom this is Genny. She's aces."

Genny rubbed and stroked on the German shepherd whose eyes lolled. "You are a very handsome dog and well-behaved. Marge is a good person. You're a lucky dog, Goggle-eyes. She should bring you over to meet my dog, Thunder. Boomer and Thunder, they sound like they belong together," she said and laughed with Marge. "And you, lady, can stop by any time to pick up some of my delicious homemade fudge," she said.

"I might do that next time I'm in Bluff City. Or you could come out to the farm. The dogs can run there. You know Mamaw and Gramps love dogs, and they are currently without canines," Marge said.

"Have you seen Angie since you've been back?" Genny asked.

"No. I stopped here before I made it home."

"While you were off training, another one of her partner's died. Slipped in the shower, hit his head, and never woke up," Genny said.

"That's a horrible tragedy. Next time I see her, I'll give her a hug," Marge replied. From what she remembered, that made three deaths, but none of them on the job. There had already been rumblings that riding with Angie Severett was a death sentence. That was ridiculous since she wasn't even around when the accidents occurred. Her first partner had choked to death on an orange during his morning commute. The second paramedic had tripped over his dog and fallen down a set of stairs, ending with a broken neck and death.

"Hey, I offered to work with her. We've both lost partners recently, so I thought perhaps two negatives might make a positive. The boss is thinking it over," Genny said with a sadder smile.

"You ladies are both positives. Don't let anyone tell you otherwise. If it didn't take so long, I'd train and come work with y'all," Marge said.

"Aw, you are so sweet under that hard shell, my friend. Thank you, but you're too good at what you do. Plus, you like to share your common sense and see it done," Genny said.

"You think I like telling people what to do?"

"I've never heard of a shrinking violet being called Marge In Charge. In my job, you can only give advice. If they're stupid, you can haul them off to jail," Genny replied, and they chuckled.

"I wish. I can only take them in if they're breaking the law. Smart or stupid doesn't matter. Sometimes I sit back and sigh and cry like you do," Marge replied.

"Hey, Gen! They're floating the body to the surface. We should get down there," her partner said. He was a big, young man with long arms and bandy legs.

"This is Angus. He's from Florida. He used to wrassle gators," Genny said.

"Hello, Deputy Cantrell. It's true, but what she means is that I played defense for the University of Florida Gators. For some reason, she holds that against me."

"They keep beating Tennessee," Genny replied with a shrug.

"Welcome. So, you're a Florida Man?" Marge said.

"Oh, please. Not you, too. I thought I left the state to escape that. People are bizarre down there, but I've come to see that they're just as strange here," Angus said.

Marge laughed. "What convinced you? The ghost hunters? The motorcycle gangs? The witches and their covens? The KKK? The Saviors of the US paramilitary groups? Or the Satanic Cults?" Marge asked.

"Hey, at least there's no alligator worship. And snakes, I am not a fan of snakes, and Florida has a lot of them," Angus replied.

"That makes two of us, and just so you know, there are snakes in this lake," Marge replied.

"Then I'm so happy that I'm not a rescue diver. I could never do what Alan Linkous and his buddies do," Angus said. Marge couldn't agree more. Bodies began to get soft when they spent a long time submerged in water.

From what they could overhear, the diver and the body were about to be pulled via lifeline ashore by the land crew. She didn't think the current would be bad right now due to the weeklong dry spell, but that was easy for her to say. There were many superstitions about a strange undercurrent due to a rerouting of the river's flow when the South Holston Dam was built on the south fork of the Holston River to prevent flooding.

She and the county paramedics descended the hill on the southwest side of the bridge toward shore and the rescue workers. She recognized several of the volunteers but didn't distract them. Ron's father, Roy, was among the group. He was a retired dog trainer who helped run a local shelter, and he glanced their way and smiled at Boomer. He stayed at her side. She brought him along because he needed to get his first taste and smells of the lake. God only knew what Boom might be chasing through the woods in the coming days.

The fog thickened as they neared the water. The mists coiled like snakes arising from the lake to slither into the sky and vanish. She was only a little bit bothered by snakes, and woe be unto anyone who teased her about it. They could kiss her grits.

"Concannon should be out here covering this. He would see that we're not scared," Genny said.

"Who is scared?" Marge asked.

"The people of the Tri-Cities, according to Cane Concannon. That's right, you've been out of pocket. He posted a chart so everyone can pick which phobia suits them. With Angus, it caused him to move away from Florida for which we are thankful," Genny said.

At Roy's instructions, the Search and Rescue workers gathered at the shore. Together, the shore crew of eight pulled on the line that swiftly hauled a diver and the drowning victim toward shore, creating a white furrow on the surface of the dark lake. It was freezing deeper down, so if Cole Dare had drowned, there was still hope. He didn't need to be body-bagged yet. Sometimes dead wasn't brain dead if the body had been kept cold.

Marge stayed back while the paramedics hurried forward. Boomer stiffened and growled deep in his throat. Marge glanced at him and then back to the water. She thought she saw something moving toward the diver, the lake churning. Boomer tensed as if he gathered to charge. She patted him to calm him. "Root," she said, telling him to stay. His butt hit the sand, but he looked at her and whined.

His white hair and mustache bright in the night, Alan Linkous stood waist deep in water while he watched Search and Rescue pull Dan to shore. The diver and drowning victim began thrashing and flailing. They appeared to be fighting something, but she wasn't sure. The two were dragged under and disappeared.

"Oh, God, no! Pull Dan in faster now!" Alan Linkous yelled.

Those hauling on the line turned, and in concert, they ran uphill. It was like in the olden days, when sailors pulled in the ropes to rescue those lost overboard and bring them topside to safety. They dragged Dan and something snarling composed of wetly matted fur, snapping teeth, and slashing claws through shallow water and onto shore. A shaggy whirlwind of sharp death, the beast attacked rescuers who were trying to help, then it found its footing and fled.

Marge drew her departmental firearm and repeatedly shot at the blur of a hairy beast while it dashed through the darkness and across the shore to leap into the woods, gone in a blink. It left men and women bleeding, and Boomer chomping at the invisible bit. The German shepherd wanted to give chase, barking and whining at Marge. Everyone else was in shock. Marge swore that she had hit her target at least once with gunfire.

"Follow," she gave the command to hunt and turned Boomer loose. Like greased black lightning, Boomer bolted in pursuit, the chase on into the woods. What she didn't want was for him to fetch. She wanted to know where it went, not have him bring it back.

"Oh, God, just like Marsha!" Genny said and fainted. Angus caught her and lowered her to the gravel.

"What did you say?" Marge asked. She wasn't going to get an answer. What did she mean just like Marsha? The comment sent the wheels in her mind spinning. Get a grip, she told herself. People were dying here. Don't think about the past. Be here now. Her training kicked in, and she assessed the scene.

Several of the Search and Rescue water crew were seriously wounded. A young man named Clayton looked gutted. He held his guts inside with both hands. Dan bled out the rips and tears in his dry suit. It looked like he had been wrestling with a wildcat or a slasher on espressos and greenies. This was all way beyond her meager first aid skills. Roy who had been injured was trying to help others even as he required bandages. Ron needed to know.

"Angus, they need your help. I'll see to Genny," Marge said.

"She's okay. She didn't swallow her tongue," Angus said. He laid Genny's head to rest then rushed over to aid the wounded. "Don't go. I need your hands," he replied when Marge looked off to where she could hear her dog's booming woofs and howls. Boomer sounded like he was still in pursuit.

Deputies Ron and Hardy rushed downhill to aid them. "What's all the shooting and screaming about. Oh, shit. Dad!" Ron exclaimed.

"How the hell did this happen?" Hardy asked.

"I'm not sure. Lend your hands and do whatever Angus tells us to," Marge replied.

Somehow, the slasher had cut every one of his rescuers, almost eviscerating two, in the seconds before fleeing. With nine injured, it was a mass casualty incident, and Angus instructed them as such. Nobody could walk on their own. Alan Linkous joined them, using his emergency training to help his wounded diving partner.

"It was a boy! I swear! I found a boy then. . . " Dan repeated until he lapsed unconscious.

Marge didn't know what that meant. She worried that Dan, Clayton, and Roy were too badly wounded to survive even with expert hands and equipment on scene. She was also concerned about Boomer, but he would have to be a smart dog and take care of himself. Marge's hands were needed to help staunch bleeding until Genny awakened and pitched in.

"Are you alright?" Marge asked her.

Genny blinked a couple of time, but then she nodded with grim determination. "I can function. Lord Almighty, I don't know how, but Dan looks like Marsha did," Genny said. That was it, and she went to work, making sure nobody bled to death, and they were successful. They kept guts, organs, and sinews from escaping bodies through gaping wounds.

About the time that Marge was tempted to go after Boomer, her dog trotted back to her. She checked him for injuries and found him soaking wet. "You've gone for a swim. Did whatever you were chasing outswim you?" she asked her partner.

Boomer whined. He looked ashamed to have disappointed her.

Marge looked around at all the bandaged and seriously wounded. "That's okay. It's probably just as well that you didn't catch whatever it was. It's fast, mean and deadly. You came back to me unhurt, that's the most important thing, you good dog, you," Marge said. She hugged on him and realized that she needed it more than he did. She guided Boomer to the wounded, and even badly injured, they smiled and touched the German shepherd, helping them feel better.

None of them knew exactly what they had witnessed, Marge soon realized. She hoped body camera footage helped, but Marge was doubtful. She had been nearby, and she hadn't been able to see clearly. To her, it looked like a small bear that had been bred with a big dog.

Marge felt inadequate. She hadn't been as much help to the injured as Genny and Angus. She had been trained to protect and yet, she had been standing right there and been unable to keep them from getting shredded or preventing the perp from escaping. She swore that her aim had been true, and yet, the maniac hadn't even slowed. She must have missed. She would have the forensics crew search for her bullets. No one else had fired.

She heard sirens. Soon, she saw flashing lights. Reinforcements arrived as two ambulances pulled into the gravel lot. She pitched in to carry and load the wounded Search and Rescue workers. It didn't look good for Dan and Clayton. Last August had been filled with the funerals of Marsha, deputies from both counties, game wardens, and TVA agents. She hoped it wasn't starting again with these folks right here.

****

Much later, she was driving home again, just a couple minutes away. She passed the entrance to Maraders Marina and turned onto Friendship Drive, driving downhill to its marina. She parked in her spot as a resident, walked Boomer to take care of business, and afterward led him to the gate. Since it was his first time here, he sniffed anything and everything.

"This is your walkway but not your territory, Boom. I have a floating house," she told him. They descended the steps to the center aisle. It smelled of oil and fuel. She turned left, away from the office, gas pumps, and chandlery, toward the floating boat stalls. A slight breeze caused the lines on masts to flap, tap and ring, while the water made a low whooping sound when it lapped at the piles.

This was one of the few marinas that didn't have nighttime music and festivities. She liked the quiet. If she wanted to get out, she could go to one of the other marinas. When there was entertainment, there was booze, which meant trouble sooner or later. She didn't miss having that in her floating neighborhood. The houseboats were located at the rear of the marina so they could avoid the traffic of daily fisherman and weekend warriors. The floating homes acted like a peninsula or a jetty to create a small bay. Houseboating moved at a much slower pace, and it was placid and sane back here on most days.

As far as she knew, nobody else was living aboard this late in fall. Her place was a modest one bedroom with one bath comprising the stern half. The aft had a porch and an open kitchen-lounge area. She loved sitting up top and enjoying the peaceful lake at night. She had grown up on a farm, and this place made her feel like she was on a short vacation, away from it all. Her houseboat was a modular built by Metroship out of Orlando. She hoped one day to buy a Salibration out of Powell, Tennessee where they made custom houseboats. Hers had looked like a rental until she added her own decorative touches.

Her home floated three stalls down on the left, facing the tree-lined cliffs of the shore. She had only taken a few steps when Boomer bristled. They might not be alone after all.

"Shush. Easy boy," Marge said.

She noticed the houseboat next door, the Shilo's summer cabin, a gorgeous two bedroom with a luxury lounge and modern tech kitchen crafted by Sunstar out of Monticello, Kentucky. She watched as the teakwood-walled craft called Z by its owners shifted and rocked. She recognized the motion as someone climbing onto the stern. She had a key to their boat and considered surprising the burglar, but first she checked her phone for a text or email from her seasonal neighbors. They usually informed her of when they were coming, or when they were letting friends or family use it. She found no such notification. It was not the time to call them. Even so, they might have simply forgotten.

She commanded Boomer to stay and went to her houseboat. She couldn't see anything, but she thought she saw movement on the back deck. Something large exited the water. It hunched low at first and then stood. She turned on her flashlight and trained it on the shadowy figure, only to discover a well-built, naked man holding a bleeding and soaking wet cat in one hand. He looked surprised and then blinded. The cat looked annoyed.

"Hey now, that's not neighborly," he drawled. His accent didn't sound local.

"I'm so sorry. My sincere apologies. I thought you might be an intruder. I haven't changed my mind, even if you are nude," Marge said. She grabbed the towel draped over a chair's back and tossed the terry cloth sheet across the water to him.

He grabbed it with one hand and carefully set down his cat. Marge stayed focused on watching his hands because he was ripped like a swimmer with broad shoulders and a muscular chest. "Thanks. Many apologizes, dear lady. I didn't expect anyone to be awake, and my cat bein' in danger was an emergency."

"This ought to be good," she said. He didn't sound drunk to her.

"Rica went fishin' and tussled with a turtle. Shelled bastard got her on the hind leg before she showed her claws. Say, do you know a good vet that I can call in the mornin'?" Despite his words, he sounded sober. "By the way, my name's Rhett Archer. Are you holdin' a gun on me, because it sounds like it?"

"You know what that sounds like? So, it's happened to you before?" Marge asked. She wanted to hear this.

"Yep. Usually, though, I'm on the other end. Well, I used to be, and not in my birthday suit. You know, dad gum, my memory is a sorry piece of work sometimes. You must be the incomparable Marge Cantrell. Jean and Randall Shilo mentioned you had a hair trigger, or was that a quick trigger? See there? I assume they forgot to let you know that I was goin' to stay at their place for a piece. I left a note on your door, I think it must've been two days ago. I lose track of time now that I'm retired and writin'. Anyway, my note must have blown off or you would know that I'm Rhett Archer, Texas Ranger, recently retired," he said, although the last sounded just tarred as in weary.

"Your mother named you Rhett?" she asked. So far, everything he said chimed as the truth. She hadn't gotten that pain in her neck, even when he said incomparable Marge.

"Yep. She and my pa loved old movies. They saw *Gone with the Wind* on their first date at a movie house in Longview that had retro Tuesdays," Archer said.

"Saying you're a former ranger is audacious, but any successful squatter or burglar would do their research or check the Shilo's Facebook and Instagram accounts," Marge replied.

"Those are some good points, deputy. Let's see, Jean warned us about the raccoon that likes to sit on the deck. Rica will deal with the varmint. Randall mentioned that you sang in the shower early in the mornin', so he recommended industrial-strength earplugs."

"You're kidding," Marge gasped. Something didn't jive. She had a wonderful voice. Her family often sang together at home and at church, or they used to before her father's death and Marsha's murder. Marge felt the pain in her neck. He was jerking her chain.

"You're right, I am, and he didn't. Randall said you sing when he plays guitar, and you sound purdier than a nightingale, but it's still way too early in the mornin' even if an angel is singin'," Rhett Archer said. The retired Texas Ranger must have big balls to bust her chops while she held a gun on his privates. That did sound just like Randall who was a night owl musician, loving to play his rhythm guitar long after midnight. He hated to rise before, gasp, 10 AM. "Listen, I was awful sad to hear about your sister. I lost a brother who was a damn fine Ranger. Jean said you two, you and Marsha, were almost inseparable," he said.

"Okay, I've heard enough to convince me that you know the Shilos. Nice to meet you, Mr. Archer. How long will you be here?" Marge asked. She clicked off the flashlight.

"Thanks. A couple of weeks at least. Randall said it was quiet and gorgeous this time of year here. I wanted to see the leaves of autumn that all y'all are famous for. I'm workin' on a cop thriller piece of fiction, so I wanted a peaceful spot where I could try and channel Tom Clancy or one of those Pattersons. Jean said you might even show me around the area, if you have the time to spare," Archer said.

"I just got back to work, so I don't know what my schedule looks like," Marge said. Just what she didn't need: a writer next door looking for ideas. At least he was fit and good looking, even if he was from Texas. She hadn't been impressed with any of them during her previous encounters. Texas Rangers thought they were better than everyone else, much like the FEDS, or the inspiration for Chuck Norris, on TV, *Walker, Texas Ranger.* As long as they caught the bad guys, her grandpa said. He was more tolerant than she was, but then he had a male perspective, even if it was more expansive than most, God bless his soul.

"Uh, I'll be appropriately dressed the next time we meet," he promised.

"Good call. As far as a vet, call Dr. Marci May. She's the best in town, and she's nearby. Tell her I sent you. Good night, Mr. Archer."

"And a good sleep to you. It's been embarrassin' but a treat to meet you, Marge Cantrell. Come on, Rica, let me bandage your leg," Archer said.

Good luck with that, Marge though. She returned fore and called in Boomer. He had stayed right in position despite smelling the cat. After what she had seen earlier, she was heartened that she had a dog for company and to guard the place while she slept.

Four

A Reunion of Five Blood Brothers

It would soon be Halloween, a season of the supernatural in spooky stories and dark tales, and yet Knives' thoughts dwelled on science and fishing, although not the science of fishing. He ignored the feeling of being observed to flick the pole and sent the hook, line, and sinker through the night into South Holston Lake with a splash. He wished he could swallow what had happened here two months ago as easily as the old saying, but he was a show me by science kind of guy. He had worked hard to earn that doctor in front of his given name, Stephen Curran.

Knives loved this lake, mostly located in Tennessee and partly in Virginia, completed and filled in 1950 to prevent future disastrous flooding along the Holston River and to generate energy through a system of earthen dams via the Tennessee Valley Authority. South Holston had been the only one built. Its creation had displaced residents along the river but brought outdoor recreation and even peace to those who experienced its sprawling beauty and quiet coves set among the forested foothills of the Holston Mountains.

The lake was just one of the plethora of reasons that Knives loved living in Bristol. Despite having a population of around 40 thousand living in two states, people remained small town friendly. Folks in this Appalachian city loved the outdoors, antiques, their dogs, railroads, pro wrestling, auto racing of any kind and music, especially country or gospel. Trains and tunes were two of the big reasons Bristol existed. He thought the people of Sullivan and Washington counties were hardworking, salt of the earth kind of folk.

A rapid clip of loud sounds made him jump. It reminded Knives of staccato gunfire, but then he realized it was just the industrial-sized bug zapper frying insects. With hills of trees and rolling green came bugs. A big moth had been drawn to it, and it was being electrified, the frying lasting for long seconds. The flickering glow cast odd shadows that seemed to thrash about. The air stank of charred protein. The sound shouldn't have startled him, and yet he felt watched like a target, not by the dog or his friend, but by something else. He kept thinking he saw movement out of the corner of his eye. He wished that he could blame his blood brothers' history of punking and pranking each other, but he had felt this way since so many friends had died last August.

The lake was connected with sorrow, tragedy and death. He felt like he had lost pieces of his mind here, so it no longer felt peaceful. Whether literal or figurative, ghosts resided here.

He drew a small pocketknife and cleaned under his fingernails. Known as Knives to his blood brothers, co-workers, and neighbors, he couldn't visit Maraders Marina without suffering PTSD flashbacks. The chandlery, bar, restaurant, and apartments on the second floor had been rebuilt after the fire and explosion had destroyed them. So, this wasn't even the same building, he reminded himself. It just looked similar to the original. The marina floated in the same place as before, a tree-lined cove near the 421 Bridge and Friendship Marina. Only the bar name had changed to The Wolf's Den.

Too near for comfort, he heard a howl. It was a dog, not a wolf, he told himself. He refused to have flashbacks about that night. He focused on his breathing. New place. New day. New ways. He affirmed.

Even now, he couldn't joke about the wake that had reduced this place to ashes. None of it had ever been resolved to his satisfaction, the hows or whys. Had there been psychedelic Kool Aid mixed with the beer?

Although he knew better than to trust human observation while under duress, he had been an eyewitness to friends getting killed by wolves. It had never been explained, so it stuck in his craw. Then, the next night, it had been almost as crazy, boating out to Cemetery Ridge to watch his friends dive to the bottom of the lake where they deployed dynamite to demolish a haunted, submerged mansion.

What madness had possessed them? He was a body fixer, not a mental health professional. He thought Dillon still owed them all answers.

The next day, many things had returned to normal, the town breathing a sigh of relief. The investigation into John's missing body had ended abruptly, dropping all charges against Knives, and yet, his blood brother's body had never been recovered. The county sheriff and FBI were stumped but at least Knives was no longer to blame.

He hated those things were unresolved. Science often found a solution followed by better and better methods.

Knives had tried to return to normal. Doctors saw death weekly, but it was different when it hit home. Denny, Spider, John, and Walt, God rest their souls, had died, their spirits passing beyond. He hadn't processed it, yet, and he doubted his friends and the community had gone through the needed stages of grief. It was all too raw and fresh. He prayed his dead friends received some kind of explanation in Heaven, because it didn't seem to be forthcoming on earth.

Nearby, it sounded like a large marble dropped to the deck. He watched a huge black spider scuttle across the planks as the eight-legged sought a place to hide. He didn't want one of those in his nightmares. Thankfully, he didn't suffer arachnophobia.

"So, you returned your Spyder?" J-Man asked. UT hat on backward, his newly bearded and bear-like buddy was fishing off the dock, too. J-Man wore his company logo on his shirt, Beck 'n Call. Jay, the man who could fix anything, had set up four extra poles and empty chairs in memory of their deceased friends.

"Yes. It seemed excessive," Knives said. He had loved driving it at first, but now, he had developed trepidations. He was all right looking like a good old boy in his pickup heading out to fish. He needed to get a good dog.

"Hey, Knives, are you all right?" his friend asked.

"No, not really. I feel watched, even judged, and I was pondering what truly happened here. Will I ever know?" Knives asked. The night seemed to suddenly hush as if everything were listening to his questions. The sense of being hunted intensified, feeling like pin pricks across his neck and shoulders, even running down his arms.

"It was a strange night. Someone must have spiked the punch. If it makes you feel any better, I feel watched, too," J-Man replied.

Knives couldn't explain it, but he could literally see fear in J-Man's words. Somehow, he had developed synesthesia. It was a perceptual phenomenon in which stimulation of one sensory or cognitive pathway led to involuntary experiences in a second sensory or cognitive pathway. In his case, it seemed his hearing and vision combined. He had no experience with anything like this until recently. His peers called him Knives because he excelled with blades and cutting to the point or the root of the problem. Now, one of the ways that he ascertained someone's health was by listening to them speak and watching their words, their color, form, and movement for signs or symptoms.

Knowing what caused J-Man's fear was different. Knives knew the amygdala went to work at the first thought of fear, alerting the nervous system, kicking in adrenaline and cortisol, and pushing blood into the eyes to see better and the hands and feet so one could run or throw punches. The hippocampus searched for clues, the decider on whether to be thrilled or scared. Someone frightened executed poor decisions unless they were experienced in such situations.

"Honestly, I think I know what I saw, but I don't know what to think about what I saw, if that makes sense," J-Man said, his words jagged and frazzled with paranoia. "That said, we both know Pete and Walt weren't killed by wild dogs. Everyone thinks they were killed by a pack of feral canines. That's bullshit. They weren't there." He punctuated it with a disdainful snort and adjusted his spectacles as if that would help him see more clearly.

"Well, they don't look like anything special on video. So, what do you think?"

"I think we both know we saw something strange and inexplicable. Or we're just denying the truth of what we saw," J-Man said.

"I'm wondering if we suffer from Post-Traumatic Stress Disorder."

"PTSD? What they used to call Shell-shocked? Hmm. I could be. What's your point? That you agree with Concannon?" J-Man asked sharply. He raised a bushy, questioning eyebrow and stroked his beard.

"What we have is not paranoia or a phobia. Our reactions are a normal part of the human condition considering what happened.

Listen, I would appreciate it if you would honestly tell me what you think happened that night Walt died, and this place burned down to the water."

"Hell yes, I think those dogs were freakin' werewolves or something similar, something out of legend. So did Desiree, Troy, and Tommy, and coincidentally, I will point out, that two of the three conveniently had silver shot loaded in weapons. I wondered about that, but things were kind of chaotic, and I was just grateful someone was prepared and loaded for not just bear but werewolf," J-Man said with a tight grin. His words seemed to blaze white when he spoke his truth. "Knives, isn't the supernatural just something science has yet to explain?"

"I think that quote was about magic by Asimov, but that thought works. Have you noticed any changes in yourself over the last two months?" Knives asked.

"I have trouble sleeping. I keep seeing things out of the corner of my eye. When I do sleep, I often have nightmares. The lack of good sleep is making me jumpy, even paranoid. I struggle with the feeling that something awful is going to happen, you know, for the other boot to drop. I'm going to crash the truck or my boat," J-Man said. His copter had crashed into the lake on that horrible night in August when they had lost blood brothers.

"That's anticipatory anxiety or even cherophobia, fear that what happened in the past could happen again. Regardless, it could be a symptom of PTSD," Knives pointed out.

The bug zapper scorched a slew of insects, mosquitoes, flies, and moths.

"Does bright sunlight hurt your eyes?" J-Man asked. He frowned at the zapper.

"Yes, but my night vision has improved. Right now, I see the fish quite clearly."

"So do I. That doesn't help me catch it. Have you had your eyes checked?" J-Man asked.

"Yes. The optometrist seems to think I must have grown more rods in my eyes, as strange as that sounds. We usually have a 120 million in each eye that aids us with night vision. Mine is now considered exceptional, where before, my night vision was average. Color and detail by day are about the same, so I guess I have about the usual seven million cones, but something has changed."

"I have sharp night vision now, too. I don't need a flashlight, unless I want to see color. I get headaches, suffer bad ones unless I wear dark glasses. That's why you see me in shades unless it's night. I never had headaches before. Less light is definitely better."

Knives shook his head. "That sounds like photosensitivity. J-Man, you really should have your eyes examined."

"And my head, too, right? Fine. I will. Do you have trouble getting warm at night?"

"Yes. I suffer acute nocturnal chills and hyperhidrosis, night sweats. I've had tests run and my blood checked for a variety of ailments and diseases, such as Lyme, but so far, thank the Good Lord, none apply. I'm grateful for that. Still, there are certain nights when I can't get warm even while sitting in a hot tub of 104 degrees."

"That sounds familiar," J-Man replied and shivered. He reached in his pocket and pulled out a Hot Hands chemical glove warmer packet. "One in each pocket. I take my temp. It's normal."

"Anything else? Are you turning into a werewolf during full moons?" Knives asked.

"Ha. You have a strange sense of humor tonight. I wasn't bitten. Were you? Ok. Listen, I see light around people, a glowing oval. Well, not just people. Dogs, cats, all animals," J-Man said. Even speaking calmly, anxiety caused his words to be ragged. If Knives didn't know better, he would say J-Man's adrenal glands were working even now, releasing cortisol. Was J-Man scared to be here? Am I? Knives silently wondered.

"You see an aura around living things? Fish and reptiles?" Knives asked.

"Yep. I'm not on candid camera or a punking show for sadistic doctors, am I?" J-Man asked.

"No, of course not. I'm looking for explanations and answers, so that we can regain our health. I am not making any judgments here."

"Okay. Point made. For all we know, there's something in the water, and that would make it a public health crisis. Knives, I can tell by looking at someone if they're healthy or if they're sick, if they're vital or feeble. I met a great aunt a couple of weeks back. I just knew she wasn't going to last the night, her light flickering. The next day, she died. It's like the light around them is some kind of health meter. Plus, I see ghosts. The other night when I was out here fishing, catching trout hand over fist, I saw Walt's ghost. Tall and skinny, humming to himself like he does when he's thinking. There was no light around him," J-Man said.

"That would mean he isn't resting in peace," Knives said sadly. Walt had saved Knives' life. Anytime he thought of that, he tried to make sure he was spending his time wisely, helping people, and making sure the sacrifice of a life had been worthwhile. He now kept a live-in-the-spontaneous-moment attitude. He still looked to the future but less optimistically than before. Those gifted should use the gift for their fellow man. He had almost gone into biotech and tools, but he believed that service to others was important.

"Speaking of ghosts, did you hear that they are going to have a Halloween concert in East Hill Cemetery? There's a song, 'Bang your head, wake the dead', isn't there?" J-Man asked. He had almost died there, killed by someone who looked like their deceased blood brother John. His body was still missing.

"Both the city and the county need money, and it will make bank, so yes, I can. Even so, I'm not going," Knives said. He had unpleasant nightmares about the graveyard. He had been there, searching for John's body when he had been attacked and knocked unconscious. He didn't believe Troy and J-Man's story that John had been undead and tried to kill them all.

"I heard a generous donor is bankrolling it, including several big cash awards, like ten thousand dollars, but you got to be present to win."

Sarge, the new dock dog, let out a howl. Knives jerked, alarmed by the sudden noise.

A bespectacled and goateed gent of middling age wearing a head-lamp, a *Leave it to Beaver* shirt, and waders stomped onto the dock. The reptile hunter known as the Snake reached down to rub Sarge's ears. Ken 'Snake' Siksay smiled as he received happy tail wagging in return. He nodded his head in greeting to them as he used a cobra-tatted arm and hand to open the door to the bar and restaurant. He peeked inside and said, "Hey, Tommy, I got your snakes, all three of them, one of them a copperhead. Big sucker."

"Oh, man, Snake. I can't thank you enough. You are my go-to-guy when it comes to snakes. Just as you advertise: Siksay and snakes go away. I can't stand them. I don't know how you do. I'm just glad you do. Hey, guy, do you relocate ghosts, too?" Tom Marader asked. Speak of the devil, Knives mused.

Tom's spoken words were powerful, bright, and bursting with vim, vigor and vitality even as they raced. Whatever J-Man suffered from, Marader was untouched by it. Come to think of it, Marader sounded healthier and stronger than anyone Knives had ever met, including college football players. How could that be?

Snake opened the door to let the muscular young man step out-side. Marader ran a hand through a wealth of wavy blond hair that he didn't have years ago. He could be the poster child for Rogaine, except he didn't take it. Often almost dying made people lose their hair or go gray. It seemed to make Marader's grow like weeds. He happily paid the snake catcher in cash and a 24-pack of Nehi soda.

"No, sir. No ghosts, no gators, and no drunken gents," Snake said.

Knives didn't suffer ophidiophobia, but he disliked snakes when he was fishing or waterskiing. He liked them eating critters in and around his yard.

"I'll give them a good home away from people, and thanks so much for the Nehi! You're a great guy, Tommy, I don't care what everyone else says," Snake said. He gestured over his shoulder and left.

An older gentleman in blue work clothing with scorched and burned marks approached. It looked like he might have singed the left side of his mustache. His gloves were tucked in his belt, and he appeared soaked with sweat. "Mr. Marader, I'm done welding."

"Excellent, Ron. Have a good night. I'll see you next week," Marader said.

Mr. Sneed winked at Knives, waved at them all and departed. Knives had treated Ron Sneed for burns incurred while welding at one of the other marinas. He had been one of thousands of workers displaced when the Raytheon plant closed so long ago. Even in a sprawling town of nearly 40 thousand people, there were only a few degrees of separation as most residents personally knew of or knew someone who was acquainted with said individual. East Tennessee was not the sticks that city people believed, although there were parts of Appalachia nearby that still lived in the last century.

"Busy around here," J-Man said.

"I'm getting ready to open back up soon. Anybody need a beer? If so, come and get it yourself, I'm not your waiter," Marader said.

"But we are!" shouted two voices.

The door pushed open and two very attractive young women, a blond and a ginger top, pushed past him to sashay outside. Neither of them was Desiree, Elle, Sandi, or Heidi who had likely returned to their colleges for the fall semester. Knives was astounded by the beauties Marader attracted. He claimed it was his animal magnetism. The young women were often exceptionally intelligent which beggared the question of why they were here. Marader was not subtle.

"We are at your service, gentlemen," the athletic blond said. Her words smelled of peaches and shimmered like a rising sun on the water. Her name tag read Staci Thompson and sat atop a well-filled, I Heart Bristol shirt. With a winsome smile, she looked like a pinup cheerleader, but she was probably a psychologist conducting a study on the psyche of males around water or the loss of male brain power when young women wore skimpy beach attire.

"Gentlemen? Man, I feel old," J-Man said. They were going on twenty-nine. Knives felt like he was approaching forty.

"You two went to high school with my older sister, Amelia," Staci informed them.

"You guys hold your age well," the other young woman chuckled. Like many with fair hair, Ginger looked as if her skin never saw the light of day. While leaning against Marader like a feline, she ran a hand through her auburn tresses. Her shirt read Virginia Intermont Nursing: We nurse beer. "What are you thirsty for?" Ginger asked and listed off what was on tap and in bottles.

Don't take the bait, Knives reminded himself. The women out here had supernatural powers to go along with intelligence and bodies by Venus.

"Ginger. Staci. You gals don't actually start until tomorrow," Marader said.

"I thought this might be more training, you know, dealing with difficult customers," Ginger chuckled.

"What kind of customer service is that?" Staci asked. She scrutinized Knives and said, "You look like a pale ale drinker, while you, J-Man, are an amber ale guy with Coca-Cola on the side."

"I feel like I've been scouted," Knives said.

"What's your point?" J-Man asked.

"Ladies, are you flirting again?" Marader asked.

"Never, boss. I prefer to think of it as advertising," Staci chuckled.

"I just do it to make you, envious. I am yours, boss," Ginger said and rubbed up against Marader like he was a scratching post.

"Everyone, this is Miss Ginger Bethel, a pole dancer extraordinaire, a fabulous cook, and a helluva boat mechanic. How lucky can a guy get?" Marader asked with a grin.

"I'm beyond envious. I'm jealous," J-Man said.

Knives managed to remain silent. He had yet to see anyone hold Marader's attention for more than a year, and six months was pushing it.

Ginger blushed but laughed delightedly. "I have six brothers. Don't worry. They're not like your friend, Dillon. They know I'm a red-haired, blue-eyed vamp with sharp teeth and claws. I can take care of myself," Ginger said with a predatory smile. When Marader reached for her, she slipped away to hurry inside.

"That woman will drive me crazy," Marader said

"Hey, what about me? Bawk?" It came from inside.

J-Man and Knives stared questioningly at Marader. "I inherited a parrot from my uncle who died last week. She's amazing," he said. He went back inside and returned with a green parrot on his arm. "This is Kia Mia. Good evening, pretty girl."

"Kia is pretty girl. Staci is pretty girl," the bird replied.

"I see you've been working with her already. What do you say, pretty?" Marader asked.

"Let's spend the night together. I like it on top," Kia replied. The bird then laughed like a crowing raven.

"My uncle owned a couple of waterfront bars at Virginia Beach. Kia came from there," he said.

"Oh, this is going to be fun," J-Man said. For a moment, the gloom lifted. Knives smiled. This is how this place should feel, he thought.

"Hey, when are you going to bring Sarina out here for us to meet? From the way you described her, she sounds hot," Marader said.

"What?" Knives asked and blinked. He didn't recall mentioning her. He tried not to mention women around his friend.

"Isn't she the honey who has honeybees and runs the pharmacy?" Marader asked. Knives nodded. "Maybe it was just your subconscious talking to me," his friend said and shrugged.

They heard a vehicle on gravel. Shortly, the sound of a car door shutting echoed in the cove.

"Is that your new mechanic?" Marader asked J-Man.

"Browny can't be here tonight," J-Man replied.

Marader inhaled deeply and grinned as if he had caught a whiff of after shave and motor oil. "That's Jambo."

Sarge announced their blood brother. Jamie Boy, now a man, petted on the boxer who stood up like he wanted to dance. The dog could usually put his paws on a person's shoulders, but Sarge only reached Jambo's pumped up biceps.

"Hey, everybody. Y'all missed a great show. I'm glad nobody was on the road this time of night, because I can't drive 55!" Jambo said and winked. He ran a hand through his curly rings of hair and gave everyone a huge, broad-toothed grin. His words contained none of the shadow or paranoia that affected J-Man's spoken words.

"Stay alive, drive 55," Kia said and crowed.

Knives glared at Jambo. "Just because you're jazzed is not a good reason to speed."

"Ah, Dr. Killjoy is with us tonight," Jambo said, invoking Troy's name for no fun Dr. Curran. "I'm glad you weren't at the concert. It was probably bad for my hearing."

"You should wear musician earplugs. Do, and you'll thank me when you're fifty," Knives retorted.

"How was Bethany?" Marader asked.

Jambo smiled. "She and Justen Hobson were amazing. We also bumped into Elke and Dillon. I invited them out to our late night gathering to fish."

"I doubt he'll show. He's got better things to do," Marader said and smiled. "What do you guys think of the place? I'm getting close to having a reopening party. I even have new staff," Marader said. He gestured to Ginger and Staci. They smiled prettily and waved.

"Is that the big news?" Jambo asked. Nonplussed, he seemed to have met them.

"I think that's big news. But it's not The Big News, although it could be, since I've been closed for two freaking months," Marader railed, obviously delaying the sharing. He enjoyed being the center of attention.

"The big news is I'm pregnant," Kia said. They all looked at the bird who stole the attention from Marader.

"Now that's news," Knives agreed.

"She didn't hear it from anyone that I know," Marader stammered.

"Come on. What's the point? Is there really news? I thought we were here to fish and discuss what happened when the marina went up like a Deep Purple song," J-Man said. He looked to the ladies. "You know what happened here?"

"Oh, yeah. The ghosts chat about it," Ginger said. Marader gave her a look.

"Ladies, you are not helping," Marader said. In a huff, Ginger left. Staci blew them kisses.

Knives felt he needed to step in and say what he wanted before they were lost in the woods. "Changing the subject for a minute, have any of you suffered any odd symptoms or changes in your body since the wolf and terrorist attacks?" Knives asked.

"I want to hear the big news," Jambo complained.

Marader puffed up. "Okay, then, I am having a grand reopening. The bands are signed and lined up, including, if you can believe it, Justen Hobson. Todd Young and the Coveralls will open. Man, I love, Todd. I am so stoked. To answer your question, the only trouble I'm having is my sister. Um, Madi is back in town," he said and sighed. His words were tangled and discombobulated, eagerness, resignation and worry mixed together.

"Hey, did she bring *The Myth Huntress*' cast with her?" Knives asked.

"What do you know about her show?" Marader asked.

"All the nurses watch it. They love that she's a local, successful woman employing and empowering other women. Some wear a I heart Madi button," Knives said. He made a heart shape with his hands.

"Oh, man. Don't let Madi know that! Her head is already way too big," Marader said.

Knives noticed the temperature fall like a cool front blowing in. Nothing seemed to move around him, the air dead calm, and yet he felt the chilling breeze. His hairs bristled, rising on his arms and the back of his neck, an instinctive fear sounding an alarm. He looked to the shore at the dark shadowy places where the wolves had hidden before attacking them.

"Look, do you see Walt? There he is, again," J-Man asked. He pointed past Jambo to the corner of the walkway at the edge of the restaurant.

Knives blinked. He couldn't believe his eyes, but he kept from rubbing them. Now he would have to admit to J-Man that he was also seeing disembodied spirits. A colorless image of Walt, sans legs, stood there staring at them, disgustedly shaking his head.

The ghost vanished when Dillon rounded the corner. He walked almost soundlessly. All of them jumped, surprised to see their blood brother. Why hadn't Sarge barked a greeting?

Dillon stood tall, fair-haired, pale, and handsome, a well-built guy who had excelled at martial arts and journalism. Girls had always been drawn to him. His charisma and warm smile emboldened people to relax and share.

"Good evening, my friends. Is this where you drown your fishing blues with beer and whiskey?" Dillon said with an easy smile. His words were unlike anything Knives had seen, fearless, shadowed, even moonlit, and yet bursting with power like a guy on steroids. His voice seemed too large, taking up too much space, and yet it lacked the warm glow and healthy vitality that he saw in Marader's speech. Was that caused by Dillon's illness?

"Bring me another Bloody Mary!" Kia sang out.

Dillon raised a questioning eyebrow.

"Meet Kia Mia, the chatty parrot," Marader said.

"Dillon man, you move like ninja," J-Man said.

"Thank you, J-Man-san. I'll try not to act like one, since they're the bad guys," Dillon replied and smiled. "Why do you look like you just saw a ghost?"

"Probably because you just walked through Walt," Knives replied. He fought the urge to run to his car. What was wrong with him? He had the sense that even the shadows were shrinking, cowering under Dillon's presence. How odd, his rational mind spoke up.

Something about Dillon engaged Knives' fight or flight reaction. The fearful feeling of being trapped grew stronger. He had a similar sense when he had walked in on a bear while he was ransacking the

Curran family cabin. Knives breathed to remain calm even as his endocrine glands released adrenaline. Hormones were a challenge to battle, ask any teenager. The best way to deal with it was to distract it. He mentally counted and thought of warm colors, bringing down his heart rate and blood pressure.

"Sorry there, Walt. Glad you're with us in spirit. Please guide us earthbound fools. I think it's time to relax," Dillon said. His words carried calming weight.

Knives' fear vanished. His heart rate and breathing dropped. He finally relaxed, not understanding why he had been frightened. Did seeing Dillon set off his PTSD for some reason?

"You still look deliriously happy. Where's Elke?" J-Man asked.

"She's in the lot waiting for me. She has calls to make, but she promised me at least twenty minutes of male bonding time before she comes to join us. What's up?" Dillon asked.

"Dr. Killjoy thinks I suffer from PTSD," J-Man said.

Knives decided to forge ahead. "Jambo, are you having any health issues or weird symptoms?"

"Nope. Why do you ask?" he replied.

"Does bright light bother you? Do night chills? That kind of stuff?" Knives asked. While Jambo looked at him questioningly, Dillon stared. Once again, Knives felt the urge to run.

"No, just some trouble sleeping. Some night's I take Ambien," Jambo replied.

Knives nodded. "You never dove down to the house, did you?"

"Thank God, no. The stories are frightening enough. This is one time I think it's more than okay to live vicariously," Jambo said. He had been called Sir Sleeps-A-Lot. He had been the guardian of the boat.

Knives gave it some thought. "How about you, Dillon?"

He smiled wanly. "I didn't dive either."

"You look tired," Knives said.

"Maybe it's tired blood. My condition hasn't changed, just my attitude. Honestly, I'm still adjusting to the night life. At times, I get depressed and want to punch something. Elke is the key reason that I'm not stark raving mad."

Knives thought he spoke his truth which was subjective. He couldn't tell the difference with his synesthesia. "I worry that those of us who went diving were exposed to toxic chemicals. I have tested my blood. I would like to test J-Man's, yours, and Marader's," Knives said.

"I'm in," J-Man said.

"You don't want mine?" Jambo asked.

Knives shook his head. "You didn't dive and have no odd health issues. What do you say, Dillon?"

"I didn't go diving, either," Dillon said.

Knives just knew he was hiding something. "So that night when the marina went up in smoke, were you there, you know, here? Troy said you rescued him," Knives said.

"I wish I had been there. As far as I know, he rescued himself," Dillon said.

He sounded genuinely pained, even regretful, but the words were hollow. They were lies, Knives realized. Why would he lie about being here? Knives blinked. He believed him, despite seeing the lie tinge to the words. Knives wondered why he felt so conflicted. Dillon had always been trustworthy.

"So, you want us to give blood, sort of like we did when we became blood brothers?" Marader asked, referring to their shared past.

Knives flashed back. It had been Jambo's 16th birthday, and they had celebrated with a deer hunt and a fishing campout. While sitting around the bonfire, Spider had suggested they become blood brothers, cutting themselves in the palms of their hands and then shaking to comingle blood. Looking back, it had been foolish, but it had forged even stronger bonds between them. Now, their numbers were nearly halved. Those remaining needed each other.

"Excuse me. That's not a good comparison. This is under much better-controlled conditions. I am a professional with the proper training and equipment to take blood."

"Bloodsucking vampire," Marader teased him.

"What about you? Are you going to give a sample?" Knives asked.

"Why not? You might discover the secret to my animal magnetism. I could bottle and sell it," Marader howled.

Knives sighed. He didn't roll his eyes. He figured this is what it was like raising a teenager.

"So, what is The Big News according to one Thomas Marader?" Dillon asked.

"My sister, Madilyn is in town, and she brought her Myth Huntress crew. Look out, world, I am going to be on TV!"

Knives remembered Madi, the Mad Marader, who was anything but a Dumb Blond. She had excelled in volleyball, softball, and track while earning a degree from UT in media and communications. The women of *The Myth Huntress* were smart, educated, athletic, adventuresome, and beautiful. It was a show about curiosity, discovery, and women empowerment. He was all for it, Knives mused, before he realized why they would be here. He kept his profanity to himself.

"What's she investigating? The ghosts at Tennessee High?" Jambo asked.

"That's a good idea but not it," Marader said.

"Wait, don't tell me," Knives began. He hoped it wasn't, but he knew where the myth huntress was going. She would be diving deep down to Von Damme's ruined mansion where death waited.

"Not THS. She is going to base her show right here, at my marina, even before the grand opening. How cool is that? My place is going to be the setting of a *The Myth Huntress* episode. There are going to be hot-looking women galore," Marader said.

"Are they going to explore why this place burned down? Investigate the wolves attacking?" J-Man asked.

"No, that's not it. Guys," Marader said. He seemed to think it was obvious.

Dillon suddenly had murder in his eyes. A vein popped out in his forehead, one that showed up when he was furious. His hands clenched and unclenched as he appeared ready to punch or strangle somebody. Knives understood the feeling. He didn't act on it. It seemed like Dillon might. Kia sensed it, too, and flew up to land on the roof.

"They are going to explore the ruins of Von Damme's mansion, aren't they?" Dillon snarled and confronted Marader, getting in his face.

"Whoa! Back up, pal. You need a breath mint, and listen, buddy, I only let the ladies get that close. And yes, she is funding a diving expedition to search the place with ROVs equipped with cameras. I don't know what else. Right here will be command central."

In a blur, Dillon seized Marader by the throat. Kia flew off. "Police brutality!" she cried.

"Idiots," Dillon hissed. He started to choke Marader.

Who could blame him? Knives blinked and took a step back. That wasn't right. He felt repulsed, shocked by Dillon's speed and viciousness. He knew he should stop his friend, especially when Marader's eyes bulged, and his face reddened.

"You must make her stop," Dillon snarled. Waves of rage radiated from him.

Knives, Jambo and J-Man converged on Dillon. They tried to pry him loose, but Dillon was astoundingly strong. J-Man and Jambo failed to move him. Dillon hip-checked Knives loose. He lost his grip on Dillon's wrist and staggered back. Marader kicked out. Dillon shifted, and Jambo took the foot between the legs. He dropped to the ground, groaning, and clutching himself. It was easy to forget journalist Dillon was also a Black Belt.

"Damn it, Dillon, let go," J-Man snapped. He draped over Dillon, attempting to overbear and drive him aground.

Marader tried to headbutt Dillon but smacked J-Man. He staggered back a step, lost his balance, and fell into the lake.

"Dillon, c'mon, let go of him. It's not his fault his sister's doing this. You know how sisters are," Knives said, referring to Silke. He grabbed a deck chair, getting ready to hit Dillon behind the knees to take out his legs.

He didn't even notice Knives. Dillon kept his hold, still squeezing. Marader's eyes rolled back.

Knives reared back. Damn it, he was a doctor, not a brawler.

"Dillon, dearest, no fair using your kung fu grip on your friends. Peace, my love," she said. The atmosphere instantly changed as Elke arrived. Her words were commanding and irresistible. Despite being shadowed, they sparkled and glittered like diamonds in the full moonlight. Her presence swept over Knives, who set down the chair even as Dillon calmed and stepped back.

Everything about her seemed perfectly amazing. A tall, blue-eyed blond bombshell of a woman, she could have doubled for the actress, Charlize Theron. Knives felt a testosterone rush and a lustful yearning. He couldn't take his eyes off her. He was going to need a dip in the lake to cool down.

"Marader, man, I sincerely apologize. Tom, wow, what can I say? I lost my mind," Dillon said. As he walked away, he glared at his hands like they were traitors. Elke held out her hands to coax him along.

"Aw. Ah. Ha. I've never done that, have I, buddy? No worries, pal. I'm a fast healer. No talking about *Fight Club*, remember?" Marader said with a wink. "I know you think I'm being a greedy idiot, and sometimes I am, but not today. I tried to discourage Madi. She told me if she couldn't use this place as a base, she would pay Lakeview or Painters Creek. Then I would have no idea what she was up to, or down to. Besides, she's my sister. I might not be able to stop her, so I should look out for her, right? I don't want to clean up her messes, but I will help her pick up the pieces. What? Don't look so shocked, okay?"

"Aw, you were right. He has a big heart," Staci said to Ginger. They swooned and then giggled with each other at some inside joke. That lightened the mood.

"I can't blame you for that," Dillon said. Their friends' deaths had affected all of them.

"You can try to talk her out of it. She will be here tomorrow afternoon. The myth huntress and crew plan to start recording with a night dive, for atmosphere, you know. She wants you to be there, Dillon," Marader said.

"Oh, really?" Dillon asked. Being around cameras could be problematic.

"Oh, yeah, man. She wants to pick your big brain about what happened. You are writing a book about what went down. I was going to call you tonight with the invite, but here you are, so, you're invited, if you don't try to strangle me, again. Speaking of invitations, she's going to offer you a contract, Knives, to be the doctor on scene while they dive. Are you ready to be elbow deep in babes?" Marader asked.

Knives blinked. Was he? No and yes. He was curious what they might find. "I would like some answers, so, yes," he replied and glanced over at Dillon.

Marader turned to Dillon. He closed his eyes as if he were exerting his will not to lose his temper. "I'll be here and do what I can to discourage her. I'm going to call it a night. I'm not feeling well. I wish you all a better night and good tomorrow. Fortune in fishing," Dillon said. He waved as he departed, and Elke took his arm, sliding comfortably close to him as the couple vanished around the corner and into the night.

"Wow. That's pure honey there," Jambo said.

"Don't let your wife hear that," Marader said.

"She agrees. She would be jealous, except I love her as she is," Jambo said.

Marader chuckled. "That's why you stay married."

"Elke Swearington is somethin'," Knives affirmed. Her words had a similar feel and appearance to Dillon's vocalizations. And yet, they were both unlike anyone else that he had heard in the last month. What did that mean? "I swear, I've never seen Dillon move so fast."

"He's working out again, and it shows," Marader said. If his throat or feelings had been bruised, he showed no sign, swallowing more margarita without a problem.

"Bo knows. The Shadow knows," Kia said. Marader held out his hand, and the bird flew back to him. He stroked her head and back, and she stretched and shivered with delight.

Knives opened his doctor's black bag. It sat next to the tackle box. He wouldn't want to open the wrong one for taking samples. "Now, who is going to give blood?"

Knives wished Dillon would change his mind. That's when he realized that he had scratched Dillon while trying to peel him off Marader. Under his fingernails, Knives now possessed a DNA sample of Dillon's. Would it tell him what Dillon was hiding?

"Knives, do you want to hear something funny, and I mean strange, not ha, ha?" J-Man asked.

Knives nodded, wondering what it could be.

"That reminds me of a joke," Kia said. They waited, but the bird said nothing more.

"You know what I was saying about seeing glows? There aren't any around Elke and Dillon. None," J-Man said.

"What does that mean?" Jambo asked.

"I don't know. Everyone else has one, including Sarge and Kia," J-Man said.

Knives wondered what Dillon's DNA sample would tell him.

Speaking of the dog, the boxer whined as he pranced like the dock was hot under paw along the water's edge. He started barking, each utterance sounding more frantic. Knives couldn't read dog speak, but he didn't think it would be necessary.

"Sarge found something in the water. A person," Marader said. He hurried over to the dog and peered into the lake's waters. "Yep."

"What? He found somebody?" Jambo asked.

Knives took down an extendable hook from the wall. He had an unpleasant feeling he was going to need this.

Marader dragged Sarge away to hand the dog to Ginger. Returning to the water's edge, he cocked his head as if he were listening. "Oh hell, yeah, I see him. If it's a person, he's probably drowned," Marader said. By his words, he was certain the individual was dead, and something was wrong. He accepted the hooked pole from Knives.

"How come I keep finding bodies? And don't say I have the nose for it," Marader snapped.

Knives stepped next to his blood brother and peered into the lake. The body floated oddly as if it were out of balance. Was that blood in the water? Was he missing an arm?

Marader reached out and hooked the body. He slowly drew the corpse toward them. As it neared, Knives could smell blood and death. He steeled himself, even as he prayed it wasn't somebody that he knew.

One arm splashing, the body rolled over to bump into the dock. Along with missing an arm, the man's head appeared to have been crushed. His once bulging eyes had been eaten away, and his nose and tongue were missing.

"He'll need to be identified by dental records," Knives said.

"Shit, I know who this is," Marader said. He pointed to the remaining arm and its exposed tatted bicep. Inside a lightning bolt it read Mac.

"What the hell happened to Macdaddy? Oh buddy, he looks chewed up," Jambo said.

Knives tried to guess the size of the creature's bite and thereby its jaw. Whatever the beast, it was big. "We need to call the county sheriffs' departments. Let their people on the lake know about this, and so they can inform Mac's family."

"This wasn't the Oktoberfest Vampire. We have a freakin' lake monster on our hands! I knew it!" J-Man said. Next, he might claim to be clairvoyant.

Knives didn't need a crystal ball to foresee that this was only the beginning.

Five

Gifts of Life

"You need to sustain yourself. You're starting to lose control," Elke said. Behind the bright twin headlights of a classic, red and white '58 convertible Corvette, she deftly handled the wheel while she drove north on VA 75 to Abingdon in southwest Virginia.

It was the governmental seat of Washington County and sat about sixteen miles east of Bristol, Virginia. The most direct route was Interstate 81, but Dillon and Elke were coming from South Holston Lake, so the curvy route was still shorter.

Abingdon's historic district held numerous residences, and the place was famous for being the home of the Martha Washington Inn, the Barter Theater, and the beginning of the Virginia Creeper Trail. According to Elke, the town of a little over eight thousand people was also home to a large community of ghosts. Dillon had often heard it said that this part of southwest Virginia was ignored by the state government, out of sight, out of mind. That helped make it a good haven for vampires, despite the area's strong belief in Christianity. Where there was light, there would be shadows, too. A church or religious center could be found on many corners.

Such places of giving were needed, as unemployment was currently high, leading to all kinds of self, spousal and drug abuses.

"You could have broken Tom's neck," Elke said, as if she had caught his thought or read his eyes.

"You're right. At least he can take it," Dillon said. His blood brother had experienced a different kind of supernatural transformation. It hadn't killed Marader, but he was a primal creature and only partly human and less during full moons.

"Your other friends, besides Troy who is out of your reach, can't take such an angry force. I shouldn't have let you talk me into stopping to chat with your friends. We should have come here directly before The Bloodlust pushed you to shove and choke."

"Yes. I'm a slower learner than I expected. I was hoping you and the vulture bees would sustain me, but it's like dealing with starving and raging hormones at the same time. It's hard to think and act rationally," Dillon admitted. Eating candy sweetened by the carrion-loving bees' honey always helped him focus. It was really too bad that it hadn't been enough. Their honey tasted like sweetened raw meat and lasted forever even better than immortal vampires.

"Well put. It's important that you realize it. That's why we continue to practice, and why you must feed to sustain yourself. You have pushed your limits and your luck."

"I know. Afterward, we must do something clever to stop the myth huntress from diving," Dillon said. He didn't want to lose his humanity. What he was about to do seemed the most humane. Was he rationalizing this?

"I agree. Do you mean compel Madi? Or perhaps buy her off?"

"Can you peer in her eyes to tell which one will work?" he asked with a laugh.

Elke chuckled. "Where is your journalistic integrity?"

"I am trying to keep people alive and us together, Key," Dillon replied.

Elke smiled warmly. "I like the sound of that."

Dillon let the night air rush over him. It helped blow away some of his anger at Marader and the foolish myth huntress. He decided to focus on something else. He played with his density, trying to float in the car. This was so much better than taking the tunnels to travel. He reveled in the wind and his beloved's voice while Key told him about his victim and her life.

"At 85, Darlene Flicker, is in agony every moment and more than ready to leave her body. Due to a stroke, she has difficulty speaking and communicating. She grew up on a twenty-five acre farm after the TVA took two hundred acres for the dam from her parents in Wyatt Hollow. When chickens were killed, Darlene was responsible for gutting and fixing them for supper. On a more delicate note, she took piano lessons and played for the Sunset Village Baptist Church, as well as singing choir at Sullivan East High. She loved to march in the band and twirl guns. She taught Sunday school and 8th grade. She remarried and the second time was a charm, lasting over fifty years. She has three grandsons and three grand stepchildren, one son and two daughters. One of them, Sheyanne or MacKenzie, gets married in two days in Kingsport. Darlene has lived in this area all her life. She feels fortunate to have made it this far, but she wants a little more and to finish on her own terms. Here's an interesting tidbit for you to chew on. She's a charter member of the Southwest Virginia Investigators of the Paranormal."

Dillon thought it ironic that she had found what she had been seeking just before the end of her life. Could he really end a life? "I feel like Dr. Kevorkian."

"You are doing more than helping her end her life. You are helping her end her life in the manner in which she chooses. You will gift her with a swansong, a golden seventy-two hours of joyous farewell. Make no mistake, what we get is precious. What we give is unique. No medicine and no doctor can do this," Elke said.

"I hear you. Something else has also been bothering me. Can Destrange just walk out of the shadows any time?" he asked.

"Yes, he could appear any time or anywhere there is no threshold, and there are shadows or places of never light," she said, tight-lipped. No place they could go, except their own home, was safe. The shadow walker could attack almost anywhere not a religious site or personal home.

Elke followed the signs to parking on Partington Place near the Martha Washington Inn and across from The Barter Theater. She cruised by the fountain and the LOVE sculpture to find an open space to park in the hilly lot.

"This is our kind of place. Ah, I see that we have company. Our shadows are here," Dillon said. He nodded to the Cadillac pulling into the lot and parking nearby. The driver, Big Al, tipped his cap. Desiree sat in the front seat. She threw him a brief smile.

"I feel like a stroll before we see Darlene." Elke said.

"Something happened here. You knew about this, didn't you?" Dillon asked. He pointed out the flowers decorating the area around the LOVE sign and fountain, making it look like a memorial. He could sense the residual fear as a panicked heartbeat, reminding him of the murderer in Poe's *The Telltale Heart*.

"Yes, a young runaway died here last night. He bled to death from dog bites," Elke said.

"And you're thinking it was a feral grayling? Or werewolves?"

"That's why I want to speak with the Haint Mistress before I speculate. Shall we?" Elke asked.

Arm in arm, Dillon and Elke strolled to Main Street. Near the historic courthouse, they headed east on the hilly sidewalk. Main Street was part of Lee Highway, an auto trail that had connected New York to San Francisco via a southern route before interstates were built. Several roads intersected here, US Routes 11, 19, 58 and

State Route 75. The black top road and brick walkways seemed to undulate past churches, law firms, tea shops and restaurants. They followed the sidewalk for about a half mile to a rustic, wooden façade.

From inside The Tavern, Dillon could hear the ghosts shuffling around. Low murmuring reminded him of hushed gossip. He couldn't tell if they were secretive or worried or both, but he could tell that they were agitated. He noticed that next door waited the Frost Funeral Home. He couldn't help but wonder if the deceased souls wandered over for spirited company. They might find solace, but they didn't seem to find rest in the old building.

"The Tavern is Abingdon's boarding house for spirits. I have tried to speak with them before, but they are skittish around me. I suspect one of our ilk has abused them. Ah, there's a woman who might know what happened," Elke surmised. She guided Dillon up the street to what looked like a tour in progress.

A buxom, dark-haired woman wearing a black cape and long dress strolled the sidewalks with a group of gawking tourists behind her. She seemed to float along as she chatted into a microphone about the spirits living in a building where they served a different kind of spirit. One could lead to seeing the other. Since 1779, The Tavern had been many things, a home, a boardinghouse, a bar, and even a hospital during the War Between the States.

Dillon recognized the Haint Mistress of Abingdon. He wondered what she would think if she knew vampires lived here as well as ghosts. She and Elke exchanged broad smiles. The Haint Mistress waved her over, turned off her mic and said, "Heya, darlin'. Good to see you out and about. How are your allergies?"

"Good for today. Usually better in fall and winter."

"I hear ya. I contacted you because last night someone was loved to death. It happened by the sculpture near the fountain where a runaway teen drowned. He had dog bites on him. The really odd thing is that the ghosts claim the dog isn't alive."

"That is strange. Ghost dogs don't usually bite anyone."

"It's a conundrum, all right. That's all I got. Good luck, dearie. All right, everyone. I apologize for the break in the action. Let's, oh, I need to turn my mic back on. There! All right let's keep walking this way," the Haint Mistress said. Like a pied piper, the ghostspeaker led her flock to see the historic town's haunted sites.

"How do you know the Haint Mistress? Is she a big art collector, too?" Dillon asked.

"No. She's a ghost whisperer. She has excellent senses and has been helpful with difficult spirits. The Haint Mistress claims some of them are quite chatty. Over the years, ghosts have provided me with important intelligence," Elke said.

"You think lightning will strike twice?" Dillon asked.

"Yes. It often does, in nature and supernature. Ferals find a hunting ground and if it's fertile, they frequent it. If there is some kind of vampire hound, well, that really upsets me. We must put it down immediately. Now, pay attention when you walk, dear. Even at midnight, people drive like maniacs on Main Street. No need to flaunt your immortality by getting run over," she told him.

"I was hoping to see the renowned ghost horse," Dillon said. He listened but didn't hear any sign of the infamous spirit stallion that rode through downtown on some evenings.

"He prefers to linger near the Martha Washington. I'll try to call him," Elke said and whistled. "Perhaps he will join us on our walk. Perhaps not. It is four blocks to the creek and railroad tracks. We can walk around them or cross the rails and jump Town Creek. It's less than a mile either way, and it's a beautiful night."

"You're hoping to find the trail or flush out the killer?"

"And enjoy walking with you," Elke said. She smiled and guided Dillon to Court Street, heading southward. Two blocks later, past

Park Street, Dillon sensed company. He was disappointed that he didn't hear the thundering hooves of the ghost horse, instead, he heard a heartbeat pounding. He smelled nervous sweat and rank illness on the night air, along with oil, gun powder and whiskey. Dillon glanced toward Elke. She rolled her eyes.

Seeming to move in slow motion, the addict jumped, actually stumbled, out in front of them, gun in hand, hoping to surprise and spook them. He seemed startled, too. "Don't . . ."

In a blink, Elke snatched the gun from his hand.

" . . . move," he told them, threatening with his bare hands. "I'm serious," he said, his empty fist shaking. He still hadn't noticed, so Elke made a showy display of handing the addict's weapon to Dillon. With a predatory smile, he packed it away into his jacket.

"Tonight, I shall perform a public service. Stand right there, Jack," Elke said. When she smiled at the shambles of a young man, he stood bedazzled. She stepped closer, placing a hand under his chin and lifting his head to stare into his eyes. The meth head was little more than a husk of a man, the soul buried deep. She had to reach through the haze of addiction. "He has something to live for, a kid, and good parents, but he's a mess and can't afford the money for counseling or detox. How lucky you are, Jack!"

He had encountered a compassionate vampire. Dillon didn't know if there were any others. Was he just so smitten that he didn't know he was doing something wrong? Ending a life? Life was precious. Who was he to end it? Dillon, bringer of death?

Elke seized Jack's head in both hands, bringing her teeth to his neck. Dillon smelled the coppery tang of blood in the air and held onto The Bloodlust even tighter. The first time that Dillon had witnessed this he had been disgusted, as it seemed savage until he saw the results. She had experimented with cleansing people over the years. Hoyt, who had once been a doctor and still served her in this capacity, had assisted her in conducting the study. Using the carotid artery worked the best, better than tapping into their wrist. The femoral worked well, but biting into someone's thigh seemed animalistic, she insisted. Dogs bit people in the leg.

Dillon turned his back and slowly surveyed the area, making sure the coast was clear. He didn't hear anyone or smell anybody on the wind. This would be over in a minute.

A cool breeze slowed everything to stillness, then a ghostly stallion galloped up the street, its ethereal mane and tail trailing St. Elmo's fire. The purple lightning crackled as the spirit trotted by, but it seemed to pause long enough to give Dillon a long look. He swore it winked at him.

"You nudged him out into our way. You knew he needed help, didn't you?" he asked the horse. It whinnied, so he took that as a yes, and gave an eye roll meaning of course.

Dillon pondered if they were the only supernatural protectors of the place. Were there ghost dogs too loyal to pass on? He didn't see anybody or anything else nearby as Key finished her unusual charity work. Even so, he sensed the stare of a predator although he couldn't pinpoint its origin. The Bloodlust felt strong. It could be his own hunger attempting to overwhelm him.

"There," Elke said. She wiped her mouth and grimaced. "Ugh. Meth. I need a glass of wine. Go home, Jack, and stay clean. Love your family. You despise recreational drugs, booze, and cigarettes. No chaw or dipless either. You are careful with prescriptions. Start a new, smarter life," she told him. Jack looked back, his spirit no longer at the mercy of his mind and body, and flashed a grin. With a firm stride, Jack walked away to a new future.

His bright eyes had shined with adoration, and Dillon knew he would listen. Elke's words would come back to him time and time again, reminding and reinforcing. Dillon had met a man at the Bristol Public Library who she had rehabilitated. Ramon had looked great, was employed, happy and chatty.

"You just saved a life and a family," he told her.

"There goes another masterpiece. It just needed a lot of cleaning up. Still does. We are helping our community. Remember that when you give your gift to Darlene," Elke said.

Although Dillon was tempted, they decided not to make a scene and jump Town Creek. Ten peaceful minutes later, via a circuitous walk down three streets to reach the other part of Court Street, they reached their destination. The brick-walled, one-story Abingdon Home for Seniors in the Elder Spirits Community sprawled out into windowed wings at the end of the road. An illuminated fountain decorated the entrance. Elke used her parasol as a shield, and they avoided getting splashed.

Without makeup, there was no reason to worry about cameras. There was no threshold either. Destrange could be here. Dillon and Elke pushed through the front doors of the assisted living center to the flower-adorned, white-walled lobby and the unmanned information desk. She smiled, took his hand, and guided him down the left wing where flute music trilled through the air.

The tune sounded very familiar, pleasant company to the coughing, wheezing, gasping, and resounding, sometimes chortling, snores. If you were sleep singing, you were breathing, he thought. Death hung heavily like a haze over a refugee hospital. It was simply a matter of time.

"Feel fortunate. You will never know this. Never confuse the two i-words, immortal with invulnerable. You can be destroyed."

He could clearly recall how easily the vampire hunter had slain the rogue vampire. She had been obliterated by a paintball gun loaded with garlic and blessed water.

"I would hate to end up living forever wishing I had died with you. It would leave me embittered," Elke told him.

Hand in hand, they continued along the hallway. He eyed the paintings of pastoral landscapes and colorful floral gardens, examples of life in this place of dying. She paused at the door of an open room where an elderly couple slept in single beds, and yet they held hands across the open space.

Elke strolled past the room where the music was being played. Even before Dillon peeked in, he knew who it was. Master Cosmo continued to play his flute for the woman wasting away in her bed. Dillon didn't want to intrude on his sensei.

"Mr. Urich, I didn't sense you there. You are making late rounds. Good to see you, Dillon," Master Cosmo greeted him.

Dillon had not visited Master Cosmo since returning home. He had planned to, but then life and death intervened, turning his world upside down. They greeted each other with an embrace. Dillon's hands and heart warming up, he felt exceptionally pleased to see his old mentor. Fears and tension slipped away from him.

Dillon realized that Master Cosmo no longer possessed the aura of a powerful and healthy man. His mentor had once felt willowy, strong, and resilient. Now he was brittle like an aged reed. His shoulders sagged, his arms were thinner, and his swarthy skin had wrinkled like old leather. His dark eyes remained bright and attentive, though, so he still had his mind. There was no fear, and yet it struck Dillon that his mentor was here easing the pain of others even as he was facing the terminal failure of his body.

"I was saddened to hear you have been ill. Challenges and change come to us all. It is our reaction to them, the Seen and Unseen, which influences us the most."

"You look like you have seen better days," Dillon replied.

"You could always see clearly into the heart. I have ripened beyond my prime. I think there may be some twists and turns left on my journey, but I can almost see the end of my path. The day that knows my name is too swiftly approaching. It happens to all humans. Do you still follow the Ways of the Living Sword?" he asked.

"Yes, and I have refocused on them to aid in my healing," Dillon said.

"I thought I could see it when I read your articles. My favorite was your work on alternative healing."

Dillon had almost forgotten about that. He had finished prior to returning to Bristol and dying. There were weeks that he couldn't recall. It seemed nearly dying affected the brain cells and recent memories. Who knew what transforming into a vampire had done to his recollections now that he had a supernatural brain and senses?

"I apologize. I should have visited you sooner, had I not been so self-absorbed."

"Do not concern yourself with such thoughts. I spoke with your mother. I know you have been through much change and loss."

"I'm still adjusting to living the night life. I miss the sun and my friends," he said.

"Aw, there is no replacing good friends and loved ones, but you are greater than the darkness. I see the light that shines from within you. I see it even now as I did back then. I foresaw you would be destined for great and simple compassionate deeds. It is that way for all who carry Shadowsbane. Push away your doubts. Now is your time. You must be the light in the darkness. As my student, you were always exceptionally bright among many radiant lights here. It is not how we die that is as important as how we lived daily. Dying is rarely of our choosing. Living is all about choice and consequences, as are all good hero and character tales. At least I keep telling myself that. I doubt I will go out fighting a dragon to save the town like in the stories of old," he chuckled.

"I am trying to make a difference and be a light."

"As we both are, including now by bringing Darlene a gift," Elke said when she stepped into the room. Master Cosmo's expression barely changed, but the light in his eyes shifted, gleaming as if he were facing a competitor.

"This is my love, Elke Swearington. She saved my life."

"I can see why you were absorbed. We all need angels to help us along," Dillon's sensei replied.

"That's the truth. Darlene taught my grandmother. They thought the world of each other, so I wanted Dillon to meet her," Elke said.

"Gratitude is a powerful emotion. Life is precious and short. Our time races toward the end as if gravity has seized it and us. Make the most of it, what you have been gifted. Dillon, please, call me, soon. My number is unchanged," Master Cosmo said.

Dillon was sure that his mentor had sensed a difference in him. But how much of the truth could he discern about Elke? When Dillon was younger, Master Cosmo seemed to have magical powers and mystical insight.

"Goodnight. It was a pleasure to meet you, sir," Elke said.

"And a wonder to meet you, Ms. Swearington. May y'all's love outlast the ages, and peace be with you," he said.

Once back in the hall, Elke introduced him to a pretty and powerfully built woman with short dark hair and mirthful eyes set in a round face with apple cheeks. Her skin was milky and flawless. Elke had thralls and agents all over the region, including in elderly care centers. "Good evening, Mistress."

"A beautiful evening to you, Amelia," Elke said and introduced him to the night manager.

"It is a pleasure. Come meet Darlene Flicker. She has been looking forward to this," Amelia said and briskly led them farther along the hall into room seventeen.

"How long have you worked here, Amelia?" Dillon asked.

"It depends. Under the names Emily Nutt and Amelia Nutterson, thirty years."

"You don't look a day over thirty-five," Dillon said.

"Thank you, kindly. It's all that wrestling on my nights off. I do some local WWF. I'm Killer Stare. My sister works at the hospital.

Nurse Mandy Nutt wrestles, too. We like to confuse people," she said with a chuckle. She opened the door and announced them. "Darlene, Dillon and Ms. Swearington have come."

Frail Darlene, her aura dim, shifted restlessly in a hospital bed. The room was decorated for her recent birthday with heart-shaped balloons and well-wishing cards standing up to be seen. By the number, Darlene was greatly loved. She smiled weakly and gurgled a greeting. Dillon gently took Darlene's hand. Her grip grew stronger. Her eyes brightened even as her smile widened.

"Good evening, Darlene, my name is Dillon."

"Are you a vampire?" she asked. Even now, Darlene was still investigating.

"Yes, I am. I'm here to assist you in bringing your life to the end of your choosing, if, that is what you want," he said. The old woman nodded. He looked through her eyes into her soul. He wanted consent to take a life. "Do you know what I am asking?"

"She is a vampire, too?" Darlene asked, nodding toward his lady love.

Elke bowed, and as she lifted her head, her features changed. She had aged greatly and not well, looking like Darlene's twin sister. Her smile grew beautiful and remained so when Elke returned to her chosen and ideal form of Venus incarnate.

Darlene's eyes were bright. "I have an answer to my question. Yes, there is the supernatural. There is more than we know."

"Yes, there are beings who thrive in the dark that shun the sunshine, but not all shun the light."

"No contract to sign. No word to give. No soul to give, right?" Darlene said.

"Keep your soul. You'll want it in the Afterlife."

"You have seen it?"

"Yes. My best friend and I have lived to talk about it. It is timeless there. No reason to hurry," Dillon said. Even now, he could see his father's hand falling away as Dillon returned to this world into the arms of Elke.

"Amelia said I could dance at Sheyanne's wedding. Is that true?"

"Yes, you can dance for at least 72 hours with vim and vigor, perhaps as many as four or five days, and through it all, you will require no sleep. But when that time ends, it will be the final rest for your body. I know not what happens to your consciousness," Elke replied.

"I want time and freedom from pain. Life is not about suffering," Darlene managed.

"I see that you are a devout Christian, a believer in Jesus and God. Are you sure about this? I don't want you to do something counter to your beliefs," Dillon said.

"Like someone evil would care if I was certain or a Doubting Thomas. Listen, young man, I prayed on it. I was given a vision of what you would look like, and here you are the spittin' image of what I saw in my mind. I take that as a sign of affirmation," Darlene said.

"As you wish. I'll be gentle," Dillon said. He had never done this, but he had watched Elke when she had sustained herself on a patient in a facility in Kingsport. She had been kind and gentle and a great comfort to Marla. Dillon had watched her grow stronger. He had met the formerly infirmed woman and danced with Marla at her family's reunion. She had considered Elke a miracle, the time a blessing. The gift of existence, the woman's blood, still sustained Elke a month later. She had been testing the theory that freely given blood, especially the last of a person's life, sustained a vampire longer.

"Life is about quality, not quantity. More moments that take your breath away instead of the number of breaths you take," Marla had told him when she saw that look in his eyes.

"I can die helpless in bed or dance my way into the grave. What would you choose at my age? I am sorry that I will not be able to tell my friends the truth about vampires," Darlene said.

"You will be compelled. You will have no choice if that helps."

"It does, thank you. I hate keeping secrets from them. You are handsome, young sir. Will you kiss me?" Darlene asked.

"Of course," Dillon replied. He kissed her softly on the lips, feeling them tremble.

"So handsome and charming, you are. I felt tingling all the way to my toes," Darlene cooed.

He took her hand and kissed it, too. Instead of intruding immediately on the carotid in her neck, he bit into her wrist. A venom in his saliva numbed the victim's flesh making this painless. Some of his blood and saliva would replace hers, temporarily and supernaturally empowering her. He moved to her neck and nipped her flesh, his teeth finding her carotid artery. Her blood tasted wonderful, heady, a jolting liquid like tequila spiked with lightning, leaving him thunderstruck and nearly lost on the rising tide of power. He reluctantly forced himself to slow and savor it so that he would do no sudden harm.

During that time, he communed with Darlene and learned about her life, its triumphs, and tragedies, along with her despairs, her ecstasies and her loves. As a child, she played outside all day and in the barn, running all over the farm and in and out of an old black and white log house. Dogs, chickens and more chased her. Her hands spun guns and flew across the keys of a piano. Her voice swelled to fill the church and school auditoriums. She married with smiles and divorced with tears, and then she remarried with tears and laughter. Kids were born, matured, had their own kids who had kids. Those recollections filled him with life as well, human life. Right now, his hands thrummed and shook. Darlene's body trembled. He felt suffused with power and drew back. He needed no more. He could leap a building in a single bound, he mused. He wouldn't be surprised if he positively crackled with zest and zeal! This feeling was incomparable to anything he had ever experience before.

Dillon glanced over to his beloved. It was almost as good as sex with Key. Almost. She smiled knowingly and winked at him. That empowered him, too.

Darlene's blue eyes blazed bright with life. "Is that it?" she asked, slurring a little. The wound on her wrist was already healing. From what he'd seen, for a few days, perhaps several, she would have an accelerated metabolism, allowing her to regenerate tissue damage.

Elke smiled. "You should be feeling fabulous soon. It takes a while to work through your system, but by daybreak, you will feel restless and spry. You'll think you can perform cartwheels, and if you want, you can. At that point, the clock is ticking. Do whatever you wish in these final days."

"Cartwheels? Seriously. Oh, no, of course not. You're pulling my leg," Darlene said. Already, she spoke more coherently. Dillon grinned. Darlene returned his smile. "I'm talking more clearly, aren't I?" she asked and laughed. "I have never felt this good. It reminds me a little of being pleasantly tipsy."

"That is what a healthy young body feels like. Your strength will grow, and your flexibility will return. You'll surprise yourself and others. Remember, no mention of us," Elke said.

"I will only speak of angels bringing miracles."

Nearby, the woman in the next bed stirred. Her eyes opened, looking into Dillon's. He could see her envy and well wishes for Darlene.

"That's my friend, Mary Lou. She is stuck in a broken body, too. She might be next," Darlene said. She glanced over to Mary Lou who acknowledged the possibility.

Dillon saw pleading in her eyes and took her hand as she wished. Their connection was electric, a jolt of white lightning coruscating between them. Mary Lou's eyes widened to briefly bulge before she smiled, sighed, and fell asleep. Dillon released her hand. Her life aura appeared brighter than before. Did that mean he had taken life from Darlene and given it to her friend? He didn't feel any lessened. *What am I becoming? And would it get him killed?*

Once outside, Elke asked the same question. "Why do you have the glow of life around you?"

"I have no clue. Did I take some life from Darlene or Mary Lou?" Dillon asked.

"It doesn't work like that. You gain energy and thereby the ability to handle The Bloodlust and its power. This could be a problem. Vampires don't have life auras. What is Dragomir going to think?"

"That I'm unique? A conundrum of a vampire?" he asked.

Key's laugh sounded nervous. Her phone made a bing sound, so Elke checked for a text message. "Desiree is loitering around the fountain. That girl is heart-broken and looking to fight," Elke sighed. Arm in arm, enjoying each other and the moment, and yet still on alert, they strolled back toward the parking lot. They reveled in the night and basked under the moon waxing toward full. No ghost stallion, guided tour, or mugger interrupted. It was just the two of them.

"I love you, Key," Dillon said.

"I feel it, and I hope you know I love you beyond words. That said, I wish we could just go home and love each other, but we are running out of time. It would be unwise of us to need a second summons to appear before Dragomir at The Bristol Hotel. I don't understand how you can be who you are and have your heart chakra aglow. I will point out to Judge Dragomir that this is a testament to your ability and readiness to walk in both worlds, straddling that line with me," Elke said. She couldn't hide her concern despite her optimism.

"*I Walk the Line* comes to mind," Dillon said.

"That was Johnny Cash. He was from Arkansas. June Carter was from nearby, Maces Springs. She was a gifted and loving lady," Elke said.

They both heard it, a scream starting only to be cut off. Dillon listened closely, picking up the sound of shoes scuffling. He and Elke exchanged glances. They heard a deep grunt. It sounded like Big Al, also known as Mr. Thick, taking a hit. His garbled shout alerted them to a supernatural attack.

"Desiree's found more trouble than she can handle," Elke said and moved so swiftly that he literally ate her dust. She dashed up the deserted street to the fountain and fell upon the struggling pair. She punched the bald vampire in the back, shattering his spine. He released Desiree who yelped when she yanked her arm away. One eye was blackened, and her nose appeared broken. Desiree was angry and irrational.

Dillon waited, instead of charging in, just in case there was a second vampire. Besides, of the two of them, Elke was far better and more experienced at fighting vampires. With a fountain full of moving water capable of killing them, they must be careful. He checked on Al. Elke's large chauffeur was groggy and rubber-legged from a blow to the head. His jaw looked crooked, broken likely, and a nasty knot had already formed on his forehead.

His mouth didn't work right. Dillon sensed the intent of the bodyguard's question. "Yes. You drew out the target. Good work," Dillon said. Al grunted back. "Catch your breath and balance. I will protect her if she needs it."

Elke appeared to have the combat well in hand, then, seemingly out of nowhere, a large dog charged to launch at her. Dillon had been told canines avoided vampires, but this one leapt into the fray. He sprang to intercept the Dobermann. It was faster and almost slipped by him, but he managed to shove the black dog to deflect its attack, so it missed Elke. Up close, Dillon realized the Dobermann had no heartbeat and gave off no heat. It wasn't alive. Really, undead dogs? What next? No! He didn't want to know.

Dillon fought like his life and Elke's existence depended on it. The dog whirled on him, slamming into him. He grabbed the undead beast's jaws and held them apart, preventing it from biting him. He wasn't accustomed to dog fighting, but his sensei had always advised him to improvise. He brought his knee up into its throat and released its jaw, letting it smack shut against its skull. He followed by pounding a fist down atop the dog's head, hoping to stun it.

The undead canine rammed him, knocking him back a couple of steps. He kicked it in the chest before it could spring, pushing them apart. As it eyed him, Dillon slipped out of his jacket, ready to use it like a bull fighter would deploy a cape.

The Dobermann lunged. Dillon evaded, stepping aside, but instead of guiding the black dog on past, he snared the beast's skull. He used its momentum to whip it around, using its big hindquarters to crash into the feral vampire's hip. The impact shook him, and Baldy released Elke.

Dillon dropped the dog and used momentum to jump-kick the feral vampire. The bald darkwalker crumpled, bumping into the wall of the fountain and its cloud of mist. Where spray landed on him, the droplets ate away Baldy's skin like a rapid flesh-eating disease, and he screamed.

The wind shifted and forced Dillon back. He popped open his umbrella to protect him, keeping it between him and fountain.

Dillon's retreat gave the bald grayling time to recover and rise. Baldy never truly regained his footing, though, as Desiree bludgeoned him with a Men at Work sign. The force of her angry blow sent the feral vampire over the edge into the water. Dillon turned to avoid the splash. Even as the feral vampire began to melt, he tried to escape, so she struck him repeatedly, breaking the sign over his pate.

"It should read, Women at Work!" she raged.

The undead Dobermann rebounded and snapped at Dillon's throat, but he was ready this time. He shoved his umbrella into its mouth to gag it. That took all the power out of its bite, but the weight of the canine overpowered him, driving him to the ground with the beast atop his chest. He hadn't listed undead dogs as one of his potential downfalls today. Sunshine, yes. Moving and holy water, yes. Quikmar daggers, feral graylings, and vampires on PEDs were part of his new life's equation, if this could be called life. The undead dog was incredibly strong. He struck it several times in the side of the head, but the black dog scratched him with its claws, tearing into his clothing and flesh. He kneed it in the chest, breaking the beast's ribs. It refused to relent and snapped the umbrella. He was in trouble.

The beast lunged, forcing him to twist unnaturally to dodge. He could move double jointed if he so wished, but he didn't have to evade long.

Elke drove the quikmar-coated bone dagger into its throat. The supernatural creature shuddered, and then it went into spasms, its legs kicking.

Dillon shoved the dog off him and hopped afoot. "Thank you, Key," he said. He looked at his mangled arm. Fortunately, he had just slaked The Bloodlust. He willed his flesh and sinew to heal, and his undead body began to repair itself. This would not happen if he had been dunked in the water like the feral vampire. "Undead dogs? How bad is that?"

"An abomination which is why it must be destroyed," Elke said. She tossed its spasming carcass into the fountain where the flowing water sloughed away fur and flesh, even its bones eroding. Soon the undead canine's body softened to jelly and diffused into the liquid.

"How are you, Desiree?" Elke asked.

"My left arm and my nose are broken, thanks to a lousy headbutt. I hope I don't have to pay for that sign," she replied.

"Have Hoyt look at you. Then you have my leave to take a vacation for two weeks. You have become reckless and need time to regain your perspective," Elke said. Desiree just nodded. Elke took exceptional care of her people.

Al looked aggrieved, like his beloved Buffalo Bills had just lost the Super Bowl, again. The bodyguard and chauffeur had failed in protecting Elke. Al would be overprotective for a while. He tried to apologize. Elke held up a hand. "Hoyt will need to examine you as well," she told her chauffeur. She patted him on the shoulder. "Thank you for protecting me and doing my will. I am sorry that any of you have been hurt. My love, you were splashed. Water burns heal slower than others," Elke said, running a finger along Dillon's cheek. It burned in a different and more pleasant way now.

She seized him and fiercely kissed him. Any lingering signals of pain were overwhelmed by pleasure.

Life and death happened every day, every moment, at your feet, next door, around the corner, down the street, somewhere in the world. Together, could two undead immortals bring more joy to life? Would they even get a chance?

Six

Dragomir and his Entourage

About half past three o'clock in the morning, Elke and Dillon returned to Bristol to face fate. She turned her Corvette onto MLK Boulevard which took them to Bristol's historic downtown and State Street. Many homes and stores were decorated for the holiday with Halloween pumpkins, bats, witches, ghosts, and skeletons still illuminated despite the late hour. It was his hometown where he'd been raised, mostly on the Tennessee side, though, in Tara Hills, and graduated Tennessee High. Go Vikings! He was just like this town, he mused, half and half, vampire in body and human in emotions and intellect.

Dillon prayed he was Spirit in action, regardless. He felt good about what he had done for Darlene. Was that because he felt well-nourished and strong? Was he developing a vampire's brain and heart? Would he completely lose his human perspective?

On the radio, Johnny Cash sang, "I went down, down, down and the flames went higher. It burns, burns, burns, the ring of fire."

No, he wasn't on the road to damnation, although some said the Good Intentions Paving Company could be a difficult company to manage. Dillon hunted, but he slew vampires and their thralls, not humans. Thralls had once been human, his conscience reminded him. Troy was a thrall. What a story this would make, a quiet inner voice nagged him. Help me solve problems, not tell stories, Dillon replied.

The railroad ran along the left side of the road. Dillon hoped they were on the right side of the tracks tonight. Elke had been here when the trains were the lifeblood of the town. She had told him that those waiting for potbellies or transferring from Virginia to Tennessee rails were easy targets. They were seen as temporary sustenance passing through town.

Elke finally pulled in to park at The Bristol Hotel in the valet lane outside its front doors. Back in 1925, the seven-storied, brick and stucco hotel had been built by Hardin Reynolds, cousin of local tobacco magnate, RJ Reynolds, and named the Reynolds Arcade. Before that, the place had been started by Theodore Swann, only to go bankrupt, leaving a hole in the ground. Decades later, Dillon wasn't sure when, it was turned into the Executive Plaza, an up-scale business building for attorneys, financiers and their like. More recently, the building had been transformed into Bristol's first boutique motel. The brick walls, stucco, and the Roman-arched entryway remained to add character. Some of the fifth-floor rooms had balconies. Display windows surrounded the ground floor giving it a storefront feel.

A young man yawned, noticed who was driving, perked up and dashed out. "Good evening, Ms. Swearington!" he exclaimed when he opened her door. He didn't even notice Dillon was there. That was fine with him.

"We won't be long, Colby, perhaps an hour at most," Elke said. She tipped with cash and a genuine smile. Colby the valet was in heaven on earth.

Once through the front doors, Dillon kept his head on a swivel. An attack could come from any direction, the right and the restaurant, or the left and the front desk. He heard only one heart beating. At this ungodly hour, only the desk clerk was awake. Destrange wouldn't have a heartbeat and could simply stroll out of a shadow. That notion kept Dillon on high alert.

He reminded himself to keep his body in Attack but his mind in Abiding. He could feel his hackles rise. He held onto himself like a leashed animal. He refused to let fear make him behave foolishly or recklessly. "This seems like a very public place for a meeting," Dillon said.

"It's neutral ground of sorts. Long ago, my kind stayed here often when it was the Reynolds Arcade. It was close to the train station, Virginian's naughty red-light district, and State Street parades. While it seems public, it's long after hours, and vampires are masters of the quiet kill. We need no silencers."

"You slay me with your smile and renew me with your kiss," he replied.

"You are mine. I will not let someone else choose your fate when fate, dare I say the Almighty, distinctly brought you to me to decide," she said and smiled fiercely.

Elke guided Dillon into the elevator. He wasn't claustrophobic, but it felt too small. He could die here, and yet, he was already on bonus time. He should have died months ago when he stepped on that cursed nail. Thanks to Elke's kiss of the vampire, he had survived to thrive by night.

As the elevator ascended, Elke fervently covered his mouth with hers, kissing him as if this might be a farewell. At the third floor's ding, she stepped back and gave him a killer smile. "Remember, when you live long, it changes your perspective. Over the years, you've interviewed many powerful and influential people. Keep that in mind. You will soon be in the presence of a being with less morals and more power than a United States senator."

"Less morals? Really? Mafioso?"

"That would be a good way to think of the Rulers of Night. A loose association of tribes composed of tighter knit families. A few are truly close emotionally, but most are alliances made for strength and power. I have been building a family here. I have agents, thralls, and vampires in high and low places throughout the area. Some are just good friends. The Rulers of Night protect, judge, and execute our own if necessary. There is little else that they adjudicate. When it comes to safety and protecting our secrecy, we can be as cold-hearted as humans," she replied.

"How should I address him?" Dillon asked. It was easy to insult some people of power.

"Judge Dragomir. He's sensitive about it. I haven't seen Dragomir since I was given the assignment as a sentinel of the lake and the city," Elke replied. She worried her beautiful lips. His love didn't say it, but she was concerned about the light in him causing their destruction.

"You know that Dragomir showing up at the same time as the myth huntress isn't a coincidence."

"Of course not. Judge executors are always attended by body-guards, in this case five, and a seer named Dawnstar. Now, be on your best behavior. Speak when spoken to and be respectful. Look him in the eye. He will want to read your eyes. The first few moments might decide our fates."

"No pressure on making a good first impression, is there?" Dillon said. He let the urge to fidget pass. He would be calm, collected, and careful.

"You are fortunate beyond words, but then, so am I," she agreed, and then she sweetly sang. "I was words without tune. I was a song still unsung. A poem with no rhyme. A dancer out of time. But now there's you. Nobody loves me like you do. What if I never met you? Where would I be right now?"

"Safe?" he asked. Those words deeply touched Dillon. He recognized them from *Nobody Loves Me Like You Do*, written by a Tennessee High graduate and Nashville Country Music Hall of Famer, Dave Loggins.

"Love is never safe. Love is reckless," Elke said. She tried to hide her concern over what was to come.

"I love you, Key, with all my being," he said, and they kissed for what might be the last time.

The elevator pinged for the rooftop and its restaurant.

When the doors opened, Dillon and Elke strolled out together into the open air of the rooftop restaurant. "My love, focus on our business here of staying alive and with each other," she replied.

The rooftop restaurant was sectioned off by glass partitions, creating seating areas with center tables decorated with fiery fountains and glowering Jack-o'-lanterns. The flickering light made the whole restaurant seem to sway while the shadows cavorted. One could get the impression there were ghosts present, but he didn't feel any. The bar was empty with all seats available.

Had he expected an orgy of sex and vampires feeding? There were no heartbeats. It seemed as though this would be a private meeting. Everyone here might be kin now, but they might be the enemy, too, one of Elke's executioners if he failed the acid test. Dillon counted three areas of darkness that seemed to defy the electric and firelight.

"There are at least six of our kindred here. One is misting, probably the one called Painter. He's concealed among the cigar smoke. I love his art because of the way he handles light and shadow, show-ing how they give shape and life to objects. I have two of his pieces in the hallway," Elke said.

"The one of South Holston at sunset," Dillon said. It was a peace-ful piece. He relaxed, knowing he would lose any fight. He must show strength by not fighting. Thank you, Master Cosmo, Mom and Dad. Of course, they had never been facing a superior vampire who held your fate in his hands.

Out of a shadow, a portable wall masquerading as a man dressed in a dark suit, tie, and black hat stepped to stand before them. He made Big Al look normal-sized. "Good evening, welcome to the presence of Judge Executor Vlade Dragomir. Ms. Swearington, how marvelous to see you, again. Good work on returning Von Damme to his watery grave. You have my vote for Vampire of the Year. If RON had a magazine, you would make the cover," he chuckled. It sounded more like a grumble of distant thunder.

"Ah, you are delightful, Mr. Mones. Thank you. I had help," she replied, nodding to Dillon. "This is my beloved, Dillon Urich. He and I were summoned to the presence of Judge Dragomir. Dear, this is Simon Mones, Dragomir's Fist."

Dillon understood that to mean bodyguard or right-hand man. Dillon nodded in deference to Mones. His name rhymed with bones or moans. "You remind me a little of the Kingpin of Crime," Dillon said. The large vampire chortled. "And frankly, you look more like the judge's hammer than a fist. Is Judge Dragomir two-fisted?"

"Oh, absolutely! The judge likes to toss my weight around and keep another fist ready to throw," Mones replied. He tipped his hat. Bald and mustachioed with a goatee, he looked like an elite bouncer. Simon Mones was built like a wrecking ball with pillars for legs and railroad ties for arms. Dillon noticed a hint of a dragon tattoo on Mones' arm above the wrist.

"Sometimes, the boss throws a dagger," Mones said, gesturing back to a very tall vampire with piercing blue eyes, bonfire red hair, an 'I would love to devour you' smile, and a body that would certainly slay mortals, all sheathed in a little black dress. She waved with fingernails that resembled talons that could easily peel flesh from bone.

"Mr. Mones is a successful horror novelist, screen writer and film director," Elke said. He frowned at her as if to say, call me Simon.

"I thought I recognized the name. You co-wrote *Monsters*, right?" Dillon asked.

"You know? Well, I am flattered. Write what you know, they say. But for us to write about us, it needs to be stand-up comedy or pulse-pounding fiction," he chuckled.

"I should write about dancing," said the vampire with hair the color of fire.

"Kate over there is a killer diller. I don't know the rest of the entourage," Elke said

"They are mysterious, dear Elsa. What you found certainly looks scrumptious. How's tricks? And what's with the name change, honey?" Kate asked.

"Sharp. I am no longer Elsa. I have become Elke," she said.

"Excellent. Stay sharp and thrive. Good work on Viktor. His draconian ways should stay buried. He will not be missed any more than Dirk DeVault. Someone should thank that vampire hunter for destroying the cronies at the Twilight Paradise. Such isn't necessary here because we have Ms. Swearington, the Von Damme stopper," Kate chuckled. A stiletto appeared in her hand. She spun it to trim her nails.

Elke's eyes were diamonds, and her voice was harsh. "It cost many lives. Sadly, Von Damme's taint will continue to spread as long as his bloodthirsty followers run amok," she said.

"Amok. You have been sleeping with a writer. That's obvious. Running amok. That sounds like fun! I wonder if there's such a thing as dancing amok. Mortals come and go like a song in the dance-a-thon of existence. Are you any good?" Kate asked Dillon.

He nodded. "Elke's an excellent teacher," Dillon replied.

"You're confident. Good, you'll need it," Kate said. She threw the stiletto at his heart.

He caught the handle of the dagger before it struck him. "A keepsake? Good for nail trimming?" Dillon wondered. Kate laughed uproariously. She couldn't talk so she waved for him to keep it.

"It's not hers. It's Stiletto's. She's here somewhere in a glittery dress and high heels, all dressed to kill. She likes to think that she coined the term, but in her case, it's literal," Elke said.

Dillon set the thin blade onto the table. "You can have it back," he said.

"Good call. It's never good to carry around one of Stiletto's knives because it's usually stuck in you," Mones said.

"Oh, I'm not so bad. Admit it? You like it when I walk on your back, Mr. Mones," a female vampire said. She appeared as the smoke and fog gathered to form a woman much as Elke had described, if you added butterfly tats along the outside of her arms. They seemed to take flight when she moved. Her blond hair was severely pulled back, and her eyebrows looked devilish above impish eyes. Her lips were as red and tempting as candied fruit. "Every great story needs a woman in heels, whether they be high heels, well heeled, or boot heels. Aw! A spider," Stiletto exclaimed. With incredible speed, she pulled off her right shoe, spiked the arachnid dead on the heel, and replaced her footwear in one fluid motion. "I'm fine, really. Just not a fan of eight legs."

"I think heels of spider killing would work as an advertising ploy. Spiders are one of the top fears," Dillon said.

"Better than Dreamkickers, that's for certain. How about night-mare stompers? I like to kick tails and take names in my dreams," Stiletto said.

"Is that why you didn't like the spidery woman who interviewed to be a bodyguard?" Mones chuckled. Stiletto smiled and nodded. Mones tilted his head as if he had heard a voice. "Ah, Judge Dragomir will see you now. Come this way," he told them, and then the stylishly tailored wall glided toward the darkness.

Dillon was glad he didn't say walk this way because he couldn't amble like a Grizzly bear on steroids. He was buffeted by tremen-dous power, an invisible wind, as they drew near the judge executor. Dillon's hair didn't stand up, but the energy reminded him of when he had witnessed ball lightning on the ceiling fan moments before a bolt lanced and shattered a neighbor's oak. He prayed that wasn't the case now where he ended up blasted like the tree.

"If there is a later, I look forward to chatting with y'all," Mones said and departed, leaving them with the judge executor.

Upon seeing Judge Dragomir, Dillon's first thought wandered to the Norse tales of the pale-skinned, Dark Elves. His long white hair fell to his shoulders, making him look slender but never fragile. A bejeweled diadem kept the hair out of his golden, feline eyes. They flicked around the room, taking in everything with a single glance like a bored tiger. To offset his predatory air, the dangerous beast was clad in dapper, modern trappings. His black silk suit had red pinstripes that looked like veins running through a body. To com-plete and compliment his attire, Dragomir wore a blood-red vest, tie, and kerchief with a shirt the color of ashes.

The judge executor moved with astounding speed to close the distance between them in a blink and seize Dillon by the jaw. Even ready for an attack, he barely saw Dragomir move. Dillon knew better than to counter. It would have been unwise to show defiance.

He would lose any fight here, and it would kill him twice, his own life and Elke's.

Judge Dragomir glared into Dillon's eyes, seeking truths, and reading him. He allowed it. It was better than fighting or sniffing each other's crotches. He felt a headache coming and grinned through it.

"I miss the days of mud streets when they built bridges to cross above traffic and keep their boots clean, when the blacksmith shops were along the river, and the streetwalkers and their johns frequented the Virginia side. The train station is a shell when it once was a smorgasbord of travelers. The state street trolley or whatever it was called once delivered humanity to this place. All were easy pickings, and when I say that I mean discrete and plentiful pickings. Does that shock, you? No, I see it doesn't. Tell me, Wordsmith, why should I let you live? You possess a living aura. That's quite strange for one of the undead. If you are even undead and one of us," Dragomir said.

Dillon had thought about this all evening. On the drive from Abingdon, he and Elke had discussed and debated what might be his best answer. According to her, Dragomir disliked wasting tools. Almost everything had a use. He relished chess, sword fighting, hawking, gardening, and the Ultimate Fighting Championships.

"I glow because Elke loves me. Who am I? You ask. I am an enemy to your enemy, and an ally to fight Goran, Butcher and Destrange," Dillon said.

Dragomir blinked as if he'd been startled by the words. "Ah, I see you have just fed The Bloodlust, and yet, that does nothing to explain the how, or the why of the glow of life about you. Your claim, it's Elke's love, is poetic. I am sure she appreciates it. As for you being an ally. Don't be ridiculous. You are a neophyte and inexperienced. Elke keeps you alive or you would have been hunted down like those you have already slain. For culling them, I commend you," he replied. Dragomir studied Dillon like a bug pinned under a microscope. Dillon felt memories flip by. He couldn't control his thoughts and didn't try. He needed his experiences, thoughts, and actions to be an open book to survive.

"What is this? Who is this man killing a vampire?" Dragomir growled.

That was not what Dillon expected to be asked. "Miles Jasper, if that's his true name. It's the name on the side of the tow truck. As you can see, he is lethal."

Dragomir cursed. His grip tightened.

"Who is Miles Jasper?" Elke asked.

"He is a very dangerous and inventive vampire hunter. Too many of our brothers and sisters have entered his cab and never left. Others have their cars towed to wrecking yards that are trapped and deadly. He has slain dozens on the spot with a paintball gun loaded with holy water bullets. He helped destroy a casino full of our kind. I'm sure you heard about the Twilight Paradise in Las Vegas. There are always reports of his death, and unfortunately, they have always proved to be erroneous."

Dillon looked to Elke. That is what had happened in the alley behind the Down Home.

"I am surprised that you survived," Dragomir growled. He released Dillon. "Do you think he sensed a kindred soul in you?"

"He didn't think Jasper noticed him," Elke said.

"I see," Dragomir replied. The silence stretched long while his stare bored into Dillon's memories and poured over them. The fight played and replayed. "I see you have considered writing about us. What do you say for yourself, Wordsmith?"

"I concluded that a war would serve no good purpose. Isn't that one of the things you were trying to prevent Von Damme from starting? A widespread curse or plague would draw too much attention, even back then. Now, it would draw the WHO and the

CDC. What if vampires are considered a virus and they attempt to eradicate or vaccinate?" Dillon asked.

Dragomir nodded slightly, a mild conciliatory gesture to his good points.

"I don't understand the life aura, but he walks the Shadowlands and serves our cause," Elke said.

"So, this is your consort?"

"Yes. I'm fortunate."

"He possesses delusions of remaining an active good citizen of the community as well as ending the threat of Von Damme. How noble," he said dryly and paused. "This should prove interesting. Only a few have been successful living in two worlds. It may lead you to fail supporting the Rulers of Night. If you are found treasonous to your supernature, Elke will suffer your fate and punishments, too," Judge Dragomir told them.

"And I would have it no other way. As you know, I function in two worlds. Because of it, we knew when Von Damme escaped and had success in containing him even before the cavalry arrived, thanks to my human allies," Elke said.

Judge Dragomir smiled thinly and said, "Deception is the vampire way, the way of existence. Those deputies who followed Von Damme concern me. Are there any in law enforcement who were involved that are still alive?"

"I have yet to find anyone else in cahoots with Von Damme and nothing about Goran, Butcher or Destrange until earlier tonight, when Dillon caught a glimpse of the Parisian in Johnson City," Elke said. "We suspected at least one of Viktor's lieutenants remained here because someone is stealing remnants of Von Damme's mansion from antique stores. I'm curious what they, whoever it is, hope to find."

"Viktor Von Damme was a maker. He didn't just tap into the Shadowlands for his own power, he turned its essence into potions and arcane objects. Anything found could potentially be powerful as you well know," Dragomir said. He seemed to grow taller as he looked down his nose at Dillon.

"Are you aware that *The Myth Huntress* and her crew are planning to dive to the ruins and explore?" Elke asked.

The judge nodded. "I am. Do nothing at this time to hinder her or them. Let them explore. I am curious as to what they find. If you have an agent, place him among them."

"Dillon will be going. They have requested that he join them."

"Perhaps the boat will sink and solve some of our problems. Wordsmith, I would like to hear what you knew about Von Damme's escape, your blood brothers' actions, and the subsequent destruction of Manse Von Damme. Then I shall decide what further will be done with your friends who know too much," Dragomir said.

Dillon managed to bite back his protests. He began his tale with Tom skiing and striking a body and discovering six abandoned pine box coffins. He had experienced it firsthand, prior to stepping on a cursed coffin nail on Cemetery Ridge. After that, he had dreamt of what was happening to Troy through shared blood, he assumed since Troy possessed one of Dillon's kidneys. It had been several nights before Dillon had returned to his blood brothers, saving Troy and others from the werewolves and the fireball of Maraders Marina when its propane and fuel tanks exploded. He recounted Deputy Burt's betrayal and the trap at J-Man's house by deputies that had led to the capture of many blood brothers and their delivery to Von Damme's lair. It replayed through Dillon's thoughts, and Judge Dragomir could see them.

"And Desiree foolishly dragged Bane through the Shadowlands. She made an unwise and emotional decision. It could be what caused the damage to the area," Dragomir said, only a hint of threat in his voice.

Troy had accomplished much, especially not dying, by flying in on a wingsuit, along with Desiree, to rescue those imprisoned by Von Damme. After being caught and tortured, Troy had freed himself to anchor a shadow gate, just as Elke had programmed him to do. He knew how to destroy the master vampire, so Elke had sent him to seize TNT, take Von Damme's fire opal necklace and the bloodthirsty jewelry box to the submerged mansion and blow everything to Kingdom Come, including the master vampire when Von Damme had returned underwater during his last gasp attempt to repossess all his power. Everything in the mansion had been infused with Von Damme's evil spirit. With Denny's help and sacrifice, the master vampire and his evil house had been mostly demolished. They hadn't considered what chemicals and toxins they might have released.

"Do you believe Von Damme is destroyed?" Judge Dragomir asked.

"No. I'm keeping an open mind, a reporter's mind. Just because we haven't been the target of his revenge doesn't mean that he isn't recuperating or re-gathering power, if that's possible. Witnesses saw Zane washed away to nothing. Troy claimed that he almost decapitated Lyla when he threw a rope tied to an anchor around her neck while the boat was moving. She was yanked into the lake where she might have been destroyed. Her demise is far less certain than Zane's," Dillon said.

The judge pondered and paced. Finally, he turned to them. "It's likely that some taint of Von Damme's spirit remains. Elke, your charge remains unchanged. I see no reason to end your watching duties since threats remain. Wordsmith, what do you suggest I do with Mr. Bane?"

"He is Elke's thrall," Dillon said and turned to his lady.

Elke smiled. "Leave him be until I need him again."

"He may reveal us."

"Troy Bane is still mine. He's just on loan to Silke. He would do anything for us, so keeping him quiet will be easy," Elke said.

"Love does strange things to people. Regardless, I have decided to have him eliminated," the judge told them.

Dillon barely managed to hold back his voice. It threatened to scream out. This must not be. They had been through so much, and he loved them. Troy and Denny had done more to stop Von Damme than the Rulers of Night. Likely, the superior master knew this without being told.

"History has shown that once someone has killed a vampire, it is difficult for them to stop. I have lived long enough to know history repeats itself. If my continued investigation reveals it, we may be adding the names of Dr. Stephen Curran, Mr. Jay Beck, and Mr. Jamie McGillis. I have agents who will be questioning those living in this area. I'm conducting an independent investigation, because the council is concerned that your love for this place, God's Country as it's sometimes called, might lead you to make less than objective decisions, perhaps even ill-conceived ones."

Dillon threw a glance at Elke. She understood that Troy's death would kill his sister, too. This must not happen.

"May my consort speak?" Elke asked.

"If he wishes to provide a reason to keep Troy Bane alive, he may speak. If he only wishes to beg, he may remain silent instead of wasting his breath and my time."

Elke bowed. Her eyes held love for Dillon and confidence.

Dragomir stared down Dillon. Neither flinched.

Dillon's mind continued to whirl. What was it that the Superior Master had just said? "Did I hear you clearly when you said that skilled thralls would be needed in this situation and perhaps others? Then killing Troy would be the waste of a resource. Elke and I can bring him back here whenever we want, whenever we need. He has unique skills, experience, and talents. He might have his uses since our trouble is still underwater, where none of us can go," Dillon said.

"An illness to your mother would bring Troy Bane and your sister back, even help keep them under control. I see. He loves two women, Elke and Silke, even you, so controlling his tongue will be possible. For the moment, I will delay my decision to contemplate what you say and see what opportunities events have to offer," Judge Dragomir mused.

Dillon hoped he hadn't traded his mother's health for Troy's life. Actually, his mother would approve, because Silke would be devastated, emotionally, and rebellious if something happened to Troy. A command might come to eliminate Silke, too.

"If I may be so bold, what has Dawnstar seen?"

Dragomir turned cold eyes on Elke. "That I need to be here. That we will be tested. That something new is rising. Our main goal is to ensure that even if the authorities suspect that the supernatural is involved, nothing will point to the existence of vampires or RON. Do I make myself clear, Wordsmith?"

Dillon bowed. "Crystal clear, sir."

"I understand you are skilled in the martial arts. I see raw talent within you."

Dillon said nothing. Elke's eyes glittered. The judge rarely praised.

"I wish you to strike me. Hit me if you can. But who would you hit?" Judge Dragomir asked. He transformed into an elderly woman with a big smile. Was that Betty White? "You wouldn't hit a funny old lady, would you? Or a man with glasses?" The master vampire shapeshifted, his flesh and bone moving at the powerful whims of his will to become younger and male, taller and less hippy. He put on his glasses to look like the spitting image of the actor Jeff

Goldblum. With another claymation like shift of his form and body, he took the form of Judy Garland in Wizard of OZ. "Is this over the rainbow?" Dragomir asked.

Dillon stood in a ready pose and studied the judge, letting him return to his dark and light Elven self. He radiated power, almost vibrating with it. He would already be in motion regardless of where Dillon attacked. Usually, he would look for weaknesses and openings, but he doubted there were any in the normal sense. Live and learn didn't seem like quite the right mind set.

He simply obeyed and tried a jab, a heart strike. His hand passed through mists, chilling his fingers. A leg sweep whiffed. Like a ghost, it seemed the judge executor could control his density. Dillon was envious. He had been trying to do the same.

Stepping back, Dillon bowed. "I cannot touch you."

"You would do well to remember this. You are on probation with the Rulers, as would be any vampire during their Gray Year. I encourage you to be steadfastly one of us. Keep our secrets, and we will tolerate you. Cross us, literally or physically, expose us by accident, betray us in word or deed, and we will destroy you. It is that simple for all neophytes. It is a more complicated now because there is a civil war in progress, making it a dark time for even vampires. Such a war is bound to spill over and complicate life for humans. I suggest you fight your human nature of sharing secrets, basking in the sun, relaxing in the water and such foolishness. I wish I could say it was a pleasure to meet you, Wordsmith, but you yearn for the sunshine. Only time will tell if the light of the moon and stars will be enough to keep you sane. As you have learned, the darkness is more than the absence of light. I believe you will make a disappointing vampire. Listen to Elke, and you will find yourself staying above water. I sincerely hope there's no reason for us to meet again until next year. Until then, I place my watchful eye upon you," Judge Dragomir said.

With his left hand and forefinger, he drew in the air, his fingernail leaving a blazing trail like a shooting star. A wide-open eye burned for a moment above Dillon, and then it vanished. He felt it settle upon him, leaving him under observation, or at least tagging and tracking in some ancient GPS way. He planned to ask Elke about it later. For the moment, she appeared unperturbed as if she were expecting this to happen.

"Now I can find you anywhere, anytime. May the Darkness embrace you," Judge Dragomir said.

Elke gave Dillon a small smile. She could find him anywhere, too, always knowing his whereabouts. It seemed like he might survive this encounter after all. He didn't relax, but it wouldn't have mattered.

In the blink of an eye, Dragomir seized Dillon. He was flung like a hammer toward Cumberland Park. He cleared the street below, heading for the trees. His momentum carried him over statues of a girl and boy playing instruments for a crowd. Any moment, he would lose said Mo and begin to fall. He curled into a ball and rolled until he faced down, and then he opened his body to spread eagle, holding his jacket outstretched. He mentally focused on lightening his mass. He prayed being desperate was the nudge he needed to succeed; otherwise, this would hurt. Now would be a good time to sprout angels' or bats' wings. He hadn't mastered the act of changing shape, either.

In a second, he would strike the helicopter monument display. He twisted to avoid it, grazed the side door by dragging his palms along it, slowing him like a monk from legendary tales, and hit the ground with a bone-breaking impact. His ankles and femurs fractured, pain lancing through his hips. He tumbled several times before coming to a stop where he sprawled in agony.

***

Elke watched Dillon fall and tried to relax. He would survive. It could have been much, much worse. Dragomir had gone easy on her consort. The judge could have commanded one of his bodyguards test Dillon. Or Dragomir could have toyed with his mind, implanting commands. She had seen him do that before. The watchful eye would itch as a reminder that he was under observation and on probation.

"Elsa, I don't see how he will be able to turn away for those things he loves and survive. Farewell sun. Goodbye writing," Dragomir said.

She turned a critical eye on the judge. "Are you saying he can't write about anything? You allow your bodyguard to write fiction."

"Ah, you have a good point. Keep him away from the subject of us. We get far too much press, thanks to Cane Concannon. We may need to do something about him."

"He may get himself killed without our help. He believes we are associated with Satanic cults. If he's pushed in that direction, that could solve our problem. Vlade, what about Dillon's book on what happened in August and the Six Finger cult? People are expecting it. It will be a perfect time to spread misinformation and reinforce what we want people to think," she said.

"So, it will be fiction?"

"The nature of the villains will change from those powered by The Bloodlust to those in a cult who lust for blood," Elke said.

Dragomir was quiet for a time. "Near truths are even better than half-truths tied together by white lies."

"We are simply calling the terrorists by a different name and giving them a motivation that people will understand. They can understand people going crazy, and *Psychology Today*, a magazine, has written articles about people's obsession with vampire myths," she said.

"Are you saying, like rock stars, people want to be like us?" Dragomir mused.

"They believe being immortal means being invulnerable, untouchable, and having more time. They don't think that it's more time to watch those you know and love die, or things change from the way you like it to whatever the hell it is now."

"It is our nature to prefer the simplicities of the past where anonymity was easier to keep. Your visits are always informative and insightful, Elsa. It is one of the many things I like about you. I still question your choice of consort, but then, I'm prejudiced. Whatever he writes, I must read it first," Dragomir replied. Elke felt like she had won a small victory for her beloved.

"Have you told him about you and Viktor? Why you were taken? About your mother? Why you wanted to stand watch here to make sure that if he returned you would defy him, again?"

"He knows that Von Damme's return, or anything tainted by him, will only bring ill fortune."

"You were made by him."

Elke hated that thought, and yet, she kept convincing herself she had grown beyond her maker's plans for her and turned the tables on him. "I was changed by him, and then I transformed myself, my old friend. Dillon understands enough. He knows that I loathe Viktor. That Von Damme killed my mother, my friends, and my neighbors who tried to save me. I have yet to tell him that she was a witch. I have been the death of so many who loved me. Dillon lives because he loves me," Elke replied.

"Well, he was dying to meet you, wasn't he?" Vlade Dragomir said with a smile.

"Old jokes can be bad jokes," Elke smiled.

"Elsa, your consort deserves to know the truth. What you are hiding might be holding him back. You are not like others. In truth, I don't believe anyone is like you. You have been transformed beyond what is considered typical for our kind."

"No, but Hoyt and I share enough to be steadfast. And you, sir, are not one to speak of the truth or of collecting secrets. Dillon knows vampires are secretive, and I will bare my soul in time, but now is not the time. There is already way too much for him to learn and take in all while feral vampires, old enemies and werewolves are trying to end us. Dillon thinks he should be flying and at least halfway to kicking your ass," Elke said.

"Ha. Good. Well, you know how we are. Our obsessions become part of us and our powers. Elsa. Elke, I actually care about you. I would be greatly saddened if I had to oversee your final end," Judge Dragomir replied.

"As would I," Elke said.

"How many ferals have you slain?" Dragomir asked.

"Tonight made thirteen. There were a half dozen roaming during the Rhythm and Roots concerts back in September. We thought we were doing great until the Oktoberfest Vampire poked the media's beehive. I have agents working on it," Elke replied.

"Excellent work. Contact me again when you have news about *The Myth Huntress* and what they discover. Most likely, they'll find death. You, your agents, and Dillon are charged with ensuring that the death these Reality TV folks bring back with them neither incriminates nor harms us."

"Then, as you say, little has changed, except you. There is an air of Von Damme about you. Why? What do you have of his, you secret keeper?" Elke asked.

"You are much more aware than the others," Dragomir said. He removed a glove, and now she could see that he wore Von Damme's signet ring on his right index finger. It was seductively beautiful, silver to bash werewolves, red rubies to cage the darkness. Without light, the ruby could look so dark it appeared as black as dried blood. The signet ring had given her and others the idea to use the necklace to entrap Von Damme. She had bad memories of the ring and what it could do, including what it could unlock. She was displeased to see it again.

"That is dangerous to wear, especially here. Knowing Viktor, you might set off some prearranged emergency restoration procedure," she said. The ring worked like a key to Von Damme's version of Pandora's box, or worse yet, boxes.

Vlade frowned. "That is a disconcerting thought, I agree, but it resonates with Viktor's other creations. I thought it was time that we find out if anything is set off."

"I see. You are searching for what?"

"Whatever it is, if there is anything, I will be drawn to it, whether it's in an antique store, someone's home or auto. Ah, this place used to be my old stomping ground. Once, liquor, women, marijuana and gambling on racing, dice and cards were legal. Then, the righteous made anything that was fun illegal. Some even wanted to outlaw singing and vertical dancing, to say nothing of doing the horizontal Salsa. Sex should only be for the survival of the species. Religions are such a hindrance. Fortunately, despite the holier than thou, Bristol has returned to its roots. I believe we can convince the powers that be to build a second casino. The Gambling Guild would give me a significant finder's fee, and it would give our kind a place to sup with a high turnover menu," he mused.

"I can live with that, as long as we don't return to the times of slaves or women being seen as inferior. Can you convince them to clean up the dump? It could be discouraging visitors."

"I will look into it, although, I smell fear here," Vlade said. He gazed into the ring.

"Does it whisper the future to you? You know, my friend, drawing on the ring's power might open you to some trick or trap of

Viktor's. I can't emphasize too strongly using the utmost care with it," Elke warned him. She wanted to scream at him.

"Yes, I can tell you wish to shout that I am a fool. I almost never wear it, but this should give you an indication of how dire this situation might be," he said.

Elke sighed. She had expressed her reservations. "I don't expect someone seven hundred centuries old to be foolish. Were you truly worried about Dillon?" she asked. He said nothing, but she got the impression Dawnstar might have portended something to cause him to be concerned. She wasn't going to learn anything, so she might as well return to her concern. "I was just curious why you're drawing darkness now. Are you suspicious of me?"

Dragomir looked a little unsettled. "No, and I am not drawing power," he began, and then he realized she was right. He was pulling in the darkness. Frowning, he discontinued the process. The judge and Dawnstar shared a concerned glance.

"My dear, Vlade. You are reckless to wear it. Remember, anything Von Damme created is toxic and insidious. He didn't build it, but he warped Hoyt's house. Viktor crafted that ring you wear from blood, darkness and who knows what from the Shadowlands. Look at Hoyt and me. May I go?" Elke asked.

"Yes. Just remember to stay aware and beware, Elke. This Miles Jasper is an exceptionally skilled and dangerous vampire hunter. During his last foray into our world, he massacred many of the Gaming Guild's leadership. Dillon may not be so lucky next time," Judge Dragomir said.

"Perhaps we can lead Jasper to Goran or Destrange, even the Oktoberfest Vampire," Elke replied.

"That would be poetic justice. I appreciate what you've done in culling the ferals. Whatever way works, take care of whoever, or whatever is encouraging too much media coverage. Farewell until we meet again," Dragomir replied.

She fumed all during the elevator ride. Dragomir was wise and experienced and yet he was a fool to play around with Viktor's signet ring. It could open doors that should remain closed forever. He had been warned by his seer, she assumed. She would hope for the best and prepare for the worst.

Elke didn't want to greet Dillon in this black mood, so she must calm herself. She could lose her mind and control of her emotions when she thought back to how Viktor Von Damme had ruined her life. Now, she smiled, as she saw a chance for joy in the darkness. She would have been dead now if Von Damme hadn't turned her into a vampire, so she never would have met Dillon. That long, harrowing, and lonely road had led her to him.

***

If he had been human, Dillon would have been dead in minutes from internal bleeding. At least he hadn't broken his neck.

With a shaky hand, he rubbed his dirt over his wounds and let the soil from his burial site work its healing magic. He gritted his teeth, steeled himself and aligned the bones in his limbs and drew on the power of The Bloodlust. It helped that he had just fed. Bless you, Darlene, I hope you're dancing up a storm. The dark regenerative energy surged through him like a wind-driven wildfire to revive him. For a moment, he was blinded by heat and acute agony as if his pain receptors were being amped to the max, and then, just like that, the nearly unbearable was gone. He was a little weary, but he felt all right.

I hear you, Dillon thought. This was a warning from Judge Dragomir. Dillon Urich was a rag doll, a child's toy.

It seemed the fates of those Dillon loved were tied to him. Toe the line or else. He would need to be very careful, a master of the martial arts. Was he to going to be used as an attack dog?

Dillon heard a heartbeat. Suddenly, there really was a dog sniffing him since he was lying on the ground. He didn't want to have a cop or a drunk stumble over him. He realized he couldn't just lie here while he waited for Elke to return to her car. He knew better than to go tough guy rushing back into the building.

He climbed to his feet, petted the mutt, and then he jumped atop the helicopter monument where he would convalesce in peace. He wished that he could dull his body's pain amplifiers while he healed. He reminded himself that he should be grateful that he was still alive, still here, and that Dragomir had agreed to delay his decision to kill Troy. For the moment, that saved both his blood brother and Silke.

Come to think of it, this was looking more and more like a win. His breaks and bruises were healing. It was a reminder that he must master altering his form in many ways. He must be able to shape change and to mist. It was so alien that he had avoided those transformations. That was normal for graylings, Elke had told him. She could get her features to flow like warm clay. He wondered about her true appearance and decided it didn't matter. He loved what he saw behind her eyes and the soul that guided her actions.

***

Leaving the hotel, Elke wanted to vent her frustrations. Where was a gang of street thugs to beat up? She didn't detect any heartbeats. Oh well, she couldn't complain about law enforcement, schools and parents doing their jobs and duties. She reminded herself that the easy-going pace and serenity was one of many reasons she loved this area. She wrinkled her nose, thinking the funk from the dump seemed at odds with the ambiance the city wanted to present to tourists.

She walked along the path taking her into Cumberland Park and to the helicopter monument where she sensed her beloved. Dillon dropped to the ground to embrace her. She was more relieved than she could express. He drew her into the shade of the trees and shared a steamy kiss. She felt glad to be alive. She wasn't alive, but she felt so. Perhaps the definition of alive needed to change.

"Lovely friends you have."

"Dragomir is an associate. We work together because it suits our own ends and needs, like working with the government. I'm delighted that he didn't kill you," she said, and he thrilled her with another soul enlivening kiss. She loved the taste of him. She was supposed to have enthralled him, but he had enchanted her. She was living, not just watching, and waiting for something to go wrong, although, she was doing that, too. It was her charge to watch for the evil taint of Viktor Von Damme.

"No, he just threw me off a roof."

"I would have jumped after you, but it was a test. If you had landed badly, you would only have felt like you wished you were dead. You would have healed. Your timing to feed couldn't have been better. If I had saved you, he might have slain you right then and there, and I would be bereft of your kisses," she said, encouraging more kisses. Carnal pleasures were another way to unleash her angry energy. "We survived the evening, and your best friend still lives to see another day. Let's go home. It's late, and I should check your body for scars," Elke said with a lascivious smile.

Seven

Supernatural Antique

The next day, when the skinny, hollow-eyed fisherman in the flannel shirt walked in, a chill wafted from State Street into spacious Grand Antiques. Bessie's booth was near the front, but she thought maybe the air conditioning had mistakenly turned on. The inane thought that death had just walked in came to mind, partly due to the old roadkill stench overwhelming the aroma of strawberries.

Bessie McCracken adjusted her spectacles. Maybe the man just looked like death warmed over, a skeletal figure with the appearance of a starving refugee. He was probably hungry and would enjoy some cobbler. She liked to treat all customers kindly, even the odd ones. They were all God's creatures, unique in their own special ways. She was glad, however, that Mr. Cane Concannon wasn't here looking for news of the weird. She was angry at him for claiming that the people of this city were scared.

Next door, the birds made a racket at Parris Exotic Pets. Behind Bessie, her sweet little dog started to growl. The din was so loud nobody could hear themselves talk, let alone Deputy Marge Cantrell. The Sullivan County deputy had crossed the state line because she was interested in supernatural and paranormal scuttlebutt. Deputy Marge had brought along her well-behaved K-9 partner who ignored Martha Mae's bark. Her Chihuahua was likely feeling intimidated. She had already put up with Carol's cat in the store. What more could Martha Mae take? The birds squawking next door sent her howling.

"I'm sorry about that, Marge! I'm going to check on the uproar! Make sure there isn't a great escape going on from my store," April Parris said. She bolted out the open door.

"Knock yourself out, girl," Pamela said.

Bessie had a big crowd today. Halloween brought them out of the woodwork, her husband joked. In attendance were seven members of the Southwest Virginia Investigators of the Paranormal and Kathy Worthy, from the Chamber of Commerce, and a pair of drop-in guests, Deputy Marge and her K-9 companion, Boomer. She kept expecting Kathy Barlow-Weaver, but so far, she was a no show. Bessie hoped Kathy's bookstore was too busy to leave. Even without her, there was plenty of space for many more guests and customers. The antique bazaar was a former Grand Furniture store, a sprawling, wide-opened warehouse with high ceilings that had been turned into an indoor flea market. Dozens of booths filled all three floors, stretching from wall to wall. People and ghosts had been known to roam the aisles. The spirit of Donna Cunningham in search of treasure was mentioned most often. She had been certain that her quest would end at Grand Antiques.

"Of course, April's leaving when I was about to take a group photo," Sheilah grumbled and lowered her camera, letting it rest on her shirt covered with images of purple roses and a button: God Has This. The short, red-haired woman was adorned in a variety of fancy stones found during her rock-hound outings. They complemented an ornate cross that she wore. She loved to explore the Mountain Empire and take photos of its history and the newness of each day. She carried a sidearm, just in case, and it now sat on the table near the cobbler since it wasn't comfortable to sit while wearing it. She claimed the skin on her forearms itched because the hair bristled when spirits were near. Sheilah Becker's local landscape calendars, Blue Ridge Ways, were a popular seller each year at Christmas. Around here, some people still wrote on paper calendars. Others collected them.

"They sound frightened, if you ask me," Pamela said. She had beautiful eyes that changed from gray to green to blue depending on the weather and to vivid purple when she sensed spirits nearby. When Pamela moved her head, her cross-shaped earrings flashed. Since the day Pamela Comber's granddaddy had died, a long-time and beloved minister from State Street Church, she had been highly sensitive to supernatural vibrations, becoming a ghost whisperer. Despite all the time that she spent smiling, she had few laugh lines. Today, she frowned like she had a bad taste in her mouth. It wasn't due to her extraordinary cooking. She had baked the cobbler for today to go along with Bessie's blueberry muffins. Sometimes, she said, a bad taste meant the supernatural was nearby.

The SVIPs held their meeting with afternoon tea, homemade cobbler with a dollop of vanilla ice cream, and talk around an old picnic table covered with a checkered picnic cloth. It wasn't smart to think on an empty stomach. Poor decisions were made when one was in a hurry or hungry, yes, they were. There would have been more mouths to feed, but the Powers, Rhonda and Emmett, docents at East Hill Cemetery, couldn't make it today. They all missed their calming presence. Even rambunctious pets and animals were peaceful around Rhonda.

"They sound scared, too," Sandee Fayette agreed. She tapped her cane on the ground. She said it was a diviner of supernatural and paranormal stories. Pen in hand, bifocals atop her head, and a pad sitting on her crossed right leg, the long-time local kept the notes and minutes on their meetings. The white-haired reporter was the senior of the group, using technology from multiple decades. Next to her phone on the table sat an old-fashioned, miniature tape recorder. She worked for an internet media site called Unexplained Phenomenon. Sometimes automatic writing took charge of her hand. That meant the spirits had something to say.

"Does anyone else feel that?" Rebecca Arnett said. She had the clear voice of a county dispatcher, so she had been on the receiving end of many calls about strange sightings. The pert-nosed, tatted, and spunky paranormal investigator tilted her head and adjusted her glasses as if that might help her see and hear more clearly. She still had the glow of youth and the thrill of exploration in her crystal blue eyes. "I think we're having a visitor. Hey Suz, wake up." She gently shook the woman sitting next to her. Suzanne Stewart had fallen asleep in the store's wheelchair. Their friend hadn't looked well lately.

Her glasses probably forgotten atop her head, blue-haired Carol Snowen rocked near the warm stove while she petted on her cat, Mia, who had her eye on Boomer. They both seemed fond of her shirt, Bill Hearts Me. A retired teacher and native of Skull Hill, Carol had also retired from visiting haunted houses and cemeteries due to a knee injury. She used to have visions in such places, but her mind was at peace now since she no longer frequented restless places.

The non-investigator, Kathy Worthy, had been hard at work promoting Bristol for over a decade. The middle-aged, former hippy with the charming, folksy way thought that even the ghost chasers should be represented in city matters. Her shirt read: Yay, baby. It's Bristol! Her button promoted her latest idea: Treat East Hill Cemetery. She had been calling for 'out of the box' events to bring the community together. They had been debating the wisdom of this one since East Hill was haunted. It seemed too soon for such a celebration after all the August deaths. And yet, many people loved the idea of Bethany singing and performing outside the Slater Center across the street from the historic cemetery. Kathy sported a pair of purple and gold Dreamkickers because Bethany's footwear was stage tested and as comfortable as a warm hug. Bessie loved her three pair. Kathy had spread the news that Bethany was in final negotiations to open a designer shoe and purse boutique on State Street. A Bethany Boutique would raise Grand Antiques profile, too. That conversation seemed forgotten now.

"Brr. My blood is running cold. You know what that means," Rebecca said with a shiver.

"That you're coming down with a bug or ghosts are nearby. Aw, shoot, I got cobbler on my new shirt," Pamela said. She wiped up the clump from where it had splattered on her aqua colored blouse.

"Hey, your eyes have gone purple, so it must be a ghost. Oh, I feel it now," Sheilah said. She rubbed her arms and the back of her neck. "Donna, dear, is that you?"

"I don't think it's her, because I hear an angry buzzing, like loud static, instead of voices," Rebecca said. She winced and touched her ears. All the investigators were sensitive in some way, clairvoyant, able to see the supernatural or predict the future, seeing good luck or ill fortune ahead.

Bessie didn't claim to have any special abilities, but she found it interesting. Sometimes, Ms. Swearington found it intriguing, too.

"Hey, is that you, Mr. Rixs Frederick?" Deputy Marge asked.

Under a red Budweiser cap, the man held his head at an odd angle. His deeply sunken eyes were dull with exhaustion. His beard stubble seemed to hide his features like a mask. Bessie hadn't recognized Rixs. Mr. Frederick hadn't been here in a long time and had lost too much weight. Rixs looked over at the ladies, offered a tooth-gaped smile, and doffed his hat. "Yes, ma'am, deputy," he replied in a raspy voice.

Bessie's sweet little dog barked once, and then Martha Mae hid under her covers. Her shaking rocked the basket.

"How can I help you, Rixs?" Bessie asked. She expected him to say he was just looking around or perhaps searching for something specific. On sale for Halloween, they had everything from a coffin to witches' gear, including hats, brooms, boots, even a cauldron, and an actual framed death certificate.

With gnarled and stained fingers, Rixs reached into a shoulder satchel that she hadn't even noticed. His herky-jerky movements alarmed her at first, but she relaxed when he drew a dark cape from his bag. He spread it on the counter, and the silken garment sprawled out like a panther's pelt. The black cape appeared to be new with red-embroidered initials, VVD.

Bessie smiled and her excitement pushed away her chills. Elke Swearington had asked her to keep her eyes open for anything associated with the underwater mansion of Viktor Von Damme.

"I caught this fishing deep. I thought it might be worth some cash," he mumbled.

"You thought right, sir. Let me take a closer look at it. Is that all right, Rixs?" Bessie asked. He nodded. "Would you like some cobbler?"

"Heh. Yes, ma'am. That's very kind of you. I've been arguing with myself about what to do. Burn the cape or get money for it. I really do need the money," Rixs said. He rubbed his belly and stiffly shuffled over to the gathering at the picnic table.

Sheilah cut a hunk of cobbler, placed it on a plate, and handed it to him. "It's a little juicy and gooey," she told him.

"Thank you, kindly," Rixs replied as he reached for it.

Boomer leaned out, his nose following the dessert dish. When the dog smelled Rixs, Boomer's nose wrinkled, and he scooted away. Deputy Marge patted her partner. "Rixs, have you been fishing recently with Mac?" Deputy Marge asked. He grunted in reply, his mouth full.

Bessie picked up the cape and ran her fingers along it. The silk was cool and seemed to squirm. She immediately dropped it and let it lie. It didn't move. She was getting jumpy, she told herself. With a deep breath, she picked it up again. There was nothing wrong with it. Had he washed it? There was no sign of sand from the shore or stain from the lake. She took it, again, and snapped it. "It seems very well made. Durable."

"Did you know Mac was found dead floating in the lake?" Deputy Marge asked.

Rixs swallowed, tried to speak, and then he shuddered twice before his knees buckled. Boomer darted aside so he wouldn't be fallen upon. Rixs thrashed about, having what looked like an epileptic seizure. Deputy Marge rushed to his side. She leaned back as he began to beat himself in the face. "Bessie, call 911."

"He's sick. Oh, God!" Sheilah gasped and reeled back. She had just handed the man a spoon. Her expression was easily readable. What if he was contagious? Was she next? Sheilah looked like she was having trouble breathing. She bumped into a bookcase of old Hot Wheels, Big Little Books, a collection of *Dark Shadows* on VHS, and a 2nd edition Monopoly game, knocking it all over. The bookcase fell into a coffin full of old clocks and a collection of signed William Hill novels for sale. It pitched forward, scattering the books and sending time tumbling. Sheilah clutched at her throat. "Walls . . . closing in."

Sheilah's eyes rolled back, and her knees gave way. Kathy caught her, struggling to keep her upright. Sandee stepped in and helped guide Sheilah to a rocking chair.

Carol Snowen jumped up. Yowling in surprise, Mia leapt off and darted for cover. With her eyes rolling up into her head, Carol pronounced, "A great shadow shall fall upon this city, feasting on our fears! They are here, nearby, there, and everywhere!" Her eyes closed, and she crumpled into her rocking chair.

What was going on? First Rixs, then Sheilah and now Carol. Was everyone going to pass out? Bessie couldn't help but wonder if she might be next. She suffered chills and goosebumps at Carol's dire prophecy. She had heard about them after the fact but never experienced one live. Bessie snatched up her phone. She felt like she was dialing in slow motion. The air grew thick and suffocating with death. Bessie found her lips and mouth were dry. Her galloping heart made it difficult to think.

At that moment, the door opened. Reverend Bob St. Martin strolled in. The air changed with his smile and laughter. "Good day, everyone! I thought I smelled scrumptious strawberry cobbler, and I couldn't resist," Rev. St. Martin said, now frowning. "Oh. What's going on?"

"Divine timing," Pamela breathed and chuckled.

"Don't start," Sheilah told her. Pamela could get laughing when nervous. Once she and Sheilah got started, it would go on and on. They could laugh themselves to death.

"Pray, Reverend, or give medical assistance if you know it," Bessie said.

"I have been blest and trained during my years of service," Rev. St. Martin said. He scowled. He drew a cross from his pocket, and placed it on Rixs' chest. He spasmed upward, his back arching, and then he dropped limp and boneless.

Deputy Marge checked his vitals, first feeling for a pulse at his wrist then neck. "His heart stopped," she said. She positioned him, and began chest compressions.

A wickedly cold breeze whipped around, catching a mirror. It began to fall forward. Bessie could never move fast enough to catch it. Even so, her eyes were locked on it. That's when she saw it, whatever it was. She only glimpsed its shadow in the mirror as the dark creature fled into the back room. As it passed, the pieces atop a stone chess board danced, and a collection of silver spoons quaked, one falling to clatter on the floor. The mirror struck and shattered.

Suddenly, the air warmed, and the pressure seemed to drop. Bessie sighed and relaxed, no longer clenching her teeth and easing her grip on her phone. That's when she noticed the dispatcher named Andressa was asking if anyone was there. She sounded a lot like Andressa Elton who went to her church. They discussed what was going on with ETSU all the time but not now. "Hi, Andressa, how are you? It's crazy here. I need an ambulance to Grand Antiques. Maybe two. Three people have passed out," Bessie said.

The cape remained lying there. To her, it seemed abandoned.

Something fell, slamming onto the counter. The impact caused the skeleton to lose its head. Its skull landed hollowly and bounced across the floor. One of its skeletal arms went flying and wheeling through the air. A hand detached and landed in the cobbler, splattering those nearby.

Bessie gasped, trying to catch her breath while putting her hand over her heart to calm it. She was going to kill her husband for that decoration's placement. Mr. Dennis thought it would add the perfect air to the SVIP's meeting. He had been perfectly right and wrong, so now he was in trouble. She might be calling Andressa later about dispatching an ambulance to the McCracken's address.

The door opened as April returned. She stopped a step inside the door to gasp as her hands went to her face. She began having a sneeze attack. That's how her body reacted if there was a ghost present.

It was too loud for Bessie to hear herself think. She picked up her dog to quiet Martha Mae. After a deep breath, Bessie apologized to Andressa and answered the dispatcher's questions.

Eight

Doctor to the Stars

Trying to shake the feeling of impending doom, Knives stood on the dock while he fished and looked out on Holston Valley and the placid, green waters of South Holston Lake. He paid close attention in case there was another body. He had suffered enough surprises.

Last night, he had waited for the authorities. Nobody had mentioned the Oktoberfest vampire, or any kind of lake monster, but he knew the Tennessee Wildlife Resources Agency had been called because Marader had mentioned getting a visit from one of them. Knives kept his speculation to himself. The bites had not looked like a shark's but appeared reptilian like those of an alligator. Had someone dumped one in the lake?

He tried to enjoy nature, taking in the trees' leaves with autumnal colors. A patchwork quilt of harvest hues, the deciduous trees blanketed the slopes and rolling hills. The flat water gleamed with sun sparkles to create a pastoral setting, adding to a picture perfect day for boating on the lake. As always, he prayed for the best and prepped for the worst, expecting knowledge and insight would appear as needed.

He wondered if Dillon's DNA results would fit the bill. Knives had called in some doctor favors to speed up the process, but at best, he would know tomorrow. He didn't know what to make of J-Man's contention that there was no light of life glow around Dillon and Elke. Knives felt it likely that J-Man's brain was playing tricks on him. He would suggest that Mr. Jay Beck get a brain scan. Seeing auras wasn't only present in concussions. It could be the sign of a more serious injury or disease.

Life was fragile. So much could go wrong, as last night's corpse washing up on shore reminded them. Whatever had killed Mac was still out there. Seize the moment, he told himself, and yet keep a long term view. After August, he didn't need reminding, but he felt as if he were being clubbed over the head with yet another warning to take nothing for granted.

Knives looked forward to meeting the myth huntresses and her crew, as well as watching them map the bottom of the lake near Cemetery Ridge. He shivered, trying to shake it off, but the fear of something about to go wrong any minute relentlessly plagued him. He had refused the offer to dive, but he would join them as the onboard doctor. Humans being human, especially on a boat and scuba diving, suffered mishaps and accidents. His mind started to list them: embolisms, cyanosis, drowning, hypoxia . . .. The list was lengthy.

He didn't think the myth huntress would find answers. More likely, her investigation would cause trouble and problems.

Even so, he hoped the memorial would give them all some closure. The myth huntress and her crew had offered to place the stone monument among the ruins.

For a moment, Knives sensed Spider's presence. It was an in your face sensation, a soulful scream of what in the hell do you think you're doing? Spider didn't want them to dive. Bad Juju, he had said. Knives didn't believe in such, but Spider had been uncannily prophetic.

A raven cawed and flew over, its shadow touching him. It caused him to shiver. If Spider were here, he would say something deep like Odin had ravens.

Her hair a whirlwind of golden blond, Staci stepped outside. To him, her stance seemed suggestive. She posed with her Dream-kickers like it was a Bethany advertisement. He could use some nightmare kickers. He had obviously been working too much. His hormones were working against his better judgment. On the other hand, he noticed that she was reading one of Jayson Humphrey's true crime books: *Bite of the Red Widow.*

"Can I get you anything, Dr. Curran? A hot toddy? Or maybe bait? Are you catching anything?" she asked. Staci's blazing words sashayed along like a woman's rolling hips and left a trail of steam as they slowly faded.

"I'm not really trying to catch anything. I'm woolgathering," Knives said. He was going to need a cold swim, soon.

"Since it's water, I thought you would be pondering. Last night's floater made me skittish. How about you, Doc?" Staci said.

"I'm watching the water more carefully than usual," Knives replied. He seemed hypersensitive. Footsteps on the wooden boards caught Knives' attention.

"Hey, good to see you, buddy! Here for an episode of smokin' hot women boldly dive where we lame bros fear to tread water?" Tom Marader chuckled. As usual, his words were fiery, but this time Knives heard and saw undertones of icy fear. Marader wore sunglasses, a dazzling smile, and a beer foam mustache.

"I am here if needed. I hope I am not," Knives replied.

"Yeah, I know you like to get paid to watch," his blood brother jested.

"Topless bikini contest every Wednesday. Women get in free. Drinks 2 for 1," Kia added.

"Dr. Voyeur. Who knew?" Staci asked and peeled with laughter. With a grin, she darted back inside.

Marader rolled his eyes. "At least my insurance is updated and paid in full. Go, Girl Power. I'll lean in. Anyway, Madi's using me."

"Baby, use me until I'm all used up," Kia sang.

Knives recognized the old Bill Withers song. "Where have I heard about the joys of friends with utility? Hmm. Hey, that sounds like a family Marader motto," he told his friend.

"Yeah, I learned it from her. She is doing a kind deed by recording and live streaming the memorial. Plus, I owe the Rentzels. The rebuilding of this place happened fast. I added extra security cameras here and at the new cabins," Marader said as he gestured to the marina building.

"Bawk! Code blue. Call security!"

"This bird cracks me up. Madi's going to love having her words of wisdom in the background," Marader cackled.

"Did you mention that a chewed up body floated in here last night?" Knives asked.

"Yeah, of course I did. Madi laughed a little and said it added spice to the setting. I sat through the security footage from last night. I didn't see squat. I still sent it to Deputy Marge Cantrell, just in case she has eagle eyes," Marader said.

"Shark bait," Kia replied.

"Thanks for reminding me that we'll be constantly on camera. The staff at the hospital would never let me live it down if I embarrass myself, or call someone the wrong name," Knives said.

He couldn't help but think agreeing to do this might be a bad idea. To leave it to someone else seemed like shirking a duty. There were times it would be nice to have less of a conscience. And to be honest with himself, he wanted to be there when they found whatever there was to discover. He didn't want to see an edited version. Being there versus only seeing via streaming or recording was not the same. He had seen the video from below and even visited the place. There was no comparison in experience or understanding. He couldn't even explain it to friends or family without thinking illogically and using trite, evil haunted house references.

He understood his observation would affect the observed as well as the observer, and yet, he felt like it was something that he must do. When he aided someone, he knew there was a ripple effect, the *It's a Wonderful Life* influence.

Sarge started barking. The boxer worked as an early warning system.

With a hum and whine, an aerial drone flew over the chandlery and hovered. The machine played the adventurous opening musical score to *The Myth Huntress*. When the theme song hit a fanfare note, the drone's bay door opened. Glittering confetti rained. The propellers spread it across the dock.

"Here's some biodegradable confetti to celebrate kicking off the search! Yeah! With the Myth Huntress arriving at South Holston Lake, the secrets of Von Damme's mansion won't stay hidden much longer. The clock is ticking on misery, I mean, heh, mystery. The clock is ticking on that mystery," a young, Hispanic narrated as he backed around the corner. The muscular guy wore a purple and gold Lakers #24 Bryant jersey. The cameraman swung the lens around to focus on Knives and Marader. When the big guy turned, his wealth of jewelry shimmered and gleamed from his hands, wrists, ears and chest. Knives blinked, blinded by bling, and donned his sunglasses to cut the glare.

"That's Juju Castillo, Madi's muscle. Yeah, I watch the show," Marader said.

Knives couldn't avoid seeing TMH. The nurses at the hospital loved it. They swooned over Juju and wished that they were a myth huntress having an adventure. Knives knew experiences were one of the many reasons why people needed doctors. You could sprain your thumb playing video games, but real adventures usually involved pain to gain.

From what Knives understood, Juju handled the heavy loads and glinted and gleamed as eye candy for the female audience. *The Myth Huntress* was a woman empowering show, so why wouldn't they have good-looking guys to work as pack mules? They could have their pick of muscle.

"Hey, buddy," Marader introduced himself to Juju before turning to Knives. "This is Dr. Stephen Curran. We call him, Knives, because he's such a cut up."

"Bad juju?" Kia asked.

"Ha. Silly bird! Juju Castillo is the best juju ever. I bring these ladies mas bueno fortuna," he replied. His perfect, winsome smile seemed Hollywood-made for the camera. His words pulsed with a Salsa beat and colorfully cavorted through the air as if they were attending a fiesta. In the background, Sarge began to howl.

Juju Castillo was followed by three women, one blond Caucasian, Madi, and two of ethnic backgrounds. They were circled by the cavorting dog. Zhen Hinode was lithe, plainly dressed and of Asian descent. Roxy Gearhart was muscular, clad in Star Wars apparel, and possessed skin pigmentation the hue of rich coffee. As beautiful as they all were, Madi was the charismatic, physical force of the three. If one was a red-blooded heterosexual, it was natural to look. He appreciated smart women who stayed healthy and fit. From what he knew from the show, Zhen worked the scientific angles, and Roxy dealt with the electronics, especially the computers and drones. All of them strolled with confidence like they owned the place.

"Oh, girls just want to have fun," Roxy sang. Gearhart's words cavorted through the air and flashed with the colors of a dance floor.

"The foxes are here. Release the hounds! Who let the dogs out? Who? Who?" Kia announced.

Madi stared at the bird. "Is that our uncle's?" she asked. Her brother nodded. "Is Kia your herald?"

"Ha. I like it," Marader chuckled.

Suddenly, the boxer stumbled. Sarge scrambled but tumbled, lost his balance and fell into the lake. Madi dodged, but Roxy was splashed. They all laughed together. Juju grabbed the dog's collar and hauled it onto the dock. Everyone backed away to avoid the shaken spray of water.

"Thanks, man," Marader said. He smacked Juju on the back, almost sending him into the lake.

"Brother, what a menagerie! You're looking good. Wow, all that hair. Dare I ask?" Madi asked while they hugged.

"I've let the animal in me out," Marader replied and gestured to the bar sign: The Wolf Den.

"It's nice of you to warn the ladies and your customers. When did you get the dog?"

"He wandered in and made himself at home. He's a surprisingly good mouser. Good to see you, too, sis."

If Knives hadn't known her, he would have thought that she was the smart and beautiful, athletic girl next door. Unfortunately, her eyes and expressions reminded him too much of her brother. The Marader family genes were reckless and dangerous, he mused.

"I knew at least one of your annoying blood brothers would amount to something. Thank you, Doc, for joining our exploration party. Accidents happen. It's part of what makes Reality TV interesting. We angle for serendipitous mishaps and pronoia, the belief something great is going to happen."

Knives studied her optimistic words. They were strong, rich in sunshine which hid some fractures. Her words weren't as confident as she would like. Like his buddy Troy, she had endured some exceptional plastic surgery. He could see the signs along her hairline. He recalled she had been in a bad traffic accident, and a surgery had left her with a metal plate in her skull.

"I'm glad you're being careful. The ruins are deeper now than when I went diving. That's pushing the edge of recreational and normal scuba diving," Knives replied.

Madi studied him as if she were trying to read him. "I totally agree. It's why we hauled a Remotely Operated Vehicle to a salvage party."

"ROVs. I like them and robotics. Spare the humans the physical trauma," Knives said.

"I hope you don't have to work at all, Doc. If all goes as planned, you can stand around and look good. But you don't care about that, being on our show, do you, Doc?"

"Being on your show will make me a celebrity. You have a devoted audience at the hospital."

Madi smiled, having come to some understanding. "You have no interest in being a celebrity doc, right? You're still trying to learn the answers to what happened. We are both seekers. Secrets call us to be solved," she said, her words shining with a golden light as they rang with truth.

Knives felt uncertain what to tell her. Some of what had happened seemed akin to a drug-induced nightmare. He didn't want to sound crazy. He never expected to find wolf skeletons down below or encounter prophetic ghosts. He just hoped to understand why his friends had died. He wanted to ensure that it didn't happen to anyone else.

"*The Myth Huntress* brings the truth to light," Knives quoted the show's motto. "It's nice that a home grown product has done so well. People believe just because you grew up in a small town that you think small, or that nothing of interest ever happens here. You and I know that's not true."

"The truth? Bawk! You can't handle the truth!" Kia told her.

"We may have to remove your bird from the set," Madi said.

"First amendment rights!" Kia flew away from her and landed on the roof.

"You're a bird," Madi laughed. "I appreciate that, Doc, thanks. Some think we're hokey, all show and no product. I thought it was way beyond time for me to work in my home town. I had planned on investigating ghosts in Abingdon, but this is so much juicier, right? It's the tale of the submerged mansion of a rich, moonshiner that is the site of the deaths of several people, including one of your friends who blew it up, along with himself, using dynamite. I apologize. That came out heartless and tactless."

"A Marader trait. I'm very familiar with it. Thankfully, it's not contagious," Knives said.

"That's God's truth," Roxy laughed.

Madi forged on. "Legal documents tell us Von Damme was called into court on several occasions, leading us to believe we might find some interesting contraband along with a wine cellar and stash of aged Appalachia moonshine. But to begin, we are going to use sound science prior to the dive to get a lay of the land, plus find the perfect spot for the memorial marker," she said. By Madi's words, this was a physical and intellectual joy for her.

"We could use more science," Knives agreed.

"There is superstition. Writings on the wall," Roxy sang. Her words were so bright he needed these sunglasses. Sarge began to howl along with her. The dog eventually stopped on cue when Roxy quit singing.

"That fabulous soprano is Ms. Roxy Gearhart. She's ex-Navy and an outstanding ROV mechanic and pilot. She can fix anything except relationships," Madi said.

"Ouch, girl! I forge onward. Grove is in the heart! The depth of hula groove moves us to the nth hoop. We're gonna groove to Horton Hears a Who-who," Roxy sang and danced.

"Wow. A female J-Man who can actually sing. She's full of Deee-Lite. That's great, really great. I call that an upgrade, even if it comes with glitter, sequins and disco," Marader said.

"I can sing anything, man," Roxy said. She stopped dancing to strike a pose, showing off her Star Wars shirt of Lando Calrissian and the Millennium Falcon. Her glittery gold leggings made her look a little like C-3PO.

Kia let out a wolf whistle. Everyone looked at the bird. "What're you lookin' at, buddy?" Kia asked.

"Zhen Hinode is our zoologist and botanist," Madi said.

"You are my sunrise, my only sunrise," Juju sang.

Zhen spared him a satisfied smile, so he stopped. "Good day, gentlemen. I like to think of myself as an explorer of the Seen and Unseen worlds. Did I hear you say that this place was newly built?" Zhen asked. Her words appeared different, doubled, even echoing as if she were speaking with two voices. Knives couldn't remember seeing anything like it. "Madi, your brother's place already has a ghost, maybe more than one." Her words were very different than anything that he had seen before. Her verbiage and even her vocables were doubled, the same words set atop each other like two voices trying to speak as one.

Knives and Marader exchanged looks. "Friends of ours died here," Knives replied.

"That was Walt and Pete, right? They died in the fire?" Madi said.

Tightlipped, her brother nodded.

"I hear others died angry, howling and snarling," Zhen said. Her eyes seemed far away. Whatever she was seeing in her mind, it was not them standing on the dock.

Marader and Knives glanced at each other. Was she talking about the wolves that had attacked them in August? Knives wondered. It fit her description.

"You already met, Juju Castillo. Schleper. Gofer. Porter. Weapons expert. And all around muscle," Madi continued.

"My hands are both lethal weapons and instruments of bliss and relaxation," Juju said.

"Castillo's proud of his guns, plus Juju is an expert in jiu jitsu and Vodou," Roxy teased.

"Hey, that's workplace harassment. Just because my mom's from Haiti doesn't mean I can conjure zombies or stick pins in dolls, although I am tempted to start," Juju said.

"With Halloween so near, I thought we could use a little *Thriller*," Roxy said, and they cackled together. She moonwalked, getting close to the edge of the dock before spinning around. Juju scooped Zhen into his arms, and they performed an impromptu Tango. They moved passionately and purposefully about the deck until Zhen broke into laughter.

Sarge started barking and turned his attention toward shore. They hurried upon hearing the backup beeping of a delivery truck. Sarge bounded along with them.

"So what's being delivered, your bags of outfits?" Marader asked.

"Don't be inane, brother. That will be Levon with the Deep Trekker truck and their new, experimental, tether free ROV. It's more like an underwater drone. We plan to use its LIDAR to scan the lake bed," she said.

Knives had read about it. LIDAR was a surveying method that measured distance to a target by illuminating the target with laser light and measuring the reflected light with a sensor. Differences in laser return times and wavelengths could then be used to make digital 3D representations of the terrain. The name LIDAR, now used as an acronym of light detection and ranging, was originally a combination of light and radar. "Reading the terrain like a bar code?" he said.

"Exactly. The computer program creates us a map. That will make it easier to dive, wasting less bottom time. I'm sorry to say we don't have a mini sub, but we shouldn't need it. I spoke with Alan Linkous, your mentor, Levon, and asked him to come along. Unfortunately for us, he is already doing a Search and Rescue mission on Boone Lake, but he gave us advice and the depth numbers, twenty-five feet to Cemetery Ridge, one hundred and twenty to the mansion and one hundred and eighty to Brown's Bottom and a little more to the old river bed. He said add twenty more feet when the lake is full, so we should be thankful it's not that deep. Then we'd be forced to exclusively use ROVs or Tri Mix which would mean that we couldn't talk to each other while diving. I have a hunch that may be important where we're going."

"We are prepared for any eventuality that we could think of. We even have a portable ground penetrating radar device," Roxy said.

"And each of us is certified," Madi said.

"We know about certifiable around here," Marader said.

Knives gave her his wait and see smile. He kept quiet about his sense of impending doom. No fear of the future, no chronophobia, here, he mused.

"I see your speculation, Doc. We took specialty classes on salvage diving. We only expect to use Tri Mix if extended bottom time is required, or we find caves that we want to explore. If that's the case, we will make sure the local expert is with us. Linkous has a wealth experience, probably diving SoHo more than anybody. As he recommended, we will set up mini safety tanks and lines along the way as needed."

"This isn't our first underwater rodeo. We have wet suits that are warmed by motion and glow in the dark," Roxy said with a grin. "We're going to shed some light on the ruins and its mysteries."

"Let's get going. We're burning daylight," Madi said.

Nine

The Myth Huntress and Crew

Madi felt more than ready. She was eager and a touch nervous. Since the accident, she barely felt fear or thrills, one of the reasons she was the myth huntress. She hadn't told anyone, but this could be a make-or-break episode for the future of the show. *The Myth Huntress* needed a serious cash infusion.

They had planned the underwater episode before their main sponsor had gone bankrupt. She had been lucky to connect with Deep Trekker. She didn't want to be Debbie Downer. She had stowed away that annoying voice. She was no Pollyanna, nor was she Negative Nellie. Instead, she was Madi Marader, exploring and bringing knowledge to light. She didn't need the Ghosts of Failures Past to look over her shoulder. They carried empty liquor bottles and stupid choices as baggage. She could use a good man, though, but she was far too busy and didn't want to get sidetracked. If *The Myth Huntress* show tanked, she would have too much time on her hands. Thankfully, she didn't expect any of her brother's once gawky friends to be attractive, although the Doc, a tall, cool one, was easy on the eyes. Well-spoken and possessing a good smile, he would make for great TV. She hoped the same could be said for Levon Crossette.

She and her crew took the gangway ashore to meet the Deep Trekker employee. She shook hands with the lanky, curly-haired young man with the eager smile. His gray shirt read Blink-182, his hat, Tennessee Tech, and a Taco Bell wrapper stuck out of his pocket. He still held his drink, a Mountain Dew, named for this part of the country.

"Good to meet you, Levon. Y'all, this is Levon, born and raised here and now out of Richmond. He's our liaison with Deep Trekker," Madi said. She had only spoken to him over the phone.

"Hello, everybody. I'm thrilled to partner with y'all for this adventure. Deep Trekker has some incredible gear, and I brought the latest in cableless ROVs. I look forward to showing it off," he said, his big smile broadening. It made him look even younger. Madi had been assured that he was the best onsite consultant to watch over the ROV.

"Do the Dew," Juju said. He exchanged a fist bump with Levon. Juju liked promoting one of their sponsors.

"I'm so grateful to Deep Trekker for partnering with us," Madi said.

"The pleasure is mine. I love the beach, but, wow, I'm excited to be home. Go Vikings! I used to kayak the river almost every summer weekend and camp somewhere along the shore," he said. She figured he had been in elementary school when she'd been in high school.

"So, you're familiar with this water?" Roxy said.

"Oh, yes. During high school, I worked for Alan Linkous and Adventure Diving. He's a great guy to work for, and the job was a cool job. I was with him when we found a school bus with portholes and a six-foot catfish that knocked off my mask. Whew! My parents and brother still live in Bristol, so it's a bonus that I get to see them, too," Levon said. He was effusive for an engineer. He reminded Madi of the gregarious host of the show *Adventures Beyond.* He had the right look, avid curiosity around his cool blue eyes, to be part of the crew of *The Myth Huntress.*

After the accident and subsequent surgeries found some damage to her amygdala and hippocampus, Madi had been unable to identify people's expressions and moods much like someone with Autism. She needed to retrain her brain, so she had taken a class in Micro Expressions to detect lies and deception. The course covered all the subtle forms of reactions, from rolling the eyes to snobbery, disbelief, sexual arousal, lying, gratitude and so much more. Fine muscle movements were associated with specific emotions. Knowing this was extremely helpful when interviewing people. Some people lied as often and as easily as breathing. She had been offered jobs based on her skills, but she craved adventure. YOYO. You're only young once, and the accident had left her fearless, although definitely not reckless. She had used her new skills to select Zhen, Juju, and Roxy.

"After reading the specs, I can't wait to get my hands on it," Roxy added. She possessed the mind of a tech wizard to go with the soul of an explorer. Weary of discrimination and sexual harassment, she had left the Navy after her first tour of duty where she had quickly become a drone master. Her time in the military had left her with a strong dislike of males, and she loathed authority figures. Roxy had interviewed Juju several times before agreeing to work with the easy-going dude from California.

Levon chuckled and smiled proudly. "You'll be impressed. I have no doubts. Cemetery Ridge has been a local legend for a long time. I used to fish the area, so getting a peek underwater will be very cool.

Speaking of myths, maybe we'll see the Dark Lady while we're out. I've never seen her," he said with a wink.

"She's been avoiding me, too," Madi joked. She knew of the Dark Lady, the ghost of a beautiful blond who wandered the shores of the lake looking for her lost lover, or her missing son, depending on which version. Dillon had obsessed over her. She was certain he was over it by now.

She didn't have time to dwell on it as another vehicle, a van with WCYB News on its sides, rolled into the gravel lot. Good, it should be the reporter, Rae Kirkland. *The Myth Huntress* could always benefit from good media coverage.

Rae exited wearing a dress of fall colors with dark leggings and sandals for easy removal for boating. She had a friendly face, perfect for conducting an interview, and she was an attractive brunette if she needed to be a talking head. She had provided photos and been one of the few to share her story of being trapped in the basement of Von Damme's mansion. Rae had even drawn a map of the place, both the upstairs and what little she could recall of the basement. She believed there were entrances to surrounding caverns or other rooms. It was one of the reasons Madi had been willing to explore.

Based on her research, Von Damme had been a collector of rare artifacts. He had reportedly smuggled diamonds and even gold, back when it was illegal to own it. Well, she could dream. Rae had taken photos of strange objects in the basement that gave credence to the writings. Some of the images were blurry, including one that looked like a doorway with amphorae, ancient Greek vases, book-ending each side. In others, there had been laboratory equipment and jarred specimens. That the house was allegedly haunted and murderous added irresistible spice to the story.

Doc and Tom knew Rae from Tennessee High having graduated a year apart. The boys greeted her warmly and exchanged hugs.

Madi realized her hometown had been through a grinder. Despite Rae's smile, her expression was haunted by fear. She didn't even want to be here. And yet, she could not resist her journalistic urge to discover and report the truth. It was her job and her life. Madi liked her.

"Good news, crew! Rae is going to be embedded with us for our adventure," Madi began. She instantly knew she should have chosen her words better.

"Oh, yes! I have waited for this day! The bedding will go on all week, right? What more could a single male marina owner ask for?" Tom asked.

His attitude hadn't changed, it seemed, but Madi didn't understand the physical differences in her brother. His eyes and facial muscles were no longer readable, seeming to move in ways that she had never seen before, like he had alien jaw muscles. She looked for signs of plastic surgery. And what the hell! Did he have teeth extensions? He was certainly hairier. Last she had seen him, he was balding. The Rogaine must be working. He was much more muscular, too. She hoped he wasn't taking steroids or testosterone supplements.

"Ah, Tommy, I love you, and I hope you'll change some day. Hey, everyone. I believe I know everybody here," Rae said with a broad but nervous smile. The reporter shook hands and embraced the crew, kissing on the cheek as TV personalities do, and mugging with them for a group shot. She pointed to her broad-shouldered and large camera man who stood back and recorded it all. "Meet the best video photographer ever, Lan Caster."

The bespectacled graybeard in the Indiana Jones outfit tipped his Indy hat and kept recording. Besides being a mutton-chopped, ponytailed, and out-of-shape fifty-something Harrison Ford, Caster looked like he could have been playing bass for a retro hippy band.

His vest pockets bulged, and he carried a satchel with a sticker: Come to the Dark Side. We have cookies!

Madi loved it. Cameras were everywhere. Stars were born, empowering others to ask questions and seek answers. Life was good. Now, if they found something valuable, life would be prosperous. "Let's get to work."

With a hand from Levon, Juju and Roxy unloaded and uncrated the drone. Madi figured her brother's staff, Ginger Bethel and Staci Thompson were just sexy and not much help, but they stepped up and together they easily carried the orange, cigar shaped ROV to the shore and set it in the lake where it floated. Either it was light-weight, or they were stronger than they appeared with those slim physiques, lucky nubiles. They seemed innocent until she saw the gleam in their eyes. Why did her brother like man-eaters?

Levon thanked Ginger and Staci who fawned and flirted with him. Staci looked like the girl next door, but her hand lingered on his forearm. Madi had no difficulty reading the girls' expressions and intent, and yet, she still didn't trust them.

Levon beamed as he said, "This ROV can do what we need without us being there. It has a depth range of 500 feet and 40 square miles before it runs out of juice. The ROV is both battery and motion-powered, moved by prop for the long haul, like when we're using LIDAR over large areas or need to travel to a distant site. It has water thrusters for tight and close up work. The three-sixty window, the two-hundred-and-seventy-degree camera sweep and the one-eighty pitch angle allows Rover to see in front, behind, above, below and all points in between. The LED lighting system tracks with the cameras. When we're recording, we also deploy side facing cameras and lighting systems to improve visibility and viewing. The ROV also can be deployed with retrieval claws, vacuums, sonar, infrared, thermal scanners, LIDAR and more. It's sturdily built and tough, essentially an underwater robot constructed of cast aluminum both anodized and epoxied."

"I'm not calling it 'Rover'. I dub thee, Diva," Roxy said. Using a computer tablet, she remotely steered the ROV, much like a drone, to the far side of the marina where Juju placed two securing dock lines on it. When Roxy cut the engine, she grinned and celebrated with a little jig.

Madi had bumped into her operating drones during contests around the DC area. They had hit it off immediately. Roxy was almost a local, born in Knoxville, raised in Roanoke, Virginia. She had earned her engineering degree at Virginia Tech in Blacksburg. To be sure they could coexist in each other's space, they had gone biking, backpacking, and climbing together. Roxy was almost as fearless and talented as the highly skilled pilot named Naomi in *The Matrix* trilogy.

One of their goals was to show women could be smart, beautiful, adventurous, and financially independent while making a difference in the world. *The Myth Huntress* audience wanted drama, suspense and the sense of exploration that led to the investigation and culminated in a discovery. They rarely learned little, at worst, only that there was nothing to find at said mythical location. A null result was valid in science and educational studies but only so-so entertainment. Even so, they all learned something by eliminating an option. It wasn't like they were spending decades in search of Bigfoot. Other times, *The Myth Huntress* scored. The best shows had been along the Killer Highway in Canada, the vortexes of Sedona, Arizona, and the ghost town of Bodie, California, where there was a bonanza of interactive spirits. Zhen had enjoyed a field day, so to speak, as Hojo found kindred spirits.

At a little over five feet, Zhen was a mixture of grace, beauty and brains with unseen strengths, both in science and supernatural matters. She was a stickler for methodology and possessed incredible and annoying patience. She spoke several languages and could converse with the dead.

A show always looked better with characters in the scene to help tell the narrative, bringing the human touch, and to look marvelous while maintaining a sense of humor and teamwork and, of course, adding conflict and drama. Each one of her crew had been reviewed, and her audiences surveyed, for their appeal.

As for Madi, her smooth voice, physique and daring smile said, yeah, I'll break the rules to find the truth, made her highly watchable. Boo-yah!

They were ready to get back to work after a short break when a large black SUV with darkly tinted windows drove into the lot. Madi didn't like the look of the Yukon. The vehicle seemed intimidating and officious with its blue, federal government plates. Madi shouldn't be worried, as all her paperwork was in order with the county to explore, dive, and excavate the site. She had expected the Tennessee Valley Authority to be a problem, but they hadn't hindered her, yet. Tom said they thought any treasure found on the bottom was theirs. Two of their men had died in August during a diving operation conducted by Search and Rescue. Any male who had gone inside the mansion during the mission that morning was dead. Only Raquel Sterling lived, and she wasn't talking.

"What is this, Grand Central Station?" Tom groused, then her brother cursed under his breath as the doors opened and a man and woman in matching suits exited the Yukon SUV. She amused herself for a moment, thinking of them as *Men in Black*, but more likely they were Feds. Juju and Caster already had their cameras out to record the moment.

The man was tall, dark, and serious, with broad shoulders and a clean-cut look. The woman stood lean and almost as tall in low-heeled boots. Both tried to hide their expressions behind neutral facades, but Madi noticed his reluctant curiosity and his partner's eagerness by the tiny muscle movements in their faces, as well as their well-practiced body language. The pair of agents introduced themselves as Bond and Kaye, and then they presented IDs for Madi to study. "What can I do for the FBI?"

"It has come to our attention that you plan to dive the site that a group of terrorists revered as an unholy site, the mansion once owned by Hoyt Wilhelm and later by Viktor Von Damme near Wreythville, next to Cemetery Ridge underneath this lake. You are well aware that two TVA agents died there, federal agents on federal property?" Agent Bond asked.

Tom nodded. "Yes. They left from here with Search and Rescue that sad day. Why? Oh, you're not talking to me, are you?" he said. Tom smiled. For once, he wasn't in trouble, or the reason the authorities were here.

Madi read Bond's expression as stern, but by the look in his dark eyes, she had a sense that he wasn't one of those by the book investigators. He was open-mindedly inquisitive about what had happened here.

Madi gestured to the Deep Trekker equipment in the truck. "That's true. I have the required paperwork from the county, and as you can see, we're just unloading equipment. Is there a problem, Agent Bond?"

"You were aware the site is under investigation?"

"Yes, but I have permission to enter," Madi replied. She hoped he wasn't going to be a prick. By his facial expression, she feared the worst.

"From the county and the TVA, yes, I've seen your paperwork. I have copies. But, upon further review, the FBI has decided to change that."

"What? Why? Are you telling me that we can't dive?" Madi asked, growing angry. Her heart wanted to seize. She had been afraid something like this might happen. It would mean financial ruin for her show.

"Well, it all depends," Agent Bond said, being cagey.

Madi realized that they wanted something. Agent Kaye leaned forward. Her dark eyes and the flesh around them revealed that she was excited about something. Madi had seen that look in the eyes of those around her. Kaye possessed the spirit of adventure and wanted to dive, too. So that was it.

"On what?" Madi asked. With a flash of insight, she thought she knew the answer.

"What you are doing there. If you are simply placing lights and the memorial stone, that's all right because you won't be entering the ruins. But, if you do plan to search the ruins, you must be accompanied by an agent of law enforcement."

"Who? You? Are you a diver? For your information, you're the wrong gender to be a myth huntress," Madi said. She was extremely unhappy about this new development. This was too much reality for Reality TV. Usually, they only had pushback when they were on foreign soil. Negative Nellie had known something like this was going to happen. Madi quieted her mental knee jerk reaction. Patience solved problems.

Agent Bond lifted a questioning eyebrow toward Juju.

"He's eye candy," Madi replied. Juju beamed proudly and flexed his muscles like a body builder. "Are your pecs ready for Prime Time?" she asked.

"That is a good question, Ms. Marader. Listen, we both believe in the truth being brought to light," Agent Kaye said, quoting Madi's show's motto. She appeared bemused by Madi's comments. "I am a master level instructor in scuba. I've worked Search and Rescue, as well as salvage and recovery, and I'm a forensic scientist.

I would be diving with you. Agent Bond here does good work as muscle and eye candy from what I can tell from the ladies' and some men's reaction if you need a strong back."

Agent Bond shook his head. "I feel harassed," he said. Bond did not, though, Madi observed.

"Listen, Ms. Marader, I'm not here to cramp your style. My job is to observe, take measurements, photos, and samples, and frankly, to be of assistance to you and record our findings. Before working for the FBI, I worked for the TVA," Agent Kaye said.

Madi could see that she thought that was her job. Depending on her superiors, that could be subject to change. But if Madi didn't include the agent, they wouldn't be able to dive, and the show would go down the drain, flushed and forgotten. No, she refused to let it die. Her show must go on. "What sport did you play in college?" Madi asked.

"Softball at ETSU. Go Bucs! I'm from near Johnson City. How about you?" Agent Kaye replied. At least she had been involved in a physical team sport.

Madi blinked, thinking the freckled agent looked too young and green to be in the field. Her smile would make men weak in the knees or cause them to run for cover. "I played volleyball at UT. Spike 'em, Vols. Welcome to *The Myth Huntress* crew and show," Madi said. She shook Kaye's hand and then explained their plan.

"Sounds solid," Agent Kaye said. She looked to her partner. "I'll get my gear out of the trunk."

It could be worse, Madi mused. They were still allowed to dive, but now her crew had a government mole. She hated red tape, and it would be difficult to keep their discoveries a secret.

Ten

Reality TV

For the next hour, Madi and her crew prepped. Sarge enjoyed an excitable time barking and encouraging them. Roxy and Lan Caster arranged the cameras all over, attaching them to different posts around the dock, some on the second-floor balcony, others more distant, giving a different view from where the houseboats sat anchored. Juju, Levon, Agent Kaye, brother Tom, and his two eye candy gals unloaded the rest of the gear: wet suits, tanks, and more, setting up for the nights and days to come.

Madi was excited about the OTS Guardian full dive masks. This would be so much better than sucking off a regulator. Without a mouthful, they would be able to communicate over radios. It was more comfortable, offered improved visibility, and allowed regular breathing. They could be hard to equalize, but they had practiced.

Zhen took water and air samples, establishing a baseline so she could compare and look for toxins or other contaminants close to the ruins. Above ground, the demolition of a house would leave debris. Underwater, it slowly drifted away with the currents, not the winds.

Roxy worked in the bar's lounge where she connected the broadcast images from Diva to the tablet to the large screen TV. "Mads, it's looking good. We'll be ready to go soon."

"It's Show time!" Kia sang. The parrot watched them closely.

"You control by remote?" Rae asked. She took notes while Lan Caster lumbered here and there, changing angles, and shooting video.

"Yes, ma'am. With Diva untethered, we don't need to be close by or haul a bunch of cable. By my calculations, unless we pick up a headwind, it'll take Diva fifteen minutes to reach the dive site," Roxy said.

Levon pushed through a door to exit onto the marina where he removed the land lines to let the ROV float.

"It's the final countdown!" Roxy sang. Ginger and Staci joined in.

On one of the screens, Levon gave her the thumbs up signal to get going.

Roxy stopped singing and said, "Thanks, ladies. Good news, Mads. Diva and all systems check out. We're green for launch. What say you, myth huntress?" she asked and looked over to Madi who nodded. Roxy grinned and tapped the button on the tablet's screen. They could hear the props spin, and water churned to splash.

"Make it so. Ahead slow," Madi suggested. She was more of a fan of *Star Trek* than *Star Wars*.

On another screen, they watched Diva motor away from the dock. It looked a little like a surface torpedo as it plowed by the No Wake buoy and out onto the lake. Roxy increased the ROVs speed, and it motored swiftly into the main channel of South Holston.

In the corner of the large screen TV, a sonar map displayed no obstacles and scattered schools of fish. It was exciting that the ROV and the connection were working and boring at the same time. More than a quarter of an hour of green water passed by with the occasional viewing of a school of trout, bass, or sunfish. Most of this, they would edit out for the show. Viewers had no idea how long and tedious the moments between discoveries could be. She shielded their short attention spans from the long haul.

Suddenly, a large chunk of driftwood, more than ten feet long, showed up on the screen. Roxy steered around it. As Diva turned, the log pursued. The distance shortened, and Madi could see the truncated tree was not really a tree, as it had four stubby legs, scattered white spots, and a white reptilian eye on each side. What looked like an alligator swam past Diva. A shred of flesh was hanging between the huge reptile's teeth.

"That's a freakin' gator. Did I miss something? Are we not in Tennessee anymore?" Madi said.

"We don't have gators," Agent Kaye said.

"Well, as they say, seeing is believing," Roxy said.

"Do you think it hid in a Florida tourist's yoga pants and escaped here?" Juju joked.

"Take your pants off," Kia announced. Madi glared at the bird. She was thinking of having her brother relocate it. Kia slowly sidled away from her and whistled.

"Isn't that something? I'm glad I'm not diving," Doc said.

"Who do we call? I am not skiing, swimming, or diving with that monster in the lake," Tom said.

"I will notify the TVA. This could be the reason that man washed up dead on your dock last night, Mr. Marader," Agent Kaye said. Wasting no time, she took out her phone and began dialing.

"Well, we thought it had to be a lake monster of some kind. That qualifies," Tom said.

"We didn't bring any equipment to deal with alligators," Madi said.

The alligator nudged Diva, reptilian-eyeing it before swishing its huge tail and swimming on.

"This will make the news, at least our news. Florida Gator tours local lake. Let's just make sure none of us acts like Florida Man," Caster said.

"You have a gator wrestling background, don't you, Lan?" Rae asked.

He snorted and coughed. "Kills me just thinking about it," he finally said.

"Not exactly the kind of news I wanted to make," Madi said.

"It is sensationalistic. Myth huntress and intrepid crew encounter gator," Roxy said.

"What a croc," Tom said.

"Crocs are found in Africa. The US has alligators," Staci informed him. The ladies all laughed.

"What, was I the only one that didn't know that?" Tom asked.

"I want a TV audience, not rubberneckers or treasure hunters. I can imagine locals turning out to get a look or photo, worse, even a selfie, with Holly the Holston Lake monster," Madi said.

Thankfully and soon, Roxy announced. "We've reached the dive point."

"Ah, now things get exciting," Madi said.

"I think gators are exciting, up close and personal," Doc said.

"Ever dealt with gator bites?" Madi asked. She tried not to think about moray eels. She bore scars that would make her more careful.

"No. Shark bites, yes, when I worked a stint on Virginia Beach. You should have hired a Florida doctor."

"I must admit that I didn't prepare for alligators. At least it's not bothering Diva. Roxy, commence diving," Madi said.

Tapping and sliding her fingers on the tablet, Roxy steered the ROV deeper. "Aye, aye, captain."

On screen, the light dimmed, absorbed by the water, and the lake grew darker, so Diva's lights shone brightly. The ROV passed through a trash layer, the junk sitting atop the colder water and unable to sink. Roxy spent extra time surveying it. She liked to use their show as a platform for protecting the environment.

"Depth gauge is good at one hundred feet. We're getting close. The temperature continues to drop. Pressure increases as expected. Diva is running smoothly and sending data," Levon said.

The ROV motored through a small school of parrotfish. Everyone in the room stared at each other. Those were tropical fish. What were they doing in freshwater?

"Hey, are those clownfish?" Agent Kaye asked.

Madi blinked. Orange and white with a touch of black, it sure looked like Nemo.

"Next thing you know, we'll see a shark," Tom said.

"Be quiet. *SharkFest* is broadcast during the summer," Madi said. Her irritating brother was wrong. They didn't see a shark, but Diva encountered a curious sea turtle the size of airport luggage. The creature shadowed the ROV as if it were kin while the drone zeroed in on the GPS coordinates.

"The saltwater and tropical fish won't last long between the cool temperature and a lack of nutrients," Zhen said.

"Haunted house ho! We're here," Roxy announced.

The ruins seemed to slowly crawl from the murk into view. The left and front sections of the mansion had collapsed, leaving less than half of the river stone building. The copper roof rested cockeyed, slanted, and bent. It had slid when the lower structure had collapsed. One of the chimneys remained, giving her the distinct impression that it gave them a defiant finger.

As Diva's cameras drew closer, details emerged. The damage looked fresh, the stones and wood untouched by algae with no sign of the green slime. A couple of chairs remained intact in what Rae had mapped out as the grand foyer. The winding stairs had collapsed and stretches of banister sprawled across the broken tiles. A section rested atop a broken crystal chandelier. Stones glittered like patches of vain hope from scattered points throughout the gloom.

"Prepare to engage LIDAR," Madi said. Time to get mapping, she thought.

Roxy set up Diva, programming the ROV to move back and forth above the ruins. As the drone repeatedly passed over the broken structure, the light bounced back, giving them an idea of depth. Roxy arranged for the topography map to cover the lower half of the screen while the cameras stayed on the half-demolished mansion.

A pot of coffee and a Coca-Cola later, they had an image that they could view from the top or the sides. Diva held her position while they studied the terrain of the lakebed, the scattered river stones, and the remains of the dynamited house. They compared it to Rae's hand drawn map.

"Much of the grand foyer and the study were blown out," Rae said.

"That must have been ground zero," Agent Kaye said. She pointed at a dark spot in the middle of the room.

Madi squinted. She could see a gaping hole in the floor. "What lies below?"

"Oh dear, God. The basement," Rae breathed. She covered her face with her hands. "I was certain that we were going to die down there. I wondered then if any story was worth dying for."

"I've heard Troy talk about that," Tom said.

Roxy steered Diva downward. Using thrusters to maneuver, the ROV searched from the top down.

They saw little of interest upstairs, except for a skeleton in a bed. The Doc and Rae had seen the scraped shutters before. It looked like someone had tried to claw their way out with their bare hands. Madi wondered if someone had been inside when the gates of the dam had closed, and SoHo had been born, rising to drown those trapped within the mansion.

Diva descended, bringing additional light to the first floor and lakebed. The study, where books had been scavenged, along with a jewelry box and some other relics, no longer existed. All that remained was a dark crater. Focused light revealed it to be, as expected, a hole in the floor to a cavern beneath the lakebed.

"Shall we go down the rabbit hole?" Roxy wondered.

"Not yet. Stay here. Let's see what else we find," Madi said.

Roxy nodded. Diva maneuvered out in a widening circle. The camera lens lingered on a hunk of twisted silver. It might have once been a box with a lid. Her brother tensed and scowled. She didn't need to be a face expression reader. His entire body screamed.

"You recognize that thing, don't you?" Madi said.

"Oh, hell yeah, do I ever! I made the mistake of bringing the jewelry box to the surface. It sliced up my hands. It's the poster artifact for not bringing shit up from that place. I'm sorry the TNT didn't do more f-ing damage and blast it to smithereens."

"Thanks, I won't have to bleep that," Madi said.

"My precious," Doc whispered.

Tom frowned. "Come on, I wasn't bad. Hey, WTF?"

Madi was thankful for more small favors, but her brother was right with his acronym assessment. Picked clean of flesh and white, the sight of a grinning skull jarred them all. Diva continued to cruise, its lights gleaming off more white craniums, these with pronounced jaws and longer front teeth. Everyone had thought that only one person had died in the blast, but obviously there were more, perhaps a half dozen. Madi wasn't sure what to make of the skulls with vampire teeth. It was like a mausoleum had exploded. Would they find more bodies below? Mummy crypts? She was disappointed that they had yet to find anything valuable. Even so, this might be their best show ever.

"I believe this warrants our investigation," Agent Bond broke the stunned silence.

"Not what I expected to find. Our forensic experts will have a field day. There must be a half dozen of them," Agent Kaye said. Not surprisingly, she was keenly interested.

"Is that why they call it Cemetery Ridge?" Zhen asked.

"I had forgotten. They were wearing cloaks," Rae said quietly. She exchanged a look with Doc. His perplexed expression said that he didn't remember a roomful of skeletons until now. Agent Kaye was obviously angry and dismayed, and Madi realized she had interviewed both Doc and Rae. Now, the FBI agent felt they had been holding back, but it was obvious to Madi that they only remembered the trauma by revisiting it. Their minds had tried to be merciful and forget.

"There was another one in the grand foyer, hanging from the balcony. He was dressed like a butler or valet," Doc said. Madi could see him replaying it in his mind.

"Look at those teeth," Zhen said. She pointed at the large incisors.

"What do you think? Six Fingered Hand whackos or Cult of the Vampire?" Caster asked what they were thinking.

It seemed the only reason someone would have their teeth altered. Madi couldn't think of any other reason. From Agent Kaye's reaction, the cults were on her radar. She obviously wanted the skulls brought to the surface for forensic testing.

"There are tribes in Africa and Indonesia that sharpen their teeth," Staci began.

Not an airhead, Madi thought. All in all, Madi counted eight skulls. Six had elongated canines, their teeth reminding her of Hollywood bloodsuckers.

"Why wasn't this mentioned?" Agent Kaye asked, looking at Rae and Doc.

"Post-traumatic stress, I would say," Doc said.

"I still don't sleep well. That place houses an angry spirit that haunts me even now," Rae said.

"It's haunted? Like this marina?" Zhen said.

"Far less friendly. I think psychotically possessed would be more on point," Rae said. Tom gave her a look. "What? You've never been inside, so you have no earthly clue what I'm talking about, Mr. It's Too Cold," she admonished.

"Let's find out what other secrets lie below the ruins of Von Damme's mansion," Madi said.

Using the thrusters now for tighter quarters, Roxy steered Diva into the dark gap in the floor. It was bumped aside as a strange fish with a light dangling in front of it swam past.

"Was that an angler fish?" Levon asked.

"I didn't get a good look at it," Madi admitted.

"They have a bioluminescent light to use as a lure on the end of a line to catch fish in the deep sections of the ocean where the sunlight never reaches," Levon replied.

The ROV's lights pushed back the black of the depths and revealed a cavernous basement. Bottom feeders and brightly colored tropical fish scattered, taking cover, and stirring up sediment. Among them floated two half-eaten carcasses. One of them was a four-foot catfish, while the other was a large angler fish. That answered Levon's question, but it made Madi wonder how gigantic the fish might be down here. Bigger fish ate smaller ones. The catfish grew to monster-sized at six plus feet. How gigantic would something be that ate big catfish? She chided herself and reeled in her imagination.

The water clarity hampered their ability to visually judge the size of the space, so Roxy activated the sonar. Everyone heard the pinging. Soon, an image appeared, as well as processed numbers.

"175 feet by 80 feet with multiple, I count four, possible branches. I'm collecting water and mud samples," Roxy said.

"Try the LIDAR," Madi suggested. With the sediment settling, the clarity improved.

"Firing phasers," Roxy joked. Laser beams fired out in all directions.

"You are mixing your space operas," Caster chuckled.

"Hey, did anyone else see those shadows jump?" Levon asked.

"Stay focused, folks. Roxy, let's take a slow cruise around the basement," Madi said. She glanced over at Rae whose eyes were wide, even as she talked into her phone. Already, she was reporting the gator and the skulls to the local media. It would likely be posted on their website, mentioned on the local evening news, and in the morning paper, fitting the Halloween theme. She realized this wasn't what the public needed with concern about the Oktoberfest Vampire.

Roxy powered up extra bright lights for Diva. As the globe of brilliance expanded, the shadows shrank back. Tropical fish mingled with native trout, bass, crappie, and catfish who darted away from the intrusive light.

The basement lit up, the LED beams refracting through the glassware. The light illuminated the walls covered in cloth tapestries and even a fresco of a field of barley and hops, next to one with rolling hills of grapevines.

Diva passed through an area dedicated to geology with tools and a large display of rocks. The chemistry section looked classic with test tubes and old Brunson burners. On the shelves were labeled bottles and vases, including, ammonia, baking soda, sodium, vinegar and more. Some, like yeast, could be used in brewing and baking. Others, like concentrated arsenic and stinging nettle, had medicinal purposes. The cages were filled with the furred skeletons of different animals left to die.

"I don't remember this," Rae said.

The section of the basement narrowed. The walls were unadorned and black, making the area darker. Along the right, part of the wall and ceiling had collapsed.

"The temperature is dropping rapidly," Roxy said. She had the drone pause over what looked like a stone table, one with green manacles.

"Is that some kind of sacrificial altar?" Juju asked.

"Don't jump to conclusions," Zhen reminded him.

"When do I ever do that?" he asked. Zhen rolled her eyes.

Roxy guffawed. "Every woman loves Juju," she teased. He waved a chiding finger at her.

At Madi's direction, Roxy turned Diva's attention to the tunnels. The narrow one that the ROV investigated led to what looked like a trap door on the ceiling. They measured the direction and distance to check the corresponding point on the lakebed.

A little wider tunnel led to a wine cellar. Barrels lined the wall. The racks stood in the center.

A nearby niche held what looked like a submarine hatch. A fallout shelter, she mused.

A larger tunnel investigated by Diva led them to a hallway with many closed, windowless doors. Each had a peephole. From a peg on the wall, a rusted set of keys hung still.

"I thought you said Von Damme made and ran moonshine," Zhen said.

"It appears he had a darker side," Madi replied.

Diva was propelled into another cave. Suddenly, light bounced across the walls and ceiling. The floor gleamed, covered in what appeared to be a pile of coins. It looked like the treasure had spilled from a large, broken vase, an amphora.

"That looks Greek to me. They were usually full of wine or olive oil," Madi said, pointing to the remaining one.

"That looks like gold and silver. Think it was a large piggy bank?" Juju asked.

Beyond the vase stood what looked like a black and gold rectangle. Thin black pillars stood on each side as if they were framing what could be a tall mirror. It was much like the photo but clearer.

"What the hell is that?" Tom asked.

"I don't know. I remember being here," Rae said. She looked to Madi who nodded. "I took photos. It looks like a mirror."

"It could be a door," Juju said.

"There's no handle or knob or keyhole. No sign of hinges," Agent Kaye said.

"A pocket door? Isn't that what you call one that slides into a wall?" Juju asked.

"We are just guessing. I want a sample coin. Roxy, engage the robotic arm and scoop. Get us a couple of coins," Madi said.

"Here we go. Now you'll see some cutting-edge tech," Levon said.

"She's not R2-D2, but Diva's amazing for the early 21st century. What do you suggest?" Roxy asked.

Feeling comfortable in his element, Levon smiled. "You could also use the vacuum tube program, pulling water in, opposite the thruster action," he said.

"That may be next. I want to be picky instead of sucking up a bunch of junk," Roxy said. She tapped her tablet screen. On the large TV, Diva extended an arm. This appendage ended in a filtering scoop.

Suddenly, the screen jiggled and rolled as Diva spun. The last image on the screen was that of the large open maw of a giant snake, then the image went dark followed by static.

"WTF?" Roxy asked, managing not to cuss out loud. She paced while she worked the remote control in an attempt to reconnect with the submersible remote-controlled vehicle. For the moment, the ROV sat unresponsive one hundred and twenty feet down among the ruins of Von Damme's mansion on the bottom of South Holston Lake.

"Yeah, what was that?" Madi asked. She noticed that Levon looked pensive.

"See if it's broadcasting," Levon suggested.

Roxy shook her head. "Not squat. Nothing in or out."

"With it inside the cavern, we can't do an emergency ascent. It's a problem with being untethered," Levon said.

Madi looked around the room. "Well, we were planning a night dive. Now we include equipment retrieval to our goals. So Levon, what do you think that thing is? I've seen moray eels up close. I have the scars to prove it. They have double teeth. That thing looks more like a snake," Madi said with a shudder. She had a painful history with eels, and while she wasn't afraid of them, she wisely stayed distant of them.

"I think it's a northern snakehead on steroids. They have been referred to as Frankenfish before the movie was made about genetically modified salmon. These real lake monster things come from Asia. They have no predators. If one ate the angler fish, well, it's tough," Levon said.

"Thanks. Words of inspiration, everybody," Roxy said.

"I brought modern spear guns with us. They are called bang sticks! They're sort of like underwater shotguns," Juju said.

Despite the lake monsters, *The Myth Huntress* crew looked excited. This was going to be a helluva show, boom or bust, Madi thought. This could vault *The Myth Huntress* to lofty ratings.

Eleven

Haunts

The sun shining bright on the snow dappled the mountains in the distance, Troy carried an axe as he strolled toward the pile of log rounds. He noticed his dogs lying unconscious and rushed to check on them to see if they were alive. He was relieved to find them breathing.

A shadow touched him, growing larger, blotting out his world. He looked up to see Silke walking toward him. Her eyes were wide, her throat in the claws of the werewolf behind her.

***

Dillon jerked awake. The nightmare left him full of rage and frustration. He grabbed his smartphone and looked for messages. There were one new call and two texts, but none of them were from his sister, Silke, or his blood brother and best buddy, Troy. What had happened? What was after Troy now?

Elke looked so at peace while meditating. Dillon knew she would be disturbed that he was worried about his sister and his best friend, so he quietly slipped out of bed and dressed. Vampires didn't need to sleep, but they needed to rest their minds to retain their sanity, and it helped keep The Bloodlust in check. Sleeping atop their own dirt, even under the mattress, was helpful as well.

Even so, this afternoon he was sorely vexed, as his love might say. He wanted to break something, which was ill-advised when one was surrounded by priceless art, magnificent sculptures, and a plethora of antiques. A vampire could acquire a large number of unknown masterpieces over the centuries. Elke had helped broker sales and bought some herself. One by Monet had been given to her in appreciation for her role in entombing Von Damme in his mansion. According to Elke, numerous galleries were owned or funded by vampires. She swore she was low key compared to some of the others.

Dillon felt juvenile, a teen with raging hormones, fast hands, and a mouth to match. A snarl almost escaped his lips. He palmed a small bag of his dirt, and it took the edge off his anxiety, allowing him to get a grip. He had been told all graylings carried a rage around inside. It is what made their first year so extremely dangerous.

He dialed Troy's number while he stalked down a hall decorated with landscapes by Monet and Turner. According to Elke, many had been legitimately consigned. His beloved leaned toward artists who focused on how changing light affected the world, so the room held works by Van Rijn and Chagall. The term living room seemed ironic, now, although the art brought it to life, one could say.

His call went to voicemail. Dillon left a message, hung up and tried Silke. She didn't answer either, so he sent her a text, waited, and paced. No responses. There was nothing he could do from here. How much could he trust the nightmare? It had ended inconclusively.

There were two new texts, one from Madi Marader. It read: Welcome to *The Myth Huntress* crew. See you @ 8 PM at MM. Bring gator repellent & FBI tolerance.

Gator repellent? What did that mean? FBI. Fantastically Brilliant Intellectuals? More likely, the Feds were now involved with the dive. Elke had been concerned the Feds would continue their investigation. She had tried to subtly redirect them. Dillon had been interviewed by Agents Bond and Kaye. They had granted him access to the terrorists' bunker set deep in the woods in an old magnesium mine that had been used by Von Damme as a headquarters. Dillon had been there before but acted ignorant.

For months, the local sheriff departments, the TVA, and the FBI had wanted to dive the ruins, but the frequent rains had stymied them, raising the lake level, making the dive deeper and the visibility low. Dillon had been hopeful the ruins were buried. Now, some reality show glory hounds were going to explore the danger zone and its caves. It sounded like the FBI would ride shotgun.

Dillon and other parties thought it would be for the best if people remained ignorant of events. To know the truth, that vampires walked among them, would scare the life out of human beings. Sounds and shadows would startle them. They would grow as fearful of neighbors as they would strangers, if they knew the truth: vampires ran amok feasting on humans, could survive the sunlight, and change appearance to mimic people that the victims trusted. Panic would run rampant.

Fools! Dillon silently cursed. Why would anyone go back to the ruins? They sought the truth? He realized that he was still angry with Marader and his sister, the myth huntress. Von Damme's unholy manse had already murdered a handful of people and led to the deaths of more. Dillon had lost dear friends. He might lose more. Had he lost Troy and Silke, too? Unless he flew to California, all he could do was wait for word.

The second text made his heart skip a beat. It was from his previous paramour, Gina: In town. I'll b @ Holston Dam @ sunset.

Meet me there. The lake via the dam had been the first place he had taken her during her first visit to the area.

Dillon didn't like the idea, but if Gina came looking for him, it would be worse. He would take the tunnels to where they exited near the dam overlook. He could arrive after the sunset before she gave up and left. Besides, he could say farewell, just in case Judge Dragomir deemed him a danger.

He decided not to text Gina. He would surprise her. Dillon did text his beloved about what he was doing and asked her to join them. Elke would not like him meeting with his ex, but Gina excelled at nosing around and uncovering secrets. If he couldn't deter her, she might cause enough of a stir to bring deadly attention to herself and them. Surely Elke would understand that. Putting away his phone, he headed for the underground door to the limestone caverns.

Dillon passed through the downstairs common room where Jayson Humphreys and Justen Hobbes lounged and brainstormed. He refused to embarrass Elke in front of her vampire guests. He didn't want to hear his fit reprised in song or text.

Who knew Swearington Lodge would be a resort for artistic vampires? The real genius behind Justen Hobson was staying with them while his doppelganger played the venues around the Tri-Cities. The original singer/guitarist was a songwriting and musically skilled vampire crafting songs from the ages. Just last night Dillon had encountered Hobbes' human proxy, Hobson.

Reclusive, bestselling author Jayson Humphrey also hung out here. His last book, *Bite Me*, had been a mega hit with its combination of wit, sardonic humor, and gritty true crime drama. The stout vampire didn't wear glasses when he wasn't doing a public appearance. He read aloud Cane Concannon's rant about vampires carving off some of Bristol's population. "And yet, he doesn't believe the

Oktoberfest Vampire is really a vampire. It's just a wannabe vampire. I think he's right. What do you think, Dillon?" Jayson asked.

"I am loathed to agree with Concannon on anything, but I agree with you," Dillon said.

"I like how you didn't admit to agreeing with him," Justen said.

"Are you going out to catch the sunset?" Ella asked, her eyes sympathetic to his plight. Elke had a gorgeous double stand-in. He never confused Ella for Elke. The beautiful woman who Elke had saved as a child was still a lesser version of her benefactor. Ella performed daily business and social duties for Elke, giving her the perfect cover. Somehow, after nightfall, Elke Swearington grew exponentially more bewitching, people said.

"For the longest time after I became a nightwalker, I would set my watch to witness the sunset. It's not odd at all. For me, you get a glimpse of your past, of who you were during those days walking in the sun. I believe that shapes us as vampires. What do you think?" Jayson Humphrey asked. He never looked up from his note taking.

"I savor the day's end and night's fall. It brings back memories that inspire songs, some of longing and others of anticipation. Those feelings are natural even among some of the supernatural. I know werewolves have those emotions," Hobbes added. He plucked several notes that sounded like tears falling.

"Aw like a moth to the flame. I understand. It helps me remember before. Keeping in touch with humanity helps me write in ways that my readers can relate. For you see, art transcends life, but if they can't feel it, then I've failed," Humphrey said.

"Just don't get burnt, Dillon. My mistress would be an enraged goddess, and there would be hell to pay for all," Ella said.

"I will be careful. I just can't sit still. See y'all, later," Dillon said. He didn't feel fit for company, and it seemed everyone else was up early, by that he meant pre sunset.

"Excuse me, sir, I believe you are forgetting yourself," the valet said as he set himself between the exit and Dillon. Edgerton offered an umbrella and a satchel.

"Thank you, Edgerton, but I'm taking the cave route to the dam," Dillon said. Had the entire staff come to see him off? He would think that they would be glad that he was out of their hair.

"Sensible," he replied. Bertram Ainsworth Edgerton continued to hold out the satchel and umbrella.

"Hold your damn horses, or I'll jerk a knot in your tail. You listen to Bertram Edgerton. His opinion often ain't worth two dead flies, but this time he is doin' as our mistress wishes. You're likely to arrive before sunset, but she would be sorely put out if you went up in flames," Doris said. Her frown would have scoured pots and pans. She set her shoulders and stood next to the valet. Elke had taken both with her from Von Damme's estate. Doris Belle was the longtime head housekeeper of Swearington Lodge and carried her broom as if it were a lethal weapon. Before that, she had run the Summer Creek Resort. She and Edgerton frequently disagreed, bickering like a sister and brother, except when it came to Elke's wellbeing. On this, they stood united.

Dillon felt hotter than a blue blaze, and yet, he had learned quickly that it was pointless to argue with them. Elke had said they knew more about being a vampire than he did. It wasn't their fault that he was angry. He thanked Master Cosmo for his lessons on letting anger drain away. He knew that he made lousy decisions when he was furious.

"I know you wish things were different, but as my daddy used to say, you can wish in one hand and shit in the other and see which fills faster," Doris said. She often offered folksy sayings and such wisdom garnered from her eighty years. She might look fifty with steely eyes, frown lines, and her hair cropped short. He had only seen her smile when Elke or Ella was around.

Dillon snorted, and then he couldn't help but laugh. It helped counter his fury like spraying water on a bonfire.

Doris glanced at Edgerton. "Did I say somethin' funny?"

"Never, my dear. It's inconceivable. Perhaps he thought you stuttered," Edgerton replied stiffly.

Dillon took the portable sunshade and bag of goodies. "Fine. I'll take them and use them as needed. You have done your duty. Thank you for looking out for me," he said.

"You're looking agitated, governor. Anything I can do, sir?" Edgerton asked, one eyebrow raised.

"I don't think so. I'm restless. I need to move. I'm concerned about my friend and sister in California, and I can't do anything from here," Dillon said.

"That explains why you're as nervous as a long-tailed cat among rockin' chairs. That Troy Bane is enough to send anyone prayin' to the Good Lord. Your sister is a sweet, saintly soul. How could she fall for such a reckless spirit?" Doris asked.

Dillon coughed and shook his head in disbelief.

"As far as I know, you haven't done anythin' to humiliate the Rulers of Night, at least not yet. Just keep dancin' and don't step on anyone's feet," Doris said.

"I sent Elke a text, but if you see her first, inform her that I'm going to Holston Dam to meet my ex and convince her to leave town before she kicks the hornet nest," Dillon said as he paused in the open doorway.

"That sounds like a bit of a sticky wicket, if I may say. Be discerning. To be a worthy mate to a Swearington, you must learn to be, as well as act, cool, calm, and collected while making the right decisions. Good luck sorting, sir. Cheerio," Edgerton said.

"Lord, love a duck. Check the wind before you spit," Doris said.

Were vampires supposed to ooze James Bond charm while they spat? Sometimes Edgerton's and Doris' words held wisdom similar to those spoken by Dillon's sensei, Master Cosmo. He would tell Dillon to shed his anger, taking it off like a coat and leaving it behind. It didn't bother the other person and would only hinder him, perhaps making him ill. The godly power within him was how he reacted to it.

Dillon closed the door behind him and entered the limestone caverns. During his early, disquieted days, he and Elke had wandered these caverns. She had been exploring them for half a century or more. She claimed there were still places that she had yet to discover, and occasionally, rock falls, rushing water, and collapses changed the terrain.

Moving underground had opened up a whole new world for him, including giving him another way to get lost. So, the trick was to know which underground passage ended where. There were many tunnels, and two months roaming them wasn't long enough to memorize them. He knew the route to the dam because Elke often brought him this way. She enjoyed the view from the overlook, too, and she remembered what the Holston River Valley had looked like before the dam had been built. At that time, Cliff Island had loomed over the river valley. Trains had run along tracks through the valley to several summer resorts built next to the flowing waters.

Dillon heard someone coming. Who else would be down here? He smelled hand lotion and recognized it was by Avon. He knew who this was. "Crista?"

"It's just me, that little old Head of Security. I'm checking the cameras. One needed fixin'." Crista Humphrey said. The big woman with the broad shoulders and mighty laugh ambled toward him. She looked to have put on some muscle.

"Have you been working out, Miss Crista?" Dillon asked.

"So, you can tell that I've been doing squats?" she asked. He knew the punch line was coming and waited for it. "Well, I've been doing sets of diddly squat. I've never felt better," she laughed. Dillon was still amazed that a devout Christian worked for Elke, but Crista thought Elke fought on the side of Jesus and angels. The Lord worked miracles through faulty humans all the time in the *Bible*. It was certainly possible in her mind for the Almighty to do the same through the supernatural. Having a son who was a vampire likely skewed Crista's perspective just as loving Elke altered Dillon's point of view.

"Your jokes are a crime. Has Jayson written about them?" Dillon asked.

"Lord, I can see why Ms. Elke keeps your around. So, don't take no wooden nickels or strolls in the sunset, you hear?" she said. With a wave, she headed for the door to the lodge.

"I'll be careful and watching for Destrange," Dillon promised.

"You have light grenades?"

"Yes, ma'am," Dillon replied. That seemed to placate Miss Crista.

The Bloodlust in Dillon hadn't been completely satisfied with Darlene's offering. Elke had said it might be like this for a while, as the desire to stalk and hunt prey was powerful, as though there was feline energy in the dark power from the Shadowlands. So far this evening, Dillon was losing his cool. He hated to lose, and he didn't want to lose his intellect or his humanity.

Dillon was trying to straddle the line, or be like the state line, on the border of two states. Who knew being undead was so complicated? It was deadly to those that he loved. Snarling, he kicked out and booted something solid, not a rock. It clanged metallically as it bounced along the cave floor.

When the object stopped tumbling, Dillon picked up the battered miner's lamp. He didn't need light anymore. Now, as a night walker, Dillon saw perfectly without light. The lamp looked old and used, giving off the aura of a hard-working personality. Why hadn't he seen it before? They had been this way many times.

Or had they? He looked around. This passage struck him as unfamiliar. He realized this wasn't the route to the South Holston Dam overlook. This tunnel and others like it wormed through limestone and shale of the Appalachian Mountains. Some stretches of the caverns had been used during the American Civil War. When he was a kid, he had heard stories of passageways through the rocks that snaked under the lake. Bristol Caverns, the popular attraction, was not far from its shores. As far as he knew, most cave entrances in the Tri-Cities had been blocked to protect the public.

The lamp hopped out of his hand and dropped to the ground. Dillon stared at his fingers. Was he getting clumsy? He flexed his left hand. It seemed all right. He reached for the battered lamp. It tumbled away.

Getting irritated, he pounced on it. It dodged his first strike, but he caught it with both hands on the second try. He opened it and peered inside. Along with dirt, there was a partly burned candle. Elke liked antiques and mysteries, so he pocketed it in his jacket.

Dillon reoriented and doubled back through the cavern. He felt followed and stopped. He listened for footsteps. He heard nothing corporeal. A presence grew, invading his senses and crowding the cavern. He calmed his mind and readied his body for an ambush or attack. He sighed, disappointed in himself. It had been unwise to rush off alone. There were at least three vampires who wanted to destroy him. If he wasn't thinking clearly or was weak, he would be easy prey.

Dillon took a left turn at the T in the tunnel and headed uphill. He sensed the open air, sunshine, and water around two more turns. Only a fool rushed into danger, he recalled the words of his sensei and Elke, too. The sunshine didn't want to kill him. It simply worked like a fatal allergic reaction. Fortunately, he had an umbrella.

Up ahead, the day waned, falling toward twilight. It was the time for crepuscular creatures, those who lived on the edge between day and night. Predators often thrived during this time when prey came to the watering holes. Would Von Damme's followers hang around Bristol?

"I am aware of you," Dillon said to the presence invading his personal space.

"Give me what's mine," said the ghostly voice.

Dillon blinked. What did that mean? Give him respect? Give him privacy? He sensed the growing pressure, likely an attack. He studied the old miner's lamp. "You want this?"

"Hey now, I don't want no fighting. I just want what's mine. You certainly don't need it," the voice said. A faint glow spread into a hazy mist that formed into a ghost wearing a broad-brimmed hat. The ethereal being carried a walking stick and yet possessed no lower legs. "What's a wayfinder without a light to guide him and his charges?"

"One who can see in the dark," Dillon replied. The Bloodlust pushed his sarcasm button, too.

"Aye, that be true, but to inspire others to follow he must use light, even if it's the light of insight sent from above."

"Or teach them to see in the dark. Were you a preacher?"

"No, sir. I was a teacher at the old, now underwater Holston View School. It used to have the view of the mountains and the river. My father was a preacher, though. We explored these caves all the time. Know 'em like the back of my hand. The name is Phineas, Phineas Jacobs. Friends call me Phin or PJ. I don't see many vampires mooning over the setting sun. Usually, they're so happy their tongue is slapping them aside the head while they're dancing, figuratively speaking, not actually cavorting."

"Cavorting does sound unvampirely," Dillon admitted. He could imagine what Edgerton would say to such an indignity, especially having your tongue hanging out smacking something other than its lips.

The wind carried into the tunnel, bringing a familiar sound. Dillon cocked his head, hearing a vehicle approaching the dam. The exit of this cavern opened on a hill overlooking the South Holston Dam visitor's center. He could see it in his mind's eye. On one side, there was the beauty of the lake surrounded by fall foliage. On the southwest side, way down below, the power plant, towers, and the Stophel Cemetery headstones set near the Weir Dam stood among the yellow and russet-leafed trees along the river.

Dillon handed the lamp to the ghost who accepted it with a wispy hand. "I apologize. I didn't know it was still someone's property. I was hoping it might be a magic lamp that would solve all my problems," Dillon said and smiled wanly.

"Well, isn't that somethin'. Not every night you hear a vampire apologizing. Listen, you look lost. You need the lamp more than me. It has often led souls to safety, even out of damned Wreythville."

Staying in the shadows, Dillon peered outside. He could see the far end of the dam of boulders and earth. Why did he feel drawn here? A sense of nostalgia? Longing for his old life?

A gray Blazer drove up Holston View Road running between the Halloween-cloaked trees to slowly roll toward the dam. The sport utility vehicle turned into a small lot near a gravel road where a sign read: Employees Only and was closed off by a chain. The road split, north leading down to the shore at the base of the dam, while south followed along the hillside to the fenced and walled spillway that plunged two hundred and fifty feet. The SUV parked across from the illuminated flagpole and Old Glory. Nobody immediately exited the car. It could be lovers or partiers who visited the dam for privacy, or an amazing sunset view of the lake and the rolling slopes of the Blue Ridge Mountains.

Dillon's attention turned to the daylight, its waning strength, and the low angle. His life was bordered and bound by sunlight, shadow, and darkness. How had he, a seeker of truth and light, come to live in the darkness? Why was he alive when his blood brothers Spider, Denny, and John were all dead? Because of Elke, Dillon Urich breathed, if not exactly living by modern scientific standards.

How could Dillon be at home and yet not feel at home? After more than two months, he hadn't been able to release his love of the sunlight. Even now, he watched it gleam off the surface of the water. People came to this area to soak in the true leaves' colors, only visible just before the leaves died and fell away. Was he like that?

"Why did you pick up my lamp?"

"My Beloved likes historical treasures," he replied.

"Vampires feel love? Get out! You're pullin' my leg, sir."

"We do. Elke is the key to my inspiration," Dillon said. She had brought him back to life. She was the key to his survival. Thinking about Elke inspired passion, song, dance and adventure, all reasons to keep going even if he couldn't bask in the sun or hang out with his mortal friends without trying to kill them or feed off them. He had been tempted before, and he couldn't always control his anger.

"In nature, only seven percent of the world's species are monogamous. I can only imagine that for beings who sustain themselves on the blood, fears and suspicion of others, love would be exceptionally rare. How interestin'. I didn't think that you'd have a choice. One look and you're hooked, you know."

"Yes, I do. Die in the light or live in the dark with the bedazzling moon," Dillon smiled. He had been swept away. He loved her spirit despite her dark supernature.

Another vehicle stirred the air as a red Mustang cruised across the dam to park in the observation deck visitor's lot, closer and below Dillon's vantage point. A woman exited the car, a tall, lovely blond that he immediately recognized. Her beauty and sexy sashay called to The Bloodlust. Gina was young and vital and unable to resist him.

She carried a bundle of something. She looked around, locked the car, and then she strolled along the sidewalk to the road crossing the dam. For a moment, she stared down the rocky slope to the gravel shore. Gina glanced back like she sensed Dillon's attention, before briskly striding across the dam.

Dillon had phoned her, told her about his malady, and in a twist of fate, bad fortune leading to serendipity, that he had found the woman of his dreams. He would be staying here for the foreseeable future. He would even have to quit his job or seek a transfer locally to Bristol, Johnson City, or Kingsport.

Obviously, that phone call had not convinced her. What was he supposed to say? Hey, sweetheart, I'm a vampire now. Stay away. That would have brought her running to find out if he was suffering mental health issues, or what made him tick. He was far from adept at compelling, or at what some called hypnosis or charm chat. Dillon felt it had something to do with how vampires affected human chemistry. Could he use it to convince Gina to return to Texas and have a wonderful life under the blazing sun of the Lone Star State? He thought he would let Key do it. She would relish it.

"She seems sad. Do you know her?" Phineas asked.

"She's my ex," Dillon said. She still looked great, vibrant, and full of life. He stopped himself before he salivated.

"Oh, I get it. Vampires and humans wouldn't mix. How could the human resist? Heck, people have trouble resistin' a dearth of normal daily things like booze, cigarettes, good-lookin' honeys, and gamblin'. Oh dear, I hear the locals have opened a casino. Is it true?" Phineas said.

Dillon nodded and kept his eyes on Gina. She used her phone to snap photos while she sashayed across the dam and turned onto the gravel road, descending toward the lakeshore. In the fading light, she was radiant. Once she stood next to the water, she unwrapped the bundle to reveal yellow roses. She began plucking petals and tossing them upon the lake's surface. The wind carried her words. "He loves me. He loves me not."

Dillon's heart lurched. He had to slow its beating.

The car door of the Chevy Blazer opened. A stooped, gray-bearded man deployed a cane to walk while he carried a plastic bag to the trash can, and then he limped out onto the dam road where he started taking photos with his phone. Dillon disliked the way the man kept glancing at Gina. He didn't seem so old in those moments. His aura shone brightly, full of life for a senior citizen. From underneath his jacket, he pulled out a skull mask to wear. It matched his skeleton bones shirt, displaying the sternum and the ribs.

She didn't sense the danger. She kept tossing rose petals. What could he do?

"Gina!" Dillon shouted.

She stopped, turned, and finally noticed Skullface approaching her. He no longer limped as he strode down the ramp, and he carried the cane as a weapon.

"Go the hell away! I sent a photo of your car and license plate to the sheriff," Gina yelled.

The stalker advanced angrily toward her, even as she backed away, stumbling but managing to stay afoot. Her only escape routes were climb up a slope or to go swimming.

Dillon barely kept himself in check. The mind controlled the body, thought before action, unless he used No Mind. He wasn't tuned into his physical form well enough to manage such a mindless feat. He must do something. "Stop it, man!" Dillon commanded, uttering a powerful compelling.

The stalker paused, just standing there. Gina took advantage of the moment to spray a can of wasp killer. The chemical splattered into the holes in the mask to burn his eyes. Skullface screamed and staggered back.

She tried to run past, but her assailant stumbled into her path. They collided, and she shoved herself away as Skullface blindly tried to grab her. He snagged her coat, so she kneed him in the crotch and yanked free. She danced back, still trapped.

"You bitch! You'll pay for that," Skullface screamed. He kept himself between her and the road.

Dillon glanced westward. Light still blazed through the trees. It wouldn't be long, but it could easily be too long, too little, and too damned late.

He blinked. What was that? What the devil?

Behind the stalker, the water swirled then churned. Something was rising from the depths.

A skull poked from the water and peered through a dive mask. Water dribbled out and ran down its cheekbones. Dark eye sockets began to gleam with an eerie red radiance at the sight of the people. It spat out a clump of algae and seemed to grin. Acting like a predator, it slipped from the lake to crawl ashore.

Twelve

Dam Skeleton

Neither Gina nor Skullface noticed when the full-sized human skeleton clad in scuba gear reached dry land. Despite its lack of muscles, the skeleton unfolded to stand and kick off its fins. A haze clung to its frame and drifted behind like a dark cloak floating on the breeze. The skeleton shook, flinging algae loose as though it were sloughing away dead skin, and shambled toward Gina and her attacker.

What the hell? Was that Bonz, the keeper of the bottom of the dam? Dillon wondered, mentally agape. Bonz wasn't made of real bones, but hard plastic covered in muck and green slime. Dive students used this place to take their open water scuba certification tests. Bonz's gear was a reminder of how deadly diving could be. Was this beast a creation of Von Damme's? Or a creature from the Shadowlands?

Feeling helpless, Dillon waited and watched.

Gina finally saw the skeletal terror and shrieked. The half-blind stalker grinned, thinking he was the reason Gina panicked. He stood there palming his cane while Bonz rattled closer. Skullface finally heard the noise and glanced over his shoulder. The man performed a doubletake even as his red and raw eyes bulged in disbelief like a cartoon figure, and he spat a loud string of profanities that would have been bleeped out.

While Bonz stalked closer, the monster tossed its dive mask into the lake and detached the weight belt to deploy it like a flail, swinging at Skullface. The man staggered back to avoid bludgeoning. He backpedaled as the skeleton advanced. Bonz's cloak drew tighter, wrapping it in a dark, gauzy robe.

Dillon searched for a pattern to the shadows. He could safely dart through them and reach the giant turbine on display. The huge impeller sat near the road on this side of the dam. Being closer to Gina would save him seconds when the sun was finally obscured. He donned his wide-brimmed hat and zipped up his long jacket.

The sun seemed to hang timelessly in the sky. The wind calmed. Powerful and yet helpless, Dillon watched until he couldn't stand it any longer.

Leaving the cave, he darted through the patches of shade. With the sun set low, the shadows grew heavy and long, reaching across the dam. Sunny stretches remained, though, and he assiduously avoided those, some uncomfortably close, while he dashed toward the turbine to hide in its shade. He took refuge on the northeast side of the six-foot diameter cylinder of giant metal fan blades.

Gina screamed again. Her stalker cursed. Dillon heard bones rattle and crack. He had no choices that he liked. He would have to cross through the sunbeams. Thanking Edgerton, he opened the umbrella and rushed toward the parking lot, where there was cover, shade, and a much better view of what happened along the shore.

Dillon smiled grimly. He was almost there. With a few more steps, he would reach cover.

A sudden gust of wind blew through. It ruffled the trees' branches and autumn leaves, some falling away. Patches of dark shifted to open up more space for the sun to shine through. The umbrella fought and twisted in his hands. While it was heavy duty constructed, so it didn't fly upward, it moved enough to let a ray of sunshine past its protective shade.

A searing pain staggered Dillon as a flash of radiance caught his left hand. He tumbled into the parking lot to hide behind Gina's parked Mustang. He checked his wrist between his glove and his sleeve. The skin was blackened and cracked. The pain was unlike anything he had ever suffered, worse than any burn that he had endured. This seared him to the core and caused his soul to roil. The sun, once worshipped, was now his nemesis.

Dillon spread some of his dirt on it, the powdered limestone and shale of his rebirth dulling the agony. He stayed in the shadows even as he re-positioned himself near a tree. Through a haze of pain, he looked down on the bizarre scene taking place along the shore.

Skullface swung his cane, striking Bonz and rocking its head. It blocked the second blow, fracturing its forearm. Using its other hand, it snatched the cane and ripped it from the man's grasp. Bonz grinned as the animated skeleton attacked relentlessly, battering Skullface. For a moment, it seemed like brother was pummeling brother.

Once Gina's stalker lie stunned, the creature seized both sides of his head in its claws, knocking off Skullface's mask. Now that Bonz wasn't fighting, the swirling dark cloud gathered in its chest like a giant black heart. Its eye sockets gleamed with a sickly red light. Dillon caught a cold, spiky scent on a dusty breeze. It reeked vaguely familiar, but he couldn't place it. What was this thing? Dillon blinked. And was that an Adventure Diving bumper sticker stuck vertically to its sternum?

Bonz leaned over, its jaws wide, coming unhinged like a snake. The monster swelled as it consumed the man's life, sparks of light like fireflies were sucked into its maw and set ablaze. They sounded like firecrackers as they were devoured and snuffed. Dillon could sense a life ending, the loss of prey. The stalker's life aura faded, vanishing with a wink as he died.

Weeks ago, Dillon would have freaked out, even been terrified. Now he was galvanized. "Gina, run!" he yelled.

His voice carried the power of desperation compelled by caring. She turned to flee, scrambling her way up the rocky slope of the dam, attempting to reach the parking lot sixty feet above. The stones were loose underfoot. Gina lost her balance then slid part way down.

Bonz finished feeding and discarded the fleshy bag of bones that had been a man. With fiery red eyes, the animated skeleton set its sights on Gina to slake its thirst. Rocks tumbled from underneath its bony feet as it pursued.

Watching would kill Dillon almost as certainly as stepping into the sun. He must do something. He checked the satchel's contents. He didn't think a flash grenade, nor a smoke bomb would work in this case. What else could he throw? His knives would do no good here, so he grabbed two stones and hurled both. The first splashed in the lake. The second was short, clattering down the slope of the dam. He had never been a good pitcher.

Dillon hurled four more stones, imagining hitting Bonz in the chest. The first was short. The second flew too long. The third rock struck a glancing blow to its clavicle, knocking the skeleton back a step and into the fourth thrown rock that cracked its skull. Part of the plastic cranium fell away. Algae and mud oozed out.

Unimpaired, Bonz charged.

Gina screamed. "Dil!"

His name was cut short when Bonz seized her. At first, it appeared to be smiling, but its jaw continued to drop, now ready to swallow her whole.

Dillon looked to the west. The sun sank. It would be thirty seconds, and yet that could be the difference between life and death.

A true hero would have gone anyway. He started to rush out and heard Elke's voice in his mind.

"Stop. Listen. Think. And always come back to me."

In that moment, Dillon recalled, like a first responder, that if he destroyed himself, then he would be unable to help anyone. That monster might roam and kill others. For all Dillon knew, it was Von Damme coming back from beyond. Damn him! Dillon ground his teeth knowing that he must wait.

Bonz held Gina face to face as if ready to offer a deadly kiss, drawing the last of her life force. She sagged as the dark aura swelled around the skeleton. Sparks sputtered in the thing's maw.

Finally, what could be too late, damn it, the trees completely shaded the top of the dam from the sun's deadly yellow light. Like Dillon had been fired from a rocket launcher, he hurtled down the rocky slope. He seized Bonz by the neck, forcing it to spit out a few sparks that fell back onto Gina. Dillon used momentum to drag the thing downhill. He threw it aground and jumped atop it, cracking its ribs. With surprising strength, it kicked Dillon away, sending him toward the lake.

No! Panic grabbed him. The water would maim if not destroy him. He twisted as he spun, throwing his jacket open wide and angling it to work as a sail. He floated past the shore and over the water. He had always wondered if vampires could glide on the wind. If he wasn't flesh and blood, he should be able to make himself lighter. For two months, he had been practicing with little to show for it.

A sudden gust of good fortune pushed him shoreward enough, so he landed on the rocks. One shifted, and his left foot dipped into the lake. He yanked it out before the water soaked through his boot. He kicked Bonz in the right hip, driving it back.

He scooped up the Skullface's cane and took Bonz down with a low sweep across its knees. He beat on the skeletal monster, breaking its Adventure Diving bumper sticker-covered sternum, and shattering ribs. The monster grabbed the cane, yanking Dillon close where it tried to choke him. He could hold his breath, no problem. That's when Dillon realized he was trying to fight a creature of darkness as if it were a human being. That was stupid, a big fail there.

Bonz seemed to realize the same and stabbed him in the chest. Dillon deflected it, or the broken rib would have skewered him through the heart. Instead, it painfully lanced through his shoulder.

He darted back, freeing himself, and wondered if whatever animated Bonz was vulnerable to sun light. They were in the dam's shadow, and yet, the sun had yet to set. Dillon spotted a patch of red-gold, crepuscular brilliance beaming between the tree tops, far above the top of the dam. In one swift move, he dipped and took the skeleton in both hands to heave it skyward.

Bonz flailed and rattled as it hurtled up seventy feet into the air where it met the sunshine. A great flash blinded Dillon.

A moment later, when he could see again, Bonz crashed nearby on the shore. Pieces of once animated plastic shattered like a clay pot. Dillon turned, letting them strike his duster, the coat protecting him. He put a small piece of plastic in his pocket for investigative and testing purposes. The journalist in him still lived. But did Gina? He heard a last heartbeat then an agonal gasp.

Dillon feared the worst as he rushed to Gina's side and knelt. He knew without checking that she wasn't breathing. Her life glow faded. Where was his blood brother, Knives, when he was needed? Dillon willed himself to slow down and eased Gina onto her back. He found her heart's position, vitality, and strength. Too much force when compressing her heart would kill her, too. According to the America Heart Association, enough air remained in her lungs and system to bring her back to life.

When he touched her, his hands warmed. The tingling seemed familiar, but he didn't chase that thought, remaining focused on Gina. He checked inside her mouth. She had swallowed her tongue. He figured that he was imagining the blue-white lightning flowing from his hands into her body while he repositioned her jaw. His fingers were close enough to her carotid to sense its stillness.

Gina jerked alive with a gasp and a shudder. Her heart thundered as it returned to beating.

Her scent overwhelmed him, more savory than any meal. What a horrible thought, and yet, she was so beautiful that he could devour her like a sweet. He had lost that battle before, wondering if two investigative journalists should become a couple. They had been good, but Elke had left Dillon thunderstruck, as well as bringing him back from the dead.

White and blue light crackled and danced around Dillon's fingers. His hands and arms tingled pleasantly, much like a numb limb coming back awake but without the stinging needles.

Gina coughed and surged to suddenly hug him. He embraced her and watched the lightning flow along his arms and into her. His body felt electric and burgeoning with lust. Their touch might be a live wire, but even so, it paled in comparison to how he felt when Elke simply spoke his name. His hunger for Gina wasn't caring. It was The Bloodlust.

He wondered how Key was doing. Was she mad at him for bolting? What was this lightning? What would she think of it?

Gina's eyes gleamed with trust. "Dil! You saved my life! My hero. I like when you stand up for the common man and woman. What was that thing?" she asked. There was nothing common about Gina. Her eyes went in and out of focus. As she recalled, she grew confused.

He needed to ground her to reality, but in doing so, he would be lying to her. He could feel another step down the slippery moral slope. He would lie to save her sanity. "He was a predator. Every woman is going to applaud you for what happened," Dillon told her.

He had no idea if losing sparks would affect her. He studied her aura. It appeared ragged; its glow pockmarked. Whatever had attacked her had done damage, but he had no idea what kind or how to heal it. He hated being so ignorant. Of course, if he had still been human, they would both be dead. That was just another reason to celebrate his vampire supernature. Huzzah!

"I killed him?"

"I didn't see. He was dead when I reached you. How do you feel? Should I call 911?" Dillon asked. Could he have changed Skullface, turned him down the right road like Elke? It hadn't even crossed his mind. Gina stared at him while he pondered. Abusing her trust made him feel awful. And yet, it would only get her killed if she started investigating the supernatural around here. Going public about vampires would be dangerous and deadly. If people ever took Concannon seriously, RON might deal with him. Dillon thought it was a lose-lose situation.

She gave him a long look. "I feel good, considering what happened and what I saw, or think I saw."

Dillon remained patient.

"A walking skeleton. It murdered that awful man and came after me."

Dillon patted her hand. "You're thinking of his t-shirt and mask," he said and pointed. The dead man's mask rested on the ground and face up to the sky. The eyes were as empty as Bonz's victim.

"Oh. Yay. That makes more sense than what I remember. Whew! We should contact the county sheriff. This was not how I expected to see you again," she said with a little laugh.

"Where did you expect to see me?"

"At some art house auction, I guess. Not finding me on my backside."

The first time that he had seen Gina, she had been riding atop a mechanical bull in a Houston honky-tonk involved in the sex slave trade. She had seduced everyone in the room and made herself a target, before getting thrown by the bull. It had all worked out, and she had saved hundreds of young lives from abuse and horror. She was a true hero.

She yawned. "I wasn't working on a story.

"What are you doing here?" he asked.

"Saving you," Gina said.

"Have you found religion?" Dillon asked.

She snorted. He knew her as realistic and practical. She had explored and written about religions. She had said it was a great place to learn about politics and prejudice.

"I don't require rescuing."

"When last we spoke, you sounded delirious," she said. There was love and adoration in her eyes. The Bloodlust boosted his charisma.

He caught her hand and lowered it. She wasn't his lady anymore. He had strong feelings for her, but that love seemed like a candle compared to a bonfire. Perhaps a wildfire would be more appropriate, he mused. "My mother said the same. I'm in love, likely head over heels stupid," Dillon said.

He could tell Gina was doing better. Her aura was less ragged, much smoother, and at least half the pockmarks had vanished. Her scent improved to that of a healthy female. She would make a fabulous meal, and she wouldn't mind. After he feasted, he could influence her and send her away. She wouldn't disobey him. Wouldn't that be better, even safer, for all concerned? Mixing his blood with hers would even strengthen her immune system. Dillon shook himself. The Bloodlust was always rationalizing its need.

"You sound irrational, I agree, and you look pallid, but good, even healthy despite your coloring. I never thought you would look so handsome and dashing as a Canadian, eh, but I was wrong. Plus, you have that twinkle in your eye," Gina said. She smiled flirtatiously, hinting about later.

"That sparkle is Elke. It doesn't change the fact that I'm very happy to see you well when I thought you were badly hurt. Much has changed. I am ill but not contagious. I don't know if I'll ever bask in the sun again," Dillon said. He showed her where the sun had burned his hand between his glove and jacket. The flesh appeared seared, dry, and cracked. She gasped. "This is what the sun does. It's a side effect of my medication. It's Elke's love that has sustained me through this dark time. I still have fits of rage because of what's happened, how unfair it is, how cooped up I feel, how much I miss the sunshine and so much is closed at night. You would think I was a pariah. I can be pathetic," he said.

"Tell me about her and the situation, then we can figure out how she's using you. If you like that long term, and if it will turn into love," Gina said. She caressed the burn on his hand.

Dillon blinked, recognizing his own words, even if paraphrased. He had always been concerned in any relationship about motivation. Why was he loved? Chemistry? Because he was incredible? Or because somebody wanted to escape their current situation? No longer wanted to live with their parents? Or they thought he had money and would create a good life? For safety? For prestige? Or the clock was ticking on motherhood? Protection from their ex? Protection from the male population in general?

Were they good together, making each other better and the best of themselves? Had he applied this rationale to Elke? He nodded to himself. Definitely.

"When you went missing, I was going to come back and search for you . . ." she said.

"But you were in the Australian Outback," he said.

"Where I caught a virus. I was too sick to travel, but I kept up with the news reports, and by the time I was almost better, you called me. I'm so sad for you, and I felt like I let you down. I wish that I had been here for you."

"No, you don't. You might have died, too," Dillon said.

Three close friends had been murdered, but unlike Dillon, had not been revived by supernatural means. Only by the grace of Elke had he and Troy survived what lie beyond here and the Shadowlands.

"From what you said, if that woman hadn't saved you, you would have died. Sounds like the Florence Nightingale syndrome to me," Gina said. She yawned and snuggled into him. "I am warm and tingly. I feel better already."

"Time to call the authorities," Dillon said.

"I guess I must. I have a civic duty."

"Yes, and I expect Elke, my love, Key to my happiness, to be along any moment," Dillon said. He looked northwest, toward the cave, for signs of Key.

"You are inseparable?" she asked and yawned.

"Almost," Dillon said and smiled.

As if his thoughts and desire had summoned her like the goddesses of yore, he sensed Key's presence. His beloved was here! Knowing so empowered him.

Elke Swearington strolled through the twilight like everything in it should bow to her. The owls hooted, reminding him of catcalls. Her blond beauty was both drop-dead daunting and captivating. Right now, though, she looked infuriated and ready to bite nails in half while she strangled him.

Thirteen

The Shadowlands Run

Even mature vampires could have anger issues. A murderous gleam shone in Elke's eyes. Dillon didn't need to guess what she was thinking. Key was jealous. Anger, passion, and fear had crashed together into a tempest. Her hair stood out, and sparks danced along the ends. She held a white-knuckled death grip on her parasol as if she were about to skewer Gina.

"I thought you were in danger. If you weren't, you now are," she said. Key had sensed he was in trouble and had come to fight for him. Dillon felt a fierce pride. They were connected.

"Gina, meet my moon and stars, my key to happiness, Elke Swearington," Dillon said. He smiled at his love, hoping to defuse her rage, and then he looked down to Gina who had fallen unconscious. He looked back up to Elke. "Awe of you knocked her senseless, Key."

She crossed her arms, but his comment drew a wan smile that didn't reach her eyes. "Here I am worried about you, and I find your former lover asleep in your arms," Elke said coldly. Key gazed into his eyes and soul. "She has sown doubt."

Dillon put his jacket under Gina's head and left her to rise and kiss his beloved. "About what?"

"Us. You and I."

"She forced me to rethink, but I am yours, Key. I'm thrilled you're here. I love you, and I'm way too clueless about the supernatural."

"What do you mean?" Elke asked with a crossways look.

"Something dark crawled from the lake and attacked her. It took over a plastic skeleton and killed that guy who assaulted her."

"You should have awakened me. We would have faced this together."

"I apologize. I had no idea this would happen. I had a nightmare about Silke being held captive, and I can't reach Troy, so I wanted to break things. It seems like I'm far from done managing my anger. Then, I got a text from Gina wanting to meet me at the dam. I'm not in love with her, and yet I care for her. I wanted to put the kibosh on her digging into your background before she started."

"I don't like it that y'all continue to share a connection," Elke said. Her eyes looked at his wrist, and she hissed. "And you were burnt by the sun trying to rescue her, you knucklehead," she bemoaned as she gently took his arm and examined it. She frowned. "It's why I love you. Now, what else has happened? Tell me, why do you glow?"

"What do you mean?" Dillon asked.

"Why do you possess an aura like a human when you are a vampire?" she demanded, her voice rising.

He looked at his hands. They retained a pale glow. Why? What had happened to him? He wondered. "I have no earthly clue."

"Hells Bells, she's done something to you," she said. He had never seen Key this distraught, not even when they were preparing to trek through the Shadowlands to battle Von Damme. "Tell me what happened."

He rubbed on more dirt while he recounted the fight: how Bonz ate the sparks of the attacker's life, Gina's flight uphill and Bonz trying to drain the life from her.

Elke's frown deepened. "That sounds like a specter, except they don't possess inanimate objects to attack. It should not be here. From what I understand, the Inuit Tribe in Alaska was one of the first to report such creatures of darkness. They called them Tariaksuq, essentially night people. During the long dark, they stole life and bodies from the living. Those of the Orient and East Asian called them shadow ninja. In Ireland and Scotland, they are offspring of an evil elf called the Fear Dorcha. Von Damme's thirst for knowledge was boundless, and he trucked with shadows. He even had a living shadow that did his bidding, a shadow assassin if you will, that he named Cloaker," she replied.

"That is frightening. I recall Doris mentioning to watch the shadows for feargrabbers," Dillon said.

"I think you mean feargorgers, but yes, she would. She escaped Von Damme's household with me, along with Edgerton. Feargorgers is the colloquial name for the Shaden, short for Shadenchill or Shadenchilde, depending on your source. It's a creature of shadow that feeds on fear and grows stronger, amplifying the fear of any around them. Von Damme captured one and then bound it. We don't know how he did what he did," Elke said. She licked her lips a little nervously while she studied the dead man. She lifted him and then softly elbowed him in the throat, cracking and crushing his windpipe. "That's how he died. Is there any evidence of the skeleton?"

"Pieces of plastic and Bonz's gear," he said.

"Could have been lost by anyone," she said and kicked the fins into the water. With a gloved hand, she tossed the weight belt in after them. "We need to check the news and online for any strange sightings. See if we can get any dope on them."

"You know that term nowadays has other meanings, from marijuana to a slang term meaning cool or very good," he said.

"I'm sorry for slipping back into the slang of my time. I meant scoop, of course. Stop busting my chops. I apologize for busting yours, but you deserved it," she said.

"I did. Could there be more specters?"

She nodded. "This time of year? Easily. Now is a time of long, dark shadows. Fall is a powerful season for anything empowered by the Shadowlands."

Dillon felt he knew so little. "Are there many types of shadow creatures, these Shaden?" he asked. He was continually disturbed to find out there were more monsters hiding in plain sight.

She nodded. "Specters are fear devourers. The feargorgers scare their victims to death. Did it grow as it ate the sparks?"

"Yes, it did. I didn't notice much in the way of physical wounds, but her aura appeared badly damaged," Dillon said.

"It looks better than expected. Considering what you've told me, it should be much, much worse. That thing was eating her life force, not just feasting on her fear. She should be catatonic. Specters cause psychological pain, nightmares, and anxiety attacks, and such. Pass out in the wrong place, say while driving, and you're dead. She's in for a rough time. Counseling would be a good idea. Scientists claim there is no such thing as darkness, only the absence of light. But then, those who are living rarely experience the Shadowlands and survive to speak of it."

"Troy hasn't been the same," Dillon said. He knew the truth of her words. He had no love of the land of never light that gave him supernatural life.

"Troy Bane was fortunate to have come back from death and the Shadowlands at all. That man must have a legion of angels in this world and the next watching over him. Same for your sister. Stop worrying about them. I have someone observing them. What we will do for love can move us beyond our nature," she said. They kissed long like a slow burning fuse, and he breathed her in, feeling her love strengthen him.

"Now, my firefly, did you start to glow before or after combat?" she asked.

"After. When I touched Gina to find a pulse," Dillon said. He suddenly recalled touching Darlene and mentioned the lightning might have started then.

"Hmm. How odd. You should have no human life within you, just your spirit, will and the power of The Bloodlust and darkness to sustain your flesh."

"Do you think I steal life from people?" Dillon asked.

"It is an aspect vampires can gain but is usually the domain of those less in this world of light than you. I think it unlikely, and Gina looks better than expected."

Dillon placed his hands on Gina's shoulders. Again, the blue-white lightning coruscated along his arms and through his hands. It seemed to originate from the center of his chest where his heart chakra resided.

Elke's eyes were wide. He could see himself in them, and he looked like electricity ran through him. "I'm not sure what you're doing, but she looks much healthier."

Dillon agreed. His ex's aura was less pockmarked, smoother along the edges and brighter.

"Ready to be touched?" he asked Key.

"By you? Always."

Dillon removed his hands, held them up for a moment as if he were letting his palms cool before he placed both on Elke's arm.

No lightning. The tingling happened for a different reason. His passion for her touch felt pleasant and galvanizing.

"Try one hand on each of us," she said and braced herself.

At the same time, Dillon touched Gina and Elke's arm. It was like connecting a circuit. Gina thrashed. With a yelp, Elke jerked back from his touch.

"I apologize. That obviously hurt. I take it this isn't normal for a vampire," he said.

She shook her arm. "This is certainly not what we need right now. Most vampires leave their prey mobile, so they can stumble home in pleasant euphoria. It lessens suspicion and cuts down on cab costs," she teased him.

Perhaps he had been forgiven. "It does sound like less effort," Dillon mused. He studied his ex-lover's glow, noted her breathing and checked her pulse. They all seemed very normal like she was sleeping. He decided not to call 911. "I'll carry her to her vehicle. I never thought she'd follow me here."

"You are quite a catch."

"Said the lady who dragged me into her boat," Dillon replied, thinking back.

"I would do it again, of course. We are destined to be together."

"I knew that before you did. Us being together really delights your household staff," he said.

"They will learn to love you, as I do, or they'll leave me. Edgerton is Edgerton to everyone. I know they are concerned that you'll be unable to control your journalistic tendencies and write about us. They envision you blabbing to the whole universe on Facebook, Reddit, YouTube, etc. Someone could do more damage now than ever before."

"I don't plan to keep a journal, nor write a vampire hand maiden's tale," he said. They shared a smile. "You have looked into my eyes, into my heart and soul. I see no reason to write about vampires. It wouldn't be helpful, and there are far bigger problems in the world and in this region."

"I know we talked about going to New York City for a while, but there is so much to do here."

"You'll get no argument from me, Key," Dillon replied. He checked Gina's pulse and breathing before he easily hoisted her onto his shoulder into a fireman's carry. The contact continued to be electric during his short, direct trek upslope and between the rose bushes to the overlook parking lot. He searched Gina's purse, found her key fob, and used it to open the car door. "I told her that her attacker had died in the fight. There are no cameras to dispute that."

"That was wise. It could be dangerous for her to get involved, especially with a Judge Executor here. He travels with his own executioner."

"About Gina, I'm not sure my compelling is strong enough to make her forget Bonz. Will you do it?"

"Of course. If someone loves you, they can ignore the compelling," Elke said.

"Truly? That explains my mother. But as for me, I can't ignore yours."

Elke's smile inspired him. "You love to make me happy. I will send her home. It works well when someone is just waking up. She is already confused and dazed by the trauma, so it should be easier than normal."

Dillon placed Gina inside the car and rechecked her vitals. He thought she would awaken any moment. By her aura and flesh tone, she appeared quite healthy. He ignored his vampiric blood urges, kissed her on the forehead and left her stirring with the keys in the ignition making a dinging noise. "Go ahead. I think she's waking up," Dillon said.

"Gina, nod, if you can hear me," Elke said. Her eyes changed as she charmed, her pupils turning red and their irises black. Her silken and seductive voice was irresistible, a whisper and command. It nestled lovingly inside her ears, and Gina nodded.

"You were attacked by a man in a skeleton mask at the dam. You defended yourself and during the struggle, he stopped fighting, so you ran. You remember nothing else. You don't even remember getting back to your car. You want to leave town, and go back to Texas, as soon as possible. There is nothing for you here. Now wake up and dial 911."

Gina's eyes snapped open. Her mouth dropped into an "oh my God" expression as she glanced out through the windshield to the dam. She seized her phone and tapped in 911.

Elke slipped away to join Dillon and took his hand. The invigorating energy of passion surged between them. "Excellent. She will forget she saw you and the skeleton. Dillon, I don't like her influence over you," she said.

"I just don't want to see her hurt," Dillon said. He didn't want her getting caught up in this supernatural world.

"Listen, my love. It is anger, frustration, and desire that gets graylings killed. Stay calm," she said.

He nodded. That made sense. "What else has gone wrong?" he asked.

"In Von Damme's diaries, I read that he was working on several dangerous alchemical projects and believed that he had successfully completed them. In one, he wished to poison the local people. In another, he wanted to curse them. The universe is a better place without him, if he is truly gone. Less Von Damme, more beauty, more art, and more love," she replied hotly. Her eyes were bright and brimming with passion.

Dillon had the sense that she had left something unsaid. She hated Von Damme with a fervor surpassing even Dillon's, and the undead maniac had killed a trio of his best friends. "Sounds like you know him," Dillon said.

"For a time, he held me captive," Elke replied bitterly.

Dillon hadn't known that. It was a little bit of a bomb, but he shouldn't have been surprised. They stopped walking so he could hold her close. He waited for her to say something more, but after a companionable time, they continued on in silence. She would share when she felt like it. Sharing was not normal for vampires.

The steep rocky slope did little to slow them as they neared the cave. Dillon felt himself growing stronger as the twilight faded, and the night deepened. At the entrance to underworld, Elke paused and turned to him. "I have been a little lax about helping you embrace being a vampire. You do not know enough of the Shadowlands to appreciate the origin of our supernature and how to manipulate it, which might be one of the reasons you have trouble changing shape or misting," she said.

Dillon still tried to wrap his head around both. With practice, he could eventually look like anybody or transform himself into an animal. He was still working on diffusing his body to be carried on the winds like a mist.

"We could take the tunnels back to the lodge, but an educational trip through the dark realm seems to be in order. Besides, if we're lucky, we might pick up a clue as to why a specter came through near the dam. You recall that the border is porous in spots, yes?"

Dillon nodded. Areas of perpetual darkness were connected to the Shadowlands. Caves were the most common, so occasionally a gopher, mole, bat, or other small animal or insects would wander into the realm of perpetual darkness. Last time, he had run into a swath of glowing moths. They had been descended upon by black-birds the size of eagles who plucked the moths out of the air and devoured their lights. The shadow birds had grown larger.

The darkness hunted the light, empowering itself by extin-guishing life. If he had been taking notes, that thought would be capitalized, underlined, and added to the axioms. Neither Elke nor Dillon felt that way. They had wondered aloud if they were of two minds, day and night, bicameral vampires, so to speak.

"Ah, this is the place," Elke said and stopped. She scraped her fingers across the stone to begin to open a shadow gate. Using her blood and saliva, she drew an archway on the wall and breathed on it. That section of rock faded away to reveal a black cavern somehow darker than pitch. The doorway drew in light, dimming the surrounding area. Dillon swore he felt a slight breeze, air drawn into the Shadowlands. He wondered if that is where ill winds originated. From what he had learned, vampires could only open gates to where they had been or were being invited.

On two prior occasions, he had traveled the dark realm. He didn't care for it, reminding him of a post-apocalyptic wasteland. With a slate gray and cloudless sky, the land of no sun was a pale and grim reflection of earth, similar in topography but different due to the lack of vegetation. The scattered trees had been leafless, usually black or white, although a few had brown nettles or spines. Mushrooms sprang up here and there where gates had been open at one time or another. Most buildings blinked in and out of existence, depending on their age. Long term structures like the dam or a bridge carried over to this place, becoming a feature of the terrain. Elke figured things needed to be three decades or so old before that happened. In the meantime, such structures faded in and out of existence in a ghostly manner.

"Many supernatural creatures call the Shadowlands home. You should be familiar with it and its denizens. Such knowledge will help you survive. Come stroll with me through the valley of death," she said and took Dillon's hand. "The judge, you, and I, all undead spirits, are connected to this realm. We draw energy and strength from this place."

"The Bloodlust originates from here?"

"Yes. Our thirst and hunger for life does. The Bloodlust gives us supernatural powers diminished by sunlight. We are near immortal, can charm mortals with our eyes, compel them with our words, see in the dark, open shadow gates and walk the land beyond, track like a bloodhound, hunt like a panther, change our form and appearance, and more, using superhuman speed, strength, and endurance. Depending on the individual and time, even more unusual talents occur, like shadow jumping or outright flight. Blood as sustenance strengthens our connection. Sunlight, naturally moving water, holy water and powerful symbols can break it, as can losing our heads or piercing our hearts with green wood. We need to see how you interact with the Shadowlands. See if anything has changed."

"I just don't seem to be learning enough fast enough."

"Even the masters took years before they were ready to paint masterpieces," she said.

Dillon nodded. He knew they were strongest at the dark of the moon and during winter when the days were shorter and the sunshine weakest, its light at a shallow angle. He followed her through the dark doorway, past the toadstools into the shadow realm. The ground felt hard underfoot. Gray rocks instead of dirt and plants created a stony amphitheater around this end of the lake. The wealth of trees blanketing the mountains had been replaced by tall charred-looking snags, or sickly, white-barked runt saplings. Tendrils of murky black drifted among them like a foul smoke. No sign of autumn here. It seemed worse today, darker. Down below, the lake basin was empty, looking like the South Holston River bed before the dam had been built. Elke had told him there were no sources of water in the Shadowlands, although some liquids slipped through along the border.

"You still have an aura, and it is brighter here," Elke said.

Glowing with stolen life, he was the cause of her shadow. Instead of green energy, his heart chakra radiated the blue-white lightning. The palms of his hands gleamed with the same, coruscating light.

"You shine in the darkness," Elke said. Her voice held worry.

"That sounds like a bad thing. So why do I shine?"

"It could be your irrepressible character and spirit. I will consult Hoyt," she said.

Dillon laughed, and she joined him. It was a foreign sound here as it rolled off rocks and around dead trees. He got the impression the joy jarred the Shadowlands and its denizens.

Suddenly, the shadow of a large dragonfly appeared. It flew in short, sharp jabs as it devoured the insects, flies and no-see-ums that had followed them into the Shadowlands. Most ground level atmosphere contained many living bugs that people didn't see. The insects burst afire as if they were colliding with an electronic bug zapper.

Two ants crawled nearby, their lives making them look like grounded fireflies. Shadow spiders rushed out to swarm and tear them apart limb by limb. By feeding on the light, the spiders and dragonfly grew larger. The winged beast swept down with its jaws extended to snap up a smaller spider and flew off.

Dillon watched warily. The black dragonfly returned to hover nearby to observe him. Did it debate on whether he was too big to eat? He was about to take his umbrella and discourage the beast to leave when it zipped away. "My glow attracts them," he said.

"Your life energy is obvious and a contradiction. We should hurry. We are near our exit. Come on," Elke said. She took his hand and then guided him ahead, running across the slate slope through the black woods. This wasn't a whole lot different than some parts of the burned area from the wildfire on the south shore.

"As I have told you before, we vampires share many common traits, but each of us has different skills and talents, since we were all human once upon a time. Some of our kin are greatly enhanced by the transformation. For example, humans who were innocuous and inconspicuous can become vampires who can be invisible."

"Like in the eastern tradition? Can any of the three that we're chasing do that?" Dillon asked.

"Not that we know of. Von Damme could have transformed them. With his alchemy, he would have altered them to make them more effective for his own means. All of them are lethal."

"Did Von Damme recruit any Shaden minions from the Shadowlands? He seemed like a domineering overlord type."

Elke's face went stony, and her eyes lost their shine, going matte black. "Yes. Along with Cloaker, Von Damme drew monsters from here. He believed if one fed on enough life, it gained some sentience stolen from its victims and would move separately from the pack, an independent predator. From what I heard from Desiree and Troy, I think at least one of the Shaden, along with some ghosts, inhabit the mansion. Von Damme's enthralled shadow could leave him and sneakily do his will. As far as I know, we have no clue what happened to Cloaker," Elke said and shivered. "We feared that he might unleash a shadow horde of feargorgers upon the locals. Shaden can cause scare surges in the frightened, feeding on their panic. Humans can literally scare themselves to death. We are typically untouched by the fear mongering, but a group working together is dangerous for us, much as eight ants can kill a spider by tearing it apart by its limbs," she said.

"That's an unpleasant mental image. You give such an uplifting pep talk."

"I apologize my love, but they are the antithesis of everything we believe in."

"I understand. So, everyone who went diving could have been affected by his strange concoctions?"

"If they had leaked out, that is true. So far, Desiree has shown no ill effects."

"But she's your thrall, and her chemistry is different. From what Knives said, it sounds like he and J-Man have been altered."

"Trauma can greatly change people. Some suffer Post Trauma Stress Disease, others experience Post Traumatic Growth Experiences. The sense of their place in the world and time shifted, their perception, ideas and wills examined, re-evaluated, and forged anew into something stronger, like you," she replied.

The invigorating feel of the dark realm roiled over him and yet also made him edgy and a touch anxious. "Is it me, or do the Shadowlands feel turbulent today?" Dillon asked.

"It does feel unsettled."

"Do you think it's because I'm here?" Dillon asked. He watched a bright white rabbit bound by. He blinked. It must have fallen down the wrong hole. It was not wearing or carrying a large watch.

Elke was bemused by his study of it. "As I've told you, vampires are far from the only type of supernatural creatures. Among them, there are many types of spirits. Haunts, poltergeist, and haints get the most attention because they act up and interact with humans. With practice, you can feel their presence before you see them, a rippling in the shadows, one might say. And speaking of shadows, there are several types of Shaden, which also includes glooms, specters and wraiths, all of them feargorgers."

"There aren't any undead skeletons?" Dillon asked in jest.

"Not that I am aware of, but then again, I'm still considered young. Isn't that nice? Stay alert and ready to defend us," Elke said. She spun her parasol. "Do you have any light with you?"

"Besides my hands?" he asked. She nodded. "I carry a penlight and laser pointer. In case of emergency, I carry a flare and flash-bangs in my pocket. They have yet to equip smartphones with those apps."

Elke slowed enough for him to see the carcass of a fox. It looked like a fresh kill, like it had dropped dead in its tracks. "I once saw a bear running wild, confused, lumbering about, and then the ravens descended in a black cloud. They were followed by what looked like a flying dinosaur, a winged creature like a pterodactyl, and it consumed them. The darkness feeds on light, but it also devours itself. Destrange and Von Damme both fed on it directly. The practice is unusual and dangerous, as darkness must be matched with blood to sustain The Bloodlust," she said.

With those words, Dillon focused more, using will to help him hurry through the Shadowlands. He tried to call on the darkness to empower him and push him faster.

"Catch me if you can," she told him. Her laughter rang, and the world seemed to rock back, letting her run like the wind. He chased her full out until she slowed for a bank of fog. She smiled and nodded to his hand. "Look. Your burn is already better," she said.

"Healed by darkness?" he asked. He tested his wrist, finding that it felt as good as ever.

"Yes, it is another reason to visit the Shadowlands. Its darkness revitalizes us. We can draw it about us like a healing cloak. It can be accessed where there is shadow and found in places of never light."

"Darkness and dirt," Dillon mused. He kept pace with her through the long shadows cast by the dead and charred-looking trees. She cautioned him on avoiding the thorns and spines. Here, the trees appeared to be bug-infested, lightning-struck, or old and dying. The Shadowlands' bugs attacked him like a swarm of mosquitoes and tried to feast on him. He had wanted to test a theory. Now seemed like the right time. He turned on his laser pointer. It emitted a hard red light. He swung it like a lightsaber and after two misses, struck a shadow hornet, slicing it in twain. It vanished.

"Nice. What a novel idea," Elke said.

"*Star Wars*," Dillon replied. He sliced up others. One got too close, so he grabbed it bare-handed. He crushed it in a fist of light. The shadow hornet vanished. The sensation had tickled. Squishing two more gave him a jolt of invigoration, but he had no time to dwell on it, for they weren't alone.

He spotted a glow ahead and thought it was an animal, perhaps even a porcupine by its size. She guessed it might be a big cat, perhaps a wildcat. They were both wrong.

The nimbus of light belonged to a toddler, a young boy of two or three. He saw Dillon and started crying. Both stubby arms reached up. "Dah, dah," the toddler said.

"He must have crawled through a small gap. He is in great danger," Elke said.

The boy cried loudly. The woods rustled, despite having no leaves. The rocks shifted and grumbled. Dillon thought he heard distant thunder.

"That is the sound of power. It is one of the many ways kids go missing. I've heard of it, but never seen it. We must help him," Elke said. She started to pick up the boy.

He screamed and reached for Dillon, who after a moment did the humane thing and took the toddler in his arms. Dillon wished he had someone to comfort him.

A bellow sounding like a wildcat assaulted them. No words needed to be exchanged. Dillon carried the child as they fled toward the nearest gate. They kept the dry lake on their right. He was curious if they could cross the river valley here. He figured she was heading for a bridge. Elke's smile bolstered his spirit and encouraged him. He tapped into the dark power of his supernature to match her speed.

In his arms, the toddler broke out into laughter. Dillon laughed along, a rolling, feel good chuckle. The realm blanched.

Then, the darkness recovered from the shock. The Bloodlust howled as loud and angry as a storm bent on destruction. He realized the hunger was stronger here, inspiring him to run faster. He tried to ignore the scent of the child in his arms. The Bloodlust tried to convince him that he was carrying a baby piglet. It even smelled like a sty.

"What destroys shadows?" he asked.

"Undiluted sunlight, copious amount of water, and strong will-power in life will do the job."

"You don't think my touch was sunlight, do you?"

"No, it would have burned me earlier. As unlikely as it sounds, we are one of the kindest and most discerning of supernature," she replied.

A dark hawk swooped in on them, attempting to peck the child. Dillon sliced it with his laser pointer. Elke clubbed two more with her amazing parasol of bludgeoning. Ahead, the dark fog thickened. To avoid it, Elke turned downhill toward the lakeshore.

"What do you mean? We're like snowflakes?" Dillon asked, amusing himself. He was starting to feel a touch of fatigue. The baby giggled, and Dillon grinned back.

Elke chuckled. "We are similar to each other, but no two vampires are alike. Some develop odd skills and talents. Others have talents that are enhanced. Some gain strange powers. It could explain your blue-white lightning. A defense mechanism, perhaps," Elke told him.

He heard wings above, flapping, and a harsh croaking.

"Ravens! I wouldn't be surprised to see shadow dogs or cats. To them, the boy would be a great source of sustenance," Elke said.

They reached the road and ran along it to the bridge. As they crossed it, the birds swept in to assault then. Their slashing claws weakened and slowed Dillon, as he couldn't deter them all, but he struck any who threatened the boy. His eyes were wide, so he might be traumatized.

"Shut your eyes, love," Elke said. She dropped a flash grenade. It erupted with light.

Dillon saw stars despite closing his eyes. When his vision cleared, all the shadow ravens had fled. He could hear their cries. Elke grabbed him, and they raced to shore and continued along the eastern bank. A chilling scream lashed them. It tried to paralyze them. Dillon had stopped while Elke staggered on. He shook it off to keep moving.

"Well, that's just hotsy totsy. That was a banshee," she said with sarcasm.

A sudden roar like a jet engine swept over them. The wind shoved into them as it sped past. Dillon staggered.

Elke's eyes widened. "Make tracks and shake a leg. That was something drawn from the abyss of the Shadowlands. Shadow tigers only venture this close when they sense a feast of life," Elke said. Like a longshoreman, she cursed Gina.

A cold, rotting breath wafted over him. A second roar knocked him forward. He let go of Elke's hand to protect the child and tumbled almost gracefully to roll to his feet. He tucked the boy in the crook of his arm and drew out a flash grenade, in case his laser pointer failed.

"It's going to catch us in those moments while I open the gate. This went higgedly piggedly fast," she said.

"Downhill swiftly, I'll agree. No worries. I'll be ready. Are we on the lam?"

"From the long arm of The Bloodlust," she replied.

When they reached the exit, where the mushrooms had massed, she pulled him onto the shadow gate stoop. Nightshade plants grew here. Feeble light leaked around the edges.

The banshee wailed and attacked. Dillon had a child in one hand, and the laser pointer in the other. He stabbed and struck home. The banshee's scream died with it in the flash, but its death echoed like a shotgun blast off the barren rocks of the Shadowlands.

Almost too late, Dillon realized something larger followed the banshee, either moving a little slower or waiting to see what happened. If it was that smart, it was more dangerous. Jaws wide, claws ready, it lunged at Dillon, who reeled, dropped the grenade, and rolled away. Despite his back to it, the flash blinded him. The Shaden's roar deafened him.

Elke pushed through the shadow gate, dragging them with her. Dillon kept an undead grip on the boy, and they exited into the courtyard of her poisonous garden. Some plants were only deadly when extracted. Others were toxic shortly after touching them. It didn't seem to bother the half dozen guard dogs which came bounding through the flowers and plants to greet Elke.

The Dobermanns might as well be mastiffs, coming to waist high on Dillon. Each of the pack seemed more wolf than dog, and Elke had named many of them shadow in different languages, Sombra, Ombre, Varjo, Skygge, Itzal, Dell, and more, except Bolt who had a white streak across his face and along his back. The dogs bumped into his legs and leaned against him for his attention. He patted each of them and had to keep one-eared Thunder to four on the floor. He and Bolt were brother and sister. They were two of Theresa Killian's favorites. The dogs sniffed the toddler and frowned at the smell.

It was good to be home, although, in truth, anywhere with Elke was home. Sometimes the lodge seemed too large and stuffy, and yet, he knew its staff and defenses protected them.

A roar blasted from the shadow gate. The dogs' hackles rose, and they growled in their throats as the hounds backed away before surging forward to bark furiously.

Elke slammed the door and sealed the gate.

"Well, that was just ducky. Something is amiss with the Shadenchill, the Shadowlands, or both. I could use a giggle water," Elke said.

Dillon could use a drink of alcohol, too, to change the taste in his mouth and numb the visceral feeling inside. His soul lurched as his imagination made leaps and bounds, thinking about the poor dogs and cats that wandered into the Shadowlands. The little boy hugged Dillon and laughed even as he cried. "It's all right now," Dillon said. What of others who stumbled into the dark realm? The ones who hadn't been fortunate enough to run into helpful vampires. How many had disappeared and died there? Everyone was imperiled if shadows and dark creatures began to reach out and grab people, or even worse, if said monsters left their homeland and crossed the border into the living world.

"Yes, I could use some liquid courage," Dillon said. Whoever thought vampires couldn't be scared or worried would be wrong. Staying young and beautiful forever as one of the undying wasn't as easy as it sounded as predators abounded.

Fourteen

A New Task Force and the Old Farm

Run! Run! Roland encouraged himself. He left the meadow of Sugar Hollow behind and headed uphill as he dashed through trees' shadows and patches of light. The flickering disoriented him a bit, and he stumbled but kept going. He could hear footsteps. On his heels now, they were getting closer. They would soon be breathing down his neck unless he kicked into a higher gear. It wasn't much farther to safety and sanctuary.

He was parked at the hilltop, where he was camping, and had run down into the wide-open space of the flood-controlled area in front of the dam. He liked to pretend someone was chasing and nearly catching him for motivation. It helped him prepare for his triathlete events. He had bicycled earlier in the day. He loved this area, especially this time of year when the humidity dropped.

Roland could see the top of the hill, the light shining brighter through a break in the dense foliage. Something grabbed him by the shoulders and yanked him off his feet. He was thrown back, where

218

he landed flat on his back, driving the wind from him. Pain lanced through his neck, and then Roland blacked out.

***

What a day, Marge thought. It hadn't gone as planned, but that was part of being a deputy. There were no groundhog days, and it was never boring. That certainly pertained to last night, too. She hadn't expected to meet a handsome buck-naked man next door. Right now, she was officially off the clock, and she looked forward to venting on her grandparents and getting Grandpa's take, but she would omit her encounter with the buff, Rhett Archer. She had trouble getting him off her mind all day.

"So, what did you think of your first day, Boom?" Marge asked. He yawned. "Yes, this morning was boring compared to last night. I know meetings are long and dull but necessary."

Her companion sighed.

First thing this morning, Marge got a call sending her to Maraders Marina. Last night, a body had washed up there. She had wondered if that might be Cole Dare or perhaps whatever Boomer had been chasing but no such luck. The corpse had been called Mac by most, his full name Kelly MacDonald. He had been chewed upon, missing an arm and parts of both legs.

Maraders Marina was near Friendship and in her county, so she knew the owner, Tom Marader. He was a savvy businessman and womanizer, thinking he was a gift to heterosexual females, although she had never heard of any kind of abuse. He just loved them and left them, as the country songs like to bemoan.

She had been assigned to interview him. A couple of strange things had happened before and during. After parking, she and Boomer ambled downhill to the gang plank. She had recognized the brash owner, a good-looking almost thirty-something blue-eyed stud. On Marader's arm was a slinky female with bright red hair tied in a ponytail.

Boomer started barking ferociously. He didn't want to get any-where near them, the whites of his eyes showing, until the woman sat down and laid on her back. Marader knelt and looked Boomer in the eye. He whined, slunk forward and then rolled onto his back. Marader and the young woman named Ginger rubbed on his belly telling Boom that he was a good doggy!

Marge had stood open-mouthed. Boomer had given a stern warning, and then he had played follow the leader and rolled over. Ginger had claimed to be dog whisperer. She had told Boomer to go back to being protective, and he had returned to Marge's side.

The interview hadn't been helpful. They had found the body after midnight during a reunion of friends. She knew Knives. Dr. Curran was solid. She knew of J-Man. He had a reputation as being honest and a civic do-gooder, flying organs from hospital to hospital. Another Eagle Scout, she mused. Earlier visitors had been the antique and arts dealer, Elke Swearington, and the journalist, local boy goes out into the big world and does well, Dillon Urich. It helped that people knew and loved his mother who was a nurse.

"So did wild dogs really attack y'all?" Marge had asked. She had heard stories about the August fire and deaths.

"No dogs. It was werewolves. Snarling furry monsters of teeth and claws. Sons of bitches killed Pete and Walt that night. We shot them, but it didn't hurt the bastards until we used silver. Dimes in a shotgun really fly," Marader said. At first, Marge had thought that he was jerking her chain, but he wasn't joking. He didn't believe he was lying. She had a gift, a sixth sense, which let her know if people were being disingenuous. Liars caused her pains in the neck, literally and figuratively. She would be frowning before she realized it. "Did you see any werewolves last night?" she asked.

They said no, but Marader and his young lady were BS-ing. Marge wasn't sure what to make of that. Why would they be lying through their teeth? She knew about witches and many locals believed in ghosts and Bigfoot, but few gave credence to werewolves. And yet, what she had seen last night, could that have been a werewolf? She asked if they had seen any animals run by. They spoke the truth about not seeing any critters.

All day, Marge had kept wondering about last night. what Dan and Genny had said. Dan was adamant he'd rescued a boy. Genny believed Dan was ripped up like Marsha. Was there a connection? Marge kept picturing her kind-hearted sister being clawed to death by a furry ball of fury. What could she do about it? Well, working on the new task force might help. She could dream, right?

Team Marge and Boom's second stop, even before going to the office, was at Painters Creek Marina. A houseboat owner had gone missing. Charlie Clarke's door had been found open, blood inside and out, and his Yorkie, Miss Lucy, was missing, too. From the blood smears, Mr. Clarke might have been dragged into the lake. By road, it was six miles between Painters Creek Marina and the 421 Bridge, but by water, it was about two miles. Could the thing that had attacked Search and Rescue last night, also have attacked Mr. Clarke? She taped off the entry to the houseboat as a crime scene and called forensics. She would leave it up to the TVA to decide if a warning should be issued.

Too soon, the media might try to connect this event to the Oktoberfest Vampire.

Their third stop was a visit out to Shady Valley, Tennessee to the local landmark, Backbone Rock's arch. She wanted to see at least one of the Oktoberfest Vampire's murder scenes that would be discussed at the meeting. Of course, there was no straight route, taking twice the distance to drive it. Almost suddenly out of the trees, there was a long spine of dark, lichen-covered limestone with a man-made arch that the two-lane road used. Once, trains had steamed through on rails instead of pavement. Empty parking lots sat on both sides. To the east, a creek ran around the end of the finger of stone and through the woods. With the sun's light on them, their leaves appeared red-gold and gloriously afire, giving her a morning boost.

Marge had let Boomer roam. She always had tingles and chills walking where someone had recently died. The dying leaves rustled like whispering, and she wondered if it was mental, or if she sensed the echoes of the victim's last agonal breaths.

At first, all Boomer had found were an empty French fries' container from the golden arches and an empty Payday candy bar wrapper. He loved peanuts. Soon, she found him whining and pawing at the ground. She found a crucifix on a chain, except when she studied it, the symbol seemed inverted. That called to mind Satanic cults, though it wasn't the Six Fingers cult, but likely another group of lunatics. The unholy symbol seemed to give off electrostatic jolts despite her gloves, shocking her. She couldn't stuff it in a small evidence bag fast enough. She dropped in onto the floor mat of the cruiser.

"Thanks, Boom. You're a good dog, literally digging up what could be evidence. You're such a police dog!" she told him. His wagging tail shook all of him from nose to toenails.

Her dog's mood changed instantly with the arrival of a reporter as he walked up the road. She recognized the handsome, annoying, and charismatic Cane Concannon, a certified PIN with the potential to cause a migraine. Most considered him to be a blowhard, a crackpot, or a story spinner, not an observer. He floated the idea that both city councils were controlled by vampires, the members being mouthpieces for the bloodsuckers draining the very life out of the community. How else could you explain the dump? The casino? Like a good guy, he wore a white jacket and hat today for the cool morning weather. Marge had never been comfortable around him. He seemed too slick sometimes. Her neck told her that he believed that he was telling the truth. An even more helpful intuition would have told her the truth, not just if her suspect was lying. Oh well, she was still thankful.

"Deputy Marge. So good to see you back. Hardaway is no fun. Now the Oktoberfest Vampire should be shaking in his boots."

"Concannon, do you somehow know that the perpetrator is a he? Are you withholding evidence?" she countered.

"No, but I enjoyed the way you used our vague English language to create further confusion. Just what I've come to expect from authority figures," he said. Humor flashed in his gray eyes.

"I strive to be effective in my communications. Listen, I'm just back on the job a couple of hours. I likely know less than you do about what's going on."

"Vampires is what's going on. You better learn quickly. The police and deputies might be next."

"What makes you think that?" she asked.

"The Oktoberfest Vampire is attacking physically strong men and women."

Marge chuckled. "I appreciate that you don't buy into the out of shape, donut eating stereotypical cop."

"Alright. So, you don't know anything about the Oktoberfest Vampire, yet. But I heard you were there last night. What can you tell me about the bridge jumper who almost drowned and yet still managed to slash up an entire SARs unit?"

"It was dark. I wasn't close. I'm not sure what happened."

"Wasn't your sister killed in a similar manner?" Concannon asked.

"Are you trying to piss me off?" Marge growled. Boomer sounded much like her.

"Whoa! My apology. I'm trying to be helpful. If pissing you off worked, I would volunteer. I've heard I have some talent in that area. It would be work, but I would try for the good of the community," he managed with a genteel smile.

"I love your stand-up comedy routine, Concannon, but would you please keep it to the stage?"

"I respect the dead. They're still around and can screw with you. Listen, I heard about a new task force assigned to deal with the supernatural after what happened in August. I hear you're a member. Are they serious?"

"I don't know yet. I'll meet with other members later and see if they're gravely serious or dead serious."

"I know you don't care for my opinions, but in this case, that won't be enough. Y'all need to be undead serious. When you are, you can come talk about it on my show," Concannon told her.

Boomer barked. "You said it," she told her dog. She had no interest in being on The Concannon Retort. The man could debate for hours without taking a breath like Louie Armstrong lingering on a blaring, trumpeter's note. "That reminds me that I need to get back to work. I'm behind. I don't like working with only part of the puzzle. You, sir, can go be the burr under someone else's saddle blanket, and have a nice day," Marge said.

He stared at her as if he just knew that she was hiding something. In her cruiser, the Satanic symbol seemed to be vibrating. She wondered if it was calling to Concannon, encouraging him to stir up fears and trouble.

Later, Boomer still wasn't as happy while waiting for her to be done with her meeting. It had lasted almost two hours, her hand hurting the entire time, and Boomer had been forced to cool his doggy jets. There was a lot to unpack from today, which is why she wanted to bounce it off her grandfather. Boomer was a great listener, but he lacked years of experience, and he had a tendency to nap on her. There was nothing like a big doggie yawn in your face when you were having a serious discussion to break the mood.

She had gone to Grand Antiques, knowing that the investigators of the paranormal were meeting and eating delicious desserts. The cobbler and muffins were to die for, so to speak, but she hadn't expected three people to collapse, and yet such things happened. She had been trained for it. Even so, when she thought back on it, her skin crawled. There had been something wrong with Rixs Frederick. She had talked to him at the boat ramps, and even after hitting the sauce, his eyes had never looked like that! It was creepy. His eyes and expression seemed to shift back and forth between being thankful and utterly compassionless, looking at them like they would soon be victims.

Rixs had been the complete opposite of Ranger Archer. Stop that, she told herself.

She was looking forward to reading the county coroner's report on Frederick. Carol Snowen had been hospitalized and was doing all right. She predicted she would recover. The doctor agreed. The paramedics had released Sheilah. Marge wondered if she had suffered a panic attack when Frederick had collapsed. That had been a wild scene with the domino chain of health emergencies.

Marge took Exit 7 off Interstate 81. She knew this route well, having spent summers and holidays at the farm. Now she visited her grandparents on off days, especially ugly lake days. Grandpa was a retired High Sheriff of Washington County and gave excellent advice and long, warm hugs. Mamaw was a retired baker, except she was still home baking much of the time. Her cooking seemed to hug you, too. Gardening, making jams and canning were her passions.

On the way, she told Boomer all about them. He looked impressed and then pleased when she mentioned that they adored dogs. They were currently without a canine and debating on whether to get another. She warned him about the mean mouser named Chester. Boomer's arrival sent all cats scattering from atop the front porch to underneath it. She warned that Chester might plot revenge.

While Marge removed her gear and tools of the trade, she marveled at the old place. It always seemed smaller than she remembered, despite having three bedrooms and a great room around a big stove and hearth. Marge loved the old-style farmhouse and its front porch looking out over the hilly green property. The fog mingled with the smoke from their chimney to create a haze.

As soon as she opened the door, a pungent wall of vinegar assaulted Marge. She held her nose as she went in. Mamaw was pickling, again. Boomer couldn't hold his nose. He hesitated then followed Marge inside like a good trooper. His nails clacked on the hardwood floors. Soon, his courage was rewarded with snacks and Mamaw smothering, so Boomer didn't mind having watering eyes.

"It is so good to see y'all. I wasn't sure when y'all would be back," Mamaw said, although Marge had told her several times. Her grandmother claimed her mind was getting foggy, and yet she was seeing more clearly as death neared. On a farm, life and death were encountered and discussed daily. They hugged. "Oh, you feel tense. You need to unload on Grandpa, so you'll be able to eat without getting indigestion. The lasagna will be ready in thirty minutes. Get yourself sorted out by then. He reset the targets if you need to shoot something."

That sounded like a good idea to Marge. "It's not that bad, and I've only been back one day," she said.

On the way to the barn, Boomer scattered the chickens without chasing them, making a clear path for her. From the loft, the cats glared daggers at her dog who thought he was feline-proof. She heard the sound of toy trains running. The tracks ran all around the barn, up and down various levels and crossing bridges and beams above. The engines were modeled after those that had run through this area. Potbellies were one of the reasons Bristol existed. The N&W #18 Engine was running today. It had been the last train to provide passenger service to Abingdon, Roanoke and beyond into southeast Virginia. Amid the movement and sound of two trains, they found Grandpa changing the oil in the tractor. He wiped his hands clean before he embraced her for a long time. Boomer tried to squeeze into the hug.

"This is Boomer. He's searching you for drugs and snacks," Marge said.

"A shake down, eh? It's so good to have you back in town and with a partner as loyal and true as they come."

"Yes, every day is a dog day," Marge mused. Funny, she thought. After her sister had died, it had been doggone unpleasant. Boomer made it easier.

"Ha. We've missed you, and I'm sure the good people of Sullivan and Washington Counties did, too. It went to Hell in a handcart while you were gone. It dearly missed the Cantrell sisters. And this vampire nonsense," he said and lifted his eyes to the heavens. He continued to ruffle Boomer's ears, earning doggie grins.

"I'm back, but I'm not sure I'll ever recover from what happened," Marge said.

"We all dearly miss Marsha."

"I feel like I'm missing a limb."

"I hear you. I would say missing a light. My days aren't as bright. How's your mom doing?"

"Maybe crying a little less. Not sleeping too well. I get that. If nothing else, she's glad she's in Florida. She feels like we do, but the days are warmer and seem longer, so the nights seem shorter than here this time of year. I think that helps. Nothing really does, you know. The not knowing sucks eggs," Marge said. She wanted to punch and kick something. Boomer snuggled up to her like he could wiggle her grief away.

"We know how you feel," Grandpa replied sadly, and he did. They still weren't sure what had happened to her father, their son.

"All we can do is put one foot in front of the other and do what God puts in front of us. Tell me about your first day back," he said.

She decided not to tell him about chatting with Concannon. "I spent part of my morning attending a meeting with agents from the world of acronyms. FBI, TWRA, VCO plus VA and TN PD."

"Sounds like a party to the letter. What, no ATF?"

"Not yet anyway. It's a booze and smoke free party where we share weird stories like we're trying to scare each other. Seriously, though, it's a task force to look into supernatural and paranormal events as a subdivision, you could say, of the terrorism and cultists task force."

"I'm surprised it's been organized. I would say it sounds like a witch hunt, but well, we've both been there and done that," Grandpa said.

"I guess it's another grouping of nuts and whackos. I'm coordinating Washington County with the Sullivan County Sheriff's department, animal control, all four police forces of the Tri-Cities, TVA, Tennessee Wildlife and Virginia Conservation agents."

"Did you say animal control?" he asked.

Marge nodded. Animal-loving Whitney Thomlinson had shared that department's information. Marge had worked with her at various times, from removing exotic snakes to dealing with rambunctious bears. Whitney was one of those lucky, natural born blond beauties that would look good in a burlap bag. She had a canine encounter with a big dog go poorly, and she'd been bitten, leaving her arm in a sling.

"Yes, there has been a jump in wild dog and wildcat attacks in both counties, and more in the city than usual, not to mention the damage to trash cans," Marge said.

"That's reason to be concerned. Say, who else got volunteered into this? It sounds like a potential career killer."

"I know. They volunteered me while I was gone," Marge said. She mentioned her friend, Betsy Tankerson, her counterpart for Washington County. With all regards to the singing Commodores, brick houses could not move like Betsy who would have played linebacker if the NFL allowed women. She could run a 4.8 second forty yard dash in all that gear. She had started as a firefighter, but the helmets and breathing apparatus made her claustrophobic, so she became a law enforcement officer for the county. She had a sleepy-eyed look and talked with a drawl, so folks thought she was slow and shocked when she was shrewd. Marge loved her like a sister.

Grandpa nodded approval. "Just be glad it's not someone like Hardaway."

"There's Andrea Wilson from the mounted police division," Marge continued. Via horseback, Andrea and Bonnie Rainbow patrolled the states' city streets and especially their parks and rolling hills. There had been recent issues in cemeteries, so they patrolled those, too. Bonnie had reported seeing a ghost horse at East Hill.

"Lucky ladies. I did that for several years. I loved it, working like a real sheriff, I imagined, until my back started bothering me. A full day in the saddle is not for an old man," he said. Grandpa blamed his back issues on a gun heavily hanging on one side of the body. She had never told anyone the story of the witch who had spat curses on him. That's when his back had started to act up.

She saw a chiropractor for her back and hips. She'd had to change because the first had been sexually harassing his other patients.

"There's also Boatwright from Tennessee Wildlife," Marge continued.

"I knew his father. He was a very good man, a by the book guy."

"His son is the same. I'm not familiar with the new Virginia Conservation agent. He's new to the area, so he will be playing catch up. He's replacing the agent who died on the boat dynamited by terrorists," Marge said. Grandpa didn't recognize the name either. She gave him the names of the city police liaisons, too, but he was unfamiliar with those sent by Johnson City and Kingsport. He noticed that the task force was heavily weighted toward females.

He was familiar with Janie Kochs of Bristol Tennessee PD. She was a tall, powerful woman with dark and laughing eyes, making her resemble Wonder Woman's bigger and intimidating cousin. Janie loved MMA fighting, trained in it, and liked having your back. She was a Godsend.

"Was she sweet-talking today or being intimidating?" he asked.

"Glaring, frowning and biting nails in half with every word. I think she was short on her coffee intake, although I'd brought her a big cup from Trailblazers. She wasn't pleased with the FBI. On the other side of the line and spectrum, they sent Officer Jack Gill from VA PD."

"Oh, ole slow walkin', slow talkin' Gill. Slo Mo is thorough. Those two are like Yin and Yang," Grandpa joked.

"I think he lulls criminals to sleep. He wasn't a big fan of how the FBI has handled things, either, but he wasn't as vocal as Janie," Marge said.

"Everybody thinks they have a better way of doing it. And nobody really likes outsiders coming in to clean up their mess. We like to take care of our own houses."

"Grandpa, I have seen how you take care of the house when Mamaw goes to Florida. You definitely need an outsider to come in and clean up. Anyway, both agents have local ties to the area," she said. Marge mentioned that Agent Bond was from Bluff City and that he was one of the four local and formerly troublesome Bond brothers. Grandpa remembered them well. One had vanished years ago, his disappearance never solved. Marge figured that might be the reason Denzel had joined the FBI. His taller, copper-topped partner, Agent Kaye, grew up in Johnson City where she had been a softball star at ETSU. Now she was a forensic scientist working for The Bureau. "I've been gone for a while, so I just listened."

"What can you tell me about the victims?" he asked.

"As far as we know, the first was found at Backbone Rock. He was a weekend warrior and triathlete kind of guy who was fishing alone at the wrong place at the wrong time. They think he was killed the prior day, maybe late afternoon. Like the others I'm going to tell you about, he bled to death out four holes in his neck along the carotid. Except, there were no signs of bleeding out which makes the media think it was vampire. There are no cameras up there. So, we have no idea."

"Someone could have laid out a tarp or dragged him into a van or the bed of a pickup. Any signs of struggle?"

"Not according to the coroner. There was no bruising of any kind. If nothing else, someone wanted it to look like a vampire."

"You said there were other victims?" Grandpa asked.

"Yes, two others, similar MOs. An ETSU football player was murdered in Buffalo Mountain Park outside Johnson City. Another, a young body builder, a female age twenty, was found murdered not far from Jay's Dock on Boone Lake. Speaking of digging up. Boom found this," she said, showing him photos of the inverted cross. It had been stored as possible evidence.

"When I touched it, it shocked me and burned me," Marge said. She showed him her hand.

"Sweet Mother Mary, if that don't beat all! It looks Satanic. Make sure that doesn't get infected."

"I treated it."

"Have a doctor look at it, please. You can never be too careful with that stuff. You know, what sounds strange to me is that these were all strong, young people. Didn't you mention a football player, a body builder, and a triathlete?"

"Exactly. The frail and weak are not being preyed upon. It doesn't make sense, yet. But that's another link. We discussed putting out a warning for tough gals and strong guys. Don't go it alone. Partner up. We thought that we would be laughed at. If we find a dead MMA fighter, I guess that would tell us someone is murderously pissed at badasses," Marge said.

"I heard an ad about bodybuilders flexing and posing down at the Cameo," he said.

"Really. I hadn't considered that. I'll look into it, and any place where tough guys hang out," she said. They had considered martial arts and boxing facilities. "Andrea shared her concerns about East Hill Cemetery where there's a pack of feral wild dogs," she said, thinking back to Marader's and Ginger's comments. "I was just looking into things at the meeting of the Southwest Virginia Investigators of the Paranormal when it got weird and three people collapsed while having cobbler," Marge said. She was telling him about it when the dinner bell rang.

"We better not tarry," Grandpa said. On the way though, he slowed down. "Mamaw's been off a little bit."

"She seems fine to me," Marge said.

"She's been seeing Marsha's ghost around here. She thinks that maybe I'm supposed to help solve her murder," Grandpa said.

She took his hand. "We all process trauma differently."

"That's what the counselor said. He said it would pass. Today she hasn't mentioned her once."

"I would be happy if Marsha showed up and led me to her killer," Marge said.

Over dinner, Marge noticed Grandpa was right. When she asked Mamaw if she was burning a lavender candle, she replied, "Oh, that's just Marsha. She came back with y'all. I wondered where she's been. I hadn't seen her all day. Have you been smelling lavender all day?"

Boomer found a blanket that Marsha had quilted. He sniffed it and curled up with it.

Marge ate too much delicious lasagna. The food at the training facility had been blandly commercial for her taste. When Mamaw started asking if Marge had found any interesting prospects for dating, that she was approaching spinster with a gun and badge age, Marge took Boomer out into the foggy night for a walk. She knew better than to even think about Rhett Archer with Mamaw around. Besides, what could she say, he had a great butt, a good bod, a strange cat, and a Texas drawl? She had made calls earlier to the Gregg County Sheriff's department. Everyone had been willing to talk about what a fine and neighborly deputy that man had been. Archer was a darlin', one in a million, and dearly missed. What had happened to him was sad but not out of the norm: getting shot forcing him to retire.

Marge could smell the funk from the dump as the evening winds shifted. She wished Bristol would get their act together. She had seen signs: This city stinks. Some had joked that they were creating zombies there. Nearby was an old sign: Don't Gamble on Our Future. The poster hadn't wanted a casino built, but it was happening. The town had voted aye. It shouldn't make more of a stink, at least not literally.

Despite the different air, the farm looked much the same as it always did which brought back warm memories. When Grandpa couldn't make enough money farming to support his family, he had joined the Conservation Police as a mounted officer. Mamaw had taken care of the family farm business of pigs, chickens, and cattle, along with a huge garden. Marge's mom and two brothers had helped run it. As a youth, Marge had free run of the place, all seventeen acres of woods with creeks that backed up to Sugar Hollow, a sprawling woodland town park in Bristol, Virginia that also worked to abate flooding. Growing up on a farm, knowing the circle of life, was good training for being a deputy.

She used her phone's Ring app to make sure that the video camera was working. Grandpa had upgraded security by installing cameras to go along with the alarm system. Retired sheriffs still had enemies.

It might be her imagination, but the feeling of being observed grew stronger. Something had set Boomer to sniffing the air. He stiffened, now on alert. Marge couldn't believe it. The air changed, and it was like they were standing in a field of lavender, the scent overpowering the reek of the dump. "Yes, that's my sister's perfume," Marge said. Only late blooming flowers like fire wheels, flea bane, asters and sunflowers remained. This area was known for laurels and not lavender. Boomer whined, briefly danced as if he needed to go outside to pee and then doggy grinned and dashed away. His wagging tail seeming to propel him faster.

"Boom! Root!" Marge said. Her commands were no good, like he'd gone stone deaf. He had never acted like this during training. What had gotten into him? She jogged to follow, feeling the lasagna heavily in her tummy. Then she saw it. He was following a figure in a white dress with blond hair trailing behind her while she ran. She vanished into the woods, heading uphill toward the back of Sugar Hollow Park.

The tree limbs were beginning to look skeletal, shedding more of their leaves in the last windstorm. A few scattered pine trees remained nettled and prickly if you bumped into them. Owls hooted. A pinecone fell and tumbled downhill, at least that's what it sounded like. She felt stickiness across her face and neck. She wiped away the clingy spider webs. Sometimes they snapped to wrap around her as if they were futilely trying to slow her progress. This was not the Mirkwood of Middle Earth, so she wasn't worried about giant spiders, even if the goosebumps on her arms crawled around at the thought of arachnids.

As if lit by the moon, Marge saw the woman now and again and wondered how she was avoiding all the strands. Boomer ran lower, so he wouldn't hit the same webs, but the woman should be clearing the way. Calling to Boomer was a waste of breath that Marge needed for running. She dashed out of the woods onto a grassy gravel road and stopped before hitting the wall of weeds along the wire barrier. The primitive road snaked into the rounded hills along the fence that separated them from the park. She had ridden it on horseback, an ATV, and a pickup when they had replaced the gate a couple years ago. The grass and leaves had been flattened with a pair of tire tracks. She would have to ask if Grandpa had driven up here.

Marge decided that running off unarmed wasn't the smartest thing to do. Besides, driving would be faster than walking, and she'd have all her equipment, including a back seat for Boomer. She hustled back to the cruiser. Hearing his bark change to rapid fire concerned her.

With her gun in one hand, she steered the cruiser up the road into the forested hills. The route had obviously been driven recently, the grass flattened and bent even before she motored toward the peak and its campground.

A black dog at night was a stealth dog, but Boomer's eyes gave him away, glowing in her headlights. When she parked and exited, her partner darted through a gap in the fence. On the other side, he pointed at the body of a male runner sprawled face down. The blond woman was nowhere in sight, but the smell of lavender mellowed the stench of death.

After checking for a pulse at his wrist, finding none and his flesh to be cool, Marge rolled him over. He was stiff as rigor mortis had set in. There was no reason to call an ambulance. He was a big guy, over six foot two and wearing lightweight shorts, a long sleeve quick-dry shirt and running shoes. She wondered what happened. The victim's neck appeared bruised, and she found four marks, the bite of a big snake, a nasty lover, or the Oktoberfest Vampire.

She called in the homicide to dispatch, and then she called Grandpa, so they wouldn't be worried about her. In a pouch around the dead man's neck, she found a driver's license for Kevin Abramowitz who resembled the corpse, several hundred in cash, a military dog tag, and a Ford truck's key fob but no mobile phone. He had been murdered and not robbed. She cooled her heels and waited for reinforcements.

They arrived shortly. Concannon seemed like an ambulance chaser as he followed it into the campgrounds. They found nothing suspicious or helpful inside Abramowitz's trailer. The poor guy had been out running for his health, training for races, when he had been murdered.

Concannon was certain it was the Oktoberfest Vampire. As crazy as it sounds, Marge was keeping an open mind. That was always best for investigative purposes. Besides, a human believing that he was a vampire was still a danger to society. She hoped that she didn't need to get in the mind of a vampire to catch one.

Fifteen

The Normal World

Driving Dad's old truck brought back good memories of camping, fishing, and hunting. Cruising the curvy, undulating, and shoulderless Old Jonesboro Road brought back a flood of recollections that Dillon pushed aside. Living in the past, whether it be times with his father, God rest his soul, Gina, Denny, or his blood brothers would only bring longing and regret. He was Elke's, she was his, and that meant the world to him.

His mother had called and asked him to drive her to visit Candy Woods who suffered pulmonary fibrosis. Candy had been placed on hospice at home, which meant Mom's best friend only had a short time to live. Mom had sounded spooked on the phone, so doing a welfare check was in order. Luckily, he didn't need to be at the marina until eight o'clock.

He turned off the radio. The news reported thieves who would record the sound of car fobs opening doors and later use it to gain access. Another story had covered how in-home devices could be accessed by bad guys if the original password was left unchanged.

It seemed not only vampires were hunting. All day, humans preyed on humans. Who was harder on humans? Humans or vampires?

No wonder Mom sounded scared. Fear mongering seemed to be coming from everywhere.

Dillon had repeatedly failed to convince his mother to leave town. He worried that she might be a target, but he couldn't exactly say it, so he implied a criminal element might seek revenge. Still, she wouldn't budge. She loved it here, and her friends lived here. Bristol was home.

Dillon rolled down the window and let the breeze in. The humid air felt alive, unlike the dead winds in the Shadowlands. The earthy air carried the smoke of dying leaves, pine trees, wood fires and burnt tobacco, along with the stinging scents of scorched rubber, diesel fumes, and engine exhaust. All were tinged with the odor of wet dogs, horse droppings, and scorched pumpkins. Was that blackened marshmallow? He smiled. After visiting the Shadowlands, the sensations of the real world were welcomed but nearly overwhelming at times.

He smiled broader, thinking about escaping the Shadowlands with the child. Doris had taken the toddler into town and claimed to have found him in Sugar Hollow while walking her dog. Police had already reunited the kid with his overjoyed parents. Doris Belle would have been famous except she had asked to remain anonymous. Dillon and Elke were also unsung heroes. When he recalled the kid's laughter, Dillon beamed.

It muted the memory of the shadows caterwauling and the scream of the banshee. People would panic if they knew what was on the other side of the shadows. He and Elke wanted to cleanse themselves, so like desert dwellers, they had rubbed oil into each other and then used a scrapper to remove it and the stink of the Shadowlands. He still tingled from it and their lustful lovemaking afterward. That's likely why he had a brighter outlook.

The new world that he lived in still felt bizarre, so old habits helped bridge the divide and ease the change. Driving to visit his mom, doing something normal, felt comforting.

With his night vision, he drove with only the parking lights on through Goosepimple Junction, where a scarecrow had been placed to hold the signs, and beyond until he reached Middlebrook. A half-dozen grinning Jack o' lanterns greeted him. He turned left into the duplexes where his mother had moved after Dad had passed on three years ago.

Dillon parked and exited the truck, breathing in the night. Someone grilled steaks and played the banjo. Geese murmured and squabbled down on small, Middlebrook Lake. A neighborhood cat stared at Dillon then realized it had been spotted and slunk away. It recognized a fellow predator.

He tucked his registered Glock and a bag of goodies under the front seat. He didn't want his mother to freak out over guns and grenades. He also didn't want to leave them behind. His mother might be a target, too. She didn't know it, but she was under the watchful eye of one of Elke's agents.

He laughed when he saw that Mom's front door was adorned with a squashed witch, her legs sticking out from her flattened hat. The Jack o' lanterns were ceramic, since her kids were long past the age of carving, although he had enjoyed that part of the holiday. Dillon was about to dial his mother when one of her neighbors strolled up.

"Hey, how's it going?" Kim Hampton asked. Short, blond, and also a lover of the martial arts, Kim lived across the street on the shores of Middlebrook Lake where she and her husband operated an Airbnb. She was a dear friend of Elke's and kept an eye on Mrs. U for them.

"Everything is easier and wonderful when you're in love."

"Isn't that the truth!" Kim replied.

"How about you and Mike? How's life?" Dillon said. That had a different meaning to him now.

"Good. We've got company. They're here for a Barter Theater performance and the East Hill Cemetery Halloween event. I have never understood people's fascination with graveyards. There are more ghosts and interesting beings found away from the cemeteries," she said.

"Truer than I ever would have believed," Dillon replied.

"You'll be glad to know there's been no suspicious activity," she said. Her driveway camera recorded the front of Mom's duplex.

"That's very comforting. I appreciate what you do," Dillon said.

"She's a neat lady, and it's comforting to have a nurse across the street."

"Well, she'll be gone for a little while. We're driving over to see her best friend who's in hospice care," Dillon said.

"Then I shouldn't hold you up. Good to see you."

"Good to be seen. Tell Mike hello."

"He wants to know when you'll spar with him," Kim said.

"He has a death wish, does he? I'll give him a call soon. Have a good night," Dillon said. He dialed his mother's phone. "Ding. Dong. Dillon, your ride for this evening, has arrived," he told her.

"I'm glad it's not a chariot. It's chilly out. Wait a moment, and I'll get the door."

"You might need to hold back Molly."

"Don't be silly. She was just in a mood last time," his mother replied.

Dillon sighed and stuffed doggie treats in the laces of his shoes. He had planned to win Molly back by appealing to the Dachshund's stomach and love of back rubs. He rang the doorbell and waited.

He heard Molly ferociously barking like a big dog on the other side. Dogs hated vampire energy. Last time, Mom had to lock the dog in the backyard because she kept growling at Elke. He had come prepared this time with the Dachshund's favorite treats. Let's see how scared she was of him now, with treats on his feet and in his pockets. He dropped a cookie to the ground. He kicked the dog snack inside when the door opened, and the treat landed atop Molly's digger paws.

Dillon smelled fear. The scent wafted over him, along with that of peachy hand cream.

"Dillon, dear!" his mom said and beamed a smile that lit up her face and her relieved green eyes. She looked so much like an older, mature Silke with apple cheeks and her auburn hair touched by a little gray. Redheads went gray early, he had read. Being a nurse, she believed in good physical health. She jogged and did yoga, so she would be able to play with her grandchildren one day.

On the threshold, his mother hugged him, and he embraced her. The scent of her fear lessened, and his hands became warm and tingled. Again, the blue-white lightning ran along his arms to now surround his mother, giving her an extra glow. She looked brighter and stood straighter. Even so, he stepped back and broke contact. The body lightning vanished, and the tickle left his hands and arms.

She stretched and smiled. "Ah, my back popped! That's much better. It's good to see you, dear. The area has grown dangerous. I don't want to take any unnecessary risks."

"Why? What's wrong?" Dillon asked. He noticed her handgun on the table near the door. She could shoot. She and Silke had gone together to the range to practice, but his mother was a long way from a gun-toting mama.

"There was a home invasion yesterday in Edgefield. A crucifix didn't ward him off, the news reported, so it wasn't that vampire-themed serial killer. He isn't doing break-ins, yet. This sounded like more run of the mill crime that still kills or traumatizes. Anyway, I'm glad you're here," she said.

That neighborhood was due west of Middlebrook Lake. Last week, he had read about two burglaries on Country Club Road. How had that not been on the news? Perhaps old fashioned breaking and entering wasn't as compelling as high-tech robbery. "Remember, you can always call the Hamptons. Mike's a really big scary guy, and he's trained in the martial arts, too. He'd likely have someone whupped before they knew it."

"Thanks for reminding me. I have baked some zucchini bread for them. I need to take it over. Ah, look, Molly still loves you."

The Dachshund sniffed his shoes searching for more treats.

"She loves those things more than life," Dillon said

His mom nodded. "Last year, I watched her scare off a pit bull who coveted her treats."

"That's bravery. Hold the bag, and she should protect you from any home invaders," Dillon said.

"She gives me fair warning. Did Elke come with you?" Mom asked, looking past him.

"No, Key's getting ready for out-of-town clients, and last time Molly wouldn't let up, which is why I came pre-treated," Dillon said. This could be the last time he saw his mother. If so, he has been blest with two months of unusual bonus time.

"That's nice, dear. Are you wearing makeup tonight?" she asked.

Dillon nodded and rolled his eyes. "Yes. I had my face painted because I will be on camera. Elke offered me a spray tan. Should I have gone with that? Am I ghostly pale?" he asked. He had worn TV cosmetics before so his face wouldn't gleam during reporting or interviews. It was no big deal, but his mom liked to tease him. This time, Edgerton had worked on him. The valet had excellent hands, having painted Desiree and Ella over the years while the beloved girls matured into young women. "Or is my nose shiny?"

"You are as handsome as always, and a younger version of your daddy when he hadn't seen the sun all winter," she chuckled and gestured for him to enter. "Well, come in. That autumn wind is chilly, and I need a few moments to get ready."

With her permission, Dillon was able to cross the threshold. Vampires needed to be invited into any place with a strong attachment, the home being a castle and all. Mom and Pop businesses could be like that. It made him realize that this was no longer his home, especially after Silke had covered the windows and doors with blest crosses, ankhs, crucifixes, and angels. Vampires keep out! He didn't blame his sister. She should hold a grudge against vampires for what had happened to her and Troy.

"You are looking fit," she said. Mom smelled of peaches and peppermint.

"I've stepped up my martial arts workouts," he replied. They were no longer practice. The sessions were for when he was assaulted. Even Edgerton thought he was an easy target. He, Doris, and the others had a betting pool on how long he would last, despite their valiant efforts.

"Master Cosmo called. I heard he was sick with bone cancer."

"I saw him. He didn't look well."

"I'm so sorry to hear that. We're all down here only as long as the Good Lord allows us to be. Master Cosmo has been a great role model. He worked with the youth and the Scouts. Dear, do you want to take any of your old gear with you? It's in the spare bedroom closet. Take a look while I get ready," his mom suggested.

Dillon had never had a permanent room here, but Mom's possession of it felt strong. She had moved after Dad had died falling off a ladder. Dillon couldn't understand how he and Troy could survive so much when Dad had broken his neck while working around the house. Mom couldn't live there after that. Dillon had planned to stay here upon his return for the reunion, but then he had died and been revived as a vampire. He had even left his sword,

Shadowsbane, here when he had gone boating and jet skiing on the lake. He didn't see it anywhere, so he pulled open the closet door.

He reacted swiftly to catch the sheathed katana slicing toward him. Silke had likely stuffed it here. He took Shadowsbane in both hands and sighed. Once, they had almost been inseparable.

He drew the blade and memories washed over him, of receiving it from Master Cosmo for winning the No Sword competition. Dillon smiled, recalling standing on the short podium, and taking the sword in both hands, unsheathing it, holding it aloft and letting the light strike it. He had earned it by working the better part of the day evading sword strikes, thrusts and jabs and disarming his opponents. All entrants fought the same sword wielders. Dillon had succeeded with everyone but Master Cosmo. His sensei's sword moved snake-strike fast.

Despite winning the sword, Dillon had only been given possession of it when he could take it from his sensei's hands or graduated high school. He was often reminded that the Way to Heaven frowned on using weapons to kill, and yet, a sword could be life-giving, if by killing great evil it saved many lives.

Dillon found himself with extra free time when Troy had started dating Raquel. The other blood brothers had helped by attacking Dillon with rubber swords. For a time, he joked that they were acting like Cato, attacking him at any moment or pulling pranks. Did that make him Inspector Clouseau? Dillon mused. He had practiced until he finally, a bit luckily, disarmed his sensei just two weeks before high school graduation. Even to this day, Dillon thought his sensei had experienced an off day.

He silently thanked Master Cosmo for forcing him to continue to improve, to be passionately curious and to study the situation and setting. Some called it knowing the room. It had served him well in meetings and interviews. He needed to do better at that when dealing with supernatural creatures. And yet, how could he gauge what he barely comprehended? He felt like a supernatural as a second language learner, and he wasn't learning fast enough!

If it was a holy sword, Shadowsbane didn't burn him, Dillon mused as he slowly unsheathed the short blade. With only a little knowledge and less experience, he needed a surprise and an edge. He hoped that the katana would save many more lives than it took. In his life now, the sword would be mightier than the pen since he couldn't use his writings against vampires.

Elke's household staff often reminded him that vampires were predators. Nice guys wound up truly dead, reaching their final end early. Seen as competition, new vampires were rarely welcomed with open arms. Dillon had been lucky with Elke, a one in a million shot. She had saved him, nurtured him with passion and trained him. She fought exceptionally well with her parasol, so he had teased her about her lethal umbrella sword, then he seriously told her that he felt fortunate that she was on his side.

"We are one side. Our side," she had replied and kissed him fiercely.

Dillon had heard the whispers by Elke's staff, and some not whispering by Doris, that he was here today and gone tomorrow. He would prove her wrong. Somehow or some way, he would learn to straddle the line. He vowed that he would walk in two worlds at once like strolling down the middle of State Street, one foot in Virginia and one in Tennessee, and still stay true to Elke and to his family.

He followed the scent of hot cider and fresh baked pumpkin pie to the kitchen. He didn't need to eat, but he still enjoyed the taste. His mom handed him a steaming travel mug of apple cider and noted the katana.

"Are you taking that with you?" she asked. He nodded. "Once, you carried that everywhere, at least in your car. I was afraid you would take it to Tennessee High."

"Master Cosmo cautioned me. He said he would take it away if I did something foolish. It never was in the car when I parked at school. I was toast if the forces of darkness showed up there."

"And now ten years have passed. Well, your father often said life is change. Embrace it. You are here and healing, and that's wonderful. I miss Silke, but she is with the love of her life," she said and sighed happily. She wrapped a scarf around her neck.

"Have you talked to Sis recently?" Dillon asked. He helped Mom with her jacket.

"I think it was just two days ago. I can't believe you threatened all her potential paramours and drove off others."

"Well, it seems I was overly cautious and wrong about that," he replied.

"Thank you. Did you ever say that to Silke?" she asked. He nodded. "I believe you're maturing some more. I wish Elke had come along with you. I love the way you two smile at each other. Did Silke get along with Elke?"

"She was so angry with me, I couldn't tell," he replied. His sister already had shot him in the foot when she had confronted him about interfering in her romance. He had never seen her so livid. Troy was crazy to love her, but such passion had brought him back to life.

"She wants me to visit them out there," Mom said while she checked to ensure her phone was in her purse. She tucked it under her arm and headed for the door. "Now Molly, stay."

"Denny's church is setting the memorial stone Sunday. I wish I could be there," Dillon said. God only knew what placing a blest memorial to Denny on the ruins of Von Damme's cursed mansion would do.

"I think I might go. It will remind me to be grateful that you're here. I was worried that I'd lost you. That was awful, so many of your close friends dying," Mom said. She opened the door and ushered him outside.

"Is that where those new gray hairs are from?"

"Oh, it's time to get a new perm, is it?" she said and locked the door.

"You look beautiful with a dash of maturity," Dillon replied.

"Are you saying I would make a good grandmother?"

"No, but that is true. You aren't expecting me to propose any time, are you?"

"I would advise against it. It's only been two months."

She noticed the truck, Dad's truck. "Oh, that brings back memories."

"I think Elke and I should experience all the seasons, a year together. That gives her time to grow weary of me and change her mind," he said tongue-and-cheek. And yet, he experienced a twinge of doubt. Why? Was it what Phineas had said? He couldn't resist Elke, so he was helplessly in love with her. What did Elke want him for? He sensed she was hiding things from him. Doris told him it was a vampire's nature to be secretive. It kept them alive.

"How are you feeling? Besides your skin tone, you look fit. Is ripped still the right term?" she asked. She felt his biceps before he opened the passenger side door for her.

"Yes. As long as I don't dwell on missing the sunlight, I'm good. I have Elke. It's odd, though, getting accustomed to being indoors by day and changing my body clock to being active at night," he said. He paused, thinking that he had heard an odd noise. A moment later, a firework exploded overhead. Dillon tensed until he heard the neighborhood kids cheer. He climbed inside the truck.

"I'm so delighted that I could do a happy dance. I thought you were going to obsess over the Dark Lady until nobody would have you. I thought you were lucky to have Gina. Oh, she called earlier today. Did she reach you?"

"She's been texting me," he replied. He had been ignoring those for the last hour. "I admit to being thunderstruck. I know that shocks everyone."

"It takes time for family and friends to adjust when we are no longer a central part of your universe. I know your father would be walking on air."

"You think so?" Dillon asked.

"You brood less. Smile more. You are present more, instead of thinking about the last story or the next story or who you need to see or even be. I feel you're really here instead of dreaming about finding the Dark Lady of the Lake."

Dillon laughed. "I can lean a little in the direction of OCD," he said. His current compulsion was the same as back when: Elke.

"It makes you a great reporter. Dear, I love seeing you weekly, but I'm concerned about your skin condition. I know you miss the sunshine."

"I do. The doctors are still in the dark. They are certain that it's not porphyria. I'm still waiting on the results of tests taken last week," Dillon said. His blood was checked weekly by Hoyt. Elke made sure everyone at Swearington Lodge stayed healthy, nourished, and educated. They all were supposed to be good members of the community.

"Do you think the terrorists might have released some sort of toxin? A poisonous gas or virus?" Mom asked, paling a bit. She voiced one of his concerns.

"Well, if so, I'm the only one that it affected this way. They checked to see if there were any other cases reported like mine, and there haven't been any," Dillon replied. Elke and her kind didn't want feral vampires. There were already too many rogues in the area. He pulled to a stop at the sign exiting Middlebrook and waited.

An old bomber, a car from the sixties, drove by. It might be a dark green Goat, a GTO, but it was the driver that caught his attention.

He was costumed and wore cosmetics to look like the villain, The Joker. The driver suddenly turned, grinned bigger and winked.

"Is that what's bothering you?" his mom asked. She could tell something was off.

Dillon blinked. The Joker was already gone, driving off. Halloween, he mused, not amused. He was trying to keep from being maudlin. He couldn't tell her about the vampires, but he could tell her about Madilyn Marader. "No. Tom called me. His sister, Madi the myth huntress, and her TV crew plan to dive the ruins. That's where I'm headed after we visit Candy."

"Where Denny died? Oh, my. Diving to that deathtrap sounds like a dreadfully awful idea," his mom replied.

"I agree. Something always goes wrong. I will join them later tonight. No worries, Mom. I'll just be watching from the boat. No diving for me," Dillon said. He pulled onto the road. They had shared many holidays with the Woods and their seven branches at their house on countless occasions, so this felt normal as well. He didn't take it for granted. Life was short. He was driving, and it was a night for paying close attention.

The Dodge Ram pickup truck that drove the other way, perhaps following the Joker, was driven by a skeleton. He gestured with one bony thumb up. In the passenger seat, Elvira waved. Dillon drove by a house themed as a haunted graveyard with tombstones, inflatable ghosts, and mechanized skeletons rising. That seemed auspicious. The next house was cheerily decorated in harvest decor with pumpkins, multicolored corn, and a cornucopia full of dried squash to celebrate Thanksgiving.

Mom called ahead, so they were expected. Phil, Candy's jolly and bespectacled husband who had often played Santa Claus, ushered them into the brick and wood frame two story house. Dillon crossed the threshold and felt his way through it into the protection of a loving home, where many hugs were exchanged. Dillon couldn't recall the last time he had been embraced so much. He was thankful and grateful that Darlene had sustained him; otherwise, he might not have been able to endure the touch of family and friends.

With help from a male hospice worker, Candy rose unsteadily to her feet. Mom's best friend wore a nasal cannula connected to oxygen. Simply standing and embracing were enough to leave Candy breathless. Dillon could tell by her dim aura that the thirteen-time, silver-haired grandmother's vitality was low. Her time was running out. She suffered from a lung ailment, unable to process enough oxygen. Knives had explained it. Dillon only recalled that the tissue in the lungs had hardened. Mom continued to hold onto Candy's hand as she sank back into her lounger. They all gave Candy time to recover. In her eyes, Dillon saw that she knew the end was near. Her usually flush skin looked as pale as Dillon's.

He had known the Woods for what seemed all his life. Mrs. Woods was a retired schoolteacher from Holston View Elementary and Vance Middle School. She had over a dozen grandkids to watch and fuss over. Her family hailed from California, but they had lived in Bristol so long they were naturalized locals. He asked Phil about all the kids, the seven trees of the Woods, and they sounded like they were thriving. He had just missed seeing bombastic Paul who was his financial manager.

Brenda Dunn from the public library was here, too. The kindly, salt and pepper-haired librarian with the big glasses was knowledgeable and helpful. She and Dillon had once discussed a secret cave under and next to the library. He had planned to do research, but then he'd died, and his life had been turned into a passionate romance, a horror novel and vampire boot camp jumbled all together. "I haven't forgotten," Dillon told Brenda.

"I know you've been busy. You have a new lady, and you moved back to town," Brenda said.

"What is it you love about Elke?" Candy asked.

Dillon beamed. "Ah, I won't sing a song because I don't possess a good voice. She is a kind soul, a beautiful person, and a gorgeous woman. I like the way she looks at the world and sees its beauty and life despite all its warts and death. She is successful and uses that to be proactive in our community. She's so amazing it's a challenge to think of anything else sometimes," he replied.

"Well, I think that sounds wonderful. New love is really somethin', especially when it grows into old love. I'm delighted that I lived long enough to see you happy," Candy said. Dillon hugged her. She squeezed him and laughed. "There is a lot of life in you for someone who was so sick."

"I wish I could share it with you," Dillon said. He realized a moment later, after he said it, he could, but it wasn't long lasting relief.

"You energize me just by being here, Mr. Eight," Candy said. She referred to him as her eighth child. Silke answered to the name Ms. Nine. "I feel safer, too. Did your mother tell you there was a break-in next door?" she asked.

That explained why he sensed a current of fear beyond terminal illness. Nobody here was a stranger, especially not Darlene who walked out of the bathroom. Dillon hid his shock at seeing the dying woman with whom he had exchanged gifts. She looked radiant, her skin aglow and her eyes bright. Only those who knew her would have recognized that she was the same woman as the one in hospice last night. She had been weighed down with entropy. Now she nearly danced on air and appeared thirtyish.

"Dillon, this is Darlene. She has taught many of my kids, and we're still friends," Candy laughed. That led to a coughing fit. Her aura blinked. Her time might be even shorter than they had all assumed or wanted to admit. He was glad that they were here now, especially Mom, since there might not be a later. He had forgotten that might be true for him, too.

"It's hard to believe you were on your death bed, Darlene. I'm delighted to see you," Mom told her, and they hugged. "It must be a miracle."

"Oh, yes! I was visited by an angel. Because of all those kids I taught, he gave me seventy-two hours to say so long, farewell, auf Wiedersehen, goodbye," she finished with song. "My granddaughter is getting married tomorrow, so I am going to dance until I drop. The meter is running." She laughed loud and long. Candy managed to laugh with her. Phil, Dillon, and Mom just stared at them. The hospice worker acted like this was normal for the situation, perhaps even healthy.

Darlene turned, took Dillon's left hand, and began to dance a shag. He humored her, joining her in cutting the rug, so to speak, bringing a smile to everyone's faces. He should take Elke dancing. "Your son can really dance," Darlene said.

"He didn't get that from me," Mom replied.

"I'm a fancy shincracker. She's the cement mixer," Dillon said.

"Where did you hear those old terms?" Mom laughed.

"Somebody made sure that I learned to read," Dillon replied.

"You know, most angels here on earth don't even realize that they're angels," Darlene said.

Dillon mused, if he was an angel, it was a fallen one, and yet, he felt warmth, caring and love from everyone.

"Angels help you either make the best of a situation or see the silver lining. I have been praying for some relief. Listen, y'all, some angels you find in the light. Others find you in the dark. Now, don't be sad. I've lived a good life, and I'm getting to boogie out on my own terms," Darlene said. She acted like she was talking to everyone, but Dillon sensed that she was speaking directly to him. "Really, I am grateful. I was literally and figuratively dying to get out of that bed!"

"Well, if you see that angel again. Send him my way. I'm hoping to make it to the Halloween concert at East Hill with the kids," Candy said.

Dillon didn't dare meet anyone's eyes. He closed them and breathed, tasting too much perfume and worry, heavy with insecurity.

A knock on the door brought in five well-wishing visitors and the smell of berry cobblers and key lime pie. Dillon didn't know these ladies, although he had seen them before. They almost looked like members of the Red Hat Society, except one's hat was turquoise. Two looked like they could be grandmothers, while two others, a redhead and white blond with big blue eyes, were in their mid-forties with short-hair and fashionable, layered clothing. A younger gal wore a Parris Exotic Pets t-shirt covered with the images of tropical birds. A blue parrot rode on her shoulder and stared at Dillon. He wasn't sure what birds thought about vampires.

"These are my friends and fellow paranormal investigators, April, lover of birds, Pamela, she who bakes deliciously, Rebecca blue eyes of dispatch, Sheilah our photo bug, and Sandee, our secretary and minutes taker," Darlene said with a smile. All the women seemed to stare at him.

Dillon felt a jolt of alarm. She was warning him. This could be trouble. The bird slowly hopped to April's shoulder farthest away from Dillon.

"I don't see Grandma Carol or Suzanne. How are they?" Darlene asked.

"Thank the Almighty, Carol is out of intensive care and in a normal room. She collapsed earlier today. Suzanne isn't feeling well, so she stayed home being taken care of by her hubby," Sheilah said, talking out of a corner of her mouth. She obviously loved purple, all her clothing and accoutrements, except for her red hat, matched the color of royalty. She noticed Mom's and Candy's baffled expression and summarized what happened at Grand Antiques.

Dillon needed to let Elke know about this. Could it be another feargorger? Grandma Carol's prophecy concerned him, too.

Before the ladies served up cobbler, Sheilah offered to take a photo of them all and arranged them for the best lighting. Thankfully, Dillon wore cosmetics. Phil took his turn photographing with his and other cameras in phones. When the images were viewed, Dillon was in them. Well, it was a good test run for being on the boat. He had the ladies gather, and he captured their photos, including Phil who proclaimed to be a very fortunate man. Dillon understood and felt the power of gratitude.

"Dillon, Candy told us that you are writing a book on what happened out at the lake with the terrorists, the vampire cult, and such. How is that coming along?" Pamela asked. She took off her turquoise-colored hat and fanned herself. "It's warm in here?"

Mom cut the key lime pie, and Phil handed out plates. Dillon turned down dessert. He didn't want to get any on his jacket or shirt. "I think it's coming along well. I might learn more after this week, after something I can't talk about unless I want to be sued, occurs," Dillon said.

"Oh, now that sounds tantalizing," Rebecca said. Her voice was strong, her smile was beautiful and if he wasn't careful, she would be charmed by his vampire supernature.

"What do you think of the Oktoberfest Vampire?" Dillon asked to distract and dissect. While he listened to the replies of the paranormal investigators, he studied their eyes, trying to fathom what the ladies really meant. Also, he wanted to discern if any of the paranormal investigators recognized him from a description, but Darlene had kept her word and their secret, staying hushed about the details and the appearance of her angel. I'm an angel of death,

Dillon told himself, and yet, seeing Darlene smiling and dancing made him think of the toddler that they had rescued, his laughter, and that changed Dillon's mind.

"I'm more of a believer in ghosts," Pamela said. All the ladies nodded in agreement with her.

"On the way here, we saw Mike the Bear's ghost. I usually see him near the Bluff City highway, and it's been a long time since that," Sandee said. She smiled at Dillon and returned to note taking.

"You have the most amazing eyes," April sighed.

"Thank you, kindly. I get them from my mom," Dillon said. He hugged his mother.

"Hey, I heard *The Myth Huntress* folks and the FBI are diving the ruins," Sandee said.

"There are no secrets in this town," Dillon's mom mused. He managed to keep a poker face.

"Ah, those daring women. I wish I was young enough to dive," Pamela bemoaned.

"I'd go!" April said.

"A haunted house on land is spooky enough. Being under water in one, brrr," Sandee replied with a shiver.

Dillon chatted a while longer before he checked his watch. "Ah, I have to run. The boat leaves at eight, and well, you know what they say. Farewell," Dillon said. He kissed Candy on the forehead and embraced her in what could be a legnthy good-bye hug. Neither knew how long they really had. Nobody did. Sometimes the unknown seemed bigger than before.

"Thank you, dear, for bringing me," his mom said as they left the house. She took his hand in hers, and they strolled along.

"Candy will be greatly missed."

"Yes, dearly and by so many. We all have our different ways of making our lives worthwhile. We all want our lives to mean something. Raising good kids means a lot to the world. Along with being a nurse, it has made my life worthwhile. I feel like I gave the world a gift of two great kids. You have already made it better with your investigations and writing and Silke with her education and hands. I miss her hands. I am over the moon thrilled that you have also found someone to share your life with! We never know how much time we have, so make the most of it. I wish I had realized that earlier," his mother said.

"I love you, Mom," he said and kissed her on the cheek. "I promise to use all due caution, and I'll send you a text when I return to shore," Dillon said. He glanced at his watch. He had enough time to drop off his mom and reach the marina on time.

Sixteen

On the Surface with Reality TV

"Yep, it's still dead in the water," Roxy Gearhart said, her voice carrying over the few feet of lake between the boats roped together. Anchors had already been lowered to the deep to keep them in place over the ruins of Von Damme's stronghold.

Dillon experienced a heavy sense of impending doom. Despite it, he thought that he must be here. He hoped, with his supernatural sight and journalistic insight, that he might see bad things coming and avert disaster. Yeah, he could dream. He was trying to do more than keep his head above water. He had watched the video of the gator in mild disbelief. What was his hometown coming to?

He was joined in the filming boat by Zhen Hinode, Rae, Caster, and Marader who captained Maverick. The divers, Madi, Juju, Levon, Agent Kaye, and Roxy occupied the dive boat that Knives piloted. Like satellites, two drones flew around them and recorded. Caster controlled the red one while Zhen guided the silver drone.

Roxy fidgeted in the navigator's bucket seat while she futilely tapped her tablet trying to regain control of the submersible ROV named Diva. The white of her swimsuit looked bright against her dark skin, vanilla and chocolate, ivory and ebony. Ms. Gearhart sensed Dillon's gaze and looked up to meet his eyes. A small smile dawned on her face and a mutual, animal, supernatural attraction kicked in. Her heart rate increased, and she perspired as hormones flowed to alter her thought patterns.

Dillon looked away. A vampire's long stare could work as a wordless invitation to prey. He must restrain his supernatural charm. Turning down his charisma is not something he thought he would ever need to do.

Dead in the water, she had said. The tech's words were truthful in more ways than she realized, Dillon mused. Not to mention that the water was as deadly as acid to him. Now, he must master his own mind and its fears. He used his two decades of martial arts training, deploying No Mind, to deal with his newborn respect of the living water. Be like water, he thought, recalling Bruce Lee.

How reversed his life had become, Dillon mused. For all his life, he had loved the water, especially this lake, almost as much as he loved the sunshine. Now he must shun both and yet treat it as natural. Now he enjoyed the beauty of the lake as normal without washing his face in it. He also surmounted his worries by reminding himself that this was necessary to protect his family, friends, and neighbors. It would shield Elke, as knowledge was power.

He would do anything for Key, including wearing the cosmetics, hair paint, and colored contact lens. Nobody here had looked at him twice about wearing makeup, except Knives who had rolled his eyes. He and Marader might be the only ones au natural. Dillon and Rae had shared a knowing smile. It was part of the business.

"Dead in the water, you say? Did you find bodies? Or just coffins?" Rae asked. She referred to the fateful camping trip where

Dillon and his blood brothers had found floaters: a murdered body and six caskets. The scent of her fear and dread were powerful tastes on his palate. It reminded him of the vibe coming off J-Man.

"Reporters and writers," Madi replied with a wry grin. The blond-haired and brash lead myth huntress was enjoying the delay and the need to dive. It added to the tension, creating suspense and an air of mystery. "She meant dead on target. All right y'all. Suit up, my fellow adventurers."

Less than an hour ago, Dillon had arrived on time at Maraders Marina for his Reality TV debut. He had been greeted warmly by Knives, Marader, and his sister, Madi. Her crew paused in their last-minute checks as they secured the load of equipment on a red and white Mastercraft named Maverick and a blue and white boat dubbed Bluebird. Dillon had met Agent Kaye before and greeted her cordially. Elke had influenced Kaye and her partner during the interview, steering them away from the truth. Madi's involvement had brought them back into the picture

Dillon sensed something unusual about Madi, but he couldn't figure out what. Her aura was normal, but he could not read her eyes. Even so, he saw she was not impressed by him. She constantly frowned at him, like he might be her ex in disguise, or appeared to be trying to figure him out which concerned him. He might not have verbal compelling powers, but women still found him irresistible, except in this case. Madi was clearly unfazed by his aura of charm. It didn't bother him ego wise. But he wondered why she reacted differently than other females. How would she react to Elke?

He wondered if something had changed in him until Madi introduced her crew. Roxy Gearhart, the voluptuous ROV commander, gushed when she met him, her eyes alight with lustful desires. Dillon could see it confused Roxy, because she hated men, having been abused by them. Even so, she was willing to make an exception for Dillon. That was proof that his vampire charm remained.

Zhen's reaction confirmed it. Ms. Hinode had dedicated herself to science, to understanding the universe, especially about ghosts and spirits, but she was willing to kiss Juju farewell and have Dillon's baby. He could see that in her arresting eyes. She had an unusual presence, as if she were larger than she appeared.

Madi had mentioned Zhen was a ghost whisperer. As if Dillon weren't pale enough, Zhen had lovingly powdered his face so he wouldn't shine under the lights. He had been forced to fake sneezes to get her to stop.

"Hey, I could use some powdering," Juju had replied. Mr. Castillo frowned at Dillon, and in those eyes, he saw that the big man cared deeply for Zhen. Juju's initial response had been wary and defensive, as if he respected Dillon but expected him to be dangerous. He watched Zhen with jealous eyes and glared at Dillon.

"Juju, you would just shine right through it," Zhen said. Juju replied with a pleased grin and a chuckle.

Oh, the perils of being too charming. Dillon felt crowded by Zhen's presence, like she took up the space of two people. For a moment, when he looked deeply into her eyes, two pairs gazed back at him. He sensed the strong will of a warrior, reminding him of Master Cosmo. He would have to mention this to Elke. It seemed like Zhen housed a guest spirit or was unwillingly possessed.

More than once, Levon Crossette had taken a step back to appraise Dillon. Deep down Levon unconsciously sensed a predator and an alpha male. That kind of reaction was normal. Lan Caster kept his distance, for better filming angles, obviously. His bushy beard bristled, and his smile was nervous.

Dillon had left Shadowsbane upstairs, locked in Marader's apartment. A sword wouldn't protect him from Rae Kirkland's stare. To keep away the night chill, she had donned a stylish hat, looking a bit like an old-fashioned reporter. She had promised to corner him and get some answers when they were done here. He could see that she didn't really want to be here on this boat. Fear had taken deep root, but it didn't stop her. That was the courage of conviction. She was another truth seeker who loved her job. He felt both lessened and emboldened by her moxie.

She had almost died in Von Damme's underwater mansion, but she was still here to cover the myth huntress' exploration of its ruins. She shared Dillon's concern that whatever lurked down there was resting, not vanquished. The two of them had been childhood friends and neighbors. She had been inspired by Lois Lane and Erin Brockovich. He could see in her eyes that she wanted to ask him questions, but this was neither the time nor place with the microphones recording every sound. He wondered if Gina had contacted Rae, one reporter to the next, to get a better idea of recent history. If so, that would create even more problems.

To be silently honest, he disliked the poorly named Reality TV. This was a modern version of *In Search Of: the Loch Ness Monster*. They didn't need to conduct an In Search Of: Vampires. The dark-walkers were living among people in local communities. People just didn't realize it. Many vampires liked being mistakenly identified as ghosts. Who would have thought?

On the way, they passed a familiar boat. John Hogan and Chance Oliver tipped their caps at them. Hogan had been fishing in the same spots back when they had been out here daily in the summer. Chance was an avid fisherman and the drummer in the local band, Todd Young and the Coveralls. Wow. Ten years seemed a different lifetime ago. Dillon reminded himself that he wasn't even human anymore, so even more had changed.

At Dillon's side, Rae groaned. She rubbed the temples of her head to ease an ache. Dillon touched her on the shoulder. The blue-white lightning danced between them. Rae looked up and smiled gratefully. "Relax," Dillon told Rae, using a bit of compelling. She at once settled back on her heels. The tension left her shoulders as they dropped a bit, and she forced a smile for him.

Madi flinched and glared at Dillon. What had caused that? He wondered.

"I'm okay. I'm nervous. I get flashbacks and chills. Knives said it's a little post trauma distress. I can feel like I was down there again," Rae began and started to shake. She had been trapped underneath the mansion with two other divers. "After that day, I became quite paranoid about shadows. It reminds me of being a child afraid of the monsters under the bed or in the closet."

"Now you're sounding like Spider," Marader said. He shrugged when Dillon glared at him. "You're looking paler than usual. Are you getting motion sick?" Marader asked.

"No, I just have a bad feeling about this," Dillon replied.

"Admit it, you were going to say sinking feeling. Oh, God, sometimes I really crack myself up," Marader chuckled.

"Spare us, Tommy. Hey, Dillon, whatever happened to those journals Spider was reading?" Rae asked him.

"There are journals?" Madi called over. Her eyes brightened at the prospect. She had pulled her wet suit half on, her long legs covered. The neoprene looked lined with clear rhinestones that were LEDs. She glared at Dillon before she continued to work the suit up along her lean and shapely torso.

Dillon looked over to Roxy who smiled. Her eyes flirted while she dressed, doing a shimmy for him.

"I thought they burned in the fire. They would certainly help me write my book," Dillon lied. How easy that was becoming. It just rolled off his tongue.

"Spider read them. There were journals in his van. Evidence," Rae said.

"Agent Kaye?" Madi asked.

"I've read the translation of one. From what I can tell, Von Damme was arrogant, abusive and drank and smoked too much which might be why he believed himself to be a vampire," the agent replied and finished with a derisive snort.

Dillon said nothing. This was news to him, that the FBI had one of the Von Damme's diaries. Elke had more than a half dozen of the German's writings. According to her, his experiments were widely varied, and he made alchemical potions to aid himself and his lieutenants, Lyla, Zane, Destrange, Goran and Guy 'Butcher' Boocher. They had been doused in and consumed many chemical potions, transforming them into only God knows what. At least three of them remained on the loose and dangerous. Only Zane had been confirmed as destroyed. Lyla could still be out there somewhere, the femme fatale of the group. That was five. There had been six caskets of the Six Finger Cult. When Dillon had asked, Elke had just shrugged.

"Journals, eh? I need to find those and read them. Then I might know why everyone refuses to talk about this sunken place. The Silver Goddess declined our request for an interview. Jay Beck told us to bug off. Mary Beth Rentzel is scared of her own shadow and won't see us. I hear she's supposed to be at the memorial, though. Who would know where those notes are? Silke Urich told me to go to Hell. And so it goes."

Each of the divers had chosen a bright yellow buoyancy compensator. The full-face masks and fins were trimmed in the reflective color of warning signs. The divers would be able to speak to each other over the radio, he realized, by having air pumped into the masks instead of breathing through regulators in their mouths. He would have liked that. Dillon found himself irrationally envious.

Recalling that she had almost died down below, Rae's pulse bounded. Her fear grew. Dillon felt it swell like a great balloon of panic. It spread to touch almost everyone. Trying to be nonchalant,

Juju blew a large bubble of gum then inhaled it, trying to even out his breathing. Roxy and Agent Kaye also had elevated pulses, eager for adventure. Levon rubbed his hands together while his heart thundered.

Only Madi acted excited but remained inwardly calm. Her heartbeat steadily, unfazed by it all. What was different about Madi?

"Bang sticks, anyone? Just in case Tick Tock shows up?" Juju asked. He and Levon carried at least two spear guns set in tubes astride their air tanks. Juju handed out the metal tubes, showing how to use the underwater shotguns. Levon distributed flares. "You got to be ready for dangerous predators," Juju told Dillon. The man was reacting to fight instead of flight. He was brave, because Dillon could smell the stink of fear in his sweat and see the shadow of doubt in his dark eyes. Love made him stand his ground.

Suddenly, Dillon and everyone else found themselves tossed about as the lake heaved beneath them. Dillon grabbed Rae and the side of the boat to stay aboard. He stared over the portside at the water, wondering what leviathan was rising. When a giant bubble burst into a stink, he instinctively ducked back as water splashed.

Potent with the reek of rotting flesh, maggots, and feces, the gut-wrenching gas caused Rae to retch. Leaning over the side, Zhen joined her. Marader still sat in the captain's chair. One hand held his nose while the other clenched the steering wheel.

Knives frowned, having endured worse. "Would anyone like a peppermint? It can help calm the stomach," he said.

"No thanks. I'll be okay. I apologize for embarrassing you, Hojo," Zhen said. She wiped her mouth and chin clean with a towel.

Roxy wore a winsome smile, undeterred and happily doing her thing. "I'm a little green, and it's not easy being green, but I'm fine and not leaving Diva down there with ghosts, no, no, no. I'm going down, down . . ." she sang.

Zhen took an empty vial out of her kit and leaned over the bow to obtain a sample of lake water. "Some of the gas should linger in the water and tell us something."

"Remember, there's a gator around here," Marader said.

Rae stepped back while suspiciously glaring at Dillon and then everyone else. Her eyes widened, and she paled. Her fear spiked to panic, sending her heart racing. "Oh, God. Oh no. Not this," Rae breathed. Dillon read her lips. She began to hyperventilate. "Monsters, all around me!"

"Rae," Dillon started to compel. Was she talking about him?

She staggered away from him, lost her balance, and fell over the side into the lake. Gasping, she began to frantically swim away from the boat.

Dillon started to leap after her and stopped. Such a foolish action would end him. "There's a damsel in distress. This is a job for Super Lifeguard," he said and looked over to Tom Marader who yanked off his shirt and dove after her. Dillon stewed, while he helplessly watched Marader swim after Rae.

Dillon realized he should be looking for a gator. "Anyone see Tick Tock?"

All the lights made it easy to discern if the surface was being disturbed. He saw nothing, and nobody called out.

Marader swiftly caught Rae.

"Something grabbed me!" Rae screamed. She fought and thrashed.

"Hey, Rae. It's me, babe, Tom Marader. I'm here to help."

She punched him in the nose.

"Ow. Rae, stop it! You punch like a girl," Marader replied, blocking her blows. He caught one arm. She screamed like it was bloody murder, continuing to struggle. She dragged them both underwater for a moment. Marader kicked powerfully and pushed them above the surface for air. "Rae, you're safe, lady. Come on, we're friends," he told her. She tried to bite him.

"Rae, you're safe with friends. Relax," Dillon called. He put every ounce of compelling into it.

She quit fighting and fainted. She would have sunk, but Marader held her head above water. Juju and Levon lifted Rae into the boat, setting her on the padded sun deck.

"Wow, Dillon. That was powerfully somnambulant verbiage. I'm calling 911. She should be evaluated at the hospital," Knives said.

They discussed who would stay and who would go back. Marader agreed to drive blue back and leave Maverick with Madi and Dillon. Caster wasn't feeling well and wanted to be checked out, too. The rest stayed for the diving.

Dillon's sense of dread grew stronger. The divers had yet to get in the water, and they were already having problems.

Seventeen

Dive to the Ruins

"Showtime!" Madi said while she watched the recording boat, now turned medical transport, speed off toward shore to a waiting ambulance. She adjusted her wetsuit and shifted the tank on her back, trying to get comfortable. "What kind of myth huntress would I be if I let this stop us?"

"Alive to hunt another day?" Dillon asked.

"Well, you only live once," Madi sighed. She mustered a winning smile despite her uneasiness. That stench had almost caused her to throw up, but she refused to puke on camera. Time playing sports, acting in the theater, and battling against her alcoholism helped her now. This was nothing compared to what she had felt like when drying out. Besides, the show must go on. Looking good and confident under pressure was half the battle. She exchanged a glance with Roxy who avidly wanted to dive the haunted ruins. This is what they lived for!

So, this situation couldn't have gone better if Madi had planned it. Back in the day, magicians arranged for shills, usually women, to faint in the audience. As part of the original plan, Madi and Roxy had arranged Diva's failure, except she had not initiated the ploy. According to Roxy, a real accident had occurred.

What they hadn't planned was the giant bubble of putrid gas bursting in their faces. She knew lakes turned over, and it was autumn, but the stench reeked of open graves. It reminded her of excavating bodies while looking for vampires outside of Boston. She hadn't expected Rae to flip out. That certainly was must-see TV.

She looked over to Dillon. He appeared fit and moved with the uncanny grace of a white tiger. His eyes gleamed like a cat's as he watched them. The fierce, young martial artist had matured into an exceedingly handsome and devilishly charismatic investigative journalist. He had taken on an inscrutable look, making his expressions a challenge to fathom. She heard it was an early lesson from one's sensei to never give away one's strategy by expression or body language. And the eyes, oh, one must control the eyes. When had he become, dare she say, dangerous? Handsome men were a pain in the neck. She would ponder it later. For now, she must stay focused on safety and the show.

Madi positioned herself for the cameras. "Listen up, my intrepid companions. We are about to embark on an adventure to a place one hundred and twenty feet deep, ruins shrouded in death and cloaked in mystery. Just two months ago, five people died down there. Others were driven to despair and depression so powerful that they died shortly thereafter. A holy man felt so strongly about the evil there that he died while demolishing the place using dynamite. It will be interesting to see what we find and learn. Are you ready to dive the haunted ruins of Von Damme and Wreythville?"

Of course, they heartily replied affirmative, except Agent Kaye who was reserved. That's why the rest of them were here. It's why they were myth huntresses and hunters! They hunted in the dark and carried the truth out into the light of day. Besides, it's what she paid them to do, and they loved it! Avid and Gung Ho could have been Roxy's and Juju's nicknames.

Levon seemed just as pumped, giving her a broad smile and two thumbs up. Dillon might have eaten a lemon based upon his reaction. Zhen still appeared pale, queasy, and disappointed. Juju kept glancing at Zhen. He didn't trust her staying with Dillon, so Juju wasn't happy going. Madi would have to nip this in the bud. She had warned them.

"Stay focused. Due to our altitude, the depth is a little deeper. We have only a scant ten minutes of bottom time which is more than recreational tables recommend."

"I'm former Navy. We had our own tables," Roxy said.

"Let's make it count. Go in, get Diva, and then jet. See if we can keep it under ten. Juju, get an idea of the best places to set up the light stands. I'll take samples since Zhen isn't feeling well enough to dive with us. Questions? Everyone have their bang stick?"

"I'm carrying a WASP knife, too," Juju said

Madi carried such a blade. It was a knife and syringe that injected the attacking beast with 800psi of gas that would freeze internal organs and force the predator to rise to the surface. The bang stick worked like an underwater gun, one shot at a time. "We'll meet at fifteen feet," Madi said.

"No gators in sight," Levon announced.

"And none on sonar," Dillon said, studying the fish finder.

"Diva, baby here we come," Roxy said. She tapped her wristwatch computer; the Blue Tooth connection activated the LEDs in her wetsuit. They began to glow bright green. It showed off her curves and made her much easier to see and record. No wetsuit was flattering, but it could have been worse. She still had a female shape. When she slipped into the water, she glowed like a bioluminescent dolphin. Juju turned on his wetsuit, emitting red. He started his camera rolling before he dropped back into the water with a wide splash. Levon activated the camera attached to his chest strap, adjusted his tank and mask before intentionally falling back off the boat.

Madi's wetsuit emanated a golden glow. The difference in color would help viewers identify them. Levon would look like a dark shadow. She handed down the extra bottles of air, including a trio with octopus regulators for their decompression stop. That way, after building up too much nitrogen, they could hang there and exhale it until their blood regained a healthy percent of oxygen. Roxy swam down to secure them to the anchor line. While below at the site, they would hook up a shot line for a direct line from the ruins to a surface buoy.

"Zhen, we're expecting you to make us look amazing when we return from the deep."

She smiled back at Madi. "Count on it. I'm feeling better. I'll be fine. Hojo is with me. If I'm shaky, I'll set up a tripod or ask Dillon to record."

He nodded. His stare pierced Madi's soul. "Expect to see weird shit. It's gonna be cold. Stay ready for at least one dangerous moment," Dillon told her.

Madi felt her skin tingle and shivered. Dillon had a powerful way of speaking. She had noticed, except for her brother, that the others followed his suggestions as if they were golden. She still couldn't read him. He had a different vibe and facial expressions than any-one she had ever seen. He appeared grave now, as deadly serious as someone could be. Zhen hung on his every word.

"I will," Madi replied and lowered her mask. When she stepped off to plunge fins first into the water, the lake embraced her, ready to buoy her to ratings and a commercial mother lode. She had a special feeling about this myth hunting.

Fifteen feet below, her crew waited for her, facing outward, and floating near the decompression tanks. The wetsuits were radiant and looked avant-garde. "Everybody's breathing, that's a great start. Is everyone good to go?"

"Yep, no sign of Tick Tock," Juju said. He swam ahead and turned around, recording as they sank deeper. Roxy led the group and directed Juju by using the GPS to guide her toward the ROVs last location. Visibility was good here and lost around twenty feet. With depth, the water grew cooler and calmer.

Madi felt like she was being observed. Of course, the camera watched them, but it seemed like something hungrily eyed their lights and life. The thoughts of a gator gnawed at the edges of her imagination. She didn't get as frightened because of her brain damage. Due to the accident, she had read as much as she could about her human computer. She understood that her mind liked to believe what it imagined, but she was here to uncover the truth, not myth, fantasy or legend. Why were people dying down here? Was there something important or valuable in the ruins?

She didn't think she would get the truth from anyone. They might not even know the truth and yet believe it as such. Rae and Doc had forgotten events due to trauma. Or was something else going on? The famous Raquel Sterling, the Silver Goddess, had been there twice on search and rescue missions and declined to be interviewed. Her last whispered comment had given Madi chills.

"What you find there will cast a pall over the rest of your life."

Four of the men who had gone scuba diving with her had died. Two had met death inside the mansion. A pair of Search and Rescue divers, also law enforcement officers, had been killed battling terrorists. Rae Kirkland, Sterling's sister, Diana, and Mary Beth Rentzel had survived being trapped there, but the man who had gone with them, Eduardo, had died. Ms. Rentzel had tried to give an interview, but after heaping praise on her brother for destroying the evil place and bringing peace to Bristol, Father Dennis' sister had crumpled into weeping. Mary Beth had kept mentioning how the shadows in the house were alive, and the ghosts tormented them, making them use up their oxygen more quickly.

It seemed the mansion cursed and slew males more than females. Were all those skulls male? Madi wondered. Come to think of it, none of the women diving there had died. Rae, Mary Beth, the Sterling sisters, Desiree Sanchez, another one of his brother's gorgeous dock girls, and Silke Urich had all survived. The men had been far less fortunate. Did that mean anything?

She reminded herself to watch out for the gator. Perhaps this one was different and liked to dive deeper. Ahead, Madi spotted the wall of debris caught between different temperatures of water. She would make sure she lingered on this to show people how they were trashing their own world.

"I hate that people are such slobs," Levon said.

Madi agreed. Growing up in such a beautiful place had given birth to the outdoor enthusiast in her. Who wanted to go adventuring, hiking, climbing or spelunking through trash? She liked using her celebrity to help Mother Nature. Madi and the others pushed through the barrier of garbage, leaving the warm water behind. The weights carried them deeper into the coldest part of the lake.

"I keep having a sinking feeling," Juju said, bringing groans.

"You can get a rise out of me on the way back," Roxy replied and yawned loudly.

"Zhen is my inspiration," he replied.

Madi checked her gauges. They were pushing eighty feet, most of the way to their destination. Madi paused, checking on everyone, including over her shoulder to make sure Juju continued to track them.

"I'm going to spark a flare," Madi said. She removed a fusee from her belt, struck it and dropped it, giving them an idea how far it was to the lake's bottom.

Luck must be with them because the flare remained lit. Her group swam toward the glow, using it as a guiding beacon. After checking the GPS, Roxy made a thumbs up gesture. They continued diving deeper into SoHo's abyss toward the light, making the mysterious look welcoming.

At one hundred feet of depth, Madi paused again. This is the deepest her brother and their friends had needed to dive when the lake level was low. They all struck and dropped flares. The red light would create a spooky effect. The five fusees fell like dying fireflies swallowed by the abyss until they hit bottom. One flare landed on the broken copper roof and slowly tumbled down the side until a shredded section of metal caught the flare. Three of the others vanished, their ruddy lights snuffed like fireflies being swatted. The last flare landed on the rocks. The fusees' lurid light cast the ruins in a hazy, blood-red glow, highlighting the rounded rocks, wooden beams, and broken shutters. A sullen glare reflected off the mangled copper roof sprawled across the remains. Sediment-like smoke swirled up from the bottom to create a gloomy fog.

"I can hear Scooby-Doo and Shaggy shaking," Juju said.

"It does look like a bomb hit it," Agent Kaye said.

Madi glanced to Juju to make sure he was ready for further descent. It would make an eerie shot as the murk acted like a cloud. He maneuvered to place them in the foreground with the ruins behind them. Von Damme's mansion appeared as chilling as described. Madi couldn't exactly say why. Nothing about the ruins looked fantastic or supernatural. It must be mental. The feeling of being watched pierced her between her shoulder blades like a cold needle. She slowly circled, visually taking in the scenery.

The mansion had suffered a collapse even before the explosion set by Rentzel. Along the left of the big house, the river stones had given way, tumbling into a pile. The copper bent and sloped down to cover the debris. Some of the rocks had rolled outward like marbles and blocks across what had once been a patio. That must be where Troy Bane had been trapped and nearly drowned. Madi sure wished that she had been able to get the man to talk about his experiences.

The current caused the flares' light to flicker, so the shadows swayed and writhed. The garish illumination flashed off the scattering of skulls. Death and darkness possessed their eyes, and their teeth gleamed with bloody-red radiance. A fish darted out of one's mouth, causing its teeth to clack together.

There was no need to create drama or mood. The ruins had a spooky atmosphere straight out of Hollywood, except she could perceive an undercurrent of anger. What she sensed reminded her of the frustrated fury of her guard dog, Cerberus, when he had been wounded during a break-in. The only thing that she had to fear was fear itself making her do something foolish or reckless.

She wasn't afraid of the dark, depths, close spaces or much of anything else. The thought she might fail, again, motivated her. It was a different fear. One must be brave to pursue one's dreams. Being scared would not benefit her in any way. It would sap her brainpower and muscles if she let it. She found courage, caught hold of her imagination, and rationally studied the place.

"You know, this damage looks fresh instead of two months old," Agent Kaye said.

Madi agreed. There wasn't much in the way of algae and only a thin layer of sediment. It reminded her of ashes. The left side of the building had been blown out. Fragments of rock, wooden beams, flooring, and shattered shutters were scattered in a semi-circle around the demolished part of the mansion. Dynamite exploded up and out. What had been the grand foyer had crumbled to the lakebed. Only the right side of the house survived, perhaps a third of the mansion remained, including a few open-walled rooms on the second floor where Diva had already searched.

"Let's go lower," Madi said. She motioned for them to descend and took the lead toward the gap in the floor. The target of their rescue mission waited within. They needed to be quick, in and out. What was it about these shadows? Cast by the flares, the dark shades seemed to dash and dart from the black hole. Madi blinked, thinking she saw ink oozing up.

"Looks like Diva's leaking oil," Agent Kaye said.

Roxy started to cuss and stopped herself. "Well, snap."

"Well, dag gum, Rox. First day out and you break the new, expensive toy," Madi said.

"My deepest apologies. On the bright side, we might've found a bug in the prototype," Roxy said.

Levon laughed. "Let's take it home and fix it up as good as new," he said.

Juju hung back and floated, camera in hand, to record. Levon took the spool of line and tied it around a large river stone. He used the rescue air hose's regulator to inflate the buoy at the end of the shot line to carry it to the surface. The line unspooled as it rose. Next time, they could drop anchor right on top of this place and have a direct shot to the ruins.

Agent Kaye, Roxy, and Madi searched the debris field. They swam using frog-kicks to minimize stirring up the sediment. All the while, the skulls glared at her. They seemed similar to those paintings that watched you wherever you went. The dead sockets on a nearby skull with a broken eye orbit seemed to boldly stare at Madi. Was this a stern warning? Or were they laughing at her?

"I wonder if this was a mass suicide. There was cult activity reported in this area. I'm going to take them with me. Forensics might get some information from the bones," Agent Kaye said.

This was one of the reasons that she had accompanied them. Madi could almost hear her mind working. There had been deaths. Had there been homicides?

Agent Kaye picked up a skull, placed it in a mesh bag and then finned on to the next, lifting up a second fish-cleaned head. Part of the spine still remained until she moved it. Now it was decapitated. She collected those bones, too, bagging them.

"I don't see how Rae and Doc forgot them," Madi said and shook off the heebie-jeebies. She took heart that they hadn't seen any skulls in the basement, although there had been a stone table that looked like a sacrificial altar. "Let's go find out what secrets wait below."

She took another flare, struck it, and tossed the lit fusee into the hole. It descended with bubbling fire. The darkness seemed to split and scuttle off, staying at the edge of the light and away from the radiance. A shadow covered the light for a moment and then passed. A black ribbon continued to drift up from the gap. Roxy touched it. "It's oil. What happened to Diva?"

Since this was similar to a cave dive, Roxy tied a spool of sturdy line to a tethering point up top on a rock and then to herself. Madi and Levon did the same. This way they could find their way back.

Madi turned on the LED cluster and placed it in an expandable latex globe to create a modern-day miner's lantern at the exit. It splayed light all about the room and created a horde of skeletal shadows hiding behind bookshelves, racks, stands and tables. Some beakers and vials sat abandoned. The shadows of the fish were distorted and huge swimming to and fro across the walls. "This is bizarre. I wouldn't be surprised to see sharks, so stay alert."

"Call me if you need me," Juju said.

"Ditto," Agent Kaye said.

When Madi dropped below floor level, the cold hardened to mind-numbing. How was this water not frozen? She hated to admit to her brother that he was on target about the Arctic comparison. Even these fancy suits that turned kinetic energy into warmth couldn't keep up with the bone-chilling temps. One needed to be part penguin to dive here. Her nipples hurt, and she considered using a drysuit in the future. Alan Linkous had mentioned it would be frigid, but this felt deadly. She thought it might form ice layers on her arms when she swam.

So, with it being bitterly cold, she was startled by the number, size, and type of fish. There were large catfish, as expected, perhaps four feet in size wallowing in the mud. The tropical fish were much larger than she remembered them. The parrotfish, clownfish, and devil fish were two or three times larger than what she had seen on dives in Hawaii and the Caribbean.

The cluttered basement seemed to be large enough to get lost within. She felt the darkness pressing down on them with all the weight of the water, sixty-two pounds per cubic foot. Her mind wanted to do the calculation, then it was crushed by the thought she should be squished.

Roxy finned ahead, using the GPS locator to home in on Diva. The fish grew curious and began to bump them. They were checking to see if they were edible. With these temps and their size, fish would be starving. As the trio swiftly swam through the laboratory, the wetsuits' lights added an unearthly glow by refracting through glass and reflecting off metal. The shadows shifted, seeming to follow them at a safe distance.

Glowing and leading the way, Roxy with Levon finned past the entrances to niches and tunnels, swimming over and past the stone block and its manacles. Madi heard a sound akin to distance screams as if they were echoing from past atrocities. She reigned in her imagination.

Ahead, a section of the wall and the ceiling had collapsed. Rubble covered Diva, and she leaked oil.

"Let's get to it, Levon. The clock is tick, tick, ticking away," Roxy said. Using gloved hands, the pair worked lifting rocks to unbury Diva. Some of the stones were so large it took two divers to dislodge them.

Out of the corner of Madi's eye, the glitter of precious metal drew her. She followed the gleam to its source, finding a variety of coins, copper, nickel, silver and shining gold. She used numb, gloved fingers to snatch up a Golden American Eagle untouched by age and nature. The coin's minting date read 1854. Her heart jumped with excitement racing through her thoughts. Yay, baby! She knew a little about valuable coins. Double eagles - $20 coins - were rare and used during the Civil War era. It could be worth a very significant amount of money. Her dreams could come true. She could save her show with something like this. She scooped two handfuls of coinage, trying mostly for gold. She dropped them all in a mesh bag on her belt. It was too cold and her bottom time too brief to be picky. "I think we might be able to start that fund I was talking about," Madi said.

"What did you find? A sunken chest of pirate treasure?" Juju asked.

"Maybe just a broken piggy bank," Madi replied. Why were they here? She wondered and wandered. The trail of sparkle and glitter led to her desire. Her light caused the mirror to shine brightly, blinding her for a moment. The dark patches acted just the opposite, absorbing the light. Those areas seemed to fall away like holes in the light, making it look like abstractly carved with bas-relief.

This place was like one of the Russian dolls, where you kept finding more dolls inside. Best beginning for a show, ever, she mused. She could feel the vibrations in the water. She swam closer, thinking the ringing came from the mirror. If she touched it, what would she feel?

She drew back, barely refocusing on what else was here and now. Two vases stood like guards bookending the mirror. The amphora on the right had been broken, letting the coins spill out. Why were there containers of coinage placed here? Closer in, on each side and about a foot in front of the reflective pane, stood two short, thin black columns jutting up from the floor. The right was solid black stone, but the left had a silver ferruled top and speckles nearly a quarter of the way down the shaft. She pondered the significance as she studied the arrangement.

The sound of the moving air bubbled with the ringing in Madi's ears. She glanced over at Levon and Roxy working on getting Diva ready to surface. They had looped a BC around Diva and inflated the buoyancy compensator. The flotation made it easier for the two of them to maneuver the dead ROV.

Time was short. She used an exploration rod to run along the edge of the frame where she found what looked like a handle. She hadn't seen it on the video. She was tempted to open it, but safety came first. She touched the rubber tipped rod to the metallic surface. While it looked carved in relief, running her stick across its facade told her it was flat and smooth like a mirror. The raised areas were an optical illusion due to the contrast of light and dark. She tapped on the gold, and the metal made a ringing sound. She rapped on the dark area, and it silently splashed out and up.

"Damn!" Madi said as she bit back the exclamation. Thin wisps of darkness snaked outward like a lash. She jerked back, unnerved as it reminded her of eels and her unpleasant encounter with them during a show off the coast of Maui.

"Mads, are you okay?" Roxy asked.

"Yeah, yeah. Just spooked, sorry," Madi said. The darkness looked like a damaged section of a mirror now. She had freaked out. She still bore scars on her legs from that day and that dive out of Lahaina to the Molokini Crater. She could have died if not for Juju.

She always debated this with herself. Was it her intuition warning her? Or fear trying to paralyze her? Fear: false events appearing real. She didn't do fear. She didn't have the mind for it, she mused. Could the depth and pressure be playing with her brain?

These thoughts flashed through her head before returning to why she was here. Zhen would want to run tests. Madi used a vial to scoop up the oil, or tried to, as the snaky darkness lashed around the stick and her fingers. There was no sensation of slickness, very little sensation at all. The tendrils swelled larger and thicker as her fingers grew numb and clumsy. Her limbs grew heavy. When she shook her hands, her fingers cramped. Madi's teeth chattered no matter how hard she clenched them. Was rime forming on her mask? What was happening to her?

Her hand reached out and grabbed the handle. She pulled on it, and the mirrored panel swung open like a door. The darkness spilled out like a flooding wave to engulf her. She thought she caught a glimpse of a chamber and then all the lights seemed to go out. The only illumination seemed to be coming from her suit.

"Mads? Oh where, oh where did our dear Madilyn go? Mads?" Roxy asked, sounding worried.

I'm right here, she tried to say, but her lips wouldn't move, and she couldn't breathe. How could they not see her? She hadn't gone blind, nor had the walls fallen in. Even so, cold darkness seemed to have swallowed her.

Madi's dive alarm sounded, startling her. She shook and shivered violently. She didn't know why, perhaps some primitive survival instinct kicked in, but she took a flare, sparked it, and suddenly the darkness vanished. The cold in her bones remained, though. Madi's headlamp still worked, and she spotted everyone else's lights. What had happened? Was there a room behind the mirrored door? Had she briefly blacked out?

"Ah, there you are! I think I'm seeing dark spots before my eyes, so it's time for me to fly. I've got to let myself live! Come on, Mads. Let's rise above this before I start singing *Ridin' the Storm Out* or *Dancing on the Ceiling*," Roxy said.

Had it really been ten minutes? Madi wondered. It didn't matter. Her bottom time was done. Madi turned off the alarm and swam reluctantly away from the strange, black and gold mirrored door. With a determined, grind it out effort, Madi frog kicked as she crawled toward the illuminated globe. She fought against a current, and the water felt thicker, more like syrup, and darker, heavy with tannins. Why weren't the others having this problem?

The coins seemed to act as ballast, growing heavier the farther she swam from the amphorae. Madi kicked doggedly until spots danced before her eyes. This wasn't going well.

She heard an odd noise, something shifted. She caught movement out of the corner of her eye. Then she didn't know what hit her. Darkness gathered and briefly hovered on the edge of her vision before she blacked out.

Eighteen

Waiting on the Boat

Like most humans, Dillon had never been adept at being patient. It had helped and hindered him during his reporting days in Nevada and Texas. Now, though, he wasn't like anyone, not humans anyway. As one who walked the night and embraced darkness, he must learn to bide his time and develop the patience of a top rung predator and long-lived soul.

Except for the hum of the drone, the night seemed unnaturally still. The boat sat placidly, only shifting when he or Zhen moved. In the distance, a train rumbled through the hills and valleys.

"Relax, you prowl like a caged tiger over water. It's only been five minutes. Madi and the others reached the bottom a little while ago and will be there a scant ten minutes. I'd give them around thirty-five to complete the trip with a decompression stop at fifteen feet. It gives us time to get to know each other better," Zhen said. She had set up a mini chemist lab with beakers, stir sticks, measuring devices, small containers of chemicals, like a large pool test kit, and elbow gloves to evaluate the water and air samples. Intently working, these were the first words that she had spoken since Madi had gone below.

The drone continued to hover and record. Zhen had left it on automatic. No wonder Dillon felt watched.

He looked over at the monitor which remained dark. What was going on down there? Was this real drama? Or made for Reality TV drama? Damn it, he wished he could still go swimming and scuba-diving. He hadn't been able to go last time either.

It bothered him that they had never found the corpse, nor any sign of the original Dark Lady. Lyla might have been destroyed. Might the gator have eaten her? He could hope. Could she still be roaming the shores of South Holston? No one had reported seeing her. He and Elke had been searching and found nothing unusual.

Dillon glanced around. From all over, the cyclopean-eyed cameras stared back at him. He twitched uncomfortably under the movie make-up. The contact lens made it feel like his eyes were bugging out. He ignored it because he sensed danger. He wasn't overly attuned to spirits, but since they were also connected to the Shadowlands, and kin of sorts, he detected them much easier now. He was certain there was one presently onboard.

What about Zhen? He thought it highly probable that a ghost hung around Ms. Hinode. Was it an ancestor? A guide? A controlling parasite? It had looked back at him when he had gazed into her eyes. That had never happened before and unsettled Dillon.

"You seem uncomfortable. Most people find the water peaceful," Zhen said.

"That's usually true but not this place. It's haunted."

She smiled winsomely. Zhen was drawn to him, a moth to the flame. "Are you phasmophobic?" she asked. He shook his head. He wasn't afraid of ghosts. "Many have died here, more than you might imagine," Zhen said with a shiver.

He had heard tales from Elke about Von Damme's operation and cruelty, so he had imagined dozens of deaths. "I can feel a ghost on the boat. Do you know anything about that? Aren't you a ghost whisperer?" he asked.

"Yes, I am. One might think it a strange mix with chemistry and science."

"You are an explorer of the Seen and Unseen Worlds."

"Exactly. You sound as if you may be as well, not exactly what I expected from someone raised here in God's Country," she said, pleased at finding a kindred soul.

"Aren't you local? I thought you went to King University?"

"Yes, I did for my undergrad. It's a beautiful campus and people were so friendly there. Do you follow the Ways of Buddha?" she asked.

"I am a student through the martial arts."

"Then you are a student of strategy and deception. You sound dangerous," she said and flirted with a little eye batting.

"As dangerous as any journalist protecting those he loves."

"It is said that the pen is mightier than the sword," Zhen said.

"They can also work in tandem," Dillon replied.

"Mr. Dillon Urich, you are unlike anyone I've ever met, shrouded in darkness and yet with a heart chakra aglow. I wonder how that can be," Zhen said, and then she paused, as if she were unsure whether to continue. She inhaled and plunged forward with a revelation. "Hojo says he believes you might be a being of supernatural powers, except they don't possess hearts of light. Is this something you have developed through the martial arts? He said there had been some who mastered the shadows and could even box with them."

Dillon blinked. She could tell he was a supernatural being. "Who is Hojo?"

"The Hinode family ancestral guide. Hojo Hinode is present always, offering the wisdom of the elders. He lives up to our family name, bringing us enlightenment with every sunrise."

"How is that working for you?" Dillon asked. That explained why he saw two pairs of eyes when he looked into her dark windows to her soul. She had company, a friendly spirit, her ancestral guardian. Did he know a vampire when he saw one?

"Fairly well. Sometimes he can be like a doting grandfather, other times he's like an annoying brother. Did you have any brothers?"

"No, just an annoying sister. She's in California with the love of her life, my best friend. The world works in strange ways but it's working for them," Dillon replied.

"You have an air of love around you. That's another reason Hojo is confused."

"Well, I saw my mom earlier, so I feel extra loved, and Elke and I are as one," Dillon said. Key seemed to fully bloom into his mind, taking over his thoughts. Gina's words came back to him. Was Elke using him? She was irresistible, so he wouldn't even realize it. Was it true that their fates were intertwined? He felt that to be true. He would like to be certain. Key might have kept him alive to use his friends to destroy Von Damme. Dillon admitted he liked being used, as long as it wasn't hurting those around him, and yet, several of his friends had died. Even so, it could have been worse, far worse. Was he rationalizing? It would have been worse if he had died. Nobody would have been there to help Troy and their blood brothers. They didn't see it that way. He had been too late to help Pete, Walt, and Spider.

"I'm sure that you attract your share of honeybees with your darkness and heart of gold. Hojo tells me of supernatural predators that use similar tactics."

"No worries. I have a queen bee."

She laughed delightfully. "Madi can also tell there's something unusual about you."

"Oh," Dillon asked, surprised again. If they had picked him out, who else had? Was he doing such a poor role of playing human?

"We are not fooled by appearances. I know because I can see with Hojo's eyes, his hindsight, so to speak, and his history of experiences available to me. As for Madi, she reads small facial movements to decode expressions. You, sir, can look as inscrutable as a stereotypical Chinaman, your face perfectly still, even the flesh around your eyes. That really bothers Madi because she reads faces."

"I use Botox?" he asked.

"Cute. You are not so vain. Madi told us about your blood brothers. You are not what I expected. Not at all."

"Almost dying will do that to people."

"You know how to tap into the Unseen World. That makes you seem beyond natural and charismatic."

"I may be dangerous, but nobody here has anything to fear from me," Dillon said.

"That is comforting. Do you know Reiki?" she asked with a wan smile.

The name sounded vaguely familiar. "No, I don't think so. Who is he?" Dillon asked.

"Reiki in Japanese means healing. It is a way of balancing oneself with the Universal Life Force," Zhen replied. She studied him for a moment, then a timer chimed, and she checked the results of her testing.

He was full of light? Would that be his chakras? Or even the Cristos, what the Greeks had called the Christ spirit? Arranging himself in the lotus position on the back bench, he tried to find peace of mind and body. He quested for a memory of Reiki. Had Gina mentioned it?

Zhen made a noise like she had discovered something.

A towel dropped over Dillon's head. He yanked it off.

Zhen screamed as her lab kit leapt up. It splashed into her face and splattered all over her. "My eyes! I can't see! There's a fierce spirit with us," she coughed.

No kidding, Dillon thought as he deflected a fin tossed at him. The lights blinked on and off as the horn honked. Dillon watched closely, looking for what he assumed was a disembodied spirit. The boat began rocking as if large rollers were striking the portside.

"Hell's bells, they're calling to you," AC/DC sang when the media player turned on.

Ready this time, Dillon caught the bottle of sunblock thrown at him. It opened and spewed all over his face and into his eyes. Now he was temporarily blind, but he had already been unable to see the mischievous ghost. The wind made strange peeling noises as it rushed around the boat.

"Hojo? Hojo! Can't . . . breathe! Hojo, help!" she gasped.

Using the towel, Dillon wiped his face. His sight remained a little blurry.

Zhen was moaning and holding her eyes.

"I'm going to rinse your face," Dillon said. He poured water onto a different towel, and then he warned Zhen, tipping her back to douse her. He wiped her eyes, her mouth, and her nose to clear them. The hand that touched her tingled and grew warm.

The song playing changed. "So come on, come on, do the loco-motion with me!"

A flip-flop struck the back of his skull. Dillon glanced back just in time to see a free-floating oar swing around at him. He grabbed it, but nothing was holding the other end.

"Hojo says it's a demon!" Zhen said. She could obviously breathe which was a big improvement. Her eyes still looked red. He handed her another bottle of water. "It's scratching, clawing and biting. And it's laughing," Zhen bemoaned.

A splash announced the boat's plug as it flew from the drain hole and onto the padded sun platform. Dillon wasn't sure what it was until the large, stout and flat-ended screw bounced off his shoe. He could feel a subtle shift in the boat as it began to take on water.

They were sinking.

He started to curse and took a long, deep breath. He couldn't reach down and plug it. If he did, he would lose an arm as the water acted like acid. Perhaps the bilge would keep them afloat. Dillon flipped on the water pumps. Water shot out from the port and starboard near the stern of the boat.

"Zhen, how are you doing?" he asked.

"My head spins. Hojo is frantic!" Zhen shouted. She stood and wobbled. Dillon guided her to sit.

An invisible Tasmanian devil dashed around the boat. A package of straws emptied, spilling them. They became caught in the frenzied swirl. Towels tangled themselves, and clothes tumbled into the water. Cushions spun around and suddenly popped up, ejected like the boat doubled as a giant toaster.

Ignoring the chaos, Dillon dropped to his hands and knees, searching for the plug. Another towel covered his head. He didn't bother removing it. He could find the metal stopper by feel, as it was cooler from its time underwater than the temperature of the carpet. The ghost demon battered him with a life vest before it switched to a rubber glove. He rolled in time to miss the hurled fire extinguisher. It landed dangerously close to Zhen who jumped, shaken by the impact.

Again, the song changed, playing another sock hop song. "Really somethin' when the joint is jumpin' when they do the Bristol Stomp!"

"Hojo, please!" she cried.

Dillon felt the carpet getting damp and cooler. The bow of the boat rose, even as the stern slowly sank. The bilge pumps were overmatched by the incoming flow. If he didn't find the plug soon, they would be in trouble.

"Is the boat listing?" Zhen asked.

"The ghost pulled the plug. Ah, I found it," Dillon said. He located it underneath one of the seats against its metal base. Did he dare trust Zhen? Her hands looked shaky, and her rheumy eyes still watered. That was a no. What now? Sinking was not an option. He would lose an arm first. If he started the boat and kept them moving, it wouldn't sink. That wasn't a good option, either. They were anchored. He must stop the leak sans losing an arm.

An idea struck him. It was lying in front of him, one of Zhen's gloves. He immediately slipped it on. When he seized the second glove, it was also grabbed, becoming a tug of war. He was ready when the glove snapped back and evaded it. He felt a foolish hint of pride and victory.

Dillon moved to the dashboard and reached underneath to remove the ignition fuse. Now the ghost couldn't start the boat while he was trying to plug the drain hole. At the stern, Dillon leaned over, pretending to reach down. He felt a shove, but he was braced for it, knowing it was coming. He had vowed to Elke that he would return to her. He swiped with a rubber glove and struck something. There was the screeching of an enraged animal, perhaps a monkey. This felt like monkey business. He jabbed and thought he punched something. He didn't dare try with the other hand, needing it to anchor him.

"Dillon?" Zhen asked.

"I'm putting the plug in now," Dillon said. He waited, even as the boat continued to slowly sink. He feinted reaching down again. This time, he remained unmolested. After another fake, he reached down with an open, gloved hand to find the plug hole barely within reach. He breathed a sigh of relief, feeling no burn, so no issues with the glove's integrity. He held onto the boat with a death grip as he screwed in the plug.

It slipped out of his grasp. The plug fell away.

He panicked, but with his reflexes, he managed to snatch it. This time, he meticulously screwed in the plug, and it stayed put. Maverick stopped taking on water.

"Done," he said. He dried his glove with a towel before peeling it off inside out. That had been close. The bilge continued to pump, spraying water out the sides to help keep them afloat.

"How are you doing?" he asked Zhen.

"I am breathing much better, thank you. And I can see a little bit," she replied.

"How's Hojo?"

"Baffled. He says it fought like a demon's pet."

Dillon shook his head. This kept getting better. He reminded himself that Hojo had an ancient perspective on what was happening. Did cultures have the same supernatural creatures only called by different names, or were the beasts various monsters?

Keeping an eye out for the gator, Dillon found an extended grabber and began plucking clothing, towels, and vests out of the lake. He noticed bubbles. Moments later, Dillon saw lights beneath the surface at the closest decompression stop. The ball of illumination in the dark green brightened when the divers ascended into view. The wetsuits made Roxy, Juju, and Madi easy to locate and identify. So many lights, Dillon thought, counting five headlamps and the cluster of LEDs on Diva. An inflatable ring lifted the ROV. Good, he thought, everyone seemed to be moving of their own freewill.

"They're surfacing," Dillon said.

"I'm supposed to record them, but I still can't see clearly. Will you?" Zhen asked.

"Sure," Dillon said and picked up the camera. Several had been dislodged and tossed about the boat. He didn't know if they still functioned, but this one worked.

Near the surface and rising, Juju waved at him and gestured the OK hand sign. They didn't need his help. Good. While he moved to the stern, Dillon continued recording. Juju and Levon tied and secured the ROV to the ski platform. Diva appeared to have taken a beating, dented and scratched. So much for technology and using an underwater remotely controlled drone, Dillon mused. He was starting to wonder about the others when Roxy and Madi finally surfaced nearby. They clung to the teakwood slats for salvation and a well-earned rest.

Agent Kaye reached air last, but her smile was the broadest like she had been released from confinement after a long time of being wrongfully imprisoned. Dillon wondered about that passing thought. She had found evidence. She would be hailed. What did that mean?

"Man, it's great to see everyone. Diva looks the worse for wear," Dillon said.

"She isn't the only one. I think Madi took a hit, too, atop her head. How are you, Mads?" Roxy said. She had one hand on her boss, guiding her along the ski platform to the ladder.

"A little addled and dizzy," Madi said. She looked the worse for the dive, now pale, her lips blue. Dark circles defined her blue eyes making them look like sunken treasure. She touched her head and winced.

"You almost blacked out. It's a good thing you're hard-headed," Roxy teased.

"Levon and I dragged your butt ..." Juju began.

"And the rest of you," Levon added.

"Out of that cold basement. It makes Pacific waters feel warm, you know," Juju said. The Californian shuddered and rubbed his arms.

"Thank you, for enduring the cold for me," Madi said.

"No sweat. You would do the same," Levon replied. The Deep Trekker employee slipped out of his tank and kicked out of the water onto the deck.

"It doesn't seem right to need to rescue the host," Madi bemoaned.

"It's a special episode then," Dillon said. He reeled from the stench and sat back onto the boat's sun platform. The reek wafted from more than just Levon. Dillon smelled lubricant oil and other unpleasant aromas from Roxy, too. What had they been marinating in? He recalled Zhen had found something in water before the mini lab had been trashed by the malicious ghost.

"How about you, Agent Kaye? How are you doing?" Levon asked.

"All right now. I think I might've been slightly narked, but it went away about halfway up," the FBI agent replied.

Dillon knew she meant nitrogen narcosis. Rising closer or to the surface removed the cause and symptoms. "Well, no one died. That can be seen as a success considering where you've been and the circumstances," he said.

"Take a look at what I brought back. The boys and girls in the lab are going to have fun," Agent Kaye said. She hefted up a net bag holding more than a half-dozen, dripping skulls. All looked to have canine teeth but one.

Dillon blinked. He didn't understand. Vampire skeletons should dissolve. Dillon tried to perceive if the wrongness wafted from the skulls. He couldn't tell. The stench of the Shadowlands seemed to be everywhere.

Roxy eyes sparkled playfully. Her beaming smile brightened the night as she climbed out of the water and atop the platform. "Dillon, why are you splattered with sunblock? And Zhen, have you been crying?"

"Yes. We had a poltergeist here. It yanked off my goggles and wrecked my lab. That's when acid splashed in my eyes," Zhen said.

"How are you?" Madi called out.

"Dillon poured water over my face, so I'm much better now. Hojo claims it was some kind of demon spirit. He tried to scare it off, but it didn't leave until Dillon slapped it."

"You slapped a ghost?" Juju asked. He removed his BC, putting it on the platform, before he hauled himself out of the water to sit next to it. "Is that what I heard?"

Agent Kaye didn't sneer. Perhaps her time down there had changed her mind.

"I was trying to put the plug back in," Dillon said and briefly explained the encounter. "So, we're still afloat, but a lot of stuff is wet or trashed. Hey, you're bleeding," he said to Madi. He watched as a rivulet of blood slid down the side of her face and along a cheek. He handed her a dry towel to staunch the trickle.

She dabbed at the wound and frowned at the bloodied cloth. "I guess that confirms it," she said and pressed the towel against her skull.

"You're hard-headed but not thick-skinned. It's why we love you, Mads. You know, Doc should look at your head," Roxy said.

"I don't have double vision, but I do see sparkles. I am not imagining this," Madi said. She grinned big as she heaved a net bag containing coins onto the wood platform. It landed with a heavy, thunk and rattling jingles. The wet coins and a hunk of silver gleamed under the lights from inside the mesh bag. "We found these and more near the broken amphora."

Dillon watched Madi carefully, trying to read her. Her life light seemed dimmer than before. He glanced around at the others. The same was true for Agent Kaye and Juju. Roxy and Levon appeared normal. What did this mean?

"Let's get loaded up and head back to the marina before anything else happens," Juju suggested. His muscles rippled and gleamed as he gathered up his gear, followed by the others' tanks. He passed them onto Levon who started securing the bottles of compressed air. The last thing they needed was for one of the tanks to fly around as a missile.

Agent Kaye exited the lake's waters to place the skulls in a cooler. Dillon noticed that while the FBI agent was preoccupied, Juju had also brought up a skull. He kept his back turned while he hid it within a soft-sided cooler and tucked it in a compartment under one of the bow seat cushions. What was that all about?

Finally, Madi boarded with help, Roxy pushing and Levon pulling. Weariness made her look almost twice her age. She would not be happy about how she looked on camera. Madi turned off her wetsuit, and she seemed to darken, too.

Out of the corner of his eye, he studied Madi's vitals with a predator's sense. Her heart beat too rapidly, her pulse on the verge of racing, and her body temperature was lower than anybody else's. He thought she might be affected by shock, but her wan aura concerned him. Agent Kaye and Juju seemed to have lost light and energy, too. Or had something in the basement fed on them? He contrasted it with Zhen. Her lifeforce seemed as bright as ever and as radiant as Roxy's and Levon's.

"Don't look so grim. Danger is my business," Madi said.

"Cool McCool?" Dillon asked.

"John Craig, salvage diver, and a TV show host," Roxy said. She was the last one into the boat.

"Ha. I laugh in the face of danger," Juju quoted, doing his best Simba.

Dillon was unamused. "You'll be going back?"

"Based on what we found, you bet," Madi said.

"As long as Doc says it's okay," Roxy said.

"You're not worried it will collapse on you?" Dillon asked.

"Sure I am. We can take precautions. Put up some barriers. Anchor some nets. I want to see if anything is behind that golden mirror. I found a handle," Madi said.

"That's interesting. Why don't we scan it? You know, use GPR, Ground Penetrating Radar? It doesn't work on metal and won't identify bone, but it would work on the limestone. We can see if there's any space behind it," Zhen suggested.

Dillon was here mostly to observe and report. He listed off the things to tell his beloved: civil war coins, a golden door, and vampire skulls. The dead and Troy would have said the collapsing ruins were a gilded death trap baited for treasure hunters, the curious, and truth seekers.

"Y'all reek. What mess have you been into?" Zhen asked.

"A chemist and moonshiner's basement," Agent Kaye replied. She sniffed herself and shrugged.

"Does anyone else feel slimy?" Roxy asked. She rubbed her fingers together then smelled them. She frowned.

"Yes. Diva was leaking," Levon said.

"I hate to say it, but y'all stink to high heaven. It reminds me of the stench from the gas bubble," Dillon said.

"I hope I can get the smell out of my wetsuit," Roxy said.

"I pray I can get it out of my hair. Let's get going. We can pull Diva along. Just make sure it's secure. Y'all can tinker with it back at the marina," Madi said.

"Aye, Captain Marader," Levon said. He double-checked the lines for towing the buoyant ROV.

Zhen handed her an ice pack and bandage which Madi reluctantly placed atop her head. "This makes me colder."

"Bitch, bitch, bitch," Zhen said with a smile.

Dillon found a comforter and wrapped it around Madi. She replied with a smile that didn't reach her eyes. Madi kept her gloves on and removed a silver hunk of metal from her net. There was no oxidation at all, as it remained shiny and sharp.

Dillon blinked, recognizing it. He said, "That's the jewelry box that Tom obsessed over." It had once housed Von Damme's evil immortal soul. It should have been destroyed by the TNT. Did this mean the master vampire was still a force of evil? It seemed lifeless enough. "You do like to live dangerously. Your brother will be pissed."

Madi grimaced, and Dillon wished he could read her eyes to know what she had seen and what had gone wrong. Five had gone diving and three of them had come back altered, not just mentally or emotionally, but physically. Did it have anything to do with the skulls?

"Let's go add some family drama reality to the show," Madi said with a Marader grin.

Nineteen

Deputies at the Dock

Madi couldn't shake the cold and her nagging doubts. They numbed her enthusiasm, as she felt frozen to the core. She couldn't stand the ice pack, her skull hurt, a headache was growing, and her vision was blurry; otherwise, she was fine. Put me in, Coach. She didn't recall anything hitting her. She might be lucky that she already had a metal plate in her head.

What did you expect, Loser? One of her nagging voices said, likely Negative Nellie. The coins are probably counterfeit, Debbie Downer chimed in. Madi was already tired of the Queens of Life's Half Full. Hot coffee did little to warm her. Her hands hurt, even in gloves after she stuffed them under her arm pits. The night wind seemed to cut through her windbreaker and clothes, so she was thrilled when Dillon finally slowed the boat for the No Wake buoy. She could see the many glaring lights of her brother's marina. Whoa to anyone in between her and a hot shower.

On the dock, her brother paced. She wasn't in the mood to deal with his melodrama. Tom would be upset about the jewelry box, if he discovered it. She should be able to distract him with gold. That or sex worked on just about everybody.

She suddenly realized there was light around everyone. Each had a freaky full body halo like colors in the clouds around the blazing sun. She thought she recalled hearing them called auras, the glow of life around people. It made everyone stand out in the dark like thermal radiation, even herself, she noted, looking at her hands. She studied Dillon. His glow was different, mostly centered in his chest like a lantern instead of full-bodied blaze. What did it mean?

"Well, everyone is alive and Maverick's in one piece, that's a good start," Tom said. Looking for damage, he scrutinized the boat as it puttered closer. With a foot, he stopped the boat inches short of the dock. While Levon tied the front, Ginger used the aft rope to tether the back to a cleat. Her face screwed up as the wind changed. Sarge had come out to greet them, but one whiff of them sent the dog scurrying in the opposite direction.

"What's that God-awful smell?" Staci asked. She frowned and held her nose. From a distance, Sarge whined in agreement.

"Oh, that smell. Smell that smell, that smell of death that surrounds you," Kia cracked, then the bird flew upwind.

"Us. Parfum de Ruines," Madi said. She didn't blame Staci or the animals. They smelled like that putrid gas bubble.

"Es muy apestosos," Juju said and waved a hand before his nose.

"Yes, y'all are a sorry group of stinkers. It won't sell," Staci said. With her eyes tearing up, she stepped back to get relief and breathe untainted air.

Tom frowned and held his nose. "Y'all need delousing. Use the outside shower and liberal soap. I'll bring out bleach if you need to kill the stench."

"You are so thoughtful, bro," Madi said. She watched her brother tilt his head and frown. Was it the smell or something more? She tossed a cold wet towel at him. He caught it, but even so, the cloth whipped around and slapped him in the face.

Doc walked out, put away his phone and helped them unload.

"Hey, Doc, any Rae news?" Madi asked.

"The paramedics had to sedate Rae when she became combative. Madi, your eyes don't look quite right," Doc said. He offered her a hand to help her step onto the dock, so she took it.

Now with firm boards underfoot, Madi hurried to the outside showers where she cranked on the hot water and stepped under the steaming spray. "Ah! I needed this. That's better. My eyes were crossed because I was chilled to the bone. I'm delighted that you're a cold-water pansy, brother. Come on, Rox," Madi cajoled.

"Doc, don't let Mads avoid your question. She took a blow to the head. Hit by a falling rock," Roxy said. She joined Madi under the hot spray and began soaping up.

"Then she should be fine," her brother said.

"Madi was dazed. I had to pull her along for a while," Levon said. He and Juju unloaded bags, fins, and masks onto the deck.

"I'm better now," Madi said, putting her fists on her hips and trying to look fierce while standing under the hot water. A sneeze ruined the bravado moment and made her ears ring.

"I could use a cold brew. It seems like forever," Juju asked. He smacked his lips.

"Yeah, we have to hurry because we'll be diving again in fourteen hours. That only gives us a couple of hours," Roxy replied with a smile. Juju's nod appeared serious and knowing.

"After we no longer stink, we can have a little celebration and watch the video. Do some show and tell," Madi replied.

"What are you celebrating? Did you find something interesting?" Tom asked.

"Pirate treasure," Roxy joked.

Tom tensed and scowled. "Hey, something feels off. What else did you find?" he demanded, his face flushed. He suddenly sprang into the boat and landed next to the net holding the hunk of silver. "Damn it! I knew it!" He looked ready to grab it and heave it into the lake, but then he managed to stop himself. He stared at his hands and crawled out of the boat. "You can't keep it here."

"Why?" Madi asked. Juju moved nearby in case she needed protecting.

"It brings back reminders of this place burning down," he snarled. His hair bristled, and his eyes took on a wild look. "I recommend getting rid of that unlucky hunk of silver; otherwise, you'll have nightmares until you do."

"You sound a little crazy," Madi said. Neither of the girls, Ginger or Staci, batted an eyelash. Juju looked ready to put him in a restraining hold. Tom ignored him. Her brother had been known to enjoy fisticuffs.

"Yeah, I guess I do. I think it's a lodestone that drags you down and draws bad luck to it," Tom replied. He ran a hand through his unnaturally full head of hair.

Fury welled up from deep, and Madi snapped. She was in charge here, not her brother. She was older and obviously knew better. "Listen, bro. Do you want me to go elsewhere? If I don't do the show from here, we'll hit the road and do it from someone else's marina, Lakeview or Friendship. You aren't the only duck on the water. Want someone else to get the business and free advertising? Well?" Madi asked. Her anger warmed her up a little. She was proud of herself for not cussing. She really wanted to set a better example. Profanity could make you sound ignorant and stupid.

"Hells bells, I need a drink. By the time I'm finished, that piece of crap better be where I can't see it or feel it," he said and stalked inside. The door slammed behind him. With a glare at Madi that needed no interpretation, Ginger paused to visually dagger Madi before following her brother.

"Caw! I have spoken," Kia piped up.

Madi couldn't have said it better. She was ready to strangle Tom. She pushed back the red haze of a temper flare up. Her brother really knew how to push her buttons.

"Well, that was heartfelt and real," Dillon said.

Madi laughed to release her anger.

"Who does your brother think he is?" Roxy asked.

"You're wasting your breath. He isn't rational about this. He would have punched one of us, but when it comes to females, he's a lover, not a fighter. He even lost this argument," Dillon began.

Doc nodded. "Think of it as a justly deserved fear. I wasn't happy to see its return either. I'm thankful there's no jewelry in it," he said and finished with a shudder.

"Oh, okay. Fine. I'll check out Diva and get to work so we can send the ROV back down soon," Roxy said. Madi gave Roxy a long look, shocked by her agreeability. That was odd. Roxy rarely reacted in such a deferential manner.

"I'll give you a hand," Levon said.

Agent Kaye strolled away to make a phone call. Madi assumed she was calling her partner. She prayed they would be allowed to return to the scene of the crime. Where was Agent Bond? Nosing around? Did Tom have anything to hide?

Doc evaluated Zhen, finding her airways unharmed and her eyes slightly burned. He recommended drops and seeing an optometrist and a dermatologist. After Madi toweled off, he checked her eyes and how they reacted, and then he tested her reflexes and asked questions to ascertain the functioning of her memory, or so he said. She passed with flying colors, having escaped concussion protocol. Doc suggested that she continue icing, refrain from alcohol, and to use acetaminophen, not NSAIDs.

To Madi, Juju seemed unconcerned about Zhen's condition. Madi wondered if he was being resentful. "So, Doc, your advice is to drink plenty of water, take two aspirins, etc?" Madi asked. He nodded. "Why are you looking strangely at us?" she asked.

"Going to that place changes people, usually to their detriment. I'm thrilled to see everyone alive," Doc said.

Agent Kaye finished her call and joined the discussion. "My partner's on his way," she said.

"What happens now? Will there be diving tomorrow? I promised to help set a memorial stone," Madi said.

"I am aware of tomorrow's ceremony. As of this moment, I don't have any reason that would hold up in court to prevent the event. You aren't entering the crime scene. I leave the issue of the gator up to locals and the TWRA. I say this with a caveat. It could all change based on the water test results."

"And what you find out about the skulls?" Dillon asked.

"I would be surprised if we hear much of anything about them before late next week. For all we know, they've been there for seventy years," Agent Kaye said. She returned to the boat and retrieved the cooler full of the bone heads.

"I could run tests on them," Zhen offered.

"No, thank you. They're considered evidence. Dental records will tell us who died, if they had records. Parts of Appalachia were lagging back then coming out of prohibition and World War II," Agent Kaye said.

They turned at the sound of cars arriving. Kaye likely expected her partner, but instead, it was a different law enforcement vehicle, this one from the Sullivan County Sheriff's department. Madi knew her hair washing was going to be delayed a little while longer. A second law enforcement cruiser pulled in to park next to the first. A brawny man with a square jaw and a stocky female exited their vehicles, nodded in cahoots with each other, and then they proceeded up the gangway ramp.

"Grand Central Station," Kia said.

"Ah, Deputies Hardaway and Cantrell," Agent Kaye said.

"Hide the hooch," Kia said. Madi frowned at the bird.

Sarge approached with a wagging tail. Deputy Hardaway ignored the boxer, but Deputy Cantrell scratched him behind an ear.

"Wow, Deputy Marge, long time no see," Tom said.

Madi wasn't surprised that he was on a first name basis with a deputy.

"It does seem like yesterday," Deputy Marge replied. She nodded to the FBI agent. She wasn't resentful, but Deputy Hardaway frowned, his expression scornful. What he thought FBI stood for shouldn't be printed or aired around young ears.

"Good day, everyone. I'm Deputy Hardaway. You know Deputy Cantrell. She's dogging it today," he said.

"And every day. This is my partner, Boomer."

"Boom, boom, out go the lights," Kia said.

Sarge and Boomer greeted each other. They walked around and sniffed each other like dogs do. They got along fine, but the deputy called her dog to heel. "We are here for statements about what happened to Rae Kirkland earlier tonight," Marge said.

"Should we call you myth hunters?" Hardaway asked.

Roxy bristled. Madi thought that he must be ex-military security. His accent sounded like he had called the northeast home. Madi could see that Deputy Cantrell watched him with silent disapproval, but what was a woman supposed to say? Hey, you northeastern idiot, we don't do it like that around here?

"No thanks, that would be calling a lioness a lion, and we all know who does all the hunting work," Madi replied.

"I can help. She's my sister, and I was there. I can answer your questions while they wash off the stink. Believe me, you'll thank me later," Tom said.

Hardaway took a deep inhale and frowned. He looked a little green around the gills. "I'll thank you now. After you, Mr. Marader," the deputy said, gesturing towards the door to the restaurant.

Deputy Marge glanced over her shoulder. "Nobody shower and run off now, hear?"

***

Madi hadn't wanted to leave the steam, but she didn't want to keep the law waiting, either. The deputies had questioned everyone else by the time Madi made her grand entrance. She apologized.

"You smell much better, and you don't look half-drown and frozen," Deputy Hardaway said kindly.

"I've never understood the blue or black lips fashion look. It's nature's sign you're cold and almost hypothermic," Deputy Marge said.

"I remember you. You pulled me over for speeding ten or eleven years ago."

"I was young then. It's good to hear your memory works. I've pulled your brother over since then. Tell us what happened," Deputy Marge replied.

Her blue eyes scrutinized Madi. It reminded her a little of herself. The deputy was looking for tells. "Is this really about salvaging? About finding buried treasure on the bottom of the lake?"

"No. It's about finding out the truth of what happened and why. The coins are a part of the puzzle," Madi replied.

Deputy Marge looked doubtful. "Who doesn't need money or a treasure? Even billionaires still seem to need it. You know, the TVA might claim some rights to them. It's on Federal land," Marge said.

"I know. I've left a message for my lawyer."

"I don't want news of this getting out. We don't need more people here and down there hunting treasure only to end up drowning or as gator bait. I know you're trying to stay quiet about it until you can get your hands on the rest," Deputy Marge said. Madi nodded. "I'll note it in my report. Anything weird happen while y'all were down there?"

"Weird? What do you mean?" Madi asked.

"Anything not normal or extraordinary?" she asked.

"Not really. Just a strong feeling of being watched. I kept thinking I saw something out of the corner of my eye. We are diving at the edge of recreational diving. I could be seeing things. To be honest, everything seemed squirrelly down there. I walked into an open door into a darkness that ate light. They had no idea where I'd been," Madi said.

Deputy Marge looked exasperated, like she knew Madi was lying but not about what. Madi wasn't lying about anything. She reigned in her imagination.

"We'll talk more later. Be safe now. My sister was murdered not too far from here. The killer was never caught," Deputy Marge said. She stood up to leave and adjusted her utility belt.

"I'm sorry for your loss. I hope you find whoever did it. That's why we have Juju here. He's our personal security," Madi said.

"If you've found rare gold coins, you may need more than Juju. I'll have the cars put this place on patrol and stop in for safety checks," Deputy Marge replied.

Madi nodded. Tom would be thrilled about that.

Madi eventually met with her brother, Dillon, and the two FBI Agents in the bar. They didn't look upset, just a little impatient, except for Ginger. She still looked ready to tear out Madi's eyes.

Madi was cleaner, but she still felt like Debbie Downer. Saying less would probably serve her best. Despite her excitement, she still felt a cold lump inside that needed thawing, so she requested a hot coffee with a dollop of cream when she really wanted it with Kahlua and rum, but she had been down that dead end road. No more car wrecks for her. She sipped it slowly, enjoying her brother's savory, French roast, and brewing impatience.

Roxy winked. She looked ready to go. Juju wasn't anywhere in sight, but Zhen slipped quietly in to join them.

"Where would you like me to start?" Roxy asked.

"How about with Dillon and Zhen top side while they are waiting for us?" Madi asked. Did she imagine it, or did Dillon tense? Why would a good-looking investigative journalist be nervous about being on screen?

Tom killed the lights, except for the beer and booze signs at the bar. Roxy had it set up so the video played on the bar's big screen TV. These images came from the camera set at the bow of the boat. Dillon was sitting in lotus position. Zhen worked at her miniature lab, a sight Madi had witnessed many times. Her eyes widened, and her lips twitched with curiosity. She had discovered something, making the huh, this is interesting sound.

"Did you find something?" Madi asked.

"As we thought might be a possibility, there are contaminants in the water. I don't know which ones yet. Same is true for the samples you brought me," Zhen said. She carefully watched the screen. Hojo would be scrutinizing what happened next, too.

Her goggles suddenly lifted up, pushed to her scalp, exposing her eyes. Like the boat was hitting a big wave, the portable lab launched upward, its contents splashing into Zhen's face. She clutched at her eyes and stumbled back as she screamed. Abruptly, the wind picked up a towel, and only a towel, and tossed it over Dillon's head. Next, a bottle of sunblock flew at him and opened, squirting in his face. Roxy loved his shocked reaction so much that she played it back and forth repeatedly. They watched as he wiped his eyes, washed

Zhen's face, and coped with an invisible assailant throwing things, honking the horn, and flashing the lights.

Madi didn't know what it was, but something looked wrong about Dillon's face. She couldn't say what, and she didn't want to stop the video now, but she would check later. She watched Agent Kaye. Nonplussed, she didn't seem surprised by any of this. In fact, she appeared bored, like she had seen this a million times. Her eyes glazed over. Unlike her, Agent Bond leaned forward, keenly interested.

"Did you see it?" Tom asked Dillon.

He shook his head. "I saw Spider's ghost, earlier, but not this one. It laughed a lot."

"Why did you use gloves?" Madi asked.

"I was concerned there might be chemicals in the water," Dillon said.

Madi wasn't sure that was the truth, or at least the complete truth. Everyone else seemed satisfied with it. They watched, surprised, when Dillon seemed to strike the poltergeist. She didn't see it clearly because she had been studying his face in the video. Was it shiny and reflective in spots? It seemed that a part of it was ghostly, fading in and out.

"I don't understand how you struck it," Roxy said.

"That makes two of us. Maybe it was the wet glove. Maybe it's that I know Kung Fu," Dillon replied, tongue-and-check. He was so charismatic Zhen and Roxy accepted it.

"Great! Wonderful! My boat is haunted," Tom bemoaned.

"I can see if I can talk to Maverick. What? Can't you smell the ectoplasm?" Staci asked, looking around. She appeared serious to Madi.

"You know, I remember hearing stories about a noisy, playful ghost when I was a teen. A screaming wind would show up on a calm day, blow stuff out of the boat and break things. I figured kids were just making it up to get out of trouble when things went wrong on the lake," Madi said.

"Wasn't that off the Painters Creek Marina?" Staci asked.

"Enough. You've kept me waiting long enough. What's the deal? What did you find? Hmm?" Tom wheedled.

Madi showed him empty hands. Using one of her bar-learned magician skills, she leaned forward and drew a coin from his ear and handed the Double Golden American Eagle to him. "Who knew you were a slot machine. It's about time you paid off," she said. Roxy was laughing so hard she gasped for breath and then bellowed some more.

Her brother ignored them while he studied the coin. "Wow. It's from around the time of the War Between the States. I didn't know they made any coinage worth twenty bucks. With the price of gold, it's worth a hell of a lot more than that now," Tom said. His eyes glinted, eager to hear more.

"If it's authentic, it could be worth anywhere from several thousands to a hundred thousand dollars. If we find a 1933, it's worth several million," she said.

Tom's mouth dropped open. "Sweet!"

"They had been stored in an amphora. When the collapse happened, the rockfall damaged one. I brought back two small bags. Most are American. Some are foreign coins," she said, sleight of hand producing Canadian, Mexican, and Italian coins. "I found eight double eagles."

"Did you say eight?" her brother asked. She could see him doing the math. His wide grin almost seemed feral as well as overjoyed.

Madi nodded. This would save her show. She would be able to run on her own dime and have more control. She felt empowered despite being tired. "I'm afraid, if I have this evaluated locally, word will get out."

"If it does, we'll have treasure hunters coming from all over. We don't want that," Agent Kaye said.

"And perhaps worse, burglars and thieves," Agent Bond said.

"Can Diva bring them up?" her brother suggested.

Madi nodded. "When she's functional and working again, probably. I don't know if the other Greek vase is loaded or not. I didn't even think of it. My brain was half-frozen. I was so stupid. I want to check the other amphora, plus explore behind the mirror. I found a handle and have the impression it swings like a door. I don't think Diva can open it, but we can try. How is Diva?" she asked

"We can't repair all the damage with what we have. Levon has already ordered parts. They'll be here tomorrow," Roxy said.

"Oh well, we will make do. Load my camera. Start from when I enter the basement," Madi said. She wondered how accurately she recalled events.

The headlamp beams seemed wan, grayed, and grainy until the light struck the coins. They gleamed like the fiery sun breaking through the clouds. Everyone gasped.

"There are hundreds," Tom said with a lottery-winner grin.

"Will you go diving with me to get them?" Madi asked. He hemmed and hawed. She loved seeing his brain debate wealth versus the joys of bitterly cold water.

The camera swung to take in the golden door, the two black columns, and the amphorae. Madi could have heard a pin drop. There was no ringing, so she mentioned the sound. In the video, when she tapped the mirror, it made fragile rapping sounds. That moment caused her to have a flashback. She was there, again, feeling the black eels crawling up her arms and burrowing inside.

She waited and watched, hoping to see the door open. Her camera went black like a blue screen or darker. There was no image and no sound.

"How bizarre. That's about the time I lost sight of you. I figure you were behind an amphora," Roxy said.

Madi rubbed her arms. Had the snakes and the door been her imagination? She looked up to notice Dillon carefully watching her. She recalled his comment that something would go wrong.

"You're going to be rich and famous," her brother told her.

"Fame puts you there where it's hollow. Fame, what's a name?" Roxy sang and laughed.

Dillon didn't even chuckle. He was inscrutable, and she couldn't tell what he was thinking or feeling. He certainly wasn't happy and celebratory like the rest of them. It was almost as if he were waiting for the proverbial other shoe to drop, for something bad to overshadow the good. Why did she find him so mesmerizing? She asked herself.

"Maybe we'll do a documentary, too. What do you think, Dillon?" Madi asked.

"The idea has merit," Dillon said and glanced at his watch.

"Got a hot date?" Tom asked.

"Yes. Elke has a meeting with a client tonight. So, if you'll pardon me, I must be going. No worries. I will tell no one but Elke about your discovery," he said.

***

When they were the only two left in the room, Roxy replayed the video for Madi. It took more than a couple of times through, but eventually they both saw it. Part of Dillon's face was missing around his eyes where he had wiped away the blobs of sunblock. They could still see his eyes but not his eye lids. The flesh around the eyes, along his nose and a little of his cheeks, were missing. At first, they thought it was just the recording, but the transparent sections of his face remained invisible no matter how he turned. Was the sunblock a camera block?

"I think there's more to Dillon than meets the eye, even if we are seeing less of him there," Roxy said.

"I think he's hiding secrets, too. He knows more about that place than he's telling us," Madi said.

Wearing a smile, Zhen returned. She flipped the gold, double eagle coin at Madi who caught it. "It's the right percentage of gold and copper. I think this one is for real. The date works, too. The little P is for where it was minted, in Philadelphia."

Madi jumped up, ignored her negative voices, and danced her happy strut. Roxy sang, and they linked arms, spinning each other around.

Zhen waited patiently.

"What? Did I dance prematurely?" Madi asked.

Zhen sighed and frowned. She was unhappy with Juju. Madi had seen that look before. "No. It's not that. Did you know Juju brought back a skull and kept it from the FBI?"

"What? Oh, crap! What was he thinking?" Madi asked. She had to talk to Juju about this right now. His actions could jeopardize tomorrow's dive. With a full head of steam, she went looking to confront him.

She checked his cabin. He wasn't there. She searched the floating docks and then rechecked the marina, store, and restaurant. She couldn't find Juju anywhere. Nobody had seen him. What the hell?!

Tom checked the security video. He was last seen entering his cabin. She recalled seeing the window open. Had he crawled out? Or had something crawled in? His room always looked like a stuff bomb had exploded. She would have noticed blood, wouldn't she? Why had he disappeared? He could jeopardize everything. This was so different than recording any of their previous adventures for the show. Madi didn't know whether to be worried or angry.

***

Dios mio! Juju was half out of his mind. Talk about stimulation overload, he breathed. Everyone seemed to be speaking at once and so loudly. He needed a place to contemplate and figure out what to do. If he decided to do anything, he needed a plan. He had broken the law, most likely. He should feel guilty because this might get his friends and his employer in deep shit.

But Juju didn't trust the FBI to bring the truth to light. He didn't trust Dillon Urich period. He was too smooth, good-looking, and smarmy to be real. Juju had met some of his cousin's gangbangers, and he had felt more comfortable with them and their air of violence than Urich. The short hair on the back of Juju's neck prickled, his throat tightened, and his heart raced when Urich was nearby. Juju had never felt that way about anyone before, like he should shoot him before he opened his mouth to speak, and yet, he felt that same way when he looked at the skull with the canine incisors. Who knew vampires had skeletons?

Juju followed the trail down to the lake. It wasn't a beach like Venice, but the water usually helped him calm down. The sound of the waves made is easier to block out the noise of the world pressing on him. He paused, feeling watched. He looked around and found himself clutching the cooler close to him. Just taking a video of the skull wouldn't be enough. It wouldn't be proof.

The night air was cooler than SoCal and a lot wetter. He didn't care what people said about it being dry here. He was sweating bullets. It was never this humid in California.

Something darted noisily through the woods. He glanced for whatever was moving through the dark underbrush, missed a step down, stumbled and fell to his knees, losing the cooler on impact. It bounced several times before losing its lid. It fell off and aside while the skull escaped, tumbling toward the water. It stopped with a plunk, landing upright, and sinking halfway into the mud. Juju breathed a sigh of relief. It was like the thing had been trying to flee.

Sitting in the mud, the skull seemed to be laughing at him and enjoying the predicament that it had caused. Juju had put them all at risk instead of protecting them.

His mother didn't believe in vampires, but his Abuelita Rita did. Granny also believed in Voodoo. There were moments during their adventures that he thought his dear abuelita might be right. After seeing those skulls with fangs, he had grown certain that she was right about the supernatural and vampires. She said vampires had killed his grandfather. She had always been seeking proof.

What to do next? He certainly wasn't going to talk to the skull. He wasn't Hamlet, and he wasn't Van Helsing or Blade, as cool as that might be. He had wanted to be Kobe Bryant, but he couldn't shoot a basketball. He was made more for football, his body powerful enough to hit people. The vampire hunter Blade, Wesley Snipes, had been one of his inspirations to learn martial arts, the sword and security classes.

Juju heard fish jumping and the flapping of wings beating air. He flinched then realized that he was spooking himself. It was only the bats flying in and out of the lights on the nearest floating dock. The night fliers artfully navigated around the different sizes and styles of boats. Their erratic flight patterns seemed to cause the shadows to stir. Juju was not afraid of the shadows. Even so, he turned on his flashlight.

The beam gleamed off the skull. Its eyes were dark and mocking. The gentle lapping of the water caused it to rock as if it were chuckling. Juju shook himself. He was imagining things, and yet, Granny Rita, as his friends called her, had always told him to trust his intuition. Zhen had encouraged him to do the same, bless her heart.

His intuition warned him. It told him to hurl the skull into the depths of the cove. And yet, he couldn't bring himself to do it. He was a myth hunter, too, and must bring the truth to light.

He was tempted to call Granny Rita and ask her what to do. First, he would retrieve the skull. As he approached, there was a heavy splash. He assumed the fish were jumping.

When he leaned over to reach for the skull, he lost his balance as everything spun. A black whirlwind threatened to suck him down. He felt a stabbing pain in his hand as he grasped the skull. Something had bitten him.

Juju lurched back from the water, slipping, and almost falling before staggering farther up shore. His right hand throbbed, reminding him of being stung by fire ants. It wasn't that, he saw, but worse. Dios mio!

He immediately freed his hand from the fangs of the skull. The undead's bone head had bitten him, and he bled like a stuck pig. He sensed that he was going to pass out, so he sat down heavily on the ground with the skull in his lap.

Twenty

Road Emergency

Leaving Maraders Marina, Dillon processed what had happened. Driving gave him time to cogitate and process facts and speculations. Even so, he remained alert while he drove northeast, following the winding road toward Swearington Lodge. Could Destrange appear in the shadows of a moving vehicle?

He savored being in Dad's old truck, the one used to go fishing. When the air was calm, he thought he could still smell bait and black bass. He wished he could talk with his dad. What would he think now, God rest his soul, about his son being a vampire in love with a vampire? Would he disown him? Or would he suggest that Dillon bring the myths to light? Tell the world the truth about the nightwalkers?

What good would that do? The world had issues accepting LGBTQ, and they were humans who didn't sustain themselves with human blood. He expected vampires to be cursed and hunted. In his ignorance, that's what he would have done. Were there good and bad vampires?

At the moment, Dillon had no idea if vampires were a plague to humanity or lived in somewhat peaceful coexistence, like cowbirds and cattle. Were they any more harm to humans than people were to themselves? Ha. That was doubtful, he thought, recalling the news of abuse with alcohol, drugs, and guns.

How many more monstrously evil Von Damme types were there? Dillon had no earthly clue, except Elke had mentioned that none had ever been entombed like the vampire alchemist, because they didn't know how to destroy him. Had Denny and dynamite truly killed Viktor Von Damme? Or was he lying in wait? Had that specter animating Bonz been the undying spirit of Von Damme? Or just his shadow? Just. Could he have more than one? What did those skulls have to do with the master vampire? Whatever the connection, they must be destroyed. The skulls couldn't be studied. Zhen would be running experiments on the one Juju kept. The jewelry box, shredded and misshapen, had returned to the surface world. Was there anything left of Von Damme in it? Thank God that they hadn't found the necklace of fire opals. Troy had said it had been left in the jewelry box.

The valuable coins found meant for certain that more diving would happen. He could see it in Madi's eyes. She would return and erect the lighting for the memorial. Dillon thought that was another mistake. They should honor Denny without disturbing where he had died, but people wanted closure. He doubted they would get it. They could be opening Pandora's box.

At least they had seen neither hide nor hair of werewolves in the past two months. That didn't mean they weren't here; Elke had warned him. He recalled Silke and Troy's story of the werewolves attacking them near Aunt Jada's house. Dillon relocated his Glock, locked and loaded with silver bullets, onto the front passenger seat. He wasn't worried about local law enforcement. He could talk his way out of it. He eyed Shadowsbane, wondering what, if anything, the katana might do against supernature.

The road was clear, ahead and behind. Soon, turning northwest onto Green Springs Road, he had rolling hills to the left and patches of shoreline as he drove by creeks and channels on his right.

He had been on edge since seeing The Joker. He had never been bothered by clowns before, nothing like some people and coulrophobia. Still, there had been something unnerving in that driver's eyes. Suddenly, Dillon realized what it was. The Joker had no life aura, not like the skeleton and Elvira in the second car. They had been alive. What had The Joker been?

Dillon worried about his mother. She was in greater danger.

He was getting ready to turn around when he spotted something standing in the road. A person? He slowed and looked closer. Whatever it was, it wasn't alive. It gave off no heat. After a moment, he realized it was an inflatable punching dummy of Bozo the Clown rocking to and fro.

The truck's headlights touched a hand-painted sign: CLOWNING AROUND!

Dillon sighed. He was not a fan of Halloween. He wasn't sure if this was the holiday, a punking of some sort, or danger.

The next sign read. STOP CLOWNING AROUND HERE.

A clown doll with suction cups for hands and knees struck and stuck to the windshield. What the hell? Dillon wondered.

It exploded, and the windshield shattered. Dillon flinched back from the chunks of debris. His face felt slashed and shredded. Smoke billowed and swirled inside the cabin, so he couldn't see the road. He kept steering straight and braked, slowing the pickup.

The rear window showered him in glass as hands were shoved through. They seized Dillon's head and sent shocks through him. He jerked and thrashed powerlessly. His body refused to obey his will. His hands and arms flopped to his sides.

"Who knew The Joker was a human joy buzzer, eh? This is a shocking turn of events, no? Good thing there were no spoilers. I didn't want a buzzkill, but now, on second thought, a buzzkill sounds like a bang-up idea," his attacker howled with laughter.

He threw a wire around Dillon's throat, binding him to the seat and keeping him upright. His attacker leaned in further, craning around so Dillon could see The Joker. It was the driver of the GTO! Dillon could not believe this craziness. The Joker placed a locking bar, The Club, on the wheel, steering it straight, and dropped a brick on the gas pedal. The truck surged forward, hurtling toward a construction zone.

"Ah, sorry, I'm all out of lead so a brick must do. The jokes on you, newbie! And it's a killer. A bonus for you, its front loaded!" The Joker cackled. Dillon noticed The Joker's scar, actually Goran's scar. Why was the vampire dressed up like DC's most infamous villain?

It didn't matter why. The truck sped toward a front loader. The piece of earthmoving machinery had been turned, its shovel now in the road waiting like a giant lance to unhorse Dillon from his modern chariot.

"Ever dance with the Devil in the pale moonlight?" The Joker asked. "It's just a question I like to ask someone before he loses his head! Why so serious? You should be smiling." His voice changed, heavy with a Czech accent. "For what you did to my master, you will die," The Joker snarled. It sounded like, for vat vou did to my master vou vill die. "This town needs an enema! And I am just the vampire to give it one! Stick it to two states at once!" he said with a guffaw. Goran turned on the radio and departed, leaping from the speeding pickup truck.

AC/DC serenaded him. "I'm on the Highway to Hell!"

Dillon's final destination rushed toward him. He willed his body to move. At first, he felt nothing. He kept his eyes on the front loader growing swiftly larger as the truck hurtled toward it. He couldn't even duck. He would be held so the toothed shovel removed the top of the truck and his head. Elke! He had promised her that he would always come back to her. An empowering surge of strength rushed through him. Even so, he couldn't grab the sword, but he could finally move. When he reached up for the wire around his neck, he touched his throat, flesh to flesh, and it caused a spark that burned away his paralysis. He ejected the knife hidden up his sleeve to slice through the restraining wire and some flesh, allowing him to immediately fall flat on his side.

The truck barely shuddered when the shovel decapitated it. A split second later, Dillon's world came to a loud, crushing stop. The front loader rocked back from the impact of the truck, while its front end crumpled into the cabin. The dash and the protruding engine slammed Dillon and the front seat into the back seat.

Dillon hurt all over, but he was alive. He could already feel himself healing. He wiggled, trying to slip loose. Gasoline fumes stung his nose and burned his throat. He could handle the crash, even the fire, but if the truck exploded like a cheap B movie, the blast might injure him. He didn't know if The Joker was waiting to finish the job or not. Dillon couldn't hesitate.

He heard a vehicle coming down the road. He twisted to see it driving closer. The truck was dragging its muffler and kicking up sparks. He must hurry. That could be enough to ignite the spreading gasoline.

With the power of a vampire, he carefully bent metal, trying not to create a spark, broke plastic, and altered his form a little to make himself skinnier. He hurried, slipping free, until his shoe caught.

The truck passed. He yanked his foot free and rolled, expecting there to be a fireball. Nothing happened. There was no explosion. Dillon sat up and smiled. He looked at Dad's truck. Dillon couldn't give Silke any more grief about wrecking the Land Rover.

He was finishing phone calls, the first to Mom and then to Key, when an old, yellow tow truck slowed, pulled to the side of the road and parked. Instead of having a flat bed, it had a boom and crane to haul vehicles behind it. The name on the side read Miles Towing: Miles Jasper, owner, 1-800-Get-Tows. Dillon had seen it before behind the Down Home concert venue.

"I hope to kiss you in a few minutes, love, but a VH is stopping to help me," Dillon told Elke and hung up. He didn't need a tow truck, but he appreciated someone stopping for him. He kept his sword sheathed but in hand while he jacketed his phone.

The wind shifted when the door of the tow truck opened, bringing a whiff of motor oil, orange cleanser, garlic, and red-hot cinnamon jellybeans. A tall man climbed out, putting on a hat as he exited. Like before, he wore a leather bombardier jacket over a shirt with a heart. Aim here, it read. Atop the heart a crucifix hung from a necklace.

He recognized this man, the vampire hunter from last night. What was he doing here? Dillon didn't blink, although he could feel the holy objects power, and smiled in gratitude. He was pleased that he didn't come out armed and ready for combat. There was a chance that he could bluff or talk his way out of it. "Thank you, kindly, friend, for stopping for me, but I'm ok, and I just called for a tow and a ride."

"I can't believe you survived that," Jasper said. He looked at his phone and frowned.

"I am blest and lucky. I fell asleep," Dillon lied.

"Wow. You look better than I expected."

"Death warmed over?" Dillon suggested.

"Nah, you look much better than that. You're unlucky and lucky," Jasper said.

"That's the story of my life."

"Are you sure I shouldn't call 911?" Jasper asked. He didn't even look over at Dillon's truck. He was staring at Dillon like he either knew him and couldn't place him, or was trying to see beyond a disguise. His jacket pockets bulged, and Dillon spotted a knife handle.

"Really, I'm okay. I can feel all my limbs, and I didn't see stars or black out. My mom, though, she won't be happy about Dad's truck being totaled," Dillon said.

"But not your dad?"

"He died three years ago. He would be happy that I'm alive and uninjured, although my neck will probably be stiff tomorrow. It's good that I've been staying limber with martial arts," Dillon said.

Jasper relaxed. "You rolled with the punches, eh? Well, if you're all right, I'll move on."

"Thanks again for stopping to check on me. It renews my faith in God and that there are good people out there."

"Well, people have to watch out for each other, don't they? Lots of predators out there and nearby, you know, animals, thugs, and the supernatural."

"Wink, wink, nudge, nudge, say no more?" Dillon replied using a line from Monty Python.

Jasper was openly bemused. His smile and chuckle were genuine. "Exactly. You confuse me, but I'll figure out if you're part of the darkness infesting this town. I can smell the stench of evil and the reek of fear in the air."

"That was the hitchhiker I picked up. I wish I hadn't."

"Oh. Sometimes being helpful can put one in danger. I used to be afraid of the dark before I realized that I am light, by Grace, and the dark should be scared of me. Can you hear the clock ticking toward an apocalypse?" Jasper asked.

"I don't hear the clock, but I know what you mean. I see the fear in friends' and families' eyes. Things have gotten crazy these last two months with the Six Finger Cult, the deaths, and disappearances. I pray the revealing is more like an enlightening event, like the word's Greek origins and less the modern use of great destruction."

Jasper appeared to look at Dillon in a different light. "Sometimes the revealing seems destructive, getting rid of what isn't natural, but it's a big step toward healing. Often times things must get worse before they can get better. That's what is happening here. Go with Grace and Godspeed," Jasper said. He climbed back into the cab of the tow truck and tipped his hat before he drove away.

Dillon had lots of questions. Besides a vampire hunter, who was that guy?

Twenty-One

Rounds of Fear

Standing in the employee parking lot of the Bristol Regional Medical Center, Knives sensed something amiss. He felt watched, and after locking his truck, he felt followed. He saw no one, but his footsteps echoed, giving him the sense of being pursued. No, he reminded himself, his mind was working overtime jumping to conclusions.

The medical center located at 1 Medical Park Boulevard spread out into two windowed wings of four stories from a medical mall and its lobby of framed glass. Tonight, it seemed darker, hunkered down and brooding, if a building could take on a personality. An illuminated triangle stood atop the open-aired and glass-walled common space of elevators, information desks, check-in counters, waiting areas of potted plants and chairs, and hallways to different services. Starbucks, Walgreens, the credit union, and the Skylight Café had closed hours ago. Currently, the lobby felt deserted except for Knives, a custodian, and whatever ghosts that roamed the building. It wasn't the walls, roofs and amenities that made the hospital special, but the people who provided care for the community.

The piano started playing without anyone sitting there. He shivered to shake the chill out of his spine. He had heard about this phenomenon, but he had never experienced a ghostly concert. Others had checked to make sure it wasn't a sophisticated player piano. He recognized the song *Rocky Top*. Carl was singing along in a baritone.

While he crooned, the custodian seemed to vacuum in time with the music. In answer to Knives' unasked question, the long-time master of cleaning and sanitizing tilted his head. Despite being a graybeard, Carl hadn't slowed down. Usually, he was all smiles, teeth so dazzling that they illuminated his pockmarked face, but now the custodian scowled. His expression was threatening if you were unfamiliar with his genteel ways. "Watch out, tonight, Doc. Good ole Morley is acting up."

He referred to Morley, a janitor who had been electrocuted years ago. Despite the high-tech equipment with flashing lights and beeping monitors, restless spirits like Morley's were still seen roaming the halls. Until tonight, Knives had never seen nor heard any signs of the ghostly residents. Recent events had changed him from a doubter to a believer. There was always more to know about the way the world, its people, and how the universe functioned. Often it was astounding how wrong scientists could be, and how amazing and incredible the truth turned out to be.

The custodian's words were normally surrounded by sunshine and floral scents. The man loved to garden and often brought in flowers to decorate the nurses' stations. That and his germ-busting nature made him a favorite with them. Today, though, his words shivered and quaked in wan, gloomy light. "He's bound to cause problems."

"Are you cleaning up after him?" Knives asked.

"Yep, Morley scared a kid half to death. Boy blew Skittles all over my clean hall. I think Liberace is apologizing for him. He knows I'll sing with *Rocky Top.* I saw Jolene, too, so, if some expensive machines short out on floor three, don't be surprised. Jolene, stop blowing up machines! All these ghosts must be coming out for Halloween next week."

"Thanks for the heads up, Carl, and I really appreciate you for all you do. You help keep us safe from those things that can't be seen with the naked eye," Knives said.

"Killing bugs is a calling. Never give in. Never surrender," Carl replied grimly. Being a neat and cleanliness fanatic was a good trait when one worked in a medical setting. Carl might not be a trained nurse or doctor, but he certainly kept people healthy through prevention, the best medicine.

Knives headed through the employee door into the ER. The admitting nurse, Tammy Stalwart, appeared upset, her forehead furrowed. "There has been a parade of visitors to see Rae Kirkland, including the mayors. I've never heard of such a thing. Everybody wanted to know what's wrong and what we're doing about it. None of them liked my answer: everything we can," she said. Her words sort of stomped out, all frazzled and disjointed. They collapsed at the end as if they were exhausted. "Ah well, God knows we're doing the best we can. Not everyone's perfect, and not everybody's a Cowboys fan."

"Mama, don't let your babies grow up to be cowboys," Knives replied.

"Oh, that's a good one. Use country music against me. I think I need more coffee."

"Fear makes us humans malfunction, so we say and do stupid things," Knives replied.

"Some say being on TV makes fools out of people, too. With that in mind and seeing how Rae has been admitted to our care, I wonder: how was hanging out with the TV folks of *The Myth Huntress?* Was it exciting?" LIFESTAR Flight Nurse Jess Meyers asked as she strolled up to join them. Her words were frazzled, fractured and faded, like she was tired. "Don't look at me like that everybody. I'm fine as frogs' hair. Flight nurses are always fine, right? Ah, these should help," she said, popping a couple of round candies like Whoppers into her mouth.

Knives raised an eyebrow. "Was that chocolate?"

"Would you like some chocolate-dipped espresso beans?" Meyers asked.

Knives declined. He didn't need his heart racing. He worked better when calm like a mechanic.

"I'll take some. My caffeine per pint of blood ratio feels like it's only half of what I should be," Tammy said.

Their discussion had drawn a crowd of nurses and coworkers. Sharon Humphreys from Imaging had stopped in her tracks to listen. She had eyes that seemed to look right through you. Maybe she experienced synesthesia, too. Even Angie Severett and her partner changed directions, turning away from their ambulance waiting outside. The tatted paramedic and the rookie EMT hustled over to hear more. Fate had not been kind to Angie's partners. Even so, the new guy, Brandon, had been undaunted and taken the job.

Knives didn't usually work evenings, so he wasn't on a first name basis with some of them. He hadn't met Mandy Nutt or Melissa Cagey before. They appeared to rarely see the sun, and their stares were intense, as he could feel their attention dig into him.

"You would think I was handing out free chocolate bars," Knives said.

"Here! Here!" the nurses replied as one.

"I have espresso beans to share," Jess said. Nurse Meyers poured the chocolate-covered treats from its plastic container into many eager hands. Knives knew this place would be buzzing soon. Caffeine and chocolate were a Heavenly combination for overworked nurses. Was there any other kind?

"See, we Appalachia rednecks from the farm are just hankerin' to hear some celebrity gossip, especially now that you're living in high cotton," Tammy said. It seemed just a single chocolate-covered coffee bean had increased the clip of her talking. The Stalwarts, she said, had learned how to take care of people by first taking care of God's creatures great and small. Most of the nurses were dog lovers.

"Exciting is an understatement. They hadn't even started diving yet when troubles surfaced," Knives began, and they ooed. "But I apologize since I can't get into specifics. Both HIPPA and the non-disclosure contract prevent me from talking about what happened." The nurses booed. He was hit by a thrown Reese's Peanut Butter Cup wrapper crumpled into a ball. "Aw, you know Rae ended up in the water and then here. While the crew was getting ready to dive, we were exposed to some kind of toxic discharge."

"Dump the dump," someone said.

Knives held up his hands. "We reported it and took water samples. One boatload went diving while my boat returned to Maraders where the ambulance waited," he continued.

"I heard there's an alligator in the lake. Is that true? Did you see it? Genny Lionel's partner, Angus said it was an alligator, a really huge one, that attacked the Search and Rescue team," Angie Severett said.

"Now there will be the irrational fear of gators written up by Cane Concannon. I wonder what that's called?" Jess asked.

"Herpetophobia. I hate snakes," Tammy replied.

"I only saw video of it. I have no need to see it up close. I plan to stay in the boat in case I'm needed," Knives said. News of the gator was public knowledge now. He imagined it was all over the net and media. He hadn't paid attention. "They all returned safely, thank Heavens, to the surface suffering only some bumps and bruises and shivers since it's cold, darker than Shinola boot polish, and scary down there. I've told y'all about the Mansion of Doom and Death. It's now Denny's grave. I can't tell you what they found, only that they gained access to a cellar and basement. Y'all will have to talk to Madilyn to learn more."

"I knew Madi in high school," Angie said. She wasn't the only one. This was a tight knit community that valued its history and relationships. Some families as friends went way back.

"That Juju is as hot as a two-dollar pistol. Is he as buff in person?" Nurse Char McKey asked. Her words danced musically, gyrating and rolling like the bands the red-headed rocker loved.

Screaming, throwing her hands into the air, Tammy suddenly reared back in her chair. Lucky for her, Knives was standing nearby. He stepped in neatly, catching the back of her chair to keep it upright, and Tammy seated. "Lord Almighty, did you see the size of that spider? I swear they're feasting on the steroids in the cabinets. Oh me. Thank you, doctor," she said.

Knives had witnessed her arachnophobia seize her before.

Char patted Tammy on the shoulder. "You, dearie, should drink less coffee and don't have any more chocolate-covered zoomers. The jitters have you."

"I drink less than Dr. Coxswain. I think Dr. J's afraid to fall asleep. What's your phobia, doctor? Vampires in October? I don't remember what Concannon named it," Tammy asked.

"I'm leery of werewolves and avid fans of God's football team, you know, Cowboys fans," Knives joked. He was a Viking fan since he was a Tennessee High Viking's graduate.

The nurses' cackling laughter followed him as he extricated himself from the crowd to check on tonight's ER physician, the Queen Bean, lover of coffee and all things Scottish.

With glasses atop her head, Dr. Joan Coxswain glanced up from her chair where she audio recorded her reports for transcribing. He caught the end of Dr. J's comments relating to Rae Kirkland and which tests had been ordered. He looked at her coffee mug, finding it half full. On the side it said: Check fluid level before asking ???s. Her moods changed based upon caffeine consumption.

"Guid nicht," he said, trying to sound Scottish. She was wearing her button: Don't kiss me. I'm Scottish. I've kilt for less. Had he missed the memo about button wearing?

"Hey, sonny. It's been dunky's since the last I saw ye. Seriously, you shouldn't be here. You should be sleepin' or doin' somethin' fun. It's called recovery time, and it decreases PTSD," Dr. Joan said. Her eyes were large, dark, and curious below thick lashes. She had shaved the right side of her head, slicked her hair on the other side and tied the back in a ponytail with a plaid scrunchy.

"I'm here because of Rae."

"So, if I tell you what I know about Rae, will you go home? You know burning the midnight oil isn't good for you."

"After I see her and visit the lab," Knives promised.

"You are going to look less like George Clooney and more like Marcus Welby, MD, if you don't get some sleep. It's essential to mental processing. Look at me. I used to look like Kate on *Bones*, but I didn't get enough sleep and now, well, it takes coffee and audio caffeine to keep me awake, and in the morning I look like a mile of bad Scottish road."

"It's why they train us to be sleep-deprived during residency and rotations," he replied, referring to their years in medical school.

"Touché. So, here's the facts. Rae remains unconscious. Her heart rate and breathing are significantly elevated, bordering tachycardic. She's experiencing rapid eye movement and hyperventilating," Dr. Joan said.

"Like she's suffering a nightmare," Knives said.

"That was my thought. What did y'all see out there at the lake? Or is that legally classified?"

Knives thought he understood all too well how Rae had felt. His experience had not been near as extreme, but he had experienced similar symptoms. "I'm not so sure it was about seeing. She grew ill shortly after there was a gas bubble that ruptured near the boats. It made some people sick and others just nauseous."

"And you're on the hunt for what caused it?"

"Yes. I think there's reason to believe that a friend of mine and myself have been exposed, like Rae, but perhaps having different reactions. I'm going to check on my results now."

"What's going on with you?" she asked with concern.

"I have a significant change in my vision. For whatever reason, I see better in the dark due to an increase in rods. I'm also having trouble sleeping and experiencing nightmares."

"The latter two sound like they could be stress-related."

"I agree. I'm also experiencing synesthesia. People speak their words in colors. That hasn't happened before," Knives said.

"Wow. I hear that's more common than we think, ten percent of the people or more. I don't know much about it, except it seems to be the entangling of the senses. There's some thought it's a mix up in the translation of the signals from our nerve bundles. So, what do mine look like?"

"Something a rock band from the seventies would play, you know, leather-clad and studded with a lot of strut and confidence. Huh!" Knives said.

"Way cool. I like the sound of that. Hurts so good?"

He gave the nod to John Cougar Mellencamp. "The synesthesia has helped me diagnosis when people are ill. You look like you'll be able to rock on," he replied.

"Synesthesia sounds like it could be a huge bonus given to you by the twists and turns of fate," Dr. J said.

"It's rare for someone to develop it when said person never had it before. You are either born with it, or you're not," Knives said.

"Are you suggesting that perhaps Rae Kirkland is experiencing sensory overload? That she's overstimulated?"

"Now you are starting to sound wise, more like *Dr. Quinn, Medicine Woman*. I'll keep it in mind and let you know about my test results. I'm on the way to the lab now. See ya," Knives replied

"We are masters of our own fate," she reminded him.

"Be the heroes of our own story," Knives replied. Dillon had said such. Continue to tell yourself that, Knives thought. His mood had grown a little dark and pessimistic since August. That wasn't good for a doctor.

He strolled while deep in thought on his way to the elevators. When it opened, Nurse Beck, J-Man's mother, exited. With a light jacket over her shoulders, she looked on her way home. Having a mother as a nurse was not easy, Knives knew. They didn't kiss it and make it better. They examined your issue, told you that you weren't seriously hurt and to get back at it. Life was full of bumps and bruises. Get up and dust yourself off. Take care of it and move on. No whining. The offspring of nurses knew more about their bodies and how they worked than other children. If you were seriously ill or wounded, having nurses around was a blessing. It's why he brought them chocolate, too.

"Good night, Mrs. B," he said.

"Hello, Stephen. My Jay says you're going on an adventure with the crew of *The Myth Huntress*. Beware that Madi Marader. She's always been trouble. Careful, or you'll be dragged into it, too," Mrs. B warned him. J-Man's mother didn't scold him with a finger, but it sure felt like it.

Knives nodded. "I can tell you that it appears nothing has changed."

She groaned. "You take care of yourself and my Jay, too. He hasn't been right since August. Good night, dear. Get some sleep or you'll start looking like one of those walking cadaver thingies," Mrs. B said as she departed.

He was starting to look like a zombie. This was not good.

Behind a counter, he found Sarina Barrett managing late. Despite being cooped up in a lab, she possessed laughing hazel eyes and a dazzling smile like a sunrise. Her dark, curly locks were arranged with honeybee clips. She owned a small honey farm as part of her property. Just recently, the Barrett Bee Farm had received a grant to fund a project that involved bee pheromones. The best of both worlds, she claimed, running it along with her sister Karina, and her mother, Carol, who looked more like the eldest of the three beautiful Barrett sisters. Sarina always let her light shine, her faith strong. Her cross necklace sat atop her lab coat, faith and science combined. They often saw eye to eye on matters.

"Hey, Ms. Barrett. You are amazing. You work harder than your honeybees. Thanks for running the tests for me so quickly," Knives said.

"You're welcome. It was quiet until late."

"Is Bradley on vacation?"

"He wishes. He's as sick as a dog, he says. Say, you're giving off worrying vibes, my friend. I hope you're not coming down with something," Sarina said. Her words were scripted in bright, sunshine colors of calligraphy. There was no sign of fear, worry or paranoia. It was relief. He hadn't realized that seeing the negative mood of people in words had affected him so. He should have known better.

"Oh, you mean I smell worried?" he joked.

"Something like that," she replied. Her words had dimmed, as now he had concerned her.

Because of his synesthesia, he had a much better idea of what Sarina meant. "I don't get worried. I have doctoral concerns," he said. Sarina snorted derisively. If he had seen it, the snort would have looked sarcastic. "I see you understand perfectly. How are the studies going?" he asked.

She chuckled. "Well, we think we might have discovered a new pheromone. I don't want to say too much as I might jinx our find, you know," Sarina said with restraint. He could see she was about ready to jump for joy. Her words were springs lashed down. She collected herself and handed him the test results. "You, sir, are wearing a serious scowl." He forced a smile. "Ick. With that kind of bedside manner, your patients will run for the hills," she replied. Her words were big, fluffy, and huggable.

"Everyone seems on edge tonight," Knives said.

"Here at the hospital, or during the adventure with the beautiful myth huntress and her crew?" she asked. Her words were tinged green with envy.

"Everywhere. As novelists write, the fear in the air is palpable," he replied and yawned. Neurological studies showed that yawns helped clear the mind to better refocus. According to test results, he and J-Man both suffered elevated levels of cortisol, which likely meant their adrenal and pituitary glands were working overtime. It was one of the signs of PTSD and increased their chances of heart attack and other health issues. It could be countered by releasing more endorphins, such as dopamine, through exercise, sex, medita- tion and even eating chocolate. Mercy, he mused, they both should seek counseling and therapy. Knives found one expected result: there were signs of hallucinogens in their systems.

"You need to find yourself a good woman, relax, share some good dopamine chemistry. Karina thinks you're handsome, if you think you can deal with a Barrett," Sarina said.

"No worries. I have the pleasure of dealing with one on a daily basis," Knives said. After that, he only half-listened and read. What was this? He certainly didn't expect to find lysergic acid diethylamide. Why LSD? That was very 1960's.

Did this mean everyone who had been in the water had been affected by LSD? Marader, Troy, Silke and the others who had been inside the house should be tested. It could go a long way to explain events that seemed inexplicable.

Had LSD caused his synesthesia? LSD affected serotonin and neurotransmitters, which moderated thoughts, governed senses and controlled emotions and behavior. Had stress and LSD caused his senses to become entangled? Now here was some science at work, and yet, as almost always, there was more work to be done. Science wasn't static. It kept discovering new things, especially since nature, viruses, and life had a tendency to constantly change.

Why was the LSD still in their systems? What did that have to do with their sensitivity to light? Why did they see better in the dark? There was no connection with any trauma that would alter their vision in that way.

Knives wished, again, that Dillon had provided a blood sample. Something had fundamentally changed about the man. It annoyed Knives that he had no clue. He prayed that checking Dillon's DNA would tell him something. On that result, he would just have to wait. He was already breaking a few laws. It bothered him that the ends justified the means. And yet, many great leaps in science had happened that way. He had thought himself better.

Even contemplating what might be wrong with Dillon seemed to slip from Knives' mind, like he wanted to just forget it, which wasn't like him at all. Knives understood that he had recently suffered significant trauma, both physical and mental. It could affect his reasoning and memory. Diagnostic mental tests had proved that Dr. Curran was thinking clearly, and Knives brain was functioning normally.

And yet, last night when Dillon had entered the bar, something had changed. After pondering it, Knives decided that everyone had changed how they reacted to Dillon. They had let him off easy for assaulting Marader.

Dillon would have killed Tommy. Knives had seen it in Dillon's words, and for a moment, Knives recalled that he thought he might have been okay with it. He could barely remember that. What kind of thinking was that?! It unnerved and greatly concerned him. Perhaps he did need counseling. And yet, they had all said they would like to kill Marader. What in Tom Marader provoked them?

Since Dillon's illness had struck, the man seemed to carry a dark, powerful anger. If he couldn't control himself, he could seriously hurt someone. Knives realized that he could have been badly injured, so Dillon must have regained a semblance of control.

"Paging Dr. Curran, are you alright?" Sarina asked.

Knives blinked, brought back to reality. "Yes. I was wandering the winding ways of speculation."

"I told Karina you were often distracted by strokes of genius," Sarina said. Her sister was very attractive, but she wasn't any more so than Sarina. Knives noticed that her words reached out with yearning. "Did you find what you were looking for?" Sarina sighed. These words were faded, lifeless and resigned. He nodded. "Will there be more tests?"

"Likely. We're doctors. It's what we do. Take tests. Run tests. Review test results. I sometimes think my last name should be Stephen Tests."

"Knives Tests doesn't roll off the tongue, either," Sarina agreed. Her words were heavy and weighed down.

He had made her sad. That was not exactly the reaction that he had been looking for. "Don't say it again. When Rae Kirkland's tests come in, please, check it for hallucinogens and increased activity in the adrenals."

"Cortisol and such?"

He nodded. "Yes. Say, how's your project progressing?"

Sarina beamed. Her words were honey-colored and smooth-flowing. "Good. I love honey, the perfect food, and honeybees. Pheromones are quite interesting. Perhaps I can come up with something that helps people be calm when they have to speak publicly. Just a whiff, and a speaker is brave enough to pontificate and elucidate in front of a roomful of people. They won't even have to imagine everyone in the room nude. Filibuster away," she said.

"Good-bye glossophobia. Smelling something honeyed and encouraging would be a lot more helpful than imagining everyone naked at a staff meeting," Knives said.

"Oh my, that's true," Sarina giggled.

"Your discovery would be a blessing for many folks. Toastmasters might make you person of the year. Just imagine if you found a way to calm people seeing doctors and dentists, you would make our lives easier," he replied.

"Such high praise, thank you. Jeremy has been wearing cologne from Love Scents based on pheromones, hoping to get a date since I told him that he needed to change the way that he smelled. He was really . . . ew. Since Love Scents wasn't working, I whipped him up a Bee Sexy cologne. Who knows, I might have a second career in the near future."

"That's the name you're using? I like it, although I hear Aire de Smoked Filet Mignon can work too."

"Ha. Well, that and bacon," she chuckled.

"So, we're all just honeybees?" he asked, pleased that he had changed her mood.

"You sound like a Hallmark card, and I think some of us are honeybees and others are hornets, but yes, one's scent is a hugely important factor. Did you know we humans smell best to someone whose genetics have different disease immunities than our own?"

"Well, isn't that something. I didn't. It makes sense, though. It would help cut down on inbreeding, offer children more immunities and better disease resistance like with cross breeding. Interesting. How's Jeremy's love life? Any changes?"

"He has a date! In my field, there's open debate on whether early human bodies had vomeronasal organs. Several places in our noses might have been more sensitive to smell, especially pheromones, given off by people."

"Any relation to synesthesia?"

"Not that I am aware of. Do I speak in colors?" Sarina laughed.

"You do have a colorful vocabulary," he replied. His phone alerted him, reminding him to drop in and see Rae.

"Ah, you need to get back to work. And I will sally forth, too. Samples to test and analyze and such. They are never ending. Why can't people just stay well? We give them the wonders of chemistry, and chemistry is life! I don't understand why people don't see that chemistry is a collection of God's hidden recipes."

"You really are spunky and busy like a bee."

"You are adorable, I don't care what people say. Get some sleep, my friend. At least six hours. You look like you could be going on fifty," she said. Her wrinkled words were almost enough to convince him.

"From what you said, who cares about looks? The question is: how do I smell?"

Sarina breathed deeply and expressively grimaced. "Fatigued. Confused. Determined and concerned. Too much cortisol and too little dopamine, plus worried," she said and then flushed.

"Not worried. Doctoral concern. Well, you are right about tired and perplexed."

"Dare I say, the Octoberfest Vampire has been keeping you up at night?" she said, arching an inquisitive eyebrow. He could see her words were meant to be silly. "Don't worry. My sister and my besties are dressing up as vampire hunters this year for the trick or treating at East Hill."

"Whew. I'm relieved. We need them. As you know and have read in the screaming headlines that vampires are our main health concern right now. Ghosts are a close second. Any ghostbusters?" he asked, playing with it.

"Just to be clear, it was Morley who broke the test tube earlier. It wasn't me," she chuckled.

"Now you sound like the cartoon, *Family Circus*. Nobody did it! Have a pleasant night," Knives said.

"Happy Halloween. I know it's days away, but I like to start early so I can say it more often," Sarina replied.

"Hah! Year around we get to wear masks that make it difficult to breathe, and nobody gives us free treats," he grumped.

"Dr. Killjoy says farewell. Remember, live by faith, not sight," Sarina called after him. Her words carried longing and conviction.

Once back in the hall, it hit him. Sarina liked him enough that she saw other possibilities. That made him smile. What should he do about it? He was an emotional jumble right now, more than he had ever been, even as a teen, and she had sensed it. He didn't want to add his Killjoy gloom to her day. When he was better, he promised himself that he would see if his diagnosis was correct, or if he was seeing what he wanted to see. He had just been told not to live by sight but by faith. In his case, could he live by both?

On his way to see Rae, Knives wondered if she had LSD in her system. It appeared that she had suffered a mental breakdown from being so close to the underwater ruins where she could have died, but what if her issues had been chemically induced? The lab was already testing Rae's blood for toxins and chemical pathogens. Earlier, he had noted that she looked cyanotic, her lips blue and the skin around her eyes looking bruised, so he wondered if she was getting enough oxygen and effectively processing it. When she had been brought in, the answer was no. Her pulse and blood pressure had also been dangerously elevated. He expected that her cortisol levels were high, too.

As soon as he stepped from the stairwell to the hall, Knives shivered. He wondered why it was so chilly here. Mandy Nutt and Melissa Cagey stood at the nurses' station, their attention consumed by a bag of Flaming Hot Doritos and patient files on the computer screen. Snacking and updating was not unusual, so keyboards should be sanitized, and hands washed. He hadn't worked with these nurses before. They had strong personalities and an ambiance of health that reminded him a little of Tom Marader.

"Mandy, I love what you've done to the hearse. I think adding red was the perfect touch. Good evening, Dr. Curran," Nurse Cagey said. When she smiled, the coffee-haired, blueberry-eyed gal gained apple cheeks and dimples. Her words flowed as silkily as melted milk chocolate. He didn't see any stress here. It was just another day of saving lives and comforting people in need.

"Are you alright? Can we help you? Would you like a Nutter Butter?" Nurse Nutt asked. Her honey-blond hair was held pinned by a bejeweled dragon. Its green eyes matched her own. Her words looked composed of cream-filled cookies. Why was that? Was he hungry? Was what they had eaten somehow mixed with their spoken words?

"Doc? Ground control to Dr. Curran?" Nurse Cagey asked. Did she really wear a button that said: I root for the villains?

"Sarina says he has walkabouts. That's Aussie for daydreaming," Nurse Nutt replied. The dragon pin in her hair shimmered, moving in a way it appeared to be chuckling. If he started seeing Cheshire cats fade and leave grins behind, then he was in real trouble.

"I thought he might be sleepwalking. We aren't supposed to wake them," Nurse Cagey replied.

"Ladies, please don't give up your night jobs," he replied, and they humored him, laughing with him. He was starting to wonder if the lack of sleep was messing with his synesthesia. Fatigue messed with the senses, so why not with those that were entangled? It didn't have to be LSD. It could be his body malfunctioning from sleep deprivation.

From ahead, from Rae's room, Knives heard voices. Was she awake? The volume increased suddenly. Rae sounded panicked. "They're all over! Smothering me!"

Knives rushed ahead. He heard the nurses following close behind him. One minute he was hurrying, just a step away from Rae's room, and then the next, he lost consciousness midstride. This wasn't the kind of nap that had crossed his mind was his last waning muse.

Twenty-Two

After Visiting Hours

Elke leapt out of the driver's seat of the car to embrace Dillon. They kissed long and passionately like it might have been the last time. Neither of them wanted to let go. Elke would glance at the wreck and blink away tears. Who knew vampires could cry? It seemed tears didn't fall under the flowing water definition that harmed them.

"It was Goran, dressed like The Joker of Batman fame. He has some kind of shocking power that paralyzed me. The blue-white lightning saved me when it freed me. I ducked just in time."

"He can stun you? This is dismaying news. I wasn't aware he was capable of such a thing. How do you feel? Your eyes look like you've been staring at Escher's art," she asked.

"More like the final end in the face. I'm all right, really. I think I confused the vampire hunter, though. Maybe I didn't look immortal. I'm concerned about Rae. Can we look in on her at the hospital before you talk with Judge Dragomir?" he asked.

"Of course. There's time," she said and guided him to the Corvette.

While he changed into a fresh set of clothes that he'd learned to keep in the trunk, they discussed the stinking gas bubble and Rae Kirkland. "I wondered if it was some kind of air bubble from the Shadowlands," Dillon said. He told her about the amphorae and the coins. He nibbled on candy made from vulture bee honey. It helped calm and settle him.

"It is possible. Those are grounding objects to help root the gate. Von Damme delved into the Shadowlands quite often. He used shadows as servants and assassins. He did something to make them more powerful than other Shaden. You have reason to be concerned about Rae. It is even possible there were feargorgers within it, and now Rae and others are infested," Elke said.

Dillon hated the thought that he had been clueless. He had gone with the myth huntress to be helpful. "I wouldn't have noticed?" he asked.

"You might have easily missed them if they were wan. You don't have much experience in identifying them. I can feel them. By the way Rae reacted, a feargorger makes supernatural sense. Like with any artisan, you have to look for their telltale style when they don't leave initials or a signature," Elke said.

"I did notice a darkening of Madi's aura. Juju and Agent Kaye seemed similarly affected."

"You did see them! That's a tell. Their conditions worry me. Shaden can spread quickly."

"It gets worse. They found vampire skulls. How did they not dissolve into the water?" Dillon asked. He climbed in the car and buckled up, ready to go. Her confused expression turned grim while she drove on and listened to him describe what Agent Kaye had found and carried to the surface.

"Judge Dragomir used six traitors to entrap Von Damme's spirit in his mansion. Their power was tapped to bind Von Damme so that when the lake filled, it would hold and perhaps eventually destroy him. Dragomir assumed that the water would dissolve them, and it should have."

Troy had told Dillon about the ghostly visitor, Mona, who had taken him into the past to watch as the mansion had been assaulted and turned into a tomb. Elke had been there and killed Mona as a mercy, she had said when Dillon had recounted the story. "Something went wrong, didn't it? We are talking Von Damme."

She sighed. "So sad, so true. Dragomir yanked Von Damme's spirit from his body, attempting to entrap him in the fire opals of a necklace that witches crafted to cage his spirit by placing it in the jewelry box that only spilled blood would open. You know the one that Marader was obsessed with."

"Yes. Did you say the witches made it?"

"There was an alliance. The witches were upset with Von Damme for a score of reasons. They made the necklace and other accoutrements."

"Instead, Von Damme left in John's girlfriend's body. Were you involved?" Dillon asked.

"Yes. I helped them get inside the house. Elsa, my previous self, worked as maid in that place."

"That was a waste of your brilliance and talents."

"I love you," Elke effused. The moon shone dazzlingly bright upon him.

He smiled. "So, is Dragomir here to clean up?"

"That and reasons likely to be his own. We must use caution when dealing with Dragomir. In truth, we may never be certain that Von Damme is destroyed. He loved to brew trouble and distill misery," Elke told him.

"You are an artist and poet. Let's hope you're a mystery solver, too, because I'm new at this."

"Sometimes it takes new eyes to get a fresh perspective," she replied, sounding sage like Master Cosmo.

"Could he have survived as a skeleton?"

"With Von Damme, anything is possible. It is as likely if not more so, that the vampires' strong-willed spirits might remain. If so, they would seek vengeance. That said, their skeletons shouldn't have survived, but then very little involving Von Damme goes as planned. Their interactions with him must have altered their bones. They must be destroyed."

"I know. Now the bad news."

"There's more?" she asked.

"Juju took one of the six without the FBI knowing about it," Dillon said.

She grimaced and seemed to bite her tongue to hold back a string of unpleasant comments. Finally, she sighed. "It's lookin' like the hind wheels of destruction, it is, if Zhen and the FBI are allowed to study them. Even so, we'll let Judge Dragomir decide what to do and when," Elke said in an ominous tone. She frowned as she steered the Corvette into the medical center's parking lot.

On the second floor of the hospital, they encountered Nurse Melissa Cagey, a round-faced brunette with dark, laughing eyes. Elke had known Mel for a couple of decades. "Good evening, Ms. Swearington," Nurse Cagey said. The button under her collar flipped back and forth between: Joy to the World, and I root for the villains. Elke had mentioned that two of her agents were working tonight and keeping their eyes on Rae.

"How is Ms. Kirkland?" Elke asked.

"She's still restive. She was given a sedative before we came on shift," another nurse said. This Nutt looked like the twin to the night manager at the Abingdon senior care facility. She sipped from a large, takeout container from Dunkin Donuts. Her perfume seemed coffee-based, or perhaps instead of sweating, the nurse oozed espresso. If so, it wasn't enough to disturb Rae.

"We may not be able to awaken her," Dillon said.

"It is what it is, but I'm confident that she will talk to y'all. Ms. Swearington can be very convincing," Nurse Nutt said. Her hair pin resembled a glittering dragon. When the light caught it right, the piece of jewelry flickered to life. She must be a big fan of dragons because there was the tattoo of a cute little beastie on the inside of her left forearm. He breathed out musical notes. She also wore a button that flipped back and forth: I love people! I hate people.

Elke could bring the dead back to life, Dillon agreed. "Is there anything to worry about?" he asked.

"A nasty virus is going around. Wash your hands like you've been cutting jalapenos, and you need to put your contacts in your eyes to drive," Nurse Cagey suggested.

"I would scrape all the skin off," Dillon joked.

"Exactly," Nurse Cagey said. She led them to the room where she peeked inside.

Elke followed her closely, peered in, and dismissed the nurse. "Thank you, Mel. Let us know if anyone is coming."

"Sure thing, Miss Elke. Poor thing, Rae hasn't had any peace since she arrived."

Dillon waited with Elke while she studied the room. Nothing appeared wrong or different, just a space with a female patient in a railed bed, along with a chair, an in-wall dresser, and a mirror. The lights from the equipment lit the place, and the beeping of her heart rate filled it.

Rae's pulse jumped faster the moment they walked into the room. Even in her slumber, she sensed predators. Rae seemed to be fighting her way awake as she stirred and moaned.

"Rae reeks of the Shadowlands. She has been touched by something of it," Elke said.

"Add the stench of diesel and the divers smelled like this after diving the ruins."

"You mentioned they stank of the Shadowlands. I understand better what you mean, and she didn't even dive."

"But she had been diving before. I wonder if the gas bubble set her off. She thought she was surrounded by monsters. Do you see a feargorger?" he said.

Elke studied her. "Yes, and the Shaden is feeding on her fear."

"Can you get rid of it?" Dillon asked.

"I am not capable. Von Damme was able to absorb them and empower himself. At best, I can bolster her courage so that she can shed herself of it by being unafraid," Elke said.

On the monitors, Rae's pulse bounded as if she were running a race. Her breathing rushed out in loud gasps. "They're here! Smothering me! Help me, please!" she pleaded.

Dillon stepped back, letting Elke take command. He heard Knives coming toward the room. He called to the nurses.

"Sleep," she ordered Rae. Her eyes closed, and all her fear departed, leaving her limp.

Knives walked into the compelling as he entered the room. Dillon caught his buddy before he crumpled to the floor.

Elke whispered in Rae's ear. "Dearest Rae, tell me, when did you become afraid of the dark?"

"I got over that long ago, but the shadows, they're different. Ever since I was stuck in that underwater basement, they scare me. They are jealous of life! They want mine," Rae replied.

"Calmly tell me what you saw and experienced under water," Elke ordered.

Rae's eyes popped open. Panic nearly overwhelmed her as they discovered the door to the basement was locked behind them. While Diana and Mary Beth wrestled with the knob, Rae went searching for anything that she could use to remove or get through the door. She dove deeper, heading down the stairs to the basement. She thought she recalled seeing wood carving tools.

"At first, it was just bitterly cold, and scary, being stuck in someone's dark cellar in a horror story. But then, it got worse. The water seemed to grow heavier, pressing down on me. Even though the lights waned, the shadows multiplied. I thought I saw them scamper along the walls where there shouldn't be any and their shapes didn't resemble anything in the basement, at least nothing I had seen. It was like they were pulled out of nightmares."

Dillon could see it. Such shadows were deeper than the darkness. He could feel the weight of the water crushing her, the walls closing in and the blackness clinging. Then he sensed things skittering across his flesh. He resisted the urge to squash. He knew that he was feeling what Rae had experienced. The phantom sensations were generated by those disturbing memories.

"When I looked down, much to my horror, I discovered that I had these black spiders crawling on me, all those legs sharp with spines. I was poked and spindled all over," Rae said. Her hands started to dart about her body.

Dillon took one of her hands in his and held it gently. The blue-white lightning surrounded them, and she relaxed with a small smile.

"There was another time, just before the boys showed up, that I swore snakes were swimming around us. They had diamond-shaped heads and huge maws," Rae said. Despite Elke's commands, she shuddered before regaining her composure.

Knives snorted.

So Dr. Killjoy, Dillon thought. He studied Rae, now calm, when minutes ago she had been wide-eyed, breathing fast, and her heart had been about to break down. He was grateful to Elke, wishing he could have done the same.

"I shall awaken your friend. We'll find out what he knows and then be on our way. The business of RON always takes precedent, and Dragomir frowns on tardiness. Dr. Stephen Curran, wake up clear-headed," Elke commanded.

***

Knives jerked awake sitting in a chair. Had he fallen asleep? He massaged his shoulder, discovering point tenderness. Had he fallen down? He really must get some rest.

"Hey, buddy, are you okay? You came rushing in and passed out," Dillon said. For a moment, he seemed larger than life. His words vibrated, and light burst around them like pyrotechnics. The color and texture of his words had changed greatly from their conversation at the marina. What had happened since then?

"Did I hit my head?" Knives asked. He felt along his skull. The last thing that he needed was a concussion atop everything else.

"No, Dillon caught you," Elke said. Looking like a blond Hollywood goddess, the woman leaned into Dillon. Her words glowed like a neon sign.

Knives felt inspired now. Something about a beautiful woman smiling pleasantly at a man instantly improved his mood. Sarina could do that. After looking at his results, he might be suffering some adrenal fatigue, but just seeing Elke caused his dopamine levels to spike. His exhaustion fell away, left like a jacket on the chair. "So, what are y'all doing here?" he asked them.

"Looking in on Rae," Dillon replied.

"It's long past visiting hours. Did I hear a scream?" he asked. He stood and stretched.

"That was Rae. Her eyes never opened. It was like she was having a nightmare and couldn't wake up," he said.

The monitors registered that her heart rate was regular and steady. Knives checked his own pulse at his wrist. For someone who had passed out, his pulse rate beat too rapidly. Why was his heart pounding? He knew it made it more difficult to think when his heart raced. It was a main reason why people did stupid things when they panicked.

"Can we step outside?" Knives asked them. The room felt stuffy and tight. Together, they left for the wide space of the hallway. It wasn't the open expanse under the sky, but it would do.

"Is she going to be all right?" Dillon asked.

"We don't know what's wrong. Do you have any clue?" Knives asked. Dillon shook his head. "Would you tell me if you did?" Knives pressed.

"Certainly. If I knew how to help Rae and you, I would."

"In the morning, leave her in the sunshine," Elke said.

"Well, they did that in WWI with patients. It has been known to help in all sorts of ways, the sunshine, the fresh air, and not being cooped up. I can't help but think that this is related to that horrible underwater house and the cult. Does your research tell you anything?" Knives asked.

"There are still lots of holes and speculation. You know they wanted to flood the city and the surrounding region. There's some indication they also thought about poisoning the water. Like any cult, they wanted followers. They filed their teeth, drank blood, and worshipped the darkness."

"Uh. Drinking blood will make you sick. It's not digestible. But, come to think of it, Rae has mentioned the darkness closing in on her, and monsters of the dark, not in the dark. You know people can scare themselves to death," Knives said.

"Death by stress," Dillon said.

"Psychological shock can eventually kill people," Knives said.

"That's different than psychogenic?" Dillon said.

"Yes, that's a good question, though. Psychogenic has more to do with blood vessels dilating while psychological shock makes our bodies work against us, pumping cortisol, adrenaline, and norepinephrine into our systems. Our false fears become real in a sense. Initially it's good for focusing and cellular repair, but too much for too long creates paranoia and other health risks," Knives said.

"Speaking of health, are you feeling all right? You've lost weight and have circles around your eyes," Dillon said.

Knives smiled. "I've been burning the candle at both ends. Did you go through anything like Rae with your illness?" Knives asked.

Dillon shook his head. "My issues are anemia and a loss of pigmentation and melatonin. I never went diving."

"We've run a few tests on her. Right now, our best guess is something is affecting her adrenal glands. Have you had your eyes checked?"

Dillon nodded. "I lost some pigmentation, just like my skin."

"You look to have some albino aspects."

Dillon one-arm hugged Elke. She beamed a smile that would turn most men into idiots. "The good news is that I feel great," he replied.

Knives couldn't disagree. By their words, they were full of vim and vigor. What a pair.

"Will you be rejoining the myth huntress and her band?" Dillon asked.

Knives nodded. "Yes. She isn't done diving, plus, I'll be there for Denny's memorial. Will you?"

"It's during the day, so I plan to watch it live-streamed," Dillon said. He seemed to leave something left unsaid.

Something like, if I'm still alive. Knives thought. How truly ill was Dillon? Was it a cover? He certainly didn't look or act sick. Dillon seemed far healthier than Dr. Stephen Curran who at last glance in a mirror had appeared rundown and ready for a break-down. "I wish nobody was going back to that place, but they are, so

I joined them to find answers. I still don't understand a lot of what happened after we found John's body. Do you think I ever will? Will your book help?"

"Drug-induced psycho terrorists using drugs to cause terror looks like the answer. Have you run toxicology?" Dillon asked.

"Yes. We're waiting on the results. You know, I had J-Man's and my blood tested."

Elke said nothing but intently watched Knives. She raised a questioning eyebrow.

"We are both seeing better in the dark but not as well in daylight. We have headaches and difficulty sleeping. I believe we both suffer from PTSD. Our cortisol levels are elevated," Knives said.

"You need dopamine or to cry a bunch," Dillon said.

"You might have PTSD, too, buddy. Hell, the whole area is spooked over the Oktoberfest Vampire. Concannon's media ravings about phobias and the supernatural hasn't helped, either. Everyone might have some PTSD since this last summer of missing people, wildfires, and terrorists," Knives said. They nodded, but they didn't seem to be concerned. Knives found it mildly irritating.

"Doctor, I assure you; Dillon is getting his dopamine. You should seek it, sleep and nourishment as well. What else is going on? You see the world differently now. How so?" Elke asked.

Knives told them about his synesthesia, how he saw words in colors, shapes, and moods. "I still want to understand why we are experiencing changes. I don't know what's up with Tom. His test was messed up nonsense with canine biomarkers."

"Marader's part wolf," Dillon joked.

"Not funny. My sense of humor is low now. So, I'll need to get another sample from him, not a dog this time. An odd thing about our results is the presence of LSD," Knives said.

"You've been exposed to LSD?"

"My test results say we have. I don't understand why it's in my system, but it lends credibility to your theory of terrorists using drugs and poisoning the water."

Elke gave Dillon a look. "We must get going. The night is wasting away."

What was he hiding? Who was he meeting? It could possibly be a source, perhaps a terrorist? Knives mind spun on possibilities when he needed to focus on medicine or get some sleep. "Be safe."

"Thanks, Knives. You've been a great friend and blood brother," Dillon said.

Knives didn't like the look of those words at all. They were truthful, but they were driven like those judged for execution, falling off at the end as if they had been hung. What was going on? Knives wanted to ask more, but a look from Elke stayed his voice.

Knives noticed Rae remained calm, the monitors registering a normal pulse and respiration rates. Come to think of it, he felt calmer now than being around Dillon. His presence provoked the jitters in Knives like he had chugged a couple of espressos. Those rampant emotions had been balanced by Elke who almost made him swoon like a silly schoolboy. Did that mean Dillon caused him to produce cortisol, a stressful and fear hormone, and Elke inspired him to produce dopamine, the pleasurable counter to it? Or was this the LSD talking?

Knives awakened standing in the elevator. The dinging of the doors opening had jarred him back to awareness. Oh my, he hadn't fallen asleep in a hospital elevator in a long time, perhaps back during rotations in Richmond. Wide open, the doorway led to the basement. It wasn't dark, but it was dim, and one of the lights flickered like the thready pulse of a heart dying. How odd. LEDs weren't supposed to function that way.

How had he ended up down here? He hadn't hit the B button. He didn't want to be down here. He hadn't been down here since he had almost died in the morgue. Troy, God bless him, had come looking for him and dragged him to safety. That man's audacity and luck were astounding and had been a blessing to Knives. The others caught in the basement during the accident had died due to the toxic chemicals in the air. One, a colleague, Dr. Pete Sullins, had been murdered. His throat had been ripped out. The grisly killing had never been solved. Due to that, Knives no longer worked part-time in the morgue, and he hadn't returned to the basement until now.

That night their blood brother's body had also gone missing. Some said that whoever had stolen John's corpse had murdered them all by purposefully spilling the chemicals. Others, even some nurses, believed that John hadn't been dead, but he had awakened, killed the coroner and during the struggle, they had knocked over and broken the bottles of chemicals. John's body remained missing.

Once again, Knives' mind wandered back to the autopsy that he had conducted on an incredible effigy of John. Its guts had been so realistic, but tests revealed them to be something other than flesh. The results on the components had been unknown, and yet it hadn't been organic, either.

Knives shivered. The erratic lighting made the hall seem like a soundless, disjointed disco floor. The rational part of his brain said everything was fine. The imagining hemisphere of his gray matter disagreed. Something slid from shadow to shadow.

The left and right sides of his brain wondered why pushing the close button or pushing floor numbers failed to lift the elevator into motion. He wasn't claustrophobic, but Knives finally decided that this elevator wasn't going anywhere. The way things were going, if the doors closed, they wouldn't open. He decided to take the stairs.

The exit sign was dark, a safety code violation that he would report to maintenance, but he knew where to find the door to the stairs. He opened it to the emergency lit stairwell. There was no other way to go but up the flight of stairs. His mind messed with him. What if the murderer was still down here? Like a tape worm, that insidious notion wriggled through his body. His hair spiked straight from the nape of his neck. He realized that he was breathing too fast and listening for the sound of a footstep.

Get a grip, he encouraged himself. He was reacting like a kid. He refused to let his imaginings propel him into psychological shock. His brain controlled his body, not the other way around. He focused on his breathing. That he could control. As he ascended, he missed a step and fell forward, almost onto his face. He caught himself on the railing. Was he seeing spots? He needed to eat. He continued on more carefully but shortly misjudged another step. His depth perception was off kilter, so he kept a hand on the banister. He felt something drop onto his shoulder and crawl toward his neck. He reached up to squish it.

Abruptly, darkness fell like a hammer. What had happened to the emergency lighting?

Knives paused on the stairs. He saw movement in the dark. He knew his brain would create sights when it couldn't see anything. He ignored them, even the feeling of breathing on his neck and the tugging at the back of his pants.

Taking out his phone, he turned on the light. It worked, brightening the empty stairwell, so he continued ascending. The walls squeezed up against him. Wait a minute. Tight spaces and the darkness did not bother him. He had crawled under the house to fix plumbing and get rid of mice. He shouldn't have to remind himself.

Did he hear breathing? What was causing him to freak out about normal things? He was like the medicine men of yore, wandering in dark caves seeking insight. He let his hippocampus soothe things over while he checked his phone. Its light dimmed despite the battery having 50% power. In moments, it was so dark that he couldn't read it.

None of this made sense. He wondered if he was dreaming.

Could he have gone blind? Yep, he could hear breathing. A large and menacing presence pressed on him. He could feel hot breath on the back on his neck. He figured that he stood under a heating vent, except that they weren't in stairwells. He took his pulse to focus on it and calm down, heading off irrational panic. His amygdala didn't know any better. Was it False Emerging As Real? Or Forget Everything And Run? Blindly dashing up the stairs would be foolish and could be deadly.

He ascended slowly. Darkness clung like a cold, wet blanket, and oozed into his ears, nose, and mouth to fill his lungs. He suffocated, unable to even gasp. His head spun. His body panicked. He missed a step, stumbled, and blindly staggered ahead, groping for the rail no longer there, and fell headlong. Hands out, he found a wall. He spun toward it and managed to remain afoot.

He stood there, letting his dizziness pass. His mind calmed. His breathing started to settle, and then he sensed that he wasn't alone. His imagination wanted to conjure black panthers that would never have been in the hospital's stairwells, but something had ripped out Pete's throat back in August.

Where was he? What had happened to the stairs?

Knives hurt, so he must be alive. The tile floor was hard under him, so he likely had fallen, again. Twice was a bad sign. Had he gotten dizzy? Something kept bumping into him.

Ding. Ding!

What was that sound? And what was that smell?

Knives managed to open his eyes. The darkness faded. Looming over him was the robot that mechanically sanitized rooms. He must have collapsed in front of a Lightstriker cleansing robot. Dr. Joan and others had warned him that he needed sleep. He must have been worse off than he had thought.

He sat up and felt okay. He hadn't broken anything and hadn't hit his head falling on the hallway floor. He watched the robot roll onto the next room to clean. Knives felt the most settled in days, maybe weeks. Had he knocked some sense into himself?

"What are you doing on the floor, doctor?" Sarina asked. Her words were jagged and worried.

"Gathering my wits and taking stock of my aches and pains."

"Wouldn't you rather do it in a chair?" Nurse Mandy asked. When she looked at him, he thought she could read his mind. "Do you need a hand up?"

"I'll take one. Or two," he replied, as both ladies assisted him to his feet. He didn't need it, really, but it seemed to make them all feel better.

"What happened?" Sarina asked. She leaned over to inspect him, looking into his eyes. Her words were seriously frayed. After what had occurred in the stairwell, he was confused and concerned.

"I'm not sure. I think I might have blacked out in the stairwell and fallen out the door to here," Knives said. It would sound mentally unstable if he described what happened.

"That was fortunate. I don't know what being sanitized will do to you. You're already squeaky clean. At least you were before you started inspecting Carl's work. Go home and sleep. I know you don't want to be the cause of an emergency situation," Sarina said.

"You're right," Knives said.

"Oh, I love hearing that. Just for that, I'll treat and pay for a Lyft or an Uber, unless you want Mandy to drive you to your house in her hearse. You shouldn't be driving," Sarina said.

Knives didn't argue. "I'll take the ride, taxi, Uber or Lyft, but no offense Mandy, I'd prefer to stay out of a hearse for as long as possible," he said. He just might sleep with the lights on tonight.

Twenty-Three

Marge and MMA

At Sugar Hollow Park, Marge let the others, especially the Bristol Virginia PD forensics' team, do their jobs. They were skilled experts, and she would only get in their way. She had considered staying at the farm, but she needed the fifteen-minute drive and the lake to decompress. Being around water calmed her, even after last night's events at the 421 Bridge.

She was disappointed that the farm's security cameras hadn't been overly helpful. They did get an image of a black SUV, which was better than nothing. They couldn't be sure of the make or model, and the license plate had been covered. She had been madder than a hornet until Grandpa jested that it was a government hit. Marge ran with the joke and made a show of searching for electronic surveillance devices. She found a dead roach and showed it to him. Yep, they were bugged. They had shared a much-needed laugh.

Whoever had driven the road had come through a big hole in the fence from the park to access the farm road. Sugar Hollow didn't have cameras. None of the campers had seen anything, although they had met Kevin. She didn't suspect any of them to be lying, either. None of them looked big enough or strong enough to take on Kevin without using a weapon. Boomer had filled his nose with smells in hopes that he would encounter and recognize the scent of the killer someday.

***

After parking her cruiser at the marina, Marge encountered Rhett Archer dressed in a dark ensemble of a jacket, a vest, a turtleneck, and black jeans. His upper body glittered in the parking lot's lamplight, and he looked like a Rhinestone cowboy. At least his jeans weren't studded and flashy.

"Good evening, Mr. Archer. Are you headed out on a stealth mission?"

"Why, Marge. What a pleasure to see you, again. As a matter of fact, I am. How was your day? And please call me, Rhett."

"Murderous, Rhett," she replied, thinking he might take the bait. He didn't seem interested. "Do you have a hot date?"

"Not unless you are off duty and offerin' to join me on my adventure. I'm dressed in costume to do research. Do you like my hat?" he asked. It was big and black with a purple rhinestone raven.

Marge had the sense he was lying. "This late, I can't help but wonder if you're visiting cemeteries, houses of ill repute, a drug dealer, or joining a Satanic ritual, except for how you're dressed, although some prostitutes like their johns in costume. Why the Glen Campbell look?" Marge asked.

"Where I'm goin' is part costume party, I've been told. My night's as sexy as socks on a rooster."

"Do tell."

"I'm outward bound to watch illegal fightin', mixed martial arts of the criminal kind."

That was the truth. So, what was he lying about? Marge thought through what he had said. "You're not doing research. What are you after?" she said. When he remained silent, she said, "You know,

I could follow you and blow the whistle. You did say illegal fighting. Illegal being the keyword."

"You could join me and blow the whistle once you're certain. I have no jurisdiction. I'm no longer a peace officer, and this is from my source. He could be wrong. Plus, I only know where the entrance is. My source said there are underground tunnels involved, ones that run through the old city of Bristol under the new," Archer replied.

"Where is this?"

"I'm to park in the 5th Street lot. A homeless guy will provide me with further information, as long as we're in costume and say the magic word. What do you say? Come along. It might even be entertainin' before the arrestin' starts. I was serious that you impressed the Shilos," he suggested.

Marge felt that he continued to tell her the truth. "You're looking for somebody," Marge said.

He frowned then his face broke into a grin. "You must be a detective."

"Sullivan County deputies might be as good as rangers in their deductive abilities."

"The man who shot me, we never caught him. He's supposed to be handlin' the numbers tonight. He's slicker than a minnow's tail, but I got to see if I can set the hook."

Marge was looking for a supposed vampire who liked to attack strong males and females. There would be a lot of those fighting tonight. She could say she was following a lead. "Give me ten minutes. Costume, you said."

Running a little late, she returned with a change of attire and attitude. She was now fully abreast for the situation, and she still thought she might have shortchanged Dolly.

"Parton me, you sure don't look like a cop right now," he replied and opened the passenger door of his black, Ford Explorer.

"That was my intent," Marge said and smiled. She had padded her bra and donned a blond wig and cosmetics to make her look like Dolly Parton. She had to maneuver her extended cleavage to slid into the seat. "It's the new Kevlar bras. You know, if I hadn't done my research on you, I would be very suspicious."

"Good. I'm glad you checked up on me. You should. I might be a bad cop. I could be a squatter who looked up the Shilos on Facebook and decided to hang out at their houseboat for a while."

"I'd like to think they didn't complain about my singing on Facebook," she said.

"I have no earthly idea. I'm not a fan of social media. It helped me catch crooks. I'm good with that. Have you been undercover before?"

"Only when trying to attract rapists and perverts in the parks and on the city streets of Bristol."

"I'm surprised you haven't cleaned it out. I assume you're armed."

"I have more than two arms," she replied.

He nodded. "I like to gear up like James West since I can't fight like Chuck Norris, and I expect to be searched," he replied and winked.

"Oh, the glory days of the Texas Rangers."

"Don't knock it. Walker helped with recruitin'."

"It does sound more exciting than Virginia Conservation Officers," Marge admitted. Just the name deputy sheriff came with an Old West ring to it. Bristol did not need a retired Texas Ranger playing shoot out at the OK corral.

Once on the road into town via 421, Marge warned him about deer and asked him about his injury. He never took his eyes off the road while he drawled, sounding similar to the local dialect. He dropped the g on ing words. He used sorry as a description as in pitiful. There was y'all and all y'all, meaning multiple groups. He was fixin' to do this or that, and occasionally he grew flustrated. She recalled that many Appalachian settlers had moved on to Texas, famous folks like Jim Bowie, Daniel Boone, and Davy Crockett were known, having died at the Alamo, but there had been many other hardy souls who had settled what was to become the Lone Star State.

"It's spinal. I'm a helluva lot better than they thought I would be. They didn't expect me to walk again, let alone jog or boogie down. Now, I'll admit I'm still a little shaky with my right hand, so I shoot left-handed, or would if it was needed. I'm not the first deputy, agent or cop that Jake Mudder has shot."

"His name is Mudd?"

"I've called him worse. We've just been plum lucky that none of us died," Archer said. He gave her a brief summary of his own background, born and raised in Longview on a cattle ranch and playing in the Piney Woods of East Texas. He tried Engineering at Texas A&M, but he didn't cut it. He would have liked buildin' bridges, so he decided to do that by becomin' a deputy doing it through people. He had briefly moved to Dallas, but he missed the country and its woods, so he had moved back to Gregg County and its county seat of Longview. He had never married because he had yet to meet the right woman, someone who could put up and keep up with him. Bristol and Longview, which had double the population of the twin cities, had smaller towns around them and hicks in the sticks. Here, the hills rolled higher and farther into mountains, but people were just people everywhere even if they seemed to speak a different language.

"So, what can you tell me about Jake Mudder and what's going on?" Marge finally asked.

"Not much. The private detective I hired said Mudder runs a mobile fightin' and gamblin' operation. It travels the country like a carnival. They come in, set up a big top tent event in a hidden spot, draw in local wrestlers, fighters, and gamblers, and then they clean up and travel on to the next place. That's what happened at Longview. They had set up in an abandoned barn."

"They will be well-armed?" she asked.

"Yep. Plus, the fighters. They're likely packin', too."

"What a fun first date. How can we top this?" she asked.

"Hey, if you're goin' to be a femme fatale', you can't complain. Besides, I don't recall hearin' Dolly complain."

Marge replied with a frosty glare. "Don't forget what happened to Franklin Hart, Jr. The overbearing and misogynist boss in *9 to 5*," she added.

"I think we should take a selfie to remember this by in case either one of us suffers a concussion," he said.

"Do you always make such an effort to impress the gals on the first date?"

"I must admit that I've never taken one to a current crime scene before. And no, I don't use that line on anyone. I wouldn't bring anyone along that I didn't think could handle themselves and the situation," he replied.

"I can't help but think you're a bad influence," Marge said. It wasn't the first time that he had complimented and flirted with her. Boomer liked him. The Shilos considered him a son by choice, and Marge knew them to be good, salt of the earth people.

She called her good friends in the Bristol police departments. They weren't too put out of joint to be notified on short notice if it meant they could catch these clowns.

In downtown Bristol, Archer parked his Explorer at the 5th Street lot on the Tennessee side. Even from here they could hear the free concert held by Double Tap at the Quaker Steak and Lube. The cool breeze carried the sound, and the music bounced off the brick buildings to reverberate downtown. She realized that the noise would make a good cover for various illicit operations.

A homeless ragman smelling like the dump shuffled over and asked for spare change.

"Here's 77 cents," Archer said. He handed the man a dollar. "Godspeed."

The lookout pointed to the door of an abandoned building then shuffled off. They followed his guidance, and at the door, Archer said the magic word, "Godspeed." The door was opened to reveal a muscle-bound man in black wearing a Green Goblin mask. He let them inside and instructed, "Go downstairs and follow the red ribbon to the end and take the stairs up."

Archer handed a flashlight to Marge. "Shall we torch the place?" he suggested, using the British term for flashlight. Wearing cowboy boots had been smart considering the steps and walking underground. She never would have made it in heels, especially being top heavy. At the bottom of the stairs, there were two doors. She could still hear the beat of the music throbbing down here. He opened the door with the piece of red string on the knob. It had neither a lady nor a tiger on the other side and led to a tunnel under the street. Along the right wall, red ribbon ran into the darkness. The horizontal shaft was dank but smelled like a party of colognes, perfumes, cigars, cigarettes, and marijuana joints.

"You take a girl to the most interesting places. If you had warned me, I might have worn a different disguise that took up less space," she said. Who would ever want breasts this large just so your hips looked narrow?

"As long as it doesn't throw off your shootin' or your judo," Archer said. They ventured into the darkness, following the red ribbon with their lights around turns left and right. Pipes and communication lines continued to run along the ceiling above them. She was glad none of the tunnels were wet. She spotted rats in the side shafts and heard them squeaking. She thought she heard one running up above.

She felt followed. Two steps later, she felt something pluck at her sleeve. When she turned, she almost lost her balance. Fortunately, nobody was there.

"Is there a boogeyman below Bristol?" Archer asked.

"Not that I'm aware of," Marge replied.

"I have my crucifix handy, just in case," Archer said.

"I would think vampires would have better digs than this."

"My momma often said, don't do in the dark what you don't want brought out in the light, but she wasn't takin' into account bloodsuckers," Archer said.

"You believe in them?"

"I believe there are many kinds of vampires, corporate, political, emotional …."

"I call those leeches," Marge said.

"That's a good name for them. I've seen unexplainable things, too. I watched what looked like a man dodge my on-target bullets, and I was only ten feet away. You'd think he was that guy from *The Matrix* movie or somethin'," Archer went on. She wondered if he might be a little nervous.

They made another turn, pushing through clingy spider webs. Archer reached out, snatched, and squished something from her wig. "Thanks," she replied. After that, she kept feeling things drop onto her. It seemed like every second or third step. When she looked or even double-checked, there was nothing there. She plucked a few spiders and a cockroach off Archer since he was leading the way.

"These tunnels are as crooked as a dog's hind leg. You should have worn a pair of Bethany Dreamkickers," he chuckled.

"I have my backside kickers on, instead."

Another turn and Marge heard people yelling and screaming. She was momentarily alarmed before she realized it was shouting and cheering. At the sound of the bell, the voices grew even louder.

She finally saw a light at the end of the tunnel and stairs up. They ascended two flights of steps to ground level. The cavernous storage building with blacked-out windows held no engines, but it had a bunch of old empty train cars, a big top tent, a smaller tent, and Port-a-Potties with washstands. At least they weren't Neanderthals.

"No handicap ramp. That'll be another violation," Marge said. She brushed her shoulders and ran her hands down her arms. She felt like the darkness had clung to her along with the spider webs.

With all the noise, she expected to see lights, but only slivers leaked out the tent's entrance folds where two bouncer types stood watch. Dressed as Tweedledee and Tweedledum, both men stood tall and wide with bald heads, broken noses, and grim scowls. She kept her hands in her jacket pocket, ready to hit send when she noticed equipment to block cellular phone signals. Aw hell, there wasn't any service. They would have to figure out something else.

With her on his arm, Archer strode up to the tent entrance like he was expected, gave the password, kissed her for luck, and said, "I'll let you place the bets this time, babe."

Why would he say that? Marge wondered.

The bouncers stopped glaring and searched them. Tweedledum was all thumbs, and she resisted the urge to slap him. None of their weapons were found. Coming in disguise had been helpful.

In the tent, a bell rang. "And the winner is . . . Dark Angel!" the announcer exclaimed.

"You have missed most of the wrestling, but you're in luck, killer MMA bouts are next," Tweedledee said. Tweedledum snorted and laughed.

"Dearest, what was that all about?" Marge asked acidly.

"My apologies, M. I haven't kissed a lovely woman in so long I've probably forgotten how. I apologize that it was subpar. I guess what they say is true. Use it or lose it."

Fake it until you make it didn't seem like the appropriate response, either.

"But listen, you were lookin' totally ticked when you noticed that they're jammin' calls, making our phones as useful as tits on a bull. I was afraid the Dweedledumb bros weren't goin' to let us inside. I figured you didn't want to miss another Dark Angel hurricanarana or a stunner or a punt, so I hoped a kiss would surprise and mellow you. They would assume that you were upset with me, and not the setup" he replied.

If Archer was lying, he was lying to himself, too. "Good thinking. Are you a wrastlin' fan?" Marge asked.

"No, but I read up on it. I watched some MMA to see if there's anythin' I might use," he replied.

"Listen up, oh masked ones. Our next showdown is Dizzy Rae and Ja Brokaw. It's Beauty versus the Beast. Last chance for bets. Taking bets now or forever regret your missed opportunity," the announcer whispered.

Golf claps came from the nearly full stands that were left in the dark. Even so, some folks wore blinky hats or necklaces. There was a carnival atmosphere with drinking, smoking, and dancing in the seats. Costumes ranged from heroes to horrific to Hollywood stars and starlets. She wasn't the only one to dress like Dolly who was the blond of choice. The brunettes were Kardashians. Big breasts must be on the ticket tonight, she mused.

Marge doubted Captain America or Superman ever gambled on cage matches, although Thor seemed more likely. The spotlights shone down on the metal cage. She recognized the pit where locomotives and train cars could be worked on from below.

"How are you going to be able to find him in this crowd of colorful characters?" Marge asked.

"Let's find a seat first. I don't want to be knifed for standin' in somebody's way," Archer said. He found them a pair of seats in the last row. This way they could survey the whole scene. Vendors walked the isles selling booze, beer and weed. Archer bought a bottle of Bud. "I'm thirsty, retired, and it's a good weapon, and my final rationale, it will give me a solid reason to go awanderin' to the john. Perhaps Mudder is muckin' about," he replied to her look.

She declined. She wasn't retired. She was working and alcohol had never improved her aim nor her judgment. Both were very important right now. She blinked. Could that be? She would swear that she saw Jayson Humphrey, the famous true crime novelist. She devoured his work. It would be an inappropriate time to seek an autograph, she chided herself.

The bell rang, and the two females circled each other while they measured one another as if their stance or eyes would give them away. Brokaw looked like a brute who had stopped a punch with her face too many times, while Dizzy Rae was one of sexiest women that Marge had ever seen. She couldn't help but wonder if it was all real. The Latina beauty had blond streaks running through her dark hair. She was both fit and curvaceous, looking like a lover instead of fighter. Even so, when attacked, Dizzy Rae blocked and evaded like an adept pro. Brokaw grew frustrated and bull charged. The two exchanged a furious flurry of punches and kicks. Dizzy backed away sporting a grin. She looked like she had never been hit. Marge had the impression that she was playing with her food.

Most of the men in the audience were drooling. Some women were equally impressed. Archer wasn't paying any attention to the fight. His eyes focused on the crowd, searching for the man who had shot him among the faces dimly lit and shadowed. "To answer your question, from what I gleaned from interviews, Mudder has a strange air about him, perhaps it's the stench of lyin' and deceit, the touch of the Devil, some say. So, if you see him, there's usually nobody close by, and if there is, they are fidgetin', shufflin' and such."

"Like they can't stand to be with him," Marge said.

"Yeah, like he's part snake," Archer said.

Dizzy toyed for two rounds with her opponent, giving Archer and Marge time to survey the crowd. Nobody fit Mudder's description. Marge didn't see any unholy symbols, but there was a lone devil costume and a bedeviling couple among the onlookers and gamblers.

Finally, Dizzy Rae slipped a punch, nailed Brokaw with a jab to stun her, followed by an elbow punch that knocked her out cold. She hit the canvas like a sack of potatoes to a stunned silence.

"Don't that just knock your hat in the creek," Archer said.

Marge guessed not too many bet on Dizzy Rae. Did that mean she was an unknown local?

A numbers runner walked the stairs and aisles to take their bets on the upcoming fight. The Nazi vs the Masked Nobody with the odds heavily in the latter's disfavor. They were being watched, so after some debate, Marge put money on the Masked Nobody. With a name like that, he had to be fearsome, didn't he?

"I'm taking a powder break," Marge said. She was able to maneuver her cleavage without knocking anyone out. She took the stairs up to the walkway around the pit to where stairs led down to the mobile bathroom huts. She paused to light a cigarette. She didn't smoke, but it gave her a reason to loiter there.

After she studied the arrangement, she still hadn't figured out a quiet way to let the outside world know that they were here. Cops were waiting to shut down this place. She saw criminals that she knew, so she donned her amber lens glasses. They were good for dim light and hid her eyes. Ready, she strutted on her way to the bathroom. She was surprised to see Dillion Urich dressed as Indiana Jones. She wondered if he was undercover.

He strolled over. "Well, hello Dolly. You're looking well, I can tell, Marge," he finished quietly while he hugged her.

"What are you doing here?" Marge asked. She knew the reporter. She had met him long before he grew ill and returned home to stay where he had become Elke Swearington's squeeze.

"We are conducting research on the cults and looking for the Oktoberfest Vampire. We thought he might be here tonight. From what I can tell, he enjoys killing strong men and women. And there is a dearth of them in attendance tonight because the prize money is hefty and under the table. No surprise that several of the bodybuilders in town are also fighters. There's an upcoming MMA event in Roanoke, and some of them stopped here first."

"You know this how?" Marge asked. He was very, very handsome. The kind that you might think wouldn't lie to you without it marring the innocence of his face.

"I walked around and talked to folks. In my previous life, I was a reporter," Dillon replied, telling the truth. It struck her oddly, the term, previous life.

"And what are you now?" Marge asked.

"I am an observer. A slave to my passion, Elke," he said. At the moment, an utterly drop-dead gorgeous woman sashayed hypnotically up to Dillon and took possession of his arm. Ms. Swearington made Charlize Theron and Margot Robbie seem pretty.

Marge had met Ms. Swearington many times, but she had never looked this amazing. She was the girl next door beautiful by day and stunning by night. Cosmetics could work wonders. "You two look radiant together. Is there an art or antique sale tonight that's illegal?" she asked.

"No, we are just here watching people fight and looking for you know who," Dillon said.

"You make an excellent Dolly Parton, ma'am. You could star in *9 to 5*, if they were talking PM to AM," Ms. Swearington said.

"You know this is illegal?" Marge asked.

Dillon nodded. "We expect to be gone before the place is raided."

"What makes you think that'll happen?" Marge asked.

"A raven told me," Dillon said.

"We are here for much the same reason you are," Ms. Swearington said.

"Looking for vampires?" Marge asked.

"Yes," Ms. Swearington replied. "There are many kinds. I have heard interesting things about Jake Mudder, the promoter of the event."

"He's the money-sucking type of vampire," Dillon said. The announcer started opening remarks and introductions.

Elke smiled. "Deputy Cantrell, you do an excellent job. I appreciate you. You have a hunch that your friends will arrive soon, and you will forget Dillon and I are here, but you thought you saw Bond and Kaye here undercover. Look carefully to your right. There they are."

Marge looked for the FBI agents, but she no longer saw them. She had a moment of dizziness, but then she was all right. She chided herself about not being young enough for this late night, clandestine work and returned to her seat.

"I saw some old friends. They were dressed like Men in Black, you know," she said with a long look.

"I get ya. Those agents who stop aliens from fightin' and destroyin' things," he replied, and she knew he understood that she meant law enforcement. Perhaps the Feds were after Mudder, too. It sounded like he crossed state lines.

The crowd chuckled and guffawed when the Masked Nobody trotted out. The man was skinny and pale, wearing a dark mask, black shorts, and matching socks with high top sneakers. He looked like a one hundred ten-pound weakling. She couldn't see his face, but his eyes burned with loathing. He was totally confident.

In contrast, his opponent was big and brawny, solid muscle from head to toe. He rippled and gleamed when he walked, but it wasn't his physique that got her attention. The tattoo on his left bicep was an inverted cross. Could it be? She wondered. If only she could be so lucky. She breathed in deeply.

The starting bell rang. The fighters circled each other.

"Are you okay?" Archer asked.

"I'm checking for the smell of lavender," she said and explained her sister's ghost in hopes that it might unfurl his brow.

When she finished, all he said was, "Okay. I'll let you know if I catch a whiff. My momma liked lavender shampoo and soap. Well, this match shouldn't take long. The Masked Nobody must be gettin' beaucoups of money for taking the beatin'. I hope it comes with a good dental plan, otherwise he'll be eatin' corn through a picket fence," Archer said.

"I bet on him. Call it a hunch. The last fight was a surprise. People here aren't Texas tough. They're Appalachia tough. You barely have hills in Texas," Marge said.

The Nazi charged, and the Masked Nobody skipped away.

"I beg to differ. You obviously haven't been to what they call Hill Country around Austin, Texas. It's gorgeous, although I must admit that the Holston Valley and the lake are marvelous. It reminds me of Texoma, which is in both Oklahoma and Texas, sans mountains, of course. That's tornado alley land. Did you know Texas has the second longest canyon behind the Grand?"

"And here I thought it was just a dry flat lakebed. Now you're telling me it has a big hole in it, too, like a drain plug?" Marge asked. She wasn't sure why she enjoyed gigging him, but Archer seemed to enjoy it. He likely missed the teamwork and his work buddies. Nobody really understood except their peers in law enforcement.

"We have mountains to the south. Texas is so big it's more than a day's drive to get to Big Bend National Park on the border."

The Nazi charged the Masked Nobody who continued to bob and weave until he was suddenly tagged. He folded like a cheap TV table.

"So much for your hunch," Archer said.

Nobody's knees and hands hit the canvas, and then he sprang back afoot. With an uppercut, he rocked the Nazi, and then Nobody pummeled him in the gut. Marge had never seen anyone punch repeatedly so fast except someone on greenies or PCP. The barrage drove the Nazi back into a corner.

A knee caught Nobody in the side of the face. Marge heard bone break. The scrawny figure staggered around drunkenly, so wildly and swiftly that the Nazi grew frustrated by punching and missing. He finally kicked Nobody's legs out from under him. He was saved by the bell when the ref intervened.

The Masked Nobody stumbled to the corner, looked out over the crowd and grinned hideously, his teeth bloodied. When the bell sounded, he wobbled out. The Nazi struck a one-two and whiffed. The scrawny boxer countered, repeatedly jabbing the bigger fighter in the belly before the Nazi finally backed away. Marge and the crowd sensed something. Archer must have felt it, too, because he stiffened, and then all color drained from his face. He had spotted his shooter.

"That's him across the way. He's dressed like the Mask or the Green Goblin, I'm not sure which, and I must admit, I don't keep up much with fiction and wild stories," Archer said.

Marge spotted him right away. Every time Mudder shifted, people around him inched farther away despite already standing a few feet distant. It was like his presence invaded personal spaces.

"What's your move?" Marge asked.

"The bathrooms are that way. Between bouts, I'll take a break."

"Do you have a derringer in the heel of your boot?" she said.

He actually rolled his eyes at her. "I don't ask where you hide your surprises," he said.

"I'm prepared if we need to a make a bust," Marge replied. She adjusted her bra.

"I'm not sure that's what they intended with C&C permits, but I'm glad you are packin'," he said.

The crowd cheered the Nazi. He landed two good jabs, staggering the Masked Nobody. His mask was even darker now, wet and splattered with blood. His lower lip was fat and split. Blood oozed from his nose, but even so, he smiled. The brute looked to be closing in for the kill when Nobody swiftly kicked the Nazi in the ribs and followed with a knee to the gut. The Nazi blocked another kick, grabbed Nobody's leg, and tried to grapple. The scrawny fighter was like a spider. He crawled over the Nazi until Nobody perched on his back. He used both fists to pound across the Nazi's neck and shoulders, seeming to paralyze him. Nobody paused, basking in the moment before he delivered the final blow.

"Well, dang, if that don't beat all. I'm glad I didn't bet much," Archer breathed.

Suddenly, the klaxon sounded. The tent rattled, and the building shuddered from the alarm. It wasn't time for the end of the round. It wasn't the bell either, she realized. The ref and the fighters appeared confused, too. The Masked Nobody leapt free and fled out an exit. The Nazi struggled afoot and staggered after him. Mudder joined the rush to leave, dropping into the pit and racing for the open door.

"This is a fire alarm! Evacuate safely and immediately," the announcer said.

"All the rats are escapin' the sinkin' ship. Where's Mudder? Ah there he goes. Come on!" Archer said. He charged down the bleachers. Everyone else was leaving the tent and heading for exits.

Marge followed Archer, and he caught her when she stumbled and almost toppled forward. "I hate being top heavy," Marge said.

They dropped the eight feet down into the arena. Her knees would complain later, although it could have been worse. She wasn't wearing her heavy utility belt, and the wind friction from her cleavage slowed her descent. There was no one to see how well-balanced she landed. Leaving the recessed arena through a door, they entered a makeshift dining room. Stairs went up and out to the interior of the building. A ladder led down where the tunnel continued into the underground history of Bristol, the city upon which the city was built. Thankfully, there weren't catacombs like in Paris. The sound of running footsteps echoed from below.

"Mudder has to be like a damned master criminal with a secret escape route," Archer breathed.

They pulled out their flashlights and descended. Ten feet further, they reached the steps. They were damp, so Marge took them carefully. Archer slipped, and this time, she steadied him.

"Thanks," he said. He meant for the save and for following him. At a fork in the tunnels, they briefly debated, then they heard a string of profanity. They choose that way, hoping Mudder had slipped. If they were lucky, Mudder had injured himself and would be limping or crawling along.

Moments later, they heard growling and snarling. It broke into what sounded like a dog fight. They looked at each, wondering if they should continue. The ear-cringing roar of gun fire convinced them to continue their pursuit of the criminal. He was obviously armed and dangerous. "What could he be shootin' at?" Archer wondered.

The tunnel widened into an old, buried street choked with rubble and a system of sewer pipes. The air smelled stale, dank and reptilian. Marge wasn't a big fan of snakes.

Flashes of light accompanied more gunfire. The discharges briefly lit what might have once been the bottom floor of a commercial building. They heard something fall inside what might have once been a storefront. Staggering footsteps grew distant. Before their sound faded, Archer hurried inside and grunted, suddenly knocked off his feet like he'd been close-lined. She wondered what had hit him.

Her light rested on a pipe running low just inside the doorway. That would do it. She smelled blood and turned her light onto what looked like a big dog with multiple gunshot wounds. The pool of blood around it was spreading larger. It seemed obvious that Mudder had shot it. She didn't see any other dogs, but she swore that she could hear someone breathing, along with Rhett groaning.

A spider dropped on her arm, and Marge didn't scream or shoot anyone. She jumped a little. Had she heard a chuckle? Had something wanted them to come down here? She thought that she saw eyes in the dark, but when she turned her flashlight upon them, nothing was there.

"What hit me?" Archer asked. He rubbed his forehead.

"A pipe was low enough for you to walk into it."

"I was goin' to blame Colonel Mustard," Archer groaned.

"Pardon me, but this is no time for jokes. You must get out of here," an unknown voice said. A slender young woman with long pink hair and tatted arms stepped into the edge of the light's glow. "It's extremely dangerous down here right now. The dogs of East Hill are prowling these tunnels. We can show you the way out, but we must hurry. You can call me J, Deputy Cantrell."

"You know who I am. Good. We were chasing a conman," Marge said. She described Mudder.

"We saw him. He ran on after he shot one of the East Hill beasts," the tatted girl replied.

"I see. And who is this we?" Marge asked.

A young woman with a mane of white hair and a satchel of flowers over her right shoulder joined J. They nodded to each other with some urgency. "Call her Lily," J suggested.

"I'm Lily and I'm ready to get out of here. This place is teeming with … bad dogs," she said.

Marge blinked. Lily was lying about something. Marge wanted to say, my what large teeth you have. "Are y'all runaways?" Marge asked.

"Naw. Just outsiders. We have a non-biological family," J said. Her blue eyes were luminous.

"Our own pack," Lily confirmed. She had arresting eyes, too and smelled of roses.

Marge wasn't sure what she was missing, but when the hair on her neck bristled, she was ready to leave. These young women weren't lying. Besides, their quarry was long gone. "Mudder has escaped. Before we get lost, step in a hole, get caught in a cave in, or I hit my head, we are leaving," she said.

Archer cursed and staggered to his feet. He was wobbly, so Marge took one arm to guide him. Lily took the point while J dropped back to cover their rear. They shared a look like they knew something while the officers of the law were clueless. Could this be a set up? "Are you gals taking us snipe hunting?" Marge asked.

"No, ma'am. No wild gooses down here either. We're leaving, too. We just thought you might need a little help finding your way back out," J said.

"You can stay if you want. Your choice, no skin off my nose," Lily said.

The howling and baying of the hounds reached them. The group wordlessly agreed to hurry on. Lily padded quickly and quietly ahead. Sometimes J pushed them lightly from behind, encouraging them to keep up around the twists, turns and up the stairs.

"I am lost," Archer said. Marge agreed. She didn't recognize any of this.

"We aren't taking you back to the arena. This is a shorter route to fresh air."

"You don't want to meet more cops."

"We didn't want to meet you, but J convinced me that we had a moral duty since I was going to blow off my civil duty and ignore you. She's much nicer than I am," Lily said.

"What were you doing down here?" Marge asked. She couldn't help it. The dogs could already hear their footsteps. Talking would make no difference.

"We visited East Hill to place flowers on my granny's grave. I didn't think the dogs would be in the tunnels. Stupid me," Lily said. The twinge in Marge's neck said that the white-haired girl lied.

"These tunnels run to East Hill. How interesting," Marge said.

"Curiosity has killed more than just cats. If you want to flex yours, you might wind up six feet under. Or wait, we're farther under than that. Sorry, I was trying to be funny, you know, lighten the moment," Lily said.

Archer was growing tense. Marge had to admit that she was growing nervous. These gals seemed half-feral and dangerous, but then that's the way the homeless could seem if they'd lived outside too long. The pair moved confidently and secretively along the passages.

"I work with SART, the Sexual Assault Response Team. Were y'all slave traded?" Marge asked.

Lily chuckled. J just smiled and replied, "No, we'd rip their balls off." The young woman with the pink hair boldly told the truth. Her sweet smile didn't last. She was unafraid of sex traffickers, and yet there was no doubt that she was as restless as a hound with ticks and fleas about the dogs of East Hill. Marge would have to talk to the folks in animal control. This might explain the rash of attacks.

Wherever they were smelled much wetter, and the air felt damp and clingy. Archer looked at her and palmed his gun. His hand must be getting sweaty, too, and his patina of patience wore thin. Marge shook her head.

"Almost time to celebrate. We've reached Beaver Creek," Lily said. The wild pair let out relieved breaths. "Y'all can find your way once y'all get outside. I don't recommend going any deeper into the tunnels. Just walk toward the light, as they say, and you'll be in the park."

Madi heard music from the left. It grew louder, and she noticed a tall rectangular frame of light. A doorway, she realized. When Lily threw it open, it was like someone had opened their cage. Marge rushed out, lugging Archer with her. He stumbled outside, blinking in the dim light that seemed bright.

They stood in a tunnel with running water and the weak light of downtown. She thought that she knew where they were: under the city and along the canal where Beaver Creek flowed to minimize flooding. It was brighter to their left where she heard the music from the concert at Quaker Steak & Lube.

With waves and calls of farewell, Lily and J hurried off toward the music. Marge and Archer were on their own, but she knew this would exit into a park. Marge guided the wobbly Archer along the creek's bank until they reached fresh air and the outdoors of downtown. Cumberland Park and its parking lot awaited them. Breweries were on the other side of the creek. The Bristol Hotel sat south of the park. There were no black SUVs in sight. Had they been guided away? Marge wondered. Regardless, she felt safe. She had been getting a little edgy down there.

"He got away. I'm sorry, Rhett," Marge said.

"Aw, it was fun while it lasted," Archer replied sadly. He sounded like a man who would have to start all over again.

At least Marge felt that she had a lead on the Oktoberfest Vampire. She was curious about the underground tunnels, but she wasn't in a hurry to return. She would report this to the task force, animal control, and the city police.

Twenty-Four

Encounters at The Bristol Hotel

Closing in on midnight, Elke turned onto State Street, the city's main thoroughfare of shops, offices and restaurants, and headed north. They had to find a parking spot, despite the hour, due to the concert at Quaker Steak & Lube. They passed eateries and breweries that remained open for the event and numerous antique shops long closed.

Used goods stores throughout the area had been looted. The focus of the thefts seemed to be on things found on the shore or floating in South Holston Lake. Over the past two months, debris, clothing, housewares, and antiques had drifted to the surface, or been pushed ashore by the wind and shifting currents. Much of the flotsam was trash, but some people liked to have remnants of the underwater mansion. Elke and her agents purchased whatever they could find. So far, none of it was valuable, but Elke wanted to limit the extent of Von Damme's taint. After the jewelry box, there was concern that the mad alchemist might still exist and find a way to escape his ruined, underwater tomb.

"I can't stop thinking about what happened to Rae. Von Damme must have gotten a thrill out of scaring people and lording over them," Dillon said.

Elke's eyes grew flinty. "You're right. It could be something he concocted."

"Can the Shaden spread like wildfire, or like a virus?" Dillon asked. Here he was, cruising around downtown like a teen, and he no longer mixed with his hometown. Or did he? There were some odd denizens that called this green slice of Appalachia home.

"If there is enough fear, they can split or multiply. Where there are a few, there are probably many. I am unsure if more are drawn, created or generated."

"That is a problem with keeping everything secret," Dillon said. She frowned. "What?"

"I've heard that said before."

"Did Von Damme write things down?" Dillon asked.

"If it went against the wishes and rules of RON, the answer is yes. It creates quite the pickle, doesn't it?"

"One dipped in arsenic," Dillon replied. He finally voiced what bothered him most. "You know Knives is conducting his own investigation."

"Yes. I hope we can dissuade as needed, much as before."

After what had happened in August, Elke had several encounters and chats with Knives and J-Man. Neither remembered anything that would harm the vampires. J-Man simply recalled Von Damme's bat form as a swarm of bats. None of the other blood brothers recalled that Marader was more than he seemed, transformed in ways that would leave them astounded and worried. They had already wondered about Troy. The blood brothers had always been amazed that he still lived. Ending up with Silke, Troy seemed divinely lucky.

Dillon knew better, but he prayed that they would stay thrilled with each other.

"I've had second thoughts about that. I can't help but wonder what he might find. It might give us an idea what the myth huntress went diving into. Does Dragomir have scientists on his staff? Or is that why he wants the myth huntress and Zhen to poke around and run experiments?" Dillon asked. He figured vampires were anti-science. Von Damme's interest and use of it certainly had splintered the Rulers of Night.

"Good questions. Vampires are secretive by supernature, as you have come to realize. Hoyt is working on things as well. It helps him to have something to focus on. I will inform Dragomir of Knives' findings. The LSD in their bodies disturbs me. Von Damme was looking for an additive that would make the effects of smoking similar to those experienced while drinking hooch. In the meantime, they grew cannabis alongside tobacco. His mountain top tabacca was about half marijuana. He had learned that from the Cherokee and other natives who inhaled various medicinal herbs."

She parked the car on the street near Grand Antiques and waited for him to open her door. Dillon looked over to the State Street store, saw the closed sign but noted the lights were on within. Long ago, the three-story brick warehouse had been a Grand Furniture store. Now it housed an indoor flea market with a Grand Piano in the storefront display window and hundreds of booths of vintage furnishings and classic collectibles on the first two floors. The third was being turned into apartments.

Elke treasured her visits to antique stores. Strolling through history, she called it. She had quietly helped Bessie McCracken and her family open up their own place by donating several valuable items, which is why she had a key. Dillon heard a small dog bark. Elke smiled, opened the door, and rapped on the wood when she entered the shop. "That was Martha Mae, her dog. Knock! Knock!

Bessie? It's Elke and Dillon! I hear three heartbeats. One seems much stronger," she said.

Something large fell over in the back room.

***

In the storage room, Bessie McCracken was looking for a hat someone had found floating in the lake. The crushed velvet Fedora had the initials VVD on it. She couldn't find it anywhere. She had hoped to have it ready for Ms. Swearington to examine when she arrived any minute.

Bessie was ready to get home. At least she knew that Carol Snowen was resting comfortably. Poor Mr. Fredericks had died right before their eyes. Now they were all traumatized.

Sheilah said she saw the poor man's ghost depart. He had waved farewell. Suzanne said she felt death's glance.

Bessie shivered. She couldn't forget the strange shadow that she'd seen in the mirror, which is why all the lights were on, making it bright inside. The shadows were crisp, many of them strange shapes cast by the collection of odd objects in the back. She found herself glaring at the shadows now and then. None of them moved, although there were spine-tingling moments when she thought that they stared back.

Martha Mae woke up and started barking. She jumped out to protect Bessie, but each bark sent the little dog backwards. Bessie felt chilly fingers slip around her neck like a noose. She found it hard to breath, having to cough. Turning, she found nobody, but the back door stood wide open.

She hurried over to shut it. She would have sworn that she had closed and locked it. Well, after today, she wasn't surprised that she was a little addle-brained. Suddenly, she had the sense that she and Martha Mae weren't alone.

"Who's there?" she asked.

The ghost of Donna appeared and pointed behind Bessie.

"Knock! Knock! Bessie? It's Elke and Dillon!"

Bessie breathed a sigh of relief. She had been imagining things. That thought had just passed when she noticed the really big dog. With its eyes locked on Martha Mae, the beast stalked forward. Bessie grabbed a bat. When the snarling animal lunged, she started swinging to protect her little dog.

***

Dillon and Elke charged ahead. A baseball bat in hand, Bessie was sprawled on the floor, boxes and items not yet on display spilled around her. A shaky Chihuahua tried to hide under her legs.

A cool breeze rushed in the back door which bumped against the wall. Elke checked on her friend, handing her glasses to her. "Easy, Bessie. It's Elke," she said.

Dillon darted outside and looked up and down Winston Alley. He expected an attack and encountered a bored cat. Nothing had startled it. He saw no sign of anyone running up or down the alley, but there were couples and groups walking back to their cars and trucks. It seemed the Double Tap concert was over. The thief could easily lose himself in the departing crowd, but then there were many old buildings where someone could hide. He made a cursory check of the area, listening for sounds as well as looking and smelling for clues. Nothing of interest caught his senses.

On his way back inside, he found a tuft of gray hair. He stuffed it in his pocket. As he rose, he noticed scratch marks along the door frame and wall. In the past, he wouldn't have given it much thought, but now, he wondered, looking at the fur, if the intruder might have been a werewolf.

Hoping Bessie was only shaken up, Dillon returned inside. "How are you feeling?"

"I'm fine, Dillon. Don't fuss over me, but thank you for helping me up, Elke."

"Key gives me a lift all the time," Dillon said. Elke beamed.

"Look at you two. You're made for each other. You know, I may have thrown out my back swinging that bat. Y'all coming in must have spooked it. The big dog was hiding there," Bessie said. She paused in stretching her back to point to a group of spilled and crumpled boxes standing among a broken lamp and mirror. "What a mess! It must have snuck in when I took a bunch of stuff out back to the dumpster. If Donna's ghost hadn't spooked it, and y'all's arrival hadn't sent it running, who knows what would've happened to me. Whew! I bless the Good Lord for y'all and that I'm all right, yes, I am. We McCrackens are a resilient breed. Even so maybe I should sit down. Dennis will be by soon," she said.

Elke assisted her to a stool. "What about the cape you called me about?" his beloved asked.

"Let me get it for you," Bessie said and stood.

Elke steadied her as the store owner lost her balance. She guided Bessie back to the stool. "Whoa, I guess I'm not as steady as I thought. It's on the table," she said.

The cape sprawled on the expanse of wood. Dillon picked up the silk garment by a shimmering corner. The underside gleamed with symbols and runes. Elke appeared to recognize it or some of the writing, but it might as well have been Greek to Dillon.

"Those are Von Damme's initials," Elke said.

"You said you wanted to know about anything that might be associated with him and his place. The fisherman who brought it in suffered a heart attack. The strangest thing happened," Bessie said. She explained about the sudden wind and the dark figure running when Reverend Bob St. Martin had entered.

"That sounds like an awful experience and scary for Sheilah and Carol Snowen. I hope they get well soon. Bessie, you should call the police and report what just happened. You've been assaulted," Dillon said.

"By a big dog," Bessie replied, a little chagrined.

"They can report it to animal control. It's still running loose," Elke said.

"I heard Andrea Wilson was bitten when a capture went wrong. People aren't talking about the downtown attacks because they are nowhere near as sensational as the Oktoberfest Vampire's killings," Bessie said and dialed her phone. They waited while Bessie made a call to the station just up the street. She assured the dispatcher that she was safe, and it wasn't an emergency. They decided to wait with her until her husband or the police arrived.

Money seemed to appear in Elke's left hand as if by stage magic, and she placed the roll of greenbacks in the palm of Bessie's hand. She looked down, blinked, and did a double take. She wobbled, on the brink of fainting. She pulled herself together with a hand to her forehead. "You must think the cape is very valuable."

"I do, and I know you have your daughter's medical school bills to pay. You can also think of it as reminder to keep your eyes open for more such finds," Elke said.

"And hazard pay," Dillon said. He heard a truck drive up outside. A horn beeped outside. "I'll let Dennis know to park and come in," Dillon said.

***

Elke drove several blocks deeper down into the main shopping area off State Street, past the Burger Bar, and the Country Music Museum to the entrance of The Bristol Hotel. The place appeared to be jumping tonight. The local iconic cyclist, Shamas, rode by and waved. As soon as he passed, the valet stepped lively to Elke's side of her Corvette.

"Good evening, Ms. Swearington!" the young man smiled as he opened her car door.

She rose and took Dillon's arm. "You know Judge Dragomir said that he didn't want to see me again," Dillon said as he gestured for Elke to enter ahead of him. He followed her under the Roman arch and into the bistro hotel. It had retained some of its early 20th century charm with stucco and brick facades. Large windows would let daylight into the lobby, but now they only reflected the indoor electric light back at them. Since they were wearing cosmetics, they actually had reflections.

"I think he'll want to look you in the eyes after I tell him that you encountered Goran," Elke said.

"Dillon? Hey, Dillon, it is you!"

He turned, recognizing the deep voice. He had known the horror fiction writer Stephen Semones for much of his life, going back to high school. The big man with the glasses and the dapper beard wore a huge smile and a hunting hat.

"I haven't seen you in coon's ages. Are you here to investigate the Oktoberfest Vampire? Are you a believer yet?" Stephen asked with a smirk.

"Good to see you, man. I'm certainly a believer that people believe, much like those in the Cult of the Vampire," Dillon replied.

"Oh, that's just a cover up," said a slim man who joined them. He stood close to Stephen as if he were guarding him. One of Bond's brothers and a longtime friend, CJ Wills, were missing persons.

"My bud, Renn Bond," Stephen said.

"I recognize the name. Investigator of haunted places," Dillon said. He introduced Elke, and they were charmed. What else could they be? Bond no longer acted hostile toward Dillon.

"You're welcome to join us. My new book just came out. It's at Kathy Barlow-Weaver's Books Galore and Books-A-Million this weekend," Stephen said.

"Congratulations! Just in time for Halloween next week. That's fantastic news!" Dillon said.

"I wish we could, but we have a meeting with a client. Dillon isn't working, but I am. He is my plus one," Elke said.

"How is the research for your book coming?" Bond asked.

"Slow and confusing, and yet, I hope it sheds some new light on what happened," Dillon replied.

"So, do you believe there were vampires? Or people pretending to be vampires?" Bond asked.

"If you think you're a vampire and act accordingly, does that make you one?" Dillon asked.

"Ah, always asking those deep questions," Stephen said. He looked to Elke, reading her body language, and getting the message. "See you later, Dillon. You can be strange but don't be a stranger. Come find me at the Outlaw Church sometime," Stephen said. Semones guided Bond back to the bar and restaurant.

Dillon and Elke waited on the elevator. Should he suggest they hold their meeting elsewhere? Elke had assured him that vampires were the master of the silent kill. What could go wrong?

"So, they are looking for supernatural creatures?" Elke asked.

"Bond is. Stephen is doing research for fiction."

"And to think they just met what they were looking for."

"Funny. I wonder how often we're looking for something, and when we find it, we don't realize it," Dillon mused. He needed to regain his focus. "Do you think Dragomir knows about Goran?"

"He is superior, not omniscient, although he would like you to believe the latter."

Dillon was struck speechless when the elevator doors opened. He couldn't believe his bad luck. What was she doing here, right now, in this time and place? He stood still, hoping Gina didn't notice him.

"Dillon! How lucky can I get? I have been trying to reach you," Gina said. She lunged out of the elevator to embrace him, saw Elke's expression, and took a step back.

"We have a meeting with a client. How are you?" he said.

"I'm a little shaky, but I'm settling down, getting there. Hello, you must be Elke."

"Key is my stars and moon," Dillon said. He could see that Gina didn't remember her.

"We are mutually lovestruck," Elke admitted, gazing longingly at Dillon. He couldn't resist kissing her, and she smiled winsomely.

"Who are you meeting?" Gina asked. She looked a little ill. Dillon wanted this over as well. The longer they chatted, the more time that Gina had to become suspicious. She had an exceptional sense for hidden and unusual stories.

"An art collector who'd rather remain anonymous," Elke replied coolly. Dillon expected her to send Gina away, but Elke remained patient.

"What happened at the dam?" Dillon asked. He wanted to see if she remembered him at all.

"I blacked out, so I really don't remember. A guy in a skeleton mask attacked me. I guess we fought. The next thing I recall, I was sitting in my car shaking in my boots," Gina said.

"You're always telling me that you can take care of yourself. It's great to see that you're right and uninjured," Dillon said. He could see that Gina wondered if saying that had been a mistake. He couldn't tell her that it made no difference to their relationship.

"Hey, Urich!"

Dillon recognized the voice right away. It was Concannon. The air conditioning brought the scent of cigarettes and coffee. Dillon never wanted to talk with the popinjay. Furthermore, Dillon didn't want to give any support to the man's beliefs, which Dillon had once berated, despite becoming a prime unliving example.

"I want to talk to you about your book, but you keep dodging me!" Concannon said. The loudmouth rolled in from the bar on a cloud of beer and wine. He didn't look drunk. He appeared his usual, handsome, narcissistic self.

"Cane. Go away! Stay away!" Dillon said in a low harsh voice. He put all his dislike into the command. The media personality spun on his heel and fled like he saw someone who he owed money.

"Oh, so that's Cane Concannon. Yep, blowhard written all over him, right over the top of a lot of me, me, and mine. I see them in Texas all the time," Gina said.

Elke gave Dillon the nod of approval. "I apologize. You will think me rude by having to meet and run," Elke said.

"I like people who are on time and honor their commitments. Can you tell me about the book, later? Oh, God, I sound like Concannon, don't I? That's horrible. I am so, so sorry," Gina said.

"You can read an early draft when I finish. There's more digging, so it won't be soon. Good night," Dillon said. He didn't want to linger here, and yet, he wasn't looking forward to his next encounter on the rooftop, either. Gina wouldn't believe it, but just being his friend could be the death of her. Anyone who loved him would be in even greater danger.

"Now I really want you by my side. I don't trust her or Concannon. She certainly didn't go back home to Texas like I compelled. I hate to think that I'm losing my touch, so to speak, or that she loves you so very much she could ignore my command. Either could be an issue," Elke said.

When the doors opened, Dillon and Elke started to stroll out together into the open air of the rooftop restaurant. He heard heartbeats, so he expected to meet people. It looked like a costume party was underway, faux undead and authentic supernatural beings mingling. Elke was surprised and agitated to be met by four witches, each a different color, reminding Dillon a bit of the three faeries, less colorfully attired, plus one, from *Sleeping Beauty*. Their faces were youthful, but their eyes belied that truth, holding witness to the passing of many years and lives. Four sets of hawkish gazes focused on him, more if you counted the extra eyes found on the one wearing earthy colors. Dillon sensed power here, a crackling undercurrent of tension like they were connected to an electric cable.

"Well, here's a sight for my weary eyes, the prodigal daughter and her consort. This is a treat," the witch in gray said. She stood the tallest. Her blue eyes and her accent called to mind the Carolinas.

"Fortunately, he looks under control if you ask me," the one clad in blue edged with black said. From under her hat, Dillon heard a fragile heartbeat, so he wasn't surprised when a raven peeked out to examine him, too. The woman suddenly reached out to cup Dillon's chin. Her hand smelled of patchouli. "He's quite handsome. I can see why Elke is taken with him. What do you think, Alicia?"

"Of course, he's easy on the eyes. But if you look in his eyes, Donna, you'll see that he's smart, too. And that Elke hasn't mentioned us to him," the witch in the purple robe said. A belt shaped like a snake looped around her waist. She also wore a necklace of bloodstones and moonstones, cymbals for rings, and a pair of turtle shell earrings. She brought with her an air of musk, patchouli, Marlboros, and Mountain Dew. Border collie pins sat on her shoulders, watching her back, so to speak.

The earth-robed witch pinched his cheek like he was a distant relative. "He's adorable, Alicia, but he's still in the gray year, and anything can happen. If he's not careful, he could literally become a killer diller," Darla chuckled. Her face paint made her skin resemble bark, giving her the presence of an earth spirit. Curly, strawberry-blond hair draped on each side of her face like pretty vines. Black cosmetics surrounded her eyes, making them appear as deeply recessed knotholes. In her forehead sat an open third eye. Its stare was disarming. She wore a black fur stole around her shoulders that stretched and opened its green feline eyes. She even carried a walking stick carved with eyes to go with her button of an all-seeing eye.

"Good evening, ladies. Miss Becky, you're a long way from South Carolina. How's the real estate business at Bower, Boyle, and Boyer Reality?" Elke asked.

"Booming. Unfortunately, so is the undead population here, there and in between. Many of them don't purchase or rent, they just squat or live like nomads. The Carolinas, Virginia and Tennessee have come together to expedite this issue. This is: Donna, Darla, and Alicia," Becky of the 3B Reality said and smiled. Her salesperson smile lit up the gathering, literally. The next blink, the white robe under her gray began to shine brightly, the painful light peeking out from its folds.

"Turn out that . . . light!" someone yelled with a profanity to describe and condemn the glare.

"Oops! I didn't mean to do that," she said, seeing Dillon wince. He heard groans from around the restaurant. The dress went dark, and everybody around her sighed with relief. "My apologies, everyone."

"You're Dillon Urich, a Tennessee High grad and a journalist of minor renown, as well as an exceptional mixed martial arts expert. We have our eyes on you, buster, and we won't tolerate any abuse of Elsa," Donna said. She tilted a Firebolt 3000 broom wafting of sandalwood at him.

Minor renown? Abuse Elsa? Dillon didn't feel a spell, but he felt insulted. He grew warier with every word and gesture. Before he could retort, like Venus rising over the horizon, Elke gently took his arm.

"He's my man. I'm very fortunate. And I go by Elke now," Key purred.

His beloved eyes glinted with the unspoken proclamation, he's mine. Dillon squeezed her hand.

"Whatever butters your biscuit," Donna said.

"The brooms are a nice touch, ladies. Beware of drones when you're flying," Elke said.

"I feel like flying off, but I don't want to make a scene. So, the elevator it is," Alicia said.

"Good call. Some people think we're Halloween witches while others think we're with the cleaning staff," Donna said and finished with a roll of her eyes.

"Dragomir's in a mood, so be wary," Darla said. When she winked at Dillon, her eyes changed color from hazel to green.

"Thanks for the warning. So, the sandalwood didn't work?" Elke asked.

"He's greatly perturbed by all the vampires running loose, as are we all," Alicia said. She smiled prettily at Dillon who in return batted his eyes. She blinked in surprise. That used to baffle the young women at Tennessee High and Appalachian State University.

"As I said, they are even reaching the coast, running from something or someone here," Miss Becky of 3Bs Reality said.

"From us?" Elke asked.

"Or Destrange or Butcher. I have heard both their names and descriptions," Alicia said.

Mones cleared his throat. Tonight, he was dressed as Fezzik from *The Princess Bride*, meaning he had bushy hair, big eyebrows, and wore an Apocalypse Robe that burned with ethereal flames.

"Excuse us, we must get going, especially if Dragomir is in a mood," Elke said. She took Dillon's arm. He stepped out of the way and gestured for the ladies to pass.

"Keep your head, Mr. Urich. May your meeting go well, Elke, dear," Donna said. The elevator doors closed on their stern expressions.

"So, there are vampires, werewolves, ghosts and witches?" he mused. She nodded.

"Yes, they are as real as you and I. They are an important part of the supernatural community. The coven was instrumental in imprisoning Von Damme. They enchanted the fire opals," she replied.

"How are you the prodigal child?"

"My mother was a witch. I am not," Elke said.

"You bewitched me," he said.

"You are so sweet, my love. Which seems to mean you can disobey my compelling and do whatever you want if you think you're protecting me or making me happy in the long run. Not the same," she replied.

More Jack-o'-lanterns and skeletons had been added to the restaurant's holiday decor. After what had happened at the dam, Dillon kept an eye on them. Light cavorted and flickered, making the whole rooftop and furnishings seem to be on the border between real and dreamlike. Several of the separated lounges were full of costumed revelers, one looking like a fest of movie villains. He wasn't pleased to see The Joker, but this one had a life glow, as did Jason, Freddie and a person-sized, red-haired Chucky doll. The young man had the crazy look down, either that, or he was related to Jon Gruden of NFL infamy.

The bar stools were crowded with costumers in Star Wars' outfits, from Jedi and Sith to Clones and Storm Troopers. All of them possessed life auras without the darkside of The Force or creatures of the Shadowlands around them. The bar was attended by a pretty brunette with long tresses and dressed in a red vest and a white collar as if she were Vampirella from the horror comics. Even under all the cosmetics, hair extensions, and faux vampire teeth, Dillon knew her as Tammie Myles, mixologist extraordinaire. Way back when, she had served him while they celebrated his 21st birthday party out on the town. Of course, Marader had tried to hit on her. She forgave Dillon for it, though.

"Ah, one of my agents is here. Tampire is our bartender tonight. That's right, you know Tammie. She hopes to be a vampire some-day. Would you care for a drink while you wait?" Elke asked.

He nodded. It was safer to stay out of Dragomir's sight. He might be offended that Dillon was in his presence on the same roof top. "You'll find me here, at the Star Wars cantina," Dillon said. They kissed before she sashayed after Fezzik Mones to the shadowy corner of the restaurant, a section as far away as possible from Bristol's brightly lit sign shining over the railroad tracks.

Dark-haired, dark-eyed Tammie from Blountville was tidying the bar. She wore red, as usual, to go with black pants. Spills from the Bloody Mary mix and bloodstains would be equally well hidden atop those colors. She was dressed modestly for the sexy Vampirella, but it was chilly up here on an autumn night if you weren't one with the darkness. Tammie wasn't cold because a heater ran behind the bar.

"Wow, Dillon Urich. It's been half of forever since I've seen you. You go off into the big world, become a success, and forget about us who still live in your hometown."

"Not true. I came back every year."

"For a reunion with your buds, I'll bet. I'm sorry about what happened to Spider, Denny, and John. They were good guys," she said sadly.

"They were. They deserved better. I'd hoped we were over the need for so many caskets, but then we have the Oktoberfest Vam-pire. By the way, I'm no longer visiting. I'm living here now."

"Wonderful! I see you are with Ms. Swearington. I love working for her. She seems to know just what people's skills and talents are. She puts me in places where I can succeed that pay the bills, too.

It's been right up my alley, nights, tending bar, music, people and excitement. So, Bristol," Tammie said.

"You're a wonderful set of eyes and ears," Dillon said.

"Thank you kindly. Usually males comment on my other body parts below my neck. What would you have? A shot of liquid courage?" she asked.

"Do I look like I need it?" Dillon asked.

"Whiskey or tequila?" she asked without batting an eye.

"Jack Daniels, honeyed, if you have it," he said.

She slid him a shot. "This will make your tongue slap your brain," she said.

He threw it back. The warmth in his stomach rushed throughout his body. It reminded him to relax. He couldn't fight Dragomir if he decided to end Dillon. "Ah, you have a bartender's sense. What you said is all true. If I screw up, a lot of people suffer the consequences."

"Then only have that one. As a journalist, this can't be the first time that you've put your friends and family in danger," she said.

Before he could reply, Simon Mones appeared and tipped Fezzik's crumpled hat. "Good evening, Mr. Urich."

"Good to be alive. It's been an eventful evening, that's for sure," Dillon said.

Mones blinked. "Ah, you've seen Goran. That darkens it, doesn't it? Lucky you, first Destrange, and now Goran. You must be resilient."

"My eyes are an open book?" Dillon asked.

"I was stunned by him once. I recognize the ozone scent," Mones frowned.

"Sounds like I need to wear cologne," Dillon said.

"Ha. Perhaps I should be guarding your body. It does sound as if you would make good bait. I could be disguised as a bottle of Brut."

Dillon wondered if he should be laughing with the one who might kill him. But then, why not?

"If you get any closer to Judge Dragomir, I will have to kill you," a voice whispered in Dillon's ear. He couldn't see anyone, so he'd been visited by the invisible or drifting smoke with a voice. Sometimes, often times, this new world was so strange.

"That was Painter. Don't let him get your goat. He likes to be spooky," Mones said.

"Believe me, I feel like bait. You know how accepting the RON community is of newcomers," Dillon said and gigged Mones. The big man's laugh was loud and jarring. It bellowed and echoed among the downtown buildings. Birds were startled. Somewhere a heron sounded aggrieved. Tammie, Mones, and Dillon shared a look, and then they all laughed. If Dillon was going to die, laughing was a better way than most, but he wouldn't leave Key unprotected.

***

Painter materialized out of the fog and smoke to float alongside Elke. As usual, he wore a t-shirt with hot women and hot cars. She couldn't discern his features, but she knew it was him. "Be nice to my consort. He's great to me and for me. Have you been doing any new work?"

"Does the downtown graffiti count?" he asked.

"That's you they're calling the streetwise Michelangelo? I love what you did in Johnson City," she said.

"You know, me and Banksy," Painter replied with a chuckle. He guided her to the dark patch where Judge Dragomir lounged with Kate on one side and Dawnstar reclined on the other. The moonlight graced their features, their shadows darker and their faces bright with anticipation.

Judge Dragomir was dressed once again to the hilt. His golden, feline eyes seemed brighter than before.

"You are looking lively tonight, Elsa," Kate said.

"I'm in love, and my love survived a trap set by Goran. His truck didn't, but he lives and learns," Elke replied.

"I told you I have no wish to see him again. Why have you brought him along?" Dragomir asked. He gestured irritably to ward Dillon away.

"I was going to have him wait in the lobby, but too many people know him," Elke said.

"Why don't you kill his ex? That's simpler. When Gina decides to investigate us, we will have to do it anyway," Kate said. Dragomir nodded as if he were hearing sage advice.

"I thought you might want to ask him questions and see for yourself," Elke said.

"Your report will do. Being in his presence . . . pains me. So, it is true that Goran has remained in this area along with Destrange. It is well that we have come. Dawnstar has foreseen there will be an unleashing of supernatural forces in the next several days."

"Do you ever consider that they wanted you to come here?" she asked.

He nodded. "It would come as no surprise if Von Damme's minions are behind most of this city's problems. Tell me, what did they find diving today? I feel you bursting with disturbing news," Dragomir said.

"They found eight skulls in the ruins and brought them to the surface. It was night, so they survived. Two are human, and six are vampire," Elke pointed out.

He remained quiet, his stare boring a hole through her. He was not really looking at her but staring back into the past. "The skulls of the six who sacrificed?" he finally whispered. She saw a rare emotion in his eyes: concern.

Elke nodded. "What else could it be? The FBI has five of the vampires, plus two human ones. Juju kept a vampire skull without the agents knowing about it," she told him.

Dawnstar looked quite perturbed, having developed a tic near her left eye. Kate was nervous enough to begin to pace.

"I should pay a visit to the FBI agents. We are already on their radar due to what happened over the summer and the cultist's activities. I much prefer the media's reference to the Six Fingered Cult than the Appalachian Vampire Cult. We don't want to give them any proof. I think I may begin at Maraders Marina. I suspect you are right to be concerned that the woman scientist, Zhen, will run tests on it later tonight while the FBI will send theirs off to be examined. Is there anything else?" Dragomir said.

Elke pulled the cape from her large purse and handed it to Dragomir. He looked mildly surprised, his eyebrows raised, but he took it from her to examine it. "There in your hands is Viktor's cloak, but his shadow's gone. I wonder where Cloaker is now?"

"Do you recall what Viktor used to say about his shadow?" Dragomir asked.

"I do. That it could split itself."

"I believe Von Damme spoke the truth. I can see Viktor foolishly empowering a shadow to suit his needs and tasks. He thought boundaries were to be crossed and explored. This has not been the way of vampires who enjoy longevity," Dawnstar said.

Elke stared into the judge's eyes. She thought back to what Dillon had said about fighting Bonz. "Do you recognize this darkness and ruby radiance? The force animating the skeleton reminds me of curse of The Shadow of the Vampire mentioned in Von Damme's journals," she said.

"That he planned to create more Cloakers and unleash them on the people? Or the fear plague that he hoped to unleash before they completed construction of the dam?"

"If we had waited much longer, he would have. I know he was close to a breakthrough. He was raving about it. He used to rant that everyone would scare themselves to death, some kind of fear pox," Elke said.

"Yes, I have heard him say much the same."

"That's not all that seems wrong. There's something amiss in this area of the Shadowlands, too. Have you noticed?" she asked and then described what they had seen, including being attacked. Dawnstar was nodding along with Elke's words.

All here knew that Von Damme had created a doorway to access, enthrall and employ shadows. The earthen basin and coins help ground the gate and hold it in place. He had used shadows to cause so-called accidents and deaths during the building of the dam. Destrange had supervised the operation.

"The Parisian certainly could be the cause of the spreading fog that you see in the Shadowlands. He has the skill, and the Word-smith saw him. We are already looking into that," he said.

Elke figured that could be where Stiletto and One Feather were tonight.

Judge Dragomir was thoughtful before he spoke. "Viktor Von Damme was a maker. He was also a futurist or thought of himself as such. He was both trying to invent the future to fit him or prepare to deal with it if it didn't. He was quite a collector, too. Supposedly, he kept many of his prize possessions in an underground safe."

"In the emergency shelter," Elke said. Few knew about Von Damme's survivalist bunker.

"Yes. Those would be unlikely to rise to the surface, but there have been minor earthquakes in that area. Viktor didn't just tap into the Shadowlands for his own power, he turned its essence into potions and arcane objects. I have wondered if the myth huntress was inspired or employed by Butcher or Goran to bring something to the surface," he asked.

"We suspected at least one of Viktor's good ole boys remained here because someone is stealing items from antique stores, specifically various remnants from Von Damme's mansion. I think it's more than treasure hunters, and tonight a werewolf was getting ready to rob Grand Antiques when we walked in. I'm curious what they, whoever it is, hope to find. This time, they got one of Viktor's hats. Lastly, Miles Jasper stopped to help Dillon after Goran took flight. He thought Dillon had wrecked his truck," Elke said.

"And Dillon lives? He is either lucky or like a cat with nine lives," Dragomir said.

"The hunter is confused by a vampire with a heart of light. It doesn't fit his black and white perspective. Dillon's aura of life aided him in this instance," Dawnstar surmised.

"You know the myth huntress will dive for more coins," Elke said.

"The wealth is of no consequence, but the gate concerns me. It will be much more difficult to deal with."

"Madi Marader wants to open it or explore behind it."

Dragomir waved off that worry. "Unlikely, and yet, it could be that the creature you fought could have slipped through that gate if it has been left ajar. And if one feargorger can slip through, then so will other Shaden," he said.

"What would you like us to do?" Elke asked.

"Continue to watch and report to me. Now, please take your consort away before he has my bodyguards laughing so hard they lose their focus," Dragomir said.

Elke smiled. Dillon had such interesting effects on those around him.

Twenty-Five

Downtown Wolf

A little earlier, Miles downshifted the tow truck's gears, his pursuit vehicle fishtailing through a right turn at Sixth Street in historic downtown Bristol. With special airless tires, aluminum wheels, rack and pinion steering, and all its customizations, the truck handled like a Porsche SUV, but the Miles Towing Truck still had difficulty keeping up with a werewolf. Miles had been following Elke Swearington and Dillon Urich. He had been staking out Grand Antiques when he spotted the monster crawling atop the building. The wolfman wore a burr cut, had only half a tail, and green eyes that glowed like a cat's when they saw each other. With the concert just finished, Miles had carefully woven among people as he followed the lycan's rooftop movements. What had started as a creeping pursuit had turned into an all-out, balls to the wall chase.

Thank Grace for engineers, Mile's thought, as he steered to skid through a right turn onto Crumley Alley. It was much narrower, and the werewolf ran along the walls to avoid obstacles. Miles felt a little guilty plowing through them, including a small fence.

Most people didn't notice the supernatural, or preferred to ignore it, even wish it away, but not Miles Jasper. He had been born with senses beyond normal ken and had keenly honed them to detect the undead and other monsters of supernature. The only good werewolf was a dead werewolf. The same was true of vampires, except the nightwalkers needed to be destroyed to be slain, not merely killed. He used completely different weapons to deal with a feral lycanthrope as compared to a vampire.

The werewolf darted right onto Seventh Street. Miles stomped on the gas. The souped-up tow truck leapt ahead, closing the gap between it and the fleeing lycan. He might only get one shot at this. He reached out the window with his left hand and fired at the werewolf's back. It helped to be ambidextrous and a crack shot. The bullets were tracers, so he could follow their trajectory. He watched as two of them struck the target. The werewolf staggered. Normal bullets didn't bother this hairy monster or any lycanthrope, but in this case, the silver-jacketed slugs worked like hollow points.

The werewolf turned suddenly, dashing into the parking lot of Boyd's Bicycle Shop. Miles followed, Grace-bent on catching it. The truck's tires skidded and squealed, and then he corrected but had to brake to a sudden on-a-dime stop. Straight ahead a creek ran through downtown. The beast jumped into the weeds along the shore to duck under the headlights and disappear.

Miles threw open the door and followed a few steps. He saw the werewolf dart into a tunnel where the creek flowed. The darkness ran easterly. This could be a trap. Grace and common-sense caution told him that following the monster underground was a terrible idea. Miles preferred the alpine woods and the mountain peaks to goblin and troll lairs.

If he recalled his map correctly, Beaver Creek ran downhill to Cumberland Park. He had heard people call it Freedom Park due to its theme and memorials. He returned to his tow truck and turned on the collision avoidance system. It would detect anything sneaking up on him. He popped a burnt marshmallow Jelly Belly into his mouth, tipped his hat back, and pulled out his smart phone to use the tracking app. The tracers were double tracing, leaving fiery streaks in the air and inserting microchips that could be followed by GPS.

Nothing showed up on the display. He would have to drive until the werewolf returned above ground. For the next few minutes, Miles cruised downtown. He had done this earlier to get a feel for the area, its bakeries, breweries, performing arts theaters, wealth of antique stores, music venues, tattoo parlors and curios shops, including a comic book seller for the Mountain Empire. Bristol had recently embraced liquor by the drink, and that change had brought legal fermenters and more restaurants to downtown in the light of the Bristol A GOOD PLACE TO LIVE sign and in view of the large red brick, First Baptist Church. He had been fortunate to find a docent who gave him a guided tour earlier today. For a generous donation, he had been blest with holy water.

Not that long ago, but a life ago, Miles had been in love. His girl, Cindy Delaney, went to work at a casino in Tahoe, the Twilight Paradise. Too late, he realized she had received the third kiss of the vampire and had been turned into a lost soul. His grandfather had paid the price and died from her feasting, although no one else had believed that truth. Miles had found Zane Caine, and the Son of Galahad had helped Miles find his path and send Zennon on his way. Miles hadn't been able to locate Cindy to redeem her, but Zennon had avenged the loss of his grandfather. Miles' altered ego had slain fifteen vampires before exposing a convention of gambling lost souls to the sunlight and redeeming the lot.

He recalled his encounter with Dillon Urich. Miles had seen many accidents. No one living should have survived that impact, but the odd character with the dark aura of a lost soul and the heart chakra of one alive had crawled out and walked away from the wreckage.

The vampires out west would be looking for Miles. He had come here to escape on vacation, because the locals reveled in country music, auto and drag racing, plus, they had built a casino. He had attended a race just last weekend, and he hadn't seen any supernaturals. He wondered if it would be different at the Hard Rock. In such places, he often found lost souls sometimes called bloodsuckers and vampires.

The Appalachians were smaller than the Sierra, but this part of God's Country was beautiful, rolling, colorful, and homey. Bristol was here because of its waterways and railroads, thanks to George L. Carter, just one of many Carters from Virginia that made the region better through vision, labor, or song. Earlier today, he had visited the Birthplace of Country Music Museum and the old train station. Railroads had shaped the west as well, especially Reno, NV, where Miles had racked up gaming points and vampire kills.

Despite this twin cities' problems, including the funk from the dump in the air, Miles felt a strong presence of Grace in this place. He had just thought that he had been enjoying a vacation. Grace had brought him here, he realized, after what had happened in August. It must not be over and more than the Oktoberfest Vampire.

Miles missed those who had helped him save Heather Winslow, but they weren't born to hunt like the Sons of Galahad. It wasn't like he was going to call someone for help. Vampire hunting was lonely business. There was no guild or union. No Vampire Hunters Conferences in sunny Miami or San Diego. Sometimes hunters had taken on apprentices, as Zane Caine had done with Miles. From what he recalled, both from journal entries and shared memories, having a partner usually ended poorly, but then, so did being a vampire hunter. There was no retirement, but as far as he knew and felt, Zane Caine was alive somewhere and redeeming lost souls.

So, Miles Jasper worked alone because nobody else could resist the vampires' compelling powers, their awe-inspiring facades, their cloying charm, hypnotizing gazes, and commanding words. A partner would just get them both killed. Batman wasn't the only one who worked alone. Of course, he referenced the movies and not the comic books with their Robins and Nightwing. Still, in the majority of his work, The Batman fought crime without partners.

Miles' phone beeped. The tracer dot appeared on the display map at the downtown park. The dot quit moving, so he raced to investigate. He would be able to tail it when it left.

And yet, the dot remained motionless, giving Miles reason to grow concerned. He said the Prayer of Protection and the Paladins' Credo. When he pulled up in his truck, he didn't see the werewolf at first. He was almost distracted by the Indian Scout motorcycle. It was in exceptional condition, its chrome shining golden in the streetlight. Miles yanked his attention away.

For a moment, he worried that the werewolf had removed the bullets, left them, and fled. He didn't expect to find a dark-haired biker chick in Dreamkickers spinning a silver baton while she sat next to a cuffed and stunned werewolf. Miles thought that he might be bedazzled, too, sitting next to such company. She possessed a welcoming, purple and gold aura, so she wasn't a vampire. Her face wore neither sun nor wind lines from those days spent on the road. Whoever she was, he had the comfortable feeling that he knew her. He mentally shook himself. He was awed. Many supernatural creatures had such a power. He needed to be on his guard when he really felt like a grinning idiot.

"Good evening, Miles, or should I call you by your nom de plumb, Zennon? Zane Caine would be so proud of what you've accomplished. It's nice to finally meet you in the flesh," she said.

Miles tried to say something. He had nothing. Perhaps he should listen carefully.

"When I saw this fellow, his name is Cole Dare. I knew you would be interested in what he knows. It's always better to move ahead with faith and your eyes wide open," she said with a winsome smile. Miles had never seen her before. He would have remembered. Her high cheekbones lifted up her eyes, black opals that gleamed with starry highlights. Her lips were generous and kissable, and he was losing focus. Most of the beautiful women that he had met were actually lost souls and vampires wanting his blood. None of them had glowed with her dazzling light nor wore an angel pendant made of jade. He thought it seemed familiar. But then, Dillon Urich had a glow about him, too. Perhaps it had something to do with the local lost souls. And yet, the angel of stone radiated the holiness of Grace.

"Do I know you?" Miles asked. Even the art on the back of her jacket - a dragon looking in the mirror at itself to discover it wore angel wings on its back - struck a familiar chord. It reminded him of a poster he had once owned. He thought it was back in the Temple of Light in Tahoe.

"Do you?" she asked, amused. She gracefully arose, put away the baton in a holster on her hip, and offered Miles a gloved hand. He glanced at the werewolf chained with silver to the picnic table.

"Ah, you must be mischief disguised as a beautiful and adventuresome companion," Miles said. He shook her gloved hand. She just looked like a vision, and she was wearing Dreamkickers, but her firm grip felt very real.

"I'm usually trying to clean up messes," she chuckled. He swore he had heard her laugh before. It was odd, as the downtown and the world seemed to have grown quiet like they were the only ones awake.

"So, if you know my name, you know I hunt and redeem lost souls, vampires, and cursed souls, werewolves who are a blight on humanity," Miles said.

"Most are predators, I agree. But you did say redeem. Killing isn't the only way to redeem the cursed or lost."

"Truly?" Miles asked. This came as a bit of surprise, and yet, Grace showered the world with miracles every day. He knew better than to set limits on Grace, and thereby in some ways, on himself and how he could live and what he might encounter.

"Cole is just a confused, cursed soul under the control of a vampire. He hasn't killed anyone."

"Yet," Miles replied. He drew his Glock and placed it against the werewolf's head. It seemed somewhat unsporting, as stupid as that sounded, since the werewolf was bound with silver chains. It became even more difficult when Cole transformed. He was a young kid, mid-teens, with a mop of shaggy hair and a poor excuse for a beard. "You said Cole is controlled by a vampire."

"He was, yes. I brought him back when I searched his soul. There's still hope, but once he intentionally kills and tastes blood, he will be lost forever. For the nonce, there's still time."

"It sounds like you're familiar with werewolves," he said.

"Too much so. Vampires murdered my family, but werewolves are often in my way when I'm meting out justice and enacting vengeance."

"Is that your name? Justine Vengeance?"

She chuckled delightfully. "Oh, I like it! You may call me that if you wish."

"I would prefer to know your name and how you know mine."

"Call me by my given name then, Anna Nobles. People call me an angel, but I do really like Justine Vengeance. To answer your second question, I know you because I'm psychic and prophetic. It's how I knew that Cole would be here carrying a stolen artifact desperately sought by vampires and dangerous to humans. The vampires are collecting whatever they can find from that underwater hellhole. Lastly, I also know that: you feel like you know me, that you have engineered the destruction of close to one hundred vampires in Las Vegas while rescuing a damsel in distress, believe me, nobody misses Dirk DeVault, and, well you'd like to kiss me. That'll have to wait until tomorrow on our first date."

"Date?" Miles said, now confused. This conversation moved at warp speed.

Anna showed off a fedora. Her fingernails were adorned with crosses. "This hat contains such a strong residue of evil and negativity that it would likely turn its wearer into a brute. If Cole wore it, he would end up savage. Right now, he's just kind of pitiful and desperate. Wolves are pack oriented. He needs a place to belong, much as you need a companion. I know, you work alone."

"It's true."

"Well, know this, Miles Jasper, if you stay true to that pattern, you will die in the next few days. You need a partner. But I'll give you time to think about it and enact your freewill. I know you worked with people in Tahoe."

"Only to save their butts but yes, we worked as a team."

"See you can do it. Tomorrow night will be the first big test. Let's see, the local Hard Rock casino odds makers would give you a one in three chance to survive without aid."

"Godless people never factor in Grace. And you said the first time."

"Over the next few days, you could die a half dozen times," Anna said.

"And you can keep me alive?"

"I tip the odds in your favor. If they weren't so atrocious, I wouldn't be here."

"Ah, you're my guardian angel."

"Standing in, present and accounted for. I'm the first of three unusual partners that you might have," Anna replied.

Miles couldn't tell if she was serious or not, and yet, he couldn't deny a sense of awe. Could this really be his guardian angel in the flesh? "Three? I'll roll with what Grace brings me. What's your plan for Cole?"

"There's a peaceful pack of werewolves in the Tri-Cities. They will take him in. Grandma specializes in loner and rehab projects. I know that I'm asking you to trust my word, but I'm from this area. In return, Cole told me there's a big meeting of werewolves, some kind of rally and orientation for the Butcher pack, tomorrow night at East Hill Cemetery. If we don't show up, there will be more deaths than we can count on both hands. If you deal with this alone, you might die. What say you? Should we show up?"

Miles nodded. This felt so right. He should be suspicious. He said a prayer to Grace asking guidance. Something lightly struck his hat from above. He removed it, finding a nut stuck in it. A second one struck him atop the head before he slipped his hat back on. "Alright, I'm there."

"Don't scowl. We will be doing Grace's work. Cole, are you ready?" she asked him.

"Yessum. Thankee for all you've done. I'm a sorry-ass piece of work, so God bless your big heart. Oh, I meant to tell you, but my mind gets fogged, do you know why the dump stinks?"

"I do not. Pray tell," Anna said.

"Butcher promised us greater control over our curse. Most thought it would be an injection or something to drink, but it's not. It's in the everyday air y'all breathe. Don't you see? Butcher has made this a haven for werewolves. His success has attracted many followers. For example, I can change back and forth at will, not just by the light of the moon, and not if I don't want to because it's a full moon," Cole said.

"What does the dump have to do with it?" Miles asked.

"That wonderful aroma that the dump puts out makes me more powerful and in better control. There are many that think Butcher is a saint in wolf's clothing."

"The werewolf vampire behind the stink is a saint?" Anna asked with an edge to her voice.

"I didn't say so. That's just what some of the werewolves say, you know, them from the Red Fangs, Black Claws, Fastbacks, and the like."

A silver Ford truck pulled up. Both doors opened. Out from the driver's side, a beefy man with bushy sideburns and a GQ beard climbed out and lumbered over to them. His t-shirt read: Shoot Grandma! Commas & Grammar Matter. He was joined by a slender, almost Elven-looking lady with luminous, baby blue eyes, a dearth of tats, and hot-pink hair. Her smile was kindly despite what looked like canine teeth. A second young woman with wild, white hair stayed with the truck.

"Good evening. Y'all called? My names Damian Thews," the bear-like male said.

"And I'm Jami Saturday. We're here to give Cole a ride and a place to go," she said with a smile

"He needs help and a place to call home," Anna said.

"Damned straight, I do," Cole said. Anna raised an eyebrow. He blanched. "See. I was born on the wrong side of the blanket."

"That's okay. We're all kind of atypical and abnormal, and we like it. Don't we, Damian? We're sort of like the home for furry misfits. Most of us have been where you are: thrown out, abandoned, shunned, and even hunted. We can help you find a new pack," Jami Saturday said.

"I'm Miles Jasper. Are there many lycan in the area?"

Thews nodded. "Oh yeah, There's a half dozen smaller packs like the Fastbacks, the Black Claws, the Slashers, and Red Fangs. We're the peacekeepers - the Peace Pack. If Cole wishes his way ahead to be non-violent, he's come to the right place. When you get deeper into the woods of Appalachia, you can encounter werebears and tigers. They're either loners or the companions of witches. Sometimes the bears are mistaken for Big Foot," Thews said.

"Nevada doesn't have near as many lycan."

"I can't say that I'm surprised. There's a lot of desert and sunshine out there."

"How many are in your pack?" Anna asked.

"There are several dozen but less than we were. Someone has been tempting them away with false promises," Jami Saturday said.

"Would that be the Butcher Pack?" Miles asked.

"Yes. The new tribe is for the lost, confused, and violent. Those dark feelings are in all of us, but it can be controlled through nature and nurture," Thews said.

"Go in peace," Anna said. She unlocked the werewolf's cuffs and chains. He awkwardly embraced her, and then Cole shuffled off with Thews and Saturday. One less there tomorrow night might make the difference.

As she walked, Jami Saturday changed into a pink-haired werewolf, her hybrid form with two legs, making Cole break out in full-bellied laughter. Blue-colored hair created tattoo-like designs on her fur along her legs, arms and back. She reverted to her diminutive human self as the three settled in the truck. The white-haired one offered Cole a bouquet of lilies.

"Thank you. No pink, but I think I might go with white. It's more wintery and lower key," Cole said.

"Oh, we're definitely low key, aren't we, Damian?" Jami said.

"That we are, right after we celebrate Cole's arrival," Thews said. He started the silver truck's engine, threw it into gear, and smoked rubber as the vehicle sped away. His hearty laughter was the last they heard of the four lycans. The white-haired one waved at Miles.

"Low key?" he asked.

"They're wolves. Packs like to play. If they burn off energy to-gether, like puppies, they're not out causing trouble. Thanks for being understanding. Werewolves are not like vampires. Just be-cause they are cursed souls doesn't make them lost souls. So, I'll see you tomorrow night?" Anna asked Miles. She arched an inquisitive brow.

"Yes. How can I resist such a graceful offer?"

"Freewill."

He scoffed. "Meanwhile, what about the Oktoberfest Vampire? Are you hunting him?" Miles asked. He hadn't come here to hunt the murderer, but the local authorities had failed.

"No, someone else had been assigned that project. I'm here to aid you in dispatching and redeeming cursed souls. I just know, despite souls crying out for Justine Vengeance, that I'm supposed to be at East Hill tomorrow night. Whatever is happening there is paramount, and I'm here to help you survive what's to come. It sounds like the dump might necessitate some investigating, but we will deal with one disaster at a time if Grace allows us."

Miles saw no reason to argue. "Thank you. Where would you like to meet?"

"At the keeper's little green shack near the main entrance off East State Street. If I'm not there, Julia will know where I am. She's a precocious and charming young lady, and she knows East Hill like her own backyard playground. She occasionally rides with me."

Miles usually was working when he was in a graveyard. He couldn't imagine playing in one.

"You might also run into Rhonda and Emmett Powers. They work as docents. They can share the history of this place, a mixed grave of free and slaves, Confederate and Union. If asked, they will be aware of where I am. They fight the good fight, too," Anna said. She strolled over to the Indian Scout and mounted the motorcycle.

"Wow, it looks customized. Usually, they have a liquid cooled 60 Twin V, 5-speed, and 78 horsepower. Is that special suspension? This looks more powerful and yet its sleek," Miles thought. The motorcycle went perfectly with his angel, sexy and powerful.

"We're not allowed to bring our wings, and y'all don't have jet packs, yet. This is the next best thing. It has a 100 hp, and I like to jump it," she said and blew him a kiss. She donned her helmet, adjusted its visor, and then kicked her bike into gear.

"Hey, you're leaving the hat," he said.

"In good hands, I think. I know you'll take care of it for me. I'm short on time, but if I hurry, I can be in the nick," Anna said. She didn't even wait for an answer. She knew that he would destroy it. With a rumble and a roar, Anna raced away, leaving Miles wondering.

He walked out from under the tree. Even so, another nut bounced off his hat. He found himself absurdly wondering if he should shave and shower before fighting werewolves. He heard Anna's chuckle like she had yet to leave, but her ride carried her away into the night.

The downtown abruptly returned to life. The nightingales sang. Music carried from the rooftop of The Bristol Hotel. Laughing voices drifted out the door from a local brewery. A bicyclist rode by singing an Aerosmith song at the top of his lungs. "You're my angel! Come and save me tonight!"

A smiling couple with a beagle on a leash strolled through the park. A pickup truck needing a muffler roared by and off into the night.

A Bristol VA police car pulled into the lot. The window was rolled down by an officer who glared at him. "Hey, buddy. The park closed at dusk," Officer Randy told him.

"Yes, sir. I'm just back to get my hat. I forgot it earlier," Miles said. He picked up the fedora from the picnic table. Even through his glove, he felt like he was holding a buzzing hornet. He planned to do exactly what Anna suggested.

"That's a nice-looking hat," the officer said.

"See why I didn't want to leave it and lose it?" Miles asked.

"All right, then. Have a safe night," the officer said.

Miles couldn't help but smile as he drove off. Tomorrow, he had a date with an angel, and they would be entertaining werewolves. Thank you, Grace. Until then, he had a hat to burn.

He drove to the sacred grounds behind the First Baptist Church. He could feel its sanctity when he entered its space. Once parked, he unstrapped a metal bucket from the work chest on the back of the tow truck. He tossed the hat inside the bucket, and it rattled around unsettled like it was ready to jump out. The black hat also seemed to taint the metal. Tendrils of darkness tried to slither from the bucket but retreated quickly each time. Miles could feel the holiness of the grounds stand strong and push back against the evil. He didn't even want to know how a hat could be dangerous. He had no wish to become a mad hatter. Many probably already thought that he was crazy. Burn evil hats, not books, he mused.

Miles invoked the Prayer of Protection, and then he called on Grace's white light as an armor. He recited a prayer to banish the evil, and then he poured a little gasoline on the hat. He started to strike a match but stopped. Following his intuition, he stepped farther back. He struck and flicked the match.

The bucket exploded with a loud whoosh of flames that spat balls of roiling fire upward. It quit sputtering and turned into a dark column of flame twisting taller than Miles and beyond into the night. The fiery, black snake opened it maw and licked the air. Waves of hate washed over Miles, causing some nausea. This beast wanted to ruin and destroy. Anna had been right about the hat's evil nature. It had been woven out of vile loathing.

Its tongue snapped up Miles' hat and flash-fried it to a crisp. His eyebrows smoldered. The evil flames tried to encase him, but he used his crucifix to push back with the power of Grace. On these sacred grounds, his faith in the Almighty was magnified, especially against the darkness.

He stepped forward and poured holy water in the bucket, killing the fiery beast, and dousing all the flames. They vanished, leaving a stench that the wind carried off. Miles sloshed the bucket contents around and then dumped it down a city drain.

He thanked Grace for protecting him, and Anna for trusting him. Tomorrow night would be dangerous if it was related in any way to the same evil that had resided in that hat.

Twenty-Six

Judge Dragomir Investigates

Sitting in the back seat of the sedan on the way to Maraders Marina, Vlade Dragomir pondered what Elke Swearington had told him. Frankly, in two visits, he had learned a great deal from her. He was impressed, as always, but he had his doubts about the Wordsmith. For Elke's sake, he would give the neophyte vampire a chance to be whatever he would be, as long as he didn't expose them to the world. To say that vampires came in a myriad of colors was an understatement. In many cases, they were what they ate, influenced by those they had dined upon.

The Wordsmith had survived meeting Destrange and Goran. That said something about his resilience and instincts. His ex, this Gina, concerned Dragomir. She possessed no compelling reason to keep the story of the supernatural to herself.

The truth could lead to a war and public hunting of vampires. He shuddered at the thought of bounties. Vlade liked when the humans were distracted by killing each other. Let the herd fight amongst themselves. As long as they didn't cull themselves too thinly, Vlade and the other vampires would stay in the shadows. Unlike Viktor Von Damme who had wanted to meddle with the government, Vlade knew it should only be done when absolutely necessary, because it was almost impossible for humans to keep secrets. The media and others rooted out half-truths. Even those could be deadly. RON had successfully kept the news of vampire hunters suppressed, except to bankroll Hollywood blockbusters that would spread misinformation. He was certain Von Damme's eyes and fangs could sparkle beautifully in the sunlight before he drained you of life. Likely, his immediate subordinates could also operate without fatal consequences during the daylight. They were beautiful killers 24-7, as the modern culture would say.

Vlade had humans to question and perhaps kill. It all depended on their knowledge. Some people that he wished to interrogate might already be dead or have vanished. He had no idea how much Butcher had been able to cover his tracks.

None of Vlade's entourage had been happy with his choice, feeling he would be exposed to danger. Concurring, he agreed to take Simon Mones along. His bodyguard was like having twin vampires protecting you. As added insurance, Painter joined them, riding shotgun in the front seat.

Vlade knew his first order of RON business was to collect the skulls for destruction and see what everyone knew, especially the divers. Also, did they have Shaden as shadows? He pondered whose skull Juju had kept. Was it Quentin's, Agatha's, Yokic's, or one of the others? The sacrificial vampires had not wanted to give their energy, but they had been found guilty of treason against RON, some even colluding with Von Damme. Usually, the penalty was destruction, but vampire energy had been needed to stop Viktor and bind him in the fire opals. It usually took something vampire to slay a vampire. The witches added their craft to the trap. There was the question of the jewelry box: did any of Viktor's power remain within it?

Elke had mentioned that Madi seemed unaffected by Dillon's vampire charms. Perhaps it was because he was a grayling, or it might be something else, such as the metal plate in her head. It was worth being cautious.

Last night, Vlade had visited the public library where Raquel Sterling was signing books. He had learned much from Raquel's eyes. The Silver Goddess remained unnerved by what she had experienced in Von Damme's underwater mansion, and yet, she had seen nothing extraordinary. Still, she suffered the paranoia that everyone gained due to their time at the mad alchemist's mansion. Vlade wasn't surprised to find Raquel had developed claustrophobia.

On the other hand, Diana Sterling had been stuck inside the basement. What he found in her memories greatly concerned him. He saw no sign of Von Damme, thank the Great Spirits of the Shadowlands, but he saw Shaden through her feelings and senses. He also noticed a shadow gate. When Elke had told him what Madi Marader had found, her discovery of a golden and black looking mirror with vases full of earthen metals, in this case coins, that had confirmed his suspicions. He would look into the divers' eyes and see if there were signs of engraved runes.

There could be wraiths, specters, and worse. He did not want to contemplate worse. Permanent gates were forbidden because they eventually ruptured, creating craters, sinkholes, and in the distant past, entire town's populations vanishing. This would explain the Wordsmith's encounter with the Bonz creature. And yet, normal Shaden could not animate objects. Feargorgers could lead people to do stupid things. They mostly thrived on frantic emotions. In times of war and epidemic, the dark shadows grew stronger because of the intense fear.

Von Damme possessed the hubris to create a permanent gate to the Shadowlands. Perhaps, if all those who had been diving to Von Damme's ruins died, people would stay away. There were secrets buried in the rubble that the human world should never uncover. If the myth huntress unearthed it, Vlade would seize it, destroy it, or use its power.

The last thing that vampires wanted was anything that kept everyone locked up and safe in their homes. Go shopping. Go to bars. Go dancing. Just go out and do it. Humans were protected in their homes by the thresholds of love and ownership. People were fresh meat while they were outside and away from their homes. He hoped Elke ended this nonsense with the Oktoberfest Vampire soon.

Simon parked the sedan along the road before the lot. The trio moved as quietly as shadows upon the gravel as they stalked downhill toward the marina. Painter spread himself out into fog, cloaking their movements. Experienced vampires could lessen their density, so their footfalls barely brushed the ground.

He had also taught Simon how to mute sound about them by absorbing the vibrations. He had met Mones long ago when he had gone by a different name. Simon the Red had fought valiantly but failed to protect his Viking king. For that, Vlade had rewarded Simon with immortality, if he would serve and protect a new superior with the same fervor.

What a quaint place, Vlade mused, a chandlery with a restaurant on the first floor and apartments on the second. Even before they reached the buildings, Vlade could sense the presence of ghosts. Spirits haunted this rebuilt marina. It still stank of fresh paint and the Shadowlands.

He wasn't a ghost whisperer or a medium, so he couldn't ascertain the exact number of ghosts in the area, but Dragomir knew there were more than one at the chandlery and restaurant and at least two near the cabins. Dawnstar would be certain. She had told him this would be dangerous, and that he would have a confrontation with spirits from near and afar. It was just one of the reasons Simon and Painter accompanied him. Loner vampires rarely lasted beyond a century. Vlade had existed that and many times longer. He had taken extra steps to protect his own spirit earlier in the evening.

Motioning for Simon to stay, Vlade took out Von Damme's ring and placed it on his ring finger. He had removed it at Elke's insistence, but now he needed it to work as a diviner. It would be drawn to anything like itself. It pulled him toward the cabins, so he continued along a sidewalk that ran between two square wood buildings on each side of the pathway. A sign read: Cabins 1-4. A porch swing, stacked plastic lawn chairs, and a grill awaited outdoor cooks. Vlade liked his meals raw.

He passed by an empty cabin. Noticing the male gear and general sloppiness of the place through a split in the curtains, he knew it was Juju's room. There was no heartbeat. Where was the male member of the crew at this time of night?

Across the sidewalk, Madi slept. He felt the ring draw him nearer. Her curtains were pulled tight, but the door had a star on it and the words, Myth Huntress. He could hear her accelerated heartbeat and restless breathing. She might awaken any second. Even so, he paused, sensing something within, a ghost perhaps. He was unsure. It could be the auras of the coins or the jewelry box. He pondered slipping in to question her, but he planned to deal with her last. From what he had been told, she might resist and create a commotion.

He thought on the information that he had taken from the Wordsmith. An ancestral ghost accompanied Zhen who was degreed as a biologist and chemist from local King University. Women had come a long way in six centuries. Unlike Von Damme and DeVault, he didn't see them as inferior.

The old spirit named Hojo could complicate matters, making it more difficult to obtain information from the Asian woman. Vlade smiled. It had been a while since he had subdued a ghost, but over the centuries, he had forced many to surrender. This one would be no different. It would bend before his indomitable will.

***

"Don't fear the reaper! Baby, I'm your man," the radio on the table of Zhen's makeshift workshop, played old rock and roll on WOXL out of Asheville, NC. Juju had left it on this station after complaining he couldn't find any good Oldies. What was up with him? He had been annoying, really not himself.

Zhen told herself to refocus. The table held her portable lab, and she was ready to conduct tests on the skull to discover its age and composition. She started by taking measurements and taking images of them. Except for the teeth, it seemed normal enough, if you accounted for the extra hinge on the jaw. It could open wider than normal. That's when she noticed that the incisors, the long teeth, were hollow as if oral surgery in the form of root canals had been performed. They also could fold back similar to a snake's fangs.

Zhen tried to focus on her work. Men, she sighed. She preferred science, but she had sent Juju away because she had trouble resisting him and temptation. Her mind also kept wandering to Dillon Urich. What kind of man, what kind of being, was he? He was dashing and intriguing.

"A creature of light and dark. I would think him a rakshasa with a silver heart."

"Not golden?" Zhen asked. She had gold in mind since she had recently run tests on the coins. It appeared they would all be quite wealthy. Madi said they might travel in a little more style. It made little difference to Zhen. She enjoyed adventure, and what an adventure Dillon Urich would be. She chastised herself, knowing they were both involved in relationships. And yet still. . .

"No. He must perform some dark deed to survive. Beware, he is already bewitching you. I can tell. You keep thinking about him. Look at what lies before you. Do you see it? Yes. Proof of vampires! Protect it from the light, or it will burst afire come morning," Hojo warned her.

"I will run tests and be the judge of that. All right, you fang-toothed skull, give up your secrets. This should tell me something," Zhen said. She felt scrutinized to her soul. She glanced up and saw nothing amiss.

"Beware! I sense evil. The skull! It might remain inhabited. The vile in life fear moving onto judgment."

"What? There's a ghost with it?" she asked. Suddenly, the room seemed to be getting smaller, even stuffy, and she knew the windows were open. She felt a chilling breeze swirl around and realized the door was slowly swinging open. A whisper caressed her ears and neck, sliding down her spine to cause shakes and shivers of pleasure.

"Wait. I sense we are no longer alone. A dark and powerful presence has intruded on us. I am besieged. Avert your eyes and scream," Hojo said.

It was too late.

"Silence," Zhen heard. The command seized her vocal cords.

She choked back her scream and looked up. A tall man, his face two colors, was so handsome that she felt graced by his visit. She found herself so awestruck that she could barely breathe. Her heart raced like a galloping mare. At first, she thought death had come for her, and then she realized that the stranger must be after the skull. She was between him and it. His smile was compelling, but his eyes shone with the dark light of having seen more death than anyone could in ten lifetimes and remain sane.

"Begone, foul spirit!" Hojo cried. The ancient warrior spirit launched a psychic attack.

Now, it was a battle of wills, a combat by spirits, one might say. The ancient warrior might be older, Vlade mused, but Hojo had not lived more, not fought more, not battled for nightly existence so that for a time it became akin to breathing. Vlade had defeated them all, from holy men and egotistical clerics to witches and evil wizards. Before him, Hojo might as well have been Hojoito. They had been as doomed to failure as this wannabe samurai was fated to be. Fighting for your very being for centuries forged a spirit to endure, to dominate, empowering him to defeat the warrior.

With a shift of will, he tossed Hojoito far into the Shadowlands.

A strong wind struck the cabin. It creaked and seemed to brace itself for more. A folding chair clattered down the walkway. A gust slammed the door shut. Dragomir thought Painter could be having some issues with this wind.

Zhen stood white-faced, saucer-eyed, and dumbfounded. It had likely been a while since she was completely alone. Well, she wasn't alone for long, as Vlade held her eyes and then her soul captive. He didn't want her body or soul. He wanted her knowledge, but she knew so little. She had not gone diving to the ruins. She had stayed above with Dillon. Her companion spirit sensed something amiss about the Wordsmith, but Hojo had yet to identify him as a blood-sucker. Now, it might, or might not, as the Wordsmith carried himself in an abnormal way for vampires. She had seen his light, too, making her doubt Hojo.

Vlade turned his attention to the skull. There was a groove running along the right temple. He had known a vampire with a scar there. He had been one of the six that would entrap Viktor. None of them had known that the mad alchemist would be so strong. It had taken all of their willpower, draining them, to contain Von Damme.

Had the haunts in the house been angry, God-damned vampire spirits? They were not selfless. It was simply not in a vampire's nature. He picked up the skull. It wasn't Quentin. This had been Josef Yokic. "Goodbye, my friend. You never should have tried to usurp me." With that, Vlade crushed the skull. These people must possess no proof of vampires. Yokic would understand. Even so, Vlade missed him and their conversations. They had grown old and then ancient while staying in touch. Viktor had warped Yokic who wanted to return to feudal times. One was never too old to act like an idiot, Vlade had learned over the centuries.

From outside, he heard scuffling. Simon was engaged in combat and struggled with someone. How unusual. Vlade turned, but he was too late.

Out of what seemed like nowhere, he was stabbed in the back. Typically, this wouldn't bother him, but he screamed. Through the blinding agony, he realized he must have been stabbed by a quikmar blade or a vampire bone. Von Damme had created more than one way to kill his own kind.

"True death to you, Vlade. Now I am the judge, the jury, and the executioner. May God piss on you at your final end."

"Josef?" Vlade gasped. Could it be his undead spirit had survived? Lashing out, he blindly swung and missed.

The Latino with the haunting eyes stabbed Vlade again, sending him to his knees. He sensed another jab coming. He must keep his head! He moved his claws to intercept a slash to his throat and deflected the jagged white dagger made of vampire bone, losing two claws and part of a finger. Burning wires of pain radiated into his forearms. He willed himself to move to block Juju's next attack.

"You have it! Von Damme's ring!" the possessed Juju exulted. He grabbed Vlade's hand, attempting to tear the ring loose. It began to slip. Vlade made a fist. "I'll cut it off!"

Suddenly, the door burst open, smacking against the wall. Simon arrived with force and flung Juju aside. The big bodyguard scooped up Vlade and carried him outside, charging back into the cover of night.

"Thank you, my faithful one. Take me back to the hotel. I need some fresh blood and time to recover," Vlade said. It could have been worse. It could have been quikmar.

"I apologize. I was attacked by a poltergeist," Simon said. He wore no shirt, but its remnants hung around his neck. He looked to have torn it off his head.

Painter pulled himself together from the mist. "Sorry, boss. The wind shredded me there for a moment. That was freaky. Simon, way to go," he said.

"That's why there's two of us," Simon said.

Questioning the divers and visiting the FBI about the skulls would have to wait until he recovered, Dragomir realized. How had his attacker known to use such a weapon against him? With those haunting eyes, it could had been Josef Yokic. Vlade believed that the vampire's spirit had possessed the man, Juju. Dragomir wondered what else had possessed the divers.

Twenty-Seven

Dead of Night Awakenings

Morning arrived suddenly, as if Madi hadn't slept, and yet, she felt amped and eager. No time to drag. The show, her show, must go on! Time flies when you're having fun, she mused over the blur of packing, loading, boating, anchoring, gearing up and diving.

Now, again, she swam in the basement, staying wary of anything that might entangle her. She could hear her companions breathing as precious air and nitrogen bubbled away.

"You are going to screw something up. You always do," she heard Debbie Downer. Nobody else did, and that was just as well.

This time, the dive group unleashed more light to counter the encroaching darkness, deploying additional LEDs, extra flares, and flashlights to vanquish the black of SoHo's abyss. She thought that would sound good on the narration. They succeeded in turning the dark, spooky ruins into a place of harsh light and sharp-edged shadows. Roxy softly sang *Jeepers Creepers*.

Madi bee-lined her way to the amphorae while Roxy gathered coins. Madi had just minutes to explore the intact vase and poke around the gold mirrored panel. She hoped it was a vault door that led to a spectacular and historic discovery.

This morning and everything else seemed to slip away to obscurity while Madi studied the gold and jet-black mirror. The lights on it made the shadowy areas gleam like the polished stone was untouched by being underwater for fifty years.

"Loser. You will end up a huge disappointment to everyone like Geraldo and Al Capone's vault," Debbie Downer continued.

Peeking into the earthen vase, Madi discovered it was full of coins. She could hear Zhen in her head recommending that the amphora would best be studied whole. Could they bring it up intact? It must be emptied, or it would be incredibly heavy. Perhaps they could raise it by inflating a ring around it as they had the ROV. A question for later debate, she decided. She was here to get whatever she could before the others finished erecting, arranging and testing the lighting.

She used an extendable pointer to explore around the edges of what she would swear was a door. How had she opened it last time? The cold still assaulted her hand, but it was less painful. She ran the thin steel wand along the edges, finding the door inset within the wall. She saw no hinges, no lock, or knob, nothing but a flat plane of swirling black and valuable gold. Had she imagined opening it yesterday? Mirror, mirror on the wall, tell me are there any artifacts behind you at all?

"This will blow up in your face one day. You'll see."

When she gazed at herself, really stared at her reflection, she saw a darkness swirling in her eyes. She also noticed the taint in her face, and the stain spreading throughout her torso. It was taking over her entire body like a cancer. The damage she had done to herself drinking and smoking would catch up with her one day.

She had quit, so it would take longer, but it was there, lurking and growing inside her.

Then, she noticed an indentation along the edge - an area to grip it to pull it open. Was it a trick of the light? What wonders and treasure would she find behind it?

The black areas of the door changed shape, becoming sinuous and snaky. One formed a head with long fangs. She pushed that fear away. There were no eels in South Holston Lake, but then, there shouldn't have been tropical fish or an alligator, either. She winced, still feeling the scars from where that twice-damned moray had bitten her two years ago.

"No, you're not scared. Not yet."

The blackness swirled, coalesced, and gathered to slowly rise. The tendrils reminded her of a bed of eels. In a blink, the swarm of dark tentacles multiplied into a mass, circling around her. She lurched up and kicked away, but before she could escape, the eels wrapped around her legs. She felt a blinding pain as one anchored itself by chomping into her left leg. Agony blossomed in her right leg as another bite set her painfully afire. Her right arm was seized, the glove torn off as she was jerked down by the squirming darkness to consume her.

Thrashing from leg cramps, Madi jerked awake, escaping the nightmare but not the agony. Calves and hamstrings in both legs spasmed. Nearly crippling pain forced her to keep them straight and relax as all her muscles threatened to join the revolt. She had overdone it, pushed her body too far.

She controlled her breathing to slow her heart rate and then worked to relax her body. She had learned yoga and meditation, mindfulness, to help her deal with pain. It's what athletes and adventurers had to do. Her legs hurt almost as much as her post car wreck surgeries. Even so, she could deal with it. It was mind over matter, although her brain right now seemed to be fogged.

What a horrible nightmare. She hated snakes and eels.

Life can be a nightmare, one of her voices whispered. It was so quiet she could barely tell if it was Debbie Downer talking her negative nonsense again.

A cold sweat soaked Madi and drenched the sheets. She shivered, chilled to the bone. How could she be hot and cold at the same time? Her tongue stuck to the roof of her mouth when she wanted to scream. She was thirsty, tired, and cold, feeling like she had to push through thick air. Might she have a fever?

Through the haze of pain, she looked around, able to see in the darkened room. Nothing appeared wrong. Music played from Zhen's place. She liked to work nights. Juju would be guarding her, so she would be safe. Juju had not disappeared after all. He had wandered down to the lake to clear his thoughts. When he had returned, he had been calmer like he had been meditating. He had apologized for scaring everyone. He thought that he had told Zhen, but Madi figured that their companion had forgotten. Zhen's work often absorbed her attention. The world could be falling down around her, and she might never notice if she was engrossed in her portable laboratory.

A dark shadow passed by Madi's window. Fierce eyes glanced at her before moving on. She felt pinned by them, her muscles frozen by fear. Her breathing caught. She suddenly wondered if word had gotten out, and if treasure hunters and the greedy knew about their find. The coins! Thieves would steal her discovery! They had slipped silently inside while she slept and fled with the funding to save her show. The show wouldn't go on! She would be laughed at. No one would hire her with her losing record. The adventure was over. Maybe she could get a job as a talking head on TV. What fun!

What was wrong with her? Her damaged brain wasn't supposed to be able to trigger fear or thrills anymore. And yet, she was almost out of her mind with panic. Almost. She forced her attention away from it and returned to concentrating on slowing her breathing and letting her muscles get heavy. She fake-yawned a couple times and brought on real jaw-stretchers, easing her mind and her body.

A near eternity later, her legs finally relaxed. She sat up, massaged them, and then she put her limbs to work. She was stiff and felt older, making her wonder if a cold might be coming on. She prayed not. As she rose, dark spots danced before her eyes. She waited for a moment. When her vision had cleared, she took a few careful steps to be sure her balance was good.

She found the coinage safe and sound, exactly where she had left it. She exhaled, relieved. Thank God. She desperately needed the cash infusion. In the morning before they went diving, she would store them in her brother's safe.

Basking in the coins golden glow, she managed a smile, shaking off the nightmare and the haunting image of those eyes. Had they even been real? She couldn't ever remember being so worked up over a discovery. This could help her show go Big Time. This would undoubtedly change the media's tune. Streaming companies and networks wouldn't be able to say that she was just running around on escapades and not accomplishing anything but titillation by being eye candy. Her day in the sun was coming. She hadn't been this excited since before the wreck had injured her brain. Come to think of it, the doctors didn't think she would ever feel strongly again. Maybe she was healing. Doctors admitted the work they did was a practice.

Outside, she heard a cry of pain, followed shortly by the sound of something large hitting the wall of a nearby cabin.

Stumbling a bit, Madi went charging into the night. A blast of cold wind stopped her in her tracks. Once it passed, she hurried toward Zhen's cabin. The door was open, and the music continued to roll out. Little River Band sang, "Hang on! Help is on the way. I'll be there as fast as I can."

Madi paused at the door. Ahead, Zhen stood as still as a statue. A bright glow surrounded her. Nearby and on the floor, Juju groaned. Splatters of blood covered his shirt and shorts. At his feet, a bloodied rib bone, seeming to be freshly plucked from a person, sat on the ground. Something about it brought on a rare case of queasiness. Madi had to look away and put it out of her mind. Her companions were hurt.

"You're bleeding! Are you all right? What's going on?" Madi asked. Her brain still seemed to function at half speed. Was she seeing halos around people? That was one of the signs of concussions. She had suffered more than one of those, seeing auras around lights, but she had never seen glows around people like she did now.

"Not my blood, I don't think. A man was here. He broke the skull," Juju said and gestured toward the bone fragments on the ground. "When I jumped him, he tossed me aside like I was a lap dog," Juju said as he rubbed his head and winced. He patted himself, feeling for wounds. "I'm okay. Check on Zhen. She looks hypnotized."

Madi thought something didn't seem right about Juju. Or, it could be her befuddled brain. This dead of the nighttime caused her to think something was wrong. Bone fragments lie on the floor not far from the rib bone. The skull had been destroyed. Madi cussed under her breath. Her own mind wasn't really working yet. She hadn't expected to wake up and see blood.

Zhen's pulse and breathing were steady, but her eyes remained vacant like someone mostly asleep or in shock. Madi guided her to the bed where she stared into space. "He's gone! Hojo is gone!" she whispered.

"Gone? What do you mean gone?" Madi asked. Zhen's ancestral guide had always been present since Madi had known her. She had come to think that Hojo was a part of Zhen.

"I had the sense of a struggle, and then he vanished. Gone. I can't believe it. Since I was a child, Hojo has been with me. I'm . . . alone," Zhen whispered

"I'm here for you, babe," Juju said. He held her close.

"I am very fortunate. Thank you, Juju," she replied.

"Tell me what happened, and we'll see what we can do together," Madi said.

Zhen didn't say anything, so Juju spoke up. "Well, Zhen was doing her highly technical stuff."

"And boring him," Zhen said coolly.

Madi didn't want to deal with a lover's tiff. She had seen how Zhen had looked and acted around Dillon. Madi had warned her companions about getting involved. It must not get in the way of the show.

"I went outside for some fresh air. When I turned around, I saw a mountain of a man dancing by himself on the sidewalk, then I noticed another tall, white-haired dude in Zhen's room. She was just standing there staring at him, and he had the skull in his hands like he planned to crush it. I tried an Aikido hold, and the bastard slipped out of it like a greased pig and threw me. His face was odd, half white and half black," Juju said. He looked surprised to see the blood covering his clothes. Whoever he had hit must have had a bloodied nose.

Madi studied Juju who stared at the bone shards of the skull. "Are you all right?"

He looked away from it to her. His eyes seemed haunted even when he smiled. It seemed cockeyed, so not him. "Mostly. I feel like my face needs rearrangin'," he said. He rubbed his eyes and massaged his cheeks and jaw. He was starting to pick up a little of the local accent. He often did that. After a while, people wondered if he'd been born there.

"I don't recall anything at all really. I looked up. I vaguely remember someone being there. I can't really describe him. I blanked out. I'm fairly sure it was a him. Has anyone checked on Roxy?" Zhen asked. She was holding it together, thinking of others.

"I will," Juju said. He departed. Shortly, Madi heard him knock on Roxy's door. She groggily responded with a sailor's diatribe of profanity.

"I think the questions are: why is your guide gone, and why was that skull destroyed?"

"I'm at a loss. It's so quiet and empty I can almost hear my thoughts echo," Zhen said.

"You used to complain about the endless stream of sage advice," Madi said.

"Yeah, well, I wanted some quiet, not utter silence. What scares me is, what happened? Did the intruder do something to cause this, and if so, what, and how?" Zhen replied.

"You're not making a whole lot of sense," Madi said.

"Sorry. I feel like I've lost a part of me."

"Roxy sounded normal to me. What can we do, Zhen?" Juju asked as he returned. He moved closer, but she stepped back.

"Let me return to work. I need to change my mindset, and I want to see if I can learn anything from the shards."

"Had you learned anything so far?" Madi asked.

"Do you want to know that the canine teeth were hollow? There were natural holes in four teeth, two upper and two lower, the sharpest ones like the teeth of snakes to deliver venom."

"So, whoever this skull was part of had a venomous bite?" Madi asked.

"It could also be used to draw in fluid, say blood. Hojo believes in vampires. The ones in old Asian folklore can become invisible to the naked eye," Zhen said. Her words changed Juju's expression from befuddling to slyness.

What was that about? Madi wondered. All this confounded her. Both Zhen and Juju were acting weird, but then, Madi realized there was nothing normal about this situation.

"Well, whoever came in here wasn't invisible. You both saw him. We can check the surveillance video, but before we talk to anyone else, we need to agree that Zhen was testing the gold coins trying to authenticate them," Madi said.

"Otherwise, we have to admit that I took and lost evidence, don't we?" Juju said sheepishly.

Madi nodded. "Zhen, are you comfortable with that?"

She nodded. "Yes. I was running an alloy test to determine the percentage of gold. That's easier to explain than what happened to the pieces," Zhen said. She pointed to where the remains of the broken skull had been. "They just vanished. I blinked, and they were just gone. I don't know if that's good or bad. Hojo would know. I miss him so much."

Madi blinked. She didn't know what to think. It made it easier to leave unmentioned. Forgetting it would be a different matter.

Juju comforted her. "Thanks, ladies, for covering my ass. I apologize for being stupid. I wanted to prove that vampires are real. My bad. I put us all in jeopardy with the Law," he said. Zhen hugged him.

Madi joined in the group embrace. "I forgive you. Being down there gave me crazy thoughts, too. Besides, I don't want to tell my brother that you kept a skull here. He would go ballistic," Madi said.

"Does he wake up like Roxy?" Juju asked.

"Much the same. I think I'll just go brew a pot of coffee. If I'm lucky, the smell will wake him. Maybe I can convince him to call the cops," Madi said.

"I'll call Agent Kaye. She asked us to wake her if anything unusual happened," Zhen said.

"Good idea. I'll be back with coffee," Madi said. She tried to tell herself not to worry. Juju was here to protect Zhen.

Before Madi headed to the marina store, she armed herself with a gun and a can of mace, just in case. Juju was a load at two hundred plus pounds, and he had been chucked aside by the intruder. Was Zhen's attacker really gone? He could just as easily be waiting in the woods.

Her brother had given her carte blanche to use his kitchen, so she decided to brew some coffee and indulge in an early, hot breakfast. Anything warm sounded good to combat the damp, cutting wind. She hoped it died down for the morning boat trip. Once they got into the water, it wouldn't matter.

As she neared the marina, she heard Sarge barking ferociously and breaking glass and thuds, like bodies and heavy furniture hitting the floor. Was her brother fighting someone? Her adrenaline kicked in, and she hurried down and peered through the window. She pulled out her phone and started to record just as a commercial-sized bag of bar snacks landed on a table and ruptured. Pretzels, Cheez-its, Goldfish, and peanuts flew out to scatter across the floor. Sarge raced around to gobble up whatever he could, then the dog began barking again. Crazy laughter filled the room.

"Is there something strange in the neighborhood? Who you gonna call? Ghostbusters!" Kia sang, adding to the chaos.

Madi cautiously opened the door. The strong smell of tequila wafted past her. From behind the bar, a bottle of Mr. T's tumbled through the air. It crashed landed on another table and shattered. Glass and sweet and sour mix splashed out all over. Madi heard shards strike the window. The screeching laughter returned, this time accompanied by what sounded like the clanging of cymbals.

"What the hell?!" she heard her brother yell. A string of profanity not allowed on her show followed his mild exclamation.

A lime flew across the room to hit him in the forehead. She managed to hold back her laughter. A tray of lemons and more limes joined the first, all flying at him as if they had been hurled. He blocked or caught them all. He sought places to return thrown fruit to sender.

It made Madi recall Juju's comment about the intruder who was dancing by himself.

"Who's in here? Come out! You'll have scars if I have to drag your butt out here!" Tom shouted. He stood there in the dark where he glowered. The aura of light around him stretched out and flickered like a bonfire. The heat of his wrath slammed into her in waves.

Ginger Bethel seemed to slip out of the shadows and under her brother's arm. "It doesn't look like you'll be coming back to bed," Ginger said. She barred her teeth in frustration, kissed him on the cheek, turned around and left, stomping up the stairs. She appeared hotter than blue blazes.

The restaurant felt like it came to rest, the chaotic presence gone. Madi's world quit tilting, and she regained her balance. She pushed through the door into the restaurant. Broken glass crunched under her shoes with every step. She tried to avoid the pretzels and snack mix.

At the bottom of the stairs, Tom stood holding two handfuls of fruit. The bar lounge and restaurant looked and smelled like the scene of a western brawl. He glared at her. "Why are you up in the middle of the night?" he snapped.

"I'm here for coffee, and I'd like to look at your security video. I didn't know you hosted late night food fights," she replied. He was the same young Tommy. Her brother would never change.

"Did this mess happen in the cabins, too? Is that why you want to see the footage?"

"No. Zhen had an intruder who fought with Juju."

"What? When? Are they all right? Should I call a cop?" her brother asked.

She explained about the strange assailant while she started the French press to brew coffee. She made no mention of the skull that Juju had kept from the FBI. There was no reason to upset her brother now that it was gone. "Are you doing all right?" she asked. He looked more pale than usual.

Tom barred his teeth. It was rather frightening. "Yeah, at least I think so. I had a badass nightmare. The jewelry box had grown spines. They stuck through my hands. I couldn't let go."

"I apologize. I was warned about bringing the jewelry box back," she said.

Her brother dragged a hand across his face. "Don't sweat it. I've been having nightmares for the last two months. Ginger helps me deal. We have a mutual need, you could say. My nightmares are only every three or four days instead of every time I close my eyes. So that's an improvement."

"Are you asking me to stop?" Madi asked. She started shivering and drank more hot coffee. Getting warm was difficult this morning, and the Appalachian fog, just as smoky as Smoky Mountain mists, seemed to have filled her head.

He took her hand. "No. I'm just asking you to be extremely careful. That place is dangerous. You can't spend anything if you're dead. And who cares about being famous once you've departed for the afterlife?"

"I want to be famous now," she chuckled.

"You are. You are golden. Don't be infamous. For our senior trip at Tennessee High, we went white water rafting down the Colorado River through the Grand Canyon. Some rapids were named after gems. A few were named by their appearance. Mostly, they were named after the people who had died in them."

She blinked. This didn't sound like her brother. Maybe he had matured a little. She was touched, quite deeply. "Thank you for caring, Brother. That gives me strength. I thought you wouldn't give a rat's ass."

"I guess I'm getting old, and I've lost friends who will never get any older. I wish I could offer you wisdom, but I'm not that rickety, and at best, I'm growing sagacious at a glacial pace, kicking and screaming all the way to being more cautious while circling the grave. Notice that big word from sage, meaning wise," he said.

"These coins could make us rich. You won't have to impress women with big words."

"Good thing, because it's never worked! Listen, the wealth could make us marked or cursed. Could you be content with what you have on hand?" Tom said.

She hesitated. With each passing moment, she was feeling stronger and more determined about the dive and exploring the ruins. There were mysteries down there to be brought to light.

"I thought as much. Three months ago, I would have said the same. Did you call Mom earlier? If you didn't, you should call her and Dad before you go diving, again. You know, I just called to say I love you, and I'm going cave diving below a haunted underwater mansion where people have died, even when the dive was twenty feet shallower," he said.

"That sounds like a good idea, although I don't think I'll add on all that stuff at the end."

"Probably just as well. Do you want to watch the security recordings with me?" Tom asked. When she nodded, he pulled them up on his phone. She leaned in, but there was nothing to see in the video by the cabins except for Juju leaving and returning to Zhen's. He had paused only a moment before charging in. The recording of the bar wasn't helpful either. It showed the bar being trashed by an angry invisible something.

"Well, don't that beat all," Madi said. Had Zhen been attacked by a ghost? She wondered.

"Ginger keeps telling me that we have restless spirits here. It seems one of them might be a poltergeist. Come to think of it, I can see Spider throwing a fit like this, pissed about us exploring the ruins," Tom said. He finished with a string of expletives.

"It wasn't Spider. It was a ghost monkey," Ginger said. She showed up as sneaky and as soundless as a feline. She hugged her brother from behind, and he perked up. The glowing radiance coming from them reminded her of a small bonfire. "Yes, I'm serious. Don't roll your eyes at me, or I'll scratch them out."

"You couldn't see my eyes," Tom retorted.

"I can hear them. It's like pool balls clacking together," Ginger said.

Tom threw up his hands in surrender. "Fine. Madi even Zhen said this place was haunted. I think Spider and Walt hang here, but they wouldn't attack Zhen. At least I don't think so," he mused.

"I saw someone walk by my window. It didn't look like the ghost of any of your friends," Madi said and described those eyes. "I don't feel safe here."

"Neither do I since you brought that blasted jewelry box back."

"Oh, so that's it? It's my fault. It really messed with you, didn't it?" Madi asked.

"It's our fault. We never should have gone diving down there," Tom said.

"But y'all had to find out what happened to your friends, didn't you?" she asked. He nodded. "Well, I would like to do the same. I thought I was going to be able to send the security files to the cops, but that would be pointless, wouldn't it?"

He nodded. "I'll call the sheriff. Y'all are on my property. I'm not sure what else to do. This place is starting to feel like a lightning rod for trouble. A body washes up here and an intruder assaults

Zhen and Juju. I hate to ask what's next. I mean, the place was just rebuilt," Tom bemoaned.

"The cops don't need to come out tonight. I looked around. I didn't sense any ghosts or intruders. Make your call and then come to bed. It's gotten cold. Later this morning, you should also call the Haint Mistress. She's a ghost talker. Maybe she can help you out," Ginger said.

"Now that's an idea. I read about her," Tom said. He seemed to accept Ginger's word as gospel. Was she able to see ghosts? She hadn't offered to work as a medium, though.

By his expression, Madi wasn't certain that her brother would be calling the sheriff's department any time soon. He would likely be warming up Ginger's bed first. Madi knew that he didn't want to call the TVA, nor was he a fan of the FBI.

***

Madi was beginning to wonder if they would be able to dive come mid-morning. By then, she hoped that she could rally the crew.

Twenty-Eight

The Abyss of the House and GPR

This time, the myth huntress and her crew believed that they knew what to expect: the grim atmosphere, the bitter cold, and the feeling death was hanging around looking for a time to kill. They had the help of a dive master, Alan Linkous, who had been diving in SoHo more than any other human and ran a local shop called Adventure Diving.

Madi heard Agent Kaye and Linkous discuss the incident that had injured Search and Rescue workers and one of his fellow divers at the 421 Bridge. She tried to put that and the attack on Zhen out of her mind. They had discussed the latter with Deputy Hardaway and Agent Kaye. Had the intruder been a treasure hunter? Madi remembered those eyes and shivered. Had he somehow driven off Hojo?

Madi reminded herself to stay focused. Each person had a job on the bottom to be completed in eight minutes. Linkous would like them to be down there less time, more like five, but it was what it was. He believed ten minutes was way too long. Diva still wasn't repaired, and Madi felt that they were short on time. She had heard more boats heading out than usual this morning. She was worried about them being treasure hunters, but after the news of the gator being in the lake, she suspected that they were reptile hunters. Her brother wondered if the Snake was out there doing his thing.

Sure enough, on the way out, they saw Ken Siksay with John Hogan and a third guy in a Virginia Tech hat. The boat was loaded for fishing and with the Snake's super-sized reptile catching gear. He must be serious about his motto: That no job and no reptile was too big. Hogan was the Shamus of the lake. If you were out there, you would most likely see him, unless he was golfing. The hunters were a further reminder that waiting two days for the parts to come was a bad idea. Levon couldn't get Diva to accept remote commands anymore, so their only option was to scuba dive and decompress.

Earlier, Madi had taken some quiet time to talk to each one of her crew. She wanted to make sure that they wanted to do this. That it was worth the risk. Roxy believed so, and she was more cautious than Madi. Zhen wanted to go, and she was the most risk adverse of them all.

Juju was surly which was rare for Mr. Sunshine. She almost left Juju behind, but Zhen had a chat with him. Juju was rude to Alan Linkous who told jokes and freely offered good advice. Linkous acted like he was experienced with morning haters. The dive master had a white mustache, a mop of pale hair and a genteel smile. He provided the folksy wisdom of the ages, so to speak, with his decades of diving and Search and Rescue experience.

Agent Kaye was the opposite, mostly quiet, here for her own agenda. She said nothing about the skulls except the FBI would take care of them. She was more apologetic and helpful when it came to seeking Zhen's assailant. Madi felt a little guilty since Juju had taken a skull. None of them mentioned it, sticking with their cover story that Zhen had been analyzing the gold coins.

Due to the size of the dive party, they took two boats out. Maverick was driven by Tom and the Linkous' craft by his lovely partner, Kim, who was clad in an Adventure Diving hoodie. Doc and the drone master, Lan Caster, rounded out their party. Right after Dr. Curran had arrived this morning, Caster had shown up to offer his services. He was licensed to fly, so Madi hired him freelance. That allowed Zhen to dive with them. Dillon had declined due to his health and the issue with his medication causing his skin to sunburn easily.

Speaking of the good old Sol's light causing trouble, Madi wondered what was wrong with her eyes. The day seemed too bright for her, even after she donned her sunglasses. The shadows seemed crisp with sharper edges than she recalled. Her own shadow seemed too chunky for her.

"I'm surprised you fit in your dive suit. You're putting on weight. You should have stayed on the dock," Negative Nellie said.

They geared up, checked their radios and reception, and synchronized watches. Roxy would guide and operate the portable, waterproof Ground Penetrating Radar. Madi was pleased by the GPR's compactness at the size of a small suitcase. Its pulses should reveal what they wanted to know. Is there a chamber behind the gold and black mirror? Madi thought she remembered opening it, but nobody had seen her do it, and that part of the recording had only shown darkness.

Well, she was about to find out what was real and what she had only imagined.

Leaving a trail of bubbles rising as if they were fleeing, Madi, Linkous in his dry suit, and their five companions followed the shotline down, descending directly to the ruins. Throughout history, humans had gone to extremes for gold. And yet, it was more than that. Despite Debbie Downer telling her this would end in disaster, Madi craved to know more. The ruins were a tantalizing mystery set in a puzzle and wrapped in an enigma. Was it truly haunted? Was she supposed to believe in the supernatural? Frankly, she was more afraid of her show failing. She had been a selfish failure before. This time, she was doing good work. Why couldn't people see it?

"Because you're doing it," Negative Nellie added.

Why did being near the ruins bring out the worst in her?

What secrets did the skulls hide? Why had someone destroyed the one that Juju had kept? They hadn't told Agent Kaye about it for fear that she would cancel this dive. Would Madi find the answers here?

"Hey, you can say you died trying. That's worth a whole lotta nothing," Debbie Downer replied.

"Instead of catching the big fish, she's gonna end up feeding it," Negative Nellie added.

"This is going to be a God-blessed great show," Madi affirmed. She touched her crucifix, seeking strength and courage. She might be walking through the valley of the shadow of death, but she feared no evil. Perhaps that's why she had damaged that part of her brain, and why she was here now.

Once on the bottom, Juju and Levon would set up portable stands of LED lighting. The other five would descend into the cavern. Linkous had been gung-ho to see the basement. Roxy would deploy the GPR while Madi gathered coins from the intact amphora. Zhen worked as their videographer and perhaps liaison to any resident ghosts who felt like speaking up. She could also help the boys if they needed another hand. Agent Kaye and Linkous would search for more bodies and, Madi imagined, clues or treasure.

"Looks just as spooky as before," Roxy said.

"I hear whispers. This is a place with a history of pain and suffering. I wish Hojo was with me. He could tell us more," Zhen bemoaned. She had seen the video, but it gave only hints of the cold sensation of things crawling around. The ruins were gloomier despite the lights. Illumination revealed its grim base nature, its warts, and its vindictiveness in housing monsters.

Did her mind wonder if such beasts were hiding just out of sight? Sometimes they taunted Madi by slipping into her periphery. She knew not to trust things seen at the edge of her vision. "Let's get to it. Be safe. Be quick but don't hurry," Madi said.

"Anyone see any hungry reptiles or fish?" Linkous asked. He had watched the video.

"They were all in the basement last time," Madi said.

When they reached the tumble of river stones, the clock started ticking. Filmmakers often used the act of compressed time to create tension and suspense in movies. You have X minutes to complete your impossible mission or kaboom! She would use that in the narrative, that time is of the essence. There was also the ever-present danger of more collapses and aquatic predators. She preferred hyping up unlikely dangers.

Tick, tick, tick, Madi dropped the LED globe of brilliance down into the hole. Levon, Linkous, and Juju held their bang sticks ready. The light threw back the darkness, and the jumbo-sized tropical fish scattered. They had survived the night despite the lack of food, although some were pale and missing scales. Their shadows seemed to multiply, creating large schools of black fish. For the life of her, she didn't know why she had become so fascinated by shadows. She looked for the shape of the northern snakehead or the angler fish. She was relieved to find nothing of their kind. Since the dive party seemed safe, Juju and Levon put away their bang sticks and went to work on erecting the light stands.

"Are there less fish than before?" Roxy asked.

"I think so," Madi agreed. Something felt different, like the place was crowded with invisible sharks watching her every move, waiting for the right moment to strike. Although she wore a wet suit, she felt like she was being nibbled on, losing a little bit of herself with each passing moment.

"They likely ate each other. It's what fish do," Linkous suggested. He began to hook up his line for cave diving. Madi did the same, knowing they might be headed in different directions.

"And they could be dying off due to their environment. There's no salt, it's cold instead of warm, and the nutrients in this water are less plentiful and different. You can see that some are already showing signs of malnutrition," Zhen said, reminding them that they were all out of their elements here.

Could the gator be down here? Or those snakehead fish? Things had been abnormal, Madi thought. A cluster of parrotfish darted every which way, leaving behind several half-eaten corpses. A dozen seahorses raced off. A pair of devilfish swam by them, making her wonder again where the devil had all these warm water fish come from? And what was eating them? She caught a strange glint of light here and there, but when she focused on it, the illumination seemed to vanish.

They left the inflatable lantern as a beacon at the gap entrance, anchored caving lines so they could easily find their way back, and then Zhen, Roxy, Agent Kaye, Linkous, and Madi swam deeper into the basement, frog-kicking along the ceiling to reduce stirring up the sediment. Their headlamps carved slashes in the cavernous darkness. The glow from their suits widened it. Her suit shining blue, Zhen trailed a bit, recording between taking samples. Agent Kaye looked more like a Navy Seal than recreational diver.

Grandfatherly Alan Linkous looked warm in his orange, dry suit. His eyes were wide with curiosity, ready to see and explore new terrain. "Our time is short. Let's get 'er done," Linkous said.

"Time's awastin'," Agent Kaye agreed.

"Under the sea. Under the sea. Everything's better under the sea," Roxy sang quietly.

Zhen appeared doubtful, but she nodded. She was a myth huntress. Her camera and test tubes were ready. "I didn't realize there would be so many ghosts here. They are loud and angry," she said and winced. Without Hojo, she seemed even more sensitive to the spirits.

"Do you need to leave?" Madi asked.

"They warn of a predator," Zhen said.

Speaking of hunted, Madi sensed a growing hunger, and it wasn't her stomach. If anything, her gut was twisted in knots, excited and nauseous, trying to keep calm despite the adrenaline. She kept her gaze moving, looking for anything worth picking up.

Suddenly, her mask seemed to crack. It spread out darkly in eight directions. Oddly, the crack seemed to abruptly scuttle across her mask. She froze, a moment from freaking out, wondering how a spider could be there on the inside of her mask freakily near her eyes! She cringed as her eyelashes were brushed. She shined her flashlight across the glass to see and yet not blind herself.

The spidery crack in her mask was gone. Had she imagined it? It was another mystery to add to the out of place tropical fish.

Roxy pushed the case of the GPR ahead of her. "Juju, beware of Ursula."

"Who is Ursula? Is she a ghost?" Juju asked.

Roxy started laughing. "No, she's a fictional character, an octopus and a witch in *The Little Mermaid*."

"Juju, you said she reminded you of your Aunt Juanita. How can you forget? When I met her, I agreed with you," Zhen said.

"Oh, that Ursula. The depths have caused me to have a bubble brain," Juju replied. He hadn't been himself since the night dive.

Had any of them been? Madi wondered. Something about this place dimmed your hopes. Madi stayed focused, looking around but resisting the temptation to explore. Some fifty feet later, she shared a glance with Roxy as they reached an outlier of the spilled coins. Behind them, Agent Kaye and Alan Linkous had already turned down a corridor. Their bright lights grew dimmer as they explored further. Madi didn't recall what was down that way.

"There's no rockfall here. What broke the amphora in the first place?" Roxy wondered.

I did, Madi wanted to say. She bit her lip to stop it. What was wrong with her?

"What's right with you, Miss Big Fail?" Negative Nellie asked.

The divers' lights caused the gold and silver to flash and glimmer, throwing glints about the basement and off the fish, equipment, and furniture. Some of the fish shadows appeared to be cut to shards by the beams of illumination. Black, spike-haired spiders skittered among the coins, darting from under one to another. Why was she seeing arachnids? Or were they something else? The coins didn't appear to move, so she must be imagining things.

When Madi blinked, the spiders were gone. Her eyes were getting adjusted, she figured, and she wasn't as cold this time. Unless that was because she was numb. That would be worse. She wiggled her fingers and toes. They did feel better than before. Time to get cracking, she thought. It was a poor choice of words, and she wouldn't use them, as it sounded like she was breaking and entering, or nuts, or both.

Why are the coins strewn as if they had exploded out of their container?

"The lock on the gate is falling apart," a voice answered her. It wasn't Nellie or Debbie. Madi didn't like its tone. She had heard negative brain chatter before but never in such a cold voice. Screw you, she told it.

She dropped down to the amphora. She could see the coins shine, the glare spraying from the mouth of the earthen basin. She wondered if there ever had been a seal. She pushed down along the wall to get near enough to use her long-handled, rubber-tipped tongs. She plucked a dozen or so gold coins out of the amphora and picked up a few shards from the broken vessel. The pieces could be tested and dated.

Glancing over, she saw Roxy lining up the GPR device on the left side of the golden mirror.

Zhen's voice popped into Madi's memory and explained. Ground penetrating radar is a geophysical method using electromagnetic radiation in the microwave band of UHF/VHF frequencies of the radio spectrum. When the energy encounters a buried object or a boundary between materials of distinct types, say sand and rock, it will be reflected back to the surface. The principles used are similar to those of seismology, except electromagnetic energy is used instead of acoustic.

The vault door tried to draw her and hold her gaze. Inside the gold, the black inkiness appeared to be in motion as it spiraled downward. Madi felt like she was falling.

She jerked her eyes and her attention away. Idiot! She dared not get lost, again. First time had been an accident. The second time would be shameful. In the back of her mind, she could hear the clock ticking. Beat the clock! Ha, this wasn't a game show from the 1960s. She wasn't your host. Actually, she reconsidered. She was a host and damn good one. Boo-yah! She was getting ditzy.

And today was her lucky day. "How's it going, everybody?" she managed.

"It's a real gas. Never in a hundred years would I guess I would be doing this," Juju awed in childlike wonder.

"Are you feelin' groovy?" Roxy asked. She began humming.

"Yes, we are! It's going smoothly. We'll be done ahead of time," Levon agreed.

"I'll be damned. This is not what I expected to find here," Linkous said.

"Madi, you may not like what we've found," Agent Kaye said and paused. "I'm taking video of a coin minting stamp press."

Madi felt her heart sink. The valuable double eagles might be counterfeits. And yet, it could be worse. The old coins were still gold at a little over thirty-one of its thirty-four grams of weight.

Out of the corner of her eye, Madi spotted movement. The shadowy shape swam closer, growing larger. When she faced it, she found a huge, black, eyeless snakehead fish. She couldn't find her voice, though. The thing must be as long as she was tall, making it freaky big. It could swallow her head. She tried not to imagine it choking her down. As if her thoughts had inspired it, the thing's jaw unhinged ghastly wide. She hastily readied her bang stick. As if she had kicked a nest, black spiders boiled up from the amphora to crawl and cover her in two shakes of a stick. Madi tried to squish them, but they wriggled under her face mask.

"I'm going to take the first reading," Roxy said.

Madi heard the click of a button being depressed as the GPR was activated. The world shifted. The water jiggled. Light and shadow jumped and leapt about before resettling into familiar aspects. The dark, snake-headed fish was torn to shreds. The black spiders seemed to vanish.

"Did you feel that?" Zhen asked.

"Was that a quake?" Roxy asked.

"They happen here, but they're usually minor, below a three," Levon said. His radio crackled and popped.

"Yep. A river rock shifted and nearly fell on me. We probably experienced a mild earthquake. They happen around man-made lakes, but like Levon mentioned, they are usually small and most people on land don't feel them. Dogs and cats might. Hey, I've found what looks like a hatch," Agent Kaye said.

"Anybody who wants to can leave," Madi said. Again, her suggestion was met by silence. Everyone went back to work.

"I don't think so. Ha! I laugh in the face of danger," Roxy said.

Fearing a collapse, Madi searched for signs of trouble. Should they leave? She saw no signs of falling sediment. Nothing seemed to have moved, and yet, for a moment, everything seemed to have spasmed, Mother Earth suffering leg cramps. In those few moments, the creatures here had vanished. Nobody had said anything about the weird fish or spiders. Calm down, Madi thought. Get a grip.

"That was something else. The ghosts didn't like the blast of microwaves. They went from whispering to howling," Zhen said.

"So, we hurt ghosts?" Roxy asked.

"I don't know if it hurt, or if it just really upset them."

Time was racing by, and Madi felt like she was crawling as she searched the amphora. She pulled coins out, dropping silver and copper on the floor, until she found a golden skeletal key chased with copper and inlaid with black stones. It sure looked like a match to the door that showed no keyhole. When she picked up the key, everything seemed excessively bright. At the edge of this glare, she saw shapes with gnashing jaws striking and clawing at the light, writhing as their talons and sometimes arms vanished.

"All right. It has recharged. Here goes take two," Roxy said.

Again, the entire world jiggled. The shadows and light intermixed crazily like shaking a jar of oil and vinegar. Slowly, it separated and settled. The monsters with jaws were gone. Had they ever been there?

"You are losing it. The world is coming apart," Debbie Downer affirmed.

Madi glanced over to Roxy. She moved from left to right, crossing in front of the golden panel, unaware of the shadow fish darting in to nip at her. One nestled in her crotch. Within the golden door, the darkness reshaped and widened to create a gaping maw with shark-like teeth. It chomped open and shut trying to bite Roxy. Madi turned her headlamp on it. The shadow fish vanished. The mirror reflected the light, throwing it about the basement and vanquishing the dark images. What was that all about?

"You always were a ditz. After all, you're blond, aren't you?" Debbie and Nellie said.

The key grew heavier in Madi's hand. She lifted it, bringing light to it.

Madi gasped, unable to breathe or move. What in God's name, she asked as she mentally wigged out. She held a stick of dynamite in one hand and, only inches away, a flare in the other. TNT still worked in water.

"Madilyn, are you well?" Zhen asked.

"Let's blow this joint!" the voices suggested.

Madi panicked, immediately attempting to pull the fire and fuse away from each other. She didn't recall picking up a flare or a stick of TNT! What had happened to the key?

Her hands and arms refused signals from her brain, locked in shock, or time moved at a glacial pace, she wasn't sure, as both dynamite and flare trembled in her hands. Like a magnet to iron, they were drawn together, moments from bringing fire to the fuse, killing her, and bringing the ruins crashing down atop everyone.

God, no! Her show wouldn't go on!

This was madness. Even if she was hallucinating, she would not let this happened. She would not blow her future or her dreams. She had come too close to that before and had a steel plate in her head as a reminder. She was lucky to be alive to tell the tale and have a second chance. No way on Earth, so help her God, she prayed. Madilyn Marader was stronger than this mindless fear, this panic. Come on, Madi. You beat Nellie and Debbie before.

"Madi, are you praying? Is something wrong?" Zhen asked.

"What are you doing, Agent Kaye? We don't have time to mess with opening that," Linkous said.

"What we're looking for is stored under here," Agent Kaye said.

"Whatever it is, y'all will have to salvage it. There ain't..." Linkous told her.

"What are you looking for? More skulls?" Roxy asked.

Lord, Madi couldn't stop herself. The pressure on her shoulders and arms was tremendous. She felt her bones might break and that her muscles and tendons were ready to snap. The flare and fuse inched closer. It sparked and sputtered. She used every ounce of will and yet, fire and fuse still met. It caught and flared, sizzling toward the TNT.

Oh, God. Her heart seized. She couldn't speak, her tongue paralyzed, held by a fear she shouldn't be experiencing. It was all over. This Godforsaken house was going to kill them. She had brought them all down here to die. She had been a reckless fool.

Her alarm watch sounded. Roxy's chimed in louder. Their bottom time was up. Hell, their time was up!

"Third time's a charm. I'm button pushing, and then we ascend to decompress. I'm fed up with being cold, squeezed and spooked," Roxy said.

Along with the sound vibrations rippling through the water, microwaves spread outward into the limestone for a few feet and then bounced back out into the open space of the basement.

Madi felt release. Frantically, she dropped the flare and yanked out the TNT's fuse. She burned her glove and fingers, but she didn't care as long as she physically defused it. Her hand spasmed painfully and so she dropped the hot cord. Her elbow smacked into one of the black columns, knocking it loose. On instinct, she grabbed it.

Her panic drained away, and she felt like herself, but with burnt fingers and an overwhelming sense of gratitude. Her courage returned. She knew that angels didn't fear to tread anywhere. They had followed her into the darkness before and carried her back into the light.

Debbie Downer and Negative Nellie made no retort. Even so, Madi had almost led her friends to disaster. She grinned, relieved, and revived at having survived. Maybe her luck was improving. She didn't want to count on it. She tucked the TNT away in a pouch. She placed the fragment of fuse in one of the BC's pockets. She looked over to see Roxy watching her.

"Mads, how are you doing, Boss?" Roxy asked.

"Whew! Better. I froze up and got weirded out there for a minute. I'll explain once we're out of here and somewhere warm. And yeah, I'm taking home a souvenir. I don't care what my bro says. Now, I'm ready to get the bleep out of here," Madi replied while she displayed her find. It looked more like a staff or a walking stick than a thin stone column.

"Stylish and versatile, for evenings out or graveside funerals," Roxy said.

Her words seemed on point. Madi attached the bag of coins to her belt and carried the black stick while she kicked her way toward Roxy, the spider lady. Little black arachnids crawled in the shadowy recesses of her body. When struck with light, they disappeared only to reform later. How creepy. The spiders surged and shifted depending on the play of light and dark. They left the case of the GPR alone. Madi wasn't going to say anything. If Roxy didn't feel it, that was fine. Madi didn't need to make her paranoid. They were running late.

"I'm starting to think this was a mistake," Madi said.

"Say it ain't so," Roxy said.

"Zhen, how are you doing?" Madi asked her companion. She seemed to be very still.

"Do you hear the voices?" Zhen asked in a hoarse whisper.

Madi blinked. She didn't think she was talking about Nellie and Debbie. "I hear my own nagging ghosts. Are you talking about residents?" Madi asked.

"Yes! They said they were brought here to slaughter. Bled like stuck pigs! Blood for the lost souls and the damned!" Zhen replied, getting worked up.

"We are leaving now," Madi said.

"Not dead for the damned. That's not what they're saying," Zhen said.

"Crap! I'm hung up on something. Mads, my leg is caught," Roxy began.

Blinking to clear her vision, Madi saw that her partner wrestled with a chain. What the hell?! A manacle on the huge bed of rock had clasped around Roxy's ankle. They had joked this was a sacrificial altar. It didn't seem funny at all right now.

"Well, don't that just beat all?" Madi said, using one of her grandfather's expressions when she wanted to cuss a blue streak. She dropped her bag. She carried lock picks. She wasn't good with them, but she had them. "Juju, Roxy is manacled to a rock that might be an altar. Zhen's feeling overwhelmed. We need help."

"What? You did? Wait, you're goofin' with me," Juju replied.

"No leg pulling here. Bring your blow torch or whatever, ASAP," Madi said. Her fingers were mostly numb, so she fumbled with her tools.

"It wasn't for the damned. It was blood for Von Damme," Zhen continued.

"Hey, knock it off, Zhen, you're scaring us! Mads, you're all thumbs," Roxy said.

"My fingers are starting to go numb," Madi said. She caught movement out of the corner of her eye. She turned, finger on the trigger, ready to shoot whatever big underwater creature was about to attack her.

"Whoa, Madi! Hold your seahorses and that bang stick. I'm here, y'all, and I've picked a few locks in my time. I started with my daddy's candy drawer and moved up to his liquor cabinet. I got that out of my system, but I can still pick locks. I was at the top of my class at Quantico," Agent Kaye said. Close behind her floated the dive master. Linkous gave Madi the OK hand signal.

"I almost shot you," Madi said.

"I can live with almost," Agent Kaye replied.

"Are y'all okay down there?" Levon asked.

"Yes and no. Roxy is currently bound to a rock. Agent Kaye is getting out her secret underwater laser to cut through the links," Madi said.

"I wish," Agent Kaye replied.

"That would be so cool," Levon agreed.

"Aye. Things keep distracting us and finding ways to keep us down here longer. It's tempting to just keep exploring. I think it goes on and on," Linkous said.

"It doesn't look complicated, just old, maybe rusted. And yes, I feel watched. This place is creepy. Moonshine cellar. Coin stamper. That's two federal offenses. With a laboratory, there's likely drugs which makes three. We saw prison cells, so there could be even more charges," Agent Kaye said. She chose a couple of picks and began to work the lock.

Madi slowly turned in a circle. She felt surrounded. From the darkness, a large, sleek creature tail-propelled itself through the water. This time it wasn't a shadow. With scythe-sized teeth and yellow eyes, the reptile appeared all too real. "Oh, the shit has hit the fan now. Heads up, Alan! Gator at three o'clock!" Madi shouted.

With the way things were going, she should have expected this to happen. She had been trying to stay positive. She might be dreaming. She would usually use a dive pointer to keep curious fish away, but a poke with a thin metal stick wouldn't bother this monster. The black staff would work better to keep it beyond arm's length.

"They aren't supposed to like deep water. It'll drown," Linkous said.

"Speak louder, sir. I don't think it heard you!" Roxy said.

"The gators! He fed some of them to the gators for sport!" Zhen cried. She still talked about the ghosts.

"Either ole Crocker or Snapper has made an appearance, has he? Vik liked his reptiles," Juju said. His voice sounded deeper with less of his LA speech. Instead, he had gained an accent. "Wait, what's this? Could it be? I don't believe it. I thought it be lost forever."

"What's that Juju? Crocker? Snapper?" Zhen asked.

Madi was too busy to listen closely. The white-speckled alligator was a dark monster with teeth as big as butcher knives. His spots seem to have a hypnotic effect. If Madi hadn't already been fighting the urge to explore the mirror, she would have been immobilized, and the monster would take her arm off in one chomp.

"Shoot! Bang the damn thing!" Roxy suggested.

Linkous set his bang stick against its nose and fired. The detonation was a sharp crack and a bubble burst forth with the projectile. The bolt blasted into the alligator's left nostril, making it larger and bloody, ripping away a section leaving the reptile with a snarling look. The monster gator thrashed, lunging at Linkous and Madi. She used the black staff to keep her distance and the jaws away, but the impact knocked her backward into Agent Kaye. The monster lunged again and snagged Linkous' arm, tearing into suit and flesh. They struggled as the gator tried to drag him off.

Linkous stabbed the WASP knife into the gator's hide to inject it with chemicals. The beast seemed to pause, growing larger, and then it shuddered. They all expected it to float away, as advertised, but it didn't. The underwater beast seemed lethargic, moving slower, but it remained as if freezing it didn't injure the gator. It was a reptile, not a fish. That could be the difference. The gator rolled over, spinning them both.

"What's going on? What has you?" Levon asked.

Agent Kaye dropped her tools. She exclaimed with a profanity. "Shit. I'm all thumbs!" she snapped.

"Alan needs help!" Madi said. She picked up her flare and burned the alligator under its throat so it released Linkous' arm. A swipe by its big forepaw almost knocked the flare from her hand. Agent Kaye deployed her bang stick. The bolt drew blood, and this time the beast fled the pain and swam away.

Madi feared it would return at any moment, that or there might be more than one. Juju mentioned two names. That creeped her out. But then, Zhen had mentioned a third. Spot! Madi realized she was scared, and she wasn't supposed to feel frightened or thrilled. Her brain didn't work that way any longer. Then why did she feel this way? Were the doctors wrong? It sure felt like she could experience thrilling and fearful emotions again! She spotted a candelabra lying on the floor near the edge of the slab of rock and thought it might be helpful. She found a fireplace poker nearby and gave it to Roxy.

"I'm taking on water. Brr and losing air. But it's just a flesh wound. Nothing broken," Linkous said.

"Juju? What are you?" Levon gasped. His transmission seemed to have been cut off.

"Levon, are you okay?" Madi asked and waited. "Levon? Juju? Shit's hit the fan. Ah, damn, Dillon said it would."

Madi was ready the next time the gator came by. "Chomp on this, ally baby!" When it opened its mouth, she shoved a candelabra into its maw. It wrested and savaged it, bending and snapping it into pieces. Even so, it bought them more time. Agent Kaye kept working the lock to the manacles.

"Juju stop! He's gone crazy! He's got a knife!" Levon exclaimed.

To think she had gone from almost blowing them up to this. Who would have thought, and then she did think. She took the TNT in hand and stuck the short waterproof fuse back where it belonged.

"Huzzah! Here comes, Gatorcuda," Roxy said. When the gator charged in, its maw open, she jammed the iron fireplace poker into its mouth. It couldn't close its teeth, leaving it wide open for delivery. Madi lit the fuse and shoved the TNT into its lower jaw.

Its tail lashed around and slammed into her, knocking her mask off. The poker slowly bent, then the alligator used its tongue to push the metal out the side of its mouth. It looked like it was trying to work out the TNT, too. It appeared ready to pop loose, already part way out.

Madi didn't see the fuse. Had it gone out? This was a crazy way to end her show! She placed her mask so it stopped leaking, and she could breathe her last breaths.

The gator lunged and lurched. It suddenly exploded with a muffled boom into a ball of chummy meat, bones, and flashing light. The water absorbed much of the blast, but they were still buffeted by the force and swamped by gator guts.

"Yes, take that! Thank you! Thank you!" Zhen said.

"That's not what I visualized this morning when I was prepping for the dive," Roxy said.

"People will not believe a word of this. That's a helluva bang stick and isn't what I would normally advise, but it worked," Linkous said.

"I like it. So, we leave with a bang," Agent Kaye said. She continued to work.

"I didn't expect Dad jokes from a female agent," Madi said.

"We had fathers, too. Mine was a lot of talk," Agent Kaye said. She continued to work the picks. The lock fell open and away, freeing Roxy. "Bingo! I haven't lost my touch."

"I believe in miracles. Where you been, Baby?" Roxy sang. She was free to leave, so they all could get the hell out of here before something else went wrong.

Madi watched her exhaust bubbles. Up was out. She heard the sound of struggle, grunting and gasping over the radio. "Levon? Juju? We're coming! Stay aware, where there's one, there might be two gators," Madi said. She swam up and out into the lake, or thought she would. Something grabbed and wrapped around her. She drew her knife, slashing away.

"Madi. Take it easy. It's a rug. Stop stabbing and I'll help," Roxy said.

"Thanks, Rox, for keeping me in line and sane," Madi said. The rug was cold and clingy, but with assistance, Madi escaped. Even the furnishings tried to keep you from getting the hell out.

Leaving the cave was like going from night to day. The electric lights seemed harsh at first and stung her eyes, making her blink repeatedly. The other four divers followed her up into the rubble of the ruins.

It now appeared to be a movie set with a half dozen racks of portable lights. She squinted, able to make out what was happening but not why. It played out like a death struggle between scuba divers on a movie screen, but it wasn't Reality TV. It was heart-poundingly real.

***

What a difference a minute could make, the difference between life and death, Levon thought less than a minute earlier. This place seemed to lend itself to gloomy thoughts. Even so, he was loving this adventure of a lifetime! It was fantastic to dive with Alan Linkous, again. Having grown up in Bristol, Levon had heard stories about the graveyard and the small hamlets like Jacob's Creek, Summer's Creek, and Friendship buried underwater, but they had usually been too deep to explore. Why did they put cemeteries on hills?

He refocused on the job at hand. At one hundred and twenty feet, he didn't have time to waste. Every inch of him had over 65 pounds of pressure on him. It would be a little less at SoHo's altitude of 1600 feet, but by being higher in altitude they sacrificed bottom time. He finished the last connection on this final rack of lights. Good, he was getting hungry, and it didn't take any time being down here to miss good old Sol.

He paused to listen to the excited radio chatter. There had been a lot of it, but this sounded fearful. Roxy was entangled in something. Did they say chains?

"Either ole Crocker or Snapper has made an appearance, has he? Vik liked his reptiles," Juju said. His voice sounded deeper. "Wait, what's this? Could it be? I don't believe it. I thought it be lost forever."

Levon stroked to turn around to find that Juju was just floating there, staring at something in his gloved hand. The pale object gleamed in the brightness of his headlamp, but Juju acted like he couldn't see it clearly. Even so, Levon thought he heard sobbing. With all the radio chatter, it was hard to tell for sure. Levon decided this would be a suitable time to light up the place.

"Juju, I'm turning on the banks," Levon said and hit the button on the remote. He needed to test it, and he wanted to see what was going on up here and down there. In his opinion, you couldn't have enough illumination in this place.

The sets of lights flared on, brightening the lake bottom, and chasing away a little of the gloom but replacing it with murkiness. The ruins of the mansion seemed to wince, even leaning away from the lights. Levon chided himself for giving the place a persona. He wasn't a psychic, but this place felt mean and angry, a trapped and wounded animal ready to lunge and snap at anyone nearby.

Juju snarled. He swam like a dolphin, closing the distance to Levon. He carried a long, white knife that seemed to be carved from bone. Levon got too close a view as he leaned away from the blade jabbing at his eyes. It scraped across his mask.

"Juju stop! He's gone crazy! He's got a knife!" Levon yelled, and then he was too busy trying to stay alive to speak. When the stab came again, Levon seized Juju's arm. They wrestled and spun around, kneeing each other, and grappling for leverage. Juju was stronger. He yanked the knife free and jabbed, but Levon blocked it with an exploration stick. Juju was faster. He barely missed cutting Levon, but the blade nicked his air hose. A flurry of bubbles rushed out and up, seeking the surface. Levon could run out in a minute if he lived so long.

Juju lunged to stab. Levon turned, slipping the jab, and grabbed Juju's mask, pulling it loose. Juju didn't seem to notice that he was losing air. Had he forgotten that he needed to breath?

The arm with the knife seemed to move faster than it should. Levon couldn't dodge fast enough, getting slashed across both forearms. He grunted with each painful cut and feared the worse was to come.

He caught Juju's knife wrist with both his hands and attempted to wrench it free. Juju head-butted him, knocking Levon's mask sideways. It distracted him, opening him to the knife stab. Juju reared back, ready to deliver a killing blow.

Levon was certain that he was a goner. He mentally sent off a farewell to his mother and his father.

Suddenly, Juju slumped forward now limp like he'd been struck by a haymaker from behind. Madi floated there with a determined expression. She held what looked like a black walking stick with a silver tip. She had conked Juju. Madi handed Levon what he needed, the emergency extra hose with a regulator connected to her tank. He breathed, grinned, and gave her the OK hand signal. She replaced Juju's mask over his face.

"Thanks, I thought I was history," Levon said. He picked up the knife, holding up the pale, crude-looking blade set in a redstone hilt adorned in red-dyed and beaded leather. Blood oozed from the wounds on his arms where he had been slashed. They hurt like hell, but they weren't deep, closer to nicks than gashes. His suit had provided him some protection.

"Levon, breathe off my spare. Madi's taking Juju up," Roxy said. He changed to get air from her extra regulator.

"Let's go! I can't tell if Juju's breathing. We need to safely surface ASAP," Madi said. She inflated her BC, lifting her and Juju from the darkness and toward the light.

Come hell or high water, Levon was more than ready to get out of here. Alan wore the same expression. They both had been wounded. It was dangerous to tag along with the myth huntress. Levon wanted to hurry, but it was dangerous to rise faster than your bubbles. Bandages would have to wait until he reached the surface, but for now, he clamped down on both arms, crossing them, using pressure to staunch the wounds.

He was glad there weren't sharks, but he couldn't help but wonder about a second alligator. Did it smell blood in the water? That thought haunted him as they ascended, leaving the darkness for the light. He glanced down repeatedly, praying their luck would hold, but he was beginning to fear that the only fortune they would have was bad.

Was that something dark rising, following them and closing in? He tugged on Roxy to look. She did, but she only shrugged. "I don't see anything," she said.

Levon swore darkness gathered among them as they rose. He wanted to go faster, rush past his bubbles and race to the surface. He could, but that might kill him, too. Embolisms or gators? He wondered which would kill him first before they could reach the light.

Twenty-Nine

Morning Dive Aftermath

All the divers paused for a much-needed safety decompression stop at fifteen feet since Juju was breathing while unconscious. It would have been dangerous to take him up without blowing off some nitrogen.

That decompression time had given Madi long moments to contemplate. She often looked up at the sun beyond the water's surface, but she spent much of her time checking on Juju or down below and around for another hungry, monster gator. Madi could feel herself drawn to that horrible place deep below. How crazy was that? Her pulse pounded. Again, she wondered about experiencing such relentless fear. She had figured that the divers were just cracking under the pressure. Now she saw that their concerns and caution were justified. She had wanted to save her show. She could do that, even if the eagle coins were fake, stamped by Von Damme, because they were close to pure gold along with copper. Mostly, she was thrilled that they were getting out alive. She almost felt like she was crawling from the ruins of her car wreck.

Something down there affected her thinking. Had it driven Juju crazy? They were all off their rockers to dive the ruins. She should have waited for the new ROV to keep exploring. She had almost gotten them all killed. She hadn't been irresponsible, but she hadn't been level-headed either. Levon, Alan Linkous, and Juju were the ones paying the price.

"Madi, you're blaming yourself. We knew the risks," Roxy said.

Zhen nodded. "Yes. I encouraged you all to dive one more time. Dear Juju knew the place's history. Now we know it all too well. The spirits there wanted me to know how horrible it was. How inhuman and cruel Von Damme was. I can understand why that reverend blew up the mansion."

"We were warned," Madi said.

"That place was bat guano crazy and amazing. It has a seductive mystery to it. I think y'all did great, but I wouldn't recommend going back there," Linkous said.

"I owe you the cost of a dry suit," Madi said.

"He's right. Y'all were troopers. That place is deadly. It's better to let the drones explore it, if at all. There could be other gators down there. We just don't know, and Von Damme was full of surprises," Agent Kaye said.

"Horrible ones. I wish Hojo had been with me. His words of wisdom might have helped bring peace to those so abused and aggrieved," Zhen breathed.

Madi was relieved, but she almost couldn't believe that Nellie and Debbie remained silent. She sensed them brooding. They had been wrong. Madi hadn't blown this opportunity.

When the timer chimed, they headed to the surface. Tom, Doc, and Lan Caster literally hauled them out of the water. Kim almost yanked Alan Linkous out of his damaged drysuit. They weren't designed for quick escapes. Doc helped her slow down and calm down. Linkous' suit was ruined, but his arm was in far better condition than Madi had expected. He had bloody grooves where the gator's teeth had latched onto his forearm.

While Tom and Roxy pulled up the anchor and stowed gear for travel, Doc examined Juju.

"How is he?" Zhen asked. She worried her hands. She already looked as if the time in the basement's ruins had aged her. She had pale wings now with white hairs near her temple. If Hojo had been there, things might have been different. They would never know.

"Still unconscious, and his pulse is bounding," Doc said.

Madi immediately called 911, getting Andressa Elton, and relayed the specifics from Doc. While she talked with the dispatcher, Doc examined Levon. He ended up letting Roxy bandage his gashes while Doc cleaned and wrapped the dive master's arm. "A visit to the ER is in your future, Alan, but you don't need to go by ambulance," Doc told him.

With that, Alan and Kim returned to their boat. Tom and Kim fired up their respective crafts, and then they sped off, each heading for their home marina.

Madi felt, dare she say, optimistic, even as she watched a pale Juju suffer spasms underneath a blanket. She must be a little loco, but she knew he had a strong constitution, and she believed he would pull through. He was physically and mentally tough. He had survived an abusive father, a violent brother, a string of bad girlfriends, malaria while on a Catholic church youth trip, and the passing of his beloved Granny on his way to being an amazing adventure companion. She prayed Juju was well for all their sakes.

Madi didn't hear the negative voices. They should be telling her this was just like the diver named Eduardo. That meant Juju was as good as dead. Doc didn't think so, which is why she was holding it together, that and the camera. Even through the tears, smile for the camera.

"Thanks, Lan. Having you here allowed us to take along Zhen," Madi told Caster.

"Oh, ow! You're welcome. Sorry, my back's acting up. It feels a hundred years old," Caster said. The big man with the ponytail moved gingerly. He hadn't hired on for muscle, but he had been very helpful. Was his back another casualty?

Madi could relate and hugged the towels wrapped around her. She had been half-frozen and could barely move. Tom had swathed her in two warm towels. She opened her hand and looked at the locket. She had found it in Juju's hand. She had to pry the death grip open. There was no photo in it, but it read To Josef, Love Ava.

Zhen opened up part of her portable lab to test the crude, ivory knife with the fancy handle that Juju had used to stab Levon. She expected to face Deputies Hardaway and Cantrell, again. The knife would be confiscated as evidence. At least she had Agent Kaye with her to provide support for her explanations of what happened. She would give them a copy of the video, too.

They could report the alligator as dead. Did that mean it was safe? Why had Juju mentioned Crocker and Snapper? Had she killed Spot?

Madi put away the locket and used both hands to pick up the black staff. It felt special. She assumed it was made of a hardwood. She would have Zhen examine it in time.

"How are you doing, my friend?" Madi asked Levon.

He was rubbing his forearms and stopped. "I'm okay. I felt a little wild and desperate down there, too. I was afraid you were going to have to conk me next," Levon said.

"But you held it together. You don't have to go back when we set up. That's not part of the exploration of the ruins," Madi said.

"Thanks, but next time we will be riding sleds. I don't want to miss out on that just because of a couple of nicks," Levon said with a broad grin.

"I'm so looking forward to that," Madi agreed. His big smile was infectious. Madi realized that she no longer saw an aura of light around people like she had before the dive. What had changed? She frowned. Now, when she looked closely, her companions appeared to be shrouded in gloom instead of sitting in sunshine. For whatever reason, her brother looked normal, but everyone else seemed to be a pale version of their normal selves. She glanced at herself in the ski mirror. She looked like she was sitting in the sunshine. Why were others overshadowed? Juju was the darkest, and then she realized that Lan Caster shared a similar cloud of gloom.

"I hope Juju will be all right," Levon said.

"As do we all. We only like to hint that this type of thing might happen in Reality TV, not actually have it happen. Zhen, good lady, we're getting close," Madi warned. She could see the 421 Bridge.

The sound of trucks rumbled overhead as the red and white boat passed under the truss bridge. Seeing the No Wake buoy, Tom slowed Maverick. The boat settled into the water as he eased back some more on the throttle to chug in where the marina floated in the hazy cove. She wondered if one of the girls had been cooking breakfast.

"Ah, beer-thirty! We can celebrate Madi Marader, gator slayer. Or am I blowing that out of proportion?" Tom cackled.

Madi groaned. She almost felt motivated enough to slug her brother. Roxy punched him in the ribs for her. He just winced, complimented her, and bellowed raucously. Madi smiled. It made her feel better hearing him crow.

With a gasp, Zhen's face lit up with a joyous expression. Rapture danced in her eyes. Madi saw that second light and the slight shift in her friend's expression. Her ancestral guide had returned. This seemed like another miracle atop their escape.

"Hojo is back!" Zhen said and exulted. Her eyes were radiant. She looked around with those new eyes, and her happiness became muted. She saw something or someone who bothered Hojo.

"Happy dance time?" Roxy asked. She hadn't noticed the look flash across Zhen's face, so they raised their hands and bumped hips. "Yay, baby!" Zhen was less enthusiastic. Roxy might figure that she was just tired, but it was more than that. They needed to have a chat.

"That's great! What happened to him?" Madi asked.

"He fought a dangerous and dark spirit that cast him away. He says it was a beast that feeds on the blood of people. He claims it is a vampire," Zehn said. All the color drained from her face. There was an awkward pause of silence.

"That sucks," Tom laughed. Zhen double-glared at him. "That bites? Hey, I wonder if that's where those slang terms come from?" he asked, her brother unfazed. He would say that he had been glared at by more important people.

"Mads, you are truly related to him?" Zhen asked.

"Yin and Yang. They have a saying here that what can't be changed must be endured," Madi claimed. Zhen smiled. She was feeling good. Now if only Juju would join the uplifting moment by waking up and making a clever comment or quoting a movie.

"Ah, she's just matured a bit more. She'll go gray before I do, too," Tom said. He held up his fingers to show how little difference there was between them.

Madi ignored him. She was concerned by Hojo's claim. "A vampire? Really? One of the cult members perhaps?"

"That would be spooky. I hate to think there are any of those six-fingered vampire huggers still here. But hey, don't you think a cultist would have shown up on the security cam footage? It was probably a vampire. Yes, I believe in them. Before you give me shit, I'll just say that strange things happen sometimes on the quiet nights in a county bar in Appalachia," her brother replied.

"Really? Fine. This discussion is headed off the rails. Do you know someone named Josef? Or Ava? Anybody?" Madi asked. Her question drew no response. She looked at Roxy. Her brother and Zhen believed in vampires. By her expression, Roxy didn't doubt them like Madi.

Breaking the silence, Levon's stomach grumbled and rumbled loudly. "Sorry. Adventure makes me hungry," the young man admitted. Being wounded hadn't slowed his metabolism.

"You're way too tall for a hobbit and lacking stoutness," Roxy said.

"This does have a *Lord of the Rings* quest feel to it. I know we didn't have our elevensy snack," Levon said. His stomach made anything that he said after that moot.

The welcoming party consisted of an eager J-Man, a sour-faced Deputy Hardaway and a patient Deputy Marge, the anxious dock girls, and the grim-looking paramedics. She wondered if they were the same paramedics that had transported Rae. It looked like a wake waiting to happen, except that Sarge was barking up a storm, his boxer's stub working like a windshield wiper. Even Boomer let out a greeting woof. Thank God for dogs!

"Ahoy, there! Our ship has come in!" Kia announced. Ginger leapt lithely into Tom's arms. Sarge started howling. Tom paused in his welcome back hug to ruffle the dog's ears

Doc orchestrated the paramedics. To Madi, Angie and Brandon looked harried and worried. It reminded her of the look on Doc's face. What was going on at the hospital? The paramedics placed Juju on a backboard, strapping him down, and then with Levon and Tom's assistance, lifted him out of the boat and onto a gurney where they rolled him to the ambulance.

"Well, two times out, two emergency calls. Are we done here yet, Ms. Marader?" Deputy Hardaway asked Madi.

"Yes, we are. At least as soon as I talk with my superiors. You hear me, Madi?" Agent Kaye said.

"I understand. But, unlike this dive, the memorial isn't my project. You need to talk to the church," Madi suggested.

"I will have my bureau chief make that call. He's more diplomatic than I am," Agent Kaye said.

"Now somebody is making some sense. So, what happened to the big guy, your porter?" Deputy Hardaway said.

"Our security officer might have suffered nitrogen narcosis," Zhen emphasized. She was holding it together. Deputy Hardaway expressed confusion with a grunt. "Nitrogen narcosis is when too little oxygen and too much nitrogen reach the brain," she said.

"Juju's brain freaked out because he'd been poisoned by diving too deeply," Tom simplified. Madi scowled at him. He wasn't wrong. It was better than saying that he attacked Levon. "Hey, J-Man, did you bring the rock?" Tom asked.

"I sure did. It's under the bird and good to go. Mr. Chris Brown-stone and I took it for a test flight. Browny's triple checking things now," J-Man said and adjusted his glasses as if they had been jostled during said flight. Under his UT hat, Jay 'Who is the Man' Beck was a bear of a figure, his fuzzy beard adding to his Grizzly Adam's impression.

"Stand down there, Captain," Agent Kaye said.

"Okay. This sounds like a delay. What's up, Knives?" J-Man asked.

Doc returned looking calm. So, nothing further had gone wrong. "They are transporting, Juju. He remains unconscious but in stable condition."

"I've grabbed a change of clothes. I'm going to follow. I'll call you. Hojo has concerns," Zhen said. They hugged, and then Zhen rushed off.

The deputies were being patient. Madi gestured to Levon who explained about Juju becoming combative.

She watched Lan Caster futz around. He seemed a little befuddled by his own equipment. Madi shouldn't be surprised. Events had discombobulated all of them, except for Doc. He looked nonplussed, and it was only part act.

"Sounds like I should arrest Juju for assault," Deputy Hardaway said.

"I think he's been exposed to toxic chemicals. They all may have been," Doc said. By his expression, she wondered if he had been during his dives. He explained about the limited test results. They were going to obtain more water samples.

"I'll give the TVA a call," Deputy Marge said.

"Well, we do have some good news. We have one less gator in the lake," Agent Kaye told them.

"Do tell?" Deputy Hardaway said.

Roxy shared the story this time.

"And where did this TNT come from?" Deputy Marge asked.

"I don't know where Madi got it, but we saw a crate near the stamp press. There might be others. There's a lot of crap, some of it dangerous, stashed down there. Add that to the list of reasons to keep people out of there and shut down the place. Madi?" Agent Kaye said.

"I don't remember where I found it. Somewhere near the amphorae, I think," Madi replied.

"We'll need to let the TVA know. They can spread the word for the gator hunters to stand down," Deputy Marge said.

"This might not be the one we saw on the video. This monster had white spots on him. So, it might be too soon to call off the hunt," Madi said. Roxy nodded, agreeing with her.

"So, you think there might be more than one? I'll mention that, too" Deputy Marge said.

Madi desperately wanted to get the residue of the ruins off her body. Still in her swimsuit, Madi slipped under the hot water of the dock shower. The deputies could ask questions while she rinsed. She couldn't believe how much better she was feeling. It was wonderful! She could still feel guilt and gratitude.

"All right, Mr. Crossette. You're first since you were the accosted. Do you want to press charges?" Deputy Hardaway asked.

"Can I answer questions while I eat?" Levon asked. His stomach rumbled.

"If you want to hear him, you should. His empty stomach is boisterous," Madi said.

"Fine. We'll do it inside. Nobody leaves unless you get my say so. You got that? Good. Go eat, clean up or whatever. Just be here for questioning," Deputy Hardaway said. He eyed them as if his stare was enough to keep them honest and their noses' clean.

"Yes, Deputy Hardaway," her brother mollified. Both deputies glared at Tom then Madi. That was a problem with living in the town where you grew up. Your family history stayed with you, and sometimes your relatives paid the price of sharing blood. Once the deputies were busy, their backs turned, brother and sister grinned at each other.

Roxy wasn't done testing the knife, yet, having taken over from Zhen, so Madi intercepted the deputy when she heard him open the door. She met him and gestured for him to lead the way. She didn't have much to add, and she didn't expect answering his questions to take long. She was just using a delaying tactic.

It almost backfired on her when Deputy Hardaway wanted to know what she had used to strike Juju. She hadn't lied, although she had thought about telling him that she had used her exploration stick, but the event was recorded on video. It's why people wanted the police to wear body cameras. He asked to see it along with the knife. He donned gloves and stuffed the knife in a bag. He looked over the black stick, but he didn't take a second glance at it. Madi breathed a sigh of relief when he handed the staff back to her.

"You know, I find it kind of interesting that a man who wanted to kill another man used a knife when he had a shot gun, one of those bang sticks," Deputy Marge said before the officers departed.

At that moment, Madi wondered if Juju had forgotten that he had a bang stick, or forgotten what one was. How had he known about the gators named Crocker and Snapper? She doubted that going to the hospital had been a gas.

The deputies departed. With the memorial dive in limbo, Madi expected to have time to do some video editing and narration, unless Zhen or Juju needed her. Then she would come running.

After Madi changed clothes, she noticed J-Man, her brother and Doc standing around near the helipad. Agent Kaye and Deputy Marge were leaving the three blood brothers to their thoughts. Another man was cleaning the windshield of the Tennessee Volunteer orange J-Copter. She noted the large flat rock hanging under the craft's belly. She walked over to get a look at the inscription on the memorial stone.

"Any results?" she heard J-Man ask.

Knives nodded. "Yes, they're in. We suffer Post Traumatic Stress Disorder. It means we need to get counseling," he said.

"Hey, it's not paranoia if something is actually out to get you. I know what I saw," J-Man said.

"That sounds like time anxiety or chronophobia, believing that terrible things will happen."

"Your point is? I'm paying attention so it doesn't happen again," J-Man asked.

"Exactly. You're in a state of high alert for too long. You and I suffer from high levels of cortisol. It means our adrenal glands are working overtime. The adrenaline and the stress affect our brains: what we see, what we feel, and what we think. Over prolonged periods, this situation could lead to acute and potentially deadly health issues. There's still time to reverse any damaging effects," he reassured. "The test samples of water and blood lend credibility to the hypothesis that we have been exposed to toxins, perhaps hallucinogens. We'll know more with additional tests. I need to have your blood work redone, anyway, Tom. It had canine markers.

"I am hungry like a wolf, and I can ski with the big dogs, so I don't have to stay on the friggin' porch," Tom replied.

"Next you'll tell him that he's barkin' up the wrong tree," J-Man said. Tom snorted.

"Is that the memorial?" Madi asked. She didn't like what she overheard. Her brother's best friends were mentally health challenged. Not that she was one to talk. Could she trust them? J-Man was an excellent pilot, but he had crashed and burned, literally. Doc ate stress for breakfast, but eating too much of anything could make a person ill. She hoped this situation wasn't a ticking time bomb. Addicts knew about mental challenges.

"Yes. I guess this will be what they call closure, if and when we're allowed to set it in place. Honestly, I'm good with the delay," J-Man said.

Madi studied the gray stone, the dates, and read the inscription: Reverend Dennis Rentzel. Beloved husband, son, dear friend, and guiding light. After it was put in the water, nobody would see it. She understood that the ceremony was for the people who still lived.

Madi had come near dying many times, twice too close. Today, she had survived another brush with death. Not surprisingly, it made her philosophical and moody, neither of which could over-shadow her warming enthusiasm. Her fears and paranoia seemed to have vanished under the sun, along with her ability to see auras. Instead of people with lanterns inside, they looked normal, except her brother and Ginger who seemed somehow larger than life. What was she missing here? Madi wondered.

"If he hadn't blown up the place, you probably wouldn't be diving and finding gold," Tom said.

"I don't understand why he demolished the place and killed himself in the process," Doc said.

Tom put his hands on his hips but remained silent. His glare spoke volumes, though.

"Denny believed it was evil," J-Man said. He seemed to be thinking back. That night, his helicopter had crashed in the lake. A flock of birds had flown into the rotary blades, damaging them.

"I'm a believer now. Earlier, while there, I was possessed by either delusion or madness," Madi began. Away from the cameras, away from the crew, she told her brother and his friends about awakening suddenly to find a stick of TNT in one hand and fire in the other.

"I wish I could say that I was shocked. Troy used to say that place was trying to kill people and succeeding. I don't know how he got in and out four times. He's like the Houdini of death escape artists. The house even collapsed on him, and he made it out with the help of John's ghost," J-Man said.

"Why are you doing this?" she asked.

He sighed. "These people deserve closure, and if I don't do it, someone else will. At least I'm mentally prepared for disaster and my insurance is paid up. Tell you what, I'll wear a helmet, an inflatable vest, and keep scuba tanks and respirators in the back seat for us, again. This time, I've got a co-pilot instead of a gunner," J-Man replied.

"I can outshoot Jambo, you know," Browny replied. He scooted out from under the copter and stood up. He looked ex-military with a buzz cut, heroic jaw, and a mini tank for a body that wasn't quite the fine-tuned machine that it had been ten years gone.

"I'd like to see a contest someday. Madi, this is Christopher Brownstone. That's too many letters we just call him Browny," J-Man said. The nickname sounded more like Brawny.

Madi smiled. "Pleased to meet someone normal."

"Who said that? Please to meet you, too. Now I can say I met the adventuresome and beautiful Madi Marader. You do know that you got all of the siblings' good looks," Browny said.

"I keep telling him that," she laughed. "Y'all are great friends to do this."

"Honestly, I feel like we let our friend down," J-Man said.

"We are all doing the best we can. Keep that in mind," Doc said.

"So, boys and girls, do you think that knife was cursed, and that's why Juju lost his mind?" J-Man asked them. It sounded like a simple, if crazy, question.

Nobody said anything for a moment.

"No, I think he suffered a stroke and became combative, or he's been poisoned and having a reaction," Doc told him.

"Yeah, based on experience, that was my first thought, too," J-Man said, obviously lying through his teeth.

"It's in the hands of the TVA and the FBI now. I'm going to watch some film and work on some narration," Madi said.

She hadn't heard from Debbie Downer or Negative Nellie in a while. They had both been quiet since she had resurfaced. Did she really want to go back down there? Is that where they lurked? Places to explore yet remained. And yet, she had been seconds from blowing them to smithereens. Did she trust herself?

In her room, at her computer, Roxy joined her with news. "Hey, Mads. I've looked at the readings from the GPR. I'm not all that sorry to say that behind that mirror is solid limestone," Roxy said.

Madi was so disappointed. Going behind the mirror must have been an *Alice in Wonderland* hallucination, *Beyond the Looking Glass*. Well, that satisfied that curiosity. There wasn't a vault hidden there. What a fool she had been. J-Man was right about the mansion. It tempted with false promises and killed the curious and any who loved to explore.

Roxy placed the black staff in Madi's hands. "It's made of some kind of ash, I think, with silver inlaid. It's been oiled, I'm not sure with what, to make it waterproof, which darkened it. There are fractures and yet it seems solid. I've tapped it with a mallet. Zhen might think of some tests, I can call her. I'd like an update on Juju. So, what do you think about her claim about vampires?"

"Zhen is usually so level-headed, but Hojo has seen more than we have. I guess that would explain why nobody except Juju appears on the security footage. It seems far-fetched. Wait, are you talking about Dillon being in the boat with Zhen during our first dive?" Madi asked. She had almost forgotten about that. She had no idea what it meant.

Roxy nodded. "I didn't notice anything that odd there, but the video makes it look like some of him doesn't record. Zhen said that Hojo believes that he is both spirit and flesh, a borderwalker, which they say is a being with a foot in this world, the Seen, and the other in the Unseen world. I had a Cherokee sister-in-arms, and she referred to it as Above and Below. Supernatural creatures like rakshasas can alter their shape to look human," Roxy said.

"She said that? Are you thinking that the scrumptious Dillon is supernaturally handsome?" Madi asked.

"And he claims to have issues with the sun due to medication and illness. Wasn't he a Kung Fu god around here?" Roxy asked.

Madi nodded. "He was a handsome young man, and his sister is beautiful. Dillon was a giant slayer, for sure, bigger and older, it didn't matter. He was overprotective of his sister, so she never had a date because guys were terrified of Dillon Urich. I'm glad he wasn't my brother."

"You have Tom instead," Roxy smirked and then added wistfully. "Having a protective brother sounds good to me. I'll be there, if you want, when you talk to him," Roxy said.

Madi wasn't ready to put that kettle on to boil, yet, as they said around here. She had enough irons in the fire. She must be more creative in her narrative, she reminded herself. She made herself sound old using those idioms, and yet, she spoke with the voice of the region. God bless her, she had been a poor thing shaking in her fins. Even now, standing on terra firma, where she was no longer scared, she was of two minds on what to do next.

She reasoned that she should be cautious. If Hojo was wrong, it was no big deal. Dillon was human. But what if Hojo was right?

Thirty

The Nazi

After getting chewed out for wasting the department's time, Marge found a computer and scrolled through virtual pages of local mug shots looking for known criminals from last night while Boomer was patient and balancing a cookie on his nose. She hadn't needed the squeezable stress ball or the Dammit Doll to smack on the desk to get rid of frustration when she had a wonderful companion. A couple of doggie-rubbing minutes later, she was well licked and so was her aggravation. Not surprisingly, more people were pleased with Boomer than her. Whoever said this life was a dog-eat-dog world didn't spend much time around dog lovers, and Bristol was full of them.

Both Richter and Mudder had eluded the cops and deputies in last night's raid. They had apprehended twenty-two people. Most were arrested for trespassing or driving while under the influence. None of those busted had taken part in organizing the fights. The locally hired grunts had been treated like mushrooms. They had only caught small fish, letting the big ones get away. The failure was disappointing, but that was life and law enforcement. It was easy apprehending stupid bad guys. Catching smart criminals was much more difficult, but there would be other chances. Without Rhett Archer, they wouldn't have known about the illegal fights or the gambling. She almost hated to admit that she had fun on the adventure since it had been a monumental waste of resources and manpower, not to mention womanpower.

And yet, there had been a lot of hurrying to get in place, and they had mostly come up empty-handed. She hoped to change that. She had nothing on the Masked Nobody or Mudder, and she found no beauty contestants like Dizzy Rae. She found Brokaw as Terri Baker. She had been suspended and then banned from mixed arts fighting for beating up a referee. After serving a year for battery, she had been released on parole nine months ago. Baker's current address was in Kingsport. She was a small fish and probably could care less who organized the fight, just as long as she got to beat on someone. Some folks were ready to fight at the drop of a hat, and Baker seemed like one.

Marge had more luck when she checked the database for felons and those with records having Nazi and Satanic affiliations who also loved fisticuffs. Many people relished fighting, but hand-to-hand, brawling and grappling were different than using a knife or swinging a bat. Her first search hit found the Nazi. Bingo! Sometimes technology could be wonderful.

Joni stopped by from the city police. She poked her half-shaved head into their office, bringing attention and awe. The department's version of Wonder Woman sounded like she hadn't had her necessary dosage of caffeine, yet. "Hey, Marge, don't let the turkeys get you down. We had no clue until you informed us about the illegal fights. They should pull their heads out of their offices every now and then to see what it's like outside. Stay the course, sister," Joni said. She left Marge smiling.

"Ya gotta love her. Wow, was the computer actually helpful with finding someone from last night?" Ron Burleson asked, peeking at her screen. He had come in early, too. His coffee smelled like cream and hazelnuts. He had been to Blackbird Bakery again for donuts. She ignored the aroma. She couldn't keep up with Boomer and criminals if she snacked on pastries.

"Yep, it is. It found one of the guys fighting last night, the Nazi. His name is Wolf Richter. He isn't from Germany but from New Braunfels, Texas. He has been jailed in North Carolina several times for fighting, but he has yet to see prison time," Marge said.

"That could be changing depending on how the day goes and how the wind blows," Ron said.

"If he's just an illegal fighter, he might receive a slap on the wrist instead of gut punch. If we put some attention and a little pressure on him, he will likely flee. That should work to our advantage."

"Yes, it's easier to search his car for an infraction than it is to search his house," Ron agreed.

If she found something in Richter's vehicle, she thought, it could convince a judge to let them search the Nazi's house. Many things pointed to him being the Oktoberfest Vampire, but that didn't mean he was a serial killer or a vampire wannabe. Even if he was innocent of those crimes, it was probable that he had something illegal stashed at home. He was that kind of guy, not that she was profiling or anything,

Ron agreed to help. She considered him a Godsend. She was thankful that he and his family had moved back here from South Carolina after his days in the Marines. Marge let her superiors know what they were doing. They hoped that this time she came up with something worthwhile.

The Good Lord must have been with her and wanted this guy caught, Marge thought. As she turned onto Beech Forest Road near Richter's address, she saw his black SUV pull out of the driveway.

The Nissan Rogue had a Tennessee plate identical to the one registered with the DMV. He or someone looking much like him was driving. She wondered if she had been lucky enough to catch him in flight.

She followed for a while, hoping he might get nervous, but he didn't seem to notice her. This rolling, hilly area outside of the city's limits had houses built around the different branches of the river. Nearby was the South Holston River Cabins, southeast of the dam near Bullock's Hollow. She followed him along the road with the same name, crossing People Road, and taking a right turn onto Booher. They drove past the sprawling Blue Ridge Equestrian Center. Marge didn't think he'd even looked back yet. He kept bringing something to his face, and she didn't think it was his smart phone.

Just before Hickory Tree Road, his Rogue almost struck a bicyclist turning into the Cornerstone Freewill Baptist Church parking lot. She was glad God was on the man's side, and the pastor was safely off the road. She had the near miss recorded on the cruiser cam, and it was enough that she could justifiably pull Richter over. She flashed the car's lights and let the siren briefly wail.

Richter didn't run, darn it. He steered the SUV to the shoulder and parked. She waited for her back up to arrive and join her. A couple of minutes later, Ron Burleson's black and white cruiser pulled in front of the Nazi's SUV and parked there. He exited his vehicle.

Marge and Boomer approached the Rogue. It was undamaged but had weeds sticking out here and there from the bumper, trim, and a wheel well. The black SUV could easily be or not be the one that drove onto her grandpa's property near Sugar Hollow.

The window rolled down to reveal a battered and bruised face. Richter's swollen eyes glared at her from above sunglasses. She didn't feel sad for him in the slightest, except the Masked Nobody had been so scrawny.

"How can I help you, deputy?" Richter asked. He reeked of cigarettes and peanuts. She had been hoping for booze, beer or pot. Sucking on coffin nails while driving was accepted by law as long as it wasn't distracted driving. She noticed nuts sticking to his teeth. Boomer started sniffing the air and grimaced. He disliked the stench of tobacco.

"Yes, sir, you almost hit that minister riding a bicycle. "

His mouth dropped a bit, and she could see that Richter hadn't even seen the cyclist.

"License and registration, please," Marge said. She already knew his license and insurance were current. Maybe he didn't carry his cards and paperwork. Unfortunately, he was an organized criminal. He handed her his license and current registration. She began to fill out the ticket.

"Mr. Richter, I heard an interesting story at the station. There was illegal fighting and betting last night in the train yards. I heard a scrawny guy, twigs for arms and toothpicks for legs, beat the snot and tar out of a big bruiser, Aryan race Nazi type."

Richter's face went white. His scabrous lips pressed into a thin line.

"It's too bad they interrupted the fight. I wonder what would have happened next? Was there a true mixed martial arts competition with women beating the piss and vinegar out of men? I can just see this sorry excuse of a male getting KOed by a princess. I wonder if his face looks anything like yours?"

"A stack of goddamned firewood fell on me," he snapped.

She sensed that he was lying. Even so, Boomer wasn't reacting to any smell of alcohol, drugs or the Oktoberfest Vampire. It was time to let Richter go. She prayed that she had irritated him so much that he did something stupid or revealing without killing anyone. "Well, I hope you were on your way to the doctor."

"I am. I can feel myself swelling up," Richter said. He placed a cold pack on his right cheek.

"Is that from eating peanuts?" she asked.

"I don't have a peanut allergy, and I love Paydays of all kinds," he replied.

"Here I was hoping it was my lucky day to pull over the Oktoberfest Vampire," she said.

"C'mon, get real. It's daytime, officer."

"I didn't say you'd really be a vampire. Do you believe in them?" Marge asked, digging.

"I believe there are dangerous things that go bump in the night that never get photographed and only spoken of in whispers. Now, can I go to see my doctor?" he said.

"Have you been over to Sugar Hollow recently?"

"No, and I'm not the Oktoberfest Vampire. Lady, ma'am, you are really reaching," he replied.

"Yes, sir. Here's your ticket. Have a nice safe day and pay attention to where you're going, especially when you're driving. The Lord might be less forgiving if you run over one of his disciples," Marge said.

She watched Richter drive off. Boomer just sat there. Crap. She believed Richter when he said he wasn't the Oktoberfest Vampire, and that he hadn't been out to Sugar Hollow.

"And here I was hoping he would lead us on a merry chase that didn't do any property damage or injure anyone," Ron said.

"I like how you dream big," Marge said.

Less than ten minutes later, Marge received a dispatch about road rage at the pumps of a nearby Gas 'n Go. The description matched Richter and his black Rogue. The call-in reported a big guy beating up a little guy. At the gas station in the Food City parking lot, Marge talked a little with Joni who was ignoring the gawks of the staff and customers. As a tall powerful woman, she stood out, and people sensed it. When she smiled, people melted. When she glared, people froze up and thought twice.

Marge interviewed the young man's girlfriend and other eyewitnesses. Colby Crossette had pulled up to the pump. When he exited his vehicle to fuel it, a white brute had attacked and shouted, "Never, again. You hear? Never again, you skinny piece of shit!"

Marge understood his ranting while it confused the witnesses who claimed that it seemed like the perp knew the victim. Poor guy thought that he had brought it on himself.

"I said, it's my turn. First come. First serve, buddy," Colby muttered. That had been enough to set off Richter.

Marge put out an APB on Richter for assault and battery. They would catch the Nazi sucker.

Even when they apprehended him, she doubted it would solve the Oktoberfest Vampire murders mystery. Perhaps it would help them catch the traveling fighting ring.

Angie Severett, a fellow farm gal and a Sullivan County paramedic, examined Colby and found mostly flesh wounds. She patched him up. Colby would need stitches. Nothing was broken, so they recommended ice, compression, and a pain reliever before going to ER. It was so busy. Angie suggested Colby check with his doctor and see if he could get a same day visit. Before he left, Marge mentioned that his attacker had been 'whupped up on' by someone who looked a little like him.

"Great. It wasn't just me," Colby said with a smile and winced. It wasn't his fault after all.

Marge returned to Beech Forest Road to question Richter's neighbors. It was tedious work, and people in general were poor eyewitnesses. She turned up very little, except confirming that Richter had been out most nights the last two weeks and returned much later, according to the self-proclaimed insomniac who lived to the south of Richter's place. Alexa Sissy said that man had never, ever waved back at her or smiled, but she hadn't had any trouble, either.

Roy Burress, a white male retiree with the pair of friendly golden retrievers, agreed with what Ms. Sissy had said about Richter's comings and goings. Marge didn't know if that meant that Richter was out boxing, pretending to be a vampire, or beating on his girlfriend.

While leaving the neighborhood, thinking that she had interviewed everyone, Marge noticed a tall, pale figure trudging through the woods to what looked like a weathered barn. She hadn't seen him before, although by the way that he walked, his gait and demeanor seemed familiar. Regardless, she had yet to question him. He was in the neighborhood, so Marge parked and called in that she had found an extra witness to question.

She and Boomer hiked uphill through the woods to a gravel driveway. She figured she was on the Goldstein's land and followed it to the barn. The shadows were thick, and the contrast between bright patches and shade mucked with her vision. She had to wait and adjust, and too often, she thought she saw something, and nothing was there. Boomer only reacted to a squirrel with his I wish I could chase that critter bemoaning whine, but he only did it once, and after that, nothing seemed to move. It was fall, after all, and she could hear the leaves hit the ground since it was so quiet in this low-laying, hilly area downriver of the dam. She and Boomer were alone except for whoever hid in the barn. She didn't like the feel of the place, and it didn't help that her Satanic burn throbbed and her hand ached. It hadn't hurt like this before.

Because her danger sense was also warning her, Marge requested back up and returned to her vehicle. She turned her cruiser around and backtracked to the entrance to the gravel road via a driveway on the Goldstein's' property. When she had questioned them earlier, they hadn't mentioned having a son. She knocked on their door and no one answered. Usually, this wouldn't be a big issue, but her intuition told her something was wrong.

Shortly, Ron Burleson arrived, shotgun in hand and ready for bear. He had learned to trust her danger sense, too. She briefed him, and then they walked the driveway to the barn. They didn't have a warrant, so they would handle this in a friendly manner. He hung back and covered her, as well as watching for anyone trying to slip out the back, although Boomer would hear flight attempts, whether it be by bird or man. Boomer started to growl. It meant that he had caught a familiar scent. He whined to let her know. Had he smelled the Oktoberfest Vampire?

Marge knocked and announced herself as a deputy sheriff of Sullivan County. "I was driving through and asking questions about your neighbor, the big guy driving the SUV. I saw you, sir. And my dog knows you're in there. I would just like to chat about Mr. Wolf Richter," she said, stepped back and waited patiently.

Boomer's ear's perked up and the top half of the barn door swung open and out. A young man stood very tall and pale with dark hair and bloodshot eyes as black as night. Usually when you met someone who was homeless or a squatter, they didn't look you in the eyes. This skinny man seemed somewhat defiant, even protective of his turf. She wondered if anyone else was in there.

"I don't know the man you're talking about," the young man said. He looked emaciated and in need of a month of good meals. An old scar ran along his cheek.

"You don't know Mr. Richter? And who am I talking to?"

"My name's Mort, Mortimer Teivel," he replied.

"Do you live in the neighborhood, Mr. Teivel?" she asked.

"I've been living here for a while. It's safe and quiet. Nobody bothers me," Teivel said.

Marge felt that pain in her neck. "Did a big, bald guy with tattoos ever harass you, sir? Call you names?"

"No. Nobody bothers me here," he said coldly.

"Did he ever confront you on the street or in the woods?" she asked.

"No. I can take care of myself. I have for a long time."

She thought a half truth. He had encountered Richter. It probably hadn't gone well. Mr. Teivel didn't want to make a scene, most likely because he was up to something illegal.

"You know the county has shelters that can help you get back on your feet."

"I know that, but I like it here. There would be too many people there and too much noise. The Goldsteins are nice folk. They know I'm here and don't mind. I park my VW Beetle at their place. It's a classic, 1965. I can fix it myself, usually. I'm a good mechanic. Aw, heck, people lie to you daily, I'll bet. Call them, the Goldsteins," he said and handed her their catering business card.

When she called, Mrs. Goldstein confirmed it. A friend's nephew had fallen on hard times and needed shelter for a while. Mortimer was repairing their Ford Explorer and pickup as compensation.

"They vouch for you. And you've never had a run in with this man?" Marge asked. She showed him Richter's picture.

"Nope. Not a run in, walk in or sit in. From what Mr. Goldstein said, he's a mean SOB. He told me to avoid him."

"Richter likes to fight. So, he never punched you? He's been known to bully people," Marge asked.

"I told you that I hadn't met him, but he did almost run over me with his car," Mort lied and spoke truthfully. She didn't know what to make of it. He wasn't homeless, and he wasn't a squatter. He was telling half-truths.

"Have you been over to Sugar Hollow recently?" Marge asked him. She wanted to know where he was two nights ago.

"No. My car has been flustrating me," Mort said, again speaking the truth and lying. He was flustered and frustrated. Now she was starting to feel the same with this walking contradiction.

"Thank you, Mr. Teivel. If you think of something, have Mr. Goldstein give me a call."

"I'll do that. Have a nice day," Mr. Teivel replied.

At their cruisers, she discussed her conversation with Ron. He knew her suspicious look, but they agreed that they had no cause to check inside the building or detain Mr. Mortimer Teivel. He was legally on the property, and they had no reason to believe there was wrongdoing. Judges believed that twinges in the neck by a veteran law enforcement officer could work as an informal veracity meter, but they couldn't take intuition, hunches, or instincts into account under the rule of law in court. Your feeling is right. Get me proof. She had heard that often. Well, she wouldn't be able to follow his car. She believed him about his VW Beetle not working. Even so, she spread the word to stay on the lookout for a black 1965 bug.

Late in the day, there was a car chase back and forth across the county line. Marge was not near enough to be involved because she was with Boomer searching for a lost kid at Backyard Terrors Dino Park in Bluff City. Even so, she kept appraised of the situation. Soon enough, Mr. Richter wrecked his car and some property, but no one else was injured. Weapons and Paydays were found in his truck.

The county judge authorized a warrant. Marge was assigned to help with the search.

In Richter's place, they found evidence in the form of trophies from the victims. They were tucked here and there, squirreled away in odd places out of sight. In the bathroom, she found a jar with faux vampire teeth that were bloodstained. They found plenty of damning evidence, but none of them discovered any kind of journal, manifesto or plans for the next kill. Was he a spontaneous killer?

Everyone else was confident that they had caught the Oktoberfest Vampire. Marge quietly shared her suspicions with Ron and Joni. Now the media would give it a rest and law enforcement a break. Bristol was a good place to live, again, as long as the winds from the dump weren't blowing your way.

Marge had her doubts, mostly due to her own internal lie detector and Boomer's reactions. He had smelled Teivel before. That was more plausible in court, but it wasn't enough to act on.

Thirty-One

Federal Bureau Incident

With all diving on hold, it was time to drive the skulls to the FBI forensics labs in Quantico, VA. Agent Sabrina Kaye loaded the evidence cooler with the seven craniums and associated bones into the trunk of their government-issued GMC Yukon. She hoped forensics could explain at least some of what had happened to the deceased and why some had vampire like teeth. It was one way that the dead could speak.

Suddenly, she had a sense of something missing. She opened the cooler and checked the number of skulls, counting seven. They were all there, all except Yoric's. Who was he? She wondered. She must be tired. The ruins and that basement tugged at her childhood fears, giving her weird thoughts. Yoric, where are you?

"Are you okay, Sabe?" Denzel Bond asked. Den was a good guy, a great listener, understanding and a keen-minded agent. He usually worked research, but they made a good team on this *X-Files/Stranger Things* kind of assignment. Most believed a cult was involved. What they had seen so far hadn't changed her mind.

"So, so. I have a headache, and my head's clogged. I think I have water in my ears," Sabrina said. She heard poorly right now, her sinuses packed, her head feeling crowded. "And those skulls give me the creeps for some reason."

"I agree. There were too many in one place, like a mass grave. Or did you mean because they remind us that we are mortal? That could be us. We have skulls. I remember the first time my father told me that, it was creepy," Den replied, tapping on his head. "We are alive, but tomorrow we could be dead, especially in this line of business. Neither the Feds nor those in blue are appreciated right now."

"Den, thanks so much for cheering me up. I can't shake the feeling that I'm missing one of the skulls, but I don't know why. We have the right count," Sabrina said. She thought back. Did she recall seeing any others? To be honest, at some point while collecting skulls, she had zoned out.

Thinking back, she had picked up five, the last the most unique. It had longer canine incisors, and two golden front teeth along the top and bottom, giving it a gleaming grin. She had thought it had a cruel set to its eyes, close together and judging. How could a skull scowl? She hadn't even been sure of the number that she had collected. Is that why one felt missing? She could feel the bones drop away as if she had left something of Agatha behind. Why Agatha?

"Why don't you take shotgun? I'll drive. The back roads haven't changed in the last couple of decades, so they're still twisty and poorly marked," Den said.

"Doesn't your brother, Renn, still live here?" she asked. One of the four had gone missing.

"Yeah. He's a Big Foot Hunter and a famous author."

"So he believes in the supernatural and paranormal, too?"

"Oh yeah. Big time. His books are about haunted places like the Raytheon plant, Virginia Intermont College, and Tennessee High which has the ghost of a drowned girl that roams the halls."

Once in the Yukon, Sabrina relaxed. Buckling her seatbelt felt odd, though, like her fingers had forgotten. She tried to clear her head by blowing her nose, but the tissue was empty. Even her vision seemed a touch blurry, like she was coming down with a cold. She loathed being drippy and weepy. At least her voice didn't sound that way when she recorded her report.

"After an eight minute descent and dropping flares, our party of five divers reached one hundred and twenty feet. We immediately split up and performed our jobs. Roxy, Levon, and Madi, the host of the Reality TV show, *The Myth Huntress*, descended into what is believed to be the basement in search of the lost ROV. I collected the skulls that I mentioned in my prior report, those discovered by the ROV but never reported by those who had been diving inside the mansion. The sight seemed a surprise to Dr. Curran and the reporter, Rae Kirkland. I don't believe they were lying. Further questioning failed to prompt any other recollections. While there, I also searched for clues and evidence and took samples. There were obvious signs of detonated TNT, several sticks by the size of the blast radius," she began but then paused the recording. She thought she heard a thump in the back. It seemed a touch frantic and not quite rhythmic.

"Do you hear that?" she asked. Could it be coming from the trunk? Did the others want out?

"I hear it. Sounds like a flat, but we're rolling along smoothly," Den said. He slowed to the sound of another thump and put the Yukon in park. He gave her a look, saying I'll check, and climbed out of the driver's seat. The gritty sound of walking on gravel halted abruptly.

Before she knew it, Sabrina held her gun in her hand. She loved the modern guns, lighter and with a clip to hold more bullets. She chided herself for acting spooked. "What is it?"

"It was the haunting remnant of new construction: tar paper stuck to the back tire. It was slapping against the wheel well," Den replied. He returned to the driver's seat. After checking for traffic, he steered onto the road, heading toward Abingdon. The SUV brought gravel with it. It pinged against the undercarriage and rattled around in the wheel wells.

She waited until it was quiet to continue recording her report. "I found seven skulls, two of them normal without the elongated or extended canines. One had gold implants for teeth. I discovered one distant to the rest, and it was undamaged, likely out of the range of the TNT's blast," she said and paused to choose her words. Again, she heard a thumping from the trunk.

She and her partner exchanged glances. "It sounds like something is trying to get out, but we both know it can't be the skulls," Den admitted. With a sigh, he pulled over onto the shoulder. He checked to make sure that the road was clear of traffic before he stepped outside.

Sabrina reached over to turn off the ignition and joined him at the back, staring at the trunk. A cool breeze whispered by. A chill dashed up her spine to cause her to shiver and shudder. He looked at her, getting her okay, and then he deployed his fob for remote control.

The trunk popped open and something dark with claws sprang from inside. Tail flying, it landed atop Den. He screamed.

If it wasn't for the Grace of God, Sabrina would have shot him and the cat. She waited, recognizing it was a feline, an almost dead one. It released Den and bounded away.

"I almost had a heart attack," Den chuckled uneasily.

"I think that's Marader's damned cat," Sabrina said. She didn't tell Den that she had almost shot him. She joined him in laughter. She searched the cooler. Nothing had changed, and yet, she suffered a sense of longing. The strong emotion was followed by feelings of vengeance.

They had been left to die.

"For a moment, I thought something supernatural might be happening," Den said. He guffawed a couple of times.

Sabrina was relieved and laughing so heartily that she was having trouble breathing. She got a grip as darkness started clawing at the edge of her vision. She blinked. Their laughter sounded choral. There was someone else here, laughing at them. What the hell?

Under hair slicked back like a dark skull cap, a pale face peered over Den's shoulder. Swarthy eyes stared at her from deep within dark circles. His lips had a splatter of red. Was he a mime?

Her eyes widened. Den grew concerned. "What?" he asked and glanced over his shoulder. When he saw her bring up her gun, he whirled. The mime in the coal black suit moved faster than the cat, darting around to Den's side while he peered over his shoulder. The mime leered at her then stepped back in a blink as Den faced her and shrugged. "Nothing. Are you all right, partner?"

"I guess I'm not," she said. Sabrina didn't understand why she was hallucinating. "I keep seeing a mime behind you."

"Did you say a mime? Are you seeing killer mimes, Sabe?" he asked as he twisted to look as if he was wearing a sign on his back.

That's when the white-faced hallucination rushed between them, grabbed her weapon and pulled it into his belly. "Shoot. Well look at that. I am here. You are not imagining me. Shoot I say," the mime commanded.

Sabrina didn't. Mimes didn't talk. She struggled in the intruder's grip.

"You're like the others!" she snarled. Sabrina didn't know what she meant, but she knew his name, Destrange, the Parisian bastard. He was the reason that she had died. Confusion assailed Sabrina.

With a powerful grip, Destrange forced her to pull the trigger several times. The gun shot sounded muffled so tight against his body. "Ah, what have you done?" the talkative mime asked as he staggered away. He straightened up after several steps, no longer acting injured, and gestured behind him. "Ah, the stage suffers my absence. I applaud your handiwork, mademoiselle."

Behind him, Den was bent over. Blood poured through his fingers as he tried to hold in his life as he bled out.

"Don't look at me! You fatally shot him. The powder burns are on your hand. The bullets come from your gun. Pow. Poof. There goes your career. All it took was one careless moment when you were scared. Such is life, no? He's dead, you both just don't know it yet," Destrange said. He finished with a florid bow.

An all-consuming bonfire of rage overwhelmed Sabrina. Agatha wanted to murder the smug SOB. She jerked open the cooler and yanked out a sharp rib bone. Somehow, she knew this would hurt the monster. Her anger and vengeance drove her stronger and faster. She stabbed the crazed maniac who dodged too late. She buried the bone in the mime's chest. It struck with a satisfying and fleshy thunk.

"What? How?" the mime asked as he staggered back, taking the rib with him. Destrange grabbed at the wound. It bled through his claws.

"No faking this time, shadow walker. I'm in control now. The fool, Sabrina Kaye, is gone," Sabrina heard herself say. She looked down at her right hand as it reached for another rib. Sabrina tried to stop her hand and failed. She tried to blink, and nothing happened.

"Agatha. You will get yours, bitch," Destrange said just before the shadow walker turned sideways and vanished, leaving a strange, unpleasant scent. The Frenchman had slipped through the border into the Shadowlands. There were many who had said the Parisian was not all there, being half shadow but all pain in the neck.

Sabrina was alone and yet not alone. She wasn't in control of her body. Something had possessed her. She could do nothing as she relocated the cooler to the back seat, loaded Denzel Bond into the trunk and closed it, letting him moan her name while he slowly died. Bond's eyes pleaded with her, but she closed the lid despite trying to stop. Sabrina wanted to cry, but no tears came, not even a sniff, although she wept with frustration within.

She tried holding her breath. Her body kept on inhaling and exhaling. She couldn't force a blink, either. Helpless, Sabrina watched herself take one of the skulls out of the cooler. The one with the golden teeth stared with blank eye sockets and a mocking grin. She was dead and yet not gone. She placed it on the front seat. It was no longer evidence. She was staring at what was left of herself. It was a dark miracle, a twist on fate.

An overpowering desire for vengeance against Vlade Dragomir and Elsa Swearington drove Agatha on. Sabrina Kaye knew an Elke Swearington. Were they one and the same?

Who was the other person? It was like being in the passenger seat of her body. Sabrina was just along for the ride. What the hell had happened to her? She craved justice for Den, but it was a candle against the decades old wildfire of Agatha's revenge.

Thirty-Two

Wannabe Immortal

Covered in a sheet with a camouflage design, the Oktoberfest Vampire strolled onto the farmland from the city park. He could see through the sheet as he stalked through the woods toward the house. His disguise would fool a camera. If he could turn invisible, mist, or change shape, he wouldn't need a sheet to seem invisible. Those privileges were for vampires only, the Oktoberfest Vampire mused.

He reached the edge of the trees and the front lawn. One car was parked out front, and it wasn't a sheriff's cruiser. He could hear loud voices coming from the front porch. It sounded like the old High Sheriff of Sullivan County was arguing with someone. After a moment, the Oktoberfest Vampire nodded and laughed to himself at the irony. Cane Concannon was here, the master of conspiracy theories himself. Well, he was going to learn more about vampires than he wanted, and it would end up killing him, the old folks, and Deputy Marge Cantrell. The vampires would look favorably upon him for this.

***

Marge drove to her grandparents' place where she planned on bouncing thoughts and ideas back and forth with Grandpa. She had called Rhett, texted him and knocked on his boathouse door. He wasn't home, but Rica had glared at her and Boomer from the rooftop. Marge left him a voicemail, mentioned she was headed out to her grandparents' farm and its address. She was going to celebrate catching the Nazi. Rhett should come along. He could share war stories with her grandpa. She figured it wouldn't do much good, but she had tried. If it hadn't been for the cat, she would have assumed that Rhett had left town to follow Mudder to wherever the fights would be set up next. She assumed the retired Texas Ranger would go a long way to catch his shooter.

She understood his frustration. Marge had no idea who had killed Marsha. Would she ever know?

She recalled the conversation with Tom Marader. He and his girl believed in werewolves. She reminded herself to consider the source. The media had contributed alcohol as the reason those at his marina had seen human-wolf hybrids when they were really being attacked by a pack of feral dogs. Nobody ever explained why dogs had attacked them, not even the conspiracy-minded Concannon. She couldn't think of anybody on the force with whom she could confide in. She wasn't even sure that she could discuss it with Grandpa. He would think that the stress was getting to her. Whodunnit? Werewolves. Where wolves? Yes, there were wolves who were people cursed to turn into canines. Maybe it was the Masked Nobody's fault.

The world seemed crazier than usual. Well, they were all breathing noxious fumes from Bristol's landfill. Could she blame her weird thoughts and sightings on its unhealthy gas releases?

When she exited her cruiser at the farm, the fog reeked like a gas station had a sewer leak. She felt it crawl over her, thick and clingy like a damp and rotting blanket full of ants. She couldn't help but wonder what kind of effect this was having on her grandparents. Boomer looked like he preferred the odor of pickling over this. She agreed with her dog.

The air was still, just waiting for the ill wind to come. She had experienced these moments before when your subconscious knew something was wrong, but your reasoning had yet to catch up. Her father had told her it was like the sense of impending doom when you suffered a heart attack. Could that be it? She worried about Grandpa. It would be reckless to dial 911 on a hunch.

Instead, she dialed Ron. She got his voicemail, so she called Joni. "Hey, sister. I'm at my grandparents' place."

"Is there pie?"

"Likely. I don't know yet. It feels weird. It might just be the dump making me queasy, but if you don't hear back from me in five minutes, call me back. If I don't answer, call our buds in Bristol or Washington County. Tell them to be careful sending in the troops."

"I got you. I'm driving to you now, but I won't be there in five minutes or ten, not even if I break a bunch of laws. Yes, fellow officer, I was doing 90. Mamaw's pies and cobblers are that good. Okay, what time do you have?" Joni asked They were in time already. "Five minutes starting as soon as you hang up."

"Thanks. 'Bye," Marge said.

At least inside the house, it smelled like fresh baked apple pie. She would certainly owe Joni one for rattling her cage. Now this was more pleasant and homey than vinegar. She closed the door, shutting out the world. She really needed a reprieve. Boomer bristled and began a deep growl.

"Hey, Mamaw? Grandpa? Anyone home?" Marge called out repeatedly.

"We're in the kitchen, dear," Mamaw said.

"We have unexpected company. Concannon dropped in," Grandpa said with an unfriendly tone.

"I can smell his cigarettes and aftershave," Marge said.

"And a second man, this one with a gun and a mad on," Mamaw said.

Boomer bared his teeth. He began to slink forward as if he were stalking prey.

"Hey, Deputy Marge. Take it easy, I have a loaded gun pointed at your grandparents, and oh look, the safety is off."

Marge found them in the kitchen. True to Teivel's words, Mortimer held a Glock43 on her grandparents who were bound to chairs back-to-back. Concannon sat tied and gagged to a separate chair behind them. He tried to talk to her, of course.

Boomer stiffened. "Easy, boy. Rooted," Marge told him. Her dog's butt hit the floor with a thump. His eyes never left Mortimer Teivel, and the German shepherd remained as tense as a bow string with a notched arrow.

"Put him outside. He doesn't like me," Mort said. He smiled broadly, faking it, because happiness hadn't found a home in his eyes for a long time. They appeared to be cavernously dark and recessed, giving him a skeletal look. He was either thin or finely boned and tall. His black attire and knit cap made him look as pale as death.

"He doesn't like people who kill people. So, I know you're serious. Why are you here? How are you here?" Marge asked.

"I'm here because of you, Deputy Marge Cantrell. Because of you!"

"Me? What did I do to you? All I did was ask questions about Richter."

"Yes, you did, but that wasn't all. Your curiosity will get y'all killed. You see, I read your mind. Somehow, you know that I'm the Oktoberfest Vampire. Your doubt would exonerate Richter, although I'm sure such a nasty piece of crap has illegal arms and skeletons in his footlocker. That dog goes outside, now!" Mort snarled and showed his teeth. "I already locked and wedged the doggie door.

If you mess with it, or you're gone longer than thirty-six seconds, I'll blow off one of Grandma's toes. That would be sad and painful, as they are painted such a lovely shade of fuchsia. I think it would match fresh blood, though, if it came down to it. Now, your gun, put it gently on the table."

Marge drew her firearm with her fingertips and did as he commanded. His voice held surprising power.

"Good. I'm starting to count. One. Two," Mort said.

Marge pushed a reluctant Boomer outside. She returned with her hands up. It smelled like someone had broken a bottle of lavender. Did that mean her sister was here? Was Mortimer Teivel connected to her sister's murder?

"Good, so far. I'm going to search you. If you attack me, you'll be sorry," Mort said. Keeping his gun trained on her grandparents, he eased behind her. When he began to pat her down, she grabbed his left arm and locked it. She elbowed him in the face, feeling a solid connection. Marge thought that should do it, but she was so wrong.

Mort laughed and yanked his arm free, which should be impossible without breaking it, but the Oktoberfest Vampire was incredibly strong for a string bean. Swifter than a snake, Mort grabbed her neck along her right shoulder and squeezed mightily. The pinch became painful, running into and down her spine. A bolt of lightning seemed to leap off the top of her head.

All the strength fled her limbs, and her muscles went into spasms. Her knees turned to jelly. Marge couldn't stop her fall, so she hit the floor, striking her head. Streaking stars ripped across her vision. A headache washed over her in throbbing waves of pain. She couldn't even cradle or self-splint it which would have provided a little comfort. Her breath came raggedly. Now she knew how the others had been taken without trauma. A lot of good that answer did her now.

"Sorry about letting you fall, Deputy Marge. Usually I would catch you, so you wouldn't have bruises, but since I'm not killing you as the Oktoberfest Vampire, because he's in custody, I'm changing styles to old-fashioned homicide. You're probably wondering what I did to you. Yep, it's a lot like the Vulcan nerve pinch, but my squeeze leaves you awake while stunned. You could say it's my knack."

She had never heard of such a thing. Outside, Boomer whined. Could he find a way in?

"I want you to be awake while your grandparents die. It didn't need to be this way. If only you had believed me, I would have gone underground for a while. But you're the dogged kind, which is probably why they put you in the K-9 unit. Oh my! Sometimes I'm so witty that I bust up laughing. Ah, Deputy Cantrell, if you had been less persistent, I wouldn't have to kill y'all. I'll scratch something in the wall that's anti cop. That will give them motivation. It'll be something easy to swallow. Blue lives don't matter. Naw, too gentle. Blue lives ain't worth a wooden nickel? Two dead cats? Shit or shinola? What do you think? Go with the two dead cats. Consider it done. Do you think people would get it if I said four dead cats?"

Marge thought it would work.

"You're probably wondering why this is happening. First, like I said, because you won't let it, or me, go. Have I beaten that dead horse enough? Second, because I can see the truth in your pretty eyes. Yes, I can. I don't get a pain in the neck like you. I see the truth, the story in your eyes. I wonder if that's where the Moody Blues got that idea? I'm also stronger than all get out, whatever that means, but hey, I escaped your inescapable hold, so maybe that's what it means because I got out! You might ask, why am I bending your ear? I think a boring monologue is more exciting than a quick death," he said and began to pace.

"Yeah, I was a 98 pound weakling, Virginia High graduate with big hopes at UT in the fall, but then the vampires turned me into a thrall. It's like being part vampire and part human, I don't know how much, but I'm stronger, swifter, and heal faster, along with seeing in the dark like it's an overcast day. Rarely can a thrall read people's thoughts in their eyes, but I can. Yes, Deputy Cantrell, you're oh so right. I am the... Masked Nobody. Tah-dah!" he exclaimed and bowed with a flourish.

"Thank you, thank you. Usually, I kill bullies and mean, tough guys. I loved beating the crap out of the Nazi. Hey, I'm doing everyone a public service here. I don't go around killing the elderly or cops, but Marge made me do it. Right, Marge?"

Marge groaned. She wanted to talk. This boy was bat shit crazy. Her Satanic burn flared and radiated heat. Despite this, she forced herself to remain calm. Her guardian angel had always come through before. Sometimes her angel had peculiar timing.

"What's my issue? I'll tell you what my issue is. I wanted to prove a point. Not to the good people of Bristol, but to the bad vampires of Bristol. I would say evil, but they're above evil. Do cattle call people evil? I think our sign should read: A Good Place to Live for Vampires. Yes, sir, I am as crazy as a loon. Unless you're Mr. Concannon here who is a believer. Are your beliefs worth dying for? Anyway, I wanted to show that I'm extremely dangerous, both by those that I slay and the fact that if I continue, the communities of bloodsuckers might come under scrutiny. They don't want that. Hey, all I wanted to be was a vampire, a full-fledged one, and they left me to rot at the mine. They didn't think I could cut it as one of them. Who, you wonder? That's RON, the Rulers of Night. That's who."

"You're killing us because you think that she knows the truth about you?" Grandpa asked.

"Yes, I don't know how. Maybe she read the truth in my eyes or my mind. I can't have cops, deputies, federal agents or even media personalities sniffing my butt when I'm trying to negotiate with vampires. They are a secretive lot."

"You believe in vampires?" Grandpa asked with exasperation.

"Oh yes sir, they made me what I am today, and yet, I could be so much more. The blood of my victims could empower me," Mort continued.

"More crazy, you mean?" Grandpa asked.

"Speaking of crazy. Granny, were you making lavender soap? It smells like a floral shop and a bakery in here. Hell, if you got to go, it might as well smell wonderful. It's better than dying in a sewer, a back alley, or atop the crapper," Mort said.

"Our granddaughter wore lavender perfume. Her ghost is here with us now. Are you her killer?" Mamaw demanded.

"No, not guilty. I didn't do it, although I was in the vicinity."

Marge listened carefully for lies. She felt no suspicious twinges. Is that because she was numb?

"Marsha Cantrell treated me first. I was lying there when she had the bad luck of trying to help an injured werewolf named Tom Marader. He was in his human form, freaked out from the pain, and tore into her."

Tom Marader? He was a werewolf and her sister's murderer? That's why they believed in werewolves? Marge was shocked. Her first reaction was disbelief.

"It's how I got scars on this arm. I knocked her partner unconscious, Genny, I think it was, so that she wouldn't be slaughtered, too. Oz was known for his fits of rage. Wait, that's right. It wasn't Marader. Sorry, they look alike, act that way, too, so much so that they could be lycan cousins. Anyway, Oz was injured and angry at the vampires who had deserted us, leaving us to die. Yes, vampires are real. How do you think I got so I could read your mind? I'm no freakin' Amazing Kreskin. Mental, perhaps, but I'm more than a mentalist. Like Alan Parson sang, I can read your mind. I'm the real deal."

Marge wasn't sure what to think, but she was furious. Nothing that he said sounded like a lie. Her lie detector must be out of whack, or all this madness was true. How could that be? And yet, after what she had seen happen to diver Dan, Marge was leaning toward believing. Rage surged through her. It burned away some of her paralysis, as she began to feel, but it wasn't going to be in time.

"Getting involved in the supernatural is deadly for humans. And now you know. Does this knowledge give you closure before you die? Yeah, it would piss me off, too. I do wish I could have saved your sister. She was a good soul; I could see it. Then I don't think any of this happens. Old Man, you first," Mort said. He walked around to the other side of Mamaw and Grandpa, keeping her grandparents between them. The spawn of devil planned to kill them execution style.

Lord help her, Marge could finally twitch. She needed to move now. She willed her body. All it could do was shiver and shudder.

Her phone rang. That would be Joni. Marge couldn't reach it. Mort didn't care. Send help, Marge thought. How could she delay Mort and give the cavalry time?

The front door opened.

Boomer charged in. "Boomer, stop!" Marge yelled, but her dog lunged. Mort Teivel didn't shoot her dog, but he pistol-whipped Boomer. Her dog crumpled. Boomer wasn't alone. Rhett Archer rushed in with his gun. Before he could speak, Mort fired. The bullet disarmed Rhett, his gun hitting the floor. Mort followed with a blurring kick to Rhett's family jewels. As he doubled over, the serial killer kneed Archer in the head. Mort pinched the ex-Texas Ranger's neck and shoulder which caused her neighbor to fall slack and land nearby. So on their second date, they were paralyzed by a serial killer.

Mort air washed his hands. "Well, I'm gonna to have to break another good egg to cook an omelet, and do it fast, since I'll bet you called for backup," he said. Mort searched Archer for IDs. "Ah, Texas Ranger, retired. What? You were already shot and retired? Shooting you again seems redundant. Hmm? What? Your tongue is paralyzed. I could have done that with a word if I was a vampire, then I wouldn't have to sully my hands. I could command you to kill the Cantrells. Hey, now that's an idea. I could make it look like you did it. Hey, who else is with you?" he asked.

Gun ready, Mort stalked toward the front door. "What?" Mort exclaimed. Marge could hear someone calmly talking with him, but she couldn't tell what was being said.

"Archer, can you move?" Marge mumbled. Fury about her sister and Boomer being hurt surged through her, giving her feeling. He mumbled. Concannon added to the futile mumbling.

"I can move, so can Mamaw," Grandpa said.

"I love you, Marge," Mamaw said.

"I love you, both. I'm so sorry this happened. All I can do is crawl. Big whoop," Marge said, working herself onto all fours. What an accomplishment. Her limbs were wooden and loaded with lead. Rhett was so close that she gave him a short kiss, which warmed up her lips and all of her body, dopamine kicking in with adrenaline. Warmth surged through her. She had people who loved her to save. Protecting the community was never more important now. God, she could use a little more time. She would take some help, too, calling any and all angels.

"The hell you say. Piss on you, I'm not an embarrassment. Listen, bitch. You tell your masters," Mort began. He followed with a scream. It was music to Marge's ears. Perhaps an angel had showed up.

It awakened Boomer, too. He wobbled as he stood up. The left side of his face was already swelling. He looked around with bleary eyes, took in the situation, and then like he planned to take advantage of the moment and steal some pie, he placed his paws on the counter. She heard him knock things onto the floor. It sounded as if he gathered something up.

"Good dog!" Grandpa whispered.

"Ouch. Be careful what you're doing," Mamaw said.

"My apologies, light of my life. My arthritis is acting up. Lord, I could use some flexibility here," he murmured.

Boomer came over and licked Marge's face. It looked like he needed ice packs and a vet. He smelled like blood.

"Good dog, Boom," Marge said. She tried to rise to her feet, but her muscles went into spasms, and her legs buckled. She fell next to Archer. He still looked like he had been tased. Marge blinked. She had set aside her gun, but she still had her taser with her.

"If he wants to be one of the undead so badly, I'm more than happy to oblige him and start the process by killing him. He can figure out the rest on his own," Mamaw said. Marge knew that they kept a loaded gun under the table near the head of it. It wasn't there for disciplinary reasons. It was there just in case something like this happened.

She wouldn't have time to get it. Mort returned. He had them dead to rights. His eyes widened when he saw her grandparents. He fired, but he stumbled as he shot. Grandpa grunted in pain. Concannon's gasp was followed by screams. Mort fell to his knees. He shook his head as if he were clearing it of cobwebs then raised his gun.

Marge had needed those few extra seconds. She fired her taser and hit. The charge released and zapped Teivel. He was jolted, herky-jerky break dancing around, knocking over chairs and potted plants, and then he yanked the wires out. He seemed hardly bothered by the electricity, although his hair smoldered. "That hurt, and now I'm hot! You're more trouble than the brutes that I've killed.

That's what I get for being gentle. Say good-bye to life," Mort said. He smiled and pulled the trigger.

Boomer latched onto his arm as the gun went off. They wrestled for a moment before the Oktoberfest Vampire tossed her dog aside like a rag doll. Even so, Boomer had given Mamaw time.

She unloaded her .38 into Mort Teivel's body. In a tight pattern, bullets riddled his chest. The Oktoberfest Vampire wasn't wearing a Kevlar vest, but despite his wounds, he acted like those bullets had only nicked him instead of blowing holes that leaked life blood in his body. He looked down at himself, shook his head, perhaps thinking that would take until at least the morning to heal.

"I told you that I was stronger and faster," the Unmasked Nobody said.

Was he some kind of slimmed down Terminator? Marge couldn't believe it.

The blast of a shotgun rocked the house and further deafened Marge. It might have killed Mort Teivel as it blew him off his feet. The Oktoberfest Vampire looked like he should be dead. Even so, the Unmasked Nobody began to rise, making it to his knees.

"Son of a gun, I'm gonna have to shoot him again," Grandpa said. He probably couldn't hear himself think either.

With a gasp, Mortimer Teivel shuddered. All the punishment finally caught up with his brain, and it shut down his body. He collapsed into a heap.

"Thank you, Lord. And y'all, wow! Y'all have always been my heroes. Now I'm going with superheroes. Boom, you good dog, you!" Marge cheered. Boomer leaned against her, and she patted him. She couldn't linger enjoying her dog when she wasn't sure if the Oktoberfest Vampire would stay down. She reloaded her firearm, and then she hurried to secure the perp. Mort Teivel might be bleeding all over and to death, but he claimed to be a fast healer. She didn't want to take any chances. Her imagination could see the serial killer coming back from being dead like in the horror movies. Keeping her gun close at hand, she handcuffed Mortimer Teivel and bound his ankles with zip ties. She holstered her gun and turned to help the others.

"You're a good dog! I'm serving Boom premium beef any time he comes to visit," Grandpa announced. Her dog and Grandpa both needed professional medical attention. Boomer's wound made his grin lopsided.

"Pa, you're shot," Mamaw said.

Concannon tried to shout around his gag. He had chewed through some of the cloth. He coughed and spat out more. She understood that he had been shot twice and could be dying. He was energetic for someone in their last moments of life.

Even trussed up, Teivel reminded Marge of a coiled snake. Could he break the manacles? She remembered the Masked Nobody's strength. Or could he slip out of them with a serpent's flexibility? When she took his pulse, it was sluggish. She wasn't supposed to let the Oktoberfest Vampire, ha, die, although she was tempted.

"Ow. Oh, dear, honey, your hand and wrist are all cut up due to my lousy knife skills. I apologize," Grandpa said.

"Praise, Jesus, I'll live with the scars. The cuts are not bad or deep. I think the slug passed through your shoulder, dear," Mamaw said. She used kitchen towels to staunch the cuts on her hands and Grandpa's wound which she held in place with duct tape.

"Ah. Ow! Better me than you. I was thinkin' of having that shoulder replaced anyhow. Hurts like tarnation, though. If you can, cover those lovely ears and pardon my French," Grandpa said.

"I should have been an ER nurse," Mamaw said.

Archer began to stir. "I can finally move," Rhett groaned. He hadn't been shot.

While she kept one eye on Mortimer Teivel, Marge untied and evaluated Concannon's injuries. He had taken a slug each in his left bicep and his right calf, but he would live to limp another day. "They appear to be mostly flesh wounds. You're so very God-blest that the bullets didn't break a bone or hit an organ."

Concannon spat another piece of gag and cussed a blue streak before mellowing. "That's easy for you to say, you weren't shot, twice for Pete's sake! I just got finished with physical therapy last week. Now I'm back in the hospital, thanks to the damned vampires this time. I could've gotten shot in the head."

"It is big enough that it's an easy target. Say, you don't believe him, do you, about vampires?" Marge asked. She glanced over at Teivel. Had he moved? She reminded herself that she needed to stop his bleeding, too. Everyone else had been taken care of. She had no excuses, except that she didn't want to get anywhere near him again. He confirmed her intuition by groaning and kicking violently a couple of times.

"You mean that you don't?! You think he's just a lunatic and good at guessing what's on your mind like maybe Copperfield or Penn and Teller? Vampires have servants, you know. He was one of those, an unhappy one, like a disgruntled friggin' employee," Concannon said, then he spat out some expletives to feel better. "Not directed at you, deputy. You, your dog, and your grandparents should get commendations, and I think y'all are heroes."

"Thank you, Mr. Concannon. Marge, dear. Who is this knight in blue jeans?" Mamaw asked.

"Some rescue," Concannon grumbled.

"Retired Texas Ranger Rhett Archer. He's been kind, helpful and fun. He's a writer of crime dramas. I thought y'all might get along. I brought him over to have dinner and chat with Grandpa, not have a shootout at the Cantrell Corral."

"That's not OK here. It's usually a safe haven," Grandpa said. He still had a sense of humor.

"Wow, sir, I know I wasn't funny when I was shot. I'm pleased that we're alive to meet each other, folks. The bullet I took forced me to change careers," Rhett said.

"It's nice to meet you, as well, Ranger Archer. Since the Shilohs speak for you, it means you're good company and welcome," Mamaw replied.

"Marge, you should call dispatch," Grandpa said.

"I did before I came inside. I need to let them know that we're okay, though. I'm overdue to call in. The troops might be on the way," Marge said. She looked around for her cell phone. It had been knocked somewhere in the fighting. "I don't see my phone."

"I see mine," Grandpa said. He started to reach for it and gasped. He looked to Mamaw who retrieved it for him.

Suddenly, the Oktoberfest Vampire surged to sit up. With a snarl, he flexed to bend the manacles. Marge found that she was paralyzed, watching her fear come to life. Teivel snapped the metal and separated his arms.

"Oh, God save us! Everything he said is true!" Concannon screamed.

Teivel tried to free his feet. Archer tackled him, but the Oktoberfest Vampire easily shucked him. With a smile, the murderer turned on Marge. Before she could pull the trigger, Mortimer Teivel's eyes rolled, and his knees buckled. She held her fire as he collapsed, again.

"Did you see him snap those cuffs?" Grandpa said.

"Do you think he's faking?" Mamaw asked.

Marge approached, needing to be sure. Archer moved with her. Boomer shadowed them both. Marge stopped. Did she hear a horse? Boomer barked.

A pounding on the front door made Marge jump. Everyone else was startled with her. They all had been focused on Mortimer

Teivel. Would the Oktoberfest Vampire rise, again? He was no longer the Masked Nobody.

"Hey, this is the Washington County sheriff. This is a welfare check. Marge, is everything all right? Joni sent us. If you don't call her, she's going to come charging out here."

Marge recognized the voice. "Hey, Andrea! Good to hear you, horse lady. We need ambulances for one critical and two non-critical GSWs. I'm limping to the door now," Marge said.

The paramedics had to resuscitate Teivel before they rolled him into an ambulance. Marge couldn't help but think the world would be better if the Oktoberfest Vampire died.

After hugs and once she was certain that her grandparents were in good medical hands, Marge and Rhett transported Boomer to the vet. Dr. Marci May would take care of her dog.

While they sat in the waiting room, the speed of the night finally slowed down. She needed the moment to breathe. She laid her head on his shoulder. She thought she owed Rhett some heartfelt thanks. He had tried to rescue them. "That was close. I feel very fortunate. Thank you so much for accepting my invitation to dinner," she told him.

"I'll assume not all family meals are so excitin'. You know, there's never a dull moment around you, Marge," Rhett replied.

"Well thank you, kindly. Personally, I don't want to be a vampire," Marge replied. They laughed together, a tired, thrilled to still be alive and kicking giddy sensation. "Who would want to be? He was crazy, wasn't he?"

"And on drugs to be that strong."

"And fast," she replied. It still bothered her that he had known about the tell-tale pain in her neck, her internal lie detector. He had known what she was thinking, too. "So, are you going to be staying around, or trying to track down your shooter?"

"I'm stayin'. This is an interestin' place with interestin' folk. I might not get much writin' done, but I might find a dearth of inspiration," he replied. His stomach growled.

"Well, how about a peaceful late-night dinner to make up for this?" she asked.

"I think almost dyin', again, makes me hungry for life. May I kiss you?" he asked.

With that already on her mind, Marge kissed him first. It was electric. She forgot about werewolves, vampires and a creature named Oz, Marsha's alleged killer. Those were worries for later. This might even be a thrilled to be alive kiss, but she wouldn't know until later. She was delighted there was a later. She could have ended up like Marsha.

"Just some stitches and bruises, but Boomer's all right," Dr. Marci said when she returned.

Boomer was upon them almost as quickly as the sound of Dr. May's voice. He darted in to interrupt their intimate moment with his own doggie kisses.

"Oh, you know. It's rarely dull or routine in law enforcement. I think there's plenty more adventures to come," Marge said. Life was good, but there were always things to do to make Sullivan County and Bristol safe and a good place to live.

Thirty-Three

East Hill Werewolves

The Spirits of East Hill by Bethany played on the tow truck's radio, and the nearly full moon changed from golden to silver as the cemetery came into Miles' view. Dark clouds that looked like sailing ships flew swiftly across the sky, causing the moon to play peekaboo.

He had been here earlier in the day. Rhonda and Emmett Powers, local docents who had played at night in the graveyard as teens, had kindly given him a tour. He had walked to memorize the terrain. The two shared some of its history while they rode in a little canopied caretaker's cart. East Hill had been called Round Hill, Maryland Hill, Rooster Hill, and City Cemetery before the name East Hill had been accepted for the long term.

The graveyard was established in 1857 during the Civil War with plots for 101 Confederate soldiers. The Exchange Hotel near the railroad station had been used as a hospital. Around 200 more were interred later at East Hill. The cemetery became official in 1868 when two acres were purchased by a merchant named Lafayette Johnson to honor those who had died. Fifty-seven union soldiers and a dozen African American soldiers, as well as some who died without being on either side, were also buried in the 16.7 acres. A revolutionary war general rested here, along with prominent members of Bristol's past. Homes and roads surrounded the grassy knob, and just to the north sat the campus of King University.

East Hill Cemetery was supposedly haunted by General Shelby's ghost and other soldiers. People swore that they had been given historical tours by the ghost docent, Bud Phillips, once the town's unofficial historian and a prolific author. Some saw the spirit of the little girl, Nellie Gaines, who had been the first to be buried here. Miles wasn't hunting ghosts. He had other supernatural beings in his crosshairs tonight. His targets hated silver.

He slowed at the sight of the small green building near the main entrance of the East Hill Cemetery and turned his truck into the Slater Community Center parking lot. Four other vehicles were parked here, but Anna's motorcycle was not one of them. Unlike the other drivers, he didn't pull into a spot. He parked with his headlights facing the cemetery's wrought iron arched entrance.

Miles disliked the thought of innocent bystanders getting in the way. The cursed souls had been known to take hostages or angrily slay anyone nearby. The moon appeared like a warped silver dollar with the shocked face of the man minted on it. Miles had the feeling that he foresaw trouble happening here, too. Thank Grace, he was meeting an angel.

Next to the entrance stood a sign: The Halloween Cemetery Ghost Walk and Treat. Commercial Plots and Tombstones Ahead Sponsored by the Bristol Chamber of Commerce and Rotary. That sounded kind of crazy. No wonder the supernatural liked this place. The humans made deliveries!

Miles exited the truck, surveyed the terrain, and crossed the street as he began his hunt for Anna Nobles. Sections of the single hill graveyard had low stone-walls to create terraces for plots, but the cemetery had no outer barrier or exterior fences, making it feel like an open field knoll with unusual stones or an odd city park. He could see the downtown lights from here. Orbs that he thought might be ghosts were likely flashlight beams altered by the rising fog. He couldn't be certain at this distance, but shadows bounced at the edges of the moving glows.

A sudden gust rushed across the road and into the parking lot, creating a brief dust devil. Miles ducked his head, taking the pebbles on his hat, and stayed wary. He had met poltergeist and vampires with wind related talents that caused trouble. As usual after dark, Zennon, Son of Galahad, was loaded for bear, werewolf, and vampire. Yeah, he had to keep himself amused, and his mind agile. It wasn't so funny that Zennon had supposedly died at the Twilight Paradise Resort in Las Vegas. Miles mused that he might need to cut back on the sweet nectar of 7-Up and Grenadine. He resisted the urge to pop a Jelly Belly. Sometimes you had to flex your will power, he decided.

Anna had told him to meet her by the green caretaker's shed. A lone light shone, reminding him of a single candle left burning for all the souls who had decided to remain behind and continued to call Bristol home. Once he set foot on the grass of the graveyard, he sensed someone nearby at the building. He didn't see anyone there, but then, sometime between blinks, a young woman dressed in black and jeans seemed to abruptly appear at his side. She possessed a shy smile and big eyes, reminding him of a young Drew Barrymore with her apple cheeks. He hoped this thought wasn't a subconscious warning about poltergeist. In those big eyes, he spotted stars streaking above tombstones.

"Might you be Julia? Anna said I should look for you if I didn't see her. She asked me to meet her tonight," he told her.

"Oh, you must be her date, Mr. Miles Jasper. Yes, I am Julia! I'm delighted to meet you," she said and exuberantly shook his hand.

"I'm supposed to take you to Anna. She's with General Shelby and Mr. Bud Phillips. They're both ghosts now, but they love this area and the people so much that they have stayed here instead of going beyond. Mr. Bud is very worried about the city. He wrote so many interesting books. I have the whole collection. Oh, good. Here they come. Somebody listened to me. I hate it when people ignore me because I look like a kid."

"Who?" Miles asked, then he saw them. The orbs were really flashlights, and their shadows were silhouettes of people. Eight figures left the cemetery. Some hurried and others trudged along the road out. They were headed toward the Slater Center's parking area. Each of the people possessed the glow of life, although the one in the wheelchair didn't have long based on her ebbing aura. He usually didn't see that clearly, but Miles often noticed his senses becoming hyper when he neared a place of restless undead.

"Those are the ladies of the Southwest Virginia Investigators of the Paranormal. They're gettin' outta Dodge. At least they listened to Mr. Bud. The guys couldn't even see him," Julia said.

Seven women hurried out of the cemetery. The white-haired lady was accompanied by a lanky man who called to mind the character, Ichabod Crane. Seven of the visitors were afoot and one of those guided another in a wheelchair. Miles could hear the wheels grind the grit of the asphalt. The investigators were all clad for the chilly evening temperatures, most of them wearing long jackets and hats or caps. Three of them appeared to be relatives, a grandmother, a mother and a pert, twentyish daughter with pink, purple and white hair. Many of the group carried recording equipment in bags and satchels, but the short woman wearing a jacket with a purple roses design could have used an assistant. Besides being in a hurry, they all wore worried expressions, more so when they noticed him standing at the side of the road.

"Good evening, ladies. Is everything all right?" he asked, removed his hat, and stepped back.

"A blessed night to you, young man. Are you here to see if your name is on one of the tombstones? Have you been chosen?" the woman with white hair asked. From behind spectacles, her blue eyes sparkled with curiosity from a face having experienced many smiles. The tall man stood behind her, his hands resting protectively on her shoulders. "If so, now is not a good time."

"I don't know. I'm from out of town," Miles replied. They didn't seem to notice Julia.

"Oh, Sandee, he doesn't know about the fundraiser. Are you searching for family?" the red-haired photographer clad in purple asked.

"No. I'm a ghost hunter," he replied. He noticed the woman in the all-terrain wheelchair was watching him closely, trying to read his body language or mind.

"Good for you. You go, boy. Knock yourself out," the bespectacled blond said. She adjusted her aqua beret, seeming bright even in the dark of the night. Her jacket pattern design displayed books on bookshelves. Only Captain Obvious would doubt that she was a big-time reader. Her eyes seemed to be dimming from a radiant violet to a calm and lovely shade of blue. Rhonda had mentioned that some folks in town reacted to the supernatural in different ways.

"Pamela is not speaking literally. I'm Sandee Fayette, and I'm pleased to meet a fellow seeker," the white-haired woman said.

"Sandee will talk your ear off," Pamela warned.

"I apologize. I thought you might be part of the fundraising effort," Sandee said.

"They're selling tombstones?" Miles asked. This town was full of mad hatters.

"Temporary, fun-loving ones of friends and family. You can tell them what you really think before they pass," the redhead said. The photographer in purple was shorter than the others, so she was forced to crane her neck to peer up at the much taller Miles. Her hair fell in curls atop her shoulders like red roses among the purple blooms. Her glare was thorny with suspicion.

"Yours, dear Sheilah, would be She Lifted and Sought Spirits," the pretty mother said. She adjusted her glasses as if to get a better look at Miles.

"Why thank you, Rebecca. That's kind of you to say. You lift mine, too. Right now, we should be lifted out of here."

The woman in the wheelchair suddenly startled, and her blue eyes widened. Her curious smile gave way to alarm. She gasped and tugged on her driver's elbow

"What is it, Suz?" the most senior of the investigators asked. Her eyes were as steely gray as her hair, but they gleamed with love.

"Doris, we must go now! It's time. Carol would understand," Suzanne said, shaking.

"The darkness is coming?" Sandee asked.

Doris patted Suzanne's shoulder. "We are, my dear friend," she said and scowled at the others like a strict schoolteacher. She was the mother of Rebecca, so there were three generations of strange things investigators here. Doris pointed to their cars. "Ladies. Get your rears in gear."

"Well, I'm sorry to keep you. Y'all look in a hurry," Miles said.

"We're fixin' to go because Bud Phillip's ghost told us to skedaddle. He said it was about to get dangerously overrun by angry beasts. Some of our friends didn't listen to us, and they're still back there, hoping to have a supernatural moment much like you are. Ah, ladies, my chills and goosebumps are back," Rebecca said. She rubbed herself all over as if she were freezing cold.

"Ah, then I'll have other fools and angels for company," Miles replied. It sounded like there might be innocents and witnesses.

"Knowing Stephen, Renn and Jackson, yes, you'll need angels. You can't fix stupid," Doris said.

"God watches over fools, babes, and males," Pamela agreed.

"I'm here," a tall fellow said. He unruffled his mustache as if they were his feathers. If a human could take after a heron, this man resembled his avian relative.

"We weren't talking about you, Hal," Sandee said.

"The lady on the gelding is not with us," the youngest said. The daughter spun her finger around her ear as if to imply that the rider might be loopy.

"Be nice. Bonnie is patrolling the area, so it will be safe for the Halloween event. She's an officer with the city's mounted patrol. Officer Rainbow and Skippy have a job to do. We, however, are just a bunch of civilians here to visit friends that we dearly miss," Sheilah said.

Suzanne loudly cleared her throat since they weren't moving.

"You really shouldn't go in there," Pamela said to Miles.

"I have a date," Miles said. He almost said with an angel.

"With death," the woman in the wheelchair said.

"It wouldn't be the first time. Grace draws me to where she wants me," he said.

"See. Men, they never listen," Rebecca sighed. She continued to smooth her goosebumps with rubbing.

"Godspeed," Miles said. He was listening, but their guidance was for them, not him.

"Let me get a photo for your obituary," Sheilah darkly joked. Miles tried to look more debonair than any tow truck driver before him. He smiled for her and in the face of death because Grace was with him, and Anna was nearby. Sheilah handed him a necklace with a polished wooden cross. Faith and Strength were burned on the underside. "You may want this. I don't know why I brought it, except I had a feeling that I was supposed to," she said.

"Is that your momma's that I blest?" Pamela asked.

"Yep. I just have a feeling that this man is going to need it and our blessings," Sheilah said.

"Thank you, kindly," Miles said as he accepted the gift. He doffed his hat, put on the necklace, and continued on his way uphill into the graveyard. He felt their questioning gazes on his back, but the cross nestled comfortably on his chest. Did they sense what he was? The woman in the wheelchair, Suzanne, seemed to know. He had a date with death and an angel.

Where was Julia? Miles wondered. He nodded to the robed angel sculpture holding a feather, praying his guardian angels were nearby and ready to fly into action. Miles kissed the cross and tucked it back under his shirt before he strolled up higher into the bulging mound of headstones, the real ones of deceased people, not the field of fakes. Come see your headstone before you die. His would read: Grace inspired him to do it.

"You have a good sense of direction. Follow me!" Julia said. She dashed by him to beyond.

"Can you go invisible?" he asked.

"Who do you think I am, Hermione Granger, or Sabrina, the Teenage Witch?" she giggled and kept going.

While Miles followed, he was inspired by a flash of Galahadian recollection. He and the other sons shared memories that were passed down into consciousness by Grace. An older Galahad had walked, armed with repeating crossbows, into a tribal gathering of werewolves. That was before automatic weapons and silver-laced shrapnel grenades. He prayed that he didn't need them.

They reached the crest. Bud Phillips had an area named after him. Miles passed an impressive angular column of red brick with the name Smith on it. The headstone was surrounded by a low-walled plot for family members. Small palisades formed similar terraces all around the peak. Their headstones' shadows appeared and vanished with the flickering illumination of the moon. The rising fog added to the ethereal, unreal feel to it all. The cemetery came and went with the passing of clouds as if the whole hill of dead would disappear into the dark forever, then moments later, the world of light would return.

Off to his right were the tombstones and the final resting places of Civil War soldiers. Julia guided him to a fenced plot where the center grave had a metallic cover in the design of a casket. He couldn't read the inscriptions on the steel, but the headstone proclaimed it to be the burial site of General Evan Shelby.

The temperature plummeted like a Nor'easter bringing a cold front. The fog thickened, gaining form, and in a few short moments, a spirit with a commanding presence paced alongside them. He cleared his throat with a harrumph.

"General, this is Miles Jasper," Julia said.

"Excellent, dear one. Thank you. Greetin', son. I see that you are a warrior and a soldier. Not many left these days thanks to peaceful times at home, but there still be enemies among us. They look like us, but they are not us, and they prey on the weak. It's up to soldiers like us to stop 'em," General Shelby said.

"Grace has sent me, sir," Miles said. He looked around for Anna.

A ghost wearing spectacles and a pencil behind his ear popped in unannounced. He flipped open his notebook and read before pacing. "The underground caverns here were often used by vampires who fed on the metal workers employed in the smithies and the shops using Beaver Creek for water. Right now, there's a gathering of werewolves. I fear that they mean ill for my adopted hometown as downtown has just been experiencing a recovery. Who would've thought there would be breweries and a casino in the city? That's stepping way back in time. Things got very interesting after I passed away. From what I hear of the dump, it's just as well that I can't smell. You know, this could be devastating."

Suddenly, Miles sensed Anna Nobles nearby. Her presence was like a warm spring breeze full of hope and vital life. He felt sunshine from her direction, and when he turned, it seemed to radiate from her beautiful dark eyes. She had the face of an angel, the glare of a drill sergeant, and the body of a belly dancer wrapped in dark leather and wearing werewolf-kickin' boots. The leather was studded with small crosses. Set in a choker, a jade angel protected her throat. She wore two sheathed swords, one short on her back and a dirk at her left hip. When she hugged him, he felt the gun on her right hip. Her touch coursed through him like he had just brushed a live wire.

"I'm relieved that my date didn't stand me up," he said with a smile.

"Rest easy. I won't ghost you. Rhonda let me know you took a tour earlier today. They're the reason I'm here. They kept praying about the caverns under the graveyard being the lair of monsters," Anna said.

"How many monsters are there?" he asked. Anna looked to the ghost.

"At least five score," General Shelby said.

Miles gasped. He needed more bullets and grenades, a lot more. "Wow. It sounds like a convention."

"If you've come to redeem cursed souls, you've come to the right place, Miles. That's why I'm here. Plus, I sense you have another ally nearby, one that may be as important to you as I am. Oh. Time for chit chat is over. The cursed ones' meeting is coming to an end, and those men still remain in the yard and endangered," Anna said.

"I tried. They wouldn't listen to me, and they couldn't see Mr. Bud," Julia bemoaned.

Anna looked to Miles. "It's going around, isn't it? People ask for guidance, are given it and ignore it. I love Freewill."

"Sarcasm from an angel?" Miles asked.

Anna smiled and handed him two cans of pepper spray. "Please don't get me started. It has been a challenging day. Here, have these. Their sensitive noses don't like the smell. It's good for six to eight sprays."

"Much more useful," Miles said. He carried a few of what he called stink grenades. They induced nausea. They were worthless against vampires but effective against thralls and lycans.

"So, Miles, would you convince them, please? I'll cover your back with fireworks if needed. We don't have long. The pack is on the move. Go now!" Anna said.

"Be quick or be dead! Take cover!" the general told them.

Suddenly it felt too late. The metal lid of the casket lifted soundlessly which seemed a supernatural act in itself. The darkness grew underneath, rising like a pillar. A chilling wind, certainly no ordinary breeze, swept through to nip at Miles' neck and slip under his clothes to bite his flesh. He began to shake and shudder. Anna took his hand and kissed him. Loving warmth washed over him like a reviving tropical tide, and he no longer felt fear.

"Thank you."

"My pleasure. It's time to share blessings. I gave you that one to keep and now one to share. May the Lord bless you and keep you safe," Anna said. She gently tossed the blessings to Miles who felt wrapped in a warm suit of armor. Its illumination slowly faded, leaving no telltale signs to the naked eye, but he felt protected and bolstered. "You may pass it on by saying, with my will and that of Grace, I share this blessing. Now go," Anna told Miles.

They shared another brief but soulful kiss, one that men dreamt would bless them with good fortune and lead to victory in battle. Miles took off like he wore angel wings. He would see if he could gently change the gents' minds. Even if the stupid couldn't be fixed, Grace protected them, too.

***

Stephen Semones and his buddies, Renn Bond and Jackson Frey, were conducting research. Stephen planned to write a story about a revenant rising from East Hill Cemetery. He sought the character's motivation, so he had been out reading headstones. Over Bethany's singing coming from the truck's speakers, he heard a train whistle and its huffing steam. He mused that it might be the connection that he was seeking. Perhaps the undead had worked on a train, been a conductor, engineer or even a yardman.

In a few nights, East Hill would undergo a change for Trick or Treating and music, creating a family outing. He liked the idea of bringing celebration to the spirits. He hoped they reacted well. It was going to be a gathering of joy, love and remembrance, flowers and candy. Renn had played some Bethany Moore because he was a mega fan and so the ghosts would know the words when she performed her concert at the Slater Community Center.

Jackson Frey in his Roswell shirt and Sherlock Holmes hat searched for an entrance into the pyramid. Ha. Actually, he was looking at angles to set up his cameras for the filming of the upcoming Halloween event. Renn was shooting photos so they could do a before and after comparison. At times, with the peekaboo moon, the graveyard seemed as if it were winking in and out of existence. The lunar light on the fog added curtains and veils of mist to the ethereal atmosphere, creating illusionary boundaries where there were none.

Along with a highly sensitive video camera, Stephen was armed for surprises. Bristol had its share of crime, but there had been some strange deaths recently, including some not attributed to the Oktoberfest Vampire that were reported as wild dog attacks. Stephen and Renn attended the same church and felt prepared whether they encountered the homeless, feral dogs, ghosts, the undead or even human thugs.

"Guys, we've got company," Stephen said and pointed to the tall guy jogging toward them. He was armed, carrying semi-automatic Glocks in both hands, and clad in a hat and a bombardier jacket. Stephen blinked, thinking perhaps the guy was taking after his very own Gloom character but without the skull mask. The man didn't seem intent on using the guns, but Stephen warned Renn who armed himself. The air seemed to become prickly and full of hidden dangers.

"Good evening, y'all. I'm afraid that's about to change. This place is the den of a huge pack of werewolves, and they're about to unlock the gates of hell and let loose the wolfhounds. For God's sake, get yours and those you love and leave now. They could be right behind me," Miles told them.

Jackson hurried up to join them. "Those guns won't do any good against ghosts," he joked.

"Not ghosts, Jack. He said werewolves. This I gotta see. I think werewolves took my brother and CJ!" Renn said grimly. His frown became a white line of determination.

"I left the rifles in the trunk. I didn't think I'd need them while visiting ghosts," Stephen said.

"You don't. And you won't need those guns, either, unless they're loaded with silver," Miles told them.

Stephen didn't possess Spiderman's danger sense, but he still spotted a trio of suspicious characters moving low, sometimes on all fours, trying to surround them. They weren't dogs, and they weren't exactly people, either. They weren't stocky enough to be young Bigfoots. They were more lupine in their build. Upon closer inspection, he counted five wolves or was that six? Make it seven, he recounted. He had almost missed the one walking on two legs standing near a tree. The moonlight glinted off its teeth and gleamed in its yellow eyes. They locked glares for a moment, and

Stephen saw it knew no mercy and no compassion. The beast killed. Stephen knew sickening fear.

Jackson and Renn sweated bullets despite the coolness. They must sense their lives were endangered, too.

Farther uphill, fireworks erupted into the night. A golden palm of sparks slowly formed as the sparkles fell and lit up the night.

***

"I think our time has run out. Run, I'll cover you," Miles said. He knew that they had an angel watching over them.

Even before he started firing with the noise-suppressed, semi-automatics, he could imagine the phone calls to the local police about strange popping noises in the graveyard. Someone was setting off firecrackers and upsetting my dogs! That might buy him extra time before law enforcement showed up. His first four shots found their targets, causing the wolves to yelp, grab at their injuries, and seek cover. One collapsed where it remained a beast to lie motionless but not dead. He figured it was a trick.

Oh Grace, no. The fools weren't fleeing. They deployed their firearms to unleash a firestorm at the werewolves. The beasts winced and staggered back with each impact. At best, regular slugs slowed their approach. In the nearby houses, the dogs barked and howled.

"Stop it! You are just pissing them off!" Miles shouted. He was dismayed to discover that he had kicked a hornet's nest. General Shelby was correct about the large number of killer furballs. Snarling werewolves seemed to be boiling up from underground like a hive of ants.

Some were set afire by what looked like a Roman candle's fireballs. When struck, they burst into purple flames that returned the lycans to their human form. That caused the werewolves to dart from various grave plots, taking cover behind any concealing tombstone.

One of the sneaky Black Claws had slipped ahead of them. The dark-footed beast bounded in and ripped into Stephen. He wasn't wearing silvered chainmail. Miles fired a headshot and slew the werewolf before it could eviscerate the writer. "Get back to your truck!" he said.

"Ahh, err, Man-o-man, this hurts. This is a cluster," Semones bemoaned.

"Oh yeah! No SNAFU here, well, for me, anyway, but for you it's probably FUBAR. Run!" Miles yelled. He fired repeatedly, his weapon spitting fire and silver death, scattering, injuring, and killing men and women cursed to be wolves, and giving the three creative souls in the wrong place, at the wrong time, a chance to scram. Despite his shoulder injury and all the blood, Stephen had no trouble lumbering downhill.

The impudent trio shot video with their phones over their shoulders while they fled. See! This is what killed us. The writers now had something to write about, their fiction inspired by real life events, running hell-bent in the graveyard. Hell-eschewed was closer to the truth. Werewolves appeared from the shadows to cut off the creative trio.

Miles had to reload. He was quick, but the wolves would be faster getting to the men. What a pain writers could be. Did they all move like they were running in thick mud?

He remotely honked the horn on his truck. The werewolves' attention shifted toward it. That's when he turned on the headlights to blind them. He dropped the cartridges and reloaded, making the infamous John Wick seem slow. The Sundance Kid would still be reaching for his weapon.

A Red Fang werewolf leapt out from behind a large tombstone. He heard shots not fired by him. Thank Grace, thank Anna, and her aim. The beast was struck by a ball of fire and set ablaze. In a moment, the wolf was gone, replaced by a ragged graybeard who limped toward them. Anna was redeeming some of the cursed souls. The man looked shocked awake. He appeared to be having second thoughts.

Miles sprinted for the parking lot and his tow truck. It would have been wise to park inside the cemetery, if only he had known. He was blest with long legs, good lungs, and endurance spent from running mile long sprints, although it was difficult to simulate similar circumstances even while practicing parkour in the urban jungle. Nothing motivated him like being chased by Fast Back wolves. What madness had possessed the werewolves to attack en masse within the city's limits?

"Hi, ho, Skippy!" yelled a female voice among the beating of hoofs. A woman in a cowboy hat riding a chestnut horse charged the werewolves with her Colt .45s blazing. Miles blinked, watching her bullets rip into the wolves, tearing away flesh and fur. The second fusillade of silver split their attention and momentarily slowed their assault. The horse kicked out, knocking down the wolves, but they weren't rocked and knocked unconscious. Obviously, the horse needed silver shoes.

Miles paused. His danger sense or angels warned the vampire hunter. Otherwise, the werewolf lunging out of the tree would have gotten the drop on the Son of Galahad. Instead, the beast mostly missed him, its claws raking across his back. The black-masked lycan screamed when it ripped away cloth to uncover a finely made, silver mesh shirt of armor. Miles shot the werewolf in the paw, slowing it, so he could target its open maw with the spray. The cursed soul gagged and clawed at its mouth. He brained it, and the beast sprawled limp.

Miles had a moment to breathe and take in the scene. Where was Anna? He heard more gunfire. More balls of fire blazed through the night.

The werewolves swarmed the officer's mount, trying to drag down Skippy. Smelling its own blood caused the horse to panic and bolt. The rider stopped firing and hunkered along Skippy's back. "Go!" Bonnie shouted. The brown charger stampeded over a werewolf and thundered away.

The horse didn't make it far, though. It began to stagger and stumble. Too soon and within reach of the wolves, Skippy collapsed. Bonnie jumped free in time, landing on her boots, hitting the ground running but unable to keep her balance. She fell into a tuck and rolled downhill in his direction.

The pack returned their attention to Miles. With all eyes on him, he dropped a flash grenade. He saw the light despite turning away and closing his lids, but when he opened his eyes, he retained his night vision. He could hear the boom echo. Most of werewolves had stopped in their tracks, waiting for the shock and blinding to subside. He planned to be driving away in his truck with Bonnie Rainbow by then.

The surprise was on Miles. A former member of the Black Mask Pack stood up and fired a handgun, a Smith and Wesson. Miles saw it clearly, but he had never seen a werewolf use a firearm. His chainmail was designed to protect from claws and knives more than bullets. He felt the slugs slam into his chest, knocking him back and the wind out of him, but not killing him, not piercing his flesh. He wasn't bleeding. Only by Grace could this be possible.

He glanced down to see that both bullets were lodged in the cross. That woman's gift had saved him. Grace was with him.

The werewolf was stunned as well. That gave Miles time to shoot out both its knees, causing them to buckle. The beast hit the ground and lost its gun.

Miles didn't have time to ensure it stayed disarmed. He rushed uphill to help Bonnie who was trying to stand. "Easy, I'm Miles

Jasper, and I'm here to help. Let's get to my truck. It's a wrecker," he said. Bonnie thanked him and managed to jog on her own. Her glasses were broken, and she needed some guidance.

Several beasts on two legs staggered toward them. He had a silver truncheon, but he didn't want them that close. He used the pepper spray. It didn't make much noise until the lycans started gagging.

"I've got some of that," Bonnie said. She readied her own can from her utility belt.

Halfway to the truck, they encountered nearly a dozen beasts with shaved backs. Of course the Fast Backs were much swifter than the other wolves. He missed with his pepper spray, but he had drawn his half-sword. With a flick of his wrist, the blade extended to lock into a full-length weapon. He sprayed pepper, dodged and cut their way through the werewolves, slashing at legs to hamstring them. Heal that, he thought. Hamstrings were notoriously finicky. When Bonnie's pepper spray ran out, she smacked them with a silver ferruled billyclub.

Nearing the parking lot, he used the fob to start his tow truck. The engine roared to combusted life. The driver door popped open. Miles hilt-bashed a werewolf, stunning it mid leap and kept running.

He was two steps away from the truck door when a werewolf with dreadlocks tackled him. He heard one tackle Bonnie, too. The unmounted police officer landed hard. Damn supernaturals! Miles twisted to land atop the red-fanged beast. Even so, it reached up and seized Miles' throat. The lycan with dreadlocks was too strong for him. He reached for his knife as his head began to spin. He fumbled the blade away. Oh, Grace, he was on the verge of blacking out.

A silver-tipped sword stuck out of the beast's forehead. A halo of light briefly surrounded its skull. When the blade was removed without leaving a wound, the werewolf's eyes rolled up into his dreadlocks. His claws relaxed, and Miles could breathe. He shoved the wolf aside, and Anna helped Miles to his feet where they shared a passionate kiss.

He glanced over at Bonnie who was unconscious. Her attacker looked human now. "You redeemed them?" he asked.

"He is Miguel. That was Riley. They can't help themselves. Between the moon, the dump funk on the night air, and Butcher's commands, they and others have lost all ability to reason. They aren't evil, just cursed and wayward. Neither of them has killed or eaten anyone yet. Many of the other werewolves are too far gone to be redeemed through normal methods, and even I'm limited in what I'm allowed to do here and through this mortal flesh. Ah, here comes my ride," Anna said. She pointed toward the sound of the oncoming motorcycle. Julia was driving the Indian Scout. Her huge, joyful smile lit up the night. It was a wonder the werewolves had let her pass. Anna grabbed a helmet off the back of the bike as it arrived and hopped onto the motorcycle.

"Those men are in trouble," Julia said.

Anna settled on the seat. "All men are trouble, dear, but some men are worth it. And isn't your middle name trouble?" Anna asked.

Julia giggled delightfully, the sound of a kid playing with a licker dog. It was lost in the roar of the engine as she kicked the cycle into gear. Anna blew Miles a kiss as she raced down the road at what seemed a breakneck speed. Miles gave her a last glance before he put the unconscious officer in a fireman's carry to set her in the front seat of his truck. He hopped in, buckled them, and drove off to race away.

***

"Jackson, jump in!" Stephen yelled. Their friend was trailing them as they reached Renn's red Ford pickup. Stephen yanked the passenger door open and jumped into the seat. Renn was already there and starting the engine. He wasn't waiting. He was haulin' ass out of here.

The radio turned on in the middle of a song. "Goin' up to the spirit in the sky. Spirit in the sky! That's where I'm gonna go when I die. When I die!"

"I don't want to die a virgin! Ow, my sciatica!" Jackson shouted. He dove and tumbled into the plastic-lined bed of the Ford, landing among the sticks and twigs from a deadwood haul. He came up with an ax in hand.

Renn spun the wheels and smoked the tires before the pickup lurched ahead. Stephen had yanked the truck's passenger door closed just ahead of the monsters. A tatted one slammed into the side panel, denting it and breaking the glass. The beast had a big C on its arm, like their missing friend CJ.

More werewolves charged from their right, so Renn yanked the wheel left to steer across the grass, running over several fake headstones. He wrestled the careening truck onto East State Street. He floored it, tires squealing, the truck speeding eastward toward Old Jonesboro Road. "Getting permission to park in there was a life saver, man. We would've never outrun them to the parking lot. I hope that guy made it."

"Yeah, me, too. I'll thank Rhonda Powers, again, when I see her," Stephen said. She had suggested that they park in the grounds on a road where they could conveniently unload their equipment. He grabbed an old towel and held it to his shoulder to staunch the bleeding. He couldn't believe he'd just done that. He was adventuresome, but he was also a family man. Autumn wouldn't forgive him if he died in search of inspiration. What was he going to tell them about the event at East Hill Cemetery on Halloween? They had planned on attending.

"Do you think anyone will believe us?" Stephen asked.

"Not for a second," Renn said.

"I have video. Well, at least I hope I do. I damaged my phone," Stephen said. His Samsung had been clawed. It might have saved him from being hurt worse. That was worth the price of a new phone.

"I got it. Boy, do I ever have proof that there are werewolves. Move over Bigfoot for the Lycan Craze!" Jackson shouted through the back window.

"So did those guys at Maraders Marina. I wonder if they'll look like dogs in our recordings?" Stephen asked.

"Do you think the graveyard is a trap? Locals will come to be part of the lotto. I want to see Bethany Moore! She's got a great voice, plus, she's a babe!" Renn said. His eyes swept the road ahead of them, and then he glanced at the dashboard. The truck pushed past sixty-five miles per hour on a neighborhood street.

"I don't think the city council is in on it. Kathy Worthy is a straight-shooter, and this was her idea. I loved it until now," Stephen said. Now he wondered more than ever. This was more inspiration than he really needed.

The tune changed on the radio. "I live my life like there's no tomorrow… I'm running with the devil," David Lee Roth sang to Eddie Van Halen's guitar. Who had put together this playlist?

"Hey, something's chasing us. Dang! It's one of the lycans, and it's freakin' fast," Jackson said, then amended that with profanity.

"That's doesn't sound as scary as a blood-hungry werewolf wanting to rip your heart out," Stephen said.

"This is The Flash turned into a werewolf!" Jackson screamed.

Stephen felt a bump and heard the thump in the back. He turned in time to watch the red-furred werewolf rise, uncoiling from its leap into the bed of the truck. The monster had a burr cut and black fangs that dripped blood and saliva.

"Oh, God. Help!" Jackson backed up against the cabin where he hacked with the ax, keeping the beast briefly at bay.

The werewolf snatched the weapon and yanked it out of Jackson's grasp. The beast snapped the handle and tossed away the pieces.

"I hope I told my momma that I loved her last time I saw her!" Jackson said.

Stephen grabbed the fire extinguisher and turned it on, targeting the monster. He adjusted his aim for the wind, and the stream of foam splashed the werewolf's face, causing it to stop, its paws flying to its eyes. It snarled and staggered ahead, snapping like it didn't need to see or smell to kill. It knocked Jackson back and coiled to lunge for his throat.

Out of the blue, a motorcyclist sped by. Its rider snagged the werewolf by its tail and dragged it off. Stephen swore Renn's truck slowed without braking. A female voice yelled, "Get down! Look out!"

"God bless it!" Renn exclaimed. He blew by the stop sign and noticed the oncoming Jeep too late. It clipped the back of the truck, sending them spinning around like a top.

Even before the truck stopped, Renn wrestled with the wheel. He managed to steer it straight and continued to drive like a bat out of hell.

***

Meanwhile, Miles' tow truck sped downhill, heading for the city. With a thump, a black and white mottled werewolf landed on the hood. A second wolf, gray with a white snout, landed on the back where it hung onto the boom to hitch a ride. Good Gracious, he had two truck hoppers, and Bonnie wasn't awake to help him.

Miles honked his horn, hoping it would warn anyone in the truck's way and spook the werewolves. They preferred working at night and in the shadows. The supernatural didn't like the glare of the public spotlight, almost as much as vampires hated sunlight. The horn didn't startle awake the officer, and here he had been hoping for more assistance. Anna had been right about not working alone tonight.

The beast on the hood punched through the windshield. It reached for him, and he evaded, even as he dodged a strike that would have decapitated him from behind. Glass spewed across Miles as he ducked and flipped the switch. The truck had built up a charge and released it through its Faraday cage, acting like a giant taser, electrifying those who touched his ride's metal skin but leaving those inside safely grounded. The beast in front lost its grip and fell underneath the tow truck. The bouncing toppled its stunned kin in the back who landed atop Miles, pinning him. It must have weighed four hundred pounds.

Miles tried to push the paralyzed beast aside and still steer. He could hear the howling behind him, and he was driving blind. Blessedly, Grace was his co-pilot. He wondered where his angel might be.

"Uh. I'm awake. I'll drive," Bonnie said. She took the wheel, ready to steer. "I got it."

"This beast weighs a quarter ton," Miles bemoaned.

She veered, and the stunned werewolf tumbled between them, allowing Miles to sit up. He hadn't hit any innocent bystanders. "Thank you, Grace! Thank you, Bonnie," Miles said. She readied herself, opened the door and hung on. As he turned sharply, he shoved the body out the passenger door.

They would be hunting for him now. He would need to get out of town and regroup.

"Why were so many werewolves there?" Miles asked.

"I dunno. There have been dog attacks, but nothing like that!"

An old white Chevy pickup truck pulled in front of him and parked.

Miles downshifted, braked, and steered to maneuver around the makeshift blockade. The tow truck slowed too much. Werewolves attacked the tires. They were tubeless, metal wrapped in rubber. He kept driving. A light came on the dash. An alarm sounded.

"What's that?" Bonnie asked.

"The boom's unreeling!" Miles said. Cursed souls!

Miles glanced in the rearview mirror. A werewolf had hooked him onto a parked car. "Hold on!" Miles shouted. He slammed on the brakes before he was jerked to a sudden stop. Even so, the truck still yanked the blue Camaro spinning out onto the road. The hook released, so Miles hit the retract button. It reeled in a scruffy-looking werewolf missing patches of fur. Bonnie open fired.

Then two middle-aged folks in their nightwear hurried into the road, blocking the truck's path. They were led and held hostage by a pair of ruddy-haired and spiky-looking werewolves. Miles braked further, coming to a stop. They pushed the two sleepy and scared people forward to sacrifice them on the electrified frame. He couldn't use air cannons, either.

"That's the McCrackens!" Bonnie said.

Miles shifted into reverse, driving backwards. He slammed into the reeled-in werewolf and shocked it before it fell over the side. Miles saw a flash of white. The last thing he wondered before the tow truck crashed to a stop on a dime: was that a compact car that he had crushed? The Dodge Dart wedged under the back tires, lifting the truck up off the ground. Bonnie had blacked out. He tried to drive forward and found that the truck had high centered. Where was Inspector Gadget when you needed a car to jack itself up and over things?

This wasn't the lycans' way! Werewolves were rarely this smart or used tactics like this, and the mixture of tribes seemed like a rare phenomenon. They had always been one pack in his previous encounters. He hoped he hadn't run into the MENSA group of lycanthropes.

From every direction, the mob of werewolves surrounded the truck. This was going to get messy. He had tried not to hurt any bystanders, as always, but he was going to have to resort to the old standby of a hail of silver bullets. One of his ancestors had deployed a Gatling gun. Perhaps, Miles thought, he should rethink how he outfitted his ride.

It didn't seem like Anna Nobles was going to show up to save him in the nick of time. Well, Grace appeared many ways, sometimes mysteriously, and angels came in many guises. He had to keep the faith and keep looking. Miles believed that he could headshot the hostage takers. One of his ancestors had taken shooting lessons from William Tell and Annie Oakley. All of the Sons of Galahad down the line from then on remembered and practiced those teachings on targeting. Even so, he prayed there must be a better way.

The werewolves stood tense, ready to charge, but they simply stared, jaws working and salivating. He expected them to charge. What were they waiting for? Were they waiting for a signal? They clearly wanted to rip and rend him to pieces.

Suddenly, a car horn and a flash of light surprised him. The Bristol police rolled closer in a cruiser. What would the werewolves do now? They usually weren't into mass killings, but tonight, the moon was full, and it was almost Halloween.

"Stay where you are and remain still!" a female voice boomed over the bullhorn. The command hit as lightning, leaving the werewolves thunderstruck.

Miles shook it off. He would swear on a stack of Bibles that was a vampire compelling.

The black and blue-striped Tennessee cruiser rolled closer, leaving its headlights on but its light bar dark. The officer in the driver's seat looked at him as if this were nothing out of the ordinary. His partner in the passenger seat was sitting comfortably with a serene expression which was definitely out of character considering the circumstances. They both were so focused on their steaming travel cups that it could have been a coffee commercial. Those reactions spooked Miles. Did they think this gang was a bunch of Halloween fools in hairy outfits? That would get them all killed.

The back door of the squad car opened. Miles recognized the man from earlier, although he had some doubt on whether he was completely human. The guy from the car wreck was obviously touched by the supernatural, but he possessed a life aura. It looked dimmer tonight. Someone was in the backseat, but Miles couldn't see her due to the shadows. Even so, he could feel strong love there, standing out against all the feral hate seething from the werewolves.

The guy with the knowing eyes from the car wreck looked to the hostages. Dillon Urich blinked and recognized them. "Bessie. Dennis. It's going to be all right. Elke says so," he told them.

Bessie's apple cheeks brightened.

Urich confronted the pack. "Now is a good time to cease, desist and disburse, before the noise you are making wakes everyone up and brings more police. Do you feel like a slaughter? I would prefer to avoid injuring innocent bystanders. Can we do this dance another time? Just so you know, your den is minutes from being raided by law enforcement," he said.

As if on cue, lights turned on in nearby houses' windows. Porch and floodlights followed, illuminating the neighborhood. In a city this size, people noticed the commotion. In the distance, they all heard sirens. It sounded like more police were coming.

Miles was all for delaying this battle.

Leaning forward to attack, the werewolves waited, jaws dripping as teeth gnashed. He took this moment to note the similar markings and shavings of this pack. Several had close-cropped heads, while he saw two or three with mohawk style haircuts. Others had painted their faces with black masks. More had piercings in an ear or along the side of their snout. Black fangs and claws were also popular, and they appeared willing to add more red to their claws' coloring.

What had Butcher done to bring them together? Where was Anna?

Then one ear twitched on all the werewolves, and they blinked. In a heartbeat, the beasts melted away to vanish into the quiet neighborhood on the east side of the city. In the middle of the street, the couple stood bewildered as if they had awakened from sleepwalking. A bewitchingly beautiful blond vampire guided the wide-eyed and happily weeping couple back to their home. Where had she come from? Had she been the passenger?

Miles wondered about Anna. How was she? Would he see her again? Well, he would leave that up to Grace. Right now, though, he could have used someone to watch his back. He didn't know what to think of this vampire with the glow of life. He approached Miles and examined how to get his truck unstuck. With discomforting ease, Dillon Urich lifted up the front end, repositioning it before he hefted the back off the compact car. Now Miles could drive it again.

"Thank you. I don't understand, but I appreciate it," he said.

"People would have been hurt."

"You're protective of this city?"

"We all need a good purpose. I expect to be around for a while. See history."

"See it or make it? The werewolves know about you now. They'll be coming for you."

"Now I know about them and their numbers," he replied.

"Well, I don't know who you are, really, but here's my card in case you ever need my services. I owe you one. With my will and that of Grace, I share this blessing," Miles said. He handed out his card, and he felt Anna Nobles' blessing tagging along.

Dillon Urich accepted them. His eyes widened a bit like he'd been electro-static jolted, and then he smiled warmly. His shoulders relaxed and dropped. "Thirteenth Son of Galahad, vampire hunter, slayer of the supernatural, master mechanic, and the man with the hat who tows vehicles in trouble. A little bit of Blade and Tony Stark?" he asked.

Miles couldn't help but smile and chuckle. "That's on my other card." He handed out his normal card, Miles Towing. The number was different.

"No Facebook or Twitter?" Urich asked.

"Hell no. If less people know, less die. It's that simple."

"Is it, Knight of the Sons of Galahad?"

"Yes. Hey, listen to those sirens. You better release your hold on the cops and let me deal with them and the insurance companies. Go with blessings."

"Thank you. You, Sir Jasper, are a very brave man," Dillon said. He turned and departed.

"Fools go where angels fear to tread, but I haven't found that place yet," Miles replied, but he realized that Urich had disappeared. That was so Batman. Miles was envious. What was that all about? There was more to Dillon Urich and what was going on in this bi-state city of forty thousand than passed the eye test. Miles concealed his weapons, ate a burnt popcorn-flavored Jelly Belly, and addressed the police.

Up the street, Miles heard a motorcycle pull in to park. Julia and Anna waved at him.

Miles didn't know if they had any influence, but Officer Bennett was very helpful and understanding about his situation.

"Hey, where are all the wolves?" Bonnie asked.

"Officer Rainbow, is that you?" Officer Bennett asked.

"Uh, yes, Randy. It's me. This man was helping me. Wolves attacked Skippy," Bonnie said. She tried to rise but suddenly sat back down.

"Wolves?" Officer Bennett asked, doubtfully. "Wait. Let me turn on my camera."

Miles thought of Dillon. It would be best to leave him out of it since he had commandeered Officer Bennett's cruiser. Miles had a feeling he would be seeing Dillon again and he wondered how Anna Nobles' blessing would affect Mr. Urich. Why, Grace, would a Son of Galahad end up owing his life to a vampire? Miles figured that he wouldn't be keen on the answer, but he would answer Grace's call.

"I'm calling the paramedics, and then I'll need a statement from you, Mr. Jasper," Officer Bennett said.

"You should send a vet to East Hill Cemetery. Skippy was bleeding badly the last we saw him," Miles said. He looked over to where Anna and Julia had been. He didn't see them now, but he sensed that Anna had stepped in to give the injured horse a helping hand.

Thirty-Four

Werewolves Hunt Vampires

Colby Crossette stood outside and listened to the angel croon. Whatever group was singing karaoke from the rooftop bar must be a group of professionals. Sometimes he needed ear plugs but not tonight. Just another perk of working valet at The Bristol Hotel. His boss managed his schedule so it fit with his classes. He was able to slowly drive expensive cars that he wouldn't normally get to touch. One day, hotels wouldn't need valets because the cars would park themselves. By then, Colby would have his degree like his brother and a real job. He planned to be just as successful, if not more, than Levon, although getting paid to handle high tech diving gear and hang out with the beautiful and adventuresome women of *The Myth Huntress* in their swimsuits would be difficult to surpass.

Colby had briefly pondered a divinity degree, but there were too many amazing women in the world. Not long ago, that incredible honey had been here. Ms. Swearington had a figure to die for.

Had she been with someone? He didn't remember her having a companion.

As a matter of fact, he noticed that her classic Corvette sat in the lot over at the park. Ms. Swearington hadn't driven very far. He wondered if she might be in trouble. Ah, he would love saving a damsel in distress, unless he was savagely beaten up, again. He ached all over.

"Hey, Colby, you daydreaming about Ms. Swearington? Naw, I'm not thinking about her, either. Why didn't God create more women like that?" his partner asked from the doorway.

Colby shivered as a bone-chilling breeze whipped up, creating a whirlwind. He heard some of these could be EF 0 tornadoes. Leaves swirled and street dirt flew in a sudden, downtown dust storm. To avoid it, Colby stepped back inside.

He moved in the nick of time. A loud metallic crash sounded behind him. The glass in the doors shattered across his back and legs. He turned in shock to see the portico awning torn and hanging down. It was a hell of a day, so far. He thanked God for the wind warning.

"What happened? Were we hit by a falling satellite?" his high school buddy asked.

"I don't know," Colby replied. He peered out the doors and around the fabric blocking their view. Caught in the torn awning was a metal stool. It looked like one from the rooftop restaurant. "Hey, man. It's raining furniture. A chair fell off the roof."

With an ear-splitting crash, a table smashed into the street. Its top spun and rolled away while the legs bounced and tumbled. The top caved in the front bumper and hood of a Porsche. That was a tragedy. A table leg stuck in the giant upright bass guitar at the nearby Birthplace of Country Music Museum. It seemed that the party on the roof had gotten out of control. Colby called the night manager.

***

What a night, Dillon thought. He and Elke stood distantly in a shadow and watched Miles Jasper explain what happened to Officer Bennett and his partner. Elke had suggested that the cops be open-minded, kind and patient. Jasper might not end up in jail for reckless driving.

Before coming to town, Dillon and his beloved had stopped at a farm adjacent to Sugar Hollow Park where Elke had manipulated the Oktoberfest Vampire into getting himself shot. The media would love it. The grandparents and the deputy would be hailed as resourceful and praised for bringing an end to the serial killer who was supposedly in jail. There might be a book or a movie deal in the offering, he mused.

Dillon and Elke had driven to The Bristol Hotel so she could inform Judge Dragomir. Once parked, Dillon heard beautiful singing. Kate was playing with the karaoke machine again. If she sang a suggestively intimate song, watch out. There would be sex in the streets.

Before they could walk across the road to the hotel, the fireworks had begun, literally, erupting east of town. The golden palm falling and fading through the air was followed by the sound of more explosions. Dillon recognized them as gunshots. They had debated whether they should get involved, especially when it sounded like several guns were being fired.

Elke had listened carefully and frowned. She had concluded that they must intervene. "Werewolves chasing people," she had told him, and then she had commandeered a police cruiser. She had crossed the street as one neared on patrol, stumbled in the crosswalk and fell. Naturally, the police got out to help. Elke coerced the officers to take them for a ride to the source of the gunfire where the officers were already headed per dispatch.

They had arrived in time for the standoff between Miles Jasper in his tow truck and the werewolves holding hostages who were friends. Elke had acted coolly and defused the situation, although the vampire hunter had given Dillon the credit. The Son of Galahad had also given Dillon a blessing. He still tingled, but he didn't feel anything wrong. Elke had cautiously touched and kissed him. She found nothing amiss but remained suspicious.

They were talking about it when Elke held up her hand and pointed toward the city where he could see the top of the seven storied, The Bristol Hotel. Dillon wouldn't have noticed anything with human eyes, but a vampire's eyes were keener than an owl's at night. Chairs tumbled off the roof of the hotel, and he thought he could discern figures fighting. In the shadows along the walls of the hotel, werewolves scaled their way to the roof. Dillon blinked. Innocent people were staying there. Gina might still be there! He took a calming breath, relaxing through breathing. Worry and panic would help nobody. He must have a clear mind to deal with this.

In a blink, Elke bolted west on East State Street and turned right on Buford. She had to be a supernatural being able to run in those heels, he thought. If anyone had seen them, they would have doubted their senses. He figured that they sprinted as fast as motorcycles. The wind tugged at his clothing. They sped by a stunned cat sneaking across Goodson Street. A running dog, a stupid Irish setter dashing through the Sedgefield, once Virginia, Street intersection, crashed into Dillon. Fortunately, he had spotted it a moment earlier and absorbed the blow. The dog staggered into trash cans as Dillon raced on.

Elke never glanced back, depending on Dillon to follow as she crossed the tracks north of the historic train station. A blur of streets later, they reached the hotel's front door in what seemed well under a minute. In a fight, though, that could be a long time.

The cloth portico over the front door and sidewalk had already been crushed. The valets had wisely taken cover inside the hotel. One of them peered out the front doors and took video. Dillon heard something falling, glanced up and seized Elke, pulling her out of harm's way. A metal stool crashed and bounced, cavorting like a giant jack down the street.

"I will fly up. You take the stairs. Calm anyone you see," Elke commanded him. "Save your worries, my love. I can take care of myself. Right now, we must assist Judge Dragomir. He was injured late last night."

"As you wish," Dillon said. He was armed with a Glock42 with silver bullets and carried Shadowsbane in its sheath.

"I love you, Farm Boy," Elke jested back. When Key had first referenced *The Princess Bride*, he knew that such a vampire must have room for humor and romance in her existence.

Dillon had seen her transform before to speak from a body that looked like him. The first time had shocked him voiceless. It was magic that he had only seen through special effects. She had told him that was the result of almost a century of practice. He was still mentally getting adjusted to her physical changes. This time, she performed a partial transformation, giving herself black wings and weird bird eyes. "Will this look fly?" she asked.

A couch crashed into the pavement with its legs flying apart in splinters. Atop the piece of hotel furniture, a werewolf sat stunned.

"Smash his head into the pavement, then secure him with these," Elke said. She removed a pair of silver handcuffs from her purse and tossed them to Dillon. He batted an eye, even as she smiled, but he said nothing, taking the restraints in hand. He holstered the Glock. She also carried a silver collar. "I was hoping to use it on Butcher. We might learn something from a prisoner," she said.

Dillon liked that idea. He saw that the white-faced, gray wolf appeared to be slowly regaining its wits. The impact had shocked it human for a moment. Dillon recognized CJ Wills by the big C tattoo on his arm. He was one of the many listed as a missing person.

CJ's lycan fury returned, so Dillon seized him by the scruff of the neck to slam his nose into the pavement, stunning him. "Sorry, CJ," Dillon said.

Elke took that moment to lash the silver collar around the beast's neck. CJ looked blearily shocked and pained, starting to writhe. Dillon cuffed him. He dragged the thrashing lycan to the car, opened the titanium-reinforced trunk, and stuffed the werewolf inside. Using a silver baton, Dillon knocked CJ unconscious with a tap to the jaw.

He slammed the trunk shut and crossed the street to the hotel's entrance. The wide-eyed valets saw him coming and held the door open for him. Dillon rushed by like a fierce wind, giving them no time for questions. He found the door to the stairwell, pushed through, and sprinted up the steps. His powerful legs carried him up six flights of stairs.

As fate would have it, he saw a female taking the stairs up from the seventh floor toward the roof. He recognized Gina's figure immediately. Per her modus operandi, she rushed toward danger. The sound of howling and snarling was so loud it would be difficult to communicate with her. He slowed and wondered what to do.

Suddenly, the roof door to the stairwell slammed against the wall, opening under the impact of a werewolf. The wolfman tried to rise to two paws, wobbled, staggered, and tumbled down the stairs.

"What the hell?" Gina exclaimed. She started to draw a gun from her purse.

That would only anger it. Dillon charged up the stairs, gently grabbed his ex-lover, and vaulted to a lower flight of steps near the seventh floor then on down toward the sixth. The snarling beast cartwheeled down the steps to faceplant into the landing above them. They waited and wondered. Would it sense them and attack?

The beast sat and shook his head, as if that would silence the ringing in his ears. The werewolf stared up the stairs, but his ears twitched. Dillon and Gina exchanged glances. She didn't dare breathe. He could hear her heart thundering. Her eyes widened, and she stifled a sneeze.

The werewolf finally bounded up the stairs and outside.

Gina sneezed. "Oh God! Dillon! I thought I was going to give us away and get us killed. What the hell is going on here? There was beautiful singing and then chaos. I saw a couch fall past my window," Gina said.

"There's some kind of fight on the roof," he said.

"I thought I heard suppressed gunfire. I started reading those files you sent. Are you serious? Vampires and werewolves? You never believed in the supernatural before," she said.

Dillon began descending, carrying her to safety and stopped at the next landing. What she said was very disturbing and worrisome. It sounded like a plot to get him killed. "I didn't send you anything."

"Well, I got a flash drive from you. A valet dropped it off. At least the note claimed it was from you. The forgery was good. I wondered why you didn't just hand it to me, then I thought maybe you don't want Elke to know," she said.

"I have no secrets from Elke. I don't know what you're talking about."

"It's a copy of your book and some of your research on the Cult of Von Damme, aka, The Six Finger Cult. Were some of them vampires? Or did they just think they were vampires?" Gina asked. Her question was deadly earnest.

Dillon continued to descend while he tried to think this through. Why would someone send her material? Who would?

"Where's Elke? Is she up there? Did some art deal go sideways? Artists can be wildly temperamental."

"She's up there," Dillon admitted. He sure could have used another set of handcuffs. Taking Gina up there was certain death.

"Then you need to go there, don't you?"

Dillon nodded. "Yes. If you ever cared for me, you'll return to your room, destroy that flash drive, and anything else that you were just given, then leave the hotel. Don't check out. Just leave."

"What? I don't understand. None of this makes sense."

"It's a set up by terrorists to get us both killed," he said and held up a hand. "I'll explain later. Please, destroy it. I didn't write that, and I didn't give it to you. There's a horrible chance that it could lead to the deaths of those I love, including you. I must go now."

Gina seized his elbow. "You still love me."

"Love but not in love," he said.

She grimaced. "I'll do it if you promise to honestly explain all of this to me."

"I will, I promise. That will be worth our lives, too, but yes, I will explain all of this if you'll immediately destroy those files and run."

"Done," she said and kissed him on the cheek. "I more than cared for you. I loved you. I still do, so you have quite a bit of explaining to do."

"I promise, but know this, I am Elke's through and through," Dillon said. Already wasting too much time, he turned and charged up the steps. He drew his gun as he ascended the stairs.

He exited the door and visually searched the rooftop for his beloved. Where are you, Key? Aren't we connected? Shouldn't I just sense where you are? He didn't see her anywhere, but it appeared the vampires had this battle under control. Regardless, it was wise to have sent Gina away.

Judge Dragomir and a female vampire of Asian descent, Dawnstar, stood ringed and protected by five vampires, including little black dress wearing Kate and the bearded Mones. Dragomir looked bemused and vaguely bored. The vampires gave off no heat while the werewolves glowed brightly thermal in the cool night air. Most lights had been knocked over or out, but the flames coming from the gas jets at the tables remained. Dillon didn't need light to see the vampires work smoothly as a team. Even this swarm of dozens of werewolves fighting like a pack seemed to be outmatched, perhaps even overwhelmed.

Why would lycans from various packs such as the Red Fangs, Skinheads, Fast Backs, Black Masks, Dark Claws, and others make such a reckless assault? Was this a distraction? Dillon realized that there would have been two dozen more werewolves if they hadn't encountered Miles Jasper just minutes ago. He had thinned the pack. Their reduced numbers had not dissuaded them from attacking Judge Dragomir.

"What is this foolishness? Who has commanded them to be grist for the mill?" Judge Dragomir asked.

Dillon blinked. The judge looked darker than before, as though the white half of his face had grayed. His red eyes were ringed and set deeper. Dillon noticed Dragomir's stance. His wound was hindering the way that he moved. A ring on his right hand flashed an angry red when it caught the light. It seemed familiar, unnervingly dark and reckless, and reminded Dillon of the rubies in the necklace used to entrap Von Damme.

"I'll find one to question when he wakes up," Mones replied. He grabbed two lunging at him and smashed their heads together. He used them first as shields against the other attackers, then as weapons, swinging the lycanthropes like flails to batter others.

Kate the bodyguard danced better than any boxer had ever dreamed, avoiding their wolf claws, then she changed her tune to slam dancing, colliding with the beasts. She used her claws to rend and hamstring. Well-placed knees and elbows broke bones and cracked skulls and shattered joints, leaving limbs hanging askew. Even so, the werewolves fought on. A black beast with a shock of red hair in the shape of a diamond surprised Kate by healing almost as fast as she injured him. It wasn't a ruse. The lycan regenerated tissue swiftly. The werewolves had different characteristics based upon their human forms, too.

Dawnstar seemed to anticipate their movements, countering and efficiently killing by seizing and snapping spines when they stuck their necks out. Already three werewolves lie dead, the human bodies looking strange among a pack of linebacker-sized wolves.

A tawny woman turned into a tiger, outweighing the wolves. He wondered if that might be One Feather. She batted them and boxed ears. When two tried to hang onto her flanks, she leapt to the edge of the building and shook, shedding them. Down below it might be raining werewolves.

A second female in severely spiked heels had drawn silver stilettos. Four still held Stiletto's hair in place. Kicking with her heels was just as deadly as the jabs and stabs that she delivered with her thin knives. Stiletto sent one beast sprawling into the karaoke equipment.

Dillon almost didn't notice the sixth bodyguard. Painter must be misting, looking more like a drifting patch of fog, smelling like smoke, and fading in and out of flesh, alternating attacks and self-defense. The beasts grew frustrated snapping at puffs of smoke.

Where was Elke? Dillon looked up, finding her circling the rooftop. Relief caused him to relax for a moment. His night angel was beyond the reach of the lycans' claws. She pointed to a pair of huge, hairy figures trying to hide in the shadows and lie low. They remained inconspicuous to everyone else.

The smaller of the two huge wolves was covered by dark, spiky fur that resembled porcupine needles. His right eye was black with a red iris, the eye of a vampire, while the left was milky white with a blue slash through it, the continuation of the claw that had scarred his cheek to the jaw. He had won that fight in the past, but his face had lost. His canine nose appeared crooked and out of joint, making his jaw look hooked with needles. From Elke's sketches and descriptions, Dillon recognized Guy 'Butcher' Boocher. Did that mean Destrange was nearby? Or Goran?

Dillon was already turning his gun on them.

The masked lycanthrope next to Butcher was even larger, his coat silvery gray to match a lean, foxlike face possessing fierce green eyes. In its hybrid form, the dark patches of the werewolf's fur made it appear that he was wearing a bandit mask to go with a black vest, gloved foreclaws and socked paws. Foxnose grinned like a wolf out of *Grimms' Fairy Tales*.

"I tire of this playing with our food. Wolves, be still!" Judge Dragomir commanded.

The werewolves stopped moving, suddenly paralyzed, and falling like string puppets with their cords cut. They were left sprawled helplessly across the rooftop. With a few words, Dragomir had stilled the beasts. Dillon saw that he wasn't needed. That was fine by him. He didn't want to get into a brawl. For all he knew, it was old grudges like the Hatfields and McCoys.

Dragomir might be weakened, but the power of his voice had slowed Dillon. He didn't shoot when he should have already been firing because not all of the werewolves had collapsed. Two had resisted Dragomir's power, Butcher and Foxnose who reared back to throw something.

It's a grenade, Dillon assumed. He pulled the trigger. He didn't hear Elke's warning in time.

A werewolf tackled Dillon, driving him back. They struggled and stumbled. Using all four limbs, the grinning lycan shoved Dillon off the roof.

Not again, Dillon thought. He had been down this way before. He seized the werewolf's tail and dragged it along as he went over the edge. This would slow his plunge, Dillon figured. He would use the momentum to his advantage. The lycan weighed at least a quarter ton and wore some kind of armor.

"Hey, let go!" the werewolf howled as he clawed desperately to scrape Dillon off and hold on. Its foreclaws dug into the stone ledge and his body swung, his rear claws trying to rake Dillon.

It could talk! Dillon swung toward the building and crashed through a seventh-floor window. A quick glance revealed that the room was unoccupied. Whoever stayed here might be British as he saw a silvery tea pot and cups set up for teatime. Other antique items, cookie jars, salt and pepper shakers, a Coca-Cola sign, were bagged and boxed as if someone had been antique shopping. He was relieved that they weren't here now. He didn't have to protect a bystander.

"I'll claim the bounty! They will pay Darko!" the werewolf exclaimed. The lycan swung inside and charged, taking the bullets in the chest vest while he covered his face with his forearms wrapped in Kevlar bracers. The silver shells flattened on the protection. A grinning Darko pounced.

A bright flash lit up the night. Dillon heard screams of pain and felt his beloved's agony. He couldn't dodge Darko. With all four claws, he sliced Dillon up and down. If he'd been human, he would be dead in seconds. He headbutted the werewolf, smashing his nose, then Dillon whirled and slammed Darko into the mirror, shattering the pane and its frame. The werewolf spun, dripping shards, and bit Dillon's arm. He ignored the pain, but it slowed him, giving Darko the advantage. The lycan was swift, and Darko leapt behind Dillon. A shiny object flashed in his claws.

He struck Dillon with an aluminum can that crumpled. It doused him with water. He could feel the tingle, and it stung, but it didn't burn. Why didn't holy water burn him? Because he was blessed, he mused. Darko didn't know that, so Dillon screamed as his attacker expected. "Ha!" Darko celebrated, just before Dillon grabbed the silver tea pot and slugged him. The blow sent the shocked lycan reeling.

Dillon drew his sword. The werewolf's tail seized and swung a lamp to knock the blade aside enough to slip inside Dillon's reach. He couldn't jab or stab. This is why warriors of old carried dirks. Dillon felt pain under his ribs, along his left flank.

"If holy man water won't work, I have a bone to stick with you," Darko said.

In agony, Dillon kicked the beast away. As the werewolf fell back, the sharpened ivory was withdrawn. Dillon felt his side burning. The fire swiftly grew and spread.

"It's been dipped in quikmar, courtesy of Goran. He couldn't believe that he failed. Fool! But better for me. I'll rub his nose in it, and Butcher will finally see that I belong by his side as his right claw," Darko said.

Dillon could barely think as the burning worked its way up his chest. He had been stabbed with the same toxin that Elke had used to slay ferals. Supposedly, only running water could wash it away. How horribly ironic, he mused, as either would kill him.

Then his time was short to help Elke. Dillon charged and stumbled from the pain. He fell among the glass shards. He was hurt worse than he thought. He must focus.

"Destrange was worried about you. Goran said you must be a big deal. Butcher is paying a huge bounty, thank you, Dillon Urich. I might get my own pack. We'll be the Deadly Six," Darko laughed.

Stabbing up, Dillon surprised the werewolf with a dagger of silvered glass. He stabbed the shard through Darko's throat. He could start the Dead Six. Darko shrank into a short skinny male with curly hair. His armor looked many sizes too big. Dillon blinked. He had just killed someone who had once been a person. Now, there was an odd statement. Still, he wondered if the man would be missed or mourned.

Dillon shook his head. He must focus through the agony. The inside of Darko's upper body armor was silvered, meaning it could be turned inside or out, able to protect him against werewolves.

Dillon stripped Darko and painfully slipped into the vest of silvered Kevlar. This lycan must distrust his pack mates. Dillon replaced the magazines in his Glock and kept his sword ready. He cursed the pain slowing him to half speed. He could have moved faster as a human. He couldn't leap up onto the roof as a surprise attack. His injury forced him to take the stairs, which meant he had to stagger through the seventh-floor hallway. A spasm of agony caused him to stumble and slam into a door. He rested there, but he couldn't delay any longer. He could feel the dark power of The Bloodlust leaking from him. His strength and time were swiftly running out.

Elke's pain and desperation summoned him, but he didn't have the strength to move. He was going to fail her.

Thirty-Five

The Bloodlust

That door didn't open, but the one across the hallway from Dillon was cracked ajar. Someone peered out, and a moment later, Gina stood there with her beautiful eyes wide as she tried to struggle through the shock of seeing him half-beaten and on the way to his final end. "Dillon, oh my dear God! What the hell happened?"

"I'm dying. I need you," Dillon said. He didn't have a choice. He was going to have to use her. He needed Gina's blood.

"I have longed to hear that. What happened?" Gina said as she rushed over.

"A werewolf sliced me up and stabbed me with a poison. I will be dead soon. There are more wolves on the roof. They will slaughter Elke and anyone up there, and the police when they come."

"Dying? You're dying! And you said you need me?"

"Yes, I need your blood. It will give me strength to keep going, an infusion of sorts."

"A transfusion? Here? I don't understand," Gina asked.

"It's simple. I'm a vampire, one of the supernatural. I can take it with a bite," he said with a smile. He displayed his teeth. There was no time to be anything but direct and truthful.

Gina stopped and stared. She recognized something in his voice. "You said the writings aren't yours, but that doesn't mean they aren't true. Is that right?"

"Yes, and vampires will kill us to keep it hidden," he said, even realizing as he said it that those he was trying to save would kill them. "Those that want us dead, the Six Finger Cult vampires, gave it to you. Gina, you can still escape, but time's running out. I did ask you to leave."

"I couldn't. I have to know the truth."

"Now you do. I died and returned as a vampire. Just minutes ago, a werewolf stabbed me, and I'm about to pass out," Dillon said. He had just enough strength to take what he wanted. The Bloodlust surged. "Elke is like me. Now you know why you and I can't be together."

"But you need me?" she asked. His words had already affected her.

"I need your love and your blood," he said, taking her hand. He could no longer control himself. "I would give you the kiss of the vampire so that I might live."

"If you die, I'd die with you," Gina breathed.

Dillon might regret this, but if he failed Elke, he might as well be dead, and he would not rest in peace. He kissed Gina on the lips, thanking her, and she moaned as he kissed his way down to her neck. Her carotid pulsed with life, and his teeth honed in, piercing flesh, and partaking of it. The blood tasted like a honey mead, smooth, sweet, hot, and heady. Dillon could feel himself growing stronger and powerful. The Bloodlust dulled the pains and healed some of his wounds. He couldn't help but wonder if the gift of blood from someone who loved him was healing. He should be ashamed of himself, but The Bloodlust was doing what it must so he would survive and protect Elke.

Even so, he forced himself to stop before he killed Gina. Drawing back was difficult, like stopping when your body still claimed it was starving. There was so much damage to heal, too much to fully repair, and he felt that he had only put off the inevitable. So much for immortality, he morbidly mused.

Gina passed out in his arms, so he carried her to the bed. Her aura looked healthy enough to survive. Or he might be lying to himself. He kissed her farewell, shut the door, and ran upstairs, hoping that he wasn't too late.

As Dillon neared the roof access, he heard voices. The door was bent, now ill-fitting and ajar.

"Vlade, my old frenemy, we were just going to steal Viktor's ring from you, but you look so pitiful that I decided we must take this opportunity to destroy you. Now, this will mess up Destrange's plans and Goran's dramatic play for revenge, but I'm a seize the moment kind of guy."

"You bastard! How did you survive the water?" Mones asked.

"You are correct. I am a bastard. No father to claim me. As for how I survived, ask Elke. She knows. She's like us."

What was that all about? Dillon wondered. He decided that he would ponder its meaning later.

"See. They're still mouthy. That first blast didn't take enough fight out of them. Besides, except for the blond bitch, they all look golden brown, and I like my vampires extra crispy."

If that first blast of powerful light had disabled the vampires, what would a second exposure do? What could he do? One werewolf had almost killed him. He needed the element of surprise. The flash bang that he carried might work.

When Dillon reached for the roof exit door, he was immediately attacked by one of the Fast Back clan. The burr cut and back-shaved werewolf grabbed Dillon. He twisted and tried to judo throw the monster down the stairs, but the lycan snagged him by the leg. "Ow! You wear Darko's armor!"

They grappled as they tumbled, the concrete edges digging into their bodies. The armor absorbed some of the impact, but when Dillon landed on his quikmar wound, he was blinded by an internal flash of pain. He instinctively twisted to land atop the beast when they crashed onto the landing between floors six and seven. The armor crushed the werewolf. Dillon heard something crack, and the beast returned to his man form. He had killed a balding Hispanic guy with a salt and pepper goatee and tats. He wore gray sweatpants and no shoes. He could have been one of the homeless.

Dillon had never imagined, in his wildest dreams, that he would be hunting and shooting werewolves. That was not his experience in wildlife hunting. This and hunting in the woods had almost nothing in common.

Dillon was hurrying up the steps when a searing light flashed outside. He stopped and stood dazzled, trying to figure out what had happened. He felt burned, a glancing blow by the sun to lightly fry his exposed hands and face.

"Well, the second one gave them a crispy look like bacon. Just the scent made my tongue so happy it slapped the side of my head," a werewolf growled and then howled. Dillon barely understood him.

"I like mine Cajun style. Let me get my spice out, and we can set off a third," a deep-voiced beast chuckled.

"In time. Viktor's ring must be mine before it's welded to Vlade's hand," Butcher growled.

"Hey, where did Fred go? He was here a second ago," a nasally werewolf asked.

From the roof, Dillon recognized the sound of his beloved and the other vampires groaning and gasping in pain among the wolves' inarticulate howls of delight. Victory was about to belong to the lycanthropes.

Spots dancing before his eyes, Dillon stumbled up the steps to where he had dropped his gun. He wished that he had two Glocks as he readied himself to face the pack with a gun and sword. A sense of survival forced him to pause and take a breath to center himself before going outside. He must attack using his physical skills and No Mind, fighting as if it were first nature, as if he had been born to it. And he must do so ignoring the pain. He would make feeding on Gina count, otherwise he had abused her love for nothing, and he would hate himself more. Even so, he would do anything to save Elke.

Dillon refocused. These were not innocents. And yet, could he incapacitate instead of killing? He felt the weight of Master Cosmo's words along with his father's presence. He could be better. He wasn't an animal. He still had a mind, if he could be of two minds, and options that he could choose instead of wanton killing. If he let The Bloodlust rule him, he would be without a light in the darkness thereby lost. He wanted to keep his intelligence and heart, but he wanted to live through this with Elke. It was looking and feeling less likely since standing was a challenge and running would be like falling forward.

He glanced at the flash bang. The light wouldn't injure the beasts who had been setting off sunlight bombs, but the boom should hurt their ears and stun them. It would give Dillon a few moments before they overwhelmed him. He wasn't sure that would be enough to rescue Elke. Should he risk it? He was running out of time. Dillon double-checked the grenade and lost hope as he noticed that it had been damaged during his fight. Jasper's blessing hadn't helped him there, except, he was surprised the grenade hadn't already exploded. That would have given him away. He might be able to wrestle the pin out, but he wasn't sure it wouldn't blow up in his face. How much faith should he have in a blessing from a vampire hunter?

Did he have any options? Dillon wondered and prayed. Somehow, oh Lord, help me save the vampires from the werewolves seemed too bizarre for words. He wanted the blessing to help him save his beloved. He mused over his surroundings. Pulling the fire alarm would only draw attention to the building and call firefighters to their death. Nothing in the restaurant or bar would be helpful, except for the karaoke equipment. It had speakers.

He recalled how the squeal of the feedback at the Down Home had caused people to wince and cover their ears. If he had time, he could start a feedback loop. At a loud volume, the screeching should stun some of the wolves. That was a better plan than charging in. This might even give the captive vampires a chance to free themselves.

"I appreciate your work, my pack. For that, you can eat one of them. Hmm. But which one?"

"The big one would feed several of us."

"He may be old and gamey. He comes from the Age of the Mighty Vikings. Eat the kitty," Butcher replied.

"She's all fur, the scrawny thing! The Viking!" he snapped back. His words became a chant. "The Viking! The Viking!"

"Free me, cowards, and I'll give you the gift of combat!" Mones roared.

Dillon had no idea how they might be bound or constricted. He didn't have time to scout. He quietly exited into the night of jubilant and hungry werewolves. They might not have heard him even if he had been wearing cow bells. The celebrating beasts had rounded up all the stunned vampires, their bodies blackened and smoldering from the blasts of light, except for Elke who appeared sunburned and a life-sized pincushion with crossbow bolts sticking out of her body. He bristled, and then his entire being clenched. They had shot her down. One of her wings was broken and folded under. Agony etched her face. He looked away, or he would lose himself to The Bloodlust.

Judge Dragomir and his entire entourage were forcefully held as if they were about to be executed with their arms bound behind them. Mones looked three quarters dead, if he weren't already undead. Dragomir appeared partly melted, his left shoulder dipped and malformed, likely taking a hit from holy water.

The werewolves gathered around Mones. The lycans licked their furry chops and drooled.

"Come to think of it, one more blast of sunlight, and I'll just bite that ring off Dragomir's finger," the spike-haired werewolf with the scar laughed. Butcher dramatically raised a grenade overhead. "This has been a long time coming, you old geezer. Destrange will be sorry that he missed it, but he would have loathed the light show."

The Bloodlust seized Dillon. He saw red and little beyond calculating threats and ways to neutralize them as quickly as possible. He could rip through them, tasting their blood and growing stronger as he advanced to save the night. At the last moment, Dillon regained his will and reason, his body in attack but his mind in abiding, then ready, back into No Mind. He had a plan. He should stick with the plan.

He raced to the karaoke equipment. Fate favored him, as the power was on to the amplifiers, speakers, and microphone. The lycans were confused by the sight of Darko's armor. Even Butcher turned to see who was moving. It gave Dillon the seconds that he needed to grab the microphone and crimp the top. Now metal touched metal causing vibrations. As the werewolves sprang into action, Dillon opened the mic, making it hot and poked a nearby speaker. The screeching peel of feedback was ear-piercing. The cacophony echoed from the buildings. Shrieking and wailing bounced throughout the downtown and along its alleys and streets.

The blaring discordance momentarily deafened Dillon, but it was much more raw and harsher on the lycans with their superior hearing and sensitive ears. Dillon felt the seconds ticking away along with his life and strength. Even so, he recovered first and charged. He targeted the werewolves reeling near Elke. By the time those two collapsed from silver bullet wounds to their hips, he had also shot Foxnose. He had missed the gray wolf's black mask but blew off one of his ears. The second bullet struck the leader of the pack in the shoulder, spinning the lycan around and down. They couldn't hear Dillon, yet, but they knew he was here.

"Rally around Rip!" became the cry. The werewolves tried to gather near Foxnose or attack Dillon. The lycans were disoriented and discombobulated, wobbling and stumbling into each other.

Dillon immediately changed targets. He shot those around Mones and Kate. The werewolves that Dillon couldn't get a clear bead on, he blasted by shooting through Mones and Kate and into their captors. She grinned at him as the werewolves behind her collapsed. Painter was able to mist, creating a protective fog. One Feather changed into a black panther. Along with her, Stiletto and Dawnstar engaged the werewolves, but they were too late to save Dragomir.

Dillon shot Butcher, but the two slugs didn't injure him. The hybrid seemed to have the best of both worlds when it came to strengths and immunities. He threw Kate aside, dodged grabs by Mones and kicks by Stiletto to stab Dragomir in the throat, and then the leader of werewolves bit off the judge's right hand.

Butcher dropped a smoke bomb stinking of garlic. It billowed across the rooftop, obscuring everything like an eye-watering fog. Dillon felt Butcher leave. Despite their leader's departure, the lycans blindly fought on. They mobbed Dillon. He was ready for close combat. The fur and blood flew from the scored and slashed flesh of each cut. The Bloodlust sat raging, ready to join the battle, ready to give Dillon over to the feeding. Now was not the time. He was dead undead on his feet, but his love kept him afoot, and fighting as he carved a path toward Elke. He must remove those arrows.

A beast grabbed him from behind. He broke its femur with a crushing back kick to its thigh. He could fight these creatures using human martial arts! He struck with his hands, feet, elbows, and knees to incapacitate, leaving some dazed and stunned from blows to the snout and others with broken limbs, briefly crippling them.

A whistle and clap sounded. Even if they couldn't hear it, they could feel it. The werewolves abruptly retreated. Grabbing dead and downed members, they swiftly vanished over the edges of the roof. Nobody was in any condition to give chase.

Good, Dillon thought. He stumbled and collapsed near Elke. "Key. I'm here, but I'm done."

"You have saved me again, my love, physically this time. What's happened? You have been blest. You glow like a giant holy symbol," she said, surprised to see it.

"That is Jasper's blessing, remember? It didn't stop the dagger," Dillon said before the pain seized him and threw him into spasms. "I was stabbed with quikmar by Darko. This is the son of a wolf's armor. He used the bone when his holy water fizzled out on me," Dillon said. He was losing his will and focus. The world started to slowly spin.

She touched him gently. She guided him to sit so she could remove his armor. "Let me look. I have seen a lot of wounds over the years," Key said. When she saw it, his love cussed like a sailor.

"By Odin, what a terrible tragedy, it be. Dying by quikmar is worse than melting in the sun's vicious heat, it's," Mones began and finished with a very human string of profanity. He looked more dead than undead, as if he were an over-roasted zombie.

"Have you looked in the mirror?" Dillon gasped. He gazed at Key. She was more sunburnt than charred, but she had yet to remove the arrows from her shoulders and legs. "Bonus time with you was worth it, Key, tell my mom and sister..." Dillon said but didn't finish. The words died on his lips.

"I hate quikmar. The only antidote would kill him," Stiletto said.

Dillon wondered what that was just before a tsunami of pain dragged him off.

Elke watched her beloved pass out. The others thought him terminally injured, his final end minutes away as the quikmar severed his connection to The Bloodlust.

None of them were in any condition to celebrate. Dillon had saved them from their final end, but they had been sorely wounded. Dragomir suffered from the loss of his hand and more, the burns caused by the sun bombs that Von Damme had developed. They didn't destroy right away like the sun, but each blast further dimmed The Bloodlust. He would need to feed.

In the distance, she heard sirens. The police would be coming to investigate.

Somehow, the werewolves had dragged away all of their own. Was it a pack thing? Or could they revive them? It didn't matter. The only thing that mattered was saving Dillon.

Dragomir gasped in pain, but he managed to transform himself, looking undamaged. His hand had regrown, and the wound in his throat had healed. His pale side remained dark, and he looked as black as pitch with his feline golden eyes shadowed by pain. "We will deal with the authorities, then we shall require sustenance."

"That can be in a minute. Right now, everyone look around. Is there any holy water left?" Elke said.

"What? Why?" Mones asked.

"It counters quikmar," Elke said.

"It will kill him even faster. That's the irony of it. The cure kills faster than the toxin," One Feather said as she returned to her human form. Her damage remained as she appeared to suffer severe eczema, her skin red and cracking.

"He said they tried holy water on him. It didn't work."

"That's screwed up. It was probably done by a layman."

"The vampire hunter blest him. Anyone?" Elke said.

"He's been blest? Dear Odin, that ain't right," Mones said. The others didn't have to speak. By their dark expressions, they agreed with him.

"It's kept him alive so he could rescue your carcasses. Now will you help me help him or not?! You might need him to do it again someday. Look at Dragomir. This could get worse before it gets better," Elke said.

"Calm yourself, Elke. Here. They threw this at me, and it didn't open," Dawnstar said. She offered her a dented can of unopened water. Her gorgeous, almond-shaped eyes were bright, their pupils opalesque, shifting colors as they swirled. The seer knew something, and she wasn't telling.

Dragomir shared a long look with Elke before she popped the can. He might be doubtful, and yet, over his seven plus centuries of experience, he had seen many oddities in supernature. His concern was for her and what might happen if something went wrong. Dillon might thrash and splash her. She put that possibility aside.

Elke sensed his blessing like hot bubbling water. She hesitated even as Dillon's aura of darkness grayed. With a shaking hand, she poured the holy water onto his wound.

It bubbled and frothed. Dillon soundlessly screamed and slumped unconscious. Now she would need to feed her blood to him. "I must take him back to his soil and nourish him. The sooner the better," Elke said.

"As I told you," the Asian woman said to Judge Dragomir.

Elke blinked. She hadn't heard anyone ever talk to him like that except his former seer, Soni Crow who had also been a skinwalker.

She was supposedly dead, replaced by Dawnstar. Elke was beginning to wonder.

"Yes, Dawnstar, it is well I did not terminate him," Dragomir agreed.

"I'll second that," Mones said.

"I would remove the Cloak of Suspicion, but it appears that it has already been removed or negated, perhaps by that blessing. We will deal with the authorities. Go," Dragomir said and nodded. He knew that her blood was unique.

"Good luck, lady. You know where we'll be. There's a party at the beer garden. Once I get the wolf hair off my dress, I'll be ready to dance the horizontal mambo," Kate said.

"I like my dinner full of alcohol and grease," Mones said.

"First, we shall deal with the local police and pacify the management by paying for damages," Dragomir reminded him.

The rooftop bar had been trashed. Broken furniture and debris were scattered far and wide. Only a shell of the wooden bar remained. Many of the barstools had been used as weapons, now bent or mangled. Elke wondered how much had been tossed over the edge.

"Sir, I am now costumed to give credence to your words," Mones said. He had a guitar in hand. Behind him, Painter solidified enough to rock out on an air guitar. He wore an AC/DC shirt: High Voltage. After what had just happened, he appeared worn and weathered enough to be rocking around the clock and aging prematurely.

"Yes, the heavy metal rock band ruse works so well. No one has any trouble believing that metalheads would get out of control during a rooftop party. It smells like we've been drinking and spilling enough for two bands," Dragomir growled. Elke felt sorry for the police who would soon arrive.

She lifted Dillon onto her shoulder. Von Damme had cursed Elke to survive many things, but greenwood arrows were one of her banes. Stiletto and Kate seemed to relish yanking the seven of them from her body. Healing would take time. Dillon didn't have the time that she needed. She would endure.

Despite the pain in her wings, she slowed their descent enough that her landing was jarring but not bone breaking as she returned him to earth like a dark angel. She carried him to her car.

With the sirens nearing, Elke didn't take time to check the Vette's trunk, but she heard soft panting coming from back of it. She tapped on the reinforced metal and whispered harshly, "CJ, if you make any trouble while I'm driving, and I have to stop, I will rip off your head and stuff your eyes down your throat."

Total silence followed, but she could hear its heartbeat race.

Elke buckled Dillon in, started the ignition, shifted, and drove off, heading away from the sirens. She could see the headlights of the police cars approaching. Lights flashing, a Bristol Virginia PD cruiser sped by them, heading toward the hotel. She wished them well in their dealings with the heavy metal band. They were liable to be hungry and impatient. Dragomir and his entourage could take care of themselves, or so she had thought before tonight. She shuddered when she imagined Von Damme's ring in Butcher's possession, but she would worry about that later. Right now, Dillon was her world.

Thirty-Six

Hospital Shadows

At the hospital, Knives peeked in on Rae. He had heard her heartbeat jump via the monitor. It raced a half-dozen fast beats, accelerating to tachycardia like a machine gun, and then her heart stopped. The alarm sounded when Rae flat-lined, suffering a myocardial infarction. Knives hit the Code Blue call button. He physically examined Rae, finding her pulseless and breathless. He laid the bed flat, positioning Rae level.

"Death is here, I can feel it," Nurse Vickie whispered as she rolled in the trauma cart. Her dark words cringed. He recalled Vickie had sworn up and down that she had seen Death when her mother and grandmother had died, both too young, not much older than Vickie was now. With that in mind, Vickie was definitely a health enthusiast.

A second nurse, Nurse Mandy Nutt, joined them. She looked powerful, like she pumped iron and was ready to subdue a combative patient.

Knives went to doctoring. He discovered that Rae had swallowed her tongue. He repositioned her jaw to open her airway.

That wasn't enough to bring her back. Was her throat bruised? He couldn't tell for sure.

Vickie deployed the ambu bag to provide Rae with oxygen. Rae's heart refused to beat on its own, so he and Nurse Mandy hooked Rae up to electrodes. The defibrillator analyzed that she needed a jolt to restart her heart. Knives stepped back, made sure everyone was clear, and deployed the paddles to release the charge. The electricity caused Rae body to spasm and arch, but her heart didn't respond.

"Oh, God, do you see that?" Vickie asked. Her eyes were wide to take it all in, whatever she was seeing.

"What?" Knives asked. He didn't see anything. Or did he? Something dark lurked at the edge of his vision.

"Death is here! I feel its cold finality," she replied. The bottom of her words crumbled and collapsed.

Knives took a centering breath, said a quick prayer and blessing, and then he spotted it, shocked by what he thought he saw. The dark image flashed across his vision, and then it was gone, as if his tired mind were playing tricks on him. Unbidden, he could see the afterimage of dark hands crushing Rae's throat. Bright sparks danced before her face, like the stars in one's vision when on the verge of passing out. Rae's shadow grew larger, swelling even as the lights vanished. Darkness loomed over her and lorded over them all.

Hands crept around Knives' throat. He could feel them squeeze. This was only the pressure to save her life, Knives reminded himself. If they did nothing, Rae was dead, so there was nothing to lose and much to gain.

His mind kept returning to the dark figure, but when he examined it critically, he noticed nothing out of the ordinary, just a friend having a heart attack. He and Rae had known each other since middle school. They had even dated for a short time, enough to know they were cut from different cloths, bent on alternate ways to improve the world. Rae seemed too young to suffer an MI, but there might be underlying conditions. Like Death was here. He heard the echo of Vickie's words, and then he saw the darkness animate again.

Rae let go a last, agonal gasp. Her shadow swelled and drew away from her, forming a second shadow now, separate and distinct. It stared at Vickie and pointed at her.

"Dr. Curran? Knives?" Nurse Char asked. The fiery red-haired nurse joined them.

Good, reinforcements, Knives thought as Dr. Joan had arrived, too. "Roto-Rooter?" she asked.

Knives blinked. The shadowy apparition was gone. "Yes, TPA to the rescue," he said. Rae had no history of stroke or previous heart attacks. This could be a blood clot. A transplanagenic activator would clear any blockages. If this failed, they could try epinephrine to chemically jump-start her heart.

Vickie's eyes rolled back. Her knees buckled, and Nurse Mandy caught her to lower her to the floor. "Vickie isn't breathing," Nurse Mandy said. Her words were intensely dark as if they had been cut from a moonless night.

Knives didn't blink. Now they had two Code Blues. Thankfully, the cart and the experts were here with him. They would work until they saved two lives.

"An ambulance rolled in. Another is expected in minutes," Nurse Char said.

Knives kept his frustration to himself. One of death's tactics was trying to overwhelm care and resources. "Let's focus on what we can control and doing the best that we can," he replied. Death and Heaven could wait.

***

Elke pulled into the hospital parking lot and found a slot at the curb near the front doors. It was late, and the lobby appeared brightly lit but deserted. She had been to numerous hospitals, and she found this one unremarkable. It lacked warmth, the arts, and green gardens that would encourage people to live and be grateful. This hospital seemed to focus mostly on the functional.

From out of the shadows, Hoyt approached Elke. He carried an old-fashioned doctor's bag and dressed like *Men in Black*, except that he'd added a cowboy hat, making him look a little like Clint Black pretending to be a doctor. Hoyt had found a way to arrive faster than she had, despite being farther away. The long-time unlicensed physician studied Dillon's condition and his wound. She didn't like the look on either's face. One was dying. The other, despite his many experiences, had no idea what to do to save her beloved. That actually seemed to move Hoyt who could be as emotional as a stone.

A security officer checked on them and moved along with a word from Elke. She turned to Hoyt. "What do you think?"

"Frankly, dear El, I'm surprised he's alive. He was stabbed, you say, with a dagger covered in quikmar."

"Yes, he had been blest by the vampire hunter," she said. It sounded odd even to her.

"What? He's been blest! That's freakin' weird. That should have injured him, too," Hoyt said. His pencil thin mustache quivered, and his eyebrows slowly descended above his black and red eyes as he recovered from that news.

"I know. So, I took the opportunity to wash it with holy water," Elke said. She recalled how those in Dragomir's entourage had reacted to her using it to cleanse Dillon's wound of quikmar. How could he survive that and be a vampire? Because, she had almost told them, Dillon was made from her blood, and it had been altered time and time again by Von Damme's experiments. Hoyt had been poisoned much the same. It was a miracle they were sane, most of the time. What was a sane life for a vampire?

"I didn't believe that the first time you told me. The wound isn't advancing. You did an excellent job of cauterizing it. Did you give him blood?"

"Yes, and sprinkled him with his own soil," Elke said with a nod. She had pulled over to the side of the road on the way here, long enough to kiss him and provide him with her blood. It had turned him pale, lessening his gray skin. Applying dirt to his wound had made no difference. She could see his aura, which he shouldn't have, and it looked shredded and pockmarked. She had also taken a moment to peer into the Shadowlands, something she had learned by watching Viktor do it. To open a shadow gate at this moment was inviting disaster. She needed to find a cluster of Shaden, so she had driven to the hospital. Dillon required more darkness.

"Your blood has many amazing properties."

"Not by choice. At least this time it may have been beneficial," Elke said.

"You are too hard on yourself. You are nothing like Viktor despite being of his blood which is perhaps why your consort is even less like him. I agree with you that Dillon still needs a dose of the Shadowlands to rekindle The Bloodlust, but it is foolhardy to take him there now. I didn't dare travel that way. I peeked in like Viktor showed me. There are hordes of Shaden pressed against the border and milling about. I wouldn't be able to get through, so I flew here. I'm always amazed by how many bugs there are airborne even this time of year. I think I have a crick in my neck," he said and spat out a bug. Hoyt stretched and massaged the muscles of his neck. His arms still appeared a little too long from being wings.

"I'm taking him inside," Elke said. She was going to save him, or there would be hell to pay.

"Why here?" Hoyt asked.

"Find me a shadow gate or a group of Shaden, and I'll show you."

"Those feargorgers were Viktor's backstabbing spies. If I ever get my claws on Cloaker…"

"Quickly find me the most powerful Shaden here, whether it be a feargorger or specter," Elke commanded. She lifted Dillon out of the car. She was going to carry him when Hoyt brought her a wheelchair. She thanked him and seated Dillon in it, lifting up his feet to place the metal supports under them. If anyone saw them, it would attract less attention. They would be looking at her and not him. Elke just wanted to hurry. She could feel Dillon drifting away as he became untethered on his way to his final end.

It took way too long for the elevator to ascend two floors. She felt Dillon clinging to life. When the doors finally parted with a ding, Elke was pleased that her agent sensed that she was needed. Round-faced, big-eyed, and compassionate to a fault, Melissa Cagey guided them to what seemed to be an incident in Rae's room. "There's a trauma team with Rae. She and a nurse both need immediate interventions," Melissa said.

"This is the right place," Hoyt said with a nod.

"Melissa, watch the hall," Elke said. She wasn't surprised to find this. She hoped this worked and prayed to the Almighty like she always had. Prayer and art had helped her survive Von Damme. If that failed, she would be opening a shadow gate, even if she had to use a sun lamp to get through it. After her earlier visit, Elke had expected the creatures to shadow Rae. Hoyt nodded as soon as he saw the female reporter teetering between life and death, her aura choked by darkness. Her fear was going to kill her, amplified by the Shaden.

The terror had strengthened the invader from the Shadowlands and empowered the feargorger to split in twain, creating a second. That Shadenspawn had frightened a nurse to near death. The undead darkness fed on her while she died as those with medical skills tried to save her. Elke recognized Knives, and Nurse Mandy Nutt, another one of her agents here. A second human doctor named Joan and Nurse Charlotte were trying to save Nurse Vickie. Everyone sensed the vampires as soon as they entered the room and the fray.

"Shut your eyes. Stand still. Hum loudly to yourself," Hoyt commanded. His words snapped out like an invisible whip of many tails and tendrils to snag all the doctors and nurses. In moments, they were all humming. The strange vibrations filled the air with a unique melody.

"Mandy Nutt, open your eyes and attend me," Elke said.

"How can I help?" Mandy asked. The former wrestler was one of her most valued agents and a friend. Elke explained, and the nurse immediately dropped the sidebar on the bed and unhooked Rae from all the equipment. Elke rolled Dillon to sit next to the bed, and then she let Mandy put Dillon's hand in Rae's. Elke had already felt a painful jolt from such a connection. She watched the blue-white lightning form around Dillon and flow over to his childhood friend.

"What is that?" Hoyt asked.

"I don't know. Whatever it is, it helps humans and hurts us," Elke said.

Hoyt squinted. "You're right. She is healing and looking so much better, but it isn't helping Dillon one wit," he groused.

Elke could see that truth. Dillon's dark aura remained fractured. His life glow had grown, but it remained damaged, streaked, and pockmarked, at odds instead of working together as Yin and Yang as she had seen earlier. She directed Mandy to put Dillon's other hand on Rae's belly. "Have you seen anything like it?" Elke asked.

Hoyt stroked his mustache while he thought. "Perhaps in the Far East. It reminds me a little of the Kundalini, although it's considered the Fire of Life, not the lightning of life," he mused.

Nothing seemed to change. Rae's feargorger hung on. Dillon wasn't drawing on it. Elke could still feel Dillon slipping away. Her anger grew with her frustration. She tried not to think what her existence would be without him. It would be like before, walking the lake shore and just waiting for something terrible to happen, instead of living each night. She contemplated opening a shadow gate right here and now. The consequences might be a high death toll of unusual accidents, but it was worth it to save her beloved.

Only, he wouldn't think so. He might hate her. Well, at least she could deal with that. He would wonder if he was worth so much fear and death, but she thought he would help many more people if he lived. She would be able to show him that given time.

"Miss Elke, we have unorthodox company," Melissa said.

Elke heard hurried footsteps and four heartbeats growing louder as people approached the room. She smelled sage, patchouli, wisteria, and lemongrass. It certainly wasn't any of the hospital staff coming to check on a patient, but witches, she realized, coming to check on her and Dillon.

"Let them by, Mel," Elke said.

"Thank you, dear. Alicia, you are right. This room is humming and overflowing with darkness. Darla brought flowers. They bring color and life to the darkness, don't you think, Elke?" the first of the witches said as the four breezed into the room.

Elke wasn't thrilled to see Becky or the others. They might try to stop her. It wasn't a good sign that Becky had stayed in town to neglect her real estate business. Elke curbed her tongue when she wanted to tell her to go back home and mind her own business. "The flowers are welcome, even though I'm trying to stop a funeral. So, I'm a little busy right now trying to save my beloved," Elke replied.

"I can see the desperation in your eyes, and it's radiating out from you in waves. You're acting from fear and thinking about opening a shadow gate. Don't. The border is teeming with Shaden. They've been riled up into a hungry frenzy, and they're ready to run amok if they can find a way through. Once they have enriched themselves here, they will roll into Bristol and the surrounding counties. Thanks to Von Damme's revival last August and the Oktoberfest Vampire now, there's already an epidemic of fear in the region. I've wondered if Shaden have anything to do with the mass shootings, the suicides, or the increase in serial killers plaguing our beloved Appalachia," Becky said.

"You'd open a gate to save your beloved?" Darla asked. She set the basket of mums, fire wheels, and asters on the table next to Dillon. They had little scent, but they changed the air.

"You know she would. She's considering it now," Donna said. She was clad in her usual blue with a black cloak. A raven peeked from its left pocket.

"Elsa. We loved and adored your mother. Because of that, we love you. We want Dillon to survive and thrive to benefit the world and you. Even one vampire who is concerned about human welfare is a rare thing. Two seems like a miracle, but the goddess in her glory has seen to give us a bounty with a pair," Becky said. Her blue eyes held the truth of her words.

"Y'all are just saying that," Hoyt said.

"Notice I didn't say three. At least you have a sane look in your eyes today, Hoyt."

"I tried exposing him to Rae's darkness. Nothing changed for him," Elke said.

"There is a better way, Elke, although it is fraught with peril, too, but that would be more personal. It could save Dillon, but it could also damn him, feeding him such potent darkness that it creates a monster. I can clearly see that he's too full of light to survive in his current form. The energy that heals others and the blessing that protects him are killing him. He needs more darkness," Becky said.

"Yes, he does. That's why I was planning to open a shadow gate and take him to the Shadowlands. He can regenerate there, but I can see you're dead set against that," Elke replied. She bit back a snarl. The Bloodlust grew agitated in her.

"This hospital has more than its share of feargorgers. Have him feed on those. Pick the easy fruit instead of cutting down the tree," Alicia suggested. She smelled of Marlboros and nervously toyed with her left turtle shell earring. "Seriously, I count four right here. It's a feast of darkness."

Green-eyed Darla adjusted her fur stole and nodded. Frowning Donna agreed with her. Her raven cawed to seal the deal.

Elke stared them down as she pondered Alicia's words and the consequences of such actions. If Dillon could completely absorb the Shaden, concentrated aspects of darkness strengthened by having fed on people's fears, it would heal and empower him. Or it could poison him. Such darkness might make him dependent on it as well as blood to feed the cravings of The Bloodlust. Vampires were what they ate. She had no idea what ingesting that much fear would do. Many vampires, the cruel ones, reveled in it. Dillon hadn't been like that. This might eventually turn him into such a beast. She winced at thinking of him transforming into Viktor Von Damme or Dirk DeVault.

"Poison is often used in a cure, but the right amount must be calculated," Alicia reminded her.

"Viktor could do it. He could feast on them. It's one of the reasons that he kept them around. Can you?" Hoyt asked her. He knew what Elsa had been through, enslaved and enthralled by Viktor because he'd been there and suffered a similar fate. Hoyt had been backstabbed and abused.

Elke thought back to Von Damme plucking a feargorger from one of the servants. He had bitten into it, and the Shaden had weakened until it was spent and vanished. She shook her head. "I've never tried. I didn't want to be like Viktor or Destrange."

"The powerful blessing on him might prevent this, but we don't dare attempt to cancel it with a curse. By its nature though, light devours darkness. He requires a more balanced diet heavier on darkness," Alicia said. Elke knew this.

"Save Dillon and help these people shed their parasites. They're friends of his, aren't they? That would be like a two for one bonus," Hoyt said.

Elke agreed that Dillon would understand this attempt to save him. At most, it endangered him and the host of the feargorger. If something went wrong, far fewer innocents would suffer than what she was proposing even if her plans went right. Elke studied the witches who had come to support her or to stop her. She recalled how much her mother had loved being among women of her kind. Elsa had used watercolor to paint many pictures of the herbs that Mom had grown, as well as her menagerie of pets. She realized that her mother would have agreed with this path. The witches understood the supernature of Shaden. After all, they had helped Elsa escape Viktor. She would try it.

Elke knew that hearing was the last sense to go, so she leaned close to his ear and breathed words of love and command. "Dillon, my love, take what you need to survive. Take on the darkness, and we will shoulder The Bloodlust together and be better, together. I trust you. Feast on the Shaden and save your friend," she said.

Elke waited and watched. Her compelling should be enough for Dillon to start absorbing the darkness, if such a thing came supernaturally to him. Nothing happened. Nothing changed. "Dillon, take a bite out of the darkness. Consume it," she cajoled.

"He is too far gone," Hoyt bemoaned.

Elke saw that Dillon's condition continued to deteriorate. She wasn't sure how much longer he would last. "This isn't working.

I'm going to open a gate and drag him into the Shadowlands. I don't know what else to do," Elke said.

Hoyt nodded. "Of course. They are just humans. They will be gone in a couple of blinks."

"Please, wait a little longer. Maybe this will help," Darla suggested. She placed a small black chunk of wood atop Dillon's hand. "It's from the Shadowlands. I hope it works as a catalyst."

"I pray so, too. Otherwise," Elke began.

Donna's raven quorked. The witches stepped away from each other, getting ready for a confrontation. Elke glanced from them to her beloved. Dillon continued to slip away.

Was Dillon frowning at her or in pain? She was going to do what she must do to save him, as he would do anything to save her. If that included incapacitating four witches, so be it. She didn't need to share a look with Hoyt. He would follow her lead when she attacked. She transformed her fingernails into talons. Becky's robe of light could be a problem, so Elke would stun her first.

What happened next changed her mind. Rae abruptly gasped and bolted to sit upright. Her wide eyes saw Dillon, and she reached for him. At first, Elke thought that Rae was going to choke him, but her hands dropped so that she clutched Dillon's arm like it was a life saver in a sea of fear and confusion. While she shuddered and heaved, she shook his arm. His head rocked, and his teeth clacked together.

"Stay calm. Stay your gorge, Rae Kirkland," Hoyt said.

For a moment, Rae heaved as if she might vomit, but then she settled. "Take it, Dillon. Please help me," she bemoaned. Rae's eyes rolled back, and she slumped in her hospital bed.

Dillon's body tensed. The Shaden that possessed Rae thrashed as it was slowly dragged away from its host. Rae lurched violently, so Mandy stepped in and steadied the patient. The feargorger used a spiderlike tenacity to cling to Rae, but it couldn't resist Dillon's dark nature and force of will. His mouth worked, and his nostrils flared. He appeared to inhale and absorb the darkness. As he drew in more and more, growing stronger, his flesh gradually darkened to reflect what he was doing. The shadow shrank, and soon, there would be nothing left of the creature of the Shadowlands. Usually, it ate fear. Now the frightened Shaden was being devoured.

"Fascinating. Those two seem to be working together," Hoyt said.

"As we'd hoped. Where there's light, there's shadow," Becky said.

"Where there's fear, we must remember that there is hope," Darla said.

"Creatures must learn to embrace and use their darkness. That's why there are cycles and seasons in nature and in our very existences," Alicia added.

"That's it, my love. Save Rae and come back to me, my heart," Elke told Dillon. She had almost acted out of fear, but hope had arrived in time. Her beloved snarled which was a good sign. That took energy. Either Rae had evicted the feargorger, or Dillon was pulling on it. Regardless, it worked. But was it enough?

"I thought only Von Damme could do such a thing. Along with that healing lightning, I discovered something new. What a night!" Hoyt exulted. He glanced around to ensure that the human doctors and nurses continued to hum and keep their eyes closed.

Dillon had acted like a powerful Shaden in devouring lesser kin. How would this affect him? She could feel him stir, but one feast of darkness had left him wanting. The hue of his skin gradually returned to a healthier pallor, though. There was hope!

"He needs more, but you know what to do now," Becky said. She appeared relieved. All four of the witches had relaxed. Elke wasn't sure that Dillon was out of the woods yet. She would breathe easier when he opened his eyes and spoke her name.

***

Dillon swam for the surface. He could see light above. He kicked and stroked for it, worried about how long he could last without breathing. He realized that his chest wasn't burning. Was he dying?

A blink later, he sat in the passenger side of Key's corvette. Dillon and Elke left the car and strolled into the woods where the natural sounds of life died to silence, all of them holding their breath in awe of her and sensing a life stealer passing by. Dillon knew her as a life giver, even if everybody eventually died that she touched, everything except for her.

Dillon had died saving her, and now he couldn't leave, hanging close by as ghost. Had Gina been right? Had Gina survived? Had he also killed those that he touched?

The fog thickened around Elke to cloak her approach. Without a crunch or whisper, she glided by the trees with their fallen and dying leaves. She remained quiet as she approached the old but lovingly cared for farmhouse. A Sullivan County sheriff's cruiser sat parked out front. The sight of the law enforcement vehicle didn't slow Elke's stride. "Stay outside, my love. I'll be back as soon as I deal with the Oktoberfest Vampire," she said and blew him a kiss.

He wasn't a ghost! This was a memory. He wasn't dead, again, not yet. This wasn't his final end.

As Elke ascended the steps to the country-style front porch, Dillon could hear voices inside. Elke soundlessly opened the door. "Mortimer Teivel, come to me now," the goddess of Dillon's nights commanded. Her voice wasn't meant for him, and it was still almost irresistible. Dillon would use the memory to return to her.

A moment later, a tall skinny man armed with a gun hurried to the front door. His shirt was a white skull on black fabric. Dillon recognized the Masked Nobody by his aura. He looked astounded that he could be coerced and summoned. "What? What's going on?"

"The Oktoberfest Vampire must die," Elke told him.

"The hell you say. Piss on you, I'm not an embarrassment. Listen, bitch. You tell your masters," Mortimer Teivel replied. He slipped a holy symbol out of his shirt and shoved it at Elke. She flinched and backed away a step. He laughed as he forced her back further until she was against the wall. "Y'all rejected me, but I am more than enough," he said in a bitter whisper.

"I didn't reject you, but I would agree. You are not worthy of the third kiss," Elke said. She reached out to the hand holding the cross, seized it, and crushed his flesh and bone. Teivel writhed in agony, and she maintained her pulverizing grip, dropping him to his knees. "Do you know why this doesn't work on me?"

He shook his head and wept from the pain.

"Because you don't believe in God, goodness or righteousness. Can it be that God wants me to be here? My mother said that the Lord works in mysterious ways, and if you look at the Bible, all kinds of derelicts came to be in His Service. In Latin, morte means death. Your time as a death bringer is over."

Elke peeked around the corner where the hostages were bound at the kitchen table. She nodded and stuffed a business card in his shirt. "It's time. Now, go make a sloppy attack, get yourself killed and leave those deputies with a lead to that biker gang."

As soon as she let go of his hand, Mortimer Teivel seemed to have forgotten it. He brandished his pistol, screamed, and stalked toward the deputies and the old folks held hostage. "Have a trip and a hard fall," Elke suggested as she departed. She smiled at Dillon and washed her hands of the matter.

The sound of a shotgun made her smile broaden. "The people will never know that they have Desiree to thank for tracking him down. I love that girl."

"It's a nice touch letting his captors shoot him," Dillon said. Elke was a hero and a savior. She was a life saver and death bringer.

"It's the little things that make a difference. Longevity and anonymity are in the details. If he recovers and is coherent, we'll deal with him then. For now, the Oktoberfest Vampire is finished terrorizing the Tri-Cities," she said.

Elke had told him to always return to her. Dillon threw his spirit into the search for that smile and for that love.

Instead, he stumbled into a memory with Rae at a younger time and place. "So why do you want to be a reporter?" she asked him.

"To speak up for people and things that can't. I would like to bring truths to light."

"Truth shouldn't be based on perspective."

"I know, but that seems to be based on one's point of view which is flavored by experiences."

"Wow, Dillon. You sound old. It must be all that martial arts training," Rae told him.

"Thanks, I think. Why do you want to be a talking head?"

"I want to bring my positive view to things," she said.

"Cool. Do you think we'll make our dreams come true?"

"Oh yes! Just maybe not in exactly the ways we expect, but we can still be the best of whatever we are," Rae replied.

"You sound like Master Cosmo," Dillon replied.

"Thank you. So do you plan on reporting from the shores of South Holston Lake while you search for the Dark Lady?" Rae asked with a smile.

***

Elke studied Dillon. He really was looking much better, putting on some weight. This seemed to be working. She was ready to dance a jig.

"Doing it this way was better. He'll be able to sustain himself and reduce the number of feargorgers causing people to see danger everywhere and live scared," Alicia said.

Elke sensed there were other feargorgers in this room. "I believe the male doctor, Curran, has one. Knives likely caught it while diving in Viktor's study like Rae did in August, but it is far less powerful. He seems to have managed his fear," Elke said.

Hoyt squinted. "It's deeply entrenched," he said.

"The doctor has been experiencing synesthesia. It could be related."

"Indeed. I am envious. I have wanted to see people talk in colors," Hoyt replied wistfully.

Rae was looking much improved, but they were too late for the nurse. The feargorger had scared her to death. Knives was a different matter altogether. She untangled Dillon from Rae and rolled his wheelchair over to his blood brother. Dillon was groggy when she placed his hand in Knives' grasp.

"Dr. Curran, keep humming a happy song and let go of the darkness," Elke compelled. Knives hummed as Dillon tugged on his blood brother's insidious feargorger. The Shaden was rooted, having been there for what could be months. Such entrenched shadows could be difficult to expunge. "Dillon, my love, save your friend and yourself. Take your fill and then come back to me. You promised me."

Dillon reacted to her words. He reached up with his free hand, his left grasping his blood brother's shadow as if it were a sheet. Knives' expression twisted into pain, and he began to thrash. Even before Elke looked to him, Hoyt moved in. He held Dillon's blood brother, supporting his neck, so he wouldn't hurt himself. Dillon actively yanked at a flap of darkness and dragged increasingly more of the feargorger into his lap where he bear-hugged it. The invader from the Shadowlands flailed, sending out waves of fear, but the people who could feel it were humming and brimming with good vibrations. They wouldn't provide it with fear to strengthen it, so it was no match for Dillon's will and thirst. His skin darkened as he drew in the shadowy beast, and this time, his eyes lost their red tint, turning utterly black.

Elke recalled him telling her that he had slapped a ghost. He could touch the ethereal in much the same way as the master vampire, Viktor Von Damme, the being she had cursed with every breath. It was only when she began blessing her miserable situation that her existence had changed. So, instead of fearing and hating Dillon's nature, she felt blest by it. He could help people possessed by feargorgers. He might become a fear devourer.

What would it do him? Regardless, she was grateful that they would face this darkness together.

***

Dillon rushed into the classroom. He didn't know how he'd overslept. He was late for his final exam! Was he in the right classroom? Why was this test in Greek? Yes, it was a test on the Endocrine system in the human body. So why was it in Latin? His pencil broke. His ballpoint pen ran out of ink. The calculator's battery failed, so it quit functioning. He wasn't allowed to use his phone. He would have to do the math in his head. He looked up at the clock. What? He only had a few minutes left! His future as a doctor flashed before his eyes.

In a blink, he was sitting in a counseling session. The doctor across from him looked skeptical. "Vampires, and werewolves, eh? Shadows that move on their own and strangle people, you say? Hmm. Dr. Curran, I believe you need a long time off and perhaps a prescription medication to ease your anxiety."

Now, Dillon stood among the dead. All of his blood brothers had wounds on their throats or been mauled by something with claws. Their shadows lived, though, and they cackled at him. He hadn't been able to help them or save them. Burdened by regret and failure, Dillon dropped to his knees. He wanted to die. What could he have done differently?

He found himself in a stairwell. The emergency lighting went out, and the darkness closed in. Dillon wasn't afraid of the darkness. He seized it by the horns, or by the collar, wherever he could get a good grip. These were Knives' nightmares. Dillon could relate to seeing all his blood brothers dead, but the darkness appeared different to him now. He knew it, and he knew how to use it because it was a part of him.

Dillon felt himself being buoyed back into sensation, hearing first. His world was humming and abuzz. Were there bees nearby? The air vibrated with life. He opened his eyes and looked around blearily.

He realized that he was holding Knives' hand while his blood brother hummed with his eyes closed. Dillon noticed that he wasn't the only one. He was in a hospital room of humming healthcare workers and four witches who were staring silently and now beginning to smile.

He felt Key's presence. She moved into his view where her smile beamed upon him, and her eyes danced with delight. "You have come back to me, my love. We are just a couple of miracles. You have healed your friends of darkness and sustained yourself without feasting upon their blood."

"Oh, that's fantastic news, Key," Dillon said. He stood, wobbled, and embraced her. He saw Hoyt and nodded to him.

"You have absorbed feargorgers from your friends. They are well. You are well. What a surprise. Is this a happy ending? It feels odd, the taste of triumph, sweet instead of bitter, as I've heard said, but it is a welcomed change. I could get accustomed to it. So, Mister Urich, you may have more uses and abilities than we expected, and anyone imagined. I must give credit where credit is due and thank the W's," Hoyt said.

"It was our pleasure to see dark and light blend together for a better future. This has almost been as satisfying as entrapping Von Damme," Becky said.

"Supernature in harmony with nature is always the better choice," Donna said.

"I think it's time for us to go. I'm sorry we couldn't save everyone," Darla said.

Dillon barely noticed them go. He was dazed, feeling like he was in more than one body, and unsure why the witches were here. He looked over to the dead nurse. He could see that a feargorger had killed her. It left a dark stain on her throat like it had hemorrhaged while she had screamed to death. From what he could tell, it had moved to another nurse. It stared fearfully from her shadow at him. He reached for it.

"No more, Dillon. Our meter is running, and it's time for us to skedaddle. Someone will come to check on the humming concert," Elke said. She took Dillon's hand and drew him out of the room into the hall toward the elevators.

"You can stop humming, open your eyes, and move again when I reach one. Five. Four. Three," Hoyt said, following them out into the hall. Melissa stepped inside, no longer needing to watch for anyone coming by. She hurried to help even as Hoyt finished his countdown. "Two. One."

The elevator doors parted for Dillon and Elke. They stepped in, holding them open for Hoyt. He arrived, and the doors closed without anyone leaving Rae's room where they heard laughter and tears.

The same was not true when they arrived at Juju's room. They had no idea what condition they might find him in. Dillon and Elke still didn't know, because Juju's bed was empty. They checked with the nurses and their logs. Juju was gone without there being a record of it. The nurses would realize it soon.

"He escaped," Elke said.

"What do you mean?" Dillon asked.

"That there is more than one kind of darkness possessing people. If there's an open shadow gate down there in Von Damme's basement, anything could be coming through, perhaps more specters. And remember, there are ghosts down below that could haunt any diver who unknowingly brings it back. I'll explain more, later, dear. Come along, it's time to vanish into the night," Elke said. She took Dillon's arm and guided him to the stairwell. He was still dazed while they descended. Hoyt followed them silently, moving like a ghost through the lobby.

Dillon knew that he should be ecstatic that they had been able to save two out of three lives, one more if he included himself, and many more spared Elke's wrath. Even so, he knew that nurse had loved ones, friends and family that would miss her, just as he missed his deceased blood brothers and the sunshine. He hoped that they had an Elke in their lives, a bright moon or star to guide them through the darkness.

***

Knives blinked and shook off the stiffness in his limbs. They felt like they were ready to fall asleep. Had he napped while standing up? His lips and tongue were numb, too, and he felt thirsty and dehydrated. He looked around, finding Rae snoring loudly. Yay! Thank the Good Lord! Death could take a holiday. Rae's heartbeat and her oxygen levels were mid-range normal. That was incredible news, but there was still one of their own to save.

On the floor, Nurse Mandy prepped Vickie for the defibrillator. He shared a look with Dr. Joan. She appeared confused, too, but they both knew that they must help now and ask questions later.

They tried everything they could, but Vickie never revived. Knives wiped the sweat from his eyes. He couldn't believe it, and frankly, he didn't want to believe that death had taken her. That made it sound like a being of some sort instead of the expiration of the human body.

"Did you see, Death? It's like he showed up, and Vickie lost the will to live. Or did I imagine that?" Nurse Char asked.

That same absurd thought had just crossed Knives' mind. He figured that was an attempt to assuage his guilt. Someone or something else must be at fault. Dr. Joan, Nurses Melissa, Mandy, and Charlotte, they had tried everything. Something should have worked! They should have saved her because there didn't seem to be a physical cause. If they couldn't save nurses from dying where they worked, could they really save anyone? Could he save anyone? They had been helpless despite their knowledge, skills, and technology. Medicine was always a practice, but the results still counted. He couldn't help but wonder what they could have done differently.

Dr. Joan made the call to have the body relocated. They had family to notify. The hospital staff would be stunned. Vickie had been vibrant, helpful, and beloved. He was in shock, too.

"Knives? Am I in the hospital?" Rae murmured. Her flesh tone's coloring continued to improve. That was a good sign of blood flow and oxygen levels. Her words looked wobbly but whole. He took that as another good signal.

"Yes, but I don't think for much longer. You're much improved, my friend," Knives replied and squeezed her hand. She pulled him into a hug. He felt better, much better. He reminded himself not to let defeats and setbacks keep him from trying to help people. As he practiced more, he improved. If he kept telling himself that, he would feel better. Yay, thanks for the practice, Vickie. She would laugh out loud. If she was going to go, it might as well give them a learning experience. She would have wished to have seen them humbled another time, though.

"What a nightmare. Thank God y'all were here. I thought I'd died," Rae said. Her words were full of burgeoning vim and vigor, more active than she sounded. Knives thought that she would rebound quickly.

"You're a lucky woman, blessed by nighttime angels," Nurse Mandy said.

"Knives, do I look as awful as you do?" Rae asked.

Everyone else in the room laughed. Knives didn't see the humor. That could be her point.

"Doc, you do good work. You should go while you can. You can't rock 'n roll every night and party every day, no matter what the songs say. Go. I'll see to this. I've got a fresh cup of coffee running through my veins. I couldn't sleep if I tried," Dr. Joan said.

"I think you're right about it being time to go home. I can barely think straight, especially if I believe that I stared death in the eye tonight," Knives said.

"We stare down death every day. Sometimes it's more personal than other days and comes with more anguish. Go! We can wax philosophically over an adult beverage another time."

"Good night," Knives replied. A rested brain would help him deal with his PTSD. If he could return to his normal self, he might be more help to J-Man and Dillon. He looked forward to finding out what a good, long ten hours of rest would do for his body, mind, and soul. What could he accomplish with a mind clear of fatigue and fear? He planned on finding out, soon.

Thirty-Seven

Watery Death

Where are you, Juju? Madi wondered. She sat on her brother's dock waiting for news and watching the time roll by with no idea what to do next. They had spent much of the morning searching for Mr. Juju Castillo, but they had stopped when the fog rolled in bringing drizzle. That made Roxy's and Lan Caster's drones useless. They had no idea where Juju might go.

Law enforcement was looking for him. The police and sheriff departments were concerned that he might be mental and a danger to people. His photo had been shown by the media through many outlets, and it seemed that Bristol had another reason to worry. If you turned on your TV, phone or the internet, such as You're Probably From Bristol If, you saw or read that Juju Castillo was an escapee from the hospital. His celebrity status made him a target and easy to recognize.

Tom had closed and locked the gate to the place. No Media Allowed had been added to the signs.

Roxy suffered a headache and was resting. Zhen was meditating.

Madi wondered if Juju's disappearance was related to the missing FBI agents. It seemed that Agent Kaye and her partner had disappeared with the skulls. Juju had messed with them, too. Madi wasn't sure what that meant. Were the skulls toxic? She even considered that they might be cursed. Her thoughts seemed to be spinning in crazy directions.

Everything seemed stuck in limbo. They couldn't dive to the ruins. The memorial was suspended and pending and expected to go to court. So, she had no clue when they would be setting the rock to remember Denny. The truth was that nobody was eager to go back there. And yet, with Agent Kaye missing, closing the ruins as a dive site might be short-lived.

Adding to the questions, Madi wondered if the double eagles were real. It had been looking good until Linkous and Agent Kaye had found a stamping press. It was unknown if any of the stamps were double eagles. She knew the TVA and Feds were likely to claim the money and give her a salvage percentage.

Who knew what else might be found in Von Damme's basement and its caverns? She felt the curious itch and refused to scratch it. If the ruins and the caverns underneath them hid traps and monsters, what had the mansion been like? Madi shuddered at the thought.

It could have been worse for Levon and Alan Linkous, too. They could have died. There again, she realized, males had taken the brunt of the mansion's bad luck. At least they were all alive. She had pulled the fuse on their wholesale deaths. Even now, that seemed more like a nightmare. Blessedly, she didn't hear any nagging voices claiming that it was only for now. She never missed Negative Nellie or Debbie Downer.

They didn't need to nag her, though, for her to realize endangering lives wasn't worth saving her show. She had thought it had been. Juju missing deeply worried her. He had fought with something or someone who hadn't appeared on the security cameras. Or could he have attacked Zhen? How crazy was that?

Madi had been warned, but she had opened up Pandora's Box anyway. She had done it to empower women and to save her show. At what point did her cause become too much a business?

Her brother ambled onto the dock and tossed a Frisbee out over the lake. Sarge sprinted and launched himself to catch the disc before splashing down in the water. Plastic in mouth, the boxer eagerly paddled back toward shore. The rain didn't dampen their enthusiasm.

"Hey, Sis! You look very deep in thought. Do you need help getting out? I can throw you a lifeline," Tom said.

"Oh, yes. I was thinking about Juju and the Mansion of Gloom and Doom. I was wondering if going there was worth it. I was thinking I've been very selfish."

"That's deep and cold-hearted. It might be best to let snoozing haunts sleep, and man, who sounds old now?"

"Do we have to be old to be responsible?" she asked.

"Ha! No. First there's stunted immaturity then learning experiences."

"Juju was in the hospital. Now he's missing. Why?" she asked, even knowing he would have no answer.

"Strange things happen at that hospital. Troy had to save Knives when John's body was stolen from the morgue. Maybe weird shit happens at every hospital. People are strange, and the world is a far more bizarre place than I ever expected."

"I can't believe I've been considering that vampires might be real," she said.

"Are you now? The Oktoberfest Vampire was caught. He was more serial killer than bloodsucker, although the final results might be about the same. People are dead, but that killer has been brought to justice, and they found him to be human," Tom reminded her.

"Hurrah. We can all sleep comfortably at night again," she said. It sounded like a lie even to her.

"You've been having trouble, too?" he asked, concerned.

"Yes. I know. I know. You warned me not to dive. Now I have nightmares about it."

"Are you feeling guilty? I thought that part of your brain was injured. I was thinking how lucky you were to feel no regrets. Besides, I have daymares, too, if that's such a thing. If I let my mind wander, I go back down there, and I didn't even go inside that place. But that jewelry box, it messed with my head."

"Supposedly, I had lost my ability to be thrilled or scared. I think they were wrong. If Roxy wasn't around to keep me from being reckless, who knows? Dillon never went diving, right?" Madi said. He nodded. "So, the mansion wasn't the cause of his illness?"

"I don't think so, but who knows? Some people blame it for most of the problems around here, but not as far as I know. He told us that he was poisoned by the cult," Tom said.

"The vampire one or Satanic one?"

"One and the same. Evil and the Six Fingered. I hated that I had to fake being part of them for a while. The guys thought I did too good a job. Sometimes, I'm not all that sure that they trust me."

"You never told me about that."

"A bunch of the blood brothers and Silke were captured. Most of us got out alive. Spider and some cops didn't," Tom said. Her brother was leaving much unsaid.

"So do you believe in vampires?"

"Which kind? Psychic, emotional, corporate, political, or tick-type blood suckers? Or do you mean the suave and debonair vampires of movie fame? Actually, I believe in all of them. People come in all kinds and colors, why not vampires? What if this is just another strange color?" Tom asked.

She couldn't believe that she was having this conversation, and yet, she needed to dig deeper. "Zhen thinks there's something supernatural about Dillon."

"Ah yes. Dillon-san moves like water. I have never seen anyone fight like him," Tom said.

Madi took a moment to realize that was a reference to Bruce Lee. "So, you don't know what's going on with Dillon?"

"He's in love with Elke Swearington. He moved back here to be with her. Now, he can't get out in the sun, so that's not so good, but he said she's his moon and stars, whatever that means. Everybody's got a dark side, right? Anyway, he's a good guy who has had a lot of be kind and compassionate and only kick ass as a last resort Kung Fu training. He smiles a lot so she's keeping him happy in bed," Tom said.

Sarge brought the Frisbee back. He and Tom wrestled. Her brother hung the boxer out over the lake where he growled with his mouth full. Water poured from his coat. The shower caused the surface to swirl, because Sarge was slowly spinning like a really big catch. Tom finally brought Sarge back in. He tickled the dog, and the boxer squirmed until Sarge let go of the disc and dashed off. Tom chuckled, faked a couple tosses, then he threw the object of the dog's desire onto shore. Sarge raced after it by taking the gangway to land. The scrambling of his paws sounded loud.

Madi realized that her brother didn't know exactly what had changed about Dillon. "So, you said that strange things can happen in an Appalachian bar late on quiet nights," she said. He nodded. "Do you care to explain yourself?"

He let out a long sigh to buy himself time. "Well, I've just seen things hard to explain. You know, people appearing and vanishing right before your eyes like David Copperfield and Criss Angel. Customers with no reflection. That's really freaky. Women too damned gorgeous to be anything but supernatural. The last, I can deal with! Customers who don't bleed when they cut themselves. One night, a drunk guy got pissed off and turned into an angry bear. It was grizzly," he replied.

Madi couldn't tell if he was truthful or pulling her leg. "Dad jokes now? In all seriousness, when your place burned down, you were attacked by?"

"Feral canines," he replied.

"Wild dogs? Why did they attack? Were you storing venison?" she asked.

"Ha! That's a good question. Nobody outside our group has even asked that. I mean, we've talked about it, but we're fairly clueless."

"Fairly. Anyone have an idea?"

"Yeah. They were after the silver jewelry box," Tom said.

"Dogs?" she asked.

"I didn't say that," Tom said.

"Then you believe it was wolves, too, don't you?" she said. He couldn't deny it. She could read it in his expression. "You've seen them, or believe you have. Had you seen them before this?" she asked. He didn't need to answer. She could see the lie of denial trying to hide in that unusual face.

He tilted his head. "I hear a car. It sounds familiar. It might be Knives or it could be Snake. They texted me that they would be coming out," Tom said.

"What interesting friends you have. It could be the FBI. Strange that they disappeared with the skulls, isn't it?"

"Strange is to be expected when dealing with things associated with the Mansion of Gloom and Doom. Yep, it's Knives. Somebody is with him. Good. It's party time," Tom said.

"How can you think about throwing a party at this time?"

"Life is short. I'm always thinking about partying. Things are more fun with company. Some say two is company and three's a crowd but not me. I like twins and even triplets," Tom said.

Madi was disgusted by his lack of concern about Juju. "Juju could be dead tomorrow."

"So could we," Tom said.

Sarge dashed back with the throwing disc and dropped it on Tom's feet. The dog barked, urging him to hurl it again. Tom tossed it over the water.

"So, when did you see a werewolf?" she asked.

"Were we talking about werewolves?" he asked.

She gave him a long dirty look that said don't lie to me. "Tell me the truth, please, or just shut up."

"Okay. You wouldn't have believed me before, but you might now. One of those late nights," he began and hesitated. "A guy was drinking a lot of booze, easily a couple of pints, mostly whiskey plus some tequila. He refused to pay, so naturally I cut him off. That royally pissed him off. No big surprise there. I thought I could handle him, but he ripped into me. I still have the scars. Knives sewed me up."

"You're telling me that a werewolf tore into you?" Madi asked. Every clue, his tone, his expression, and his body language said he was telling her the truth. She might have freaked out earlier or called him a bullshitter. Now, she gave him the benefit of the doubt. He believed what he believed based on his circumstances. After her experiences, that made perfect sense.

"Yep. Knives thought it was a dog. Hey, buddy, I hear you!"

"My, what big ears you have!" Knives yelled back.

"I smell perfume. It smells familiar, too," Tom said as he sniffed the air.

"Hey buddy, I brought company! A good surprise for once," Knives said.

As he and Rae Kirkland came around the corner, Sarge swam onto the ramp, stood and shook. He soaked Tom who was grinning broadly. "Rae! You look great!" he said and hurried over for a hug. "I'm so glad you ignored the sign out front. This is great, really great. I mean it. You freaked me out. I was worried. J-Man will be thrilled to see you, too. He's coming over to drone on," Tom said.

"You and your parties," Madi grumbled.

"I thought you would like this. I called Jambo and Dillon, too."

"Wonderful," Madi said, starting to steam. She should have Roxy come slug him. She threw a better punch.

"The more the merrier. Knives, buddy, you look much, much better."

"I had a good long slumber."

"Okay, then. I need to sleep like that. Rae, lady, what's the news?" Tom asked.

"They're not sure what happened, but I'm better now. It sounds like I missed a bunch while I was lying in a hospital bed," Rae said.

"You're not the only one that freaked out," Tom said tactlessly.

"I heard about Juju. It reminded me of Eduardo. I miss him. I hope Juju turns up safely. I heard Levon and Alan Linkous were injured," Rae said.

"Yes, they were, let me tell you," Madi said.

"Oh, please do, plus whatever will help us find Juju," Rae said.

"See, she just got out of her hospital bed, and she wants to help," Madi said.

"I hear a truck. Hmm. It could be Brownstone's. Brawny-boy needs to have his truck's muffler fixed. I hope he brought tequila. I'll bet that he's brought a new rifle that he wants to show off. You know, some tequila might help us think out of the box," Tom said.

Madi wanted to slap her brother. And people thought she was unfeeling. Was it a Marader trait?

Sarge dropped the Frisbee and barked. He still wanted to play. He looked like such a happy, wet dog with the disc in his mouth. The water near him rippled into a wave.

The surface seemed to suddenly part and a huge, tooth-lined maw opened wide. Before anyone could move, the gator's jaw snapped shut on the dog. Sarge had sensed canine peril and lunged forward, so the alligator snatched one rear leg.

Tom spat out justified profanities. Madi echoed them. Like it would make some difference, they both saw and shouted, "Gator!"

There was another one! Juju has spoken the truth. Was this Snapper or Crocker? It didn't have any white spots. A tattered red ribbon was stuck in its teeth. Madi wished she had a bang stick or a rifle.

"You can't have my dog!" Tom snarled. With amazing speed, he sprang at the reptilian beast and tackled it. The trio tumbled into the lake where they thrashed in the water. Blood in the churning foam turned pink as they struggled, rolling over and over. Did he have a knife?

Madi was shocked. She wasn't the only one. Rae stood stunned, too. Madi had heard about owners doing crazy things to save their pets. Madi didn't know what to do. She was ashamed thinking that she should have this on video when she should be saving her brother. She looked over to a jet ski.

Knives shook off the surprise the fastest. "Where's the Snake when you need him? I need a rifle," he said and yanked the door open to the bar. Madi knew what he was thinking. Her brother kept a shotgun behind the bar.

She looked over to the boat and wondered if there might still be bang stick there. She could fire up the jet ski and take the fight to the gator. They had been in a rush to get Juju to the ambulance and then distracted thereafter, never really properly unloading the boat.

Madi jumped into Maverick and frantically searched. She could hear her brother shout now and again as he resurfaced. Sarge whined.

Madi finally found a bang stick and looked up. With a hairy handled knife, Tom repeatedly stabbed the beast, drawing blood. While the two fought, Sarge escaped to swim toward the dock. Then, Madi couldn't figure out what was going on. It looked like her brother was caught in a rug while wrestling with the gator. She looked closer. Was that another dog in on the fight? She heard snarling, then she heard gunfire from nearby. Instead of Knives, J-Man and his pilot buddy stood there. Both were armed with rifles.

"Let it go, Tom! Brawny and I got you!" J-Man yelled.

"Yeah, bro, we got your back!" Browny added.

Her brother released and threw himself backward. The gator turned on him and began pursuit. It was closing in when J-Man and brawny Browny opened fire. Some slugs hit the water while others struck the reptilian beast, slowing its advance. Her brother kept backpaddling as he swam away. He was a superior swimmer, having anchored Tennessee High's team, but the gator was in its element.

"Any time now, guys!" Tom shouted.

"I've hit it a half a dozen times, I'm sure of it," Browny said. He took aim and fired again. Madi didn't know what kind of rifle. She didn't know guns.

"Brawny, keep hitting it until you run out of bullets," J-Man replied.

Madi took the bang stick, jumped on the Jet Ski, and fired it up. She was just about to ride the Yamaha to her brother's rescue when the monster took a bullet in the eye. She saw it pop. The gator thrashed, and yet it continued to swim toward her brother. It seemed unstoppable, but when Tom darted sideways, the beast kept coasting along and past him. It took a moment for it to sink in that the beast was dead.

"Yes!" Tom cheered, throwing his arms in the air and briefly sinking. Her brother, his hair and face bloodied, crawled back onto the dock. His clothing was torn, and he had suffered clawing gouges along his ribs, but he still possessed all his limbs and looked free of bites. Sarge rushed over and began licking him. "Oh yeah, that will help. Yes, you were worth it, Sarge. You are not gator bait, buddy! I think that sucker is twenty-five feet long!"

"Someone was a dead eye shot," Madi said.

"That was me!" J-Man and Browny said in stereo.

"Crack shots! Drinks on the house!" Kia cried.

"You bet, especially for J-Man and the Brawny dude. Man, I'm glad you guys decided to show up. Hey, Knives, the shotgun was a nice thought, but you might have gotten me. It has a wide pattern."

"I was going to suggest you drag it near like you did in those life-guard classes so I could unleash a close-up blast. Sidestroke, baby!" Knives said. They all laughed in relief.

"Madi, you were right. I know. Savor those words. There was more than one gator. I didn't have any dynamite, so a knife had to do. It was a good knife. I guess I left it in that dog-eating monster. I think I may have the cobbler make us some new boots or some all-natural Crocs!" Tom bellowed.

"How can you joke about this?" Madi asked. He looked like he actually enjoyed it.

"I have all my fingers and toes. Snake Siksay has nothing on me, baby! I can't wait to show him the carcass," he replied and grinned.

"Hey, isn't that a snake right there!" Knives said. He pointed near Tom, startling him.

He squinted. There was no sign of a snake. "Not funny."

"You know, this isn't the strangest thing that has happened here," J-Man said.

"That makes two of these monsters dead. I'm not going back in the water until it's checked for more," Knives said. He helped Tom out of the water and onto the dock.

"That's as good as any excuse and better than most. I think it's time to call Agent Boatwright and the wildlife folks. He can let the TVA know. Knives, buddy, I'm fine, don't mother me. Let Ginger clean it, okay? She has a light touch," Tom said. He brushed off his blood brother's concern.

"You can stay here, be the guy in the chair, and coordinate our search for Juju. You and Madi know Bristol as well as I do. I can rig my drones up to search using infrared. I know Lan Caster can do the same. That should help us even in the fog," J-Man suggested.

"So, you were talking about a search party?" Madi asked her brother. She hadn't even considered that he would do such a thing.

"Yes. What did you think I was talking about?" Tom asked. He didn't quite manage to conceal his smile. He had been playing along. "What was I supposed to say? We're in Search of Good Juju?"

Madi went from wanting to slug her brother to hugging him. "We won't stop looking until we bring him back to us. We bring the truth to light," Madi said.

Thirty-Eight

A New Day

Earlier, from the protection of the front porch, Dillon watched the crack of dawn illuminate the dark sky out there beyond the thick branches of the trees shrouding Swearington Lodge. Had he survived almost dying, again? Or had he returned from the dead? That's what Joseph Campbell, a mythologist, said about heroes. They would return from the dead, leaving their life behind to return with new knowledge. Dillon didn't think of himself as a hero. Had he learned any earth-shattering knowledge to share with people?

Seriously, he was not competing with Troy. This death was even more unexpected than the first time. Immortal really didn't mean invulnerable. Instead of longing for the daylight, Dillon was appreciative and grateful that he was even here at all. The pain in his hip reminded him that he had almost met his final end.

Hoyt called it Oblivion where vampires belonged for spitting in God's eye for living too long. Dillon didn't feel long-lived, but being able to spend another hour, another night, any additional time with Elke was a blessing. They brought the best out in each other. It pleased him that his mom agreed. He planned to call her soon. She would be awake by now, but he doubted that she would be alert. First, she needed to have her hot caffeine with creamer fix. He had joked that she used drugs to get motivated.

Canadian geese flew in formation over the water. Fish jumped from the lake to eat what few bugs remained this late in October. Distantly, fishermen were after those hungry fish, predators eating predators. He couldn't help but think of Goran, Butcher and De-strange. They were feeding on the locals. He had encountered them each once. He didn't expect such future encounters to end in a draw. If he had any mission, besides protecting Elke and being a good son, it would be to protect people from those three vampires. He had learned that there were different kinds of vampires, much as there were different types of people. He considered Elke a good vampire, so there was good and evil found in the supernatural.

The lodge's dark hounds rushed around to the shadowy front yard. They sniffed and searched around every bush and tree as if they were even scrutinizing said shades and sticking their nose into each nook and cranny along the house. He waved to Theresa Killian and her favorite canine, Bella. The Mistress of the Hound's eyes blazed blue this morning with the hot thrill of the hunt. Her change to a thrall had given her superior vision plus a connection closer than normal between canine and master. Unlike wolves, dogs chose the friendliest and most generous to be their leader, hence, Ms. Killian. They adored her and Elke.

He needed to be more like the Mistress of the Hounds who was in love with the dark, rainy days and thunderstorms. He would skip the tats, though. Theresa fit right in at the lodge of river stone and timber, even more than Dillon. Her hounds would eat any-thing, squirrels, rabbits, mice, people, and more. Theresa had told him about the time that her dogs had taken down a mountain lion. He knew they could handle thralls and even a werewolf but not a pack of lycan. Vampires would hardly consider them an annoyance.

Dillon now seemed so far from that kid who had started taking martial arts classes and gone hunting, camping, and waterskiing with his blood brothers. Two months ago, his life had changed just before dawn on Cemetery Ridge in South Holston Lake.

The sky brightened, taking on a ruddy hue. He wondered if red sky at morning, sailors take warning, might apply here. He felt like he sailed, even raced, into unknown territory. Light and dark seemed to be at odds during the crepuscular times, starker and edgier. The crimson light slipped in among the trees, and the woods seemed to be glowering before the sky's morning light brightened. The clouds seem to have caught fire, creating flames across the heavens.

Elke was nearing! He set his cup down on the porch. She glided out the front door, settled in his lap, and passionately kissed him. He enjoyed the intimate comfort of her pressed against his body. This felt natural even if they were supernatural. That's when he realized vampires were more greatly influenced by their human pasts than people could imagine. Who they had been before wasn't totally left behind. Their memories hadn't been wiped out. His beloved was a perfect example of this. She still loved art and cared for people.

"How are you feeling?" Elke asked.

"Rode hard and put up wet, darling, otherwise, I'd be prepared for a lap dance," Dillon said. Elke laughed and hugged him. "I'm doing better all the time, and I appreciate you more than ever when I didn't think that was possible," he replied. He knew that she was worried about how much diffused light his body could handle since he had absorbed Rae's and Knives' evil shadows. Dillon was still wrapping his head around consuming feargorgers for improved health.

"I love you."

"I feel it! I still have an ache in the stab wound, but it's minimal. I'm truly grateful for this moment," he replied. They shared another soulful kiss and companionable silence full of acceptance and wonder. The barking dogs, honking geese, cawing raven, and the motorboats rumbling made it sound homey. Somewhere, a motorcycle roared by to remind them that they still lived near civilization.

"I am thankful, for whatever reason, that you were able to feed on Shaden. You sustained yourself and saved the people you care about and came back to me!" Elke said. He could feel joy radiate from her. He wondered if the other vampires were capable. Hoyt had just shrugged when asked. Nothing had been written down, so they depended on memory, and the tradition of oral sharing among vampires was non-existent. As one might expect, it was all in the dark.

"Are you worried that I eat feargorgers for breakfast? I plan to throw that in Goran's ugly mug next time I see him. You might be shocking, but I eat fear for brunch, what do you think?" Dillon asked.

"I am not worried," she replied.

"Liar," he replied.

She grinned sheepishly. "You, my dear, are getting more discerning. Yes, I am, because I've only known two vampires that could do what you did: Viktor Von Damme and Destrange, so..."

"Oh, I can see why that would bother you. Those two are darkness incarnate, and you're concerned that I might become them," he said.

"Eating darkness is different than consuming blood to gain energy. Life feeds The Bloodlust, but the darkness makes it more powerful, so that it must eat more and more frequently."

"You are also worried that there are more Shaden infesting locals, aren't you?" he said.

"Yes, my love. I don't want you indulging in feargorgers, and I'm afraid there might be a feast and smorgasbord of them in the city. I saw numerous Shaden at the hospital, far more than usual. That place is full of invaders. Between Bonz and the feargorgers clinging to Rae, Knives, and others who have been diving, I believe Von Damme's basement to be the likely point of origin. The FBI closed the dive site, but they might have shut the barn door too late."

Dillon wondered how his friends at the dock would feel about the delay in setting the memorial. Relieved? He planned to call them. "Do we go hunting shadows hiding Shaden and elusive Von Damme fanatics?"

"When you're at full strength, again, yes, we will. Rest a while. Nurse Melissa Cagey called me. Gina is in the hospital," Elke said.

"I almost killed her, didn't I?" he asked.

Elke kissed him. She knew he had chosen her over Gina, vampire over human. "You didn't, but you did what you had to do to save us. Don't worry. Melissa and Mandy are giving her TLC, and they expect her to be released as soon as her white blood count returns to normal. She will ultimately be healthier from the experience, if what Hoyt and I have learned is accurate," she said.

He recalled the methhead in Abingdon. The first bite of a vampire could be quite beneficial. After that, it could get deadly and transformative.

"I have told my staff of your heroism. This should change their minds about you," she replied.

"I could tell. Edgerton brought me tea sweetened with honey. Doris' glare was only half as scalding. I have her eternal gratitude. I noticed that there's furious cleaning and house arranging going on. Are we going to have more visitors to go along with Jayson and Justen?" Dillon asked.

"Yes. I'm glad you're sitting down."

"So, you sat in my lap so I couldn't jump up?" Dillon asked.

"Of course! I didn't want you to hurt yourself when you jump for joy when you learn that Judge Dragomir and his entourage are coming to stay with us while he heals and figures out how to get

Von Damme's signet ring back," Elke replied. He wasn't sure if she was happy about it or not.

"Wow, talk about in-laws. I can't say that I'm excited. This place was starting to feel really homey. Now we have creepy company for Halloween. Are they less fearful of me giving them away now?"

"Yes, less so. They will always be a little suspicious. Just the fact that you received a blessing uninjured baffles them. Plus, it canceled the watchful eye that Dragomir had thrown upon you. That almost made me burst out laughing! My years of experience in keeping a stoic face around Von Damme finally paid off. Dragomir was only a little irritated. He has seen stranger things than this, believe me, far stranger. Even so, you normally would have been injured by the holy water. And then, you should have died from the quikmar. In other words, you are not what they are accustomed to, perhaps at the edge of the spectrum. And I am so thrilled for it. I'm atypical, too," she said with a beaming smile.

"Which is why you love me. I'm a hybrid," he joked.

"The staff will get used to your idiosyncrasies as they have dealt with me and mine. They will appreciate you even more when the day comes, and you heal them," she said.

"Hoyt mentioned that y'all are different than typical vampires, thereby I am, too, because of your blood, the transfusion and trans-formation," Dillon said.

She nodded. "He speaks the truth. I am a product of Von Damme. For over a decade, the God-forsaken monster tested many of his draughts and tinctures on me. Sometimes I thought I would die, seeing my final end. Other times I prayed for oblivion. Now I can see why the Good Lord didn't listen to me. The Almighty had something better planned," Elke said.

"Perhaps your silent prayer was for me to come along."

"I love the way you think, dear heart."

"I've been wondering about the skulls of the six who were sacrificed. The ones brought up from the ruins. Did Dragomir deal with them?" Dillon asked. It seemed that they could cause trouble.

"He assured me that they will disappear. He is distraught, though, that he has lost Von Damme's signet ring. I am quite worried, too. The ring acts like a key to open many doors. I don't think they were all in the mansion," she said.

"So, there might be scary things like gators locked away in the hills around Bristol?"

"I'm sad to say, that and worse could be behind door number two. Von Damme had his Dr. Moreau side," she said, mixing *Let's Make a Deal* with HG Wells' classic novel.

"And here I thought that with the Oktoberfest Vampire in a coma and the gators caught, Bristol was a good place to live again. Hey, what happened to that werewolf that I locked in the trunk of your car? How is CJ?"

"Hoyt questioned him," Elke said. She saw him frown. "We didn't need to torture CJ. The dogs loved him, and he loved them, so Mr. Wills told us quite a bit about what Butcher is doing. I believe that we are going to need to investigate the caverns under East Hill and the dump."

"What's going to happened to him?"

"Granny Wolf's representative from the Peace Pack will pick him up later. I'll introduce you to Damian Thews. Someday, you'll have to meet Grandma Wolf. She and her big family are a hoot," Elke said.

"Okay. Hey, I really like how you had the deputies take down the Masked Nobody."

"Thank you. Now, people might relax a little. That should keep the feargorgers from getting more powerful. Fortunately, people don't know that Goran, Destrange and Butcher are still out there, which is why Dragomir is coming to stay here. If those werewolves had fed on us, they might have eaten the hotel guests and staff for dessert," she said.

"Vampires are coming for dinner, eh? That's scary whether they're relatives or strangers. Do we have any time to ourselves before they arrive?" he asked.

"All day, darling. We should make intimate use of it," Elke said. She stood up, took his hand, and guided him indoors before the sun broke over the horizon.

He might be immortal, but he could still feel the clock ticking. He might suffer a little time anxiety, which seemed odd for an immortal. He had grown accustomed to the darkness, but he couldn't abide evil. Good love and a little lust without blood would energize him to deal with his suspicious and dangerous kindred.

Despite the darkness, he looked forward to his future with Elke and whatever it might bring.

***

The story continues in *Vengeance of the Vampires.*

ABOUT THE AUTHOR

Thirty plus years later, William Hill is a naturalized Nevadan living in the Carson Valley. Bill is a Hoosier and a native of Indiana. He attended high school in Prairie Village, KS and graduated from colleges in Nashville, TN and Denton, Texas. He thrived in Bristol, TN, toiled and sweltered in Texas, and lived and played along the north and south shores of Lake Tahoe, Nevada. Twenty years ago, he moved to the high desert valley below the alpine basin.

Bill was a reluctant reader who fell in love with superhero comic books. Much to his teachers' chagrin, he added spy thrillers, horror, and fantasy novels to the educational required reading list. Bill earned a serious degree in Economics and Business from Vanderbilt University and an MBA from the University of North Texas, formerly NTSU. Along with working in human resources in the corporate world, Bill has been a tennis instructor, bartender, sports official, ski patroller and speaker at schools. He and his wife, Kat, love to snow ski and hike areas of natural beauty. They live at the foot of the Sierra in the blustery Carson Valley.

You will find Bill to discuss his novels and more at the Facebook group site: Fans of Dawn of the Vampire books.

Otter Creek Press Titles by William Hill

- California Ghosting
- Dawn of the Vampire Revived
- Ruins of the Vampire: Sequel to Dawn of the Vampire
- Dragon Pawns, Jules and the Runt Dragon
- Impatient Fire: Jules and the Runt Dragon 2
- Prey of the Spirit Bear
- The Magic Bicycle
- Chasing Time: The Magic Bicycle 2
- The Vampire Hunters
- The Vampire Hunters Stalked
- Vegas Vampires
- Wizard Sword